MONEY CHANGERS
AND
FALSE PROFITS

A SUSPENSE THRILLER

JANE M. BELL

DEDICATION

I dedicate this book to the memory of my grandparents
Francis and Margaret Bell. My grandma's love for writing,
mystery, humor and adventure were not lost in me.

I also dedicated this book to my three children
Colton Bell, Trevor Diaz and Annika Diaz! I will always
love all of you more than you will ever know!

CONTENTS

ACT 3 ———————————————

ACKNOWLEDGEMENTS

I must begin by thanking my Grandmother, Margaret Bell and her best friend Edyth Koerzendorfer for showing me how much fun the creative process of writing could be when I was growing up. Thank you to my children Colton, Trevor and Annika for their love and support. Thank you especially to Annika Diaz for your help in designing the book's back cover. To my best friends Carol Baranski, Deborah Ciccarelli, Jennifer Edwards, and Conna Nelson. I appreciate all of your input and feedback. I'm sure you all had many moments convinced that this project would never actually get finished. Thank you to my close friends Lisa Greenhow and Carol Baranski for their constructive criticism of this story. Thank you Rachelle Vargas King for your patience, feedback and editing talents for this beast of a project, despite your crazy busy life and schedule. Thank you to Alexandra Tataje and Jini Artega for being my religious consultants. Thank you, Joe Baranski for agreeing to be the model on the front cover. Finally, thank you to my former therapist Linda Yeates for kicking my butt gently to get this story told. Linda may for not have always told me what I wanted to hear, but she always told me what I needed to hear.

Thank you all!

ACT 1

CHAPTER 1

Detective Francis Clavering was sitting nervously in the downtown Manhattan District Attorney's office. Never a moment in his entire ten-year tenure as one of New York City's finest had his nerves been so worked-up as they were at this moment. He held his body taut in a conscious effort to prevent any noticeable outward signs of nervous fidgeting. He could feel the beads of sweat starting to flow down his back. The detective hoped sincerely that would be the only outward sign that all was not right with the normally cool, calculating, seasoned detective. He was grateful that his racing heart and the knot in the pit of his stomach were oblivious to the other men seated with him in the room. His nervous brain wanted him to bolt from that office and abort the task at hand. However, his own personal wants were not to be entertained; not now. His gut instincts would rule over this situation.

This plan was cooked up mostly by himself, with a little help from only one other accomplice. Inspector James Bentley, the commanding officer of the Detectives assigned to the Manhattan Racketeering Bureau, sat to his immediate left. Fran was most impressed with his boss' outward display of cool calmness. Bentley served many years as an undercover agent. That experience gave him one of the best damn poker faces Fran had ever seen. As far as the other detectives in the department were concerned, Bentley was the best in the business.

Across the desk from the two men sat Paul Christopherson, the District Attorney of the Racketeering Bureau, on Leonard Street in downtown Manhattan. His reputation as a hard as nails, by the book, incorruptible prosecutor had earned him respect that extended far beyond New York state lines. Fran had worked closely with D.A. Christopherson for over five years now. The seasoned D.A. ways a more senior version of himself, as far as Fran was concerned. He knew this man like the back of his hand on any given day. Today, however, was far from one of those days. The detective and the Inspector, had the utmost respect for this D.A. they worked for, yet they were both about to betray all the trust and respect that had been established over their many years of working together.

Like the man seated across from him, the one thing the detective hated more than anything else was a liar, especially among his colleagues. Yet, here he sat, on the verge of telling the biggest lie he'd ever told in his life. Lying to the D.A. was, in his mind, a horrible situation. Dragging his supervisor into this deception was even worse. Bentley embraced the plan willingly. He trusted this detective's instincts, far more than his own, or anybody else's, in his department. If they were found out, however, the impact on both of them, personally and professionally, would be catastrophic. Neither man wanted to think about those consequences at this moment, or ever.

If successful, Fran would be on his way to Munich, West Germany, in a couple short weeks. However, this was not to be a pleasure trip. Deep in his gut, he knew that this trip was extremely important to the case the entire department had been working on for the last eighteen months. The exact impact, however, was still completely unknown. All he knew was that he had to get his ass over there, somehow, some way. Failure just was not an option.

Gaining Christopherson's approval of this trip would be next to impossible. The daunting financial burden on the NYPD's already strapped budget was definitely not their biggest hurdle. NYPD just didn't send their men out of the country, no matter how hot of a trail they were on. The last time a detective ventured so far out of their jurisdiction was some 65 years ago. That trip resulted in the most brutal murder of one of the most highly seasoned officers in the history of the department. The emotional impact of a fallen comrade and the many years of work resulted in the case going stone cold following that incident. As far as the department was concerned, the risks would never justify putting the life of another man in danger, ever.

Bentley droned on with explanation, while Fran's mind began to drift, replaying the events of the months leading up to this moment...

Fran had been trailing a low-level mobster named Luca Benedetto for well over a year. His colleagues could never understand the detective's almost obsessive fascination with this particular gangster. The detective didn't quite understand it himself. Benedetto was a boring, little, insignificant piss-ant, who managed the local street gangs' narcotics hustle for the city's infamous Lanscano crime family. Benedetto was a cheapskate of the highest order. The tenth grade drop-out had his turf, rackets and routines, which Fran knew so well he could almost set his wristwatch to most of the gangster's activities.

Fran reluctantly gave up on watching his subject when Inspector Bentley needed his detective's talents elsewhere. Manning a solo surveillance detail outside the exclusive Brazilian Club in New York City. Everyone in "Rackets" knew that getting into the club was impossible. Attempts were made many years prior with disastrous results that immediately killed momentum in all mob related investigations for years. The best they could do, for now, was to note the comings and goings of various dignitaries associated with the New York Mob scene. Fran watched intently the club's entrance from a distance through binoculars. "What the hell?" He mumbled aloud to himself. He dropped the binoculars from his eyes, then raised them again. Making sure his eyes weren't playing tricks on him.

Over the coming days, his favorite gangster, Benedetto, would be seen many times coming out of the Brazilian accompanied by a man already familiar to the detective from his many years of work in "Rackets." Gordon "Gordo" Davies had a rap sheet going back at least thirty years. He'd done time in the Federal Pen and Sing Sing for forgery and dealing stolen and fake securities. He also had a very close, extensive history of working with many of the syndicate leaders throughout the country.

Benedetto would also be seen exiting the club with the Don of the Moretti crime family. He suddenly seemed to be a very important person within the syndicate, working very closely with some surprisingly high ranking New York mobsters. He wasn't there for social hour; he was there for business. After his "club business" was complete, he'd then scurry off to his usual "office."

"Why is old man Moretti hanging out with a piece of shit like Benedetto?" Fran wondered. "It just didn't make sense."

That week, the team's strategy meeting resulted in a much heated debate. A surveillance detail outside the club would no longer suffice.

"How about wiretaps?" Suggested a colleague.

"Hmmm, that's an idea." Confirmed Fran.

Bentley chimed in. "The budget will allow for one tap to be installed. My only concern is we don't really have anything to justify a wiretap on the Brazilian, and there is no way for us to get in there to help our own cause."

"No, I don't think the club is the best place for it."

"Well, if not there, where Fran?"

"I suggest the pay phone in Frankie's Lounge."

The rest of the team immediately thought the detective had lost his mind. "Frankie's, that rat infested shit hole. You've got to be kidding! You still got the hots for Benedetto, don't you Fran." Chimed in a critical colleague.

"Shut the fuck up, and hear me out, you idiot. Can any of you tell me why our friend Mr. Benedetto is all of a sudden hanging out with the likes of Don Moretti and Gordo Davies?"

The room was silent. The detective had a point. Fran continued. "Who here wants to volunteer to go undercover into the club to see what's cookin' in there?"

Bentley interrupted. "Now Fran, you know that's not a possibility."

"Exactly! Anyone here want to go in and keep tabs on Benedetto's in that disgusting, sleazy dive he calls his office?"

The idea nauseated everyone on the team. Fran's answer was implied through the deafening silence of the room.

"Yeah, that's what I thought. James, I do believe Frankie's is our best bet. Benedetto is up to something, and I feel that it's in our best interest to find out what, and soon. We already know he's managing the leaders of local street gangs and lower Mafia thugs dealing street level dope out of there. Crime outside Frankie's joint was rampant and blatant, but what's going on inside? Bugs are too risky as is undercover work."

Bentley knew his team leader wasn't going to give in. "Damn it, alright Fran. I'm sure from our prior work we can get temporary approval, but you guys only got thirty days! Thirty, that's it! Ya hear me? If nothing comes of it, I'm pulling the plug."

"Thank you, Inspector."

The 'tap was installed, and a command post was set up in a dingy basement room a couple blocks down the street. It was scantily supplied with tables, chairs, a radio and some recording equipment, headphones, speakers and microphone, coffee maker and a cot. The surveillance detail moved from the Brazilian to outside Frankie's.

Early February the 'tap finally went live. While he waited, Fran poured himself a cup of coffee, lit a cigarette, and opened up the New York Times. In the "World News" section, a headline on the lower half of the front page read, "Is Trouble Brewing for Italy's Economy?...Italian Stock Market volatility and the mass exodus of money flowing out of Italy seem to be key factors in Italy's decline after decades of postwar boom..." Fran lowered the paper, as he heard the first call come in, and the recorder began to spin. Fran listened intently, just a few blocks away.

The outgoing call was placed by Gordo Davies trying unsuccessfully several times throughout the day to reach a contact elsewhere in New York City. Fran thought it was nice of Mr. Davies to leave his name and number with his contact's secretary. Later that afternoon, a squelch came over the radio informing Fran that Mr. Davies had left Frankie's with Benedetto.

Three days after the 'tap went live, Fran ran bursting through the door of Bentley's office, sweating profusely and extremely out of breath.

"Clavering! What the hell is going on?!"

"Boss, boss, boss!... you're never gonna to believe this, not in a million years..." Fran panted, trying to catch his breath. "Our boy, Benedetto, is heading over to Germany in a few days."

Bentley looked at him, stunned and a bit confused. "Are you sure? Don't bullshit me Fran, I don't have time for this. We're all too busy for bullshit right now!"

"Yeah boss, I'm sure, I just heard him over at the post booking his plane, hotel, you know, the works!"

Bentley thought out loud for a second. "Why the hell would he be going to Germany?"

"James, I have no clue, but you and I both know it's not to chase ski bunnies around the resorts over there."

"That's true. The only thing Luca's chased in ages were goons that owed him cash." The inspector quickly drew a mental image and issued a slight chuckle. "So why do you think he's going over there?"

"That's just it boss, I haven't got the foggiest, but I think we ought to follow him over there. It has to be something big to get him to leave that shit hole lounge he hangs in so much."

"You? Go over there?" Bentley snickered sarcastically. "You've been working too many hours in that damn basement, Clavering; you need a day off!"

"I'm serious boss. Look, I don't mean any disrespect, but I was bustin' my balls for a year and a half in this fuckin' division before you even allowed me, then the team, to followed up on my first hunch on little ol' Benedetto. No one could believe he was a bigger player with the mob than he let on. But look where we are now with him and these other cases in Rackets. You have to admit, this is completely out of character for this guy. I know it, and I know you do too. We have to get over there and find out what the hell he's up to."

"Look man, I don't disagree with you." Fran gave him a slightly off, doubting glance. "Honestly Fran, I don't...You're right, this is not normal behavior for Benedetto, and I do strongly believe that you should follow your instinct on this, especially given your track record over the years. But there is no chance that this will fly anywhere but into the garbage can with Christopherson. And you know it. After that incident sixty-five years ago in Italy...forget it Fran. We will have to wait until he gets back to figure this all out."

"Listen, James, a lot has changed in this department in sixty-five years, including policies. You and I both know Christopherson. If he wants somebody or something, there ain't nobody gonna tell him no. If anyone can and will break policy, it's him."

Bentley sat quietly, thinking for a spell. He knew Fran well enough to know that he wasn't going to let up on this. He was annoyingly stubborn when he caught-on to something involving a case.

"...only because I agree with your stupid ass, and I know how much of a pain in the ass you are going to be if I don't concede on this, I will do what I can. I guess at this point we can only try. The worst that can happen is he says no, I guess."

"Thanks James!" Fran smiled, excitedly.

"Hold on there, detective, I'm not finished yet."

The smile quickly faded from Fran's face, and he suddenly looked worried.

"You know as well as I do that this can't be presented to Christopherson as one of your crazy hunches or bullshit gut feelings you got. It's got to be something he can hang a case on. How soon is Benedetto leaving?"

"A little more than two weeks," Fran replied apprehensively.

"Well, you better come up with something fast then, if you're going to have any chance of making a go at this."

"Shit, you're right." The gears in the detective's mind started turning. "I will come up with something, boss."

"You always do, Fran." Bentley reluctantly encouraged as he escorted his detective out of his office.

The detective's attention once again returned to the present. Fran, to those who knew him well, was now visibly scared. The beads of sweat continued to form and roll down his back, under his shirt. Christopherson, however, never noticed. He was still listening intently as Bentley explained the situation Fran had concocted.

"Fran, everyone in the damn division knows that one of Benedetto's rackets is that bullshit travel agency he runs with the stolen and forged airline tickets. Why the hell didn't he just use that for this flight to Germany?" Christopherson questioned.

"That's a great question, sir. Matter of fact, if he had, there's no way in hell I would have learned of his plans to leave the country."

"This is true." Agreed Christopherson, as he rubbed his fingers over his stubble studded chin. "So you think Benedetto's going to Munich to set up weapons supply lines for the Protestants over in Ireland to be used against the Catholics?"

Fran bit his lip as the fib flowed out of him. "I do know that tensions between the IRA and the Protestants have really become heated in Northern Ireland recently."

"Yes, that is true." nodded the D.A. in agreement.

"Everyone in the division, including you, knows that one of Benedetto's rackets is gun running between the states and the drug dealers and suppliers in South America, right?" Clavering continued. "Everything I've seen lately suggests that he's trying to set up a similar racket abroad. This must be a very big deal he's working up over there in Munich for him to use legit arrangements for his flight and lodging. He's not willing to risk anything disrupting what he has planned over there." Fran took a deep breath as he completed his lie.

The D.A. considered everything he was just presented. The three men sat in silence for what seemed like an eternity. Finally, the silence broke. "Alright Fran, James, I've heard enough." The excitement of the two men rose quickly... "Let me think about it."

Fran's stomach sank as he tried his best to hide his disappointment.

"I'll let you know my decision by Monday." As the three men stood and Christopherson moved to escort his visitors out of his office.

"Thank you, sir," replied Bentley.

The two men returned to Bentley's office. Fran no longer hid his disappointment. "damn it, I thought we had him, boss."

"Oh Fran, stop it. You knew it was a long shot at best. Besides, even though the chief didn't say yes, he certainly didn't say no."

"This is true, you're right. For the moment, nothing changes until he says no."

"That's the spirit, detective. Listen Fran, it's Friday, why don't you knock off early, have a few beers, and get out of your head for a while."

"Thanks boss, I certainly have been neglecting Peg and the kids since we started chasing Benedetto all over this God damn city."

"Well then, Fran, I guess I'll see you Monday Morning!"

CHAPTER 2

In the heart of Vatican City, near the Gate of Saint Anna, sits a tall building known as Saint Nicholas' tower. A place completely closed off to the majority of the people who visit the Holy City on any given day of the year. The top floor of that tower houses the *Instituto per le Opere di Religione.* For those who work and reside within the walls of the Vatican, some referred to it as the Institute for Religious Works. Some call it the IOR. However, most know it simply as the Vatican Bank.

A balding, short, rotund banker with dark thinning hair and mustache makes his way through the floors and corridors of the building and soon arrives at the foyer of the bank. A very attractive secretary acknowledges him as he enters. She cups her hand over the mouthpiece of the phone, addressing the man.

"Please, Mr. Ansios," she offers in a soft, sweet voice. "Have a seat. I will be with you in just a moment."

The man nods politely in confirmation, then lowers himself in a taught, controlled manner onto the fine leather couch across the room from the secretary's desk. Anxiously he sits, staring off into the design of the fine hand woven Persian rug under his feet. Tightly, he clutches his black leather briefcase while she continues on with her conversation to its conclusion and returns the handset to the phone's cradle.

She scribbles something quickly on a notepad, then redirects her attention to the man seated on the couch across from her. "I'm sorry, Mr. Ansios, for keeping you waiting. I didn't realize you had an appointment with Bishop Krivis this morning."

"The apology is all mine, miss. I'm sorry for barging in here unannounced. I have no appointment, actually. Do you think the bishop has a few moments that I might see him this morning?"

"But of course, Mr. Ansios, he always has time for you." She winked, then moved suggestively from behind her desk. "Please, Mr. Ansios, allow me to escort you to the bishop's office."

"Thank you, miss."

"Right this way, sir."

The somewhat unkempt man's face displays great concern as he follows behind the barely twenty-year-old girl with long tan legs, sweetly scented skin, deep blue eyes, and softly curled, gently bouncing strawberry blond hair. As she passes in front of him to lead him down a long passageway to their destination, he doesn't even notice her robust cleavage on full display in her pastel green peek-a-boo sweater or her short skirt and matching heels. He walks in silence behind her, clutching tightly in his arms, his dark briefcase with a few white papers sticking out the sides, like a frightened child grips their most cherished security blanket. At the end of the corridor. She struggles slightly to push open the oversized, dark, heavy double doors, then escorts the visitor into the chamber.

"Your Excellency," Her coy smile greets the wanting eyes of her boss, Bishop Jonas Krivis, as she and the visiting banker enter the office chamber of the IOR president. "Mr. Marco Ansios is here to see you."

The hulking, six foot six, 220 pound bank president rises from behind a large, oversized mahogany desk to greet his visitor. He transfers his smoldering Havana Cigar from his right to left hand, then extends his empty hand to the man for a vigorous handshake. "My dear Marco, what an excellent, yet unexpected, surprise."

He then turns from the man for a moment to ogle his secretary quickly, then responds with a flirtatious. "Thank you honey," he gives her a wink. "That will be all, my dear."

She nods with a half smile, then turns silently to leave the room, closing the double doors behind her.

Krivis now turns his attention back to his guest. "Scotch, Marco?"

"No thank you, Jonas. I still have a lot of work to do this morning after I leave here."

"Then by all means, let me pour you a double... Besides, you look like you could use a stiff one...On the rocks?" Krivis insisted.

Lowering his head ever so slightly, Ansios knew his protests were futile. The bishop could never pass up an opportunity to flaunt his own self-importance. The visitor's hands trembled slightly as he took the glass from his host. "Thank you, Jonas."

Ansios loosened his grip on the briefcase when he received the drink. He raises the glass in a toasting gesture, then takes a small sip of his scotch. The smooth, smoky liquor coats his tongue, and for a moment his attention is on something benign, not all his troubles floating around his head. He lowers the glass from his mouth, tilts the glass slightly, looking at the contents of the fine crystal glass with a raised eyebrow. "Mmm, that is really good, actually. Thank you."

"Ahhh, yes. I knew you'd like that one. Say what you will, you gotta admit, I have fine taste when it comes to my scotch." Krivis smiled smugly.

"That you do, my friend."

"So Marco, to what do I owe this unexpected visit?"

The banker's anxiety instantly returned. "I need your help, Jonas."

"Of course, my friend. Your problems are my problems. How can I help?"

"The Catholic Bank of Venice."

Krivis observed Ansios unconcerned. "Yes, what of it?"

"The parishioners of Venice are very upset about my recent purchase of that bank."

"Ahhh," Krivis brought his fingertips together in a diamond formation, in front of his mouth, then lowered them a little as he spoke. "Is that sale finally public?"

"Yes, yes it is, and it has me very worried."

"Since when have you ever been worried about the clientele of any bank, Marco? This is so unlike you, my friend."

"...but this situation is different, very different. The people of Venice recently learned of my purchase from the bank. They are not happy Jonas."

"Alright, but I don't understand. Why now? What's with this buyer's remorse nine months after the ink has been dry?"

"Clearly, I underestimated the backlash I'd receive from the Venetian clergy."

"The bank is now yours, Marco. It is no longer my business what you do with your bank."

"It is such a small bank. The hostile response coming from the locals in that region will be more damaging than I anticipated. It is important that I put this fire out, Jonas."

"Important?" Krivis gave a slightly sarcastic chuckle. "You've got to be kidding me. How is losing the patronage of a few local priests, nuns, and congregation causing you so much concern? Maybe I should have waited out my initial offer of that bank to Giovanni Fedora."

"You and I both know that those who control you were not about to let you sell it to Fedora."

"Those who control me? What the hell are you talking about, Marco?!?! No one controls me here, except for Pope Michael VI."

"Bullshit!"

"Excuse me?!"

"Both you and I know what a crock of shit that is, Jonas."

"You have some nerve barging in here, unannounced, asking me for my help, and then insulting me to my face, Marco!"

"Oh, stop with your childish tantrum. I'm not wrong here, and you know it, regardless of whether you want to admit it."

"I did you a favor selling you that bank, you ungrateful bastard."

"Ha!"

"You laugh at my generosity?"

"Generosity? You were only kissing my ass because Archbishop Leone pulled the plug on you selling that bank to Fedora. If anything, I helped you out."

"You must be joking, Marco. You didn't help me at all."

"Well, if I recall, you sure were in a hurry to unload that bank for some reason. Still, to this day, I don't understand why."

"And you certainly took your own sweet time completing the deal."

"It was my first official transaction with the Vatican Bank. No sense pissing off the boss on the first deal, Jonas. Even you can appreciate that kind of reasoning."

"You stubbornly demanded the blessing of the Holy Father at least three times prior to your purchase."

"Yes, the approval of the Holy Father was very important to me last July. But that was certainly not how you wanted this deal to go down, Jonas."

"What is that supposed to mean?"

"If we would have done this your way, the Holy Father would have never even known about the transaction."

Krivis took a drink of his scotch. He savored the rich flavor for a moment before swallowing. He then took a long drag of his cigar. The blend of smoke and scotch intoxicated his senses and calmed his spirit. "If the Holy Father was unhappy with your acquisition, do you honestly think he would have bothered to thank you personally for making the purchase, Marco?"

Ansios thought for a second, "Thanking me? I thought all that was for sorting out the whole library fiasco."

An amused Krivis responded with a slight chuckle. "Your assumption isn't even close, Marco."

"I had no idea that it had anything to do with the bank purchase."

"It's true."

Ansios let his guard down for a moment, reflecting. "How did I completely miss the intent of the Holy Father's gratitude?"

"Don't beat yourself up about it too much, my friend. There are far worse things to be wrong about."

"This is true, Jonas." Ansios confirmed.

"Shall we get back to the matter at hand, Marco?"

"I'm sorry. Yes, of course."

"Don't worry about it. I apologize for barking at you. You caught me in a weak moment."

"Apology accepted. In all honesty, Marco, I don't see what it is exactly that concerns you. How much more assistance can I truly offer you on this, at this point, my friend?"

"I need happy clients..."

"Ha, you already know how to keep your clients happy...at least the really important ones." Krivis chuckled and cut him off, then gave him a wink. "You have far more years in banking than I do, so I know you know how to handle the patrons of a bank. Maybe you can offer them a free toaster or something."

Ansios continued. "I'm serious Jonas, what I really need are happy clients."

"Why are you so damn stubborn about this?"

"Happy clients help deflect the attention of Italian Banking Authorities."

"Italian Banking Authorities? Oh Marco, you are always so stupid in your paranoia regarding them. I'm sure Brother Gherado Fratello can keep the banking authorities in check, or at least in the dark, while you conduct whatever operations you have in mind for your new bank."

"Jonas, I don't doubt Fratello's ability to control the situation. That's not my point here. I don't want him involved with this bank, and I certainly don't want to be owing him any favors for his services."

"Fine, fine," Krivis conceded. "It is, after all, your business at this point. So what is it exactly that you wish for me to do for you, Marco?"

"I feel that if I can somehow gain the favor of the patriarch of Venice, it will calm the outrage of my clients in the region."

"Riluciani? Cardinal Chiaros Riluciani is giving you trouble?" Krivis laughed. "You've got to be fucking kidding me, Marco."

"Yes, he is extremely angry with me right now."

"He has to be the biggest push-over I've ever met in this church."

"Obviously, you've never dealt with him when he's mad."

Krivis thought for a moment. "You're right. All that damn bastard does is smile and pray."

"I'm sure he's still praying, but at the moment, he wears no smile. He scares me Jonas."

"You? You're scared of him?!" Krivis let out a big, loud belly laugh that echoed throughout the chamber. "Bwhahaha, you've got to be kidding me, Marco."

"I can't put my finger on why, but yes, he genuinely scares the shit out of me."

"In all your years of dealing with... um, well, ya know mobsters and such, believe you me, Riluciani is not a man you should be at all worried about. Trust me Marco."

"I trust what you tell me, Jonas, but my gut says otherwise. So, what is your advice on how I should approach him?"

"Hmmm, well, you know as well as I do Marco, that the almighty Lira can appease all men, even men of the cloth like Riluciani. May I suggest perhaps a charitable gift for that stupid retard home he wants to build?"

"Do you really think that will work?"

"Well, I know it is a project near and dear to his heart. He's constantly pestering me to give him some of the pope's money for it."

"I had no idea."

"That is to be expected, Marco. He is obviously not someone you've ever worked with before." Ansios nodded in agreement. "True."

"If you knew him as I do, you certainly wouldn't be afraid of his smiling ass."

Krivis thought for a moment. "Yes, I think coming from you, it just might serve as a suitable olive branch between the two of you. Besides, you'd be doing me a favor."

"How so?"

"You will get him off my back. He can be quite annoying when he gets a wild hair up his ass."

"I will make him an offer, as you suggest. Do you really believe it will work, though? He strikes me as one who will not be happy until that bank is back in the Vatican's hands."

"I'm most certain of it, my friend. Don't you worry about the anger of Cardinal Riluciani. I will deal with that, my friend. Besides, there isn't anything he or anyone else can do about it at this point. The deal is done."

"I hope you're right Jonas." Ansios once again started second guessing himself. "Maybe you should have just waited and sold it to Giovanni Fedora."

"Nah, I sold it to you with the blessing of the pope. If that's not good enough for you, future business dealings with the Vatican may be problematic, my friend."

"You're right Jonas," Ansios sheepishly conceded. "I apologize for burdening you with my troubles, but I appreciate your guidance."

"Don't give it a second thought, Marco. Feel free to visit me anytime. My door is always open, and the drinks and advice are always free, my friend."

"Thank you."

Krivis rose and walked his friend to the door of his office. "You're welcome, my friend." The two shook hands and Marco Ansios departed.

CHAPTER 3

Francis Clavering, a big, sturdy man, stood six foot four. His dark, curly hair accentuated the handsome Irish features he inherited from his mother. Despite his large stature, he moved with an air of self-confidence and grace, more becoming of a professional athlete or a martial artist than a cop. The detective sergeant, in his fifth year with the New York City Police Department, ascended quickly through the ranks to become the commander of the Homicide Task Force, and a Special Assistant for the Organized Crime Division to the Chief of Detectives. Fran was a humble man who, if ever pressed, would always say that it was always luck, not skill, that seemed to place him in the right place at the right time. No one in the division could ever figure out how his hunches were always so spot-on. Great instincts, eidetic memory, and an uncanny ability to see through distracting chaos, and directly at the bigger picture inside a criminal mind, were all assets to his career chasing down various players in the syndicate underworld.

Margaret "Peg" Clavering, was the love of life, and wife of twelve years, and the envy of all who knew or worked with her husband. Fran knew the blessing that she was on the day he met her. He passed up full ride football and basketball scholarships and an appointment to West Point just so he could go home and marry this beautiful and smart woman. For Francis, it was an easy decision, and one that he would never once regret. When they first met, Peg worked as an investigative reporter for a local newspaper. She willingly set aside her journalism career and became a housewife upon the arrival of their first child. Fran was humbled and appreciative of her sacrifice for their growing family. She too had instincts, insights and talents that the detective would often draw upon throughout his career.

In September 1964, Fran worked in a lucrative position at a New York electrical engineering and manufacturing company. He provided well for his family. Gone were the days of his youth, growing up poor in a three-bedroom ghetto flat in New York City's Lower East Side. It was his dedication to Peg and their family that initially kept him from accepting a police department position. He had already given up all prior offers with the Department. Peg knew he had, but only one chance left before his opportunity would be lost forever.

"Fran, I know you take great pride in your work at the factory. The money it provides for the family is great, but it has also made you a complete ass to live with. You have always wanted to be a cop ever since you were a child. Your talents are being wasted working in that factory. You have to be a cop Fran, it is your one true calling, love. You have to be blind not to see it sitting right in front of you. I know those salaries aren't what they are in the private sector, but we will make it, somehow, some way. That I can promise you, love."

Fran felt guilty even thinking about changing careers. He also knew that his wife was smart and far more stubborn than himself. Fran finally accepted the police force position and never looked back. He never for a second took her for granted. Not her love, and definitely not her unwavering support. She believed in him and his calling to fight organized crime completely. She also had an unshakable, complete understanding that his work was very much who Fran was. For him, his social life, and even at times his family life, would take a back seat to his work.

Peg soon had a vested interest in her husband's work. She knew everything about his work. Listening to him share his experiences night after night during his nine years of service on the police force, she truly was his "partner in crime." Being a detective's wife, she worried, but never too much about her husband while at work. He certainly could handle himself if need be. It was also comforting knowing that there was an unwritten code within the Mob that retaliation against law men doing their duty was not tolerated.

Fran was a mess. His stomach was in knots, his temper was short and barbed, and his mind jumped from one thought to another, giving him no peace the entire weekend. Peg did her best to try to keep him calm and pull him out of his head once in a while. It was a challenging, if not impossible, endeavor. The weekend dragged on, long and heavy. He had no idea what Christopherson would decide. The chief, an older version of himself, also grew up poor in a devout Irish Catholic family. The D.A. was also a man committed to the war against organized crime.

Unable to sleep, the detective arrived to work early Monday morning. By 9 am, he and Bentley were once again sitting in Christopherson's office, anxious and terrified. Christopherson sat, poker- faced across from them, glancing at some papers from the Benedetto file open on the desk in front of him.

"I've been running everything you've presented through my head all weekend. Benedetto needs to be trailed to Munich. Especially if he is trying to get weapons to anyone in Ireland, especially those Protestants. He must be stopped! We can only afford to send one detective over there. To be honest, we really can't even afford that. Fran, get your ass over there, and you better come back with something good, or you will be stuck on shit detail for a very, very long time. You got that Clavering?!"

The detective replied, trying his best to contain his excitement. "Yes sir, I understand."

"You've got a budget of $1,000 to make something happen."

"Thank you, sir! That will be more than enough." Fran couldn't contain his smile any longer, as he quickly looked over at Bentley, who also looked pleased with the situation.

"Oh, and Clavering," Christopherson paused. "Please, please, please be careful over there. The department just can't lose another officer on foreign soil."

"Absolutely sir! You have my word on it."

The two men were dismissed from the D.A.'s office. They walked at a quickened pace. Both were excited, yet relieved to be back in Bentley's office. Sporting huge smiles, the two men spoke briefly before Fran headed back to his own office.

Upon his return, Fran immediately called Peg. She, too, was happy and relieved to hear the news, completely dismissing his nastiness from the prior weekend. Within twenty minute word had already spread throughout the department. The detective had too much to do to acknowledge any of their hazing.

Sitting at his desk, Fran began to make notes of what all needed to be done in the coming days. Glancing at his calendar, "Saint Valentine's day! Shit!" He muttered to himself. His head was so focused on Benedetto and the upcoming trip, the holiday completely skipped his mind. He quickly made himself a note with huge, underlined letters. "I'm such an awful husband sometimes..." he thought to himself.

Benedetto was leaving for Munich in exactly two weeks. Fran needed to get over there a couple of days prior. Last minute disorganization was something that deeply bothered him. Some chaos was to be expected, but he worked hard to anticipate every possible curve ball.

"Less than ten business days...," he mumbled to himself.

The days rushed by with still so much to be done before leaving the country. Fran was still in charge of the detail that managed the surveillance post. Even though he and Benedetto would be out of the country, surveillance had to be maintained. Benedetto wasn't the only one using that phone for "business operations."

Once he was satisfied with his preparation efforts, the detective took a few shifts at "The Post" a few days prior to his departure. Fran listened while Benedetto talked to another man about an overdue debt. The two men made arrangements to meet in Munich to square up the matter.

Fran quickly transcribed the conversation, then added that Benedetto was extorting money from the man and was planning to collect the money on his trip abroad. Knowing the Mafiosi's reputation so well, Fran knew that if the situation even hinted at turning south, Benedetto wouldn't think twice about killing the man on the spot, no matter where he was. It wasn't an implausible stretch of the truth, Fran thought as he continued typing the report. He brought the transcript and report along with the court order issued by the New York judge just in case he ran into any issues with his Munich counterparts.

The day had finally arrived. Peg and the children drove him to JFK airport. This was the part Fran dreaded the most. He held his wife firmly in his arms. She could feel the anxiousness in his body as he pulled her even closer.

"When I get back, I'm going to take you out for a night on the town."

"A night on the town? You mean like a date?"

"Yeah, yeah," Fran responded excitedly. "A date."

"It's been so long, love. I think I've forgotten. What's a date?" She coyly jested.

"Oh stop it." His smile held a hint of guilt. "Let me help you remember...cocktails, dinner, dancing, the works."

"Really love?!" Peg gushed, then she smiled teasingly. "dancing? You?"

"Yes, me...and you too!"

"That sounds amazing!"

"Wonderful! Then it's all planned." He held his wife tightly, and the two kissed tenderly.

"Ewwww!" came a loud chorus of protest from their children standing nearby, turning their faces away in disgust as the two continued their extended kiss.

The kiss finally broke. He whispered in her ear, still holding her tightly, "I love you, honey. Please take care of those kids for me."

"I love you too. And don't you worry about us, love. Concentrate on what you've got to do over there."

"Thank you." He said as he held her a little tighter and kissed her one more time. "I will call you as soon as I get to Munich. I promise."

"You better," she ordered, then leaned closer and whispered. "Be safe love,..." as his embrace released.

Once boarded and settled in, he instantly became soberly aware that he was now completely alone, as he had never been before. The magnitude of everything caught him up by surprise, and a huge wave of fear and uncertainty came over him. He was risking reputation and career for what? A stupid hunch. The department heads said that if he didn't find anything over there, do not bother coming back. He knew they were joking, but it was enough to allow self-doubt to seep into his thoughts. He didn't know a lick of German or anything about the city of Munich. All this compounded with his absolute fear of flying turned the calm, cool and collected detective into a nervous wreck. He ordered a whiskey and cola to help calm his nerves. Next thing he knew, he was on his fifth cocktail, very early into his eleven hour flight. No matter how hard he tried, no sleep would find him.

Noon the next day, he touched down in Munich. Groggy, hungover and very jetlagged, he was ready to check into his hotel for a shower, shave and quick call to Peg before meeting up with the Bavarian team. The Munich Police Department, however, had other ideas. They quickly whisked him through the customs gate and baggage claim and immediately into an awaiting car headed directly to Munich Police headquarters.

An extended hand and warm smile initiated his introduction to German Detective Hans Kruck, his partner during his stay in West Germany. The German detective had coordinated with hotel staff to set up surveillance operations on Benedetto and accommodations for their guest detective. His new partner was thrilled to report that they had sixteen men assigned to assist them. The exhausted New York Detective was completely overwhelmed by all the support.

The Germans were star-struck. They'd never dreamed of ever working with a "big-time" New York detective. Fran humbly tried to explain, to no avail, that it really wasn't that big of a deal. Their enthusiasm gave Fran a well needed lift after his rough, booze infused flight. All the self-doubt from the night before was now gone as he finally shifted into "work" mode.

The first order of business was to discuss the surveillance equipment. Fran was excited to see the latest technology in the German's arsenal that he had read so much about.

"Fran," Hans explained. "We're here to help you in every way possible, but we don't want to use wiretaps and room bugs."

"Wait, What! I don't understand. Why the hell not?" The normally calm New Yorker immediately exploded. "My assistant D.A. told me that German surveillance laws were similar to what we have over in America."

"They are, that is true."

"That is entirely why I'm here." Fran explained. "Back in New York, we have built a whole case against this guy and many others based on information gathered almost exclusively through bugs and 'taps."

"These German laws you speak of have been around since 1949. That was during our Federal Republic days." Hans calmly explained.

"So, your legal system is ok with these techniques, but you don't use them?" Fran interrupted, then paused, confused. "But why? What am I missing here?"

Hans lowered his head slightly in shame. "When the laws were enacted, we were still under the control of The Third Reich. I'm sure you are familiar with their reputation and history." Fran nodded respectfully, as Hans continued. "These modes of surveillance were very common tools used by Hitler and the Gestapo to keep tabs on many innocent Germans. The police departments in Germany have had a hard time losing the Gestapo stigma that still haunts us to this day."

Fran's thoughts raced as Christopherson's words ran through his mind. He needed those bugs and 'taps or the trip would be a complete bust. Back and forth the conversation went on for hours, landing both detectives in the Director's office. Fran presented his case. It was obvious to the seasoned director that the American detective was not going to back down. Around midnight, final approval came with the signature of a German prosecuting judge. Fran was visibly relieved and more exhausted than he'd been in a very, very long time. He finally checked into his room, collapsed onto the bed fully clothed, and fell into a deep, deep sleep.

7:00 AM the next morning, the American detective woke with a start. Completely disoriented, he reached his hand toward the rude noise interrupting his sleep.

"Heh...Hello." He said groggily.

"Hallo, Gut Morgan Sir," said the hotel operator, politely in her accented English. "Dis is jour vakeup call."

Fran rubbed his stubbled face, trying to gather his bearings. "Good morning miss," now a little more awake. "Thank you," then hung up the phone.

Rubbing his eyes, he stretched and yawned, while he regained the rest of his mental faculties. The sleep had completely restored him back to a human state. "Oh shit, I'm late!" He thought to himself in a panic. He quickly called down to room service for some breakfast and a carafe of coffee, then quickly showered and shaved while waiting for his breakfast to arrive. He was concerned. Peg was going to be very angry with him. His call was long overdue. He glanced at the clock in the room, then down at his watch, still set to New York City time. "One in the morning in New York. Damn it." He muttered to himself, conflicted. He didn't want to wake her, but he knew he wouldn't get another chance once his day got going. He just had to call her now, before his day got away from him.

The ringing phone jarred Peg out of her dream. She looked at the clock as she reached for the ringing phone, assaulting her ears. Her initial annoyance was quickly replaced by the comforting, reassuring voice of her husband on the other end of the line. She no longer cared that it was the middle of the night. Knowing he made it safely to Munich quelled her worrying. She was used to his "normal" crime fighting adventures. It was so commonplace that she rarely gave a second thought. Traveling to Germany was new, unknown, and concerned her greatly.

Fran apologized profusely for not calling her when he touched down. He felt bad as he carried- on over his breakfast and coffee. He then told her about the group of Munich police he'd be working with over the next several days. Peg was surprised by their resistance to the surveillance equipment, but happy the issue was resolved. With a phone kiss and an "I love you," Fran hung up the phone in a great mood. He finished dressing and headed for police headquarters.

Walking into Hans' office, his head was much clearer than it was the night before. He was ready to face his day.

"*Guten Morgen*, I mean good morning detective!" Hans greeted. "Did you sleep well?"

"*Guten Morgen!* Yes, yes I did, *danke!*"

"Your German, it's *sehr gut*. The room was to your liking, I hope?"

"I'm afraid that's about all the German I know," Fran chuckled, then continued. "Yes, Hans, the room is very nice, thank you."

Hans was still impressed with the detective's ability to persuade the director's approval the night before. Hans handed him an ornate wooden box. "Fran, this is for you to use during your stay here in Munich."

The New Yorker curiously opened the box slowly. Inside the lined case sat a Walther PPK side arm and ammunition. He admitted to Hans that he had felt a little naked, leaving his trusty .38 at home. He wasn't in the mood to hassle with security and customs on either side of the Atlantic, opting instead to just leave it at home with Peg and the children.

"Thank you, Hans. It will do just fine." Fran couldn't help but be amused by the gesture. He joked as he removed his jacket to put on the gun's shoulder holster. "damn, I feel like fucking James Bond over here."

The men in the office laughed as Bond jokes continued to circulate the office. Fran enjoyed the playful nature of the team. The mood soon shifted; it was time to get to work. Benedetto was scheduled to arrive in about twenty-four hours. Bugs and 'taps needed to be installed, tested and ready before his plane ever touched down on German soil.

"Hans, do you think it will be possible to look over your surveillance equipment before heading back over to the hotel?"

"You didn't bring any equipment with you, detective?"

"No, I thought your agency would have all the necessary devices and equipment." Fran was suddenly concerned. "You do have bugs and 'taps, right?"

"Of course we do Fran," Hans reassured. "I will have our technician bring them in."

Minutes later, the technician was at Hans' office door pushing a cart loaded with several old dusty boxes of equipment. Fran could see water stains, grease and German words on the cardboard. Fran quickly opened the first box. His stomach instantly sank. The legends of state-of-the-art German surveillance technique and equipment from the WWII era were instantly reduced to several dirty old boxes of leftover relics from the war.

What the hell was he going to do with this shit? This shit needs to be retired to a museum. "This is not going to work, Hans." Fran explained, trying to keep calm. "I need to speak with the Director again, immediately."

Within minutes, the three began brainstorming. After twenty minutes of discussion and a phone call, the two detectives were on their way to a parking garage a few blocks from the hotel. Waiting in the garage for the two men was an American CIA operative, ready and willing to help.

"I will have the technician meet you with the equipment in Benedetto's room in an hour." The operative said as he shook the two detective's hands and departed.

"Thank you. We appreciate all your help!"

Thirty minutes later, the team was bustling all over the German hotel. Especially the fourth floor. The crew set up the surveillance room. In Benedetto's room, two doors down, Fran and Hans waited.

Upon his arrival, Fran was relieved that the CIA agent insisted on including the technician with the borrowed equipment. This gear wasn't WWII era, but was most certainly outdated. Fran could not get over the size of the listening unit. It wasn't ideal, but it was all they had. They would have to make it work.

After a quick survey of the room and a bit of discussion, the two Americans felt it best to attach the device to the massage unit under the bed. Knowing Benedetto as well as he did, Fran was confident that their Mafia man didn't partake in bed massages while conducting his business. The 'tap for Benedetto's room was installed through the hotel's phone switchboard in a similar manner as it was back at Frankie's. After a few tests of the equipment, the technician, Fran and the team were all satisfied with their setup. Now there was nothing they could do but wait until their Mafiosi arrived.

Hans was kind enough to give him a short tour of Munich before the sun went down. The two detectives then met up with other members of the team for dinner and beer. He'd been running full tilt for over eighteen months. It felt good to finally have a moment to blow off a little steam.

Noon the following day, Benedetto touched down from his Trans-Atlantic flight. Detective Clavering spotted him immediately from a distance. He had shared pictures of the man with the entire team the day before. Hans radioed the description of his clothing to the rest of the team. A member of the detail would watch or listen to his every move during his entire stay in Munich. Final checks were quickly done on all the surveillance equipment before Benedetto arrived at the hotel. Inside the command post, German detectives were positioned by an assortment of recording and listening machines with attached headphones. Fran and Hans snuck into the surveillance room just as Benedetto entered the hotel elevator.

Benedetto anxiously got settled in. He unpacked his clothes and toiletries and stowed his luggage away. He then ordered a late lunch from room service. The thickset New Yorker immediately called several local numbers without success.

"Damn it!" He said loudly to himself, as he slammed the handset on the receiver following his final attempt.

As the Sunday afternoon faded into early evening. Benedetto was cranky and frustrated. He knew trying to reach business numbers at this point would be a waste of time until the morning.

Nothing could be done until he made contact. He clicked on the television, turning the dial repeatedly in an effort to find an English speaking station. He finally settled on a German news broadcast, completely clueless to what the anchor was saying. Moments later, he drifted off to sleep as the tv droned on in the background.

Two rooms away, Benedetto's snoring could be heard loud and clear through the bug placed in the room. One of the team members continued to listen through headphones while the rest of the detectives talked. Fran was pleasantly surprised to learn that the team was already familiar with the men Benedetto was trying to reach. Gunther Straussen ran a Munich branch of a Swiss corporation with questionable practices. The other contact, Hugo Franz, was picked up for questioning by the Munich Police Department in September of last year in connection to a Belgium case involving the theft of $100,000 worth of US Treasury Bonds. Many law enforcement agencies throughout Europe worked together to keep a close eye on Franz, hoping that he would lead them to the bigger organization responsible for the flood of stolen stocks and bonds throughout the continent. The only effort made to slow him down was to pull his passport. Unfortunately, yet not really too surprising, it didn't even phase him or their operations.

The next morning, the mafiosi woke up early, showered and shaved, and headed out to a local cafe for some breakfast and coffee. Benedetto returned and began calling at the top of every hour, trying to reach Straussen. By mid-morning he finally reached Straussen's secretary, and Straussen himself around 3:30 PM. The conversation was difficult to understand, given the language barrier between the two men. Straussen eventually realized that Benedetto was looking for him and Franz, and a tone of concern suddenly came over the German. In the best English he could muster. He'd tried to explain that he'd make contact with Benedetto as soon as he got a hold of the other man.

"Like hell you will," thought the Mobster out loud as the call was completed. An hour later, Benedetto couldn't contain himself any longer. Hans and Fran trailed Benedetto's cab through the dark streets of Munich to a tall downtown office building. Benedetto instructed the cab driver to wait as he entered the building. Hans and Fran followed him into the building. Fran took the stairs while Hans watched each floor light up above the elevator doors until they stopped.

"He's on the fifth floor, Fran. Straussen's office is 554." Hans relayed over the radio. "I'm on it, Hans!" As Fran quickened his steps.

Fran quietly stepped out of the stairwell and hid. He watched as Benedetto burst into the office suite at the end of the long hallway. The woman seated behind the desk screamed. The mobster violently pushed his way past the protesting secretary and kicked open Straussen's office door.

"*Was zur Hölle geht hier vor?*" A startled Straussen shouted.

"You and that fucking shit, Franz have me chasing you guys all around this Goddamn city for the last couple days."

"*Was?* Vo are vu, I know vu not, nor vat vu sbeak of," replied the man in his best broken English.

Fran inched closer, hiding behind a tall plant in the hall. He watched through the gaping doors as Benedetto walked behind the desk, grasped the man by the collar, and pulled him close to his face. "You better fuckin' know who I am, Straussen!"

Straussen's eyes suddenly went wide with fear as Benedetto tightened his grip.

"I've come all the way from New York to collect the money, $350,000! Pay up Straussen!"

"I-I-I know vu not, how I bay zomeone I know not?" Straussen stammered, as Benedetto loosened his grip slightly.

Benedetto shoved the man back into his office chair and continued to yell. "You call Franz, and you call Gordo Davies over in Philly. Tell them Luca Benedetto paid you a visit. You understand?"

Straussen nodded fearfully.

"Davies will tell you who I am, and why I'm here. Understand?"

"I call D-D-daffies and Franz, right avay."

"Good, then you pay up the money. You and Franz bring that money to my hotel room tomorrow morning. You understand Straussen?"

Again, Straussen nodded, shaking with fear. Benedetto shot him a menacing look, kicked over a large chair, and fumed out of the room past the hidden American detective, and out of the building into his waiting taxi. Back at the hotel, he headed straight for the bar. After several drinks and some dinner, he returned to his room. He made one more unsuccessful attempt to reach Franz's, then retired to bed.

The next morning, Benedetto woke with a splitting headache. Lingering jetlag in combination with his anger, and the booze from the night before had him moving painfully slow. He took a couple of aspirin, hoping for some relief. Thirty minutes later, he called down to room service for some breakfast.

Benedetto's phone rang at 11 am. The caller had a slight German accent. "Benedetto, it's Franz."

"Franz! Where the fuck you hiding? You piece of shit! I've been trying to find you since I got into town."

"Nobody told me you were coming."

"Well, I'm here now, and we have to meet. Today!"

"I agree."

"I'm over the bullshit, you hear? You get Straussen and get your asses over here. No more stalling. No more fuckin' around."

"Alright, alright, just calm down. I'll pick him up and we'll be there in an hour and a half."

Benedetto looked at the clock. "Alright, 12:30 on the nose, right?"

"Maybe closer to 12:45."

"I'm waiting Franz! No more jerking me around, you hear?"

As soon as Benedetto hung up the phone, two rooms away, Fran, Hans and the team sprang into action. Hans called police headquarters, informing the rest of the detail that it was time to assemble to their assigned posts. The technician approached Detective Clavering with a clear look of concern on his face.

"Fran, I need to get into that room."

"Now?! Why?!"

"Yes now! I need to change out the batteries in the bug. The batteries are dying, the sound is already starting to fade."

"Shit, shit, shit." Fran muttered aloud.

"If I don't get in there soon, shit nothing is about all you are going to get from the meeting between those three bastards."

"Damn it, I know," he sighed as he tried to think of a way to get Benedetto to leave his room.

He knew they couldn't use anything crazy like a fire alarm. Something like that could spook them into moving their meeting to another location. Fran paced the room, looking over at the clock as it edged closer and closer to the 12:30 meeting time.

At 12:05, Benedetto called down to the hotel front desk. The detective monitoring the tapped phone line motioned to Fran to grab some headphones.

"This is Mr. Benedetto. I'm expecting a visit from Mr. Straussen and Mr. Franz soon. I am heading down to the hotel bar. Will you please page me when my guests arrive?"

"Zertainly, sir." The front desk clerk's polite replied.

One of the detective detail dressed in overalls as a hotel maintenance worker, was stationed in the hallway, "working on a light fixture." As soon as the doors closed and the elevator car started to move, he alerted the command team. The technician gathered his equipment and tools then headed down the hall to Benedetto's room, as Fran looked on. The hotel housekeeper, working in the room across the hall, noticed Benedetto leave. She grabbed her key to clean his room quickly while he was out.

The technician began to panic as he watched the housekeeper and slowed his gait. Not sure of what to do, he looked back at Fran, worried.

"Just keep going." Fran whispered.

The technician nodded and slowed his pace even more. The sound of shattering glass echoed from the surveillance room and into the hall, startling both the technician and housekeeper. Fran came running out of the room, looking in both directions down the hall.

"Excuse me, miss, we have an emergency in here! Could you please come help?" Fran explained excitedly. The housekeeper stared at him blankly. It was clear she didn't understand English.

"*Entschuldigung, wir haben hier einen Notfall. Könnten Sie bitte Hilfe kommen?*" Hans interjected. As the woman continued to stare at them both, still confused.

Another detective poked his head out. "*Mi scusi, abbiamo un'emergenza qui. Potresti venire, per favore, aiuto?*"

"*Certo signore.*" The housekeeper smiled and offered her Italian response, while nodding at the officer.

The technician continued down the hall. As soon as she stepped into the surveillance room, he stepped into Benedetto's room, closing the door behind him.

"I was trying to put fresh water in these flowers when the vase slipped and crashed to the floor." The Italian speaking man translated Fran's information to the woman.

"*Fammi prendere la mia padella per la polvere, la scopa e alcuni asciugamani, signore.*" She replied and left the room.

"She's going to get her dustpan, broom, and some towels."

She cleaned up the mess while the Technician completed the battery change and tested the surveillance device. He let the man listening to the bug know he was finished with his task. The listener gestured to Fran that the work was done. The housekeeper finished cleaning the mess.

"*Signore, ho bisogno di correre di sotto per un momento.*" She said to Fran, as his puzzled gaze oscillated between the two Italian speakers.

"She needs to run downstairs for a moment." The detective relayed. He then turned to the housekeeper. "*Grazie signorina, lo apprezzo molto.*"

As soon as the elevator closed, Fran ran to Benedetto's room to get the technician.

Five minutes later, there was a knock on the surveillance room door. Everyone tensed up for a moment. It was the housekeeper with a new vase of fresh flowers for the room. Fran tried his best to thank her. She smiled awkwardly at him, unsure of what he was saying, then left and went back to clean Benedetto's room.

Within minutes, there was a squelch over the radio. An agent positioned downstairs alerted the team that the two Germans had arrived and were in the building. Benedetto greeted them and escorted them to his table in the hotel bar.

Straussen ordered from the bartender as he passed. *"Asbach und Cola, auf eis bitte."* Franz ordered the same for himself and Benedetto. Benedetto's unrefined palate was unfamiliar with the drink.

"What is it?"

"It's kind of like cognac and cola," Franz explained. "But better."

"Better?"

"Of course it's better," He explained with great pride. "Us Germans do a much better job than those French *scheiß kopf.*"

The men, mostly the Germans, engaged in pleasant, casual conversation, and two more rounds before heading upstairs to more private quarters. They rearranged the table and chairs for their meeting and settled in.

"Would either of you like anything to eat or more to drink, before we get started?" Offered a surprisingly polite Benedetto.

"More *Asbach und Cola* vould pe vonterful Misder Penetetto," chimed Straussen. Benedetto called down the order. Then took his seat across from the other two men.

"Alright..." Benedetto began.

"Before we start Luca," Franz promptly interrupted. "Gunther and I need to know what has become of our friends from Los Angeles, his *Kind*, and Mr. Davies."

Benedetto shifted in his chair, then let out a deep drawn-out sigh, "Johnny got thrown in jail for some gambling scam he was running out in L.A. Then his kid got really, really sick. They let Johnny out for a few days so he could go to Philly to see him.

Concerned, "He petder now?" Asked Straussen.

"Yeah, yeah. Much better. Anyways, While Johnny was out in Philly, there was a little meeting between him, Gordo and myself, trying to figure out why we hadn't seen any of the money from you guys yet. So the guy in Philly tells Johnny that it's ok to have Gordo come over and collect the $350 grand that Johnny had comin'."

Franz, confused. "But where do you come into the picture, Luca?"

"Listen you two, that's not important right now," raising his voice. "What's important right now is that you guys need to pay up what you owe Johnny and the rest. Now!"

"Ok, ok, ok, but what about Mr. Davies? What happened to him?"

"Um, well Gordo ran into a little bad luck about two months ago when the Feds caught him with several packages of hot securities."

"Hot Zecuridies? I don't Hundersdand," queried Straussen. "Stolen...stolen securities."

"Oh schtolen, I zee. Oh, zat's not kood nevs."

Benedetto was getting tired of the interruptions and questions. "Anyways, Johnny had to come to Philly again, from California to bail his ass out of the slammer... Now can we just get on with this please?!"

"Well, we did have that deal with Johnny, then his *Kind*. Next thing we know, Davies is over here trying to get the California guy's money."

"That's right." Benedetto confirmed.

"And while Davies is here, the guy from Philly, not Johnny's *Kind*, the other one, calls us and says we have no business with Davies. He was no longer part of dis deal."

"He told you what?!?! He was the one who ok'd the release of the money to Davies during that meeting! Don't bullshit me Franz."

"No, no, no I heard it with mine own ears Luca. Davies wasn't part of dis deal no more. Davies didn't believe it either until I gave him the phone so he could hear it for himself. By then he was stuck here with no money to get back home."

"That's right, then you spotted him a plane ticket and some cash so he could get home."

"Right, and he told us he'd come back for the money after he cleared up the problem, but we never heard from him. He never came back."

"You dumb fuck! He couldn't come back or call, he was in jail."

"He sdill in chail now Luca?" Questioned Straussen.

"No, he's out now, but they pulled his passport because now he's a flight risk. Anyways, while Johnny was out here we had that big meeting about getting this shit all squared up."

"I'z don't zink vu know all of vat's hinfolffed in zis Luca."

Benedetto turned to Straussen. "Like hell I don't! We were supposed to see the money mid October...but we saw nothing. End of October...nothing. November...still nothing. Davies had to harass you chumps over thirty times, and still we saw no money.

"That's because none of the Americans told us to pay him."

"Bullshit! So then after all that, Gordo has to get me involved, to see what the fuckin' hold up is. He told me he was talkin' to you Straussen, sayin' maybe your English is not so good, or somethin'. So then I gotta drag my ass over here to make you two shits make good on your deal."

A knock on the door startled the three men. Benedetto went to the door and opened it a crack to see a waiter carrying a tray with their order. Benedetto opened the door and gestured.

"Please put that on the table." He directed. "*danke.*"

"*Bitte schön,*" responded the waiter as he slightly tipped his cap and bowed slightly to the men and left the room.

The two Germans refill their glasses with fresh ice, and more drinks. The two guests would refill their glasses repeatedly as the meeting progressed into the afternoon. As the men settled back into their chairs, the two Germans could feel the warmth from the first few rounds hit them.

"I schtill don't zink zat vu know all ze deal from zee sdart Luca."

"Oh enough already Straussen, I've been in it from day one."

"Well, I think you are full of shit Luca!" Replied an embolden Franz.

Benedetto was not used to being talked to in such a manner, and was now furious. He was used to grown men pissing themselves, in fear, whenever he came calling to collect a debt.

"Now that I think about it," Franz continued. "If anything, they owe us money."

"Oh for fuck's sake Franz, what the hell are you talking about?"

"There was that big meeting in London."

"The one with Johnny, Duncan... and the Rest?"

"Yeah, yeah, that's the one. That was my first meeting with Mr. Davies. There were a lot of people there, lots of Americans."

Benedetto let out another huge sigh, frustrated. "Um...yeah."

"That's when we were all introduced to Johnny's friend...doctor, what was his name?" Franz looked over at Straussen. Both men were completely drunk by now.

"Docfador Karl Schvarz."

"That's right, Dr Schwartz." Franz continued as he looked back to Benedetto. "Well, it seemed that Johnny and the Doctor had a bit of a problem, you see."

"What the hell are you talking about Franz?"

"They had some business to discuss, but Johnny didn't speak German, and Schvarz knew no English., so I helped them out. But Johnny thought I was full of shit."

"Johnny was right, you are full of shit."

Franz continued, ignoring Benedetto's insult. "When I told him the Doc needed some stuff for his friends in Rome, he couldn't believe what he was hearing. Johnny made me ask him over and over and over again. 'Are you sure?'"

Ninety minutes passed quickly. The intoxicated Germans and Benedetto wrapped up their meeting without any money exchanging hands. They agreed to meet at Straussen's office the following day to complete their business. The three men stood and shook hands, then made a final toast to their new deal to settle an old debt. They rose from their seats, slowly, stumbling a little after sitting and drinking for so long, then the three men left the room.

Two doors down the hall, no one made a sound. Hans continued to hold an earpiece to the side of his head while everyone else removed their headsets as quietly as possible. Benedetto escorted his guests past the room to the elevator. As soon as the doors closed and the elevator car began to move, a squelch of static was heard in Hans' ear, *"Alles klar, Hans."* came word from the undercover maintenance man still "working on a light fixture in the hall" alerting the surveillance crew and the detail positioned downstairs that their subjects were once again on the move.

Frantic chaos ensued instantly. Hans reached for the phone to call Munich Police Headquarters. A cacophony of rapid German could be heard all through the room, none of which registered with Fran, except for the occasional mention of Rome, American towns, familiar mobsters, Straussen and Franz. Most were completely stunned by the discussion they had just heard.

Fran gathered his notes and things, and shot out of the surveillance room door, heading straight for the stairs at the end of the hall. He ascended two floors, skipping every-other, as each step echoed through the stairwell. He entered his room, threw everything onto the bed, grabbed the phone and started to dial. Suddenly, he froze, his hand stopped midair. Then slowly reached to return the handset to its cradle.

He couldn't call New York, not yet. He sat on the side of the bed and rubbed his face with his open hands, and drew in a big, deep breath and exhaled completely. He needed to re-organize his thoughts and notes on everything he had just heard before he could even think of calling his boss. He was exhausted and famished, he ordered some food and coffee, then closed his eyes and sat quietly on the bed as he replayed the events of the last few hours in his head. "Had this all been a dream?" He asked himself. Never in a million years could he have imagined that Benedetto could be involved in something like this. Suddenly he was no longer worried about facing Christopherson when he got home. The amount of money and stocks moving and changing hands world-wide had to be astronomical. So big in fact, the New York detective was having a hard time wrapping his head around the possible numbers involved.

Fran washed his face and decided to call Peg. This wouldn't be the first time she would help him piece together details before presenting them to Bentley or Christopherson. She too couldn't believe her ears as Fran began his review. She helped him organize his notes and thoughts while he mindlessly consumed his meal. The two couldn't help but laugh when he read about the two Germans calling Benedetto an "errand boy," seeing the New York thug's face in that instant would have really been something. As far as Fran was concerned, he had just hit pay-dirt. He couldn't believe that his hunch had actually paid off!

Fran took a big bite from his sandwich, then he stopped mid-chew, suddenly, it all clicked. He knew exactly what was going on. He finished up his call with Peg and hung up the phone. He was finally ready to call New York.

"Inspector Bentley." The voice sounded from the other end. "Hey boss, it's Fran."

"Fran, it's good to hear your voice. How's it going over there?"

"Well sir, I hope you are sitting down, because you aren't going to believe what Benedetto and his friends are up to over here."

"Um, ok, I'm sitting. What ya got?"

Every ounce of calm collected composure Fran had mustered since the two Germans left was completely gone. The information came out of his mouth like a dam that had suddenly burst, flooding the ears of the inspector. A few breathless minutes from the detective, Bentley halted the deluge.

"Whoa, whoa, whoa Fran. Hang on a second. I need to get the Assistant D.A. Thomas is here to record all of this."

An hour later Bentley and Thomas sat dazed in a state of shock. They were having a hard time wrapping their individual or collective heads around what he had just told them. What their detective had reported went far beyond anything they had expected or experienced in their many years with the D.A.'s office. So many names and leads to investigate. The report from him was so detailed and complete, neither man had but a few questions for the detective.

"Damn Francis, that is quite the information haul!" Exclaimed the inspector. As Thomas sat quietly listening to the exchange. "Great job!"

"So now what are we going to do with all of this?"

"Walter and I will need to discuss this further after we all hang up. But I can tell you this, investigating all this is going to take far more resources than just our department can handle or afford as far as manpower and finances are concerned. We are probably going to dangle this big juicy carrot in front of the Strikeforce commander. There's no way they are not going to want to be involved in this going forward."

"Those stuck up bastards Inspector? Hell no!" Fran protested.

"I understand your apprehension Fran, but we need their manpower and money if we are going to do anything with this. If you want to see this investigation continue, much less, come to completion, we really don't have a choice. Besides this now reaches far beyond the borders of our city, county, state or even country."

"I guess you are right boss, but I don't like it...not one fucking bit."

After a few minutes, Fran started to feel a little relieved that resources and reinforcements were not too far in the future. "Well, I'll continue to keep an eye on these guys until Benedetto leaves town. I will call you if anything else develops over here."

"Excellent detective, you've already done some very nice work over there." Bentley congratulated. "Finish up over there, then get your ass back over here as soon as Benedetto leaves."

"Will do boss!"

"Oh and Fran..."

"Yeah?"

"Be careful over there."

"Honestly, you guys need to stop worrying so much about me. I'm in good hands over here, I swear."

The rest of the trip was relatively uneventful. There was nothing new to add to Fran's report. The NYPD detective spent the remainder of his time in Munich in a crash course on securities trading on the international black market. He had no idea that Munich was the epicenter of the illicit securities trade for all of Europe. His hosts were more than happy to share patterns and details about how some of the different groups operated in various parts of the continent. Fran thought he knew everything there was to know about Benedetto and his rackets. He had no idea that Benedetto was essentially the American counterpart to Europe's Franz and Straussen. The men were in fact middle-men who controlled the distribution of both real and counterfeit securities in their respective regions of the world. The profit potential from these operations was enormous.

On Fran's final day, he took Hans and the entire team out for dinner to thank them for all their hard work. He remained extremely impressed with their polished professionalism displayed throughout the week. He was, however, even more impressed with their capacity to drink and celebrate the conclusion of their work together. It was a fruitful trip, to say the least, but he was missing his wife, children and his normal routine. He was ready to go home.

Hans picked him up at the hotel. On the way to the airport, Fran returned the Walther PPK. "Thanks Hans for letting me borrow this."

"Of course Fran, you're welcome. I do hope we will get to work together again in the future at some point." Hans replied, as he shook the American's hand.

"Me too Hans, me too."

With his luggage checked, he soon boarded the plane that would take him home. There was too much going through his head for his aviophobia to even have a chance. While on the plane, he went over his notes several times. More questions came to his mind. He knew that the next several weeks would have him up to his eyeballs in work. His first order of business when he got home was the date night he promised Peg before he left.

CHAPTER 4

Giovanni Fedora, the global financier, did not always enjoy a life of luxury and fine Italian suits. Growing up poor in the Sicilian region of Mussolini's fascist Italy, there was nothing he loathed more than the scourge of socialism in his mother country. During his mid-teen years, he interned at his cousin's law practice. There, he displayed an innate aptitude for mathematics and economics while increasing his knowledge of civil law and trade contracts. These experiences would shatter all notions of political innocence for the young man. Bureaucratic corruption was rampant, and a formidable source of power. He watched and learned, as "important men" routinely would bribe local authorities who awarded the building permits and contracts. These "authorities" would then frequent the law practice looking for ways to keep their newfound gains away from the prying eyes of the public and local tax collectors.

At the tender age of twenty-two, he had already earned himself a law degree from a college in Messina. He then moved north and found work as a tax attorney and accountant for large regional corporations near Milan. The removal of Mussolini by the King of Italy signaled the end of fascism and a resurgence of the Mafia in Italy. His life and family flourished as he followed and often capitalized on the economic twists and turns of post WWII Europe.

By the time he turned 30, in 1950, he had earned his first million from various real estate acquisitions. His talents in accounting attracted the attention of the Lanscano crime family of Milan. He was invited to a Lanscano "family reunion," and offered a job as laundry man for their heroin trade. Tax evasion was the appeal, and the bonus was an upward trajectory in business for both the Lanscanos and Fedora. After only a year of working with the Lanscanos, he bought his first bank and began a close friendship with the archbishop of Milan, Cardinal Giancarlo Volonté. Fedora would soon acquire another bank, this time in Sicily. This move gave his Lanscano family new, unfettered access to banking services in their home region of Italy.

In 1963, his, by then good friend, Cardinal Volonté, was elected Pope Michael VI. Fedora became a frequent face in Vatican City. Developing close working relationships with a man named Rinaldo Manna, and two other top officials at the Vatican Bank, Fedora found that Manna was a great asset and resource. In addition to his work with the Vatican Bank, Manna soon sat on the Boards of Directors of over twenty different banks and companies. Neither the financier nor the Holy City concerned themselves with tales, whether true or not, of dirty Mob money being cleaned through the Vatican Bank by Fedora.

Of bigger concern to both parties was the resurgence of communism in Italy and the appointment of a new, incompetent Italian Minister of the Treasury. The banking system and treasury soon became inundated with loss and debt. It was a one-two punch in the destruction of the Lira and the Italian Economy. Fedora would use every fiber of his being in the fight against state economic collectivism.

The following year, he partnered with Nico Novelli to create Euro Money Exchange Brokers of Milan. By their second year in business, thousands of global banks would seek out their services, resulting in over $40 billion in exchanges that year. The cash flow was nice, but for Fedora, the real value of the Brokerage came from insight and perspective. For almost a decade, Fedora had his finger on the pulse of all global money movement. He watched in stealth as nations and industries meshed and clashed. He was positioned perfectly to cash in and become the world's largest loan shark. His empire was growing faster and larger than ever before, as he freely took advantage of the need and greed of all who sought his advice and services.

Fedora met his now good friend and frequent business partner, Marco Ansios, in January of '69. The balding, little perpetual nervous wreck of a man, with a dark mustache and brooding eyes, was born and raised in the same little southern Italian town as Fedora. Ansios studied at a university, then fought for Mussolini against the Russians in WWII. In 1947, he followed in his father's footsteps and began work at Banco Generali, a little priest's bank in Milan. It is there that he, too, met Cardinal Giancarlo Volonté.

By the time Ansios and Fedora met, Ansios had worked his way up to a centralized, yet restricted position in Banco Generali's international division. Fedora found in Ansios a submissive man, with an insatiable appetite for wealth and power, not for his bank, but for himself. Fedora saw many benefits of befriending such a man in an increasing position of power at Banco Generali.

Fedora was introduced to Bishop Jonas Krivis, a few months after he met Ansios. Fedora immediately saw Krivis' absolute incompetence in economic and financial matters, and an arrogant idiot in all others. In front of Pope Michael VI and the pope's personal secretary, Krivis was a pious proletarian priest. To everyone else, he was the most graceless, vain climber of social ladders anyone had ever seen. Krivis boasted to Fedora that he would immediately fire Manna and other top Vatican banking officials who also happened to be Fedora's close friends, if he were ever in a position to do so. Fedora laughed in his face, explaining to the fool that Manna was the most worthy manager the IOR ever had. Manna was a man who commanded respect throughout financial sectors globally. Krivis could not handle being second rate to anyone and blew off the sound opinions of Fedora. Fedora knew the best way to play Krivis and take full advantage of his position, greed and vanity for his own gain.

Krivis met Ansios in 1971, a couple months prior to Pope Michael VI appointing him president of the Vatican Bank. Suddenly, Krivis directed all the financial affairs of the Vatican and was answerable only to the pope. He also knew absolutely nothing about banking and soon became a student of Fedora and Ansios' expertise.

With his new position, he now radiated even more self-importance than ever before. His posh new office was decorated with expensive art, furnishings, and beautiful, playful, young girls he called secretaries who acted like his secret mistresses. Krivis was drunk on the attention the girls gave him. Boasting loudly of being granted full powers within the Vatican Bank upon his request of the Holy Father. Everyone around him knew he was full of shit.

By the early '70s, the Italian economy was a mess with sky high unemployment and inflation. Fedora, Ansios and Krivis didn't care. Fedora and Krivis profited greatly from the money they were illegally moving out of the country. Ansios, with the help of Fedora, grew cocky with their control of the Milan stock exchange. Ansios' relationship with the Vatican Bank allowed him to repeatedly violate numerous Italian banking laws in his quest to expand his own personal empire and power. The Vatican Banks' coffers benefited greatly from the upward trajectory of Ansios as well.

In 1972, Marlon Brando and Al Pacino brought a nicely packaged Hollywood version of Mafia myth, legend and power struggle to many around the world. For many, it was their first "real" glimpse into how money and power moves of crime families operated in and around certain regions of the world. The corporate media began publishing fact punctuated by fictional pieces in an effort to capitalize on the public's growing curiosity. Giovanni Fedora initially found *The Godfather,* and the public's response to "Mafia Mania" amusing. However, he quickly lost interest once those tales started including his own personal ties to the powerful Lanscano crime family in New York and Italy.

Fedora always knew that Marco Ansios had a mind for high stakes finance operations. However, he lacked backbone and courage. Being a global power-financier, Fedora's skin was thickened by his twenty-six year rags to riches journey in Milan. Fedora rolled with the punches while Ansios ran and hid, fearful of anyone finding out what he was doing.

When the Bank of Italy filed two complaints of wrongdoing against Fedora, the vague and unsubstantiated complaints did not worry Fedora. Ansios' Banco Generali of Milan heard the complaints and other warnings from Rome. They would have no further business dealings with Fedora's banks or businesses. Ansios immediately became even more of an anxious, nervous wreck than ever before.

Fedora found great entertainment hazing, embarrassing and playing on Ansios' paranoia and fears. Public meetings between himself and Fedora before were always done at popular expensive restaurants. Those days were now over. The two men suddenly resorted to conducting their business in modest little hole-in-the-wall eateries, away from the prying or curious eyes of anyone who might recognize either of them. Ansios now lived in absolute fear that his numerous partnerships with Fedora would be exposed and sink his entire career.

Ansios wasn't the only one in Italy suddenly showing the global financier the cold shoulder. The Italian political landscape had rapidly changed, too. Left leaning splinter organizations claimed responsibility for many deadly bombings throughout Italy. The nightmare hit close to the bone when one of his colleagues was murdered in an explosion near Milan. As bombings and grenade attacks became a more frequent occurrence, it was no longer safe for him and his family to remain in Milan.

In a lavish top-floor apartment on *Rue de la Bourse* in Geneva, Switzerland, Fedora and his wife enjoyed their evening. The lower portion of the building housed the corporate headquarters of his Swiss Finance Bank. The streets around their neighborhood were empty as heavy rains of a spring storm pounded against the external walls and windows of the building. Fedora and his wife instinctively jumped when a bright flash of lightning and an almost immediate clap of thunder shook the entire building, knocking out their power.

"That was a close one," he commented, trying his best to calm and comfort his terrified wife. The raging storm made it an impossible task. With no power, they decided to retire for the evening, hoping the angry weather would soon move past them.

Around eleven that night, Fedora heard the rattling of their front door, and dismissed it to the raging storm outside. Moments later they were both startled by the heavy pounding of fists on their door. "Who on earth could be out in this storm at this hour?" Questioned his wife. As he made his way to the foyer, a flash of lightning highlighted the silhouette of a young woman through the frosted glass windows of the door.

The flame of a lit candle highlighted the facial features of the daughter of Fedora's longtime close friend. "Jelena? What on earth are you doing here? Please, please come in, child. What on earth are you doing running around alone out of that storm, my dear?"

His wife scrambled to grab some towels and a blanket for the soaking wet twenty-two-year-old. "*Grazie la signora Fedora.*"

"Uncle," she explained, trying to catch her breath. "Come, you and your family. We must go elsewhere!"

"But why? It's too dangerous to be out in this storm."

"No, we must leave now! Please, you must listen to me. It is urgent that we all get out of here." She pleaded, then began to cry uncontrollably.

Fedora and his wife dressed, then accompanied her to her hotel on the other side of the Rhône.

Once she knew her loved ones were no longer in danger, Jelena finally calmed herself. She told Fedora that she was being paid to work closely with the general secretary of a powerful Italian communist group. She caught wind that some men were dispatched to come kill Fedora and his family at midnight. There were no blood relations between the girl and Fedora, but he still held great fondness for the young lady, as he did her entire family. While they never politically saw eye to eye, he knew that she would never lie to him and his wife.

Fedora returned to his home the next morning to find the locks of his door expertly picked, and left ajar. He was careful not to touch anything as he made his way through the ransacked apartment. Most disturbing of all was the discovery of two rounds each from a .38 mm handgun discharged into his and his wife's pillows. It was no longer safe for him and his family to remain in Europe.

CHAPTER 5

While Fran was wrapping up his Munich trip, Bentley and Assistant D.A. Walter Thomas knew that the case which had kept the "Rackets" team busy for over a year had instantly and dramatically changed. The role of Christopherson's department would continue with their work, but with multiple cities, states and countries involved, the case was now beyond the New York D.A.'s jurisdiction. It was time to get the Feds involved.

Bentley and Thomas met with the chief of the Federal Strikeforce Command against Organized Crime in Manhattan, Joel Wallace and his assistant Nathan Bayer. The four men listened intently as Detective Clavering's voice sounded from the speakers of a tape recorder. Halfway through the report, Chief Wallace reached over and stopped the tape, and turned to the inspector and assistant D.A.

"Alright Bentley, Thomas, you tell Christopherson that we'll bite on this one." The chief confirmed as he looked at each of them. Then he turned to his assistant. "Bayer, you are now assigned to work with these two to coordinate this investigation."

"Got it, chief," Bayer responded as he finished jotting down something in his notes. "Gentlemen," the chief turned again to

Christopherson's men again. "We are here to support you in every way possible. Whatever it is that you fellas need? Funds, vehicles, men, you name it, we'll supply it. From this moment forward, this is a combined agency investigation."

Bentley and Thomas sat speechless as they absorbed everything the chief was dictating. They had been rejected help so many times in the past by the Department of Justice's Strikeforce. They had prepared themselves for massive resistance. They never dreamed that they'd be now working with an agency that outranked even the FBI.

"Thank you, chief." Walter responded after what seemed like an eternity.

"Yes, thank you, chief. We will need to have a pre-investigation strategy meeting to evaluate exactly what resources we are going to need." Bentley interjected.

"Gentlemen, I have another meeting to get to," the chief rose to leave the room and shook Bentley and Thomas' hands. "I trust that you three will work out the details. Please keep me posted of your needs and progress going forward."

"Absolutely sir," Thomas replied gratefully, as he escorted their guest out of the room.

Bayer was considerably younger than either of Christopherson's men. Both men felt his youth, and by default, lack of experience may not be an asset at the moment, or in this case. The way the feds conducted investigations was very different from their standard operating procedures in "Rackets." This case was only new to Bayer, not to Bentley and his team. Bayer was tightly poised and wanted to waste no time getting this investigation started.

"Can we schedule that strategy meeting for sometime tomorrow, Inspector Bentley?"

"Bayer, I'd like to get the next phase of this investigation started as quickly as possible, too. However, I feel strongly that we must wait until Detective Clavering returns from Munich for that meeting."

"When will that be, Inspector?"

"Not for another three days."

"You are telling me that you are going to delay this strategy meeting because of a detective, Inspector?" Bayer responded, frustrated. "From what I heard on the tape, I feel we have enough to get started."

Bentley did not care for Bayer's condescending tone in reference to his detective. "That's exactly what I'm saying." Bentley responded sternly. "We wouldn't even be here without all the many hours of work Detective Clavering has already put in on this case. Three more days will not make a difference at this point, so early in this investigation."

"But inspector..."

Bentley cut him off. "I want to make one thing very clear to you, Mr. Bayer. While on paper, you and I are in charge of this investigation, Detective Clavering will be the real man in charge as far as this department is concerned. Do I make myself clear?"

"Yes inspector," Bayer reluctantly conceded. "I don't agree with you, but I respect your decision."

Three days later, Fran touched down at JFK airport. He was already anticipating the busy months ahead. For the foreseeable future, he would be absolutely buried in his work. He had to take Peg out on that date now. He had no other option. Fran instructed Peg to leave the children with her sister. He missed his children dearly, but he wanted to take his bride out on the town as soon as he got home.

He laid his jacket over his arm and grabbed his briefcase from the overhead compartment and exited the plane. Outside the boarding gate, his eyes immediately locked on a familiar pair of gorgeous brown eyes. His steps quickened as he grew nearer. When he got to her, he tossed his belongings to the ground and lifted his bride off the ground with his embrace. Peg could not have been happier, as she felt his strong arms wrap around her. It had been a very long ten days. Fran kissed her tenderly, then gracefully returned her feet to the ground.

"How was your flight, love?" She whispered in his ear with her eyes still closed, completely taking in the moment.

"Believe it or not, wonderful."

"Wonderful? But you hate flying." She slightly pushed him away, surprised. "Wait, how many cocktails did that stewardess bring you?"

"None, love," he responded as she looked at him in disbelief. "I know, it sounds crazy, but with everything running through my head, I completely forget about my fear of flying."

She contemplated his words for a second. "I guess it doesn't matter. I'm just so glad you're home. I missed you so much."

"I missed you too, honey. How did the kids handle my being gone?"

"For the most part, no issues, really. Except at bedtime. The first couple of nights they missed their good night stories and kisses from their daddy."

"Mmmm, I missed those, too."

Peg smiled as she gave him one more kiss, then turned to gather up his coat. Fran picked up his briefcase and placed his arm around her as they walked together to the baggage claim area.

"I'm famished love, let's grab some dinner before we head back to the house."

"That sounds wonderful," she gushed excitedly.

He grabbed his luggage off the conveyor and followed Peg toward the car. As they were making their way towards the exits, there was a firm tap on Fran's shoulder. The detective whipped around to see his partner from "Rackets" standing there. Fran was so smitten and drunk in love, he didn't even notice the man approach.

"Hey there, my man! How the hell are you?" Stretching out his hand.

"No complaints," he responded as he shook Fran's hand. He then smiled and tipped his hat slightly towards Peg. "Mrs. Clavering, how are you?"

"I'm well, Detective, thank you." She responded politely.

Fran turned to Peg, "You remember my partner from rackets, right?"

"Of course I do. He talks about you all the time, '' she smiled, reaching out to shake the man's hand.

"Nothing too bad, I hope."

"Of course not, Detective."

"So, what brings you to JFK at this hour?"

"Well Fran, actually, you."

"Me? I don't understand."

"Yes, I was told by Bentley and Thomas to come pick you up and bring you down to the station."

"Now?! What the hell for?!?!" Responded an annoyed and confused Francis Clavering. "I just landed. Can't a man spend a minute with his wife after being gone on work shit for ten days?"

"Look, Fran, I hate this as much as you do. Believe me, I tried to talk them out of it, but they insisted that it was important and couldn't wait until the morning."

"Alright, alright," Fran replied, unable to hide his disappointment. "Just let me put my luggage in my wife's car. Where are you parked?"

"Over near the taxi stand."

"Fine, I'll meet you over there."

Fran escorted his wife to her car and placed his luggage in the trunk. He then walked over and opened the driver side door for his bride. Looking at Peg, he sighed loudly. "I am so sorry, love." He whispered in her ear as he pulled her in close once again.

"It's alright, love, I understand."

"No, no, it's not alright. You deserve a better husband than me."

"No,... I deserve YOU."

Fran kissed her again. "Rain-check on dinner?"

"Of course."

"I love you," he said as he kissed her one more time, helped her into her seat, and pushed the driver-side door closed. He grabbed his briefcase, flung his jacket over his shoulder, then headed off to find his partner.

He caught sight of his partner, leaning on the fender of the black unmarked police car. "So, what gives?" Fran questioned, with an air of extreme annoyance.

"Well, the whole department has been on pins and needles since you reported from Munich."

"Really? I thought Bentley and Thomas were going to get the ball rolling before I got back."

"They did, as much as they could, anyway."

"I find that hard to believe if they are sending you here to pick my ass up as soon as I've touched down."

"Well, everything's on hold, waiting for you."

"Me? I don't get it."

"You'll see."

When Fran walked into the precinct, there was a low audible hum, then applause as Fran's partner directed him toward a conference room. Seated at the table was Bentley, Thomas, several men with FBI badges on, and a man he had never seen before.

"Fran, this is Nathan Bayer, Nathan Bayer, this is Detective Francis Clavering." Bentley introduced.

Bayer stood and the two men shook hands, then both men were seated across from each other.

Bentley explained, "Bayer has been appointed by Strikeforce Chief Wallace to assist us in coordinating this investigation moving forward."

"I see," Fran nodded. Those in the room who knew him could hear the annoyance in his tone.

Bayer finally spoke up. "Detective, the Strikeforce has been investigating large-scale operations involving stolen and counterfeit securities for many months now."

"That's great Bayer." Chimed Fran sarcastically.

"Well it was," Bayer continued. "Up until recently. Our investigations have completely stalled out. The chief and I feel that the information and tapes you've brought back from Munich will get this investigation back on track once again."

"It'd be great to hear what you already have on this case, so we don't have to start everything back at square one or waste time duplicating our efforts."

"Well, the first thing that caught our attention from your report was the mention of Soda King Bottling Company from Los Angeles."

Fran nodded, "Ok."

"You must all understand," Bayer turned to address everyone in the room. "The Strikeforce and other federal agencies have been tasked by a congressional subcommittee to put an end to all of these operations."

"Really?" Fran interjected, "And do we have any idea just how big of an operation we are dealing with here, Bayer?"

"Our best estimates at this point is somewhere around $50 billion worth of stolen and counterfeit securities are currently circulating on the black market, detective."

Fran took a deep breath and exhaled audibly, as his eyes opened wide in shock. "No kidding? And obviously, these securities aren't circulating just within United States borders."

"After your trip to Munich detective, I think you already know the answer to that," Bayer responded in a snarky tone.

The three men from Christopherson's office shot a quick glance at each other, then to Fran, put off by Bayer's tone.

"Failure to shut all this down is putting global markets, including the US Economy at risk of collapse."

"Alright Bayer," replied Fran, once again annoyed. "What else do you got related to this?"

"We don't think Soda King is the only Blue-chip company being victimized in all this."

"Well, no shit," responded the detective in his own snarky response. "If we are talking $50 billion worth of stuff floating around every damn where."

Bayer continued, dismissing Fran's annoyed tone. "Since the beginning of this year, our agency and the FBI have noticed an uptick in the movement of these stolen and counterfeit stocks. Major corporations are either already victims or are being targeted in these crimes."

"So where are all these securities coming from?"

"Our best guess is the counterfeit's sources may be closely related to the counterfeit currency suppliers."

"That would make sense. And the stolen documents?"

"They just disappear."

"They just disappear? Com' on Bayer, you gotta do better than that."

"No seriously, Detective, when corporations or brokerage houses ship out those packages of parchment, they often disappear before they reach their destinations."

"Are these documents being shipped via US Mail? Courier? Or what?"

"Multiple modes of shipment, and every effort we've tried to halt the thefts has completely failed."

Fran looked at Bayer, puzzled. "And where does the Vatican come in on all of this?"

"To be honest, Detective, your tapes are the first I've ever heard of their involvement in any of this."

"Oh, really?!" Fran blinked in disbelief. "Someone in the Vatican orders some $990 million worth of counterfeit American stocks, and this is the first that you've ever heard of their involvement?!"

Bayer completely ignored the detective's comment. "We need to begin our strategy now, on how we move this thing forward..."

Fran was now pissed. "Let me stop you right there, Bayer."

"Yes Detective?"

Fran stood up, picked up his briefcase and jacket. "I'm going home." The focus of everyone in the room was now on the detective. The slightest of grins could be seen on both the faces of Bentley and Thomas.

"But detective," Bayer stood up and looked around the room, hopeful for some support, then looked back at Fran. "You can't go home now. There's a lot of work to be done."

"Listen Bayer, I've just worked my balls off for the last ten days and the weeks and months leading up to that trip. There is nothing in this case that can't wait until tomorrow morning. I'm going home to spend some well deserved time with my wife and family."

"But Fran..."

"That's "Detective" to you." Fran shot daggers from his eyes as he looked at Bayer. He then turned to the rest of those assembled in the room, as he turned to leave the room. "I'm going home. We'll pick all of this up tomorrow morning. Get some rest gentlemen, the real work begins tomorrow morning at 9 am. Until then, good night."

Bayer just stood in stunned disbelief, while a soft cacophony of conversations and moving chairs came over the room. Everyone in the room completely ignored him as they calmly gathered their materials and exited the conference room. Fran returned to his office to call Peg.

"That was quick," she responded excitedly. "What happened?"

"I'll explain on our way to dinner."

"Our date is still on?!?!"

"Yes ma'am! You get yourself ready. I'll have one of the guys give me a lift to the house."

"Wonderful, love! I'll start getting ready now!"

"See you shortly."

Fran hung up the phone, and he headed straight for Bentley's office. Bentley, seated behind his desk, was talking to assistant D.A. Thomas. Fran didn't even knock, he just walked right in, closed the door and sat down.

"What the hell was all that?" Fran interjected, furious. "Now Fran, just calm down." The inspector pleaded.

"Look boss, you know I'm not one to complain about my workload. I've given this damn department 110% since day one."

"Everyone in this department knows that, Fran."

"Well, it's obvious that Bayer doesn't. Is it too much to ask for three seconds to spend with my family after everything I've given this department and investigation?"

"No, not at all. Believe me, Fran, both Thomas and I were against tonight's meeting from the start."

"So then why is this little shit Bayer running the show? Who the fuck is he, anyway?"

Bentley and Thomas explained the situation. The detective was still not happy.

"Listen boss, you know I'm not one to whine about anything, but do we have to have the Strikeforce working with us on this case? I know these clowns; they are just going to fuck up everything we've all been busting our balls on for the last year plus."

"Look Fran, they have offered us anything we need for this investigation. Funds, cars, manpower, the works."

"That sounds great," Fran smiled, still annoyed. "But why do you need me here?"

"Because you are the one calling almost all the shots on this."

Fran suddenly sat up in his chair, thinking. The jurisdiction of the feds could certainly be helpful, he thought to himself with a half smile. "Well, I'm flattered, Inspector, but it's a federal case now. And I really don't understand why this meeting couldn't have waited until the morning."

"I tried to explain that to Bayer, but he insisted. He just wouldn't take no for an answer," explained Bentley calmly. "I don't like having to work with them any more than you do, but we really have no choice here. We need their funding and resources to bring this case the justice it deserves."

"But,..."

"Besides Fran," the inspector continued. "This case goes way beyond just our city, or even state now. It really is a federal case."

"So we don't have to sit back and listen to this blowhard punk?"

"No Francis, like I said, from the beginning, this is YOUR case."

Fran smiled with pride. Suddenly he felt a little stupid for laying into his boss. "If he continues to be a problem, let me know, and I will handle it."

"Oh, I think I can handle him, boss."

"That's not what I meant, Fran. I've got a direct line to the chief if we need it."

"That's good to know, but I really don't think that will be necessary."

Bentley smiled at Fran. "Yeah, I don't think it will either."

Suddenly, there was a knock on the door. Fran could see his partner's silhouette through the frosted glass, standing outside the office, ready to give him a ride home. Bentley called the man to come in.

"Detective, go home. We will pick this up in the morning."

Fran smiled, suddenly excited. "Yes sir. See you in the morning."

CHAPTER 6

A man clad in a plain black cossack and white collar approaches a younger priest seated behind a desk.

"Good morning. How can I help you?"

"I'm here to see Archbishop Leone."

"Do you have an appointment?"

"No."

"He may be too busy..."

"I'll wait."

"Who shall I say is calling?"

"Riluciani, Cardinal Riluciani."

The young priest stammered at the man. "Oh, I'm so sorry, Your Eminence, of course, Your Eminence. Just one minute while I check in with the archbishop."

The man soon returned to escort the cardinal into a chamber deep within the walls of Vatican City. As he entered, he appreciated the vintage oil paintings, tapestries, rich walnut and poplar furnishings, and immaculately woven carpets. At a large desk in the middle of the room sat Pope Michael VI's Under-Secretary of State, Archbishop Dante Leone. When the archbishop looked up from his paperwork, a sense of joy immediately came over him. He watched his secretary enter with a tall, slender yet graceful man through his office door. Archbishop Leone smiled, recognizing his guest immediately.

Leone's joyous greetings quickly shifted. He softened his tone and body language. Knowing Riluciani for as long, and as well as he did, he immediately detected something was off with his longtime friend. His beaming trademark smile was nowhere to be seen. His eyes and countenance were cold, and his gait failed to conceal the man's anger and frustration. This was definitely not a social call.

"My dearest Chiaros, how have you been? It has been so long."

"Thank you, Dante, it is good to see you again too, my friend. I am well enough, I suppose." Leone tried to light up the cardinal's spirits. "May I fix you a cup of tea, Chiaros?"

"That would be lovely, thank you."

"Of course, my friend. I enjoyed reading the book you wrote." Riluciani blushed, then responded humbly.

"It's nothing special, just some correspondence."

"Your letters to Charles Dickens, Jules Verne and others are a most enjoyable read. You would have fit right in as a contemporary for any of them."

"Thank you," Riluciani continued, blushing. "It really is no big deal...just some penned reflections, but I'm glad you enjoyed them."

Leone handed him the cup of tea and made his way back to his seat. "I did, very much, again, thank you. So, my dear friend, what brings you to the Holy City this fine morning?"

"I was hoping to see His Holiness, but he seems...to be too busy." Riluciani gave the secretary, still standing next to him, a slight smile.

Leone was so wrapped up in the reunion, he overlooked his secretary. "Thank you, Father Barton. That will be all for now."

"Of course, archbishop." The secretary issued a confirming nod, then turned to the two men and left the chamber.

Cardinal Riluciani relaxed a little. "It must really be an awful thing."

"What's that?"

"Being pope."

"Oh, I don't know. For many of our colleagues, it's all they've ever dreamt about."

"I have a hard enough time being a cardinal, Dante."

"That reminds me...congratulations!"

"For?"

"On becoming a cardinal, of course."

The new cardinal blushed again. "I'm still getting used to it, to be honest."

"You will soon settle in nicely, Your Eminence. I have no doubt."

"Please don't call me that." Requested his guest modestly.

"You are going to have to get used to it sooner or later, Your Eminence." Leone responded with a sly smile.

"Please stop Dante, later will be fine."

"Suit yourself, Emin...Chiaros." Leone teased. "So how is my new patriarch of Venice? You are so lucky to be in such a lovely city."

"The city is beautiful, but I'm still adjusting."

"That's to be expected. It's only been a few weeks."

"My parishioners insist that I should have my own boat."

"And what's wrong with that?"

"Me? Having a boat just sitting around waiting for me?"

"I've seen that junker car of yours. A boat would suit you well, my friend."

"Bah, it's an indulgence of rare use to me. Too wasteful."

"And suppose you need to get somewhere?"

"I have my car or if I truly need it, I just call the captain of the fire brigade."

"What if there's a fire?"

"We should all be grateful that Our Lord is a patient God."

"So, how are things in Venice and Veneto?"

"Physically, they are well, but her people are presently not happy."

"Oh?"

"It's true, and I just don't know how to fix it."

This concession caught the archbishop off guard. Seated in front of him was the wisest, most learned holy man of God he ever had the privilege of knowing. He always confronted challenges with the most brilliant of solutions. "You mentioned that you were here to see the Holy Father, Chiaros."

"Yes, but I have no appointment."

"Perhaps there is something that I can help you with, my dear friend. I've noticed there is a little tarnish on your trademark smile this morning."

"I need help with Bishop Krivis..."

"We all need help in dealing with Bishop Krivis, but continue."

"He's selling the Catholic Bank of Venice..."

Leone cut the cardinal off. "...for a lot less Lira than it's worth, I might add."

"Then you know about all of this."

"Yes."

"Well?"

"Have you discussed this matter with the Secretary of State?"

"Yes, he said nothing could be done."

Leone looked surprised. "Huh, Cardinal Benoît just might be smarter than he lets on sometimes."

"We all know that it is you who runs the Holy Father's Church, Dante, not Zacharie."

"You'd better not say that too loudly around here, my friend."

Riluciani ignored the comment. "You and Pope Michael are good friends."

"Yes, but Krivis is his chosen banker, Chiaros."

"And the poor of Venice? Who is their banker?"

"Blessed are the poor in spirit..."

The cardinal interrupted, infuriated. "It is not God who has forsaken those poor souls, but this Church most certainly has..."

"I don't understand. What do you mean?"

"When I first arrived in Venice, the pews there were empty, and the streets were filled with sex workers, drug addicts and all sorts of mentally and physically ill souls."

"Why?"

"To the surrounding community, these people are outcasts. They don't cast votes. They don't pay taxes. They are nothing but a burden to their materialistic society. They have nowhere else to go." Riluciani paused for a moment before continuing. "They will not be abandoned, Dante, not on my watch."

"Your work is commendable, and a blessing to all those people."

"Not without your help, it's not."

"Chiaros, I must inform you, Krivis has some very dangerous friends."

"Dangerous? You are afraid of him, aren't you?"

Leone gave a slight chuckle. "Afraid of him? Hardly."

"Then why won't you help us, Dante? Please."

It pained the archbishop to see a man he held with so much respect begging. "You want me to confront him over this little bank for the poor in Venice, Chiaros?"

"Absolutely."

"I must advise you against this, my friend."

"Why?"

"He will hold this against you."

"My only concern is God's judgment, not his."

"God's judgment is the least of the bishop's concern. He now holds the power of the Vatican Bank."

"What's that supposed to mean, Dante?"

"He has broken lesser men than you with that power. Cardinals don't even stand a chance against him."

Riluciani would not be deterred. "I wish to see him; will you please help me?"

"I can see that you already have your mind made up on this matter." Leone gave a long, loud sigh. "Fine, only because it is you. I will try, but I'm not making any promises."

"Thank you, my friend. I will pray for your success."

"You're welcome. For what it's worth, I will pray for yours as well. Have you spoken to anyone else of your outrage?"

"Just Benoît and you at this point, my friend."

"Good."

"I demand to speak to the Holy Father regarding this matter immediately!"

"Look Chiaros, I don't think you know all the details of what led up to your current situation."

"I've done my research, Dante."

"That's understood and expected from someone like you. However, there's no way for you to know everything that has transpired."

"Everything?"

"Look Chiaros, I don't like it any more than you do, but Marco Ansios became the key shareholder of your bank last July when Krivis sold him controlling interest in a scheme cooked up by Krivis, Ansios and Giovanni Fedora."

"Wait, this all happened in July 1971? But many of us are still shareholders of that bank. How come we never heard a peep about it until a couple of months ago?"

"That's why I told you, there are holes in your research, Chiaros."

Chiaros shook his head, frustrated. "Alright then, please educate me. What is it that I am missing here?"

"Last July, Krivis approached Fedora to see if he wanted to buy your little bank. Fedora then discussed the matter with Rinaldo Manna."

"Rinaldo Manna?"

"He used to work with Krivis at the Vatican Bank before Krivis became president. He now sits as vice-president of the Board for three of Fedora's other banks. It was Fedora's plan to merge your little bank with his other three in the region."

"And where does Ansios come into all of this?"

"Fedora, for some reason, insisted on Ansios' involvement in the deal. At the time, Ansios had never worked with the Vatican Bank on anything like this before and was welcoming of this opportunity."

"Ahh," Riluciani confirmed in understanding.

"Everything was all set to change hands until Fedora became distracted with some business in New York. Krivis was losing patience with Fedora, and for some reason, he was in a hurry to get this deal done. That's when I stepped in and told Krivis that he couldn't sell your bank to Fedora."

"Wait, you had direct knowledge of all of this, Dante? And you didn't tell me?"

"I apologize, my dear friend. Had I known then how this was all going to turn out, I certainly would have informed you."

Riluciani was not quite satisfied with Leone's response. "But why did you stop the sale to Fedora, then?"

"At the time, I had just received two complaints filed against him from the Bank of Italy alleging possible wrongdoing with one of his Milan banks that would have been involved in his planned merger. Roman banking officials sent out warnings to all the financial sectors not to do any further business with Fedora. I didn't want us getting tangled up in whatever mess was brewing with him."

"So how did Ansios end up owning the bank, then?"

"What I should have told Krivis at the time was that he wasn't allowed to sell the bank at all. That was my own stupid error of judgement."

"Dante, I'm not going to blame you for this mess."

"I appreciate that, Chiaros, but I still hold a lot of responsibility for your current situation, and rage."

"I implore you, please don't let this eat up your spirit, my friend."

"That will take some time Chiaros, but I digress...So as I said, Krivis was in a hurry to move the bank. Ansios had at least three meetings with Krivis that I know of regarding the transaction. Ansios, being new to working with Krivis and the Vatican Bank, did not want to go behind Pope Michael's back on this deal. Ansios was also aware that the Vatican Bank had stiffed Fedora and his London based partner in transactions back in May of '69. Ansios was not interested in becoming the next victim of the Bank's schemes."

"Wait," the cardinal interrupted Leone. "You said the Vatican Bank did a dirty deal with the Fedora banker prior to this, Dante?"

"Yes, Chiaros, many of them in fact. This particular one I mentioned was long before Krivis was crowned 'King of St Nicholas' tower.'" Leone gave Riluciani a sideways nod, then continued. "So Ansios, the perpetual nervous wreck that he is, kept doubting Krivis and his offer. 'Was he sure? Was he authorized to make the sale? Was Pope Michael ok with this transaction?' Much to Krivis' chagrin, he now had no choice but to involve the Holy Father if he really wanted to sell that bank to Ansios. Krivis knew that Ansios wouldn't move until Michael's blessing was given. The deal was finally done on 27 July, '71.'"

Riluciani's gaze drifted from Leone. His heart sank, realizing he was never going to get any satisfactory answers for himself or his parish back in Venice.

Archbishop Leone was at a loss for how to comfort his guest. "You must know, Chiaros, this type of thing is nothing new for these three."

Riluciani's anger was once again growing within him. "This is the first I've heard of these schemes. You must tell me what else these scoundrels have done?"

"Oh, there are far too many to mention Chiaros. They swap companies and shares, illegally manipulate and inflate the Milan Stock Exchange, while Krivis hides their transactions from officials at the Bank of Italy."

"But why? What am I missing here, Dante?"

"All for the purposes of tax evasion and the illegal movement of shares and money in and out of Italy."

"You lost me."

"Krivis sold your little bank to Ansios at a ridiculous low-ball price on purpose. And Ansios in turn paid off a 31 billion Lira balance on another bank."

"And what does all this have to do with the Church of the poor? In the name of all that is holy..."

Leone raised his hand to stop Riluciani mid-sentence. "No Chiaros, not in the name of all that is holy, but in the name of all that is profitable."

"And the Holy Father knows of these things?" Leone rendered a silent nod.

"Well?"

"You must keep in mind who put Krivis in charge of the Vatican Bank, Chiaros."

"Pope Michael?"

"Exactly, and at the time, it was with my full approval." Leone softened his gaze, lowering his head in shame.

"What the hell Dante?"

"I have regretted that endorsement ever since Chiaros."

"Good!" Riluciani dismissed Leone's lapse in judgment. "But that doesn't do anything for any of us now. What am I supposed to do? What do I tell my people, Dante?!"

Again, Leone raised his hand in an effort to calm his dear friend. "Patience, Chiaros. You and your flock must practice patience."

"That's not good enough, Dante!"

"Krivis will eventually expose his true Achilles' heel."

"And that is...?"

"His lust for papal praise."

"Lust for papal praise? Does he not have that already?"

"That's just how the sin of lust does us in, my friend. It only leaves one's spirit empty and unsatisfied."

"That I understand, but what is it that he really wants, then?"

"He lusts for the scarlet zucchetto."

The cardinal paused for a second as Leone's words echoed in his brain. "He lusts to be a cardinal?"

"Exactly Chiaros!"

"But what about all these banking deals? Why does he want with all of those?"

"Oh, that's simple...he wants to make money."

"But for what purpose?"

"For the sole purpose of making even more money."

"And in the meantime, my priests must present begging bowls to the parishioners of Veneto in order to continue God's work?"

"No, you must counsel patience. I've seen it in you. If anyone can teach it, it is you, Chiaros. I have to practice and apply it myself almost daily in my work around here."

"My followers will not be satisfied with that response, Dante."

"Pray Chiaros, only God can and will intervene where weaker men won't."

"I wish to speak with the Holy Father about this, Dante. Please help us. Please help me." He implored.

It was clear to the archbishop that his close friend would not return to his parish without speaking to His Holiness. Leone gave a disapproving sigh. "As you wish, Your Eminence." Riluciani was too upset to protest this time. Leone stood and moved from behind his desk. "Please wait here until I return."

"Certainly."

"Please help yourself to more tea or some biscuits. This may take a bit. I'll be back." Riluciani bowed his head slightly. "Thank you."

Archbishop Leone barged right into Cardinal Benoît's office without so much as a knock. The cardinal glanced up at the entrance, over the reading glasses resting on his nose. "I hope this is necessary."

"Krivis. The selling of the Catholic Bank of Venice."

"That transaction doesn't concern you, Dante. As a matter of fact, it doesn't concern any of us any longer."

"It does now Zacharie. Why did he let it go for so little?"

"He's an American, what can I say, from Chicago no less."

"Not exactly Chicago, but Cicero is close enough, I suppose. The birthplace of Al Capone, no less."

Benoît lit himself a cigarette and took a long drag before responding. "If you wish to have a conversation regarding Krivis, draft an agenda and contact my secretary."

"No! We will discuss this now!"

"He has the trust of the Holy Father."

"And you?"

"He has saved this pontiff's life twice already. I have better things to do with my time than to grapple with this pope's goon. But if you want to, I won't stand in your way, Dante."

Krivis enters the room unannounced. "Cardinal Benoît," he addresses, then nods at Archbishop Leone. "I'm sorry. I didn't realize this was a formal meeting. I didn't receive an agenda."

"This isn't a meeting." Responded Benoît, giving an annoyed, darting glance to Leone. "Cardinal Riluciani has visited me today. He has some questions about the sale of the Catholic Church of Venice."

Krivis smiled with his typical air of arrogance. "You should have sent him to my office, archbishop. I always enjoy the visits with the cardinals."

Benoît was not amused. "Their supplication for money is what pleases you, Krivis."

"My cardinals don't beg, they command, but sometimes, unfortunately, I must deny them. It's a terrible position for me, telling them no."

Leone was having none of Krivis' arrogance. "Not many can deny the requests of a cardinal."

Krivis gave a sneering look at Leone, then continued. "I have heard that a certain archbishop does, and often, isn't that right, Cardinal Benoît."

Leone smiled at the bishop. "I say what the Holy Father tells me, Krivis."

"I thought you answered to Benoît."

"In the end, we all must answer to the Holy Father, and God." Responded an incensed archbishop.

"The pope has placed me in charge of his bank, archbishop. To lend to religious causes in need. I...or rather, the Bank, can't help everyone, but those who find themselves so lucky, are always ever so grateful,...even the cardinals." Krivis smiled, then winked at Benoît.

Benoît was puzzled by the bishop's words and gesture. "What is that supposed to mean, Jonas?"

"Those cardinals are always so gracious with their gratitude."

Leone interrupted their exchange. "The selling of religious banks such as the Catholic Bank of Venice is not your business, Krivis."

"Raising money is, archbishop."

"I know the price Marco Ansios paid. It's rather low, don't you think Jonas?"

"These things are always so complicated to those not in the know." Krivis was quickly becoming annoyed with the conversation. "A businessman such as Ansios has already been of great service to the Vatican and her Bank."

"High risk finance is not the business of the Vatican Bank." Interjected Leone.

"Ansios has the complete confidence of myself, and certainly of the Holy Father."

Benoît could no longer hold his tongue. "So did his predecessor, Fedora."

Leone couldn't help himself. "And where is Fedora now?"

"He's busy."

"Busy? Busy avoiding the wrath of Roman Banking officials. He should be saying prayers. He should be in jail." Commented Leone.

"Prayers will not save that man." Benoît interjected.

Krivis turned to Benoît. "Which one of you would like to have the discussion with the Holy Father regarding his misguided trust and friendship with Fedora?"

"I know what you've been up to since he put you in charge of that bank, Krivis. Your friends are not innocent in your operations, and you are not innocent in theirs."

"Are you accusing me of something, archbishop?"

"Oh, I don't know…am I?"

"Innocence is more difficult to prove in cases of implied guilt." Krivis smirked.

"Perhaps I can help shed some light on your operations, Jonas."

"It may be in your best interest to stay out of the Vatican Bank's business archbishop."

"This is the Church's business." Leone turned to Benoît. "It's time for someone to start looking into the bank's finances."

Krivis was now growing angry. "The Vatican Bank is the pope's bank. Owned by the pope, for his purposes."

"That's right Jonas, it is for the pope, not Ansios!"

Krivis laughed. "My dear archbishop, it is clear that you have not heard me properly. The rest of the Vatican may have to report to you, but my Vatican Bank does not."

"An accounting audit will be done!" Demanded Leone.

"I am accountable to no one!" Krivis blurted out.

"No one?" Benoît questioned with raised eyebrows. "Must I remind you Jonas, that you are in fact accountable to the Holy Father himself, and God?"

Krivis recanted. "Of course I am, but I'm certainly not accountable to Leone, or you, Your Eminence."

"What am I to tell Cardinal Riluciani?"

"He is still here?" Replied the cardinal.

"Yes, waiting patiently as we speak, in my office."

Krivis chimed in, "Send him to my office. I will speak with him."

Benoît was surprised yet relieved. "Good, I'm glad that is settled. Now, if you two don't mind, get the hell out of my office, and get back to work."

A defeated Cardinal Riluciani would soon return to his parish and report on what he had learned. He would be frank with all who would listen, refusing to sugar coat or hide the truth of the matter. Their favorite bank was now lost to the diocese forever. In addition to Leone's advice, he would lead his followers to sell off their remaining shares of the Catholic Bank of Venice and move their business elsewhere. Marco Ansios, Giovanni Fedora and Jonas Krivis would never see another dime from him or anyone else in his parish. Not while he remained the patriarch of Venice.

CHAPTER 7

Fran headed back to his office, still pissed off from his introductory encounter with Bayer. He looked at the clock on the wall in his office. "Just enough time." He thought to himself. He grabbed his coat off the back of his chair and packed up his briefcase and headed for the door.

"Ya ready?" His partner queried.

"Yeah, but I have to stop by the florist's shop on the way home."

"Special occasion, or just because you just got home?"

"Both actually. I did promise Peg before I left, a date night. And to be honest, it may be difficult to find the time once we really get into this investigation."

"Yeah, I think we're all going to be very busy for quite some time."

"Too true, my man. Besides, with all the shit I put her through, she deserves a little pampering and a night on the town!"

"Well, if she puts up with your ass, I'd say so..."

"Yeah, you're a funny one...Here's some advice...don't give up your day job, buddy." Fran shot back in jest with a wink, planting a clenched fist softly on his partner's shoulder, then gave it a slight push.

Fran walked into the house with his briefcase in one hand and a bouquet of red roses in the other. Peg was still upstairs, working on her hair and makeup as he made his way up the steps.

"Honey," he said with a sigh, looking at her as he walked into the room. "I will never understand why you make such a fuss. You are so beautiful." He complimented as he hugged her from behind and kissed her tenderly on the neck.

"You only say that because you've been looking at thugs and your co-workers for the last who knows how long, love."

"Now you know that's bullshit, Peg." Whipping her around in his arms to face him. "You are actually prettier now, then you were on the day I asked you to be my wife."

"Oh, stop!" She blushed, then buried her face in his chest for a short moment. "So, what do you have planned for our evening?" She asked as she wrapped her arms around his neck, giving him a loving kiss.

"Let's go to that new French restaurant downtown for some dinner and cocktails. Then we can head over to your favorite dancing spot. How does that sound to my beautiful bride?"

"Oh, Mr. Romantic! It sounds so wonderful!" She gushed with a wink and another kiss. "Well, I'd better finish up my hair and makeup then, or we will never get out of here."

"Take your time, love, we've got all night." Fran said as he kissed her again tenderly.

Over dinner, the couple held hands across the table and talked while they waited for their dinner to be served. The couple smiled and laughed. Really enjoying each other's company, for the first time in ages. Dancing together, Fran couldn't help but to fall in love with her all over again. He was glad she ignored him. Her hair and makeup were perfect. Everything about her looked absolutely stunning. He loved holding her close, feeling her body dance with his, whispering in each other's ears. She was so happy. It had been so long since they had an evening, much less a moment to themselves. They both soaked in the much needed break from their daily routines.

When they returned home, Fran escorted her up the stairs towards their bedroom, scooped her up in his arms and carried her into the room and laid her gently on the bed. He began kissing her tenderly on the neck and shoulders.

"Honey?"

"Yes, my love…"

"I have something to tell you..."

"I'm listening," he whispered as he continued kissing her.

"I just thought you might like to know I'm carrying your next child." She whispered in his ear.

Suddenly, he stopped kissing her and pulled away from her slightly to look deep into her eyes as the words echoed through his mind. His eyes got wide, and a huge smile came to his face.

"Are you serious love?!?!" Gently placing his hand on her tummy. "Yes!"

"Oh my God, honey! That's wonderful! How far along are we?!?!"

"About eight weeks."

"I love you so much. You always make me the happiest man on this planet! I can't wait to meet him or her!"

The next morning, Fran was on cloud nine, with his lovely bride still in his arms. He did his best to not disturb her as he got up and got ready for work. It wasn't often that she got a morning off. The kids always absorbed so much of her time and energy. She never got a minute to herself. She was such a devoted mother and wife. Never protesting or complaining. She would never have it any other way. He had to pinch himself. She looked so beautiful as she continued to sleep peacefully in their bed. He flung his tie around the unbuttoned neck of his collar, grabbed his coat and shoes, and left the room, closing the door quietly behind him.

He arrived at his favorite diner, taking his usual counter seat. The huge smile on his face was on display for the whole world to see.

"I'd say 'somebody' had a good night!" The waitress winked at him while chomping on her a huge piece of pink bubble gum and pouring him a cup of coffee. "So, what's the word on the street, Hon?"

"Oh hey Laura, not much really," he said. Still grinning ear to ear.

"I'm sorry, darlin', but you are so full of shit this morning."

"Is it really that obvious, Laura?"

"I'm afraid so dear, now spill it! Don't keep me guessin' over here."

"Alright, fine, no more guessin.' Peg is expecting! She's about eight weeks along now. She just told me about it last night!"

Laura squealed in delight. "No kiddin' Fran! That's some wonderful news for you and your family. Congratulations!"

"Thanks Laura, we're both really excited about the news."

"You should be, hon. Between you and Peg, I know he or she will be an absolutely beautiful child!"

"Aw gee Laura, stop, you're embarrassing me."

"It's true hon, you two are such a beautiful couple." She continued. "So you gonna have your usual or what?"

"The usual, of course Laura, sounds great, but throw on an extra egg. I'm starving!"

"You got it, hon, and the coffee's on me this mornin'! I'm so damn excited for y'all."

When Fran finished his breakfast, it was still early, but he headed to the office, anyway. The reunion with his wife the night before had completely recharged his energy and spirits. His boss, handing him the reins on the investigation going forward, certainly didn't hurt either. He moved through his morning now with even more confidence and a distinct quickness in his step. Jet lag was no match for everything flooding his head. He was more ready than ever for the work that lay before him and his team.

He sat in consultation with his boss prior to the initial 9 AM strategy meeting. A knock on Bentley's door frame averted both their attention.

"Hello, may I help you?" Bentley greeted the strange man standing in the doorway. "Good morning, I'm from the FBI. I'm looking for Detective Clavering."

"I'm Detective Clavering. What can I do for you?"

"Nice to meet you, Detective." The agent approached, extending his hand. "Nathan Bayer assigned me as your new partner in this case."

Fran's warm smile quickly faded as he shot an angry glance at Bentley. "Oh really?!" Francis questioned indignantly.

"That's right, detective." Responded the excited agent.

"Well, you go right back to Bayer and tell him I will speak with him later regarding your assignment." The detective responded tersely.

Confused, the FBI agent's smile was instantly gone. "Um, well... If you say so, detective." As Fran escorted him out of the room, he had to consciously stop himself from slamming the door behind the man.

The detective returned to his seat. "Can you believe the balls on this guy, Inspector? I can already tell that this Bayer guy is going to be a major problem. He has some nerve, 'assigning' me a new partner without consulting with me, or even you, for that matter."

"You will get no argument from me, Fran. I admit, that was a pretty ballsy move. We are going to need to get some things straightened out before the meeting starts at nine."

Bentley immediately called Bayer into his office. The meeting was tense. Bayer did not want to hear what Fran had to tell him. Finally, Bentley explained that he'd be calling Bayer's boss later, requesting the chief to transfer Bayer elsewhere.

"But inspector, this is MY case, the chief said..."

"No Bayer, it is not YOUR case. This is OUR case. I was in that meeting too, remember? And this certainly wouldn't be anyone's case at all if it wasn't for all the hard work of MY Detective. I have delegated my authority to him. If he needs anything from MY department or YOURS, he will let us know. Do I make myself clear, Bayer, or do I need to bother the chief to help us come to a better understanding of our work relationship here?"

A disgruntled Bayer now had a better understanding of his role going forward in the investigation. He wasn't thrilled with the arrangement, but he was no idiot. He knew he did not want to be removed from this case. He sat in silent admiration of the work relationship between Bentley and Clavering. He was jealous of the confidence and trust that Bentley had for his detective-in-charge.

Strategy meetings over the next several days consisted mostly of Fran fielding questions, filling in details, and analyzing suggestions from the team. It took them a little longer than he had expected, but one by one he watched everything finally click in their brains. Christopherson's office had punted the ball to the Feds but kept his men on the field. Huge computers began humming, wiretaps and bugs were installed in all the Mafia hotspots around the city, and undercover agents were now working everywhere. The budget of the Manhattan Police Department no longer hindered their investigation.

The US Department of Justice was now all-in with Christopherson's office to shut down the global multi-billion dollar black market securities trade. Fran didn't like the idea of partnering with an FBI agent. He didn't like the way the Bureau operated. He preferred to stick with his "Rackets" partner. After giving the matter much consideration, he finally conceded his resistance.

"You want Lance Erickson? Really, Fran?" Questioned Bentley

"...yep, that's my guy."

"But he's nothing like you."

"Oh, I know boss. But at least I've worked with him before. He isn't the most street savvy guy, but he is a very smart man."

"I will trust your judgment on that, detective."

"Besides, we don't want some unknown FBI clown in here fuckin' up this investigation."

Bentley nodded. "This is true..."

Fran had worked a case with Erickson before, many years prior. They had similar physical features, but not much else in common. Erickson was not a New Yorker in any way, shape or form. He lacked intuition and street smarts that could only be gleaned from growing up in the "projects." Fran operated with a certain *je ne sais quoi*. He may or may not have stretched or broken procedure on occasion if it would advance an investigation. Unlike Fran, Erickson was clean-cut, straight laced and extremely nerdy. A cookie-cutter, "by the book," detail-oriented kind of guy. The type of agent that would make J. Edgar Hoover most proud. He was a great researcher, and a master at finding the proverbial "needle in the haystack" in papers and reports. The detective sensed that those qualities could prove useful as the investigation moved forward. Erickson was also impressed with the intellect and work ethic of this new partner.

Fran relished the planning and running of the investigation, but it was not what he was born to do. It was finally time for him to roll up his sleeves and get back to the trenches where he was most comfortable. It seemed like forever since he manned the listening post set up to keep tabs on Benedetto and Frankie's Lounge. He was curious what all he'd missed since he left for Munich. He walked over and cracked open the logbook. The detective was puzzled as he flipped through one blank page after another. His own impeccable, ball-breaking work ethic was expected from everyone on his team. He was not happy with what he saw.

"What the hell is all this?" Turning to the senior detective monitoring the 'tap at Frankie's. "Where are all the logs, tapes and transcripts for me to review? What did I miss while I was gone?"

"You was off in Munich chasing Benedetto, Fran. Ya know, checkin' out all da Frauleins over there. There wasn't nothin' happenin' here, man."

Fran was pissed. He threw a porcelain coffee mug against the wall, with such force, the cup shattered into a million pieces. "Nothin' happenin'? How the fuck would you know? You fucking bastards were goofing off, partying this whole time, weren't ya?"

The other man ignored the detective's outburst, then produced a smutty smirk. "So Fran, how was the Fraulein action over there?"

A searing pain followed the sudden impact of Fran's fist on his jaw. "Listen, you piece of shit, just because your wife's a bitch and won't screw you, because your shit don't get hard, doesn't mean my home life sucks. If even a hint of your bullshit ever gets back to Peg, I'm coming after you personally. Do I make myself clear?!"

Rubbing his left jaw, the man was angry, yet grateful the detective held back a little when he belted him. "Calm the fuck down, you psycho! You ain't my boss."

"Calm the fuck down? Me? We've all been bustin' our balls, well over a year now. I sure as hell hope you jack offs haven't fucked up this investigation."

"How the hell could we have fucked it up? Benedetto was in Munich with you."

"Hey dumb shit, Benedetto ain't the only one who uses that place, or that phone! Why do you think we have 'taps and bugs all over this Goddamn city now that the Feds are involved? I really expected a hell of a lot more from a senior investigator like you. These young bucks look up to you, ya know. Maybe I should talk to Bentley about transferring you back to the street beat."

The gravity of the situation finally hit the seasoned detective. "I'm sorry Fran," he said softly, as his tone quickly changed. Recognizing his fault. "You're right, we fucked up. I promise, this will never happen again."

Everyone on the team recognized the future potential for their own personal career advancement in police work that came from working this kind of case. Everything Fran had brought back from Munich, brought a new energy to everyone associated with the case. From that point forward, the lead detective never had to worry about any of his "Rackets" fellas ever again.

While monitoring the post one afternoon, Fran intercepted a frantic call into Frankie's Lounge. The caller was extremely secretive, scared, and anxious. "Listen to me carefully," explained the caller, with fear in his voice. "Don't use my name. I want you to call me back right away. Use the pay phone across the street. Hurry, this is very important!"

Benedetto's goon waited a few minutes, then dialed back the man using the exact same phone he'd always used. Completely ignored the caller's request.

"Listen to me carefully. One of 'our' cops up here in the north just told me that two fed agents were up here snooping around. Flashing their badges, goin' through hotel records, and stuff. Tell Benedetto his phone is 'tapped, ya hear?'"

Fran listened tensely to the exchange, now very concerned. A suspicious Benedetto and friends could start using other phones and sending word throughout the syndicate. It would be a devastating blow to the entire operation. Fortunately, the visiting LA mafiosi was unsuccessful in selling his paranoia to his New York counterparts.

The team really dodged a bullet, however, this could not happen again. The "Rackets" team always ran a tight, stealthy operation. Never coming out of the shadows until their case was solid, and it was time to make arrests. The pompous asses of the FBI went around flashing badges early and often, thinking that people would just spill their guts the moment they walked into a joint. He called the entire team for an impromptu meeting. Fran was pissed.

"Bayer, you and your team of fuck-ups are going to ruin this entire case."

"Detective, what on Earth are you talking about?"

He went on to explain the entire situation. "But Detective..."

"No buts Bayer, I'm going to tell you how it's going to be, or we can just throw this whole operation in the shitter now. If your FBI guys pull another stunt like this, everyone we are now chasing will scurry underground."

Both the Feds and Christopherson's division were now focused and diligently working the counterfeit and stolen securities cases. Fran continued to keep close tabs on Benedetto. Benedetto's actions would help him direct the team and resources exactly where and when they'd be needed.

Lance's research and insight, combined with the notes from Fran's Munich trip, were eye opening. Lance came barreling through Fran's office door one morning, completely out of breath, startling the detective seated at his desk. "What the hell, Lance?"

"Take a look at this!" Throwing a wrapped package to his partner.

Fran's eyes widened as he carefully opened the paper to see what was inside. "Counterfeit?"

"Every last one of them."

"Where the hell did you get these?"

"They were sent to the New York Bankers Association for authentication. Someone over in Europe opened an account and wanted a loan using $1.5 million dollars' worth as collateral!"

"Who was?"

Lance glanced at his notes. "Looks like they were joint accounts for Mateo Taverna and a monsignor..."

"No shit?" Fran immediately recognized Taverna's name from Benedetto's discussions with the two Germans in Munich.

Thomas, Bentley, and Bayer were called in immediately. All three men were impressed with the securities Fran and Lance had recovered. They repeatedly flipped through the stack, closely inspecting a couple of the documents.

"They're fakes, ya know," Fran casually informed them. "You're kidding!" Bayer quickly grabbed one for a closer look.

"Nope," confirmed Lance. "Every last one of them, 100% counterfeit."

"I have to admit, Benedetto's friends do some mighty fine work. They had me convinced." Remarked Thomas with a raised eyebrow.

Fran alerted Hans and his team about the counterfeit stocks that were just sent over from Europe. Hans reported that it was the first he'd heard of them being used. He would check with Interpol to see if there was any other activity involving the documents anywhere else in Europe. He reported a few days later that Switzerland and Rome were all he could find.

Fran was, in many ways, appreciative of the extra help from the Strikeforce. It was more than he could have ever hoped for. The recovery of the counterfeit documents clearly demonstrated Benedetto's direct ties to operations in Europe. Who was the monsignor working with Taverna? Was he the Vatican connection in all of this that Fran had been looking for? For Fran, this went beyond professional boundaries, this was personal. He had a hunch, this time stronger than the one that took him to Munich. The Vatican was the key component of the entire case. Fran's biggest frustration, however, continued to grow. No one on either team wanted to delve into if and how the Vatican was involved in all of this.

Over a month into the case, a frustrated detective walked into Inspector Bentley's office. "Hey Boss, you got a minute?" He asked as he knocked on the door frame.

"Oh hey Fran," Bentley said as he looked up from his desk. "Come on in. How's the Benedetto investigation going?"

"Well that's what I wanted to talk to you about." He replied as he closed Bentley's office door. "From what I understand, you are running a really tight ship over there. I'm not surprised, but I am still extremely proud of you. How do you like working with Lance?"

"It's taken me a while to get used to his 'style,' but he's great. He's really a smart guy. He actually loves researching stuff, and to be honest, he's really good at it."

"That's great to hear. I apologize for not attending the strategy meetings lately. Thomas and I are up to our eyeballs keeping things organized. It seems that Christopherson is going to take this case to trial himself once we get to that point."

"That's wonderful news, boss."

"I'm just glad everything is moving forward without a hitch."

"Well, not quite everything, Inspector."

"Oh? I'm sorry, I'm out of the loop here. What do you mean? Is it Bayer again?"

"Kinda, but not specifically. It's actually the whole team, to be honest." responded Fran. "No one on the team wants to investigate the Vatican and European components of this case."

"That does seem odd." Responded Bentley, puzzled. "That seems like a very important part of this case, if you ask me."

"It is, sir, from the research that Lance and I have gathered so far, Europe and especially Rome are key components in the black-market trade for the majority of these securities."

"I see, so they are more or less the demand for their supply."

"I think $990 million in fake stocks more or less answers that question for you."

"Without a doubt."

"I bring it up all the time at strategy meetings, but the team just keeps ignoring me."

"That's just weird. If nothing else, entertain the notion at least until the lead goes cold. It's Basic Case Investigation 101."

"I just don't know what to do about it. They took the meeting tapes and ran with them. But they only want to work the domestic stuff."

"So they haven't investigated any of the European characters the Germans brought up?"

"Not a single one of them. Not even with the recovery of those fakes Taverna was trying to use...Nothing."

"Well, it's not because they don't have the manpower. I've never seen so many agents on a single case before." Bentley thought out loud. "Let me talk to Christopherson about this. Maybe he will have some idea of what is going on. For now, I want to keep this between the three of us. If that's alright with you."

"Sure thing, boss."

A day and a half later, Bentley called his detective back into his office. "I brought up your concerns with Christopherson." Bentley started.

"And..?"

"He's curious, but unconcerned at this point. He said that the two agencies are hot and heavy on everything here at the moment. His only real suggestion was to give it a little more time."

"But isn't he concerned that they seem to be ignoring this gigantic piece of the puzzle?"

"He is curious, but he is pretty sure there must be a reason. I'm sorry, Fran, that I don't have a better answer for you."

"I hope you guys are right. I appreciate you trying anyway." Fran said, deflated, as he left the office.

CHAPTER 8

The warm sun sparkled like diamonds off the surface of the pool of a tropical Bahamian resort. The bitter, arctic cold that gripped his new New York home was the last thing on the mind of Giovanni Fedora. In the lounge chair next to him was his friend Marco Ansios. The two Italian men enjoyed the sun, water and bronze skinned bikinis decorating their surroundings. Sipping on cocktails and puffing on fine cigars, the two men were hard at work. A few feet away, their two spouses gossiped and chatted about fashion, friends, and a shopping excursion later that afternoon.

Fedora took a long, savored drag from his cigar, while he watched a beautiful young redhead playfully saunter past. "The weather is nothing short of perfect today." Fedora commented.

"I certainly can't argue with you there." Agreed Ansios, as he too caught sight of the girl. "It's not very often we get to ditch those suits."

"Suits are so bad if you don't skimp on the quality."

"I suppose..." Ansios' attention drifted.

Fedora noticed the perpetual look of concern once again returned to his friend's face. "I hear you paid Krivis a visit a few weeks ago."

"Yes, I did. Have you been to his new office yet?"

"Yeah, he invited me up there right after Pope Michael appointed him president."

"It's a really nice office."

"Yeah, he sure knows how to flaunt his own self-importance, doesn't he?"

"Better than anyone I know, Gio."

"Ha, like he will ever change. So, how is he? I haven't talked with him in a while."

"He seems to finally be getting the hang of running that bank."

"It's about damn time. What's it been, a little over a year now?"

"Yeah, that sounds about right."

"He sure made a mess of things over there right out of the gate."

"It seemed stupid mistakes were his specialty there for a while."

"I've known Pope Mike for such a long time. I told him Jonas in that position was a huge mistake, but he wouldn't listen to me or anyone else on the matter."

"He worked his way up to that position, Gio."

"More like he bootlicked his flunky ass into that position. He has zero business being near a bank, much less running one."

"Then why do you do business with him, Gio?"

"Because, unlike him, I'm not stupid."

"Does that even make sense?"

"Of course it does, Marco. In my opinion, the best way to rob a bank is to own one...unless you have someone like Krivis running the damn thing."

"You certainly didn't have any issues with him serving on the board of directors of our Banco Generali branch here in Nassau."

"Being on the board is one thing. Being in charge of the actual money and banking operations is something entirely different, my friend. I mean, honestly Marco, would you let him run any of your banking operations?"

"Hell no!"

"See, I rest my case."

"That reminds me, I'm very impressed with the job you've done in getting Banco Generali established here, Marco." Praised Fedora.

"Thank you Gio, I couldn't have done it without your help and guidance."

"You're welcome. The pleasure is all mine."

"Tomorrow I will give you a guided tour of our entire facility."

"I'd very much like that. I like to keep tabs on my various investments and partnerships from time to time."

"I can understand that; I think you will be most pleased."

"Why shouldn't I be Marco? I've put in a lot of time teaching you. You've certainly come a long way since I took you on as my protégé."

"Well, much of the credit is due to the skills of the instructor."

"Oh stop Marco, unlike Krivis' bosses, I can't stand a suck-up. Besides, you already had the skills, my friend. You just needed a little guidance and direction. That is all. I saw the promise of your potential, otherwise I wouldn't have even bothered working with you."

"I'm most gracious for that."

"You must understand, I'm not trying to be lazy. I just don't have the time to teach anyone who doesn't already have a certain knowledge base."

"That is completely understandable Gio, you are a very busy man. As a matter of fact, I have no idea how you manage to keep everything running so smoothly."

"Thank you, Marco. It's just what I do. You too will be here someday, I'm sure."

Their respective wives quickly became bored with all their business talk. It was obvious they were outgunned by the younger girls hanging around the resort pool. It was time for them to get out of the sun, anyway. They returned to their suites to get ready for a shopping excursion. The two men remained in their lounge chairs, talking. A pretty blonde waitress came over to chat and flirt with them for a few minutes, then scurried off to get them both fresh cocktails.

Fedora closed his eyes and turned his face towards the sun. The warm rays felt good on his tan skin. "I understand that Gherado

Fratello has been working closely with the Argentine government lately."

"Well, he was a guest of honor at the General's inauguration a while back."

"Hmmm, interesting. Why does that not surprise me?"

"Did you see him at the Roman Embassy a couple weeks ago?"

"No, I've been wrapped up in other business outside of Italy."

Ansios forgot for a brief moment about the attempt on the lives of Fedora and his wife in Geneva. "I'm sorry Gio. Where is my head? How are you guys doing, following...ya know?"

"Understandably, we were considerably shaken up by the whole thing. Things are much better since we moved to New York City."

"I'm so glad to hear your family is doing better."

"What happened in Rome?"

"Rome? Oh Fratello, that's right...He was appointed to a diplomatic position."

"Ahhh, well, that explains all the signed pictures of him and the Italian president I saw when I visited him at his villa recently."

"I'm surprised he didn't tell you?"

"He didn't even mention it, but we were having some serious discussions about Cuba and Russia providing a way for us to help Argentina and her people."

"But you hate communism, Gio."

"I absolutely loathe it, Marco, for Italy."

"But you support it in Cuba, Russia and now Argentina?"

"I wouldn't say I support it, but I certainly won't be one to fight it."

"You lost me, Gio."

"Well, I think Cuba, with a little perceived threat from Russia, could help us take full advantage of the South American people unhappy with dictators and fascism."

"And where does Cuba come in?"

"Well, if they run to Cuba for protection from Russia..."

"But why would Fratello want to push Argentina towards Cuba? He hates the communists with everything in his dark soul, Gio."

Fedora chuckled. "I wouldn't say he hates it, and his soul isn't so much a dark thing, but rather more like a fickle whore."

"Fickle whore?"

"Yeah. He doesn't give a shit about the political structure in a country, including Italy, as long as he gains coin, power, or both in the process."

"I can't argue with you there."

"Besides, Cuba with pressure from Russia would help raise the standard of living of the South American countries, especially Argentina. It's the quickest and in my opinion only way that the left and right of that country will ever be on even ground."

"Do you really think so, Gio?"

"I know so. You see, Marco, currently under the General's dictatorship, they do not have the financial backing to take advantage of their own natural resources. A better standard of living will create an opportunity for us to establish banks in South America. A solid financial infrastructure in the region can provide much needed services to the locals."

"I'm with you so far."

"These banks, our banks, will also attract international investors into their local industrial ventures for the private sector as well as for their government."

"And we will be there to reap the rewards for our 'services rendered.'"

"Exactly! While I am no fan of communism, that shit needs to stay far, far away from Italy. There is absolutely no reason why we cannot profit from the strategic use of their political setup, Marco."

"I never thought of it that way, Gio, but it does make sense. Fratello's been telling me that I needed to start working on getting Banco Generali established in Argentina. I had assumed that it had something to do with providing banking services for his Nazi Rat-line buddies he smuggled down there through the Vatican."

"Oh no Marco, this has nothing to do with any of that. As a matter of fact, I was the one who planted that little seed in his little brain. I'd be more than happy to help get that project started."

"Who all is involved with this project so far, Fratello, you and I?"

"Oh, I'm sure we can get the Vatican Bank on board with this project too without a problem."

"What makes you so sure?"

"I'll give you two great reasons, Marco. First of all, South America has more Catholics than anywhere else in the world."

"This is true."

"Second, the notion of Catholics turning to communism is a fresh and most realistic threat to the Mother Church. I've seen firsthand the damage it can do to the Roman Curia. Besides, Krivis is too stupid to say no."

"But what about Pope Mike?"

"Pope Michael, are you kidding? He's been friends with both Fratello and I long before he was elected pontiff. Fratello is just a better ass kisser than I."

"You're anything but an ass kisser, Gio."

"Exactly. I refuse to lower myself or my standards, no matter who it is. Fratello, on the other hand, could teach Krivis a thing or two."

"Like?"

"Like a little grace, for starters."

"Grace is not something one associates with a gorilla of a man like him."

"No, but it does make him a good bodyguard for Pope Mike."

Ansios laughed, more than he should have. "To be honest, I think bodyguard was his true calling."

Fedora joined in the laugh, "I think you are right, Marco."

"Did Fratello tell you he was knighted during your visit?"

"Knighted? By the Queen? When?"

"No, no, no, not by the Queen, by Pope Mike. He's now a Knight of Malta and a member of the Holy Sepulchre, Gio."

"Well, that is impressive Marco, considering that Fratello isn't even a Catholic. With that kind of influence over the pope, we will have no problem getting our banks established down south now."

"I guess we will have to start addressing him as Sir now." Ansios chuckled.

"Like hell we will, Marco. He may be in the pope's blind spot, but the rest of us can see him just fine."

Fedora hailed a waitress for another cocktail, then took a quick dip in the pool to cool off. He chatted up a couple more ladies before returning to his towel and lounge chair.

"You should jump in. The water's great!"

"I'm not that into swimming."

"This isn't swimming...more like a little 'sightseeing.'" Fedora winked with a smile. "I like the view from here."

"You really need to learn how to relax, my friend. You gotta let some of that shit go."

"I can't."

"Let me help. What you got on your mind?"

"Nothing."

"Don't bullshit me, Marco."

"Fine, fine, since you asked..." Ansios started getting an idea. "Well, maybe you can help me out a bit."

"Of course Marco, what do you got going on?"

"Well, you know I finally got named General Manager of Banco Generali last year?"

"Yes, and you seem to be doing a great job, especially with getting it established here in Nassau."

"Yeah, that was fun."

"You have a sick sense of 'fun', my friend, but continue."

"I want to do more with the bank on the international scene, but I can't. The Nassau branch was an exclusive opportunity and required so many approvals and a lot of oversight."

"Yeah, that is the drag of being a General Manager, unfortunately."

"I want more Gio."

"What do you mean, you want more? More money?"

"No, not just money, more control, more power."

"Be careful what you wish for Marco...people get drunk off that shit, and the hangover is the absolute worst...just look at Krivis."

"I'm not an idiot like Krivis."

90

MONEY CHANGERS AND FALSE PROFITS

"That you are not, my friend...alright, so what is it you want exactly, and how can I help you make that happen?"

"I want to be chairman of the board of Banco Generali."

"You'd be an excellent chairman, Marco." Fedora thought for a moment. "Well, that shouldn't be too difficult. I'm sure Fratello could get you right in, in the blink of an eye."

"No, I don't want to do it that way."

"So a corporate take over is not your style here."

"No, that's more Krivis' style."

"True. So you want a more legitimate take over then?"

"Something like that, but the challenge is the corporate charter."

"Which says..."

"No entity can hold no more than 5% controlling interest in the bank. It's a failsafe against exactly what I want to do."

"So we work around it, but under their rules then."

"That's where things get complicated...how do we do that?" Fedora laughed a little. "Oh, this will be easier than you think."

"I don't have time to campaign to eleven or twelve groups for their votes."

"Of course you don't, and you certainly don't have to, my friend. The solution is actually elegant, yet simple."

"You tease more than these damn waitresses, Gio."

"I never tease, not about business, Marco. All we have to do is get various businesses and holding companies to purchase 5% of the bank's interest."

"More campaigning?" Complained the Milan Banker.

"Nope, not a bit of it." Fedora smiled knowingly. "No?"

"Look, you and Jonas have your banks, and I have several."

"Right."

"And all three of us have several holding companies."

"Right."

"Between the three of us, I'm sure we can pull together enough 'influence' to get you elected chairman from the shareholders, wouldn't you say?"

An excited smile came over Ansios' face for the first time in months. "You make it sound so easy! Why didn't I think of that?"

"We could make it even easier if you want and get Fratello to pick up a few shares."

The joy left his face, and the concern returned for a moment. "No, I think you and Jonas' assistance is all I'm going to need on this."

"Are you sure, Marco? I can ask him if you want."

"No...I'd rather you not."

"Fine, your wish is my command, my friend."

"Thank you Gio."

"Actually, this development couldn't come at a better time, in my opinion."

"How so?"

"The timing will be perfect, as we start rolling into South American markets."

Ansios couldn't contain himself any longer as aspirations of the future flooded his brain. "Wow!

"That thought never even crossed my mind."

"I'm glad that's settled. Now I'm going to ask you for a favor."

"Of course. What do you need?"

"I've been looking over a proposal to purchase Lincoln National Bank in New York."

"That's great Gio."

"It's a very promising deal, but there's just one problem."

"And that is?"

"None of my usual partners want any part of it, or should I say, any part of me."

"Because of what went down with the Bank of Italy and Rome?"

"Yeah, those damn bastards."

"I'd love to help you out Gio..."

Fedora cut him off. "That's great! Thanks."

Ansios suddenly became very nervous once again. "But... you know I can't help you with this. Especially if I ever want to become Board Chairman. If anyone at Banco Generali ever found out, I'd be out of a job immediately. I'm sorry."

"It's alright, I understand. I just thought I'd ask." Ansios was relieved. "Did you ask Jonas?"

"Yeah, but Archbishop Leone is now watching his ass like a hawk."

"Oh?"

"Don't worry about it. I'll figure something out."

"You always do Gio."

Fedora smiled at Ansios' compliment. "Listen Marco, I need to get out of this sun for a while. Shall the wife and I meet up with the two of you for dinner later?"

"That sounds great, but who knows when they will get back from their shopping. You know how they are while they are out spending our money."

Fedora chuckled, acknowledging the comment. "You're right, well in that case, Marco, I am going to go get a massage and a bit of a nap before they get back."

"I think I will go for a nap too. We can decide when they get back."

"Sounds good. See you in a few hours."

Marco returned to his room. He walked over to the bed, took off his sandals and laid down on the bed. This trip was a well deserved, needed break. He started to relax, and his thoughts began to drift. It was the first time in years that worry didn't consume him. Soon, he drifted off to sleep, snoring.

CHAPTER 9

The "Rackets" and Strikeforce teams were now operating like a well-oiled machine. Constantly remaining one step ahead of the Mobster and his friends, every move in stealth. Everyone was pleased with their work and progress. Well, almost everyone.

Bentley, Thomas and Christopherson were extremely busy, as the case was building closer to arrests and trial. There was also a growing concern regarding their lead detective. The hunch in Fran's gut was growing into an obsession. Frustration with the now blatant, almost intentional ignoring of the Vatican and European connections in the case made him an absolute pain in the ass to be around. Most of his venting landed on Peg. She knew how stubborn he could be when one of his hunches got a hold of him. She also knew how accurate they had been in the past.

Lance knocked on Fran's door frame. "Hey, you got a minute."

"Yeah, what's up?"

Lance threw the latest copy of *Business Week* onto the detective's desk. On the cover was an Italian man in his early 50s. His black slicked back hair accentuated his good looking facial features. The man staring back at the detective was wearing one of the finest Italian suits Fran had ever seen. Fran had never seen the man before.

"What's this?"

"Bayer just threw this at me."

"So..."

"I guess the guy just moved here from Italy not too long ago. He wants us to check him out, maybe keep an eye on him."

"Maybe we should keep an eye on Bayer instead." Fran jested in protest. Bayer continued to be the most annoying thing in his work environment. The detective continued with his uncharacteristic complaint. "'Cause I don't have enough to do, keepin' tabs on Benedetto and his boys, and us and our boys at the moment...why not pile one more thing onto the lead detective...So who is this cat, anyway?"

"His name is Giovanni Fedora."

Fran opened the magazine and began reading the article aloud. "Italy's most successful and feared financier has settled on the US as his next major field of operations." He looked up from the periodical. "I do hope we have more than this magazine article to work from."

"We have been hearing complaints of fraud and possible wrong-doing from Rome and the Italian banking minister."

"Ok."

"Word is that he's also been working with Mafia groups in Italy."

Fran perked up a little. "Do we know which group?"

"I'm hearing it might be the Lanscanos."

Fran raised an eyebrow. "They are a very powerful family in the Syndicate here in our region."

"They are even more powerful in Italy."

"Alright, what else do we know?"

"He recently purchased a Roman publication called *Americans Today*."

"By the reputation of this fella, it sounds like he's movin' and groovin' a lot of that kind of business globally. Why is the *'American'* paper significant?"

"Well, it is a CIA backed paper."

"CIA? Really? Why are they funding an Italian publication? Why are they teaming up with Fedora? Maybe a better question is why isn't the CIA digging into this guy for Bayer instead of us?"

"I believe him buying it was a move requested by the US Ambassador. He thought it best if the paper stayed out of the hands of those with communist sympathies in Italy."

"So, did they approach Fedora to pick it up?"

"Those details I'm unsure of at this point. All I know is Congress has issued an inquiry on their million dollar investment that seems to have landed on Bayer's desk."

"Bayer's busy, and so are we..."

"Yeah, that won't fly in DC."

"It seems that Mr. Fedora has done work with the CIA and other US agencies in the past."

"What? Where? Here in America?"

"No Yugoslavia, Greece and other stuff in Italy..."

Fran was getting confused and frustrated. "So why can't the Feds keep tabs on him?"

"Something tells me that they want Bayer to do some kind of internal check-in on an asset type of deal. With his move to New York and us already being here, that theory kind of makes sense, at least in my mind, anyway."

"Yeah, I guess I can kind of see that. Has he ever had any operations here in the states?"

"I read that he partnered with some financial groups out of Chicago within the last couple of years, but other than that, nothing."

"Alright, so then, what's he doing here in the States?"

"That's the big question, Fran. We just don't know."

"Is there anything else that we know about Fedora?"

"Rumor has it he wants to move $100 million into US interests."

"A $100 million?! Wow, that's some dough." Fran gave in. "Fine, fine. We can scratch his itch for a bit, I guess, but not for too long. With the two of us working on it, we will know soon enough whether it's a bust or not. No matter what, though, I can't let this derail anything going on with the Benedetto case."

"Oh, and I also learned that he and his wife recently escaped a murder attempt on them in Switzerland."

"Oh really? Now that makes things a little more interesting. Sounds like we better keep a close eye on this guy for a while. I'll have my 'Rackets' partner keep tabs on Benedetto and Frankie's while we dig a little into Fedora. Do we know where he's living and working here in the city?"

"Looks like he and his wife are currently living at the St Regis, and he has an office down on Park Avenue."

"Wow, St Regis and Park Avenue! This cat sure knows how to live...Poor guy." Fran thought out loud sarcastically. "Do you think Bayer will let us put some bugs and 'taps in his office?"

"'Taps for sure, bugs may be a little more complicated."

"We'd better get busy with the paperwork then..."

"That won't be necessary."

"Huh?"

"Bayer's already given us the green light for that Fran."

"For once, he's one step ahead of me. I never thought I'd ever see the day..."

The wiretaps were installed on Fedora's office phone through the phone company's lines, just like they were on Benedetto's phone in Frankie's. An undercover agent posed as a maintenance worker and installed a listening bug in the office overhead light fixture. A command post was set up in a basement nearby, similar to the one monitoring Benedetto.

Initially, a lot of Fedora's calls were to foreign destinations like London, Zürich, and Germany. It seemed that much of Europe had also heard about Fedora's banking problems in Italy. The usual lines of people and businesses champing at the bit to partner with him on deals were now nowhere to be found. Lincoln National Bank of New York piqued his interest. However, for the first time in his career, he was challenged in coming up with the capital for the investment.

The change of focus for Fran made him much more tolerable to work with. Peg too found her husband a lot less cranky. She found his evening recaps on Fedora a wonderful and interesting change of pace too.

"Hey honey?"

"Yes love?"

"Have you seen this *New York Times* article?"

Fran moved behind her, placing his hands on her pregnant tummy. He looked over her shoulder while she looked at the article. "No love, what does it say?"

Peg read the financial section headline aloud. "Italian Tycoon Hosts Bankers and Investment Managers Luncheon."

"I bet he's trying to get someone here locally to help him buy that bank. He sure seems to keep striking out everywhere else."

Peg kept on reading the article, half listening to her husband's comment. Suddenly, she stopped and looked directly at her husband. "Honey, you're not going to believe this..."

"What's that?"

"I used to work with the guy who wrote this article..."

"You're kidding? Did you like him? How was his work?"

"He was one of our best reporters. I worked with him on a couple of pieces. He was always such a joy to work with, a very thorough researcher."

"Hmmmm, I wonder if he'd be open to a chat with Lance and I?"

"I'm sure he would be. Just don't ask him to reveal his sources, or he will drop you like a hot penny."

"Well, it'd be hard to get anywhere in that business if y'all started doin' that."

It only took a couple of shifts for Fran to become engrossed with his new person of interest. Fedora certainly had a lot more interesting friends than Benedetto ever did. Fran felt almost naughty as he manned the post, listened in on conversations between Fedora and the United States Treasury Secretary, or even President Nixon himself. There was an awful lot of talk about some sort of scandal involving the Watergate complex in DC. Fran and Lance brought their findings to Bayer. Bayer, hearing these things, tried to scale back their operations. It was an impossible task. The bulls were already in the China shop.

"Remember Bayer, this was YOUR idea." Fran couldn't help but throw a verbal jab and the Strikeforce leader.

"Listen...Detective, this administration has enough going on without the two of you adding gas to the fire."

"That's not our fault..."

"No, it's not, but that's beside the point here."

Fran had a feeling where Bayer was going with all this, and he already didn't like it.

"Fran, Lance, I am giving you an order. You are to only focus on Fedora's operations here in New York. You will not be following any of Fedora's connections or activities involving anyone in the Nixon administration. Do I make myself clear?"

"You really like doing half ass shit, don't you Bayer." Fran just couldn't help himself as Bayer left the room.

"How the hell do you work with that guy, Lance?" Fran was now pissed, back in his office.

"What do you mean?"

"He's not interested in looking into the Vatican and European stuff with the counterfeit securities scam, and now he doesn't want us digging into the shit we are finding here at home involving our government."

"Yeah, he puzzles me too."

"I mean, this was HIS little side project that he gave to us. It's almost as if he doesn't want to get his little nose dirty or something, Lance. I mean, you've known him for a while. What is it with him? Is he lazy, or just stupid?"

"I don't think he's stupid. I don't think he's lazy either. Just unsure in his decision-making processes. He's certainly not used to being challenged by someone like you. He probably doesn't want to chance ruffling anyone's feathers that he may have to work with later on in his career."

"I don't agree with his work ethic, but I guess I can see that. But that still doesn't explain his actions about the Vatican and Europe."

"Yeah, that one stumps me too."

One morning, Fran was listening down at the Fedora listening post when a foreign call came in. "Giovanni, my friend, how are things in The Big Apple?"

"Frustrating Jonas, very frustrating."

"Really? How so?"

"I'm trying to purchase Lincoln National Bank, but no one wants to partner with me right now."

"Hmmm, have you spoken with Marco?"

"Yeah, he can't help me right now. Besides, he won't do anything with me at least until we get him into that Chairman of the Board position at Banco Generali."

"Yeah, he was saying something about that last time he and I talked."

"I'm disappointed and frustrated after all I've done for him. But in all reality, I guess I can't really disagree with him right now either. Him becoming chairman will be very important as operations start moving into South America."

"So, what are you going to do?"

"How about you? Surely you can lend an old friend a hand."

"Sorry Gio, no can do."

"And why not? You've never said no before..."

"They are watching me like a hawk over here right now."

"Really? That's never concerned you before, either."

"Well, it's different this time."

"Different?"

"Yeah, it seems that I've ruffled a few feathers around here when I sold that Catholic Bank in Venice to Marco last year. Now the Vatican Secretary of State's office is thinking about conducting a financial audit."

Fran perked up immediately at the mention of the Vatican.

"Yeah, it sounds like its best if you lie low for a while until that all blows over."

"It's certainly cramping my style over here."

"Hey, I heard the Rinaldi Group in Milan was up for sale."

"Yeah, I've heard that too."

"I'd sure love to get my hands on that conglomerate. What do you say Jonas, want to go in on it with me?"

"I already told you, Gio, I can't."

Fedora pressed further. "Who says this has to go through the Vatican Bank, Jonas?"

The caller and Fran were having a hard time understanding where Fedora was going with his idea. Suddenly, everything came into focus for both caller and detective. As the conversation continued, Fran figured out that the caller, this Jonas fellow, was actually part of the Vatican Bank. Fran's hand was cramping as he frantically wrote down notes from the conversation. It seemed like it took forever for the two men to wrap up their call.

"Peg!" Fran was having a hard time figuring out his next move. "First, I must call Peg!"

"Hello?"

"Hi Honey..."

"Fran?! Is everything ok?" She replied while looking at the clock.

"It's never been better, love! Listen, I need you to get hold of that old colleague of yours at the 'Times. Have him meet me at my office as soon as he can. I have a scoop for him!"

"What's it about?"

"I'll tell you later tonight, love!"

"Damn it, Fran, you can't do that to me! You are such a tease."

"Sorry, love, I gotta go. See you tonight. I promise I will tell you everything then!"

"Asshole!" Peg said to herself as she hung up the phone.

Fran's next call was to Munich. If Fran and Lance could not derail what Fedora and the caller had planned, it would directly impact banks in West Germany. Hans had a colleague who did a lot of work in Rome. From him, he learned a little more about the Rinaldi Group. He also learned more about Fedora's caller, including his identity.

A knock on Fran's office door frame announced the arrival of the reporter. "Hi, I'm Robert Henson from the *New York Times*. I'm looking for Detective Clavering."

Fran stood to welcome the man, and directed him to a seat across from him, next to Lance. "I'm Detective Clavering. Please come in. Would you like a cup of coffee or tea Mr. Hinson?"

"No thanks, I'm fine, Detective."

"Please Mr. Hinson, call me Fran." Fran instructed, then turned his attention to Lance. "This here is my partner, Detective Lance Erickson."

"It's nice to meet you, gentlemen. I was told to come here by an old colleague of mine named Peggy. She said you might have some information for me, but she was very vague."

"Yes, Peggy is my wife." Boasted Fran.

"Ahhh, of course...I thought that might be the case. There aren't too many Claverings around these parts, these days, ya know. What a lucky man you are, detective, having her for your wife. I really miss working with her."

"Oh?"

"Absolutely. She was one of the best investigative journalists I'd ever worked with until she left the profession."

"I will tell her you said that, Mr. Hinson."

"Please do Fran, oh and please, call me Robert."

"Thank you so much for finding some time for us this afternoon."

"It was no problem at all. I actually didn't have anything on my schedule today. Tuesdays are usually slow days for news."

"I read your article the other day on Mr. Giovanni Fedora's luncheon. I was wondering how long you've been reporting on him."

"He's actually kind of new to me to be honest. My boss asked me to keep tabs on him when rumors started up that he was interested in purchasing Lincoln National Bank."

"I see," responded Fran. "Have you been reporting on Lincoln for a while, Robert?"

"I've been keeping tabs on it for many years now."

"That's good to know."

The reporter pulled a fresh notepad and pen out of his briefcase. "So what do you have for me, gentlemen? Peggy sounded like the matter might be urgent."

"Mr. Hinson, I mean Robert...Are you by chance familiar with the Rinaldi Group in Italy? More specifically, in Milan?"

"I can't say that I am, detective. Most of my work is stateside."

"Ahhh, well, it just so happens to be the biggest holding company in all of Italy, and probably most of Europe at the moment."

The visiting reporter made a note on his notepad. "So what's going on with this Rinaldi company?"

"There are rumors that Fedora is working on a partnership with Bishop Jonas Krivis, President of the Vatican Bank, to purchase it."

"The Vatican Bank is going to do a joint venture with Fedora?"

"Not exactly. This is a deal just between Fedora and Krivis."

"But not the Vatican Bank?"

"Exactly."

Hinson was confused and concerned. Then he stopped completely. "Hold on a minute, Fran. You said this is all based on a rumor?"

"It's less of a rumor, and more of an idea in the planning stage at the moment."

"And what is the source of these rumors, or plans?"

"That's a bit of an ironic question, coming from an investigative reporter, wouldn't you say, Robert?"

"What do you mean by that, detective?"

"Turn the tables for a moment...what if it were me asking you that question?"

Hinson smiled. "...Yeah, I see your point."

"Let's just say, 'I heard it through the grapevine,' and leave it at that."

"So was it Gladys Knight? Or one of her Pips?"

Fran chuckled at the reporter's quick wit. "Say Robert, do you, by any chance, have any press connections in Germany, Italy, or other parts of Europe?"

"I most certainly do, detective."

"Good, we need to stop this deal from going down."

"But why? How?"

"I have an idea..."

Fran explained everything to the reporter. The idea bothered Him. "Look Fran, I will do what I can to help you guys out in order to stop this deal from going through, but I can't risk my reputation as a journalist by publishing rumors."

"I understand your reluctance completely. Now that I think about it, you may want to use a pen name for this piece."

"Oh? Why?"

"These are very dangerous people, with lots of very dangerous connections. I'd feel awful if they came at you after this hit the press."

"Why would I be in danger with material based on rumors?"

"By the time this hits the press globally, it will be 100% fact..."

"How can you be so sure, Fran?"

"Let's just say Gladys told me..."

The reporter did as the detective instructed. Contacts were made abroad. Everything was primed and standing at the ready just waiting for the detective to say go.

The sound of the bedroom phone woke Fran and Peg with a start. The detective sleepily reached for the nightstand. Anything to stop the obnoxious noise coming from the damn thing.

"H-h-hello." Fran said in a groggy voice.

"Hey Fran, it's Hans. Sorry to wake you up at this hour. I just thought you'd like to know..."

Fran laid in bed, rubbing his eyes and head, trying to gather himself enough to converse. He looked at the clock. 2:48 AM. He still wasn't awake enough to even know who the caller was.

"Who is this again?"

"Fran, it's Hans. You know from Germany. Should I call you back later, at the office?"

"Oh, sorry, Hans, I was in such a deep sleep. No, this is fine. What's up man?"

"We just got a call from a bank over in Dachau. Fedora and Krivis have a meeting with them next Tuesday."

Fran racked his brain, still trying to wake up, while Hans continued to talk. "Oh and the president of the Bank said that they want to discuss American Securities."

Fran responded now, more awake. "Excellent! Do you think they will try to use only one bank, or several, to get this done?"

"I honestly don't know. $100 million is a lot for such a small bank to deal with...but then again, that is probably exactly why they selected this bank instead of another. I will certainly let you know if I get an alert from any other banks in the area."

Something clicked in Fran's brain. "Wait, a second... did you say $100 million?"

"That's what the bank president in Dachau said."

"That's an interesting number. That's the exact same amount that Lance told me Fedora wanted to sink into US investments."

"That is interesting."

"Lance and I will dig a little more into that. I will let you know if we find anything on our end."

"Sounds good Fran."

"This is going to go down, just as I had hoped. I will start the wheels in motion with our reporter as soon as I get to the office in a few hours."

"Is there anything else I can do from here, Fran?"

"There is no way in hell I will be able to get over there right now. There is too much going on at the moment. I will find out their lodging arrangements. Can you get a surveillance team set up so you will be ready to roll?"

"No problem Fran, we're on it!"

"Excellent! damn I wish we could get a bug or something in that bank for their meeting."

"I will see what we can do. By the way, you will be happy to learn that we've updated our equipment since you left. I'm sure they'd love a chance to play with their new toys."

"That is great news. I will give you a call in a few hours from the office."

Fran hung up the phone. He rubbed his face and stretched and thought to himself... "Six days...That will do nicely."

CHAPTER 10

The day finally arrived. A global network of reporters started publishing the press release Hinson prepared under the detective's guidance. In West Germany, Hans and his team had eyes and ears on Fedora and Krivis as soon as their feet touched West German soil. Everything was going according to plan.

For this trip, Krivis traded in his white, starched priest's collar for a nicely designed suit. Fedora, as per his usual, was dressed to the nines. The two men entered the West German Bank carrying an extremely overstuffed briefcase without a care in the world. They were led to a conference room. Seated at the table across from them sat the bank president, and one other gentleman, an undercover man from Hans' team who was wearing a wire. It was a very long and tense thirty minutes that passed. Suddenly from a surveillance car, through binoculars, Hans watched as Fedora and Krivis came bolting out of the bank, and hastily retreated to their waiting cab. The two men were upset, in a hurry, and empty-handed.

In a well-furnished hotel room in Dachau, Fedora paced the floor, while Krivis sat in a high-back chair reading a newspaper article.

"Jonas, what the fuck just happened?"

"I have no idea, Gio, but this is bad. How the hell did the press find out about the counterfeit stocks? How did they even know we were going to use them? Here? Today?"

"I can assure you Jonas, it wasn't on my end."

"Nor on mine. No one involved was ever to discuss them, ever!"

"Looks like we have a leak somewhere. A very big leak."

"There were so many involved in the production and logistics of the documents, tracking down who and where is going to be difficult. Honestly, it could be anywhere...Germany, Austria, Switzerland, US..."

"Wait a minute, didn't one of your guys run into some trouble with some of them in Switzerland a few months ago, Jonas?"

"We did make a mistake in Switzerland, yes..."

"...and Rome..."

Krivis made a deep sigh. "Yes, there too."

Fedora became heated. "I thought you said you were going to be more careful this time."

"I was being careful, otherwise you'd be sitting here with someone else, not me."

"What the hell's that supposed to mean?"

"I never had any intention of going anywhere with any of those securities myself, especially after the mishap in Switzerland..."

"...and Rome...You've been president of that bank long enough, Jonas. You shouldn't be making these kinds of mistakes anymore."

"Huh?"

"Everything that happens in the Vatican is confidential, but nothing is a secret. Hiring out your dirty work like that has exposed you and all of this to the world!"

"Like I don't know how secrets travel within Vatican Walls. I already told you they were watching me. Why do you think I'm sitting here with you instead of Taverna, Gio?"

"Because Taverna is in jail, from the last fuck up, you idiot."

"No, that's not what I meant. And there's certainly no reason to be calling me an idiot."

"But you are an idiot."

"Look, I get that you're pissed right now. This really throws a monkey wrench in both our plans, especially your purchase of that New York bank that you want..."

Fedora threw the nice crystal glass of water in his hand at the fireplace, glass shattered everywhere. "Son of a bitch!" The thought had completely slipped his angry mind until Krivis reminded him.

"That's why I'm here, Gio."

Fedora just turned and looked at Krivis with a crazed look in his eyes. "What?"

"Look Gio, you can be pissed at me all you want, but remember, this whole thing was your idea in the first place."

Fedora gathered himself a little. "Yeah, I know." Calming himself slightly. "There's no way we could have anticipated our current situation."

"Oh, of course we could have...once again we just got too sloppy. Now I have to come up with another plan, if I am going to pick up Lincoln National Bank."

"If it's any consolation, I don't even want to go back to Vatican City right now. There's no way to stop word of this from getting everywhere, especially back to Pope Mike."

"Yeah, you are going to have to swallow hard and do some serious damage control."

"What are we going to do now?"

"You are going to lie low, lie, and kiss ass."

"And you?"

"I will figure it out. I still have two cards left in my hand. I was just hoping I wouldn't have to use them quite yet."

"And those cards are?"

"Fratello, and some 'family members' over in Milan."

Krivis knew exactly where Fedora was going. "Yeah, I can see this may be a difficult decision for you. I'm sure Fratello would love to help you, you just gotta say the word."

"Oh, he would love nothing more than to partner with me in a heartbeat."

"You mean we never had to expose ourselves with this Rinaldi thing? Why didn't you just go to him in the first place, Gio?"

"You know me well enough. I won't be controlled by the likes of him. Every ounce of his wealth and power has come via blackmail. I will never be one of his pawns. EVER!"

"You use blackmail too."

"Mmmm, sometimes. But that is where we differ. Blackmail isn't the only arrow in my quiver. For me, blackmail is a tool to be used only when necessary. We all know what he does to those who are disloyal to him after he's helped a brother out."

"Maybe it's time you joined Marco, me and the others. Come on Gio, it's not so bad."

"Not so bad? He's got every damn one of you guys by the balls in that P2 Masonic lodge of his."

"He's never done me wrong, Gio."

"You've yet to be in a position where you owe him a favor."

"Have you?"

"Ha, no, I won't stoop to that level."

"I stoop to no one..."

"Bullshit! You kiss the ring and ass of the pope and that Goddamn secretary of his."

"Oh stop it, you bastard."

"See, you don't even bother to deny it because you and I both know it's true. The last thing you want to do is fuck up your position of power in that bank."

"So, what are you going to do?"

"I will have to think about it...I've made it this far on my own. I have never once stood on the back of anyone. I owe no favors. The last thing I need is Fratello's blackmail hanging over me, controlling me."

CHAPTER 11

A few days passed. A large, heavy package landed on Fran's desk from Munich. Fran was giddy as he listened to the surveillance tapes and read the notes from Hans and his team. Fran and Lance were pretty tight-lipped about what was happening in Germany. Especially after Bayer demanded that anything that led to the Nixon Administration was off limits. Fran had zero respect for Bayer or how he ran investigations. As far as the local and federal teams were concerned, whatever was going down in Europe was not part of the Benedetto investigation. Fran and Lance decided this would be a good morning to invite District Attorney Christopherson to come check in on the team and the investigation. The two men walked into the daily strategy meeting of 'Rackets' and Strikeforce a few minutes late. The large, heavy box landed on the oversized wooden conference room table with an authoritative thud.

"What the hell is this?" began a clueless Bayer.

"$100 million in counterfeit stocks," explained Fran.

There was an immediate buzz in the room, as members of the team postured and positioned themselves for a better look as some of the boxes' contents were removed.

"Where on Earth did you get these? New York Bankers' Association again?" Questioned Bentley.

"Not this time, Boss. These are from Dachau." Responded Lance.

"Where?" Commented one of the team members.

"Dachau, West Germany. It's just outside of Munich." Continued Lance.

None of them could believe their eyes. The quantity and quality were impressive. Bayer couldn't help himself. "So, how did you two end up with this haul?"

"It seems your friend Giovanni Fedora made a little trip recently. He is trying to find some capital for his latest investments here in town... He was attempting to open a joint account using these at a bank over there..."

"Oh?" Responded Bayer.

"...with the president of the Vatican Bank." Explained Fran.

Everyone in the room gasped upon hearing the news. Soon the room erupted into muted, excited side conversations. Bentley, Thomas, and Christopherson smiled proudly at their detective, and each other, with their own comments amongst them. Fran and Lance continued throughout the meeting to field questions about the haul.

An unmistakable look of concern came over Bayer's face. That was the last thing the Strikeforce commander wanted to hear. As the meeting continued, Bayer's anger and frustration grew. His plan to distract Fran from his obsession with Europe and the Vatican with Fedora just backfired immensely...for the second time.

Following the meeting, Lance and Bentley, Thomas and Christopherson were seated in the Detective's office, while Fran stood behind his desk. Bayer popped his head in the door. "Hey Fran, you got a minute?"

"Sure Bayer, what's up?" With a proud smile on his face.

Bayer was hesitant. "I was hoping for a conversation in confidence."

"Whatever you've got to say, I'm sure will be fine with Lance and the rest of the men here in the room."

"Fine," Bayer conceded. He was anything but pleased with the situation. "You and Lance are not to investigate the Vatican or their bank president. Do I make myself clear?"

Bentley would not have believed what Bayer was saying if he hadn't heard it with his own ears. "You want them to ignore this Bayer?"

"Yes."

"But why?" Questioned the District Attorney.

Bayer bit his lip, then answered. "Orders from DC."

Fran knew immediately that Bayer was lying. He couldn't hold his tongue any longer. "Orders from who?"

"That doesn't matter at the moment."

Christopherson chimed in. "It matters to me, son...and my department, too. My Detective, with the help of your agent, recovers $100 million of the counterfeit securities from Germany, with the Vatican Bank president's fingerprints all over them, and you want them to just ignore it? I've heard that you like to run things that way. Does the chief know this is how you do things?"

Bayer was now more uncomfortable than ever. He knew he should have waited until he could speak to the two detectives alone. "That won't be necessary, D.A. Christopherson."

Fran couldn't restrain his comments any longer. "Listen Bayer, around here we don't do things half ass like you and your boys do. You were the one who put me and Lance on Fedora. You didn't like it when we found out his connections with Treasury figures in the administration and Nixon himself. You told us to ignore all that. So we did."

Bayer tried to interrupt, "But..."

"I'm not finished yet...Now you are pissed because we did as you asked and found some of the counterfeit stocks from Benedetto and his boys in the hot little hands of not only Fedora, but the Vatican Bank president too, in EUROPE. No Nixon investigation, No Europe and No Vatican investigation. What's your deal, man?"

"I only do what I'm told from the Strikeforce chief, Detective."

"My God, man, have some balls. You certainly think you do when you're telling me and Lance what and what not to do. We did what you asked of us...it's not our fault if you don't like the results."

Christopherson finally chimed in on the conversation. "Why exactly did you put these two on Fedora in the first place?"

Again Bayer bit his lip again before answering. "The US Treasury Department received complaints from the Italian Finance Minister's Office on the guy. We knew he was setting up shop here in town. I thought it'd be a good idea to keep an eye on him."

"Did you ask the chief for permission first?" Continued Christopherson sarcastically.

Bayer was now pissed. "Starting immediately, Lance, you are to continue watching Fedora. Fran, you can return to the Benedetto listening post. Do I make myself clear?"

Christopherson, Thomas and Bentley interjected their protests.

Fran soon interrupted them. "Fine. It's about time I check in on him and his friends again anyway."

"Good. I will see you gentlemen in the next strategy meeting, if not sooner." Bayer turned and left the office.

"Why did you give in to him, Fran? That is so unlike you." Commented a confused Bentley. "Let's just say I have a hunch...and leave it at that."

Lance was confused. The rest of the men were now worried.

It was now April. The residents of New York were enjoying a pleasant spring day. Across town, the phone rang, disturbing the usual drone of television, jukebox and conversation inside Frankie's Lounge.

"Frankie's..." Said the guy as he picked up the phone.

The caller responded in a very thick British accent. "Is Benny in?"

"Who ya lookin' for, man?"

"I'm sorry, Luca Benedetto is the chap I'm lookin' for..."

"Oh yeah, sorry, let me get him for you." The man cupped the mouthpiece of the phone. "Hey boss, telephone for you."

Benedetto was talking up one of the barmaids. He really didn't want to be interrupted. "Who is it?"

"Some guy with a funny accent."

"Alright, alright?" Benedetto thought out loud, as he waved the girl away, walked over and grabbed the phone.

"Benedetto here..."

"Hey Luca, how you been?"

"Oh hey...I'm well. How about you?"

"I really can't complain much."

"It's been a while."

"Yes, it has, too long."

"So Duncan, what can I do for you, sir?"

"I'm coming to New York in a few days, and I am in need of your help if you've got some time."

"Sure thing. What ya got?"

"I have some money I want to use to start a connection in some South American trade."

"South America, really? What's wrong? Securities got you bored already?"

"Oh, fuck no. That's a fun and pleasant ride through the countryside, Luca."

"I wish it was on our end."

"Really? Why, what's going on?"

"Oh, don't worry about it. I'm taking care of it."

"Whatever the problem is, I'm sure you are the man to set it right. Look man, I will be in town in three days. I will call you when I get in."

"Sounds good. Do you need someone to pick you up?"

"That'd be great! I'll be on British Airways flight 460 from London. Arriving at 3 PM Tuesday."

"Ok, I will pick you up then," scribbling on a notepad. "I am looking forward to it."

"Me too, Luca. I will see you then."

"Alright. Later man."

The two men hung up the phone. A few blocks away in the dingy basement post, Fran was monitoring Benedetto's line. His attention immediately locked on to the conversation as soon as the caller's name and securities were mentioned. A British man named Duncan and securities, was familiar, but he couldn't make the connection. He rushed back to the Leonard Street headquarters and frantically flipped through the transcripts from his Munich trip. Finally, his eyes locked on the name Duncan Hughes. Benedetto and Franz were talking about the big meeting in London. Duncan was one of the guys at that meeting. Was it the same guy? How many blokes named Duncan, from England, involved with securities could there be in the world? Fran was pretty sure that Duncan Hughes was the same man mentioned in Munich, but he had to be sure.

Prior to Hughes' arrival, Fran could hear Benedetto arranging a big meeting at Frankie's with his boss and Gordon Davies. If Benedetto's boss was involved, it had to be for something big, very big.

Upon Hughes' arrival, Fran paid his hotel a visit requesting to see the list of registered guests, but not tipping who he was looking for. Duncan Hughes' home address was listed as London! One final check with Interpol, and he'd be convinced. He didn't care about Bayer's order to ignore Vatican connections. He was not the man for that assignment. He just knew if, given the chance, he could get something out of Hughes.

Hughes would remain in New York City for a month while his host made various arrangements. Benedetto was on the phone constantly. Counterfeit currency was obtained from mobsters up in Buffalo, then the two men and one of Benedetto's goons traveled to Miami to get Hughes hooked up with the South American cocaine trade. Unbeknownst to them, Fran and his "Rackets" team were never too far away from them. Satisfied with the initial introduction and transaction, Hughes was off to the races immediately placing another order, with an even bigger transaction in the works.

Fran followed Benedetto and his underling back to New York, leaving another "Rackets" man to keep an eye on Hughes. Hughes would make contact with Benedetto daily to keep him abreast of the developing deal. Ten days later, Hughes called in to report that he had just struck an 82 kilo deal with the biggest cocaine supplier in all of South America. Arrangements for cash and logistics were now in the works. Benedetto once again dispatched a henchman to Florida to assist Hughes.

Benedetto remained in "The Big Apple." He had bigger problems on his mind. His trip to Munich in late February had not motivated Straussen and Franz to pay up, or stay current with their contracted payments. Benedetto was over it, and so was his boss. It was time for another trip to Munich.

At the next strategy meeting, both Bentley and Bayer ordered Clavering and Erickson to intercept Hughes' huge cocaine shipment.

"With all due respect, gentlemen, Erickson and one of the 'Rackets' boys can handle that assignment. I need to head over to Munich again, and I'd like to take a backup with me this time."

The room was suddenly quiet as all eyes focused on Fran.

"Munich? Again? Our work over there is done, Detective." Bayer responded, confused.

"Well, clearly Benedetto's work over there isn't."

Bentley replied curiously. "What do you mean?"

"Benedetto's going back to Germany, and this time he isn't flying solo."

"Why? Who's going with him this time?"

"He's going with HIS boss."

"Who's his boss?"

"His 'Uncle Al.'"

Bentley's eyes suddenly got wide, but Bayer was still missing the connection.

"Who is 'Uncle Al?'"

"Alessandro Moretti." Chimed in Bentley.

Bayer finally put the pieces together. "Alessandro Moretti, you mean the number two in command of the Moretti crime family?"

"Yup, that's the one." Fran confirmed.

Bayer and Bentley looked at each other, stunned. Everyone in the room knew that the senior Moretti Consigliere almost never traveled far from home anymore. There had to be a very good reason for him to join Benedetto on this trip abroad. Both supervisors quickly conceded.

"Alright Fran, so what's the plan?" Began Bentley.

"Benedetto and Moretti leave for Munich on May 17th. We need to get there two to three days beforehand to get everything coordinated and set up with the Munich team."

"And what about Duncan Hughes and the huge coke deal?" Bayer interjected, concerned.

"Erickson, you can join Gonzo in Buenos Aires," Fran directed. "Gonzo's Spanish speaking skills may come in handy chasing Hughes and his coke dealer friends all over South America."

"Got it," Erickson confirmed.

Fresh from his meeting, Fran called to book travel arrangements for himself and his partner. He then alerted Hans and the Munich team of the developing situation. Hans would set up their lodging as he had done on the previous trip, excited to be working again with the American detective. Fran sat staring at his calendar, tapping his pen on his notepad nervously. He was dreading his next call.

The phone rang, 1..., 2..., 3 times. "Hello?"

"Good morning, love."

Peg instantly picked up on the dread in her husband's voice and suddenly became worried. "Honey? What's wrong?"

"I'm heading back to Munich in a few days, with my partner this time."

"You're going with Lance this time?"

"No, my partner from 'Rackets.'"

"Um, ok." Still not understanding her husband's apprehension. "When do you leave?"

"We leave Sunday morning at 6 am."

"Alright, the kids and I can drop you off like before. Will your partner need a ride too, love?"

"No, his wife has him covered." Fran was still holding back.

"But you still haven't told me what's wrong, dear."

Fran took in a big breath and sighed into the phone. "Sunday is Mother's day."

"Mother's day?" She replied with a slight giggle. "That's what's got my big New York detective all in a bother?"

"Well, yeah, I thought you would be mad."

"Love, after all these years, I'd think you'd know me better than that."

"Well, the kids and I were gonna take you out for brunch and everything...ya know, the works."

Peg smiled, "Well then, I guess we will have to do all that on Saturday then, won't we? In the meantime, I'll start getting your suitcase ready, love."

He was instantly relieved. "I really thought you'd be mad at me."

"Oh, I'm sure I will be sooner or later, but over this? That's just stupid, love."

Even after all the years he and Peggy had been together, her support and understanding still amazed him. "I honestly don't deserve you," he thought to himself, as he hung up the phone and got back to his work. He hated the timing of this trip. He also knew that there wasn't a damn thing he could do about it.

The rest of the week was a blur for himself and his partner as they prepared for their trip. The other detective had a visible pep in his demeanor. He'd never traveled outside of the United States before. Fran had to elbow him a few times to keep his head focused. Even though Hans told Fran that the Munich PD had updated their surveillance equipment, he would not arrive in Munich empty handed. In addition to their luggage, listening bugs and phone 'tap equipment would travel with the two Americans to their destination. He was determined to avoid every damn one of the frustrations of his last visit.

Sunday morning finally arrived. The two detectives were kissing their families goodbye. Fran was grateful for his wife's love and support, but it still didn't make leaving her and the children any easier. He pulled her in close to him and placed a hand on her tummy. "One of these days, I'm going to take you to Europe, love." He whispered in her ear.

"Sh, don't worry about me or those kids, ya hear? You focus on what you gotta do over there, honey."

Still holding her tight. "I don't deserve you." He whispered, as he kissed her.

Peg pushed him away slightly, "Oh, will you shut up already," she said with a wink and a slight smile. "Get on that damn plane, Francis."

"Yes, ma'am!" He returned the smiling wink, reaching out to hug and kiss his children. "Oh and Fran," Peg interrupted.

"Yes, ma'am?"

"Be careful over there, love."

"Of course, love."

The two men walked toward the gate and boarded their plane.

This trip to Germany was already nothing like his prior trip. His fear of flying was a small fraction of what it used to be. The two New York detectives settled into their rooms and grabbed a quick bite to eat. It was finally time for them to meet up with Hans and his team to get the surveillance room set up and the 'taps and bugs in place.

When the two mafiosi arrived, Benedetto was on the phone, immediately demanding that Franz and Straussen come to the hotel room right away. It quickly became obvious to all parties involved that this meeting was not going to be anything like the last. The initial meeting was brief salutations, followed by all four men heading out for a nice dinner. Seated at a nearby table, the two American and two German detectives sat within ear and eye shot of their targets. The gravity of the situation was on full display at that table. Franz and Straussen were terrified, visibly shaking in fear. Benedetto was pissed that he had to make another unplanned trip to Europe. Moretti, on the other hand, sat at the table completely oblivious of the other three men, smiling and absolutely enjoying his dinner.

Several minutes after dinner was served, an old time New York acquaintance of Moretti approached the table and sat down. Over dessert and coffee, the two old friends were enjoying their time reminiscing. Half an hour later, the table guest escorted the senior Moretti from the establishment for a tour of the German city. The other three men returned to the hotel room.

To Benedetto, there was only one thing in the world more important than his money, and that was his Uncle Al and his money. Franz and Straussen were holding up both. Benedetto was out of patience. He would not accept any more delays or excuses, and both Germans knew it. Franz and Straussen were out of time, but their bigger problem was that they didn't have the money. Straussen offered payment in precious stones and jewels. Benedetto balked. He and Al were there for cash or blood. Finally, in a last ditch effort to square up their debt with the Americans, Straussen proposed shares of a real estate development he had in Spain, still in the building phase.

The two Germans sat on pins and needles as Benedetto contemplated the new offer. He would have to present it to Moretti for approval, but if the real estate offer was legitimate, the men stood to make well over $1 million each on the offer. At this point, Benedetto was pretty sure that this was the best that he was going to get from them. He certainly knew that he wasn't going to get the $350,000 from them. The next day, Uncle Al gave his blessing of approval, and the deal was done without bloodshed or further fanfare.

Fran called Inspector Bentley back in New York with a report. Bentley updated his detective on the latest developments back home. The team had heard from an informant that on Saturday, Hughes and Benedetto's henchman were going to Philadelphia to pick up a narcotics shipment from Davies and then return to New York City. Fran sensed that nothing else was going down in Munich. He left his partner there to keep working with Hans and his team, just in case something came up and caught the first flight back home.

Hughes and his accomplice were pulled over just after they crossed the Goethals Bridge and turned toward Staten Island. The henchman was convinced that the men in unmarked cars were hijackers there to steal the cocaine. His tough guy facade had vanished into a whimpering lump so scared that he pissed himself. His partner in crime was a complete polar opposite, well dressed, quiet and stoic. A complete search of both men and car revealed 10 kilos of cocaine. Both men were booked into the infamous Manhattan jail known as the Tombs, charged, and separated from each other.

Hughes' accomplice was a rotund button man for the Lanscano syndicate. He didn't waste any time spilling his guts. He was immediately ready to make a deal. Leniency on charges and witness protection were his demands.

"Have you ever heard Benedetto say anything about Rome?" Fran asked, continuing his interrogation.

"No, never," the sweating man replied with a blank stare in his eyes. "How about the Vatican?"

"No."

"Are you sure?" He pressed hopefully.

"He's been doing some stuff over in Munich, but nothing in Italy that I know of..."

The grilling continued, and Benedetto's bird continued singing. By the time Fran and Lance were done with him, he was a big, fat, sweaty mess. The New York detective was seasoned enough to know his canary was telling the truth. They were glad to have more on their case against Benedetto. This witness was going to help Christopherson put Benedetto away for a long, long time.

Hughes, on the other hand, wasn't saying a peep. Fran got word from an informant that Hughes was no stranger to this type of situation. Hughes knew exactly how Benedetto handled squealers. He waited patiently for Benedetto to send him a good lawyer and some smokes.

Hughes, stewing in his cell, was the last thing on Benedetto's mind. Benedetto and Uncle Al were still over in Munich, being shown the town and countryside by Franz and Straussen. After two weeks, Hughes had had enough of nicotine withdrawals. One of Fran's fellow investigators came running through his door.

"Hey Fran, I just got a call. Hughes wants to talk with you." He said, excitedly, "Boy, is he pissed! Benedetto left him high and dry without a lawyer or cigarettes."

Fran knew Hughes was a chain smoker. A couple weeks cold turkey was all it took for Hughes to turn. Fran grabbed a carton of Salems from his desk drawer, Lance and Assistant D.A. Thomas, and headed to the jail.

The three men seated in the interrogation room were absolutely shocked when Hughes was escorted into the room. The Brit who took his fashion and appearance very seriously looked like shit. Wearing his jail jumpsuit, his hair was a mess. He had a few days of stubble growth on his face and was sweating profusely. Hughes sat at the table.

"You got a fag?"

Fran took out a fresh pack of Salems, peeled the plastic and foil from the pack, shook a cigarette from it, stuck it in his mouth, and lit it. Hughes watched longingly. He then took a big, long drag, then blew the smoke directly into Hughes' face. Hughes inhaled deeply. Fran then backed away. After a few more drags, he handed the cigarette to Hughes. The addict eagerly grabbed it with his shaking hand, put it to his mouth, and smoked it all the way down to the filter.

Fran shook another cigarette from his pack and handed it to the Brit. "You wanted to see us?"

Hughes was in no hurry as he relished his second cigarette. After several minutes passed, he finally responded. "Benedetto."

"We've heard of him."

"You want Luca Benedetto; I'll give you everything you want to know about that cheap ass son of a bitch." Hughes continued with anger and betrayal in his voice, and smoke curling out of his mouth as he spoke. "After every fucking thing I've done for that God damn bastard, THIS is how he repays me? I'll show that fucking bastard!"

Fran threw a new pack of cigarettes and some matches onto the table. The addict removed the plastic and foil from the package as fast as he could, his hands still shaking, but less than before. He lit himself another cigarette, took another big drag, and held it for a while. The smoke again curled as it flowed from his mouth.

He detailed everything about the South American drug deal that Benedetto had set up for him. The detectives now knew who set it up, who was running it, and even the source of counterfeit cash. Between this and his accomplice, Benedetto was done in this town. Hughes then started talking about a scam that almost bankrupted the government of Panama. This too was something that Fran remembered being discussed by Benedetto, Franz and Straussen in their first meeting, but he was having trouble connecting all the dots.

Fran kept the cigarettes coming while Hughes continued for over two hours about the various rackets that kept Benedetto busy. Hughes was not seeking leniency or a reduction of his charges. All this songbird wanted was a constant and reliable supply of smokes, nothing more, nothing less.

He took another long drag from his cigarette. "And of course," he paused. "You must know about the deal with the Vatican, right?"

Fran, who was pacing the room taking in every single word Hughes uttered, stopped dead in his tracks. Thomas and Erickson turned to look at him as he turned toward the smoking man. "No, we haven't heard anything involving the Vatican." Fran fibbed.

"I'm impressed that they have managed to keep all this under their hats," Hughes half-muttered to himself. "I will tell you exactly what Benedetto, a west coast mobster and an Austrian Doc had going on...EVERYTHING."

Fran quit pacing and sat down at the table across from their British guest. Notebook and pen at the ready. He didn't want to miss a single word Hughes had to tell them.

"Well, the Vatican, it seems, had managed to get itself into a sticky and awkward predicament. Overextended with its finances, they cooked up a dubious solution to their problem. They consulted with some shady characters from the banking and investment sector to get their bank back in the black." Hughes explained as he smoked one cigarette after another.

The two detectives and assistant D.A. were stunned. This was the break Fran had been looking for since he got back from his first trip to Munich. If Fran didn't know any better, at moments, Hughes seemed quite satisfied with his revenge campaign against Benedetto. By the time he was finished, Hughes had fully implicated Benedetto, Franz, Straussen, and a whole host of others.

"Their schemes really are global." Hughes continued.

"So how deep is the Vatican Bank involved?" Asked Fran.

"From what I understand, the Vatican was seeking over $990 million worth of counterfeit US corporate bonds. Everyone who knew anything of it wanted a piece of the action. Dr Karl Schwartz was the one who approached the Los Angeles man, and the two of them then brought the deal to Benedetto. He is the guy with direct ties to the Vatican and their Bank." Said Hughes.

"Do you know what companies they hit?" Fran questioned.

"Mostly blue-chip companies," Hughes continued. "Soda King USA, American Industrial Manufacturing, Business Computer Corporation, Deutsche Automotive Manufacturing, US Telephone Corp and Electrical Technology Corp were all hit for sure. Benedetto's stock portfolio would shame any of the greatest Wall Street investors. And if he needed more to back one of his scams, he'd just steal or forge more." Hughes divulged.

The days following the Hughes interrogation, Fran and Lance were the talk of the office. The information Hughes and Benedetto's minion provided started a daily parade of characters being brought in and charged. Both Christopherson's men and federal agents had nothing but praise and accolades for the two detectives. Many loose ends in seemingly unrelated cases suddenly came together. As a result, D.A. Christopherson and his federal counterpart would now be able to bring charges for the theft of almost $20 million in blue-chip securities against Benedetto, Franz, Straussen and others. Christopherson knew that the $20 million was only the tip of the iceberg, but it was all that was needed to put Benedetto away for a long, long time.

The FBI was pleased to see that the conclusion of the case was now in sight. Fran argued and insisted that the investigation was not over. What about Schwartz? What about the Vatican Bank? Even with all the information and details that Hughes provided them, Bayer and the Feds still ran interference. How could they just ignore $990 million in stolen and counterfeit American securities? What the hell had become of our justice system? The only response he could get from the FBI was they had spent enough time, energy, and resources on the case already. As far as they were concerned, their work here was complete.

Tired of beating his head against the wall over the Vatican Bank leads, once again Fran was back in his supervisor's office. Bentley was stumped, too. This time, going to Christopherson was not an option. The D.A. was up to his neck preparing for the Benedetto trial.

"Look Fran, I know you are frustrated. I have a hunch we haven't heard the last of this case even if the Division and the FBI think their work here is done. Look, you've been working your ass off since long before that first trip to Munich. You should take some time to recharge and catch your breath, and frankly, to spend some time with your family."

"I'm fine sir, really I am. I'll get through this." He replied.

"Take two weeks off. You and your wife could use a vacation with the family. And frankly, after all you've done, you certainly deserve it." Bentley implored.

"I've got work to do, boss."

"Damn it Francis! Quit being so fucking stubborn!" Yelled the inspector. "Get the hell out of here and don't come back for two weeks! That's an order!"

"Well shit, sir, I guess I'm going on vacation." He conceded. "See you in two weeks, then."

Fran left his boss' office. He had to admit to himself that his family life had been on the back burner during most of this investigation. Back in his office, he was just about to call Peggy with the great news but opted to surprise her instead. On the way home, he stopped by the flower shop for some roses for his bride, then rushed home with great excitement.

Fran walked through the back door, like he had done a thousand times before. His smile quickly faded; something was wrong, very wrong. It was a beautiful spring day, yet the children were all playing inside. The children explained that "mommy was sick," and had been in bed all day. He sent the kids to the neighbor's house to play, then proceeded up the stairs to their bedroom. He found his wife curled up in a fetal position in their bed, with all the shades drawn. She was crying. He suddenly was now very worried. His wife was the toughest woman he had ever known. To see her lying there in that state had him beside himself.

"Peggy? What's wrong? Are you feeling ok?"

"Oh Fran," she turned to reach for him, then grimaced in pain, unable to stop the tears from flowing.

He took her in his arms. He could feel her shaking in his embrace. "Shhh, shh, shh it's ok love, I'm here now." Holding her tightly against him.

"N-n-no, it's not." She once again winced in pain, grabbing her belly.

"I'm calling the doctor. We need to make sure the baby is ok."

She grabbed his hand so tight she was hurting him, as tears flowed down her cheeks. "I-i-it's the baby."

Fran pulled back the covers. There was blood everywhere. "What? What about the baby?"

"I'm pretty sure I lost the baby about an hour ago..."

He pulled her close to him again and held her tighter than he ever had before. He had no idea what to do at that moment, other than to hold and gently rock her in his arms. His thoughts raced through everything that had happened over the last several days. "I need to get you to a doctor right now."

A few minutes passed before she regained a little control over her emotions once again. "I started having cramps...while you were gone in Germany," she forced out, then began sobbing uncontrollably.

His heart sank. "Oh my God, honey...Why didn't you tell me?"

"You were so busy with your work, love, I didn't want to bother you." She said, heaving.

"Bother me? My God Peggy. You will never bother me, ever. Please don't ever think that, and please, please, please don't ever do that again love. Ok?"

She looked at him and nodded, as she once again started to sob uncontrollably.

"Can you tell me, exactly what happened, love?"

She wiped her tears as best she could, as she continued her short breathed heaves. "The cramps started Monday night. I thought it was because I was doing too much, so I came upstairs to lay down, and the cramps stopped. I didn't think any more of it until this morning."

"This morning?!"

"Yes, I got really dizzy. I couldn't even stand up the room was spinning so much. Then I started having really bad pains in my belly. The pain was so bad I wanted to throw up."

"Oh Peggy,...You should have called me." He interjected as he took her hands in his.

"So I crawled from the bed to the bathroom. Honey, there is still blood everywhere..." Once again Peg began bawling uncontrollably.

Fran took her in his arms to comfort her again. "Shhhh, Peg I love you more than you will ever know. We will get through this, I'm just sorry I wasn't here when you needed me."

"It's ok Fran," wiping her eyes and nose with a tissue, heaving. "How could either one of us have known?"

He knew she was right, but that didn't make him feel any better. He was now more than ever grateful for Bentley insisting that he take a couple weeks off work. Over the next several days, he would nurse his bride back to health. He continued to kick himself for being so consumed in his work when his family really needed him. He also made a conscious decision to not chase the Vatican case any further.

CHAPTER 12

Summer was approaching the middle of July. New York City was having its worst heat wave in decades. Giovanni Fedora and his wife joined some friends for the curious observance of America's Independence the week before. The fireworks, parades and festivities impressed the Italian natives. The heat and humidity, however, were another story. Summers in New York differed greatly from those in the Northern and Southern regions of Italy.

The failed corporate takeover of the Rinaldi group by Fedora and Krivis using counterfeit American Stocks, was quickly fading from the Italian's mind. He didn't become the richest man in the world by dwelling on failures for too long. The only lingering concern of the incident was exactly how the press learned of their plans. He was confident that the leak must have come from someone inside the Vatican. As far as Fedora was concerned, that was more of Krivis' problem than his own.

Fedora still had his sights locked on Lincoln National Bank in New York City. A financial world that was spooked by the Italian Finance Ministers before was now absolutely cold following the incident in Dachau. Fedora was due to change up his *modus operandi, anyway*. It was now time to be more covert in his financial moves.

Tapping into two of his international holding companies in Luxembourg and Liechtenstein, Fedora finalized the $40 million purchase of controlling interest in Lincoln National Bank. At the time of purchase, it was one of the largest banks in the US, holding just under $4 billion in assets. If it wasn't the most difficult transaction of his career, it certainly ranked up there of anything recent. He sat in his new office, alone, celebrating his success with a fine cigar and a nice crystal glass with a double shot of single malt scotch.

The press circled like hyenas, giving a lot of attention and fanfare to Fedora and his latest acquisition. On the following day, the bank's officials announced its trading figures for the second quarter. The public was deeply concerned about the 28% drop in value from the year before. Unbeknownst to everyone, including Fedora, the bank was actually on the brink of bankruptcy as the ink was drying on the deal. Fedora didn't care. In interviews with reporters, "The savior of the Lira" would draw on his important connections in the financial world to rescue the failing bank.

The first "important connection" to arrive in the salvage effort of the troubled institution came from the world of organized crime. All the dominating families in the syndicates were pleased. Gone were the days of moving money to Italy to be laundered. The volume of laundry and fees associated with such services was impressive. It was the shot in the arm that helped turn the bank around quickly.

With the new and improved status of Lincoln National Bank, other reinforcing connections from around the world were ready to step up and help, too. Curia cardinals in Rome started working with the bank, followed by Pope Michael VI and his bank situated within the walls of Vatican City. Italy's Prime Minister and others from Rome soon followed suit. With a Nixon ally at the helm, many in the administration moved their banking operations to Lincoln too. The US President and his Treasury Secretary were both extremely impressed, but not surprised by Fedora's work.

Some of the most powerful financial institutions in the world soon came knocking on Fedora's door. Intimate banking relationships were forged with major banking institutions in Chicago and San Francisco. Outside of the US borders, London and Paris came calling. Fedora couldn't have been more pleased as his new bank continued to grow bigger and stronger.

A man named Gherado Fratello took it upon himself to further help in the recovery work of the large New York institution. Fratello told all who would listen that "bank vaults always opened to the right." Suggesting that success in banking, finance and ultimately power could be found among right- wing leaders and sympathizers. In the past, he served in leadership positions in the Spanish Civil War and German SS Divisions during WWII. He also served as a spy for both Italy and Germany, reporting intelligence to both leadership commands. He was very successful in his craft. His wealth grew substantially while stationed near an Italian town where Yugoslavian national treasures were reported to be hidden.

Another source of wealth for Fratello was operating Vatican "ratlines" to help some of his colleagues from Hitler's SS ranks who sought to avoid the Nuremberg Tribunals following WWII. Like Fedora, he too was a close friend of the Nixon White House and other NATO leaders. He worked closely with the American CIA throughout Europe to help stop the spread of Communism. The double agent, however, was not committed nor loyal to any of the anti-communism efforts. The work he did for the CIA and other spy operations gave him strategic intelligence. Fratello would then use that knowledge to help him build and fund even more robust fascist regimes all over the globe, especially in South America.

In the early '60s he joined a Masonic Lodge and quickly earned his third degree. His Grand Master, at the time, encouraged him to recruit influential men to bolster the organization's membership throughout Italy. Fratello was extremely successful at his task and soon became the Grand Master of his own lodge, which he called P2. P2 quickly morphed into an ultra-secret clandestine society, Masonic in name alone.

As Grand Master of his P2 Masonic Lodge, Fratello had eyes, ears and influence everywhere. Soon, he wielded more power than most global leaders did. He was very good at making problems vanish into oblivion through his global network of lodge members. Membership had privileges for its brethren, sometimes.

Members, from time to time, came to join willingly through personal acquaintance. For others, more nefarious techniques were used. Prior to joining the lodge, a recruit had to demonstrate his loyalty by presenting to the Grand Master compromising documents and information. These documents not only implicated themselves, but other potential member targets. New members willingly joined when presented with their own misdeeds. This form of blackmail was extremely effective in the successful growth of the lodge, and Fratello's power. Fratello was particularly ruthless to those who owed him money, or favor, demanding more and more "interest" for services rendered if it suited him. Deserters quickly became brutally silenced examples. A decade after its formation, P2 had branch lodges in multiple continents. Argentina, Venezuela, Paraguay, Bolivia, France, Nicaragua, Portugal, West Germany and the United Kingdom. In America, many of the P2 members were also high-ranking members of the most powerful Mafia crime families. The Mafia/P2 were especially influential in the New York, New Jersey and Pennsylvania regions of the US.

Fratello traveled the world playing his international game. The man collected souls like a chess master collects his opponent's pieces on a board. Moving pieces into strategic positions, while sacrificing others like pawns. The more valued the target, the more he coveted it.

He had a most impressive collection. In his mind, the rooks were law enforcement officers, judges and government secret service agents. His knights were military generals, admirals, and other high-ranking military commanders from many Army and Navy units from multiple countries. Of course, his bishops were actual church bishops and a few cardinals who held top positions within the Catholic Holy See. His queen was the pope himself, and his kings were the prime ministers, dictators, presidents, and other leaders of countries. The pawns came from all walks of industry. Doctors, lawyers, cabinet members, politicians from every persuasion except communist, newspaper editors, television executives, and of course executive officers and board chairmen from an expansive array of industry, especially banking and finance.

At times, his game was played, for the pure sake of entertainment. He loved to test the reaches of his amassed power. However, no moves were ever executed without great thought and planning. The loss of life, limb, liberty or happiness by his pieces was a worthwhile sacrifice as far as he was concerned, as long as it advanced his personal wealth, power or both.

It had taken many decades for him to rise from a lowly department store sales clerk to one of the most powerful men in the world. But there was always one piece that always seemed to elude him. The missing piece that would truly complete his chess board. That man was Giovanni Fedora.

Fedora was a very different type of chess piece. In some ways, very similar to Fratello himself. However, in some ways, the two men were polar opposites. Fedora watched Fratello operate for many years from the sidelines. It didn't take him long to have the man completely figured out. Fedora was smart, and always strategically four or five moves ahead of Fratello. As far as Fedora was concerned, Fratello had three major, yet easily exploitable weaknesses: emotion, greed and blackmail.

Fedora enjoyed living a life of luxury. Fine suits, cars, homes, food and art were fun embellishments. However, he never felt the need to flaunt titles or position. Fratello, on the other hand, displayed his greed for power, wealth and position to the public whenever an opportunity presented itself.

Emotions and frustrations were another major weakness for the Grand Master. Fedora didn't have Fratello's military background. Nonetheless, he was a master of strategic planning. Obscuring Fratello's ability for rational thought and execution, emotion and frustration quickly incapacitated his ability to alter and adjust once a plan was set in motion. If there was any type of hiccup in one of his brokered three way arms deals between Libya, Italy and Argentina, his plan would often unravel quickly. He went to great lengths to plan ahead and resolve issues before they became problems whenever possible.

If he didn't have what he needed, he wasn't above falsifying documents. It was just one of the many tools in his blackmail arsenal. Fratello was a quite skilled blackmailer. Fedora, however, was an absolute master. Rule number one in the art of blackmail is to never put yourself or your fate in the hands of another blackmailer. Fedora didn't have the Freemasons to support him, even if for Fratello it was in name alone. Fedora didn't need them. He was a self-made man, with a self-made empire.

Fedora didn't need the Mafia or the Catholic Church either. However, those carefully chosen alliances certainly made his operations much easier. Of course, many of those Mafia and church pieces were also in play on Fratello's board too. Such assets gave Fedora a stealthy perspective on Fratello's operations and plans. The Mafia was useful for those few tasks that the church just couldn't or rather wouldn't involve themselves...which weren't many considering some of the questionable scruples of men like Pope Michael VI, Cardinal Benoît, and Bishop Krivis and others running the church. Even for those in the know, it was not easy to see where exactly the Mafia ended, and the church began, especially under this pope's reign. Neither Italian financier cared about such blurred lines.

Fratello knew that Fedora had a gaping hole in his portfolio. He felt he could collect his most coveted yet elusive chess piece to date by bringing South American businesses and regimes to his New York bank. Fedora wasn't fooled. He knew exactly what Fratello was trying to do. He decided to test the waters. How far would Fratello go to get Fedora into his Lodge? Soon a parade of rulers from Argentina, Paraguay, Uruguay, Venezuela and Nicaragua came through his bank doors escorted by the Grand Master.

Fedora loathed socialism and fascism, especially for his mother country, Italy, or any country he called home. For other countries, however, doing business with fascists was a preferred joy. One-man dictatorships were so much easier than democratically elected governments and their officials. Such forms of government often created an environment of intrinsic, or rather implied, honesty. While no form of government could ever be completely honest, checks and balances made things complicated in a business world. All their committees, inquiries and controls took a lot more time and energy. As far as Fedora was concerned, that much honesty and oversight was bad for business. Especially if that business was banking.

CHAPTER 13

Fran returned to work from his two-week vacation in a completely different mindset. The timing of this respite couldn't have come at a more opportune moment. Fran's time off helped the entire family cope and bond following Peggy's miscarriage. The break allowed the detective to catch his breath, too. Moments of reflection resulted in a promise to his family and himself to be more of the father and husband that his family deserved from that point forward.

Late July was ready to fade into August. Families all over the state were ready for the last month of Summer Vacation. Fran's work environment was a constant buzz. Thomas and Christopherson, Bentley, "Rackets," Bayer and the Strikeforce team were all bustling about, preparing grand jury cases related to the upcoming Benedetto trial. Fran's work regarding Benedetto and his associates was more or less over. Fran's head became clearer as Benedetto and his buddies' glory days in the syndicate began to fade.

Fran was impressed, and in some ways disturbed, that Fedora finally came up with the funds to purchase his bank. "I wonder how the hell he did that?" He muttered to himself as he read one of Robert Hinson's articles in the *New York Times*. He would continue to keep tabs on Fedora's New York activities. Restricting his points of interest to anything stateside. Even his co-workers noticed and were curious about the detective's obvious change in character.

The last summer month flew by quickly. The Benedetto case was finally completed. All of his cronies had been rounded up, and Fran was given the privilege of personally serving Luca Benedetto his subpoena. He walked into the dirty, musty dive known as Frankie's Lounge, wearing his pressed button-down shirt and summer suit, and his badge on full display. His name was well known throughout the syndicate by now, but somehow, his face and voice still remained a mystery. There was no doubt in the minds of anyone in Frankie's who this man was once his feet crossed the threshold.

Detective Clavering had finally come to pay Luca Benedetto a face to face visit. Benedetto was seated at the bar, sipping a cocktail. Fran sidled up to a grungy, empty red bar stool next to the Mafia *capo*. Benedetto's gaze remained fixed, as he swirled a cocktail stirrer around the glass.

Without looking up, he muttered, "So...you're Clavering?"

"That I am. Who wants to know?"

"Barkeep, a drink for the man seated at the bar," Benedetto pepped up and barked at one of the girls behind the counter.

"I don't want a drink." Fran declined sternly.

"I insist," Benedetto ignored. "A beer for the hard working Detective Clavering here."

The woman behind the bar pulled the draft brew as Benedetto had commanded and placed it in front of Fran on a cocktail napkin.

Benedetto smirked as he watched. Fran methodically picked up the beer and began moving the frothy mug to his lips, then Fran stopped. He pulled the mug away from his face and proceeded to slowly pour it all over the bar top. "I told you, I don't want your damn drink. I would never drink with a worthless fuck like you. You can shove that beer up your ass!" His final move, he left the mug sitting upside down on the bar in a puddle of beer.

Benedetto's fists instantly clenched, and he began to turn red from the neck up. "You fucking son of a bitch! Waltzing in here all cocky, like you're some sort of god or something. Well, I got news for you, you fucking bastard! You're a dead man! You hear me? A DEAD MAN!"

"I don't think so, Benedetto." The detective remained calm, yet firm. "Here's a parting gift for you from me and my men in the division." Fran then reached into his jacket pocket, then grabbed Benedetto by the wrist, slapping the subpoena in the criminal's hand. Fran then calmly rose from his bar stool, turned and casually strode out the door of the dive bar.

Fran enjoyed Trick-or-Treating with Peg and the kids. Plans were being made for the Thanksgiving festivities at Peg's sister's home outside the city. Soon the family would be on the hunt for the perfect Christmas Tree to fill their home with the scents and spirit of the coming Christmas holiday. At work, Fran quickly immersed himself deeply into his next assignment.

"Hey Clavering, call for you on line three." Fran heard a voice shout from down the hall.

His attention returned to the present, lowering the report he was reading, as he mindlessly reached for the handset. "Got it, thanks!" He replied, then turned his attention to the caller on the phone. "This is Detective Clavering."

An accented voice on the line responded. "Hey Fran, it's Hans calling from Munich."

"Hans, my God man, it's been ages! How the hell are you?!?!"

"I'm well, I'm well, and you...the family?"

"I'm not too bad, considering the circumstances." Fran chuckled. "Peggy and the kids are doing well, too. They're still putting up with me, too."

"That's wonderful news, Fran."

"What's new with you and yours?"

"Things are wonderful, but the weather is cold here."

"Well, it is almost Thanksgiving."

"Thanksgiving? Oh yeah, that's not one of our traditions here."

"It's my favorite holiday, really. I will have to tell you about it sometime. So what else is new?

I'm sure you didn't call just to discuss family and holidays."

"Um, well no, not exactly."

"Ahh, just as I suspected. So what can I do for you, Hans?"

"Well, I thought you might like to know that the Austrian Police raided Schwartz's compound in Salzburg the other day. They got him sitting in a Salzburg prison cell over there."

"Oh, really!" The detective exclaimed, excited. "What did they pick him up for?"

"They got him on fraud, but there should be more coming soon," Hans continued. "It looks like this time the charges are going to stick too. Not that he still won't try to weasel out of some sort of deal."

"Interesting, but I'm not too surprised, really."

"Did they get anything good in the raid?"

"I don't know yet. They have a lot to still comb through."

"Alright, well, keep me posted if you hear anything that might help our case over here."

Fran's mind suddenly started racing. He was conflicted by the promise he had made to his family, especially Peg, and himself, that he wouldn't pursue this any further. But he couldn't ignore this opportunity. He was certain that both Christopherson, Thomas, and Bayer would be interested in what Schwartz had to contribute to the Benedetto case and others that they had in the works. For Fran, the fascination Schwartz held was that he was the lynchpin in how the Vatican was connected to the fake securities affair. This most certainly would be his final opportunity to pursue any kind of tangent involving the Vatican. New assignments were already awaiting each member of the "Rackets" team. Their talents and skills scattered to other divisions in the department, once the present cases wrapped up. It was now or never.

"It's a long shot, Hans, but I have to get my ass over there. Let me run it by my bosses and the Strikeforce fellas. If I can manage the approval, do you think you can help me out again? I sure could use your interpretive skills."

"I will run it by my supervisor Fran, but I'm pretty sure it won't be a problem on our end. They are very impressed with your work. Especially after the Dachau thing a while back."

"Great, I will be in touch as soon as I find out something, one way or another. Keep your fingers crossed that it all works out."

"Alright, I will. We'd love to work with you again."

The New York detective hung up the phone and sat for a moment at his desk, tapping his pen on the paperwork sitting in front of him as his mind raced. How was he going to get approval for this trip? No one else in the office gave two shits about Europe or the Vatican, or either's possible involvement in any of Benedetto's schemes, except for him and maybe Christopherson. The D.A. was already swamped with work from the Benedetto case. First, he needed to get Bentley on his side. Once again, he found himself knocking on his boss's door frame.

Bentley looked up from his desk. "Francis, please come in. What can I do for you, this fine cold day?"

"Good morning, sir, I just wanted to let you know. I just got a call from Hans over in Munich."

Bentley put his pen on his desk as he cocked his head to the side with a "What now?" look on his face.

"Hans told me that the Salzburg police in Austria have Dr. Karl Schwartz in a holding cell over there."

"Dr. Karl Schwartz?" Fran could see that Bentley was having a hard time finding the relevance of the name.

"Schwartz was the guy who approached Benedetto about the counterfeit stocks order from the Vatican last year."

"That's right." Bentley recalled. "Hmm, I see...Let me guess, you want to go over there and interrogate him about the Vatican Bank's involvement with the fraudulent securities deal?"

"Well, um, yes...and while I'm at it, I'd be happy to see if he has anything to add to our current cases against Benedetto and his friends." Replied Fran.

"Of course you do, Francis. Well, we can't present this as just you going over there to chase down the Vatican connection, but I'm sure you knew that."

"That did cross my mind"

This will have to be ran by Christopherson and Bayer. It will be up to them to approve this one, as you probably already know."

"Yeah, I figured as much, sir. But I must interject that I feel strongly, if we don't take advantage of this opportunity, we will never be able to resolve exactly how the Vatican's involved with all of this."

"Do you have any ideas regarding resources you will need, and details like that?" Questioned the "Rackets" chief.

"As a matter of fact, sir, yes, I do."

"Alright, I don't need all the details right this minute, but I expect you to have all your shit together when we talk to the D.A. and Strikeforce team."

"I promise, chief, my shit will be spit shined long before we go talk to them." Bentley chuckled. "I will see what I can do, detective, but no guarantees."

"I understand, sir. I just appreciate you having my back on this once again."

Fran returned to his office and work. He was hopeful, but doing his best not to get his hopes up too much. He braced himself for the very real possibility of disappointment. He went home that night without a call from Bentley. After what had happened at home during his last trip to Europe, he was extremely reluctant to tell Peggy about the call from Hans. She could tell that something was troubling his mind, and she hated it. He finally explained, and once again, he was amazed at how supportive she was of him. She was more concerned about how long he'd have to wait for an answer than about him taking another trip to Europe. Her only hope was that he wouldn't have to wait too long for a response.

Mid morning the following day, Fran was called to Christopherson's office. He ran as fast as his legs would carry him, all the way to the D.A.'s door. He was caught up by surprise, walking into the room. Seated around the room were his immediate supervisor, Bentley, Christopherson, Assistant D.A. Thomas, his partner, Lance, and Bayer.

"Good morning Francis." Bentley welcomed. "They have some questions for you regarding Schwartz and other details regarding your potential next trip to Europe."

Fran suddenly became nervous; his answers could easily make or break the approval of this trip. He fielded their questions, briefing them on the background he and the Munich team already had on Schwartz. Bayer was still hesitant about approving the trip, as Fran continued talking.

"Sir," Fran looked at Christopherson, ignoring Bayer. He was very careful with his words, completely avoiding any suggestion of the Vatican. "I understand your trepidation, but Schwartz is one of the key people in this entire fraudulent securities case. He was the one who got Benedetto involved in the scheme in the first place. My greatest fear is if we miss this opportunity to interrogate him, we will be missing some vital information regarding this case."

Christopherson lit himself a cigarette as Fran's words rattled through his brain. He quickly interjected, with smoke clouds swirling his head, cutting off Bayer as he was opening his mouth to speak. "I see your point Francis, and I agree with you. Do you really think he will talk willingly?"

"Since I've never met the man in person, I'm unsure exactly what to expect. I only know what Duncan Hughes has told us about him. But I'd feel better about the success of the trip if I arrived with something in my back pocket to help entice his cooperation."

"Yeah, that makes a whole lot of sense. The last thing we need is for you to get your ass over there and he clams up. Any ideas of what we might dangle in front of him?" Christopherson continued.

"How about immunity from extradition for his involvement in relation to the Benedetto case?" Suggested the detective.

Christopherson and Bayer sat silent for a short while thinking.

"We can authorize that," responded Bayer, conceding all of his objections, while looking over at the District Attorney. "Does this guy speak English?"

"If he does, it's extremely limited." Replied the detective, surprised by Bayer's response. "So you will need an interpreter then..." Asked Christopherson.

"No, sir,"

"I don't understand Fran, are you fluent in German?" Questioned Bayer.

Fran let loose a slight smile. "Oh no, of course not...but my German counterpart, Hans Kruck, with the Munich Police Department certainly is. He and his department are already standing by, ready to support this trip any way they can. He was actually the one who called to alert me about Schwartz's arrest in the first place."

"Well Francis, sounds like you have all your bases covered," said the D.A. "You can go to Salzburg. Oh, and Detective...Please be careful over there."

"Yes sir! Thank you, sir!" Exclaimed Fran, doing his best to contain his excitement.

The meeting was adjourned, and Fran sprinted back to his desk. He called to book his flight, then he called Hans to inform him of his travel arrangements. The two men were looking forward to working together once again. Hans would take care of his hotel arrangements and reach out to the staff of the Salzburg prison to coordinate the upcoming visit. The detective's next call was to Peggy. He couldn't help but think about what had happened during and right after his last trip. It was the furthest thing from her mind and quickly put his mind at ease. She offered him love and support, like she always did. "I'll pack your suitcase, love!"

A few days passed, and Fran was once again on a plane flying to West Germany. His lifelong fear of flying had now vanished with the frequency of his European jaunts. Hans picked him up from the airport, treated him to dinner, then dropped him off at his hotel. The next morning, Hans picked him up, issued him his trusty Walther PPK and the two international friends began their two-hour drive to the Salzburg Prison. On the way, Hans gave his American partner some of the history his department had dug up on Dr. Karl Schwartz.

Fran looked through Schwartz's file pictures and documents, shaking his head. "This is not good..."

"What?" Hans was confused and concerned as he drove. "What's wrong Fran?"

Fran smiled, then chuckled. "It's all in German. I can't read a word of this."

Both detectives laughed, then continued their discussion detailing the impressive reputation of the short, round, dark-haired, thirty-six-year-old Vienna native. His rap sheet went back less than ten years, yet the contents were nothing short of legendary. He was a master in the art of the swindle.

Schwartz had his hands in almost every illegal con game known at the time. Of particular interest to the New Yorker was his activities involving stolen and counterfeit securities and currencies.

When the two detectives arrived at the historic Austrian prison facility, they were given a brief tour of the facilities then ushered into a room. The two detectives sat at a cold metal table as they watched a prison guard escort Dr. Schwartz into the interrogation room. The man quickly settled into the room, grateful for the break from the confines of his cell. His demeanor was approachable and quite pleasant, yet he had no interest in talking to either of his visitors about anything criminal. The two detectives could see right away that he was a very charming personality. They now understood how he duped so many of his victims so easily. Schwartz talked in circles, not really saying much, especially with the Austrian authorities still in the room. His trial was still pending. He certainly wasn't going to help the Austrian authorities with their case against him. Hans quickly picked up on what Schwartz was doing and politely asked their Austrian hosts to leave so he and Fran could speak to Dr. Schwartz freely in private. They obliged. Moments later, Schwartz remained conflicted about talking to his visitors. It was time for Fran to finally play his ace. Schwartz turned quickly. His fellow inmates already convinced him that he had to do whatever it took to avoid extradition to the US. He would have to risk life and limb in order to do it. Ratting out powerful people in Rome was worth the risk if it kept him out of the United States Justice system.

Schwartz lit up a cigarette, took a deep, long drag, then slowly and steadily blew the smoke up towards the single light bulb contained within the fixture suspended in the middle of the room, above the table. "My friend, Mateo Taverna, was the one who introduced me to some of the most important and influential people in the Vatican Curia. Our relationships blossomed quickly once I was finally accepted as a friend and colleague. An appointment soon was never required, and business was discussed over many dinner invitations. The situation was perfect, as I became an influential businessman in and around Rome.

I became particularly close to a high ranking French cardinal who was also closest friends with Pope Michael VI. In early January 1971. I was called for an urgent meeting with the cardinal in his Vatican City office. He was visibly distraught. His beloved missions were deteriorating and in dire need of money. The *Istituto per le Opere di Religione* (IOR), more commonly known as the Vatican Bank was a mess. To compound the situation, the rest of Italy's financial situation was hardly any better. Money was hard to come by, and the value of the Italian Lira was in free fall. The banking sector was completely unstable. My host explained that the present state of the Vatican's financial affairs rested squarely on the shoulders of Bishop Jonas Krivis."

The two detectives immediately recognized the name of the Vatican Bank president, from the failed Rinaldi takeover, with Fedora a few months back. The detectives thought it best to just play ignorant. "Who is Bishop Jonas Krivis?" Questioned Hans.

"Oh, I'm sorry...he's the current president of the Vatican Bank." Schwartz responded, then continued. "Anyway, as a result of Krivis' careless investments, the Vatican Bank had already lost millions of dollars from its treasury. The church was now desperate for solutions, perhaps something that might help the Italian economy improve too.

I was at a loss. I was excited to be called upon to help, but I hadn't a clue exactly how, nor why, I had been called to the Vatican. The cardinal coyly asked if I knew where one could get a large number of Blue Chip stocks from major US corporations to help restore the Vatican Bank to its former financial prestige."

Fran instantly perked up as Schwartz rattled off the names of some of the corporations. These were exactly the same as those victimized by Benedetto and his American Mafia associates.

"I then asked him how many securities they were looking to purchase. They were looking for $990 million worth of these stocks."

Fran and Hans immediately knew where this interrogation was going, but they continued to play ignorant. "$990 Million! Holy Shit!" Exclaimed Fran, trying not to "choke" on his sip of coffee. Fran's next question was actually a legitimate query. "Doctor, if the Vatican Bank was in such financial dire straits, how were they planning to fund this purchase?"

"I was still very confused and unsure, as that exact question actually crossed my mind, too. Coming up with that amount of stocks would be no easy task. Knowing the present financial status of the Vatican Bank, I pressed him as to how they would ever pay for them if I could even manage to fulfill their request.

The cardinal let out a huge, thunderous laugh, then smiled widely. 'My dear friend Dr Schwartz, would the task be any easier if, say, the securities were...um, counterfeit?'

I was still shocked by the amount they were seeking. Counterfeits would certainly make the request considerably easier to fulfill."

Hans interrupted the Austrian. "Did he tell you what they had planned for all those fakes?"

Schwartz nodded. "He explained that half would be deposited into the Vatican Bank to recoup the losses at the hands of Krivis and his friend Giovanni Fedora. The other half would be deposited in the Bank of Italy in an effort to halt financial collapse in Italy."

Of course, the two detectives already knew who Fedora was, but Schwartz didn't need to know that. "Who is Fedora?" Fran asked, causing Schwartz to momentarily pause his story. "Why does that name sound so familiar to me?"

"How can anyone not know of Giovanni Fedora? He has to easily be the world's richest, most famous and powerful man in finance."

Hans chimed in. "Doctor, I'm curious. That's a huge amount of counterfeit documents. Weren't they worried about getting caught with them?"

"That crossed my mind, too. They weren't concerned at all." Recalled Schwartz. "The cardinal explained that no one would ever dream of accusing The Holy Mother Church or her bank of purposely dealing counterfeit stocks. If they were ever caught, they would feign victimhood of swindlers and cons. Then the US Authorities would feel bad and obliged to make restitution for their misfortune. The plan was foolproof."

Fran and Hans were stunned, yet impressed with the ingenuity of the scheme. It seemed like the masterminds had everything figured out.

"How much was the Vatican Bank looking to spend on these fake documents, Schwartz?" Questioned the detective from New York.

"$650 million in total. Of course, the cardinal, Krivis, and the other masterminds of the plan would pocket $150 million off the top. The remaining $475 million would be more than enough to keep everyone else on board and happy with the plan."

"Wow, $150 million! That's not a bad haul. So what happened next?" Interjected Fran.

"Well, I knew there was no way I could handle that kind of volume on my own. I needed help; I knew exactly who to turn to for help... My good friends in the United States."

"Your friends in the States?" Hans questioned as he looked at Fran.

Schwartz continued uninterrupted. "Yes, you see, I met a Los Angeles man about a year and a half earlier. It was late '69, when we were both in New York. He had $100,000 worth of American Blue-Chip stocks, and another $100,000 in US Treasury notes on him, at the time."

A little over a year later, I met up with him again, this time in Switzerland. He was very worried...jumpy and scared. Once again, he had a lot of securities on him that he needed to unload. A friend of mine in Rome just happened to be in the market for exactly what the LA man had, so I took all of them off his hands.

My Roman friends were extremely pleased with what I gave them. A month later was when I had the meeting with the cardinal requesting the lot worth $990 million."

"When was that meeting?" Fran questioned, trying to recreate a timeline in his head.

"That was in March of '71."

"Got it."

"So I returned to Austria and called Los Angeles, requesting an urgent meeting with him in Switzerland. He was in the middle of some legal issues and was unable to meet until the end of April. When the meeting finally came to fruition, I took my friend, and interpreter Hugo Franz from Munich. The importance and urgency of the job could not get lost in any kind of miscommunication or misunderstanding. Four months had passed since I had gotten the request from the cardinal. I was starting to feel the pressure. There was an very real urgency to getting things started soon, or my Vatican friends might go find someone else to work with. I was still unsure if my LA connection could do the job on such short notice. Johnny remained calm, confident, and reassuring, saying that there would be no issues in supplying whatever we could possibly need.

He was absolutely stunned. '$990 million? Are you sure? What the hell for Doc?'

I explained to him in detail what the men in the Vatican wanted exactly. He could not believe the magnitude of the request.

'The Vatican? Are you sure...?'

I assured him that it was 100% legitimate, and the Vatican wants to move forward with the plan quickly. The verbal back and forth continued for well over an hour. My supplier remained skeptical; he'd never heard of anything like this ever before. He just knew it must be some sort of set-up for a sting.

The size of the job also concerned him. He was going to need help...and lots of it on this project. He was also going to need a little time to get supplies, engravers, printers and forgers together. Only then could he finally start organizing production. He needed more than just verbal agreements on in order to get started. We set up another meeting this time in London. There, I would provide proof of the authenticity of this deal from my friends in the Vatican.

The American returned home and reached out to a New York Mafia guy named Luca Benedetto. Initially, Benedetto laughed at the proposition. It took a while to finally convince the New York skeptic.

Final approval would have to come from a man above Benedetto, his Uncle Al.

Prior to our London meeting, everything was prepared and ready to go. Upon approval, production would begin immediately on both coasts. My man would oversee operations in Los Angeles, while Benedetto would keep things moving along in New York. Certificate parchment, ink and a numbering machine were all ordered. The only snag in the project was the upfront overhead and arrangements. Those provisions would require a lot of money and manpower. They got busy in the states lining up engravers, printers and forgers. I returned to the Vatican to update the cardinal and Krivis. They weren't concerned or surprised that they'd be working with the American Mafia.

On June 29, '71, my west coast contact and his son joined Duncan Hughes, Benedetto, Uncle Al, Hugo Franz and me in a London hotel suite. Some of the men were still not convinced. I answered questions, hoping to gain their confidence. Benedetto still didn't trust me; he knew my reputation.

To seal the deal, I produced from my satchel two letters that I had obtained from Rome the day prior to our meeting. The letters confirmed the details of the request with quantities, deadlines and payment details. One of the letters was written on official Vatican letterhead. The letters were passed around the room and read carefully. Finally, Uncle Al looked over the letters while we waited for what felt like an eternity.

His gaze finally lifted from the pages. "Alright Schwartz, we're in!"

A huge audible sigh of relief and elation erupted from all in the room. Well, except for Benedetto. Benedetto quickly seized control of the meeting and brought us all back to the business at hand."

"Alright, Schwartz, what needs to happen next?" Benedetto began.

"Well, if we are expected to meet the 10 September deadline, production of the first $200 million needs to begin immediately."

"Agreed." Benedetto replied curtly.

"Any missed production deadlines, the suppliers will be assessed a $9.5 million penalty as per the contracted agreement in the two letters.

"Understood."

"Before we get too far into full production mode, however, my friends in the Vatican would like to see a sample of, say, $14.5 million of various stocks to inspect for quality."

"Of course, what kind of deadline are we talking about for the samples??"

"Any time before the end of July would be fine."

"Ok, that won't be a problem." Benedetto confirmed, then continued. "And how does the Vatican want their merchandise delivered?"

"I will take care of all logistical details, Mr. Benedetto."

"Fine, fine...as long as one of our guys escorts the documents to their final destination and collects payment at that time."

Suddenly my face went deadpan. "Well, um...that will be a problem. That could jeopardize the entire operation, Mr. Benedetto."

"Well, if you think we are just going to turn you and whoever the fuck knows else loose with almost a billion dollars' worth of stuff, unchecked and unsupervised, and unpaid-for, you can forget the whole fuckin' deal as far as we are concerned Schwartz."

At that moment, the room went dead silent. All eyes were now on me and Benedetto.

Everyone knew that Benedetto could end the deal at any moment, without giving it a second thought. I could not risk them walking away from this deal.

I smiled, and responded, "Mr. Benedetto, I assure you that these little particulars can be worked out later."

"Little particulars Schwartz?" Benedetto responded with absolute glaring seriousness. "If we are to move any further on this, you must understand that there is no such thing as 'little particulars' in this transaction. Understood?"

My smile faded as I conceded. "Fine, fine...you send along whomever you wish with each delivery."

"I'm glad we could reach an agreement on this 'little particular' Schwartz."

"Me too, Benedetto." I said, relieved. "Who do you have in mind to serve as escort for the documents?"

Benedetto scanned the room quickly, then pointed at my LA man's son and Duncan Hughes. "You will be working with either of them, or both, for all deliveries."

Both men immediately perked up. They nodded confirmation of the assignment and reached over to shake my hand. I certainly was in no position to protest. With that, the deal was set, and we all went our separate ways. Everyone was pleased that everything could now move to the next phase. In a matter of weeks, the first $14.5 million shipment would be en route to the Vatican.

Back in the States, engraving plates were quickly made, and printing was operating at full capacity on both coasts. Once printed, Benedetto's master forger Gordon "Gordo" Davies worked day and night in order to meet the first deadline. His job was to apply the serial numbers, ownership dates and signatures to the documents. When the final document of the sample run was completed, Davies collapsed in a heap from absolute exhaustion.

All the documents were then carefully packaged and placed into luggage, ready for their journey to Rome. The two couriers were instructed not to give anyone the overstuffed luggage without payment, in full! I wanted to carry the documents myself to their final destination, but neither man would fail on their strictest of marching orders. They knew exactly what would happen if they failed.

Our first stop was Banco Generali. I took a few reams of the bonds into the bank for inspection. The two couriers sat nervously in the vehicle, waiting for my return and report. The bank president, Marco Ansios, was very pleased and impressed with the quality of the documents. The Banco Generali official then called the Vatican with his assessment. The following morning, we were to meet in the cardinal's office for delivery and payment.

Early the next morning, we traveled to Vatican City. I wanted them to wait outside the Gate of St. Anne, just north of St. Peter's

Square and the Swiss Guard's Barracks, but neither man trusted me. I took them as far as I could into Vatican City. The Swiss Guards would not permit them into the most secure inner confines of the Holy City. That is where I left them. I proceeded on, a little to the left of the gateway, through the high-walled Courtyard of the Triangle. I then entered the fifteenth century building known as the Tower of St. Nicholas V. Situated at the very top of this fortress-like structure was the Vatican Bank.

The bank building the day before had specific entrances and exits however, Vatican City was something completely different. They feared that I could easily enter Vatican City with the bonds and vanish; never to be seen again. Hughes and his partner issued two final orders before I left them.

Payment would only be accepted in US dollars or Deutsche Marks. At first I balked, then quickly realized that with the exchange rates, what they were, payment in Lira would amount to about 3.5 billion. Carrying that kind of volume could certainly complicate their return trip to the States. Their other demand was that if for some reason I should disappear with the merchandise and not pay them, I was a dead man, and no other documents would be coming out of the US.

Krivis and the cardinal were extremely pleased with the quality of the documents. The rest of the order was given a thumbs up. However, payment was going to be an issue. Neither the Vatican Bank nor any other bank in Rome had enough American or German currency on hand to pay the waiting Americans. Krivis carefully returned the documents to their respective packages and resealed them. We would have to travel to Turin the next morning for payment. In Turin, we were intercepted by a deputy with the Italian National Assembly. He offered to keep quiet and look the other way if he was cut in on the deal. We didn't know what to do at that point, so everything was paused."

"So what happened to all the stocks?" Questioned Hans.

"They were instructed to leave them with me until further notice."

"So, where are they now?" Hans continued.

"I have no idea..."

"What do you mean, you have no idea? How can that be?" Questioned Fran.

"On 11 August of last year, I was arrested on fraud and extortion charges. They raided my home, but found nothing related to the Vatican deal."

"What did you do with the documents, Schwartz? You have to know where they are." Fran immediately sensed that Schwartz was holding something back.

"Honestly, detectives, I really don't know. Shortly before my arrest, I gave them to my good friend, Mateo Taverna. He was the man who introduced me to the men in the Vatican Bank in the first place. I haven't seen them or him since."

Fran and Hans already knew some of what happened to Taverna. A bunch of the documents he had ended up on Fran's desk via the New York Bankers' Association several months ago.

Fran thought for a minute. "Do you have no idea where Taverna is now?"

"I have no idea, detective. He does frequent Rome, but he also travels all over Europe, too, so it's hard to say."

Moments later, the interview concluded. Schwartz had told them all he could and was escorted by guards back to his cell. The two visiting detectives remained in the room in a suspended, collective state of silent shock. The brazen boldness of Krivis and his cardinal friend was something hard to comprehend. Schwartz provided information that would fill in many gaping holes in the ongoing investigations in both Munich and New York. Their work in Salzburg was now complete. It was time for them to head back to Munich.

CHAPTER 14

Fran wasn't scheduled to leave Munich until late the following day. The detectives ventured back to Munich Police Department headquarters to unpack everything Schwartz had just given them. Of course, they knew a little about Krivis. Fran was curious about the Vatican's financial losses involving Krivis and Fedora. Clearly, they had been working together for a while. What about Banco Generali? Who is Marco Ansios? Were he and his bank important or just middle-men? At this point, nothing should be overlooked.

With these types of deals, he knew that there was no such thing as a trivial participant. Every single tangent had to be followed until all was revealed. It was also imperative to locate the now infamous Mr. Mateo Taverna. What happened to the rest of that sample order of fakes? Clearly, more than just the samples made their way to the Vatican since $100 million worth of them were confiscated thanks to Fran and Hans in Dachau. The two detectives wondered if the entire $990 million ever was delivered to the Vatican following Schwartz's arrest last August. With the financial status of the Vatican Bank and the Italian economy, it probably mattered not to the masterminds of this scheme that Schwartz was no longer available.

Back at Munich Police headquarters, Hans introduced Fran to the department expert on Italy and Rome. His name was Friedrich. The man was excited to learn what Schwartz had divulged. He had been on the trail of the Austrian swindler already for a couple of years. Their interview with Schwartz was about to breathe new life into his stale, old investigation.

"So, what do you know about Mateo Taverna? Ya got anything on him, Friedrich?" Fran started.

"Ah yes, Mr. Taverna. I actually do have a little something on him. Let me go get my file on him."

"If you, by any chance, have information on Bishop Jonas Krivis, Giovanni Fedora, or Marco Ansios, you might as well bring those back with you too." The New Yorker suggested.

Friedrich slowed his step, and raised his eyebrows, impressed with the names Fran rattled off for his additional requests. "You know that those are some of the biggest names in the world of banking and finance in those parts, Fran?"

"I know some about Fedora and have scant knowledge of Krivis. However, I've never heard of Ansios."

It took an extended while for Friedrich to return to Hans' office. He entered the room wheeling a cart loaded with several very large files. Hans and Fran sat briefly in silence, momentarily overwhelmed by the large volumes placed before them. They both stood to assist with the unloading of the cart.

"Sorry it took me so long to fetch these. I had a quick phone call to make before we got too far into any of this..."

"Oh?" Fran responded, curious.

"I hope you two will forgive my forwardness, but I decided to give my good friend and colleague in Rome a call. His name is Detective Cosimo Angelo. I've been working with him for years in Italy and Rome. He's like a brother to me, and certainly more of an expert on these three men and anything related to them, than I."

"That's great, Friedrich, no forgiveness needed. I actually appreciate the gesture." Fran was suddenly excited to hear more. "What did Detective Angelo have to say?"

"He would really like to talk with the two of you about your meeting with Schwartz, if you two don't mind." With a great big smile on his face.

Hans responded, "Shall I go get a speaker for the call?"

"No Hans, he actually would like to meet with you two in person." Fran was instantly confused. "Here?"

"No, in Rome."

"When?" questioned the New Yorker, looking at the clock on the wall, then back at the two Germans.

"Early tomorrow morning. The three of us can drive there tonight, if you guys don't mind me tagging along."

Fran felt a sudden rush of restrained excitement and anticipation. "I'd be more than glad to meet with him Friedrich, how long will it take us to drive there?"

Hans chimed in, "About nine hours, give or take."

"Oh wow, nine hours," Fran again looked at the clock, concerned. "But I'm scheduled to fly back to New York tomorrow afternoon. There's no way we would make it back in time for me to catch my plane home."

As much as he missed his wife and children, he also knew he couldn't pass up this opportunity. His gut told him that even with the new information that Schwartz had just dropped on them, and the way the investigation was going back home, his window of time and opportunity to dig into the Vatican connection on this case was quickly coming to a close. "I'm going to have to call my boss and wife to let them know. Oh, and I am going to have to change my flight, too."

"You could leave from Rome instead of here..." Hans suggested, interrupting Fran's train of thought. "I'll change your flight; you call your boss and family."

"You can use my office phone to make those calls if you want, Fran." Friedrich Offered. A surge of excitement coursed through the New York detective's veins as he left the two Germans in search of Friedrich's office and phone.

After a few phone calls, they loaded all the gathered files into a car, checked Fran out of his hotel, grabbed a quick meal, and then three detectives set out on the road to Rome. The two Germans took turns driving. The nine-hour road trip, during daylight hours, had some of the most breathtaking views Fran had ever seen in his life. Once night fell, he and the other passenger did their best to nap when they could. They arrived in Rome very early the next morning. The three men freshened up a little before meeting with their waiting Italian counterpart.

Hans and Fran were soon escorted by Friedrich into Detective Cosimo Angelo's office and introduced. The four detectives soon all sat down and started to exchange and compile their information. Fran and Hans began with a detailed report about their interview with Schwartz.

Cosimo looked at Hans and Fran. "I must commend you two on your great work getting Schwartz to spill his guts like that on all of that counterfeit securities stuff. That is going to help all of us out a lot."

"Ah, it was just dumb luck, ya know, following up on leads Cosimo..." Responded Fran modestly.

"Don't sell yourselves so short, detectives. Our investigations into those fakes have been stalled out for months. We haven't been able to catch a break anywhere."

Fran instantly perked up. "Well, give the credit to Hans. He's the one that called me."

"That's true, but it was your idea, Fran, to come over and interview him." Offered Hans modestly.

"Let's just call it a team effort, then. We just hope it helps bring these chumps to justice."

"It certainly won't hurt the investigation going forward..." Commented Cosimo. "So I'm told you'd like some background information on some of the people Schwartz mentioned in your interrogation?"

"Yes, please!" Fran replied, rubbing his hands together eagerly. "Anything you got will be most welcomed."

"Alright, where shall we begin?" Questioned Friedrich.

"Well, since Mateo Taverna was the last known person in possession of those fake bonds, as far as Schwartz was concerned, and he seems to have the smallest file, let's start there." Hans suggested as he gazed at the stack of folders they brought from Munich.

"Alright," Friedrich rummaged through the stack of files to produce a relatively smallish volume of documents. "Mateo Taverna ran an insurance and finance company in Rome and Munich. Out of his Rome office, he also ran an investment firm. A close friend of Krivis' from Connecticut was listed as president of the company."

"Oh, really?" Responded a surprised New York detective.

"Yes sir," Cosimo affirmed, then continued. "There is also a Vatican lawyer with a very successful practice that serves on their board."

"Vatican lawyer?" Queried Hans.

"He's the one that Mr. Taverna opened the joint account with in Zürich last July. The two of them took out a loan to open the account using the $1.5 million in counterfeit bonds as collateral. Those bonds were all sent by the bank to New York for a thorough inspection."

"Oh shit! How much was the loan for?" Interjected Fran. "5% of the bond's face value."

"Hmmm, I was expecting more..." Commented Hans.

"I think they were trying not to set off any suspicions among the bank officials. That plan obviously backfired horribly, since the bank they used had a policy of confirming the validity of all bonds used as collateral."

Fran's curiosity was piqued. "You say Taverna's partner in crime... literally, was a Vatican lawyer? What kind of lawyer, I mean, besides a dirty one?"

"Mostly, he represented the wealthy going through divorce and matrimonial disputes. He was a good connection to have. He was also closely connected to Krivis."

"He wouldn't by any chance have been a monsignor, would he?"

"Actually, yes." Cosimo was surprised by Fran's knowledge. "The lawyer is a monsignor with the church. How did you know?"

"Actually, I'm very aware of those counterfeit certificates. They actually ended up on my desk in New York, after the Banking Association was done with them." Fran explained. "I had heard it was a joint account. Do you know much about the other party on the account?"

"Hmm, it looks like a monsignor that I believe may be working in the Vatican's Secretariat of the State's office."

Francis and Hans instantly looked at each other, then back at Cosimo.

"That happened right after Schwartz gave him the fakes! Just before he was arrested last August." Hans commented. "Do you two think it's a pretty safe guess that Taverna replaced Schwartz in this scheme after his arrest?"

"That seems to be a plausible assumption." Cosimo agreed. "Taverna has certainly had more than enough interaction with the Vatican in the past to easily slip into that role."

Fran turned back to Friedrich. "So what is his status and whereabouts now?"

"Well, of course, he and the monsignor never saw a dime from their requested loan placed into their account. The account was closed immediately by the bank once the bonds were determined to be fakes."

"...and Taverna?" Questioned Hans. "He disappeared."

"Of course he did," Fran responded, with sarcasm, disappointed.

Cosimo continued. "Well Fran, if you knew Swiss banking officials, and how they feel about swindlers, you really wouldn't be all that surprised, my friend."

"Alright gentlemen, who shall we look at next? Just keep in mind, these men are never really very far from one another."

"What do you mean by that, Friedrich?"

"You will see, soon enough Fran...How about we start with Giovanni Fedora?"

"Alright..." Both detectives agreed. "We already know a little about him since he moved to New York earlier this year, and after we foiled his and Krivis' buyout of Rinaldi."

"That was your doing?" questioned a surprised Italian detective.

Fran looked at Hans proudly and smiled. "Yep, it sure was!"

"Wow, I had no idea. I am very impressed with your work already, Detective Clavering." Continued Cosimo.

Friedrich opened up an extensive file and took out a photograph and handed it to Hans. After his inspection, he handed it to his guest. Fran recognized the impeccably dressed man immediately. He was slender, clean shaven and of medium build, with short, dark wavy hair, dark eyes and handsome facial features.

Cosimo responded. "I heard he fled to New York City. He seemed to keep a low profile after he left Italy."

"Low profile? Working with Krivis and $100 million worth of fake bonds to open an account in Dachau, is 'keeping a low profile?'"

"Um...well...it is for him. That incident, I guess, could be a slight exception."

"I've only been looking at him for a few months now. To be honest, I really know little about his history before he landed in America."

Cosimo nodded at Fran, then began. "So this 52-year-old international banker, financier, and industrialist has to be THE richest, most powerful man in the world."

"THE richest, most powerful?" Fran challenged.

"Well, if he's not, he's pretty damn close to the top." Commented Cosimo. He pulled out several recently published magazine articles from the file.

"Italy's Most Successful and Feared Financier," read one business headline. "One of the World's Most Talented Traders," claimed *Fortune.* Fran quickly scanned another article handed to him. His gaze was quickly directed to a quote from Krivis regarding Fedora. "Giovanni Fedora is, in my opinion, a man well ahead of his time, especially where financial matters and vision are concerned." Fran continued reading aloud as Krivis expressed his absolute faith in Fedora's prophetic vision of the future, in print. Fran continued, "His ideas and judgment are sound, and I seek his advice frequently on matters of finance and investment."

"Hmmm, I wonder how Krivis really feels about this Fedora fellow," Hans jested.

"Their close friendship is no secret, Hans. Krivis considers him a master of his craft and a model to emulate. He follows Fedora around like a lemming." Added Cosimo.

"A lemming? That's an interesting, and rather odd way of putting his devotion to Fedora, Cosimo," Fran queried.

"Well, it is common knowledge around here that some of the Vatican's biggest losses have resulted from some of Fedora's investment direction executed by Krivis. This has happened several times already, and yet Krivis still has complete faith and devotion in the man."

"But why?" Hans interrupted, confused. "Isn't Krivis concerned with the solvency of that bank he's running?"

"Like I said before, Krivis follows Fedora like a lemming. He's been advised and reprimanded repeatedly, from church higher ups, not to work with Fedora, yet he refuses to listen or heed their warnings." Cosimo paused and pondered for a moment. "I suppose Krivis' actions and devotion could be motivated out of fear. If that were really the case, he certainly would have plenty of company."

"Why would fear be a motivator for Krivis' continued defiance of church officials?" Questioned Hans.

"There are a lot of very savvy businessmen and investors in Italy and other parts of the world who are very skeptical of Fedora and his business practices. Many, I'm sure, have solid evidence to justify their suspicions, but they are scared. They absolutely refuse to come forward or confront the mobster."

Fran was suddenly confused. "Mobster? You lost me Friedrich."

"Fedora's reputation for international reach and limitless power is legendary. He's a merciless man capable of doing anything he pleases, any time he wants, without fear of retribution or consequence, regardless of legality. His entire operation is similar to and rumored to be closely connected with the Mafia."

"Ahhh ha," Fran interjected. "I may not understand all this

financial mumbo jumbo, but I do know, very well, I might add, how the Mafia operates. At least in the States, anyway..."

"While he has those Mafia connections, he certainly doesn't need them. He has plenty of legitimate businesses to keep him busy and wealthy."

"Such as...?" Hans inquired, curious.

"He serves as president of seven companies, and vice-president of three others. He also serves on the board of directors for at least twenty-four others. And those are just the ones we know about. He does all this while running the largest tax law firm in Milan."

"...And now, a bank in New York...Where on Earth does this man find the time? Or even keep everything straight, for that matter?"

"Hans, my friend, that is a question only Fedora can answer...You know, now that I think about it, there is no way that Krivis can be operating because he is fearful of Fedora. There are plenty of fact-based rumors of the two of them partnering on many deals that have resulted in huge profits for them both personally."

"Jesus fucking Christ!" Exclaimed Fran under his breath.

Friedrich paused for a moment. "Shall we move on to Krivis, gentlemen?"

"Sure," all the other men confirmed in unison.

Fran continued to comment. "While I am sure that there is plenty more, I need to learn about Fedora. I think my head is going to explode if you tell me anymore about him right now. How about we talk about his partner in crime, Bishop Jonas Krivis?"

"You mean the Bodyguard?" Responded Friedrich, as he heaved another large file onto the desk.

"The Bodyguard?" Questioned a puzzled New Yorker, looking at a shrugging Hans.

"That's what the locals like to call him in Rome and the Vatican. Hang on, I have a picture of him here in his file." Friedrich quickly retrieved a photograph from the inside cover of the file and handed it to Fran and Hans to view. It was quickly, quite obvious to both detectives why they called him "The Bodyguard." The man was a real behemoth.

JANE M. BELL

"This is Bishop Jonas Krivis, born and raised on the outskirts of Chicago, Illinois."

Fran suddenly stopped and began choking and coughing. "Wait, what? He's a Goddamn American?!?!?"

"Yes, Fran! All 6 foot 4, 220 hulking pounds of him!

Fran quickly grabbed the image for a more detailed look. "He would make a better football player than a man of the cloth, if you ask me."

"You will have no argument there...Krivis was raised in the same Chicago suburb as Al Capone. He became a priest at 25, ordained by the Archdiocese of Chicago. During his college years, he studied Cannon Law in Rome, earning his degree in '53.

Following his studies, he landed himself a full-time position with the Vatican's Secretariat of State. Through his work in the Vatican, he became close friends with a certain high-ranking cardinal within the Holy See."

"Certain cardinal?" Interrupted Hans.

Cosimo issued a nod of confirmation, then continued. "In the summer of '63, everything dramatically changed for both men, more or less overnight. The said 'certain cardinal' was elected, and crowned Pope Michael VI, and Krivis, with his monstrous stature and personal acquaintance with the new pope, was immediately appointed the new pope's personal bodyguard and traveling aide."

"Well, isn't that convenient?" Interjected Hans.

"Not nearly as convenient as Pope Mike appointing him president of the Vatican Bank about eighteen months ago." Added Cosimo.

"Jesus, he's only been there a year and a half, and he's already run the thing into the ground? He's like a clumsy ox..." responded Fran.

"Krivis is nothing more than a huge, pompous ass. He isn't a smart man, and he certainly has zero business running a bank. He is just there because Pope Mike put him there." Continued Cosimo. "Fedora, on the other hand, has the financial mind and connections to make huge deals happen, and fast. According to some newspaper reports, Krivis has sunk as much as $100 million dollars of the Vatican's money into Fedora's companies around the world. The hemorrhaging of money coming from the Holy Bank would have gone completely unnoticed if it weren't for someone leaking the information to the press. Some of my sources in the financial sectors have even told me that these two have shared controlling stakes in a banking and securities firm in Switzerland.

Then there's Krivis' board of director's position at a Bank in the Bahamas. He and Fedora are co-owners with Marco Ansios of Sierra Madre International Bank in Nassau, The Bahamas. I'm sure there are more than a few shared accounts in that one. And of course there is the international holding company in Luxembourg too. However, I don't think Krivis has anything to do with that, that one's all Fedora's I think."

"Holy fuck!" exclaimed Fran. "Shit, these guys are all over the fucking place!"

"Obviously Krivis isn't your typical 'Man of God,' interjected Hans. "Obviously..." parroted the New York detective.

"I mean, his physical features don't exactly exude an air of reflective piety for one. Add to that his pomposity as he goes about the Vatican and Rome, and you get a man who is most passionate about fine, expensive scotch, beautiful women, Havana cigars, money, golf and himself. And most definitely not in that order. I suppose God is somewhere on his list, but only he knows where exactly."

Fran and Hans continued to be dumbfounded the more they learned. As seasoned as both of them were, every new revelation on this case still hit them hard, shattering long held delusions of much of what is good in this world. The truth stung badly with the details that continued to be revealed to them. All this new knowledge sent Fran's mind racing. While he and Hans were no longer solely focused on Schwartz's testimony, they were still getting an insane amount of information to keep both of their investigations moving forward. Fran felt energized and intoxicated by the hunting of these sly foxes. He wanted more, like a junkie needing a fix.

Fran turned to Cosimo, "I know it's a long shot, but do you think you can get us a meeting with Krivis?"

"It would be next to impossible for non-Vatican folks to get anywhere near Krivis. He is, for the most part, well insulated from the prying public."

"I figured it would be a long shot." Fran tried to hide his disappointment. "I really shouldn't be surprised, especially after what Schwartz told us about how even Benedetto's two couriers couldn't even grace their presence, and they had the $14.5 million of fake bonds they ordered."

Cosimo chimed in. "Speaking of Schwartz, did he say when and how much the first shipment was supposed to be, Hans?"

Hans flipped through his notes. "It looks like $100 million worth was supposed to have been delivered on 3 September, '71."

"Interesting..." Cosimo thought out loud, looking at a cut out newspaper article dated 10 September 1971. "This article from our region's biggest newspaper says Krivis and Fedora were once again partnering on huge ventures."

"That's about a week after the first shipment was supposed to arrive!" Fran exclaimed. "But why are 'those two working together again' a front-page story? I thought they were best of friends."

Cosimo continued. "Well, at the time it WAS a big deal, Fran."

"How so?"

"The two of them working together certainly wasn't anything new, but Krivis isn't the brightest cat on the block, especially when it comes to banking and investing. He became the subject of some very harsh criticisms after Krivis, under the advice of Fedora, gambled millions on some of Fedora's companies and lost."

"Like, how much are we talking about Cosimo?" Fred questioned.

"Some in the press have estimated well over $100 million of the Vatican's money."

"Shit, that's a ton of money!" Hans interjected. "How the hell does that man still have a job?"

Cosimo continued, "Well, he immediately downplayed his relationship with Fedora, claiming only limited financial involvement with him, and claiming that the two of them weren't all that close."

"Bullshit!" Francis interjected. "I guess that explains the need for all those fake securities."

"Yes, it is bullshit. While Krivis is a very pompous and stupid man, he can't be so stupid that he can't see the very crooked road he and Fedora were traveling. I mean, it really isn't a secret in these parts. I mean, the press and even the Italian National Assembly suspect that Fedora is, or was, using Krivis' bank to transfer money illegally in and out of the country to avoid taxes. Other rumors suggest that Fedora is also using the Vatican Bank to launder Sicilian and American Mafia drug money for his mob friends."

The New York detective was still thinking about the possible Fedora/Mafia connections, when there was a loud audible growl coming from his stomach. "Excuse me." Responded Fran, embarrassed.

Cosimo glanced over at the clock on the wall. "10:45 AM. What do you say we grab an early lunch, gentlemen?"

"Sounds good to me," uttered Fran. "I'm famished!"

"Good, I know just the spot! And while we're at it, we can do a little spying on the good ol' Bishop Jonas Krivis."

All three detectives whipped around in confused unison. "What?"

"We can't get an appointment with the man in his office, but we can certainly get a firsthand look at Krivis and how he operates." Said Cosimo.

"I don't understand, Cosimo. What the hell are you talking about?" Responded Fran. "Come along gentlemen, you will see soon enough…"

The four men piled into Cosimo's car and headed for the Santa Romano Golf Club on the outskirts of town. "Almost every afternoon, the bishop could be found at the country club." Cosimo explained. "We can get a table near his usual dining spot and you can see firsthand how the bishop operates."

"Wow, this will be better than wiretapping Benedetto's activities." Hans exclaimed. "I get the feeling that this isn't the first time you've done this, Cosimo."

"Oh, hell no. I've done it more times than I can count."

"Does he know who you are, or what you do?" Hans queried.

"The man doesn't have a clue, and by the end of lunch, you will understand why." Continued the Italian Detective.

"I can hardly wait!" The American responded excitedly.

The four detectives arrived at the Golf Club's *Ristorante*.

"We'd like a table with a view of the golf course, please." Cosimo addressed the hostess. "Right this way gentlemen," replied the hostess with menus in her hand.

As the four gentlemen were being escorted to their table. The hostess kept walking. "Excuse me Miss," Cosimo interrupted the procession, and gestured to a table near a large corner booth. "Could we please sit at this table?"

"Why, of course sir." Responded the hostess.

"Thank you, Miss." Replied Cosimo.

"No problem, gentlemen," she said as they took their seats and she handed each of them their menus. "I will send over your server right away."

"Thank you," responded the four detectives.

The four men weren't seated for more than fifteen minutes before Bishop Krivis and his entourage walked in. Hans, Fran and Friedrich could not believe what they were witnessing. There were throngs of beautiful young ladies just swooning over the man, like he was some sort of "A-list" movie star. Immediately after taking his place at the table, Krivis lit up one of his big, fat Havana cigars. One of the barmaids cruised by his table. "Would you like your usual Scotch on the rocks, bishop?" She asked flirtatiously.

"Of course, honey, you know what I like. It's no secret." replied Krivis suggestively, as he winked at her and blew her a kiss.

It was more of the same, all through lunch. Fran was finding it hard to stomach his lunch because of the revolting display he was witnessing. Everyone around him gracelessly flaunted themselves before him, completely catering to his every whim. The loud, obnoxious, pompous fool just soaked it all in as he puffed away on his cigar and sucked down the scotch. As far as Fran was concerned, this was no "Man of God." Following his lunch and cocktails, the bishop and his attending entourage left the restaurant to play a round of golf on the links. The four detectives paid their bill. It was time to head back to Cosimo's office.

"What the hell was that all about?" Fran asked as soon as they all got back into the car. "They acted like he owned the Goddamn place or something."

"Well actually, in a sense, he does, well sort of...oh shit, well he used to..." Replied Cosimo. "Huh?" Fran responded, confused.

"The Vatican Bank used to own that golf course." Responded Cosimo. "It's the same dog and pony show at the executive golf course across town."

"Do they own that one, too?" Hans queried.

"No, actually, they never did own that one. He just thinks his shit doesn't stink anywhere in this town. The funny thing is that while his cheap groupies fall all over themselves when he's around, the local high society aristocracy talk all kinds of shit about him behind his back. They call him *Imperatore Brutis in re.*'"

"Huh?" Chimed in Fran.

"Emperor Brutis, the King," translated the German detective, as all four of the detectives chuckled.

"Forget God, gentlemen," Cosimo explained, "if you want to know about the Roman Catholic Church, you must frequent the golf courses of Rome. You will most certainly learn more there than you will attending weekly Mass. While Krivis is the most blatant in his carousing, other men of the church often join him and his entourage. A few have their own 'attendants,' but it's not nearly as tactless and the 'King's.'"

Back in Cosimo's office, again they all looked over the notes from the Schwartz interview. They all knew that Krivis was a man of questionable morals, but this securities scheme was absolutely beyond their expectations. From that moment forward, these men vowed to bring all of those involved to justice, regardless of borders. They agreed that if they could somehow get ahold of those letters Krivis sent to the big meeting via Schwartz, their jobs would be made a lot easier.

Fran still had a little time to kill before his flight's departure,

"Cosimo, did Fedora start using the Vatican Bank for his transactions when Krivis was appointed as president by Pope Michael?"

Cosimo responded. "No, I'd say it was probably sometime in the late '50s, right after Fedora purchased a bank in Milan. Through that Milan bank, he got his first taste of working with the Catholic Church. It was a small 'investment' that resulted in huge dividends for him later."

"How so?"

"The archbishop of Milan, at the time, was trying to raise money for a home he wanted to build for the aging locals, but he was having a hell of a time securing the funding. He approached Fedora at his new bank. Fedora stepped in and raised the entire $2.4 million requested without even blinking an eye. That archbishop, at that time, was the future Pope Michael VI. The two became fast friends, and the archbishop continued to seek his advice."

Francis's eyes went wide. "So the man who was laundering cash for the Mafia with one hand and building old folks' homes for the Vatican with the other? Does this man even have any type of moral compass?"

"His only compass, which obviously has nothing to do with morals, points in the directions that will make him more and more money." Interrupted Friedrich. "His ties to this pope, at the time, got him in the door with the secretary of the Vatican Bank. He became such a well-trusted friend of the church, they appointed him to boards of directors for several Vatican owned companies. He also helped broker Vatican linked deals with banks in London and Chicago."

"This man was all over the place," interrupted Hans.

"Oh, he was just getting started at that point," responded Cosimo.

"But I don't understand. If you know about all this stuff on him, why hasn't anyone done anything to stop him?" Asked Hans.

"It's not that easy, Hans." Replied Cosimo. "While we are pretty solid on most of what I've told you, there just isn't any hard evidence."

"Do you think some of the Boards of Director positions that he currently holds are Vatican interests?" Questioned Fran.

"That's hard to say," replied Cosimo. "We know that he owns at least four banks. He has control of some 130 major corporations from at least fifteen different countries around the world."

"Good God!" Fran interrupted. "That's some serious clout."

"I'm sure most of that is his, but to be realistic, it would be very difficult to tell what belongs to him, and what belongs to the Vatican without auditing the Vatican Bank."

"An audit really should be done, but it won't." Friedrich responded in a defeated tone. "It will never happen, as long as Krivis is at the helm of that bank. Besides, even if we did get a proper report, things are so fluid with him and that bank. Within a matter of weeks, the entire landscape would look completely different."

"That's frustrating." Remarked Fran with a sigh. "I bet he's a slippery one, too."

"Nah, I wouldn't call him slippery. He is actually quite public and extremely cocky about most things. He certainly believes he can do no wrong, that's for sure," continued Cosimo. "And we haven't even gotten into his real estate holdings. His holdings and world-wide client list are just ridiculous. I mean, they don't call him 'the most ruthless and skilled financier in all of Italy' for nothing."

"And do we know what exactly he does for all these high-profile clients?" Asked Hans.

"If I had to guess, I'd say moving money and assets here and there, all around the world, in order for them all to avoid taxes." continued Cosimo.

"So he's doing all this global wheeling and dealing that, for the most part, is publicly known, even if his activities aren't always above board, right?" Queried Francis.

Cosimo affirmed, "Exactly!"

"And what more can you tell me about his Mafia activity, Cosimo?"

"We really don't have too much on his Mafia involvement, Fran. At this point, they are mostly just unsubstantiated rumors, and nothing more. Unlike his other business activities, whatever involvement he may have with the Mafia, he's been pretty stealth about it."

Fran was still curious by the possible Mafia connection. "He has all this wealth, and yet he's still rumored to be a major laundryman for the mob...I mean he has more money and power than most men could ever dream of having, yet he is still rumored to be doing the mob's dirty work..."

"Right..."

"But why? What value could those mob connections ever possess for him?"

"If I had to guess, Fran," Cosimo suggested. "Maintaining those ties secures a certain power and rank within families and syndicates. Those connections might come in handy at some point down the road in ways that we can't quite understand...yet."

"I suppose..." Fran was not satisfied with the response, but it was all they had at the moment. "When I get home, I will see what I can dig up on him from my side of the Atlantic. I have a few guys who may know a little of something about it. Especially if he is involved with any of the syndicates over there. Of course, anything I find on this cat, I will certainly pass along to you fellas."

"We certainly welcome any assistance and information you find, Fran. That's one of the big, deep, dark secrets about this guy for us."

"I will also keep my eyes on that Bank he just bought over there in Long Island."

Fran continued to scribble in his notebook. "Well, that certainly brings everything I've learned on this trip full circle." Fran replied, reflectively, as he scanned over all the fresh notes gathered in his notebook since his trip began. "You guys have certainly given me a lot of great information. A lot of additional work now awaits me when I get home. Thanks to you guys, I won't have to start back at square one, and for that I'm truly grateful."

"Well, the stuff you and Hans got from Schwartz has created lots of new work for us, too. We appreciate you making the trek over here to help us."

Hans looked at the clock on Cosimo's wall. "We probably should start making our way toward the airport. Your flight will leave soon."

Fran sighed audibly, as he also checked the time. "Oh shoot, we didn't even get to delve into Marco Ansios' history!"

Cosimo responded, "We will put together a file on him for you and send it to you. It will be informative, but he doesn't do much in the States."

"Oh, ok," replied Fran, as he looked again at the clock, and then turned to Hans. "I guess you're right, Hans. Gentlemen, I already know that I will be in contact with you in the future, if I need help, or information?"

Cosimo, with a great big smile, extended out his right hand, giving Fran's hand a firm shake. "Of course you will. Welcome to our team! It will actually be nice having an American connection going forward."

Fran and the two Germans soon arrived at the airport. Fran once again thanked his German friend for the adventure, contacts and information. He couldn't believe all the new information they had gathered on this trip. He had some expectations with the Schwartz interview, but the side trip to Rome was far beyond his imagination.

Jet lag from his quick round trip, paired with sleep deprivation, was quickly settling in on him heavily. He was ready to get home to his family and his work. Fran returned his side arm to his German partner. The two Germans dropped him off at the airport in Rome before they embarked on their own journey back to Munich.

"Thanks again, good friend." He said as he firmly shook Hans' hand. "'Til we meet again!"

"It was our pleasure." Replied Hans. "This won't be the last time we work together on any of this..."

"I have a strong suspicion you are right my friend." Agreed Fran. "I already look forward to the next time!"

Fran boarded his plane for home. He settled into his seat, ordered a quick cocktail. He smiled to himself. This trip netted so much more than he ever could have imagined. "Krivis, Fedora, Ansios, we will bring you men to meet lady justice. We will bring you all down." He silently vowed to himself as he quickly drifted off to sleep.

Fran touched down from his eleven hours plus flight at JFK

airport in New York. His head was still in a haze from his inflight slumber. He couldn't remember the last time he had slept so soundly, or for so long. It took him a few minutes to gather his bearings. Excitement and joy quickly replaced the brain fog. A huge smile came over him in anticipation. He knew Peg was already waiting for him at the gate. His trip was only a couple of days, but all the events made it seem like an eternity since he'd seen his wife and family.

He grabbed his briefcase from the overhead compartment, flung his sport coat over his shoulder, and made his way off the plane. His gaze immediately locked onto Peg's smiling face through a sea of people gathered at the gate. His pace quickened. He tossed his things aside and wrapped his masculine arms tightly around her slender waist, lifting her gracefully off the ground. The two embraced, swaying gently from side to side.

"Honey, I love you." He whispered softly in her ear. "I love you too."

"I missed you so much."

"Really?" She responded with an air of sarcasm, as she pushed him away slightly, looking into his eyes. "Munich, Salzburg, with a side trip to Rome? I find that hard to believe."

"Really," he abided. "I did. Four countries in two days is hardly a pleasure trip. While I admit that what I did see was absolutely stunning, I slept in the car for most of the drive from Munich to Rome after nightfall."

"Sure sweetie," responded Peg, still unconvinced.

"I swear, love." Trying his best to be persuasive. "I'll make you a deal...no, a promise. I will take you there someday, hopefully soon."

"You promise?"

"I promise," he whispered as he pulled her close once more and kissed his bride, then set her feet gently back on the ground.

Fran grabbed his briefcase while Peg grabbed his coat. He wrapped his arm around her shoulders, pulling her closer into him, and the two of them headed to the baggage claim. It was difficult for him to contain his excitement. He wanted to tell her everything that happened, but he knew that would have to wait at least until they were in the car. A loud rumble was heard coming from his stomach.

"Peg, are you hungry?"

"I could go for a bite." She responded.

"Great, because I'm starving. Let's grab some breakfast before heading home."

"Wow, such a treat, having breakfast with you on a weekday morning. That sounds wonderful, love."

Over breakfast, Francis painted verbal panoramas of snow-capped peaks and the Austrian and German countryside he saw on the drive from Munich to Salzburg and back.

"Oh, it sounds wonderful." Peg gushed. "You would love it."

He went on describing the road trip to Rome, what he saw of it. Again, she was overcome with emotion, listening to his verbal paintings.

"I can't wait until we go there together, love." Peg fantasized dreamily. "Me neither, love."

In the car, on the way home, the two of them were finally alone. It was finally time to tell Peg all the other stuff he had learned on his European journey. She sat beside him in a complete state of shock and disbelief. She just could not believe all that he was telling her. Schwartz's revelations, the pompous ass, Krivis, and Fedora's global riches and power, it was a lot to mentally consume in such a short time. She knew this case would mentally and physically devour every fiber of her husband, her family, and herself for the foreseeable future. She affirmed to her husband that the journey ahead of him would not be traveled alone.

CHAPTER 15

Cardinal Chiaros Riluciani was finally settling into his new assignment as the patriarch of Venice. All his life, he had always been a most learned and humble man. His many years of service to God fed his spirit, not his ego, nor the ego of those around him. He was loyal to his God, his pope, his church, and his parish, especially the poor and disabled of the community. He did things differently than those who came before him. At first, Riluciani politely declined the appointment. A position of advancement, so many of his colleagues would have been over the moon to accept. Riluciani was content where he was, in his prior parish.

Pope Michael VI had two men in mind for the patriarch position. It had reached his ears that the people of Venice preferred the other man to stay where he was. They knew little about the 60-year-old Riluciani, other than he had a beaming smile and deep local roots, but he was still their man for the job. After much prayer and reflection, the cardinal reluctantly conceded. "It is not my will, but God's. This is where God needs me now." He was not happy with his decision almost instantly. He left his prior assignment the same as he had arrived, with a handful of linens, a few sticks of furniture and his books. Only his personal library had grown during that time. His arrival in Venice was no different. Upon leaving his prior position, they presented him with a donation of 1 million lire. The patriarch gracefully declined the money, suggesting that the generous gesture instead go to local charities in need.

The people of Venice planned an elaborate welcome for Cardinal Chiaros Riluciani, as they did any of his predecessors, with extravagant celebrations, parades of gondolas, marching bands, and speeches from local dignitaries. The new patriarch hated all the fuss and quickly canceled all the pomp and celebration, opting only for a simple speech to his community instead. Riluciani learned quickly that his new city direly needed Christ's teachings, blessings and guidance. He had much work to do. His new city contained over 125 parishes that, mostly, sat empty. The city had sold its soul long ago to tourism.

He set to his work right away. They filled his personal calendar with many soirees, cocktail parties and receptions. He directed his personal secretary to cancel them all. He opted to replace them all with visits to local churches, seminaries, hospitals and prisons where he would hold Mass. If they would not come to church, he would gladly bring church to them. He declined unnecessary extravagances like a personal watercraft to navigate the waterways of Venice, opting instead to use the public water bus system. As the price of petrol rose, he gave up his beat up, old clunker of a car, and took to the streets via bicycle. He was a most unusual priest; it would take some time for them to get used to his ways.

The aristocracy didn't know what to do with the Riluciani. They disapproved of his simple ways. To them, the man who sat as the patriarch was a very important man. One who the Venetian upper-class celebrated every ounce of pomp and ceremony. They wanted to be in his orbit to fill their vain egos. It was the farthest thing from salvation one could get.

One afternoon, he and his secretary showed up unannounced at a local hospital for a visit with the sick. As word spread through the facility, administrators, doctors, and nurses soon surrounded him. He insisted the staff go back to their business.

"Please, go about your important work. I don't need to take up your precious time. I can go around on my own if you please."

"Your Eminence, it is our duty and an honor." Was the growing response throughout the hospital as the procession kept increasing.

He lived for these visits with the sick in his prior village. The growing procession made them most uncomfortable and unpleasant for him. "Perhaps I should return at a better time than..."

"Nonsense, Your Eminence, any time is perfect for a visit."

The cardinal tried halfheartedly to lose his entourage through a stairwell...it didn't work. It took a few weeks, and many explanations to educate the staff about how he liked to conduct future visits. Between the education and the frequency of his visits, he soon became a familiar, welcomed face to the staff of all the hospitals in the region. It was an exercise that filled his heart with great joy.

It wasn't just hospitals and communities, however, that needed to adjust to his ways. Some of his clergy weren't too sure about him, either. Not everyone who entered the profession had eyes to see that the "real treasures of the Church were the poor." Some in his clergy would argue that the poor didn't fill the offering plates on Sundays. Riluciani countered, "neither do empty pews...if that is all you are concerned about." This man felt that the weak, and down-on-their luck people should not be helped with just token occasional monies, but in a true and meaningful way that would really benefit their lives, situations, and futures. The parish priests who failed to see Riluciani's heart and ways soon found themselves new assignments elsewhere. The cardinal dismissed some, others left on their own accord.

Riluciani's offices were soon a popular destination for throngs of the poor. He proclaimed his door was always open to anyone seeking assistance or witness. The materially minded of the community watched as he hosted ex-cons, alcoholics, ex-prostitutes, poor people and other outcasts of society. His greatest fulfillment came from serving the mentally retarded and handicapped. His pure heart overflowed with love, while the community and many parish priests remained indifferent to these children of God. One morning, he went to give first communion to a large group of handicapped people; some of his peers disapproved and protests his actions. "These creatures do not understand what it is you are doing for them." Riluciani demanded his dissenters attend the service and Mass, too. A young girl suffering from debilitating birth defects and horrendous, painful deformities. The patriarch approached her with his biggest smile, blessed to be in her presence. Before a silent congregation, he asked, "Do you know who you received today, my dear child?"

"Yes, Our Lord and Savior, Jesus Christ!"

"Are you pleased with your decision, child?"

"Happier than I have ever been in my life, Your Eminence."

Riluciani turned to the crowd with a beaming smile and hands raised in praise to God. Then he looked directly at his protesters. "You see, my friends, they have hearts full of love, more so than many adults I've met in my days."

The local politicians were not interested in the souls Riluciani wanted to reach. As far as they were concerned, there was nothing in it for them. The poor, retarded and handicapped held no jobs, nor cast no votes. They certainly paid no taxes. These souls were nothing more than burdens on society, unworthy of their time, energy, or money. They wanted nothing of their pure-hearted patriarch's work. The local community was not interested in Riluciani's pet project, a special work center for the handicapped.

He began the project using funds from his diocese. In the past, he would have tapped into funding from the Catholic Bank of Venice. After twenty-six years of Vatican controlling interest, they secretly sold the bank to banker Marco Ansios. Bishops, monsignors, priests, and nuns soon joined Riluciani's usual court of societal outcasts. A defeated Riluciani returned from his protest trip to Rome, without good news or a suitable solution.

Gone were the days when the little "Priest's Bank of Venice" would issue low-interest loans necessary to fulfill God's work. Full rates of interest would apply to all new loans despite how noble the cause. The Vatican was supposed to protect their little church from these kinds of third party takeovers, not sell them out. It was because of these protesting clients, from all walks of life, that their little bank grew over the years into one of the wealthiest in all of Italy. It didn't matter one bit that some of the unhappy clients still held shares of the bank's stock. Collectively it amounted to less than 5%.

Neither the Vatican nor Ansios were concerned with what they had to say. Riluciani's new audience wanted papal intervention, but no help was coming from Rome. The ink was already dry. He could only advise them to move their funds and sell off their shares. The locals were left dissatisfied with the response from Rome and the advice from Riluciani. They felt that perhaps a different patriarch would have returned to them with a more palatable solution to the situation.

Following a discussion on the matter with his dear friend archbishop Dante Leone in the Vatican Secretary of State's office, he quietly began his own research probe, and learned more about Marco Ansios, Giovanni Fedora and Bishop Jonas Krivis. His discoveries appalled him.

He now knew the Holy Father would do absolutely nothing to help resolve to help the poor people of Venice. Fedora and Ansios were somehow highly respected sons of the Church, held in high esteem by this pope. From Archbishop Leone, the cardinal learned Ansios had called on Krivis multiple times to hide many transactions and operations from the Bank of Italy. Krivis opened the Vatican bank door wide to Ansios to do whatever he pleased. Tax evasion and illegal movement of money and shares were all the norm for these men. The cardinal had no desire to do business with Ansios. Ansios visited his office in a graceless attempt to improve local public relations. Riluciani already knew too much about the snake before him. Even the offer of a full funding donation to his work center would cool the fire in him. He moved all official diocesan accounts to a small regional bank. His final act of defiance was a request to get the directors of the old bank to remove "Catholic" from their name. They just waved off the "crazy patriarch."

Archbishop Leone continued to urge Pope Michael VI to intervene, but it was too late. So he began arguing for the immediate removal of Krivis as head of his Vatican Bank. The only man in the world capable of making even just a little of the situation right, responded with an agonized, helpless shrug of the shoulders. Help was not coming from Rome.

Pope Michael, however, was very impressed with the work and leadership of his appointed patriarch in Venice. He took every opportunity to publicly applaud the good, holy, wise, learned leader of a man. While en route to a Eucharistic congress, Cardinal Riluciani was a proud host to the Holy Father. St. Mark's Square was overflowing with people wanting to listen to the visiting pope's words. Crowd watched in curious silence as the pontiff gracefully removed his papal stole and placed it on the shoulders of Cardinal Riluciani. The patriarch instantly blushed, trying to wave off what his pope was doing. The crowd, however, roared their approval of such a public gesture.

In private, over coffee, the pope, who was getting on in years, informed Riluciani that the "local financial difficulties" had not gone unnoticed by him. He was most proud of the patriarch's efforts to build the work center for the retarded. A sizable donation toward the project was issued by the Holy Father personally. Riluciani was happy to accept the funds, but for Riluciani, it didn't resolve the problems that continued to plague the church's finances. Riluciani continued to pray for the Holy Father, his Church and his community. It seemed only God could correct the scourge of materialism and greed in the world, and especially the church.

CHAPTER 16

Fran arrived at work early the next morning. He was excited to be back. He was ready to roll up his sleeves and get down to business. He didn't have time during his whirlwind tour of Germany, Austria and Rome to update the team, not that he wanted to hear any argument or disapproval from Bayer. The first order of business was to brief them all of his findings. Christopherson and Lance Erickson joined Bentley, Thomas and Bayer. Upon conclusion, everyone in the room, like his wife the night before, sat in a state of silent bewilderment.

Bentley, like the others in the room, sat pensive in reflection. He knew at that moment that he had just lost his most seasoned and successful detective to something that would consume his every waking hour, and probably some of his dreams, for the foreseeable future. There was no way Fran would or could spit out the hook on this case, not now. Christopherson, a senior version of the detective, would not interfere with this new tangent of the investigation. Nothing Bayer, or any other federal official, had to say about it, would change the trajectory of this detective's immediate future.

Bentley took some comfort knowing that at least with Fedora running a bank in New York, and his rumored ties to Mafia syndicates would at least keep some of this detective's work locally focused, within their jurisdiction, or at least contained somewhat within the States.

Bentley was the first to break the long, reflective silence. "Well, I guess we know what you will work on for the next long while."

Fran smiled, confirming the innuendo of his boss' comment. "Thank you, sir! And I look forward to it, sir. I want to get these dirty ass bastards. I don't know exactly how yet, but believe you me, I'm going to put these arrogant shit heads out of business."

"I believe you Francis," chimed Bentley. "We all believe you."

Bayer sensed that nothing he could or would say in protest, at that moment would have any impact, but still he wondered... "But Fran, how are you going to navigate work in Rome, Italy, Europe, and beyond, from here?"

"I'm not working alone here, Bayer. I have some very good connections and assistance on my little team on the other side of the Atlantic!"

Bayer thought about it for a moment, then replied. "I guess you do. I can see that you are going to have your hands very full. Lance can continue to work with you on this case for now."

Bayer's support and offer surprised Fran. He expected and was ready for the Strikeforce man to resist. "Thank you. I appreciate the help and support."

The meeting wrapped up, following a few questions from the group. Fran, with Lance in tow, headed back to his office. They had to work out a plan of action. The department had an informant that they sometimes used when they needed intel on the Lascano Crime Family and other mafiosi dealings.

"Lance, send up a flare, and see if you can get a hold of Sal. I want to see if he can give us anything on Fedora's Mob activities either here, abroad, or both."

Lance scribbled in his notebook. "Sure thing Fran."

"Oh, and see what info you can get me on Lincoln National Bank and its history. I'm sure that reporter Robert Hinson, with the '*Times*, might know a thing or two."

"I'm on it," Lance continued to scribble in his little notebook.

"I think it's time I paid a visit to a longtime friend across town." Fran thought out loud.

Lance listened, puzzled, but he refrained from further questions.

The Detective made his way over to the Lower East Side, en route to The Church of St.

Raphael. The walk through the old familiar neighborhood flooded the detective with memories of the days of his youth. His entire education from kindergarten through college was under the tutelage of the Catholic Church. When he turned thirteen, he met the most influential man of his entire life, second only to his own father, Monsignor Wexford. The monsignor was a wise, pious soul. A writer, philosopher and staunch advocate for the church. In Fran's heart and mind, Wexford was the purest incarnation of what a man of the cloth should be, and the finest man Fran had, to this day, ever met. Monsignor Wexford was the standard by which Fran would judge every other man in the Catholic clergy. He was everything Bishop Krivis was not.

As he navigated closer to the church, the now grown and seasoned detective's mind wandered and question all that he had ever known growing up in the church. Could the hero of his youth and teen years be as corrupt as these other cardinals, monsignors, archbishops and bishops? Were the activities and behaviors of Krivis and the others common throughout the Church? He stepped into the church and crossed himself, then made his way to the church office. Seated behind her desk at a typewriter was the church secretary.

"Good morning sir, can I help you?" She looked up from the document she was typing and greeted him.

"Good morning, Sister. How are you this fine morning?"

"It is a beautiful day to be in the service of the Lord. Thank you for asking."

"You're welcome. I was wondering if Monsignor Wexford was in today?"

"Monsignor?" She responded, puzzled for a moment, then smiled.

"Oh, you must mean Cardinal Wexford? I can see that you haven't been here for quite a while, have you, sir?"

"Um, no Sister, I'm sorry." Fran responded shamefully, "I guess it's obvious that I haven't."

"I can tell." She responded with a sweet smile, and a slight chuckle and a wink. "Well, since your last visit, they have promoted Monsignor Wexford to cardinal, and he is now the archbishop of New York!"

"Oh wow! The archbishop of New York? I had no idea."

Again, the nun behind the desk smiled. "Yes, yes! Now His Eminence works across town, on 1st Ave. He has been there for several years now...I'd say three years at least. Do you need directions?"

"No ma'am, I mean Sister, just an address will be fine."

The nun scribbled the address on a piece of notepaper and handed it to the detective. "Here you go, sir. I sure miss working with him. He is such a sweet and gentle man, firm, but full of love and laughter. He really loves his job, the church and the Lord." She continued. "Can you please tell him Sister Caroline sends him greetings?"

"Of course I will, Sister. Thank you very much for your help."

"You're welcome, sir."

Fran soon arrived at the Archdiocese of New York, a nun escorted Fran to an office. Upon walking through the door, the cardinal stood, walked from behind his desk, and extended his hand. He squinted slightly as he scanned his memories, then his eyes suddenly went wide.

"Francis?! Is that you, Francis Clavering?!?!" He exclaimed.

"Yes, sir," Fran responded humbly. "I can't believe you still remember me."

The cardinal extended his arms to wrap his guest in an enormous hug. "Of course I remember you, and your family too, fondly, I might add. How could I forget such a fine example of God's love and faith? How long has it been, Francis?"

"Oh, at least fifteen years, maybe even twenty, I'd say."

"At least. Too long in my book."

The two gentlemen reminisced about the old days and where

Fran's different family members and friends were these days. Fran told him about his wife and children, and about his career as one of the New York Police Department's finest. Forty-five minutes passed quickly while the two men reconnected. All the formalities were now finished.

"So, my son, what brings you here to see me today?"

"Before I get into that, monsignor, I mean cardinal, sorry." Francis caught himself.

"It's alright Francis. It really has been a very long time since our paths last crossed."

"That it has, sir. I just wanted to let you know before I forget that Sister Caroline from The Church of St Raphael sends greetings."

Cardinal Wexford's face instantly lit up, full of joy, with the mention of Sister Caroline. "Ah, yes. I do very much miss working with her. She is such a lovely woman of God."

"Yes, she is quite a delight to speak with, even during our brief encounter." Fran agreed, then segued most ungraciously. "Cardinal, I'm most curious. What can you tell me about Bishop Jonas Krivis?"

The smile immediately disappeared from Wexford's face, and was replaced with an exaggerated look of concern. "I wish you wouldn't have asked me that, Francis."

"Why, Your Eminence, what is it?"

"Yes Francis, I know him." The cardinal hesitated. "What in the world are you doing running around with that man's name on your tongue, son?"

"That I can't exactly say at this point, sir. But I would like to know everything and anything you know about him if you don't mind, sir."

"I don't like speaking ill of my colleagues in the church, Francis." Wexford's gaze focused on something distant outside his office window. After an extended, silent pause, "However, I won't lie either. There comes a time when enough is enough. I will tell you, Francis, what I know, on two conditions."

"And those are?"

"First, you heard nothing I'm about to tell you from me."

"I swear to you on my grandmother's soul, Your Eminence, your words are safe with me. I promise."

"Thank you, Francis. That means everything to me. I'm tired of carrying these secrets inside my head and heart. It is eating me up inside, to where it's affecting my health, knowing what I know, and not being able to do a damn thing about it."

Cardinal Wexford walked over to a corner of his office and poured a cup of coffee for himself and his guest. He then returned to his big brown, high-backed, leather office chair, sat down, and got lost in his coffee cup as he stared, stirring mindlessly.

"What's the second condition, Sir?"

Wexford returned to the present and turned to look back at Francis. "Please be careful Francis, if you go after him and his friends. I will help you where I can, and I wish you luck. I will say many prayers for your safety and your success, my son."

"Thank you, father, I appreciate your help and support. My team and I will proceed with the most extreme caution, I promise. I'm not even going to tell them I spoke with you monsignor, dang it! I mean cardinal."

"Alright, I guess it is best to start at the beginning then, Francis."

"The beginning, sir?"

"Yes son. If we start at the beginning, you will have a better understanding of how the *Istituto per le Opere di Religione* or IOR, more commonly known today as the Vatican Bank, evolved to its present state of operations."

"You lead, sir, I'll follow."

"So the physical location of the Vatican Bank is on the top floor of the Tower of St Nicholas V in the heart of Vatican City near the Gate of Santa Anna. The tower that houses the bank is closed off to the public. Access is also, of course, closely guarded by the Swiss Guard there in the Holy City. The earliest manifestations of the bank, and even today, are very similar to the Money Changers that Jesus threw out of the temple for collecting temple fees, and other profit driven activities within the church, as I will soon illustrate."

"Ah yes, I'm familiar with that story from the bible, sir." Fran confirmed, as he scribbled on his yellow notepad.

"Good." The cardinal continued, "they established the first incarnation of the IOR or Vatican Bank in 1887 as a commission for pious causes. At that time, there was much conflict in the region between the Kingdom of Italy and the Holy See. Fast forward to 1929, The Kingdom of Italy and the Holy See finally came to terms and signed the Lateran Treaty. The treaty recognized Vatican City as an independent state under the sovereignty of the Holy See. Italian Prime Minister Mussolini, also gifted the Catholic Church 80 million in gold Lira as reparations for losing the Papal States following the unification of Italy in the middle of the 18th century. Mussolini also declared the Church exempt from taxation by the Italian government.

In the summer of 1941, Pope Mathias XII created the modern-day version of the Vatican Bank. He alone established and directed it. It was not quite yet what we now know as the Vatican Bank, but actually the pope's bank. This newly formed financial establishment absorbed the 1887 administration and eventually expanded their financial services, like managing fiduciary deposits for clergy and Vatican staff. The Vatican Bank, from that moment on, was a for profit institution, supposedly for 'religious works.'

Soon the Vatican Bank began to having serious problems with cash flow and was a hard time collecting 'Peter's Pence' from the Americas. Mathias went on a quest for new money sources to supplement the church's declining income. He relaxed the exclusivity rules for the clientele of his bank. This action morphed his personal bank into a public bank. It didn't take long for totalitarian elements all over war-torn Europe to take complete advantage of these changes and their secrecy clauses. The bank now gladly provided services to Italian fascists, aristocrats, and, after the fall of Mussolini, even the Mafia. Pope Mathias soon gained the horrific, yet dead on accurate, nickname of 'Hitler's pope.'"

"Good God!" Fran blurted out, then caught himself, "Sorry, Your Eminence."

"It's quite alright Francis, that whole situation angers me too."

"Your Eminence, since the Vatican Bank was at that point a 'public bank,' aren't there bank records subject to review or audit?"

The cardinal gave a little chuckle and a nod. "Nope, the Vatican Bank has a standing policy to destroy records older than ten years, and the Vatican Bank has never been audited. As long as Krivis is in charge of it, that bank never will be. These standing policies mean that there are no records from the WWII era."

"How convenient." Responded Fran in a snarky, sarcastic tone.

"Well, it would be, except for their ARE archived records from the secular financial world. Records from Germany and the United States show transfers of money from the Vatican Bank to Nazi controlled banks in Switzerland during that time period. There are also documents showing the stolen gold of Hitler's victims from *Schutzstaffel* or *SS* accounts to an unnamed bank in Rome in September 1943. Deposits of victim's gold bolstered the coffers of the publicly 'neutral' Church and her Bank. Some rumors even suggest that some of that gold is still hidden in one of the church's holiest shrines in Portugal, presently under the control of Masonic elements.

During the war, and for some time after its conclusion, the church once again found itself in desperate need of money. The Vatican Bank's solution was to become a major accomplice in the looting of the treasury of Independent Croatia. By '45, they had pillaged some $200 million from the poor souls of Croatia."

Fran responded in complete shock. "That's horrible!"

"It is, but what's worse, Francis, is the Croatian Nazis better known as the Ustaše, were responsible for the slaughter of 500,000 Orthodox Christian Serbs, tens of thousands of Jews and Gypsies, and banked the proceeds of their genocidal efforts through the Vatican Bank! To pour salt on those wounds, they then used the pillaged funds to finance their government-in-exile and ratlines to post-war Argentina."

"Jesus! I had no clue all that happened, cardinal."

"It's a part of our history that the church would rather not come to the public's awareness..."

"Yeah, I can see why they wouldn't want to let any of that out of the bag."

The cardinal nodded in agreement, then continued. "During the last days of WWII, British forces intercepted a Croatian treasure convoy. Deals were made, money changed hands, and the convoy continued on to Rome without further incident or interruption. Once in Rome, the treasurer of the Franciscan Order opened up access to Vatican Bank accounts. Whatever was deposited in that bank was disbursed and then quickly erased from the record without a trace."

"But how can those deposits just disappear in that bank? There must be a record subject to an audit somewhere, right?"

"Francis, you are by no means the first, nor will you be the last to ask such questions. Like I said earlier, the bank has never been audited. Yet we still know that large parts of the Ustaše treasury did end up in the Vatican Bank, and a very close relationship between the Vatican and the Ustaše continued well into the '50s.

The United States courts did their best to try to address the treasury issues on behalf of the Croatian people, but the Vatican Bank stonewalled the courts. The Vatican Secretary of State, at the time, lobbied the courts to dismiss the lawsuits. Despite all of that, the US State Department still refuses to get involved in the matter."

Fran shook his head, thinking for a minute about Bayer's reluctance to dig into Vatican ties to the Benedetto case. Then the detective returned to the present again, muttering under his breath. "Those poor people. But why?"

"At one point, the Vatican established The Jewish-Catholic Historical Commission."

"Well, that's good, I guess...Isn't it?"

"The commission, of course, could never establish exactly what the relationship between the Vatican and the Ustaše was during and right after WWII. Despite the fact that many of the top Ustaše leaders were housed inside the Vatican and other Franciscan sites located throughout Italy. The commission was eventually defunded by the church, and all relevant records were sealed."

"Surprise, surprise...Your Eminence, do you think there will ever be any justice for the people of Croatia?"

"Even though the Vatican is without records, what was uncovered by the US Government's records are nauseating and extremely damning. However, I'm pretty sure that it will never really go anywhere. The US Government knows just how damaging this scandal would be for the Catholic Church, and especially for this pope."

"I don't understand, sir. I can see this being an embarrassment to the Church, but why wouldn't the pope want to clear these atrocities from his bank, his Church and his conscience?

"Well, during Pope Mathias XII's reign, his secretary of state was Archbishop Giancarlo Volonté. He knew everything that was going on in the church at that time and did absolutely nothing to stop it."

Francis responded, puzzled. "Yeah, so?"

"Well, the then Archbishop Giancarlo Volonté is now Pope Michael VI, Francis."

Francis instantly stopped writing. He sat frozen, completely stunned, whispering under his breath. "Oh my God!"

The two men sat in the room, still and motionless. The ticking clock on the wall was the only sound in the room for the longest of moments. Each man experiences that moment from a completely different perspective. The cardinal felt relieved to finally pass on these deeply held secrets of his church and her bank. Francis, on the other hand, was visibly disturbed, upset by what Wexford had just told him? A car horn from the traffic outside brought the two men's attention back to the present.

"Francis, I must apologize. I didn't mean to shake you up with all that I just told you. I have carried it around with me for so long that I've become numb to its potential impact on those not in the know...I'm sorry."

Francis placed his pen on a canary yellow notepad on a table next to him. He took a deep breath, then rubbed his face with both hands and ran his long fingers through his curly, dark hair. "It's alright Your Eminence, I understand. I'm unfortunately getting used to these gut punches that keep hitting me as this investigation progresses. Please cardinal, we must continue."

"Are you sure Francis? We can continue further at another time."

"Yes, I admit, I don't like any of what you've been telling me, sir, but I, nonetheless, need to know everything if there is even the slightest chance of changing the *modus operandi* of this church and her bank."

"You are an ant chasing after a giant Francis, or rather David, going after Goliath, but I commend your determination and enthusiasm."

"I see your point cardinal...but we all know how the story of David and Goliath turned out..." Wexford was impressed with the man seated before him. "You're sure?"

"100% sir. Faith in God is a strong and powerful thing, but even David eventually picked up a stone and got the job done."

"Fine, I will continue, but please feel free to stop me if this all becomes too much. We don't have to do all of this in one sitting, in one day."

"Will do, sir."

"So Pope Mathias and Volonté, now Pope Michael, essentially became money changers, travel agents and landlords to some of the most notorious Ustaše war criminals. This was all before the Mafia infiltrated the Vatican."

The mention of the Mafia jarred Francis's memory. He was hoping the cardinal could expand upon what Cosimo and the others had already told him on his recent trip to Europe. "Your Eminence," Francis interrupted. "Can you tell me about how Giovanni Fedora and Krivis became associated with the Vatican Bank?"

Cardinal Wexford reacted in shock, "Francis, you know about Fedora too?" Fran nodded "Yes, he came to my attention several months ago."

"I see, well I will tell you all that I know, but, again, I must advise you. Please, please, please proceed with the utmost caution. These men are extremely powerful and dangerous. And once again, you didn't hear any of this from me, Francis."

"I appreciate you confiding in me all this information. You have my word that I will exercise the greatest of caution moving forward in this investigation, sir. And nobody but you and your secretary will ever know that I was even here."

"Very well then," Wexford continued. "From '29 until '54, the bank was under the management of one of their monsignors. Prior to Mussolini's tax exemption declaration, the bank was only dealing with small, sound, yet modestly profitable investments and everything, for the most part, was on the up and up. Following the restructuring of the bank in the middle of '42, the bank was no longer just Pope Mathias' personal bank, but rather a for profit financial institution. As I mentioned before. The monsignor decided to spend large amounts of the Mussolini compensation grant for two industrial powerhouses. A large construction firm, and a huge real estate conglomerate in Europe. The monsignor was suddenly in way over his head. By the time his financial incompetence was fully realized, the church's bank had already suffered great financial losses.

Like all things within the Vatican, though, change comes slowly, if it comes at all. It wasn't until '54, the bank finally replaced the monsignor with *delgato* Rinaldo Manna. He was not a man of the cloth nor of the Roman Curia. The then future pope, Volonté, was on a personal quest to build an old folks' home for his local parishioners. The Vatican Bank was such a mess. Manna had his hands full, correcting the mistakes of his incompetent predecessor. But Volonté was determined, and would not be denied, even if the Vatican Bank was in no position to fund the project for the foreseeable future.

That's when Volonté turned to Giovanni Fedora for help. Fedora pounced on the project and funded the entire project personally. Volonté was so pleased that his pet project could finally move forward. He also felt that Fedora's talents might be of service to Manna in the effort to get the Vatican Bank back on firm financial ground.

Fedora's new relationship with Manna and the IOR gave him access to an almost unlimited credit source. Both men, working together, soon had the Vatican Bank humming and extremely successful. The IOR soon became a very important and influential part of the Italian economy. The two economies, although completely independent, are closely connected to this day.

Over the course of the years, friendships flourished. The Manna/Fedora friendship turned the IOR into an international banking powerhouse, while fortifying their own personal secular positions of wealth and power. The Volonté/Fedora relationship flourished on an entirely different level. Their relationship was more cerebral and spiritual, and one of mutual respect. The relationship became especially meaningful when Fedora sought counsel and condolence from Cardinal Volonté following the death of his grandmother sometime in the middle of '61."

Francis scribbled furiously in his notebook as Wexford conveyed the deep, dark secrets of the church. Francis paused for a second. "Your Eminence?" he interrupted.

"Yes Francis?"

"Forgive me, but I must know, how is it that you know all these intimate details about the church, the bank, these men and situations?"

Wexford gave a half chuckled response. "Funny you should ask, but I'm glad you did. God will always provide answers and guidance when asked, son."

"Huh?"

"You see, the dark history of the church's bank has always bothered me. In my desire to do whatever I could to change it somehow, some way, I figured that in order to fix what I found appalling, I must first understand how it got to where it is now."

"I guess that makes sense."

"So I started silently watching and researching the church and her bank."

"But how can you know all this from your post here in New York?"

"I haven't spent all my time in New York since our paths last crossed." Wexford smiled and winked at Francis. "Besides, Krivis and his friends aren't the only ones who have spies working inside the Vatican, my son. And now God has sent you to me with these questions on your mind and tongue."

Wexford's behavior again puzzled Francis. "Cardinal, you are losing me again."

"Francis, I've been asking our Heavenly Father for help on this matter for as long as I can remember. And now, here you sit in front of me, seeking this information. This quest, path, or whatever it is that you are on, Francis, is being guided by God's hands. You must understand the importance of what you have been chosen to do here, son. I know it's a tremendous burden for anyone man, Francis, but this church and world need you, and we need you to be successful going forward." A huge smile came over Cardinal Wexford's face as he gazed at Francis.

Francis was stunned at Wexford's words. He was never one to believe in coincidence. Even though his colleagues always viewed him as the luckiest man on the force, always in the right place at the right time, his hunches always seemed to work out, etc. He never felt that luck had anything to do with his success. He often clung to his own father's teaching and guidance from a very young age. Memories of the senior Clavering's words echoed through his mind. "If you always do what is honest and right by your fellow man, you will never have to question the twists and turns on the road ahead of you."

"Well, Your Eminence," Fran smiled. "If you put it that way, I guess we'd better keep going then..."

"Are you sure Francis? I've already given you a lot of information."

"Yes sir, I'm sure." Francis implored, full of confidence, as he sat poised like a schoolboy, ready to take more notes. "Please continue."

"Alright then, let's see, where did I leave off?"

Fran quickly glanced at his notes, "Fedora's grandmother just died..."

"Ahh, that's right. So, not long after the passing of Fedora's blessed grandmother, Cardinal Volonté was appointed a new secretary. This new young priest was full of self-importance and an unwavering sympathy for a communist, socialist agenda. Volonté had already publicly denounced Marxism. This was perhaps one of the most important points of view that he and Fedora held in common. They were a united force in their vehement fight against the tyranny of the weak.

But this new priest would become a wedge between the longtime friends. As the cardinal and his new secretary grew closer, rumors swirled that the two had become lovers. I have known Volonté long, and well enough to know that there was no truth to those words, but there was no doubt in anyone's mind that the new priest sought to influence and, in many ways, control the man who would one day be elected pope.

As the priest chipped away at Volonté, the cardinal became more and more sympathetic to the ways of communism. Fedora watched and distanced himself in disgust from Volonté. The hurt and betrayal in Fedora grew, as Fedora's disdain for the priest grew, his long cherished relationship with Volonté turned frigid. Long chats on philosophy and the classics turned into heated exchanges on matters of church and state. Many stood in silence as the priest, through his manipulation of Volonté, worked to destroy the Catholic Church and the communists destroyed the thriving capitalism in Italy.

On June 3, 1963 Pope Phillip XXIII passed away. A few weeks later, Cardinal Volonté was elected, and became the pope he is now. But by the end of '63, Italy was moving farther and farther left, and her economy was in ruins as the balance between private and public sectors shifted to the state. As state intervention destroyed private initiative in efforts of economic collectivism, Italy fell to communistic rule. Fedora, with all his wealth and power, pledged himself to become a key figure in the fight against the evil scourge that had taken over his mother country.

In '64, Volonté, I mean Pope Michael, replaced Manna with another secular man close to Fedora.

These three men were so close, in fact, both Manna and his replacement continued to work together. The two men retained director positions on the boards of several of Fedora's Italian banks. The new pope continued from time to time to call on Fedora for advice. Fedora obliged him, but the relationship was never what it once was, so he distanced himself from the church for a while.

From the sidelines, Fedora watched, along with the rest of us, as the new pope, still under the communist priest's spell, destroyed our beloved church. It would take the pope many years to realize his grave mistakes, and by then, it was way too late. Pope Michael was deeply troubled by his now damaged church. He had no clue how to undo his mistakes, or turn his church around, which sent him spiraling into a deep, debilitating depression. Pope Michael has never been the same since.

In December 1967, my good friend and predecessor here passed away. He was by far one of the most prolific money makers the church had had. It is mainly through him that I know much of what I am telling you now. You see, for many, many years, he governed this archdiocese. It was by far the most affluent archdiocese in America, if not the western world. The real estate holdings of our New York See alone were well over $50 million. My predecessor was well liked by the Vatican. It's amazing how many 'friends' money can buy. He was religious, in the sense that he regularly sent large amounts of money to the Vatican. After his death, and my installment here, that all stopped. I could not continue the practice with a clear conscience. Especially with Krivis, Fedora, and others working in and around that bank. The pope, his Church and especially, his bank were suddenly in a lot of trouble.

Now, keep in mind that after Volonté was elected pope, Krivis essentially became the new pontiff's shadow, serving as his personal bodyguard and traveling companion. But Krivis was a hungry and restless man. He wanted more. It didn't take Krivis long to exploit his position and the relationship between the priest and his pope, watching and waiting for an opportunity to arise. The death of my predecessor was an opportunity he just couldn't let slip by him.

Krivis began to lie, and lie some more, spreading falsehoods about all of his many powerful friends and acquaintances in the Chicago and New York financial sector to the pope by way of his little communist priest. He deceived them both with great tales of how the financial world operated, expressing false contempt for the lacking social conscience of the financial communities around the world. His boasting and bragging quickly served their purpose, and his trajectory was straight up from there. By the end of 1967, he was appointed Secretariat of the IOR, and a year later, he was named to the cardinal's Commission of Vigilance for the Vatican Bank. Soon after that, the consummate liar was consecrated bishop.

In '68 Pope Michael had to face yet another financial problem. This one was very different, and more complicated. Italian Parliament voted to change the tax laws, and reverse Mussolini's generous tax exemption status, enjoyed so long by the church. The Vatican would now be subjected to dividend taxes on their stock holdings. The Church's cache of stocks would now lead to a financial bloodletting of epic proportions if something wasn't done, and soon. Pope Michael, once again, turned to his old friend Fedora for his expert advice on the matter. It was proposed that Fedora take over the two very large corporations under IOR control that I mentioned earlier. Fedora wasn't interested, suggesting that the pope's favorite little priest might have a better solution. Pope Michael sensed the hurt in Fedora, and apologetically persisted. He didn't know what else to do or where else to turn.

Fedora remained firm, stating his inaction had nothing to do with money. For Fedora, this was personal. Michael played his final card, hoping Fedora would reconsider. Corporate balance sheets for the companies were presented. At that point, Fedora could no longer decline, no matter how deeply Michael had hurt him.

The deal was now moving forward. Now the pope wanted complete secrecy in the transfer, and Fedora wanted something more substantial. Fedora's demands were a deal breaker. You see, Fedora wanted certain guarantees written into the transaction, but the Vatican Bank didn't have the amount of funds at the ready to satisfy Fedora's demands. Of course, Fedora, through his friendships with Manna and his IOR successor, already knew this. Mussolini's grant had a been foolishly squandered many years before by incompetent fools running the establishment. Fedora sadistically watched as the pontiff squirmed more. Stating that since the IOR couldn't meet his conditions, he would have to seek a partner in the deal. Pope Michael, who was already troubled at this point, was more disturbed by this development. His demands for secrecy were no longer in play. He was no longer in a position to protest. Finally, by early May of '69, to the relief of the pope, the $50 million purchase of the Vatican's construction firm, and all but 5% of its real estate conglomerate was complete.

Now Krivis already knew of Fedora's closeness to his office's chief accountant and Manna. Both men served on committees in one of Fedora's banks. Krivis asked Fedora, an extremely loaded, rhetorical question. He wanted Fedora's honest opinion of the men's work in the world of banking and finance. The new bishop invited Fedora to his office and proceeded to bad mouth them, gloating that if he were ever in such a position with the Vatican Bank, he'd can his current *delgato* immediately, along with a couple of others. Fedora, amused by Krivis' pomposity, did his best to explain how the current manager was more than capable, and was a man commanding respect in the global world of finance. Krivis didn't care, he was more interested in hearing himself talk about his own self-importance.

Krivis was working on his own little scheme to get himself promoted. His fake persona of piety and humility presented to the pope and his communist secretary, he began a most vain and graceless ascent through the Vatican social strata. By February, '71 Krivis was appointed president of the IOR by Pope Michael. From that point on, Krivis he's been even more incorrigible and impossible than ever."

"I can only imagine..." Responded Fran. "I admit I've already had a taste of that firsthand."

Wexford suddenly stopped, confused and impressed. "Wait, you've met Krivis, Francis?"

Fran couldn't help but break out into laughter that broke up the tension of the moment. "Oh, no... of course not, Your Eminence. I haven't met him personally, but I have seen how he carries on at one of the golf courses there in Rome."

"You know about his love of golf?"

"Sure do, and he seems to like cigars, scotch, and women too."

"You, my son, know more than you let on..."

Fran issued a slight nod, punctuated with a proud smile. "I guess we all have a few secrets..."

"I guess we do..." Wexford continued. "Alright, so about a month after Krivis became Vatican Bank president, a banker named Marco Ansios under the guidance of Fedora established Sierra Madre International Bank in Nassau, The Bahamas. This new bank was on a sharp, steep trajectory upward, attracting wealthy clients from around the world. Krivis' big mouth was by far the best advertising they could have ever done to attract new clients."

"What do you mean by that cardinal?"

"Krivis was a sitting member of the board for the newly established bank, Francis. His ego just couldn't allow this to remain a secret."

"Oh wow! These men are crazy!"

"I'm sure it's more greed than craziness, Francis... Greed is a very powerful drug, my son."

"It certainly seems that way, sir."

"Fedora from time to time would offer Krivis advice, especially after Italian banking laws changed. His day-to-day activities were now suddenly penal offenses. Krivis ignored Fedora, risking irreparable harm to himself, bank and pope for their involvement in black money crimes. Krivis didn't care. In his mind, he was above the stupid Italian Government and their laws. The only thing missing for this Vatican Bank president was a cardinal's rank.

"Your Eminence?"

"Yes Francis."

"Cardinal? He wants a cardinal's rank?"

"Yes, and he still does..."

"But wasn't he just promoted to bishop at that point?"

"Greed and power are intoxicating to weaker men than I, my son. But if it's any consolation, Francis, flash forward to today, he has yet to become a cardinal...and from what I've heard, he never will."

"That's only a slight comfort, sir."

"I actually feel the same way, son...but it's a start. Moving on to more recent interactions between Krivis, Fedora and Ansios...Krivis approached Fedora with an offer to purchase The Catholic Bank of

Venice. Fedora, to Krivis' surprise, did not jump at the opportunity. Fedora was busy here in the states. He was in Washington, DC at the time attending an International Monetary Fund meeting, one of Fedora's nemeses whispered in the ear of one of Pope Michael's Secretaries of State, and the proposition was immediately dead in the water.

In February of this year, the Bank of Italy issued two complaints against Fedora for wrongdoing and fraud. Shortly thereafter, Ansios' bank headquarters advised Ansios to also cut all ties with Fedora. By spring, the Catholic Bank of Venice was the furthest thing from Fedora's mind, and Marco Ansios purchased a controlling stake in the little Catholic bank for $45 million. Fedora's only response on the matter was that the only thing on par with Krivis' vanity and dishonesty was his stupidity. Shortly after all of this went down, there was an attempt made on the lives of Fedora and his wife. So they moved out of Europe to New York City."

Fran instantly stopped writing. He already knew exactly where in the city Fedora lived and worked, thanks to Bayer's little side job. "Yeah, I heard he was living and working here."

"Just don't ask me where, Francis. I don't know, and I don't want to know. The Mafia rumors that follow that man are not to be dismissed, son."

For Fran, the Mafia connection was the least of his worries. "This cat is now living in the Big Apple. That's certainly going to make my life and job a hell of a lot easier..."

The cardinal detected the excitement in the detective's voice and suddenly became worried. "Why do I suddenly regret telling you all of this, Francis? Please don't take all this knowledge and plunge into this very dangerous world without using your head and extreme caution."

"Your Eminence, if you recall, I made you two promises before we started. Yes, I'm grateful and excited, but I'm certainly not stupid. I've been chasing down Mafia thugs for many, many years in this city. The information you've just given me is going to save me and my team so much time and energy."

"Francis," The cardinal paused. "Remember, you are the only one to know where you got this information. You promised. I don't even want your team to know you spoke with me. Understand."

Francis regained his composure. "Yes sir, I completely understand. I already gave you my word. No one will ever know I was here. I swear. Besides, we already know where Fedora lives and works."

The cardinal was relieved, yet surprised. "Good, because I still have close connections deep within the church and her bank. If I hear of anything that may be helpful to you and your case, I will certainly pass it along to you."

"I'd appreciate that, sir," Fran scribbled his home phone number on a business card and handed it to Wexford. "Please call me at home if you have anything further to add, or anything develops. Just leave a message with my wife, Peggy. I will get back to you right away, sir."

"I most certainly will. I sense you will have an easier time keeping an eye on Fedora...Krivis, hiding in the Vatican will be much more of a challenge for you, but I will help you there, where and when I can. But for now, I've bothered you enough for today, Francis."

"Please, Sir, feel free to 'bother' me anytime." Fran pointed to retrieve his business card once again. "I'm also going to leave you with the contact information of the man I'm working with in Rome. His name is Detective Cosimo Angelo, just in case."

"Ok great, Francis. Sounds like you are deeper into this than you let on."

"Not really, Your Eminence, to be honest, we're only getting started. But I appreciate all the hours and hours of work and research you've already saved us. I have no idea how I will ever thank you."

"Just shut these damn bastards down Francis, if you can!" The cardinal quickly caught himself and regained his composure. "I apologize for my outburst, Francis. It's just that I've lived with this anger and these secrets for so long. If you are successful, that will be thanks enough for me. Now get on out of here."

"Yeah, it seems that I now have a hell... I mean heck of a lot of work to do."

Fran placed his yellow tablet of paper containing all his notes and pens in his briefcase, closed the lid, snapping the two worn gold colored latches shut. He stood and shook the cardinal's hand and exited the office. Once he got back to his car, he just sat for a moment, excited, yet scared. He couldn't just walk back into his office with all of what Wexford had just given him without raising eyebrows.

How was he going to get this past all the nosey jackasses back at the office without a million questions?

Fran pulled the car into his driveway and walked through the door. Peggy was taking a break from the children and housework chores to watch *The Young and the Restless* on the couch when he walked through the door.

"Fran??? What's wrong? Why are you home so early?"

"I'm fine, love, I'm fine, but I need your help."

"Me? Of course, sweetheart, I'll do what I can. What do you need?"

"I need you to do me a huge favor..." Peg sat wide eyed as he went on for some time telling her about his meeting with Wexford. "I need to get all this information over to Hans, Friedrich and Cosimo, but I don't want anyone in the office to know about any of it, at least not yet and they certainly can't know where I got all of this from. If word gets out, it will put the cardinal's life in grave danger. Would you mind, love, typing up these notes, making copies and sending them off to the guys in Germany and Italy? I really hate to bother you with this, but I don't really know how else to do this without the boys at the office finding out."

"I don't mind at all, love. It sounds a hell of a lot more interesting than *The Young and the Restless*." She smiled and winked.

"Oh geez," Fran rolled his eyes, instantly relieved. "Thank you so much, love! I promise I will take you out for dinner tonight!"

"Awww, you don't have to do that, love."

"Yes, I do," Fran pulled her to her feet from the couch and close to his body. He held her tightly, swaying slightly as he kissed her. "Besides love, I want to...you work so hard around here."

"Watching daytime soaps isn't that hard..." She winked and smiled.

"You know what I mean, and I just want to make sure that you know that it all doesn't go unnoticed, love."

"Well, thank you, love. Don't you worry about any of this. I'll take care of all of it."

"Just remember, you can't tell anyone about any of this either."

"Don't worry about it, Fran. You just get your ass back to work," glancing at the pile of notes. "It looks like you've already been gone for a while. I'm sure they are wondering where the heck you are."

Fran quickly glanced at his watch, "Shit, is it that late already... damn, you're right. I do need to hustle back to the office." Fran gave her one more kiss and rushed back to headquarters.

CHAPTER 17

Lincoln National Bank was not a new bank in any sense of the word. Established in the mid- 1850s. The bank had an excellent established foundation. In the past, times became extremely challenging for Lincoln National, like similar financial institutions, after the 1929 stock market crash and the depression that followed. By the spring of 1934, the bank was nearly shuttered because of insolvency. With less than $500,000 in deposits and only five employees, the bank had nothing to lose, so they took a chance on a new, young Irish bank executive, lovingly referred to as "Pops." It was perhaps the best, most important decision made in the entire history of that bank.

The twenty-nine-year-old bank executive, "Pops," fully embraced the opportunity that lay before him. Slowly and steadily, the bank rose like a phoenix from the ashes, and by 1962, the bank's assets were well over $1 billion. Two years later, things were still going increasingly well. It was time to move the bank literally and figuratively into more lucrative markets that would challenge the big banks of Manhattan's financial district. Many were thrilled with the move, and the trajectory that lay before the bank, especially their shareholders.

However, the vice-chairman of the board disagreed with the Manhattan move, and other decisions were executed by the bank's leadership. In the summer of 1968, the now seasoned executive "Pops" was unexpectedly removed from his position as CEO and was replaced by his Vice-Chairman. Two years later, the former CEO was removed from the Board of Directors entirely. If he had been a younger version of himself, he might have fought more to stay on with Lincoln, but the new guard was poised and determined.

"Pops" possessed 70,000 shares of the bank in his retirement account. It was in his best interest to see to it that "his bank" remained successful despite his removal. His replacement, as far as he was concerned, was not a good fit, nor was he competent to serve in his new position. The dissatisfaction and frustration went beyond the monetary value of his retirement nest egg. This was his pride and joy on the line, and all his hard work over the many decades; this was personal, on multiple levels.

From the outside, he could see exactly what was happening to his beloved bank. However, he no longer had the power, nor any influence, on the directors in charge. His removal was now complete. "Pops" did, however, know other major shareholders. It was also in their best interest too, to motivate the bank to take immediate corrective action against Lincoln's declining earnings.

In January 1972, an investment banking firm approached Giovanni Fedora. Due to actions and changes implemented by the US Federal Reserve's Board of Governors, their client was being forced to divest their 22% interest in the Manhattan bank. A carrot consisting of all or part of their $1.1 million share purse was dangled in front of Fedora. The parties involved, however, were not the only one privy to the developing transaction.

The news broke in the press around mid-February. The *Wall Street Journal* headlined an article "Italy's Howard Hughes, Giovanni Fedora, Italy's richest and most respected financier is looking to make a substantial increase in his American investments..." By late April, more press reinforced the speculative rumors. A luncheon hosted by Fedora for bankers and investment managers the following month added more fuel to the roaring rumors. Few details were given, but this Italian outsider was about to enter the very exclusive New York banking scene.

Fedora looked over the bank's balance sheets, auditor's certificate and report from the comptroller of currency. The most glaring issue was the credit losses on the books. *Bank Stock Quarterly* listed Lincoln National as having the worst record in over one hundred banks surveyed. The sellers waited on pins and needles, while Fedora took his own sweet time contemplating the deal. They couldn't afford for him to walk away from the table.

Fedora assessed that Lincoln was, for the most part, a healthy bank, containing sufficient reserves to cover any potential losses due to their previous dubious credit practices. Once convinced, Fedora's Luxembourg holding company handed over $40 million in mid-July, for controlling interest in Lincoln National Bank. The bank was boasting $3.5 billion in assets and was the twentieth largest bank in the United States. It was Fedora's vision to move Lincoln into a more international banking direction.

The press was plastered with Fedora's image and news of his buyout of Lincoln. A couple of weeks passed before Giovanni Fedora and a man named Nico Novelli were elected to the board. Fedora was obviously not a new figure to the New York financial world. However, Novelli was mysterious and unknown.

Upon the arrival of Giovanni Fedora and Nico Novelli, more than a few Italian financial institutions decided to promptly cancel the lines of credit with Lincoln National Bank of New York. A man took to the local press, and anyone who would listen, proclaiming that dark and dangerous days lay ahead now that Giovanni Fedora was now running Lincoln. Some heeded the warnings and distanced themselves from both the man and his new bank.

Curious about what he was reading in the press, the overthrown former CEO of the bank investigated the matter himself. During a visit to the Fedora residence, the one man who knew all there was to know about Lincoln advised Fedora to fire the current CEO who stole his position.

This was not solely a vindictive or retaliatory suggestion. This new man was a good public relations man but was otherwise incompetent for his position. The former Lincoln man liked Fedora and the way he did business. Fedora's vision he presented for the bank's future was realistic, optimistic and satisfying.

Fedora chose to ignore his guest's advice. The current CEO was an important man, with important friends. Some of those friends had last names like Rockefeller, Dulles, Kissinger, and Bush. In New York, the Rockefeller and the others were good friends to have. But the CEO's credentials failed to translate into ability and knowledge. Everyone in town knew that Lincoln gave money to anybody and everybody. It was that lack of discretion that caused much of their credit problems. It was also widely known that Lincoln also took money under the table. The rumors of Fedora's Mafia ties also continued to build. Fedora had no time, nor desire, to confirm or deny such accusations.

He proceeded full steam ahead with his plans for Lincoln and her future. He decided to hire a new manager to run the International Finance Department. Fedora already had the confidence of Novelli to oversee the new department head. This move allowed Fedora to turn his attention to other matters.

CHAPTER 18

Fran got back to headquarters, doing his best to not let on where he'd been for such a sizeable chunk of the day. "Play it cool, play it cool," he whispered to himself. The detective cruised by Lance's office to find him with his nose buried in the multiple piles of papers scattered all over his desk.

Fran knocked on Lance's door frame, "Ya busy?"

Lance instantly looked up as his attention returned to the present. "Fran! There you are...you won't believe what all Robert Hinson gave me!"

Fran was instantly relieved. Lance's discovery and excitement, regardless of what the information was, would make it easier for him to hide his mysterious absence from the office all day. The detective approached Lance's desk with genuine curiosity. "What ya got, my man?!"

Lance explained the entire bank's history revealed to him by the reporter.

"Whoa, whoa, whoa, Lance, slow the heck down, will ya?" Fran held up a hand to interrupt his partner, as he shook his head, trying to process Lance's barrage of information. "Wait, they replaced their

CEO and the entire board, but why? If they were doing so well, why the hell would they do that?"

"That, I haven't figured that out yet, but it only took three years with the new group for the bank's earnings to decline to a point where corrective action was necessary."

"Interesting," Fran responded, as he further processed what Lance was telling him. "And where does Fedora come into the picture?"

Lance continued to explain everything he just learned.

Fran confirmed the legitimacy of Lance's research. "Yeah, that's more or less what I heard from the guys over in Germany and Italy during my last trip. Did you find out anything yet about Fedora's Mafia ties?"

"No, I'm still waiting for our informant to call back on that."

"Ahh, the waiting game..." Fran looked at the wall clock in Lance's office. "I'll give Cosimo a call in the morning. He will be happy to hear what you've dug up."

"Sounds like a plan, Fran."

"By the way, good job on finding all of that stuff on Lincoln and Fedora. Why don't you knock off a little early today?"

"Thanks man, I just have a little more here to finish up, then I'll get my ass out of here for the day."

"Cool, I'll catch up with you in the morning."

Fran tended to a little work, then headed home earlier than usual, too. En route home, his mind wandered back to his talk with Wexford. He was curious why Wexford never mentioned anything about the fake securities deal. Did he know anything about it? With all the intimate details he had thrown at him, how could he not? Fran made himself a mental note to bring up the subject the next time he saw the cardinal.

Fran arrived home, eager to see how Peg was doing with her assignment. When he walked into the house, she was busy working at her typewriter, situated between the kitchen and the living room, tapping away as fast as her fingers would move. "Man, she types fast," he thought to himself.

"Honey, I'm home..." Fran announced with a big smile as he walked through the door.

The rapid tapping, punctuated by a distinctive "ding," instantly stopped as she looked to see her husband enter the room. "Francis Liam Clavering!" Her tone surprised the man walking through the door. "I am so damn mad at you!"

Fran quickly tried to scan his memory. What the hell did he do this time? "Why?" He responded with a sheepish, shameful tone.

"How dare you throw this at me without giving me any warning of what was in it! You're nothing but a big ass sometimes, Francis Liam Clavering."

"Huh?"

"There is some pretty messed up shit in these here notes, mister!"

Fran knew it was serious for Peg to be cursing. "Oh, that." He knew exactly what she was so disturbed about. "Sorry love. It won't happen again, I promise. I was in a hurry to get back to the office... it completely slipped my mind...I'm sorry." Fran walked over to her, took her hands in his, lifted her from her chair at the typewriter, and into his arms. "Come on honey, let me make it up to you over that dinner I promised you. Your fingers must be tired from all that work."

"Oh, my gosh!" Exclaimed Peg. "I completely forgot about dinner! I'm sorry, love, I got so engrossed in typing this stuff up."

"Don't worry about it Peg, I'm taking us out for dinner."

"All of us? The kids too?"

"Yeah, yeah, the kids too."

"But they aren't ready either."

"Don't worry, love, I'll get them ready. You go get yourself ready."

His wife was suddenly relieved. "Oh, ok, well let me finish up this one part, then I will go upstairs and get ready."

"Sounds great love, take your time."

Fran ran upstairs to get the kids ready. As he waited for Peg to finish, he then went back downstairs, grabbed a can of beer from the refrigerator, turned on the news, and sat down in his favorite recliner. He read the newspaper while the CBS Evening News droned on in the background. Fran's attention was deep into the newspaper until he heard "Rome" and "Mafia" mentioned in the broadcast. He glanced at the television from behind his paper to see Walter Cronkite speaking on the television. The newsman explained that the report was one of a series of reports on Mafia activities in Rome. Fran watched with intrigue as a reporter in Rome talked about a November 1957 meeting in Palermo. A young Sicilian businessman who was appointed financier by the International Mafia committee attended the meeting. The reporter continued explaining that the mafiosi in charge of the committee claimed that "young Sicilian businessman" was none other than Giovanni Fedora, who to this day is the money man of the Sicilian syndicate.

The reporter finished up his segment, "...from the NBC Bureau in Rome, this is Charles Faust reporting. Back to you in New York, Walter..."

Fran grabbed a pen and a small notepad sitting on the small table next to him and scribbled down the reporter's information. "Maybe Cosimo can get something from this guy that will prove useful."

For the next three weeks, Fran and Lance continued to dig and learn more and more about Franklin National Bank and Fedora. The department informant was a bust. Fran thought it was amazing how no one could nail anything Mafia related to the Italian man. Even the news reporter wasn't as helpful as he had hoped. He purposefully decided to not give either Cosimo nor Hans and Friedrich a heads up that the notes from Wexford, his wife had typed up, were on their way. He wanted it to be a surprise. Suddenly there was a knock on Fran's door frame. He looked up.

"Hey Fran, call for you on line two." Said the sergeant as he passed by the door. "Oh, ok, thanks Jack."

He picked up the phone and pushed the blinking button. "This is Detective Clavering."

"Francis?" said the accented voice on the phone. "It's Cosimo from Rome."

"Oh hey Cosimo, how's it going over there?"

"Well, I have some good news for you."

"Really?! Lay it on me, brother! What ya got?"

"Remember that man, Taverna? The one that Schwartz and Krivis were working with in Rome?"

"Yeah, of course I remember him."

"Well, I thought you'd like to know that we picked him up the other day."

"You did?! That's great!"

"Yeah, and he's singing like a bird, about everything."

"Wow, that's some great news, Cosimo. Wish I could get back over there to help you."

"Nah, don't worry about it. We got this under control. I'll send you the interrogation notes as soon as they are ready."

"Perfect, I'm sure that will be just as good. At least I won't have to grovel for another trip over there yet."

"Funny you should say that Fran..."

"Huh? What's that supposed to mean?"

Fran could hear a smile in the Italian's voice. "Boy, do I have another nugget of news for you, my friend."

"What's that?"

"I managed to get you, or rather, us, an appointment with someone in the Vatican!"

"You what?! Holy shit! That's great Cosimo! When? Where? Who with?"

"April 26th at 3:30 PM. Archbishop Dante Leone's office in The Vatican."

Fran glanced at the three-month wall calendar hanging on his wall. "Damn, that's a good month away. You couldn't get anything sooner, Cosimo?"

"No, I tried, but he is going to be traveling much of the next few weeks. Besides, I think it's actually a good thing because this gives us a chance to strategize how we want to approach this."

"Yeah, you're right. This will be a very different situation, certainly not like our usual interrogations." Suddenly a thought came to Fran, and he became curious. "Hey Cosimo?"

"Yes, sir."

JANE M. BELL

"Did this Vatican person reach out to you? Or did you reach out to him?" Cosimo became curious about Fran's questions. "He called me. Why?"

"Oh, I'm just wondering." Fran instantly wondered if Wexford had a hand in any of this. "Did he say what he wanted to talk about?"

"No, he was very vague, but he specifically asked to speak with me, which I thought was odd."

"That is odd. Did he say what he did to the Vatican?"

"He said he was the Under-Secretary to the pope. He works in the Secretariat of State's office of the Holy See."

"Under-Secretary to the pope? Oh wow! This is huge!" Fran caught himself, then instantly pretended to second guess himself. "Isn't it?"

"Well, if we don't screw this up, it will be." Responded Cosimo. "I, for the life of me, can't figure out why he called me, though."

"I guess the Lord works in mysterious ways." Fran was glad that Cosimo couldn't see the grin on his face at that moment.

"I guess...we may never know..."

Fran continued. "Yeah, knowing the reason for his call to you would certainly give us a better idea on how to prepare for this meeting."

"No doubt about it."

Suddenly, the New York detective was antsy to get off the phone. They wrapped up their conversation, and Fran returned the handset to the phone's receiver. "Right on!" he yelled as he clapped his hands loudly.

He filled Lance in on the details of the call. "Looks like another trip to Italy for you, Fran."

"Yeah, I guess I'd better start crawling again. That's the part about all of this that I hate the most."

Bentley, the chief and Bayer were not so eager to approve this trip. They gave Fran tentative approval but wanted to hear more of what the plan of action was first. He argued that a plan of action would be difficult without knowing the purpose of Archbishop Leone's requested meeting. It was Bayer, who protested the approval of this trip the most. They tabled the matter, to be revisited in a couple of weeks. Next he called Peg. He told her the news. She inquired if Cosimo had received the notes she'd sent him in the mail.

"No, I'm pretty sure he hasn't. I know he would have mentioned them if he did."

A week later, Fran had just gotten to his office and started going over his to-do list for the day, when there was a sudden knock on his door frame.

"Oh hey Jack, what's up?"

"Hey Fran, I just wanted to let you know, when I stopped to get my coffee this morning, this caught my eye on the newsstand as I walked by..." He tossed him a copy of the latest issue of *Time* magazine.

"Thanks Jack, I will check it out." Fran's voice faded as he surveyed the cover.

The piercing eyes of Giovanni Fedora on the magazine cover looked back at him with the slick grin of a sly fox. Fran glared back at the image for a minute, then flipped the pages to the article and started reading. The article profiled the Italian con with pictures of him in finely tailored Italian suits and expensive furnishing and paintings in the background. The article confirmed everything that Cosimo and Wexford had told him, of course leaving out his involvement with the Mafia, Krivis, or the Vatican Bank.

The following week, another article was printed about him in *New York Business This Week*. This article waxed poetically about Fedora, "Lord of the Lira," and how he single-handedly saved Post- World War II Italy from certain economic collapse. The accolades kept coming from every direction. Even President Nixon was swooning over him and his financial prowess. Fran couldn't help but become absolutely nauseous by this sudden and growing public relations campaign. "The bigger they are, the harder they fall," he thought to himself.

The weeks were flying by. It was now early April, and everyone was getting ready to celebrate Easter. Christopherson, Thomas, and Bayer took a break from their preparation for the upcoming grand jury case against Benedetto to discuss Fran's upcoming trip to Rome and the Vatican. Once again, seated in the large conference room, was the usual assembled cast of characters. Christopherson, Bentley, Thomas, Bayer, and Lance.

Christopherson was finally satisfied with where the next leg of the investigation was headed. "Alright Francis, you can go to Rome to meet with this Vatican Official."

"Thank you, Sir!" He once again found it difficult to stifle his excitement. "I have a feeling this will be a very fruitful trip."

"Hold up there," Bayer suddenly interrupted the momentum of the meeting with a bit of a crack in his voice. "D.A., with all due respect, sir, you do not have the authority to approve this trip."

The room became suddenly silent. The only sound in the room came from the buzzing fluorescent lights overhead and the clock ticking on the wall. Everyone in the room was now staring at Bayer.

D.A. Christopherson finally broke the elongated silence. "Excuse me?"

Bayer cleared his throat nervously. "You don't have the authority to approve this trip."

"And why exactly is that?" The D.A. suddenly did his best to not explode in that moment. "I had the authority to approve his prior trips to Germany."

"That you did, sir, but it's different this time."

"Mr. Bayer, you'd better start explaining yourself, and fast..."

"I've discussed this upcoming meeting with the chief of the Organized Crime and Racketeering Section of the DOJ, Joel Wallace..."

"And?!"

"Well, his office has responded to Archbishop Leone's diplomatic request."

Fran couldn't hold his tongue any longer. "This isn't and never was a diplomatic request, Bayer! This was a personal invitation extended to my Roman colleague and myself."

"I'm afraid, Francis, you are wrong. It IS a diplomatic affair, far beyond your jurisdiction, detective."

214

"Like hell it is Bayer!" the detective yelled, completely losing his composure. "Rome didn't call you or your boss. They called Cosimo and me! You're just pissed that I got an invitation to the Vatican and you didn't. So when are we leaving?"

"You're not going Francis."

Christopherson was now pissed. "Wait, what?!?! But why?"

Bayer calmly continued. "This is strictly a federal affair. The meeting with the archbishop will be with myself, Chief Wallace and Lance. Detective Clavering will not be needed on this trip."

"Not needed!" Bentley quickly saw what Bayer was trying to do. "How the hell can you even say that, Nathan? Fran has been busting his ass on this case for years leading up to this! Long before you were even assigned to help us. If it wasn't for him, you wouldn't even be here! Nobody knows more about this case than him. I told you from the get go, and you agreed, this was HIS case! Without him, your whole trip will be pointless."

Bayer finally responded. "He's not going. The decision has already been finalized by Chief Wallace. Besides, we need him to go back to Germany to tie up some final loose ends for the Benedetto case."

Fran was absolutely livid at this point. "Germany! I'm not your fuckin' errand boy, Bayer! Go over there and get your fuckin' shit yourself, you fuckin' bastard!"

Christopherson raised an extended hand in front of his detective, and looked directly at Bayer, pissed. "You've got some fucking balls, Bayer!"

A very nervous Bayer spoke. "Excuse me?"

"Oh, shut up, you fucking piece of shit. I see right through your little fucking game here!"

"What are you talking about, Christopherson?"

"Detective Clavering here has been trying for months to get anyone interested in investigating the Vatican connections to this case, and NOBODY, especially you with your fucking jurisdiction bullshit, would give him the fucking time of day! But now that he has managed to get himself an appointment with high-ranking officials in the Vatican State Department, all of a sudden you are interested!"

"What the hell would you know Christopherson, we've always been interested in how the Vatican was connected."

Fran's blood was now at a full boil. Just as he was about to speak, Christopherson cut him off. "I know EVERYTHING about my men, Bayer, and if you EVER lie to me or my men again, your entire career will be over! Do I make myself clear?!"

Bayer suddenly felt very cocky. "You are not my boss Christopherson! You DO NOT have jurisdiction over me!"

"You can shove your 'jurisdiction' up your ass, Bayer! Your little hijack of his investigation, just to make yourself look good in front of your bosses, will fail! Especially without the help of my detective."

"You WILL go to Germany, Clavering!" Bayer said in a firm, yet shaky voice. "Our detail will go to the Vatican, and that is final! This meeting is adjourned! Lance, come along. We need to discuss the itinerary of our trip."

Bayer gathered up his belongings, grabbed his jacket off the back of his chair, and left the room promptly, with a sheepish, embarrassed agent in tow. Everyone else in the room remained seated, stunned by this turn of events.

"He's going to go over there and fuck this entire thing up!" A still livid detective interjected. "I told you, at the beginning, it was a bad idea getting these clowns involved in this case!"

"We really didn't have a choice at the time, Fran, and you know it," Bentley, the calmest one in the room, consoled.

Christopherson chimed in, "I will call Bayer's bosses and see what I can do. You have to be on that trip, Clavering!"

Fran, now a little calmer, turned to the D.A. and responded, "Look, sir, I don't mind going back over to Germany to get whatever you need for your case. I'm more than happy to do it, and to be honest, it's the least I could do after you approved the last few trips. I just don't understand why, I couldn't just do a repeat of my last trip? You know, go to Germany and do what I gotta do there, then do another side trip and meet up with them in Rome."

"This is the Feds we're talking about here. Nothing ever makes that much sense, Fran, and you know it." Bentley continued to try to comfort the room. "Let's see if the D.A. can do anything to change the situation. For now, I guess I'll go see what they want you to do over in Germany, and when."

Fran took a big breath, "Alright, I guess that's all we can do until this all gets sorted out."

Fran had been in a rage as he went about the department since the meeting two days prior. Nobody, at work or home, wanted to be around the detective. Bayer and Lance avoided him like he was the Black Plague. The detective tried his best not to take his anger out on his co-workers, wife or children, but there were times he just couldn't contain himself, no matter how hard he tried. Peg listened to him rant. She did her best to calm him, but the point was moot. The stunt Bayer pulled actually angered her, too. The best anyone in the detective's orbit could do was to just give him space.

Bentley sat in his office with Assistant D.A. Thomas and D.A. Christopherson. He was dreading his next call. Within moments, Fran joined the three men assembled in the room. None of them looked happy, nor did they want to be there. The detective already knew that the news was not good.

"Good afternoon Detective." Christopherson began in a somber tone.

"Afternoon Sir," Fran responded curtly, then caught himself. "Before we begin, if I may...I owe you guys an apology, and everyone else I've come in contact with the last couple of days."

Bentley interrupted. "No, you don't. You know we're just as pissed about this as you are, Fran."

"Well, I appreciate that," Replied Fran in a sheepish tone, still clinging to a sliver of hope. "So, is there any good news?"

"I'm afraid not, Fran," responded Thomas. "I'm sorry."

At that moment, the entire team could feel the defeat in the man's spirit. After a brief silence... "Well, I appreciate you guys having my back, even if it didn't do any good this time. So what do they want me to do this time, ya know, in Germany?"

"This will be the final piece of the puzzle in the Benedetto case," began Christopherson. "And if it's any consolation, this work will be more for us than the Feds. We need you to go back over to Germany and see if you can convince Straussen and Franz to come over here to testify against Benedetto in our case."

Fran took a huge deep breath, "Alright, I can do that for you, sir. Knowing how scared those cats are of Benedetto, I'm not too sure how it will go. They will either want to fry him or run."

"Well, at this point, all we can do is ask." Bentley's voice faded off.

Fran reached over and patted his boss firmly on the shoulder with an understanding hand. "So, when do I leave?"

"Next Tuesday. My secretary is getting your itinerary together. Feel free to reach out to Hans and his team, if he doesn't mind serving as interpreter once again."

Fran made a note, "I will. I'm sure he won't mind. Those crazy Germans think I'm James Bond or something." The mood in the room lifted with a chuckle from the other men seated in the meeting. Fran reflected further, "It actually will be good to work with them again. It will be a nice break from the element hanging around here, if you know what I mean."

"I think we all can understand that, Fran." Bentley confirmed.

Assistant D.A. Thomas cleared his throat. "Umm, I spoke with 'Chief Screwball.'"

The other three men were instantly confused. "Who?" They replied in unison.

"You know, the DOJ chief with Bayer's nose up his ass...Chief Wallace."

The rest of the room chuckled as Thomas continued. "As you know, he won't budge on this decision."

A defeated, frustrated Fran just looked down, shaking his head, as Thomas continued. "Um, uh," Thomas suddenly became very nervous and quiet, stumbling over his words, as his gaze lowered to his shoes. "He said he wants you to help Bayer and Lance prepare for their trip to Rome."

Fran's rage returned instantly. "You can tell Bayer AND 'Chief Screwball' to go fuck themselves!"

"I can't tell him that for you." Replied Thomas.

"Well then, you go tell Bayer and his fucking boss that I said they can go fuck themselves!" Christopherson yelled at Thomas. "If Bayer wants to hijackThis investigation, he will have to do this on his own! This detective will be too busy doing work for me."

"Alright Paul. I'm sure Bayer and the chief will be thrilled..."

"If he wants to throw his jurisdiction around on this, well so can I. I don't even care what that pissant thinks or feels, fucking bastard!" Christopherson barked, then he turned to look again at Fran. "I don't give a shit what these sons of bitches say or do, Francis Clavering, you work for me, not them!"

"Yes, sir!" Fran suddenly developed a slight sideways smile on his face.

Bentley knew his detective well enough to be worried when he saw that look. "Why are you smiling?"

"Well, I couldn't help them even if I wanted to. I don't even know why the archbishop called us for the meeting in the first place." The other men just smiled, understanding his point. "We will just have to see how these guys manage without me..."

Christopherson looked at the clock, then turned to Bentley and Thomas. "Well, gentlemen, I need to get to my next appointment. I trust you two will keep me abreast of everything...Oh and Clavering..."

"Yes, sir?"

"Get your ass back to work! Oh, and be careful over there."

"Yes, Sir!" the detective confirmed with slightly lifted spirits.

With the confirmation of his changed travel plans, Fran knew he needed to get a hold of Cosimo. But before he did, he needed to pay another visit to Cardinal Wexford. The following afternoon, he found himself once again seated across the desk from Wexford in his diocese's office.

"Francis, my son, it is good to see you again, so soon."

"Thank you, Your Eminence." replied the detective, still feeling a little defeated. "You seem to have something troubling your mind today, Francis?"

The detective was suddenly transported back to the years he spent working for this hero of his youth seated before him. "You still know me so well, despite all the years that have passed."

"You are an open book to me, my son. So what's on your mind?"

"Your Eminence, there is a lot on my mind, but I didn't come here to seek counsel from you."

"Well, my door is always open to you, Francis. Always..."

"I appreciate that, sir."

"Besides, you called me for this appointment, remember?"

"Yes, That I did. You see, a few weeks ago, I got a call from my Roman colleague Cosimo Angelo, whose number I left with you on my last visit. Well, he got a call from an Archbishop Dante Leone in the Vatican's Secretary of State office. Since I haven't said a peep to anyone about our last meeting, I was wondering if you might know anything about how that might have come about?"

The cardinal seated across from Francis issued a slight smile and wrinkled his nose. "I may know a little something about it."

"Ahh, I had a feeling you might have. Why else would the Under-Secretary to the pope call him out of the blue?"

"Oh, I may have mentioned something in passing to Dante." Wexford said with a wink. "So, when is your meeting with my good friend in Rome?"

"You know of my appointment in Rome?"

"I do..."

"You would make a brilliant detective for New York's finest, Your Eminence." Fran gave a smile and slight chuckle that once again faded to defeat. "Well, we've, or rather, I have, run into a bit of a problem."

The cardinal continued with his sly smile. "And what's that, my son?"

"I can't go."

The cardinal didn't like that response. "What do you mean, you can't go?"

"Well, since I started the investigation that would eventually lead me to Bishop Krivis, the Department of Justice has had an element working alongside us here in New York. They have had no interest in how, where or if there was any connection with the Vatican, until now."

"But why now?"

"Well, now, with Archbishop Leone's invitation to meet with Cosimo and myself, they suddenly think this is a diplomatic affair between the two governments. My FBI counterpart, the Federal prosecutor, and his boss from the Department of Justice will be making that trip, and they've forbidden me to go."

"Oh no," Cardinal Wexford's sly smile was instantly gone, and replaced with a look of deep concern. "This is not a horrible development."

"While I don't disagree with you, Your Eminence, why do you suddenly look so worried?"

"I need to call Rome immediately! Nobody knows of my little chat with you except for Archbishop Leone. This change of events could expose the two of us, you and what we're trying to accomplish here, Francis."

Francis thought for a moment. Moving forward, everyone involved in this Vatican investigation must operate in complete stealth for as long as possible. "You say that this archbishop that called Cosimo is the only one in the Vatican who's aware of this meeting."

"Yes." The cardinal was now curious about where the detective was going with this.

"I never told anyone either. Even Cosimo doesn't know what this is all about. I'm wondering if we can do a little sleight-of-hand here and keep all of our noses out of the spotlight in the process."

"I'm afraid I'm not following you, Francis."

"Look sir, since we're the only three who know what this meeting is about, I will keep playing stupid down at the station. If the Feds want to hijack my meeting and make this into a diplomatic fishing trip, none of us should get in their way. All the archbishop needs to do is get someone besides himself to meet up with them."

"I'm more than certain that Dante can make that happen."

"Good, good!" The detective confirmed. "We will let them all fly blind into this, and Cosimo and I will meet with the archbishop at another time and place, without the knowledge of anyone. My gut tells me that this, somehow, some way, may actually work out to our advantage."

"While I can see how this will protect the three of us from discovery, I still don't see how this will help us, Francis."

"Yeah, I'm not too sure of those exact details yet, either. It's just a hunch."

"So what exactly do you need me to do, Francis?"

"I need you to get the archbishop to bow out of that meeting with our Federal guys, and set up another just for Cosimo and myself. I'm going to be in Munich next week working with the Munich PD. I could make a side trip to Rome perhaps...I've done it before. Worst-case scenario, I will make a private trip over there on my own if I must. Cosimo and I can work around whatever schedule works with the archbishop."

"Alright. I will leave a message with your wife when I have the details of a new meeting."

"That will be perfect, Your Eminence." Fran smiled with a gleam in his eye. "Don't worry, this will work out just like it's supposed to..."

"God willing."

"Yes! God willing, I would never reject any Divine Intervention, especially right now."

Fran returned to his office and was just about to call Cosimo with the news when he heard a voice from down the hall.

"Fran, call on line 3..."

"Alright Jack, thanks."

The detective picked up the handset. "This is Detective Clavering."

"Hey Fran, it's Cosimo."

Fran broke into a chuckle, "Oh, hey Cosimo, I was just about to call you. You must have picked up on my mental vibes."

Cosimo suddenly started yelling into the phone. "You son of a bitch!"

"Whoa, whoa, whoa, what was that for?"

"I just got a little package from the States. I don't suppose you'd know anything about it?" Fran suddenly grinned from ear to ear. "Umm, well, I might..."

"Well, the postmark says New York, and it's addressed to me personally, and you're the only New Yorker I know..."

"Alright, I fess up..." Fran paused as he got up and closed his office door. "But I need you to do me a favor. Keep that information just between you and me until I tell you otherwise."

"Why? Where did you get this?"

"That I can't say. Just know that it comes from an extremely reliable informant, my friend."

"Alright," Cosimo didn't understand what was going on, but he trusted his American cohort.

"Does this, by any chance, have anything to do with our upcoming meeting?"

"Mmmm, it might...Speaking of which, I have some bad news sort of..."

"Oh?"

"Yeah, about that trip. I'm forbidden to attend it."

"What? Why? What am I supposed to do? I don't know what that guy wants to talk to me about."

"Don't worry about it, I'm taking care of it from my end, just keep quiet about it alright. I will explain later. For now, we need to be extremely tight-lipped about all of this."

Cosimo was completely confused but was willing to follow the detective's lead. "Alright, I won't say a word about any of this or the package to anyone, I promise."

"Look, I have to go back to Munich next week. I don't suppose you could meet up with us there?"

Cosimo glanced at his calendar. "What day?"

"I leave here on Tuesday. I should be there for up to a week, so you pick the day. I'll work around it."

"Yeah, I will have to rearrange some stuff, but I can make something work. I'll confirm with Hans and Freidrich."

"Perfect! I will explain everything when I get there."

"Excellent, it will be good to see you again, my friend." Fran echoed the sentiment and hung up.

The detective next called Hans. Hans confirmed that he and his colleague, too, had received the packages Peg had sent them, and he reiterated what he had told Cosimo in his previous call. Suddenly Fran didn't feel quite so angry about the turn of events. "Things will work out; I can just feel it. Just like they're supposed to, I just have to have faith." He thought to himself.

CHAPTER 19

As soon as he stepped foot on German soil, Fran immediately got to work on Straussen and Franz. He wanted to get all the "official business" out of the way before Cosimo arrived in Munich. His assignment took a little longer than he had expected, but it was fruitful nonetheless, in more ways than he ever could have imagined. The two German cons, after a little coaxing, finally agreed to testify in the case against Benedetto, but not before they revealed more of the wheeling and dealing antics of American swindlers, mobsters, cardinals, archbishops, bishops, monsignors and businessmen in the US, Italy and other parts of the globe.

Fran and Hans' interview with Franz and Straussen revealed that the Benedetto's network reached far beyond the criminal underworld. The New York Detective was particularly interested to learn of a meeting in the spring of 1971 when Schwartz and Benedetto's West Coast counterpart was in town to prepare for the upcoming big meeting in London to finalize the Vatican deal that would set everything in motion. The hotel in which they were staying was extremely full. It was hosting a major international economic conference. Finance ministers and dignitaries from around the world were in attendance.

The two German cons noticed their mobster friend across the hotel lobby chatting with a very well dressed, tall, silver-haired American. When approached, the man was introduced as the LA mobster's "financial advisor." The man's name, however, was never disclosed. Later, Schwartz told Straussen that the mysterious American man was a very important official in the US government.

Fran's curiosity was piqued. Who was this mysterious American official? What was he doing in Munich talking with a big-name West Coast Mobster? It only took a little digging to learn that the man was actually the former US Secretary of the Treasury. Fran was sure that it was probably not a coincidence that the man was removed from his position only a few months following that meeting in Munich. While the man no longer held his position with the Treasury Department, he was still a very powerful, influential man in politics, and he remained very close to President Nixon. The New Yorker knew immediately that this would warrant further investigation, but it was definitely beyond his jurisdiction. Fran stuffed the information into "his back pocket," thinking it might come in handy to get Bayer out of his hair if he needed it at some point.

With his "real" work wrapped up, he could now focus on his side mission. The group decided it would be more private to meet in Fran's hotel room instead of down at the Munich station. While he admired the professionalism of the Munich team, he could not risk exposure by nosey co-workers in the precinct. Secrets are easier to keep in a tight circle. Cardinal Wexford had instilled in him a very guarded and sacred trust, and Fran had every intention of honoring it. The cardinal also gave him some very real-world reasons and warnings not to trust anyone. Fran did trust his European men, he had to. There was no future to this investigation without them. Despite everything he was about to divulge, he would keep his source, Wexford, to himself.

As the men settled into the room, Fran and Hans couldn't help but remark on the similarities between this meeting, and the meeting between Benedetto, Straussen and Franz in the early months of the prior year.

"Fran, should we check the bed's massage machine to make sure our room isn't bugged?"

The other two men joined Fran in a laugh before he commented with a wink. "Maybe I should call down to the bar for some Asbach and cola..."

The liveliness of the moment quickly gave way to the serious work ahead of them. The Europeans were quick to compliment the New Yorker on the information he managed to gather so quickly.

They were all extremely impressed. They knew nothing of these dirty little secrets that haunted the Vatican. The Vatican public relations corps sure knew how to bury all of their hideous truths. Archbishop Leone's unsolicited call and request for a meeting was even more impressive.

"Well, you aren't the only one with some good news to contribute to this investigation, Fran," Cosimo interrupted.

"Oh yeah, Cosimo? What ya got?" Fran inquired.

"I looked into all those names Schwartz gave you and Hans..."

"And? And?"

"...and we found nothing. Every damn one of them was fake."

The team looked disappointed. Hans then chimed in, "I thought you said you had some good news."

"Well, we managed to bring in Mateo Taverna...remember?"

"Oh my gosh, yes! I can't even begin to tell you how helpful that was. Thanks so much!" Fran issued a smile. "That reminds me Cosimo, I keep forgetting to ask you if you have ever heard of a guy named Nico Novelli?"

"He sounds familiar, but I'm not sure of the context. Why, what's up with him?"

"He's one of the new directors on the board of Fedora's new bank in New York."

"I'll see what I can dig up on him and get back to you if I find anything."

The discussion continued on for several hours as Cosimo briefed those assembled with more information on Taverna. Taverna, via Cosimo, confirmed that the Vatican was in fact involved. He also confirmed that Duncan Hughes and his fellow courier had delivered the $14.5 million counterfeit initial sample bond order. While this pleased the American, it also left him with even more questions. They needed to confirm who all in the Vatican was involved. How did it all start? Where were all these bonds going?

With the Benedetto case complete, the team could turn all of their attention to the Vatican. The men they were now after were not their typical criminals. These men had great power, influence, and protection. They were also well respected, admired and honored among their peers, church and community. The men who had "dedicated themselves" to God and the betterment of the Mother Church had committed unthinkable grave crimes. Everything they would discover led directly to the heart of the Vatican. If they continued, they would most certainly uncover the crimes of some of the most esteemed church leaders, possibly implicating even the pope. The scandal would cause significant damage to the church.

What the team could not know was whether the Church and her leaders were all rotten to the core, or was this the results of a handful of very fallible men? If it were just a few rotten apples, how would they know the bad from the good?

Fran was suddenly fully aware of what lay at their collective feet. "Gentlemen, we are at a very precarious crossroads at the moment."

"What do you mean?" Questioned Hans.

"The decisions we make here and now could very well hold global consequences. Should we simply ignore the role the Vatican and church leaders played in this scheme?"

"I don't understand Fran," responded Cosimo. "I thought we all agreed to our mission back in Rome."

"We did, but we also must keep in mind the very real possibility that no matter what we do or find, there will be little to no chance of bringing a cardinal, archbishop, bishop or monsignor to justice. There may be a very slim chance at best in Italy, but Munich and New York would never be able to bring any church official to trial. The scandals we uncover will only be mitigated by their public relations people.

I mean, look at all the scandalous material that I already sent you that's never seen the light of day as far as the public is concerned?"

"Even with Benedetto's involvement with the Vatican?" Hans commented.

"Benedetto's case is done. This goes way beyond him and the syndicate. This may even be bigger than the Mafia, if that's even possible, gentlemen."

The other three men agreed. This investigation was expanding quickly. Fran continued, "We, as investigators, have a sworn duty to follow every case, no matter where it leads. I just need to make sure you are all on board from this point forward. Because if you aren't, it is probably best to just leave it here. Because I can't do this without you guys."

Fran's European colleagues looked at each other, then back at him. "We have your back, Fran. We're all in this together now, regardless of where it leads."

The New York detective was relieved that his team was still willing to move forward. The guidance of Wexford and Leone would be crucial for moving forward. No stone would be left unturned. Even though they had their work cut out for them, come hell or high water, justice will be served.

Meanwhile, in Rome, the three-man entourage from the United States went to Vatican City to meet with Archbishop Leone. The archbishop briefly met with Bayer and Chief Wallace while Lance remained seated in the hallway outside the office. The archbishop then escorted the two men to another office, where they met with three of the monsignors on his staff. Chief Wallace did all the talking, detailing the grand jury's findings regarding the $14.5 million worth of counterfeit bonds delivered to Rome in July 1971 that were destined for the Vatican. What became of the remaining $990 million order?

The chief continued. "Our investigation has revealed that IOR President, Bishop Jonas Krivis was directly involved in this scheme and other illegal projects with Mr. Giovanni Fedora. We have indictments pending with allegations of Vatican involvement that will soon become public record and sully the good name and reputation of the Vatican. We're sure our trial will result in plenty of bad press for the Vatican and her church."

One of the monsignors, who happened to be the Secretariat of State assessor, claimed ignorance of any Vatican personnel's involvement in this or any other scheme. "Gentlemen, I'm just here to listen, not to confirm or deny anything you have to say about your investigation."

With that, the tone of the meeting quickly and dramatically changed. Wallace continued to explain that many of those involved in this scheme had already been arrested...some were even dead.

"Mr. Wallace, you claim that this Taverna fellow told you he worked directly with someone from this office?"

"Yes."

"Taverna gave you direct evidence of this scheme?"

"That's correct."

"He told you of deposits he'd made using these false documents?"

"Yes, among other proof."

"We can assure you that the information he gave you is absolutely false. These counterfeit bonds and trial deposits you mention, this is the first we've ever heard of this, and we've been working in this office for over eight years. I can assure you that the Vatican Bank does not have any counterfeit American bonds on deposit."

The Wallace and Bayer adjusted their strategy, ignoring the monsignor's last comment. "You realize that dating, we've already recovered over $114 million worth of those counterfeit documents, right?

Our evidence strongly suggests that those bonds were headed directly to the IOR. We know for a fact that at least some of them reached their destination. It would be in all of our best interest if we worked together to recover the remaining missing documents, monsignor." Bayer then presented the letters they obtained from the Schwartz raid, requesting the counterfeit bonds with listed contracted amounts of documents, payments and deadlines.

The assessor looked over the document, front and back, then passed it on to another monsignor seated next to him. The assessor addressed the two Americans. "While this letterhead does seem to be authentic, this letter is in no way indicative of any type of deal as far as we can tell."

Chief Wallace was beginning to grow impatient with the two monsignors. "How can you even say that after authenticating the document?"

"I only said that the letterhead was authentic. We have no comment on the document's content. Your document is dated 1971."

"So?"

"The office from which this letterhead came has been officially closed since at least 1968."

Both men suddenly felt idiotic, as Bayer presented a list of the types of bonds in question for the assessor to look over.

The assessor scanned the list, then returned it to Bayer, then continued. "Look, Mr. Wallace, Mr. Bayer, we know nothing about these counterfeit bonds. Perhaps Bishop Krivis can convince you two in the morning. After all, it would be his job to follow up on this matter, anyway. I'm sorry gentlemen, there is nothing further here that we need to discuss."

The two Americans were soon escorted out of the room to be rejoined with Agent Erikson, still waiting patiently out in the hallway before they realized what had just happened. Wallace and Bayer were ill-prepared for what had just occurred. The two men would have one more shot the following morning. They spent the rest of their day strategizing their approach for the next day.

The next morning, once again, Chief Wallace and Bayer were escorted into the Vatican. This time, their destination was Bishop Jonas Krivis' office. The bishop was presented with the same evidence and allegations presented to the monsignors the previous day.

Again, Chief Wallace repeated his statements from the prior day, hoping for better results. As Bishop Krivis sat at his desk puffing away on his big fat Havana Cigar, he intently listened to his guests. Finally, the bishop broke his silence. "Gentlemen, these allegations are very serious, and most upsetting. I'll answer your questions as best I can."

The two Americans felt their luck change, and proceeded optimistically, as Krivis continued, "Mr. Fedora and I are very good friends, we have been for several years now. I personally consider him a pioneer in the world of finance, and of course the wealthiest industrialist in all of Italy, if not the world. But in all honesty, my financial dealings with him are extremely limited."

Krivis continued to carry on at length about Fedora's virtues, skills, and talents. "I am not willing to divulge names in many of my answers I'm about to give. While the charges, Mr. Taverna and you allege against me, are extremely serious, they are absolutely preposterous, and do not warrant the violation of banking secrecy laws in any attempt to defend myself here."

Chief Wallace commented. "Bishop, we have been working on this case for over two years now. Would you be willing to make yourself available, should it become necessary to confront Mr. Taverna face to face?"

"Yes, I am willing."

"If necessary, would you be prepared to testify in the US Court?"

"Absolutely, but only if it is necessary and unavoidable, but I hope that won't be the case."

"Oh? Why is that bishop?"

"The only ones to gain anything out of this kind of situation would be the press."

"I'm sorry bishop, I don't understand."

"They seem to enjoy dragging us through the mud with their inflammatory pieces concerning the Vatican, regardless of whether their information is truthful or not."

The latter was of no concern to the American visitors. Wallace proceeded. "Bishop, do you own a private numbered account at a bank located in The Bahamas?"

"No sir, I do not."

"How about an ordinary account over there?"

"No."

"Are you sure?"

"While the Vatican has some financial interests in The Bahamas, it is strictly business, much like the other interests controlled by the Vatican. It is in no way anything that any one person could privately benefit, in my opinion."

"Those are not of our concern at the moment. We are strictly interested in your personal dealings."

"I don't have any personal or private accounts there, or anywhere, for that matter, gentlemen."

Krivis cleared his throat and continued. "You see, gentlemen, my position here in the Vatican is quite unique. I'm in charge and have complete control of what is commonly referred to as the Vatican Bank. I oversee all the Vatican's financial affairs. My job differs from that of any other person in finance. I am answerable to only the pope as to how I carry out my job. In theory, there are a few cardinals who oversee my work from time to time. But reality is such that I am the one who directs the financial affairs of the Vatican."

"...and your point is?"

"There are many within the Vatican Curia who view me in this position with great contempt."

"And why is that bishop?"

"It more or less comes with the territory, I'm afraid."

"What?"

"You see, I'm the first American to have ever ascended to such a position of power within the church. The entire situation has left a bad taste in the mouth of many around here." The bishop paused to reflect, then continued. "You know, now that I think of it, I was involved with Mr. Mateo Taverna on two separate occasions. There was a $100 million investment opportunity that caught his interest at the end of July in '71. He was seeking to partner his investment group with the Vatican Bank on a transaction. If it had come to fruition, it would have greatly benefitted the diocese of Rome. While the deal was complex and confidential, it was by no means anything illegal. Unfortunately, the proposal never progressed beyond the planning stage. My only other interaction with Mr. Taverna was back in March of '72." Krivis verbally danced around details, so as not to break any banking secrecy laws. "This new deal of his came via Pope Michael himself. It involved a $300 million investment deal. The Holy Father wanted me to verify the authenticity of the deal and evaluate whether it was a worthy opportunity for his money. I admit that I was not pleased with the two of them for excluding me from their discussions and breaking protocol. I am pretty sure Archbishop Leone had a hand in that one, but regardless, who was I to deny the Holy Father?

I did wonder and pressed Mr. Taverna on how he managed to present his proposal directly to Pope Michael. I knew something was amiss as soon as his name was given. The supposed point of contact was too far removed from any of the Vatican Curia's staff, and I called Mr. Taverna out on his lies. He later sent me correspondence stating that my staff was utterly dishonest and corrupt. The suggestion was absolute rubbish and lacked any facts to support his accusations. Following that interaction, I wanted nothing to do with either Mr. Taverna or any of his friends. Obviously, this made them none too happy, so they proceeded to go around town talking trash about me and my character.

The mere rumor or suggestion that me or my bank would be involved in some counterfeit American bond scheme is a glaring example of the constant barrage of slander I'm subjected to at the hands of Taverna and others. There have been no attempts to deposit any such bonds in this bank whatsoever."

Bayer handed Bishop Krivis a list of the suspected counterfeits. The Vatican Bank president was appreciative and gladly accepted the document. He said he would be in touch with American Authorities should any of them ever appear at his bank. With that, the interview concluded, and the entourage was then escorted from St Nicholas V's tower.

The following Monday, all the world travelers had returned to New York. Fran tried not to let the success of his German trip show on his face. He didn't have to fake his displeasure for long. As he read the initial report from the Vatican trip, his rage was triggered once again. He was now primed for the next team meeting.

Assembled in the room were Christopherson, Thomas, Bentley, Fran, Lance, and a few other senior detectives on the team. Of course,

Bayer was feeling smug and quite full of himself as he presented his report. He concluded his presentation on his trip. "Are there any questions?"

Fran straightened himself in his chair, and cleared his throat before he began, with a barbed tone, "You never asked any of them the right questions, the hard questions. You never pressed any of them, you just let Krivis and company say whatever the fuck they wanted with a nod and a thank you. What a waste of fucking time and taxpayer's dollars."

"Detective Clavering, it would be in your best interest to curb your attitude and tone." Responded Bayer.

"Shove it up your ass, Bayer! Well, at least you got that stupid bishop to admit to interacting with Taverna, but you've got your head so far up your ass that you didn't even know what was sitting right in front of you."

"What the fuck are you talking about, Detective?"

"Shall I call Chief Wallace and let him know that the date Krivis gave you regarding the failed 'initial partnership deal' involving $100 million was just 2 days after Taverna deposited $1.5 million in fake bonds into a Zürich Bank?"

"Nobody we spoke to knew anything about the counterfeit bonds, Francis!"

"You stupid fuck!" Fran quickly scanned the report. "This assessor, monsignor guy you spoke with..."

"What about him?"

"His name was listed on the fucking account Taverna deposited the fake stocks into."

Bayer's stomach sank, while Christopherson, Thomas and Bentley did their best to hide their smile and pride in their detective.

"Oh, and another thing, that second interaction between Krivis and Taverna was bullshit, too. That was eight months after the Zürich deposit, and six weeks after a deposit of bogus stocks was made into an account at The Bank of Rome, everyone in the banking world at that point knew Taverna was up to his balls in the counterfeit bonds scheme."

At that point Bayer just wanted Fran to shut his mouth, never to speak again, but reflexively he retorted, "So..."

"So Krivis knew, as did all bank presidents, and he still continued working enormous deals with Taverna." Fran then turned to Lance, "Right, Lance? Why didn't you bring any of this up?"

Lance had zero desire to be dragged into this discussion. "How could I Fran? I wasn't allowed in any of the rooms where those meetings took place. I was stuck sitting out in the damn hallway."

"And look at this shit about his involvement in The Bahamas."

"He denied all of that, Detective."

"Fine, he denied all of that, yet he's held a spot on the board of that bank over there since 1971! And what's this bullshit about him not having any personal accounts there or anywhere else?"

"That's what he said."

"You are too stupid for your own good! Krivis must be the only bank executive in history who carries his cash around in a tube sock then. Whose ass did you kiss to get your job?"

"Excuse me, Detective?"

"Whoever it was, it's obvious that you are better at kissing ass than conducting an investigation."

Fran felt a little better after his rant. The silence in the room was deafening. Everyone in the room knew at that moment that Chief Wallace and Bayer had botched the entire trip, and most likely the investigation. Bayer wanted nothing more, at that point, than to crawl under a rock, but he had to have the last word.

"I'm sure our visit has put Krivis on notice now that the 'cat is out of the bag' as far as the counterfeit bonds scheme is concerned. Perhaps it will be enough to get the Bishop to change his ways."

Fran broke into a loud, most boisterous belly laugh. "You gotta be fucking kidding. Right? Your cat was out of the bag right after Taverna made that first deposit in Zürich with your 'monsignor assessor' fella. He was so disturbed by the whole thing that a few months ago he and your friend Fedora got caught red-handed in Dachau...remember?"

Christopherson cleared his throat and looked at Fran. "Detective, may we now move on to how your trip to Munich went?"

Bayer was suddenly relieved that the focus was no longer on him and the trip to Rome. "It went very well, sir, much better than expected, actually."

"Oh, so the two Germans will come here and testify?"

"Yes sir! You just need to let them know when."

"Good job Fran!"

"Oh, by the way, Franz and Straussen gave me another little nugget."

Bentley was suddenly curious, "like what?"

Fran told the team of the cozy chats between the American Government Official and the west coast mobster. The Watergate scandal had already been thick in the news cycles for months. Was this yet another part of it, or something entirely different? It didn't matter, the team all agreed that the matter warranted further investigation.

Christopherson chimed in, "Francis, I want you and Lance to see what else you can find out about that."

"Excuse me, sir," interrupted a very sheepish Bayer.

"What is it now, Bayer?" Christopherson had lost all patience with the federal prosecutor.

"I will take the lead on this one, if it's involving a government official. It's, um, well...beyond the jurisdiction of this office, sir."

Christopherson thought about it for a second. "Alright, fine. Francis and Lance, get back to what you were working on before this trip."

"Yes, sir!" Fran was not keen on working with Lance again, but he was glad to have Bayer busy elsewhere. His only hope was Bayer's little failed stunt didn't completely mess up his investigation into criminal elements within the Vatican.

ACT 2

CHAPTER 20

Bayer would continue to lick the wounds of his crushed ego and reputation for several weeks. For some, having their ass handed to them in such a public fashion would have resulted in shame, bitterness, resentment, and revenge. This was a hard lesson, learned the hard way. He very much wanted to blame the New York detective for the blunder in Rome, but he couldn't. This was all on him thanks to his own stubbornness and stupidity. It had only taken the entire Benedetto investigation with the "Rackets" team for the federal prosecutor to finally see Detective Francis Clavering through the same lens that D.A. Christopherson, Assistant D.A. Thomas, Inspector Bentley and many others had been using for years.

Francis sat at his desk, pondering the future of the current investigation. Thanks to the fiasco with Bayer and Chief Wallace in Rome, Fran and his covert team would have to retreat a little and reevaluate a lot. Fran was fairly confident that what went down recently in Rome did nothing to change "business as usual" with Krivis or anyone else in the financial sectors of the Vatican. The team would proceed more cautiously until this little storm blew over, and he was given the "all clear" sign from Cardinal Wexford and Archbishop Leone.

It was beyond the detective's comprehension how anyone could hold such an elevated position in any type of law enforcement field locally on up to the federal level, while being so damn stupid. This was yet another incident to further confirm why he hated working with elements from the federal government. As much as he wanted Bayer and his boys out of his hair, he knew that that wasn't really an option. There would be no future investigation for Fran, without federal involvement. He just hoped that Bayer and Chief Wallace didn't completely screw up all their hard work up to that point.

In an effort to make amends for the mistakes made on the recent trip to Rome, he dispatched a couple of agents to Italy for the extradition of Mateo Taverna. Mr. Taverna would soon join men like Franz, Straussen, and possibly even Schwartz on the witness stand in the upcoming trial against men like Luca Benedetto, his "Uncle Al" Alessandro Moretti, and other high ranking Mafia leaders of the region. The "Rackets" and Strikeforce teams together had successfully delivered a debilitating blow to local Mob elements. Some syndicate mobsters chose to leave the city, for more lucrative rackets, far away from New York law enforcement surveillance. Those who remained in the Big Apple were put on notice. They quickly scurried into the syndicate underworld. The people of New York City appreciated the lull in Mafia violence and "influence" that permeated their neighborhoods and streets each day, regardless of how the shift of events came about.

A knock on Fran's door frame drew his attention away from his work.

"Come on, we gotta go across town and bring in a guy for questioning." Lance issued with a gesture.

"Who?" Fran gulped the last of his coffee, and put on his coat as he walked through the door, following behind the FBI agent.

Lance was scant on details. If this little "errand" came from Christopherson, he would have been on it like flies on shit. If this came from Bayer, Fran would still comply with far more resistance.

He could not tolerate any more future interference and fuck ups on behalf of the Federal elements that had infested his precinct. The two men sat in complete silence for the first several minutes of the drive. After what seemed like an eternity, Lance finally broke the tense stillness.

"Listen Fran, I just want to apologize for all that shit that went down regarding the Rome trip."

Francis had mixed feelings about future work with Lance or any of Bayers goons since the botched Rome trip. "It's ok." He responded in a distant, disingenuous tone.

Fran's tone hit Lance hard. "No Fran, it's not."

"Let's just get this over with, I have work to do."

"Fran, will you please just hear me out?"

"Fine." Responded Fran in a bitter tone, punctuated with a sarcastic sigh.

"You must know that I had nothing to do with any of that whole hijacking of the Rome trip. I had no idea Bayer was going to pull that shit. Actually, I was quite pissed about how that whole thing went down. And after we all got over there, all I did was sit out in the hall, away from all conversations and meetings."

"Really, Lance, it's ok, you have nothing to apologize for, and certainly not to me. It is Bayer who owes me an apology, not you."

Lance was relieved that his partner wasn't bitter with him any longer. "I just wanted you to know that I absolutely respect you and your skills as a detective. Shit, you've even managed to teach me a lot, and I didn't even think that that was possible. The FBI sure could use a man like you Fran."

"Oh fuck no! I'd be going ape shit weekly, if not daily if I had to work with the likes of Bayer. NO fucking thank you!"

"Yeah, I could see that being an extremely difficult work environment for you, Bayer and anyone else who might have to work around you."

The two chuckled as they envisioned Fran working as a Federal agent. The lightheartedness of their overdue conversation broke up the tension that had consumed them both for the past several weeks. Fran would need federal help moving forward as he probed further into the Vatican case, as much as he hated to admit it. There was just no way around it. All he knew was that he'd rather work with Lance than some other federal know-it-all, blow hard from the Bureau. Lance's skills and talent would be helpful moving forward. However, Lance would be purposefully kept in the dark regarding Fran's ongoing investigation into the Vatican with his assembled European team and Cardinal Wexford. He couldn't risk word of their efforts getting back to Bayer, Chief Wallace and beyond. Bayer may have learned his lesson, but to Fran it didn't matter; Fran still didn't trust him.

Bayer, in a heartfelt effort to make amends between himself and Clavering, went to Washington DC with the detective's finding from his latest trip to Germany. When he returned, he already knew that the federal response would not sit well with the assembled men from New York.

"There will be no further digging into how or why a former Nixon cabinet member might be chatting up West Coast Mobsters involved in dubious financial activities in Europe."

"Of course not." Clavering responded sarcastically. "At least they are consistent in their *MO*."

"What's that supposed to mean Fran?" The federal prosecutor immediately reacted defensively then relaxed his demeanor remembering the events of the past few weeks.

"Honestly Bayer, who in this room is surprised? I bet you talked to the same damn clowns in that circus over there in DC, didn't you?."

"Well actually Fran, this time you're wrong. This time, I didn't take no for an answer..."

"Like hell you did! We all know you left your balls back in Chief Wallace's office." The unrelenting detective continued to pour salt on Bayer's still festering wounds.

"I did not leave my balls in the Chief's office Fran. I actually took this shit above him, all the way up to the Attorney General's office."

D.A. Christopherson sat up and took notice. "Oh? And..."

"I already told you of their response."

The D.A. thought for a moment. If the Attorney General said no, there really wasn't much anyone else could do. "Well that's disappointing. Did they offer any type of reasoning Nathan?"

"Nothing with any meat on it, I'm afraid."

"Of course not..." Responded Inspector Bentley. "Surely you have some sort of theory for their decision."

Bayer thought for a moment, contemplating a response. "My best guess would have to be Nixon and Agnew..."

"Nixon! You've got to be fucking kidding Nathan." Responded a dissatisfied Bentley.

Bayer himself was now becoming frustrated with the assembled men in the room. "The best I've got is that Nixon just won re-election a few weeks ago in a historic landslide victory." Everyone seated in the room nodded acknowledgment of that fact, as he continued. "We've all seen and heard the increasing buzz in the news cycles about this administration regarding some sort of something involving the Watergate Complex there in DC. Whatever all of that is about, it seems to be gaining steam in the press. The last thing that this administration needs is someone like Detective Clavering to pour gasoline on an already smoldering fire."

Bayer made sense, even if it was not to their liking. If the A.G.'s office said no, there really wasn't much more to do or say on the matter. Bayer's body language then noticeably shifted from a man sort of sure of himself to one who was very scared. He got really, really quiet. He didn't want to be in that room. He dropped all eye contact with everyone and just looked down at his yellow notepad and nervously fiddled with his ink pen as he uttered in a completely defeated tone. "There will be no further looking into the Vatican stuff either."

Fran was confused and annoyed, but noticing the physical change in Bayer's demeanor. He decided to hold off the explosion that was going off in his head at that moment. "Why?"

"It was an order and a policy decision. DC feels that there is nothing more to be done. As far as the Feds are concerned, their work here is done. It is time for our agents to pack up our equipment and personnel and move on to our next assignments."

Chirstopherson wasn't as kind as Detective Clavering. "Come on Bayer, don't give us that shit. You're gonna have to do better than that if we are expected to abandon either of these investigative efforts."

Bayer's body language shifted a little. He actually expected that response from someone seated in the meeting. He figured it would either be Fran or the D.A. After all, both men grew up and still were devout Catholics. "You fellas do realize that President Nixon just happens to be Catholic, right?"

"Yeah, so...what's that got to do with any of this Nathan?" Pressed Christopherson.

"The American Catholics are by far Nixon's strongest allies at the moment. Alienating the Catholics still loyal to this president by stirring up some very serious charges against the highest ranking American in the Vatican would essentially be political suicide."

"Of course..." Christopherson responded. He was ready to verbally lay into the weak federal prosecutor, but surprisingly was stopped by Detective Clavering. The meeting continued for several more minutes, then the assembled were dismissed to return to their usual work.

Bentley, Thomas, and Christopherson were not quite sure what to make of their detective's out of character response. Most men working in their field would have simply done as instructed and walked away. Opting for something less complicated, less challenging after years and years of ball breaking work. They all knew that this detective was not that type of a man. This just couldn't be the hill on which their detective's years of hard work would be lain to rest.

Fran slightly pulled the District Attorney aside. "Excuse me sir, I know you are extremely busy at the moment, but I was wondering if I may have a brief word with you."

Christopherson normally would have denied the request, had it come from any other person in the division. This too was out of character for his detective. Christopherson was curious about why he was breaking procedure and protocol. Why was he not going through Bentley or Thomas first? "Of course Fran, I have a few minutes to spare. Please step into my office?"

"Thank you sir, that would be great. I promise to only take up a few minutes of your time."

The two men continued to walk down the hall, in silence, as the D.A.'s curiosity continued to grow. Bayer's excuses and explanations during the meeting left a really bad taste in his mouth. He noticed the very odd behavior of a man he had come to know very well, over the years. Something wasn't right with his detective.

Christopherson had been a D.A. for several decades. He had prosecuted some of the worst the world had ever seen. His time weathered soul had become thick and callused from his years of experience. Fran's recent work had already uncovered information regarding the Vatican that would hit anyone hard. This old man was no exception. For those who were devout Catholic, like the D.A. and the detective, these revelations were personal, disturbing and penetrated deep into one's psyche. If anyone knew how to proceed with an investigation that hit on such a deeply personal level, while maintaining a hard hitting professional, procedural path, it was Christopherson.

Fran already knew that future investigations into crimes involving the Vatican was uncertain. The momentum and opportunity had already shifted dramatically. Fran suddenly found himself at an unfamiliar, uncomfortable ethical and professional crossroad in his career. Time and experience manifests itself through growth and change. The veil of innocence that the Catholic Church counted on to hide their transgressions no longer existed for the D.A., Fran or his team. There was so much already that just couldn't be undone, unseen, or unlearned. For Fran, there would be no return to business as usual. How could he?

Were the Catholic Church and her leaders all rotten to the core? Fran had to believe that there was still some goodness and good men in the church. Men like Cardinal Wexford, and Roman Curia power players like Cardinal Leone, couldn't be the only men dissatisfied with the evil that had been going on in Rome for a very long time. Men who cared about the future trajectory of their Blessed Mother Church. Both of his Catholic "informants" were eager and willing to offer assistance and guidance, despite the very real risks to their lives, limbs and professions. A few fallible men of the church couldn't represent the organization as a whole. One of the true challenges moving forward would be identifying who the good clergy were, from the bad.

In order to move forward down this path that seems to have chosen him, Fran was going to need help. This was a deeper, cerebral need. Help beyond what might come from people like Hans, Freidrich, Cosimo, Cardinal Wexford, Archbishop Leone or even Peg. He absolutely appreciated and respected the leadership and guidance of Inspector Bentley, and occasionally Assistant D.A. Thomas but his future work, should he continue, would even be hidden from them. D.A. Christopherson was in many ways a more senior, more seasoned version of himself with thirty-six years experience on the younger detective. The highly respected opinion and consultation with the D.A. would be crucial for the successful execution of the plan that was swimming through his head.

His plan would reach far beyond boundaries of faith and religion and deep into the diplomatic and political machine of Vatican City. Unlike the United States Federal Government, Fran would not ignore uncomfortable truths, nor would he concern himself with the resulting fallout of anything he might uncover. Fran had a sworn, ethical duty to proceed, while doing everything in his power to conceal and protect those who risked their own lives in order to help him. Cardinal Wexford, his childhood mentor, already believed that he was chosen for this moment, this mission, by the divine. Walking away, and leaving everything the way it currently was, just because someone in Washington, DC ordered them to, was not an option.

Krivis and the Vatican remained crucial components in the American and European illegal, stolen and counterfeit securities trade. The bishop was still very much in charge of the Vatican's financial affairs. He also remained the point man in Pope Michael VI's security detail. Krivis was a resident and official of Vatican City, an independent, sovereign country, just like Italy. Navigating jurisdiction beyond the confines of the borders for a man from New York would be next to impossible unless they could somehow persuade the Vatican State Department to issue some very exclusive permissions. Despite every enormous boulder that stood in the way, as far as these two men were concerned, the Vatican Bank president was still an American Citizen, subject to all of her laws.

The men that were now in Fran's cross-hairs, while heavily infiltrated by mob elements, were very different from any other criminal element they had ever encountered. These men wielded great power, global influence and more importantly were incredibly well protected, literally and figuratively. The majority of the innocent world still viewed these men with high levels of respect, admiration and honor. They remained completely unaware that some of the men who had "dedicated their lives" for the betterment of the Church and mankind, had committed unthinkable, unspeakable crimes.

A short while into their private, impromptu meeting, Christopherson could finally see clearly his detective's plan for the future. He had already, half-heartedly decided that at the age of sixty-nine, it was time for the old horse to be sent out to pasture. He wasn't a spring chicken any longer, and his deteriorating health was beginning to impact his ability to continue his work to his own personal standards, even if he was the only one who noticed. What his detective was suggesting was still very much in the planning stages, this D.A. would throw 100% of his support behind him as he always had for this swan song of a mission before retiring.

Christopherson advised that Fran keep Bentley in the loop as he moved forward. The decision to involve Assistant D.A. Thomas would be entirely up to the detective. For now Fran would keep the D.A. in the loop, and provide Inspector Bentley only what he needed to know, when he needed to know it. Keeping a tight circle of allies moving forward meant that Thomas would not be involved, at least not for now. These men would proceed as they always had, following all leads and lines of inquiry no matter where they may lead. Even directly into the hallowed heart of the Vatican. Clavering's efforts would potentially reveal to the innocent world the crimes of their most esteemed church leaders. Great damage to the church seemed to be inevitable.

The New York D.A. still held two cards in his hand that he could use to assist his detective. Either situation, unlike Bayer's botched trip to the Vatican, would publicly air out some of the Vatican's most dirty laundry. The D.A. already had most of what would be needed to indict the Vatican Bank President, Bishop Jonas Krivis, and put in a formal request for his extradition from Vatican City. Such a move would most likely be ignored by Vatican officials, and be a waste of time, energy and resources. Christopherson's other option was to have a little chat with Chief Wallace and perhaps some of the men even above him. He was pretty sure that the *New York Post* and other publications would be more than interested in hearing about a cover-up story,...or two. Vatican dirt, paired with a former Treasury Secretary's visits to Europe, coming from a man with Christopherson's reputation and clout would be far more damaging to the Nixon administration than a bunch of pissed off American Catholics. The resulting public outcry from either situation or both might serve to discourage Krivis and his friends of future financial transgressions. Such pressures, though highly unlikely, might even motivate the church to take a long hard look in the mirror, roll up its sleeves and clean up its own house.

Detective Clavering appreciated the offer and continuing support of his DA. He would tuck those options into his back pocket for later, should he need them. For now he would move forward like he always had, in stealth. Judging by the response Bayer brought back from Washington, DC, going through Secretary of State Kissinger and Vatican Secretary of State Cardinal Zacharie Benoît would not be an option. Unless he and his team could somehow get permission from the Vatican to gather even more incriminating evidence against Krivis, nothing would change. Any chance of that, would have to come from someone with great power like Archbishop Leone. Fran already knew in his heart of hearts what needed to be done. With the exception of Christopherson, occasionally Bentley and anything he could get from Leone, he was done asking for permission moving forward.

"So Francis, what is it that you need from me at this point?"

Fran sat and thought for what felt like days. "I have already learned that the cardinal who first approached Schwartz with the fraudulent securities scheme passed away about the same time I first followed Benedetto to Munich. Schwartz certainly didn't give us the names of everyone involved. Somewhere down right bullshit. But there was still enough meat on those bones for us to figure out who's who in the operation." Christopherson simply offered a nod of understanding as his detective continued to think out loud. "I think it's best for me to continue working with Agent Lance Erickson at this time, if that is alright with you sir."

Christopherson was not prepared for his detective's response. "Are you sure Fran? That means you will still have Bayer looking over your shoulder."

"Look I'm not exactly thrilled to be working with the Feds moving forward, what happened in Rome still pisses me off. I have absolutely zero trust nor respect for Bayer or his superiors. However, with the global scope of what I need to do, a federal agent on board will certainly be a handy resource moving forward."

"I can see how that would make sense."

"And I'm certainly in no mood, nor do I have the time or patience to go looking for another federal fuck up to train and work with. To be honest Lance isn't that bad as far as g-men go."

"I will respect your judgment on that detective...is there anything else you need from me Francis?"

"Well actually, there is one more thing. I feel that it is imperative that Lance and I continue to keep a watchful eye on Mr. Giovanni Fedora for the foreseeable future. If that's alright with you."

"Hmmm, aren't you afraid Bayer will get in your way and run interference?"

"No, he doesn't need to know why I still want to stay on the Fedora case, sir."

"I'm not even sure I understand your reasoning here Francis."

"It's nothing all that complicated sir. Look, Fedora has already proven himself to be a man with direct connections to..." Fran caught himself, almost revealing some of Wexford's secrets. "Krivis and more than likely other powerful men in the Roman Curia. I can somewhat keep tabs on Vatican activities through my continued work on the Fedora case. Even Lance will not be privy to all that I'm doing, only what I choose to share with him, if that makes any sense."

"I'm concerned," confessed Christopherson. "This deception is so unlike you Francis."

Fran thought for a moment back to the lie that he and Bentley told him to get him to approve the first trip to Germany. A lie that was still rotting away in his mind. However, now was not the time for confessions. Fran didn't want to do anything that would jeopardize the unwavering support of his D.A. "I understand sir."

"I guess I will have to trust you know what you are doing to move forward with your plan."

"I've got a pretty good handle on it. Besides, why not use some of the Feds resources and funds..." Fran offered with a wink.

"Alright, I will have Bentley put in a request to retain Agent Erickson and keep you two on Fedora until you tell me otherwise."

"That's much appreciated sir."

Fran left the private meeting feeling better about himself and his future. Moving forward, with the help of Lance, and his support crew, he would channel the disturbed and outraged energies stirred by discoveries in the Benedetto case to accomplish what needed to be done in Europe. He vowed to himself that no stone would be left unturned, this was now a very personal quest for justice, even if the deck was already firmly stacked against him. Fran knew that these kinds of crimes just didn't stick to people in such highly privileged positions. He couldn't let that deter him. Fran had to give this all he had, with the backing of his ragtag team, and hopefully some help from the Lord God Almighty himself.

CHAPTER 21

$\mathbf{N}$ico Novelli was no stranger to the banking industry. He was also no stranger to Giovanni Fedora. The two men had known each other for at least twenty years, and worked together intimately for almost ten. Their initial business interaction came in 1964, when Novelli came to Fedora, a very desperate man.

Novelli suddenly found himself fired from his Branch Manager position that he had held at TownshipBanc in Milan for several years. His dismissal, had nothing to do with incompetence, for he was quite the wiz with economic numbers, especially when it came to international exchange. His superiors at the Milan bank were unnerved to discover that he had exceeded limits on some foreign exchange deals and executed others using unauthorized currency speculation tactics.

Fedora offered Novelli a foreign exchange position at one of his Milan banks, but the offer was immediately declined. Novelli wanted something more than Fedora's little Milan bank could offer on the global stage of finance. He countered the offer with a business partnership proposal for an international monetary brokerage company. Fedora was cautiously optimistic about the offer, the proposed business concept was nothing short of brilliant. Holding up the partnership from moving forward was a very legitimate concern. You see, Mr. Novelli had quite the speculative gambling habit. A solemn, sworn promise was made. There would be absolutely no gambling, and absolutely zero risk of loss for Fedora. With a huge leap of faith, their brokerage opened its doors the day before Christmas, 1964. Business started slow, but grew steadily. By 1966 they were handling an impressive volume of high value transactions that dwarfed even the largest bank in America.

Fedora was quite pleased as he closely observed Novelli's work over the coming years. What impressed him most was Novelli's mind for numbers and finance almost on the same level as his own. Fedora kept a close eye on the reformed addict for a while until he was satisfied that Novelli's old vices wouldn't creep back into his regular reality. It was time for Fedora to let out a little more rope.

A test, of sorts, was created when Fedora tasked Novelli to evaluate and straighten out a chaotic mess at one of his banks in Milan and a short while later a similar situation and task at one of his Banks in Zürich. Novelli worked hard at all that he was given, eventually reestablishing a strong, important sense of trust from Fedora. Satisfied that Novelli had turned over a new leaf, Fedora placed the man in administrative positions at two of his Milan banks and one of his two Swiss banks.

When Fedora purchased controlling interest in his fifth bank, Lincoln National Bank of New York City, the addition of Novelli to the bank's Board of Directors was not happenstance. Novelli may have been unknown to the New York banking and finance scene, but he certainly wasn't in Italy and Switzerland. Suddenly Novelli was busier than he had ever been before as travel between New York and Europe became a frequent part of his work.

One day, the two banking men were called to the UK for an emergency meeting with a long established banking partner. Novelli could see on the horizon a shift in speculative sectors and he already knew that the US dollar was starting to decline in value as a result. For the UK Bank, these financial changes meant that they were suddenly in deep trouble. They were now operating with an unexpected $4 billion loss. The UK bank head was now looking to Fedora for an $800 million guarantee on losses. Fedora gave them nothing but a cold shoulder. The UK bank eventually found what it needed, from other sources. Requesting that Fedora and Novelli remain tight-lipped about the details and all that was discussed, at least until the value of the US dollar rebounded. A satisfactory resolution eventually came to pass resulting in no harm nor foul for all parties involved.

As the UK situation was in its beginning stages, there was a different version of Novelli emerging. It's hard to say what exactly triggered him. It may have been the budding adulterous affair with an Italian exotic dancer, or perhaps the large numbers involved in the UK deal. The situation was just too inviting and intoxicating. It created an unfortunate moment of weakness for Novelli. Did he see something while straightening out Fedora's European banks? Regardless of the cause, Novelli once again began to get an itch. However, this one was different than any he had ever had before.

As the bitter cold of late January gripped the people of New York City, Fedora placed Novelli in a temporary executive position at Lincoln. His attention was urgently needed elsewhere. The Italian economy was doing well in all sectors of commerce. The stock market was booming, the Lira was strong against the US Dollar, and manufacturing and development was the best it had been in years.

It's hard to say if the economic boon was in any way related to the counterfeit securities scheme cooked up by Bishop Krivis and his friends. Publicly, the world would never know one way or another. However, in these men's minds, all of the credit was theirs. The rest of Italy and the world was enjoying the wave of good fortune that had come their way.

Feeling happy and confident about the economic future of Italy, Fedora and Ansios liked to blow off a little steam. Their idea of fun was playing the Italian Stock Market like a child plays with a yoyo toy. Money flowing their direction with every turn, up or down. Ansios enjoyed the game the most, almost becoming intoxicated by the art of the play, and especially the reaping of the rewards.

While a lot of economic health rests on the status of a region's stock market, there are other contributing factors too. Ansios, Krivis and especially Fedora gladly took full advantage of the windfall. Large amounts of capital were now moving from his banks to various global destinations. Favorable political parties in Italy, the Vatican, Gherado Fratello's P2 organization and Right-wing Juntas in South America all benefited from Fedora's increase in cash flow. Those who professed their disdain for Fedora in previous years, were now standing in line looking to get a piece of his pie. The murder attempt on his wife in Geneva that had brought him to New York, was now far behind him, and even farther from his mind.

Fedora, had once again reclaimed his spot on top of the financial world. From the executive suite of his office building on Park Avenue in New York City, he continued an insanely, expensive juggling act of banks, businesses, shell companies and more. He did for himself as he did for his clientele, moving shares around in a game of merge, divide and re-mergeing. Profiting, and evading taxes every step of the way.

The rose colored glasses sported by Fedora and his friends, seemed to be fashionable, but they were not corrective lenses. A nearsighted view was all they would provide those who sported them. Novelli, with his experience, thought he saw something brewing in Eastern-Block sectors, but he remained unsure, opting instead to wait a little longer to bring his observations to Fedora's attention. He opted instead to present his discoveries after evaluating Fedora's two banks in Milan and Geneva. Fedora was none too pleased after having the list of transgressions from his two banks thrown in his face.

Looking up from the reports, a verbal altercation ensued...

"You ball-less wonder, with your whore of a girlfriend, you will never be a 'real banker.'"

"Shove it up your ass Giovanni, you've got nothing on me. I've worked hard since the Brokerage opened, and kept my nose clean, which is more than I can say for you!"

Fedora broke into a thundering belly laugh. "If you will recall, you came crawling to me, when no one else would give you the time of day Nico."

"That was almost ten years ago Giovanni, nothing is the same now."

"My little junkie's got that itch again doesn't he?"

"Huh? What? No! Fuck you."

"I can see it, your eyes give you away."

"My eyes give away nothing..."

"Hmmm, maybe I should go have a little chat with, say the head of the Bank of Italy and let them know what I see in your eyes."

"We both know that that's bull shit Giovanni."

Fedora issued a sly smile like the cunning fox that he was. "It may or may not be true, but whose story do you think they will be more inclined to believe Nico?"

Novelli suddenly felt defeated by Fedora's not so subtle threat. The Bank of Italy would take his boss' word over his in a heartbeat. The result would annihilate any potential future for Novelli in the banking industry, especially on the international stage. Fedora, using his mafia training and master level blackmail skills, had Novelli painted into a very uncomfortable corner. Fedora was confident he had Novelli back under his control. He was correct before, he did see a glimmer of something in the man's eyes. However, Novelli wasn't lying in his response regarding his gambling habit. He thought to himself, "You can't lie about something if they don't ask you the right questions."

He may or may not have given into nagging impulses before Fedora's threat. He knew such a threat from a man like Fedora, was not to be casually dismissed. Fedora was correct regarding how the authorities at the Bank of Italy would respond. The confrontation changed the entire dynamic of their professional relationship. He dutifully did what was asked of him regarding the two banks. It wasn't his fault that findings were not to his boss' liking. The information certainly didn't change the day to day operations of either institution.

Fedora would make one more move to hammer home his dominance. The next blow to Novelli's ego came when he brought in a new man to run the international department of Lincoln National Bank. New energy in that department, untainted by the intoxicating lure of speculative gambling was just what the decades old New York bank needed. Fedora was convinced that the man who had sworn there would be no gambling, had finally reverted after all of these years. The new man would keep a watchful eye on Novelli so Fedora could turn his attention elsewhere across the Atlantic.

The new department head was a smart enough man, however, he didn't know the Fedora that Novelli knew. Over the years, the two men had had several fall outs. Some more serious than others, but they never resulted in any kind of sustained animosity. Something was different about this spat. The personal insults stung a little more than usual. "After everything I've done for that damn man, now he thinks I need a babysitter?" The spat, and the hiring of the new guy, pushed a few buttons. Fedora had reached a new personal low, as far as Novelli was concerned. Insulting his girlfriend just didn't sit well. This was the first time Fedora had brought blackmail into their long established business relationship.

Fedora was right, he could see something different in Novelli's eyes. Fedora just assumed it was addiction. Whatever it was, now Fedora lit a fuse and added some anger to the power keg. The two men knew each other very well. Fedora was certainly a very powerful man, but he was by no means any smarter than himself. Novelli could see weaknesses forming in Fedora's facade, that no one else was privy to. While he didn't have Fedora's Mafia training, nor his masterful skills in the art of blackmail, he promised himself at that moment that Fedora would never get the better of him ever again.

CHAPTER 22

It was a warm spring day in May. In Venice, The patriarch busied himself with opening all the windows of his office. The breezes carried scents of flowers and ocean to fill his lungs, and the singing songbirds in the courtyard brought great calm to his soul. The patriarch was opening up the last of the windows in his office, when a loud knock sounded from the door.

"Come in." Called the man. He turned from the window to see who was entering his chamber. The door swung open gently to reveal the identity of the man entering the room. "Dante Leone, my good friend! Why didn't you tell me you were coming for a visit?"

"Chiaros Riluciani!" The man smiled warmly, "I wanted it to be a surprise!"

"Surprise? A trip here, all the way from Rome that is a long way to come for just a surprise my friend...nonetheless, it is good of you to come. It is so good to see you again my friend."

"Well I had to come."

"Why? What is it? Is there something wrong?" Riluciani returned with concern.

"Oh, no no no, nothing like that Chiaros. I just had to come and see you in person, my friend."

"Well I'm most happy that you did. I see you are sporting a new color these days..."

Leone blushed a little. "That I am."

"Red suits you quite well, my friend. Congratulations on becoming a cardinal, Your Eminence!"

"I won't protest that address as much as you did last year, my friend."

"To be honest, I still don't like it."

"You have to admit, it does seem to open more doors than the archbishop's magenta."

"Mmmm, I guess,...but I've always opened my own doors."

"That you have..."

"Don't get me wrong, it is always good to see you again, but it's sure a long way to come just for a surprise visit..." Responded Riluciani humbly.

"Ahhh, you know me too well, my dear Chiaros. Fine, I do admit that I do have business further up north, but I just had to stop in and pay you a visit and let you know in person,..."

The patriarch suddenly became curious, "Know what?"

"Remember when you last visited me in Rome?"

"Even with the year that has passed, how could I forget? It was the most angry and frustrated I've been in many, many years."

"That it was. How are things here now?"

"It took some time, and some adjustment, but things are better now."

"Oh?"

"Well I moved the diocese accounts from Mr. Ansios' bank. Most who still owned shares in his bank sold them off, and also moved their personal accounts to another bank across town."

Leone smiled, hearing the news. "What a brilliant solution to such an unpleasant situation."

"Well I wasn't about to do business with corrupt men like him and that poor example of a bishop..."

Leone was caught off guard by the patriarch's response. "That's rather judgemental of you Chiaros..."

"I'm sorry, please forgive me...you've stirred up my anger again reminding me of those encounters."

"No forgiveness necessary my friend, your ire is completely justified."

"I don't like that feeling Dante, justified or not..."

"You never have, in all the years that I have known you. At least you found a suitable solution..."

"Suitable, yes, but it did nothing to stop those evil men."

"Oh I wouldn't say that..."

"What do you mean by that?"

"I can assure you that the financial issues you brought to Rome last year have not been forgotten."

"Oh? They haven't?" The patriarch was suddenly cautiously optimistic. "This is certainly all news to me, I haven't heard a word since we last talked."

"Well when you are in a position such as mine, you see and hear everything."

"I would certainly think so Dante...So what's happened since last year?"

"You might want to take a seat before I proceed."

Riluciani gracefully lowered himself into his chair while maintaining his attention on his guest. "Alright."

"Late last month, my office had a visit from two men from the United States Department of Justice."

"Department of Justice?"

"Yeah, one of them was head of the Organized Crime and Racketeering section, and another man was working out of New York."

"Hmmm, that sounds serious. What was that all about?"

"Just before I left Rome, I got the report from the FBI regarding their visit, and it's definitely not good news."

"Yeah, and?"

"It seems that they had been investigating a case for over a year, prior to their visit. The New York Police Department's work started with the New York Mafia and led them all the way to the Vatican in a case involving counterfeit American bonds that were supposedly delivered to the Vatican sometime in July of 1971."

"Oh goodness! This is serious!"

Cardinal Leone continued, "The FBI has a lot of very strong evidence that someone within the Vatican with financial authority actually ordered the counterfeits in question."

"And was their order ever fulfilled?"

"Yes, and the entire thing stinks to high heaven, and points directly back to Bishop Krivis."

"Oh my God..." Riluciani couldn't help but be in a state of shock, as he turned his gaze and shook his head. "Hmmm, should I really be all that surprised, especially after meeting him last year. How in God's name did this even happen Dante?"

"Do you really want to know, Chiaros?"

"Yes, as much as this pains me, I must know...Please continue."

"As you wish...There was a well known con man running around Rome at the time named Mateo Taverna who introduced one of Krivis' cardinals to an Austrian named Dr. Karl Schwartz."

"Which cardinal?"

Leone's response was a gut punch to the patriarch. Shaking his head in disbelief, "I can't believe he's involved in this too..."

"Yes, as a matter of fact, he was Krivis' point man for this entire scheme. Thanks to his actions and direction, the Vatican now has almost $1 billion in counterfeit bonds."

"I don't understand how you can be so calm about this Dante, doesn't any of this bother you? It sure as hell bothers me!" The cardinal immediately caught himself. "I'm sorry for my emotional outburst."

Leone raised his hand to silence the cardinal seated across from him. "No apology is necessary, your anger is absolutely warranted my friend."

Leone continued to enlighten Riluciani on the details contained in the DOJ report. As the afternoon proceeded, the cardinal's feelings towards Krivis grew colder and colder. Leone knew that his long time friend was one who was slow to anger, but on the rare instance that Riluciani was angry, it was always 100% justified.

"Dante, who all knows about all of this."

"That's hard to say, exactly."

"Perhaps a better question would be how do we stop this?"

"That too is hard to say, these types of things are definitely not new to our church's financial system Chiaros. But according to the officials from the US, many of those involved have already been arrested."

"Are those that have already been arrested, just Americans?"

"No, they have arrested some of the co-conspirators in Austria, and here in Rome too."

"Well that is good, I guess."

"Mmmm, yes and no."

"What do you mean?"

"Of course it's good that some of those involved are being brought to justice in this matter, but one of the men, Mr. Mateo Taverna, is nothing more than a first class conman. The Roman Magistrates sent the finance police to arrest him and search his home. In his safe, they found a signed blessing from Pope Michael."

"What?"

"Yeah, I was shocked too."

"So what happened?"

"Well upon discovering Pope Michael's blessing, they apologized for the inconvenience and left Taverna's property."

Riluciani gave a deep, reflective, yet frustrated sigh. "I figured that Justice's journey would end at the walls of Vatican City, but apparently I was wrong."

"Unfortunately, you are correct. Even the Americans produced a written request for the counterfeit bonds written on Curia letterhead."

"They certainly are bold in their actions, I guess we must give them that. They operate without fear of consequence."

"That they do, and have been, for a while."

"Were you aware of this scheme prior to the visit by the American's Dante?"

"Yes, I've known about it for some time. Mr.Taverna thought it a good idea to implicate me in all of this."

"Oh?" Riluciani was suddenly concerned.

"He failed miserably, and a short time later, he was arrested again. This time the pope's blessing would not save him."

"There must be something we can do, Dante."

"I really wish there was, but I'm afraid that any effort to change the current status quo of the Curia under this pope would be pointless."

"That's beyond discouraging, but if anything changes, if there is anything I can do to help, please don't hesitate to call on me. I'm not sure what or how, but I do want to be a part of placing our church back on her proper course."

"I will certainly keep you informed and I won't hesitate to seek your assistance in the future, Your Eminence." Leone smiled at the frustrated Riluciani, then continued. "I must ask you to please keep this conversation between you and myself."

"Of course, Dante, your words are safe with me my friend, as always."

"Thank you, Your Eminence."

Riluciani gave his guest a sideways look. "Dante..."

Leone smiled. "It's actually good to be able to even just discuss this with someone. There certainly isn't anyone in the Curia I can discuss any of this with freely."

"I'm the only one outside the Curia who knows of these things, Dante?"

"You are the only one who knows what I just told you. However, it seems that Cardinal Wexford knows some of it too."

"Charles Wexford? From New York?" Riluciani questioned curiously.

"Yes, that's the one."

"He's such a great disciple of Christ's love and teachings. A man I greatly respect."

"You will hear no arguments from me regarding him, my friend."

"But I must know, how in Heaven's name did he learn of all of this given his post in New York?"

"I'm unsure how detailed his knowledge of these dealings are exactly. He didn't elaborate too much, but it seems that a detective directly involved in the case there in New York paid him a visit."

"Hmmm, well that is curious."

"Actually the meeting with my office and the men from the US Department of Justice was originally supposed to be between myself and the New York detective and his Roman colleague."

"Oh?"

"Yes, actually I invited them after I got a call from Charles Wexford."

"But you ended up with a visit from these other men?"

"Yeah, I'm unsure of how that all happened."

"So what happens now Dante?"

"We will still meet up at some point. We just have to coordinate where and when. Hopefully soon."

"Oh wow, that's some wonderful news. I will pray for all of your safe travels and success in your work together."

"I appreciate it, Chiaros."

Riluciani and Leone continued their visit for another hour. The information weighed heavily on the heart and mind of the humble cardinal. All any of them could do at this point was pray for each other and for something to change. Only God and the pope had the power to rectify any or all of what was wrong with the Holy Mother Church. In the meantime, those in the know maintain their sanity by studying the trials and tribulations of Job, and having the patience of a saint.

CHAPTER 23

Fedora's good friend and protégé Marco Ansios, was having an incredible year. The fantastic financial boon enjoyed by most of Italy resulted in a significant increase in his own personal wealth. While he didn't have an executive suite in one of the world's major financial hubs like Fedora, he did finally see one of his long time dreams come to fruition. Thanks to the help of his friends Giovanni Fedora and Bishop Jonas Krivis, he finally claimed the highly coveted Chairman of the Board position of Banco Generali. The scheme cooked up during a vacation trip to the Bahamas, worked brilliantly.

The Milan native, like many born in 1920, had his younger days molded by the historical events of the times and the region. Following his studies at a prestigious Italian university, he enlisted as a soldier in Mussolini's military, fighting on the Russian front during World War II. Upon his return from war, he followed the footsteps of his father, into a career in banking. In 1947 he came to work for Banco Generali. It was through his work there that he met Cardinal Giancarlo Volonté. In the summer of 1963, Cardinal Volonté was elected Pope Michael VI.

Marco Ansios' introduction to Cardinal Volonté proved to be a significant event in both men's lives. Banco Generali in its early days was known locally as "the Priest's Bank." A Catholic Baptismal certificate was a required document in order to open a new account. At the end of each board meeting, prayers of gratitude were offered up to God for the blessing of continually favorable annual figures.

Ansios' vision for the future of his bank went far beyond that of a sleepy little Catholic bank. By the time Volonté was elected pope in 1963, Ansios had been elevated to a central manager position. Ansios soon met and became good friends with another financial layman close to the sitting pope, Giovanni Fedora. As their friendship developed, the two men came up with a plan to take over control of Banco Generali and transform it into an exclusive type of banking institution.

The other significant event of 1963, for Mr. Ansios was the formation of Banco Generali Holdings in Luxembourg. Although the shell company shared the same namesake as the Milan bank where he worked, Ansios had full control of the holding company to do whatever he wanted with it. Banco Generali Holdings had nothing to do with the bank that he managed, and was exclusively his to do with as he pleased. It would soon become a key component of his business model over the years, as he worked his schemes, and watched millions flow through his shell company. Over time, global banks by the hundreds would be conned out of over $450 million by the unassuming central manager of Banco Generali in Milan.

When Ansios finally became managing director of Banco Generali in 1971, he was fifty-one and had far exceeded the humble clerical banking position held by his father many decades before him. Any average man would find contentment from his work and achievements over the years. Marco Ansios was a banking man who did not fit that mold. The only thing average about Marco Ansios, was his height.

The mind of Mr. Ansios was an extremely creative one. The crooked schemes he came up with for laundering Mafia money, moving money illegally out of Italy, evading taxes, concealing his own criminal purchases of shares from his own bank, and rigging the Milan Stock Exchange were impressive to even his mentor Fedora at times. It wasn't above the "quiet little banker" to be deeply involved in bribery, and corruption. When necessary, he'd purposefully alter the course of justice by ordering a wrongful arrest or a contracted murder if it would help his own cause.

In 1971, shortly after becoming the managing director of Banco Generali, Marco Ansios was introduced to Bishop Jonas Krivas by their mutual acquaintance Giovanni Fedora. This new relationship, like the one between Fedora and Ansios, quickly flourished. Thanks to his long standing financial relationship with the sitting pope and his new relationship with Bishop Krivis and other Vatican men of finance, Marco Ansios soon became one of the "men of trust" known as the *uomini di fiducia* in the Vatican Curia. *Uomini di fiducia* was a very select group of five laymen that included himself, Fedora, Nico Novelli, Rinaldo Manna and one other man who was the highest ranking layman to work in the Vatican Bank. All of these men worked with and for what many in the Roman Curia called "Vatican, Inc."

In '71, Ansios and Fedora opened a new bank called Sierra Madre International Bank located in Nassau, The Bahamas. Sitting on the board of directors from its inception was the newly appointed Vatican Bank president at the time, Bishop Jonas Krivis. The new bank's name was carefully selected in a feeble attempt to throw off the increasingly suspicious Italian finance police. Their idea worked, but not for long.

As Ansios' empire and status continued to grow, so did the amounts of his profits flowing through the Vatican Bank's coffers. Through a series of deliberate, overly complicated financial moves, Ansios' Banco Generali and the Vatican Bank quickly became essentially joined at the hip. Even the most skilled public accountant would have had a very difficult time determining where one banking establishment ended and the other began. Ansios didn't mind his work efforts profiting the Vatican Bank. He never wrote it off as an expense, but rather as an investment. Many operations and deals were done jointly. Ansios used the Vatican Bank to hide his business dealings which repeatedly violated numerous banking laws. None of his crimes would have been possible without the help, full knowledge and approval of the sitting Vatican Bank President, Bishop Jonas Krivis.

Ansios' "work" with the Vatican Bank soon became a daily occurrence that went on for many many years. When Ansios purchased the Catholic Bank of Venice in July, 1971, this particular transaction was the first time Ansios had actually purchased anything from Bishop Krivis or rather from the Vatican Bank for himself personally. The purchase was simple and straightforward enough and was even graced with the blessing of Pope Michael VI himself. It was the backlash and uproar from the locals and the patriarch of Venice that caught Ansios off guard. It was enough to keep Mr. Ansios away from similar types of future deals with Krivis and his bank in the future.

When the calendar flipped to September of 1973, Giovanni Fedora, Marco Ansios and Bishop Jonas Krivis donned their best threads for a head of state gala. The men worked the room, conversing with many of the assembled world leaders. A conversation between Fedora, Ansios and the Prime Minister of Italy was interrupted by a forceful tap on Fedora's shoulder and a pointing gesture issued from Bishop Krivis. Argentina's General Juan Perón had just arrived for the festivities. His smile was genuine as he shook many hands in the room.

Upon locking eyes on P2 Masonic Grand Master, Gherado Fratello, Perón politely excused himself from an already involved conversation and moved quickly and with purpose to stand before Mr. Fratello. Many in the room watched in silence as Perón lowered himself to kneel at the feet of Fratello. It was a gesture he gave in deep gratitude, for Fratellos assistance in returning him from a place of exile to his rightful position of power in Argentina. The majority of the people in the room watched in absolute shock. They could not believe what they were witnessing.

Fratello had been observing and working the situation in Argentina for some time. He soon noticed that the ruling junta leader at the time was quickly losing favor with the people of his country. Fratello had the perfect view of the entire Argentinian political landscape. The Masonic leader moved with precision to take full advantage of what was happening in that South American country. Following a series of strategic meetings, he persuaded the sitting president at that time that the political stability of the country was absolutely dependent on the return of General Juan Perón as president.

Perhaps the man most impressed in the room was Giovanni Fedora. While he was no fan of fascist and socialist political structures for his homeland in Italy, he had to admit that Fratello was not a completely stupid man. Developing close working relationships with the men who ruled Paraguay, Uruguay, Venezuela, Nicaragua and obviously Argentina was actually an extremely smart move. Following Fedora's own recent work with the Nicaraguan dictator, it became abundantly clear to the Italian New Yorker that it was a lot easier to do business with a one-man dictatorship than any democratically elected government. All those committees, controls and oversight made things much more complicated and time consuming than things had to be. All those checks and balances translated to more honest operations on the part of those types of countries. Too much honesty was not a good thing for banking related business, as far as Fedora was concerned. From New York, Fedora's new center for operations, the closest thing he would get to any sort of South American dictator was President Richard Milhous Nixon.

While deep in the middle of one of the many conversations with the US President, a man whom Fedora had known for many years joined the conversation. The man also happened to be the head of the Italian Military Secret Service and a close associate of Mr. Gherado Fratello. Fedora and Fratello were very familiar with each other, through their mutual relationships with Marco Ansios, Bishop Jonas Krivis and several others. However, the Secret Service man was shocked to learn that Fedora and Fratello had yet to meet formally. The Italian banker had no idea that the Secret Service man arranging their initial formal introduction was already one of Fratello's P2 Masonic men. While Fedora had no interest in the Masonic fraternity, the Grand Master's reputation for blackmail was something that intrigued him a great deal.

As the two men discussed at length the aims and goals of the Masonic lodge, they learned that they had a lot in common. Especially their views regarding global economics and free trade. As the hours progressed, a frustrated Gherado Fratello still hadn't convinced a cunningly, stubborn Giovanni Fedora to join his lodge. Never in all of his years had Fratello worked so hard for so little in return. He remained a patient man, not yet willing to abandon his quest.

Their cat and mouse game continued for several months following the head of state gala. Fedora found great entertainment in observing Fratello's graceless pursuit. He would let the Masonic leader get close then back off again. This exercise allowed Fedora to learn more about this commander of men. What motivated him, and more importantly how to manipulate him for his own best interest. Ansios and Krivis didn't understand what was going on between the two men. They soon became bored with the whole affair and moved on to other things.

CHAPTER 24

The months of keeping a watchful eye on Mr. Fedora were a welcomed change of pace for Federal Agent Lance Erikson and NYPD Detective Francis Clavering. After years of dingy dives, Mafia goons, and street gang thugs from the Benedetto case, Fedora's orbit couldn't have been more different. His world was accented with ornate, yet tasteful luxuries. Even his friends and associates were, for the most part, top shelf.

Word from Washington, DC, via their minion Federal Prosecutor Nathan Bayer, meant an immediate halt to any further investigation into "former men of significance" from the Nixon cabinet. Angry and frustrated, Fran was certainly not surprised. The displeasure of the two men surveilling the New York activities of the Italian banker didn't last long. Apparently Fedora and Nixon's men didn't get the memo Bayer did from DC. Fran and Lance continued to watch, listen and learn about Fedora and his associations with different men close to the sitting president.

Fran's most trusted confidant would get an earful, often. Most saw her as a devoted housewife. However, her years of investigative reporting prior to becoming a mother, kept her fascinated and engaged in his work. There were more than a few incidents where she caught things that both Fran and Lance had overlooked. Wiretaps and bugs were the front row seats that kept the detectives and Peg in the know. For Mr. Fedora, it was soon clear, not all roads lead to Rome, a couple of those routes lead straight to the heart of DC and the Nixon administration.

Detective Clavering popped into his favorite breakfast diner on his way to work. Between sips of coffee, and bites of buttered white toast, dipped in the runny yolks of his sunny side up eggs, he looked over the morning edition of the *New York Post*. As he read, he couldn't help but issue the slightest of grins. The rest of the world was finally beginning to learn things about the Nixon Administration that Fran had already known for many, many months.

Francis found it amusing that the building Watergate mess meant that government officials including the Attorney General of the United States would now have to take another, more thorough look at the government official, introduced as a "financial advisor," to Benedetto's two German friends in Munich. His involvement in an antitrust case against the biggest communications corporation in the US was now stoking an already well established trash fire. Whatever Bayer and his boys in Washington, DC were trying to keep under a lid, on the back burner, was just about to boil over. Watergate was seeping everywhere in the nation's capital. No one was safe. Even the FBI's acting director, who had held his position since the death of J. Edgar Hoover was found caught up in a clandestine political effort of evidence destruction connected with the Watergate scandal.

Their many hours of surveillance revealed the close personal and professional relationship between Fedora and Nixon that was established sometime before Nixon's first presidential bid against John F. Kennedy in the early 1960s. Nixon, as a private practice lawyer in New York, would send many a client to his good friend Giovanni Fedora for expert investment advice and other banking services. Fedora, appreciative of the referrals, offered the president's re-election campaign an anonymous cash infusion of $1 million. The offer was rejected, but other forms of "help" from the Italian financier would be offered and accepted over time.

Fran was already developing a fairly accurate understanding of Mr. Giovanni Fedora as he watched and listened. To the world, the man could do no wrong. Articles touting the man's greatness were everywhere. Accolades and praise from American Ambassadors, the Italian Prime Minister and other global dignitaries absolutely repulsed the detective.

"Clavering, call for you on line two..." came through the chaotic bustle and drone of the busy precinct reaching Fran's ears.

"...Got it Jack." Fran picked up the handset and pushed the blinking button. "Detective Clavering here."

"Fran, it's Cosimo." Announced the voice on the other end of the line.

"Cosimo, my man! It's been a while...How the hell are you?"

"I'm well, and yourself?"

"Oh you know, the day to day typical police stuff."

Fran got up and closed his office door then proceeded to update his Italian colleague on the Fedora situation in the States. "The only thing I'm hearing about from over there is Watergate and Nixon."

Fran couldn't help but laugh as he filled Cosimo in on the connection between that mess and the Benedetto case and Germany. They both were disgusted by how the media and global statesmen painted such a favorable image of the Italian financier.

"Yeah I know what you mean, they swoon over him over here too." Cosimo weighed in, then shifted the conversation. "But I think that that love affair may be changing."

"Oh?"

Fran couldn't help but feel giddy as Cosimo updated him on the Fedora situation in Italy and Switzerland. Suddenly the detective stopped all scribbling of his notes. "Wait, what?! A $45 million debt doesn't just disappear into thin air overnight Cosimo! There must be some sort of record of where it went, somewhere."

Cosimo didn't have a satisfactory response other than the two warrants issued by the Italian Government for the arrest of Mr. Giovanni

Fedora for charges of bank fraud. Extradition orders would be slow in coming, as Fedora's friends purposefully dragged and stalled the entire legal process. As the call was wrapping up, Fran finished up his notes. He glanced at the clock labeled New York hanging on his wall. "Perfect timing." He thought to himself. The detective grabbed his jacket off the coat stand situated by his office door, and headed down the hall. As he approached Lance's office, he noticed that it was empty and that the lights were already turned off. "Looks like I'm going to have to do this solo..." Fran muttered to himself.

He arrived outside Lincoln National Bank just before closing time. Fran waited patiently outside in his unmarked car. He recognized his man immediately, as he exited the building and turned to head down the street to hail himself a taxi cab to take him home. He watched as the man passed by his car, oblivious that he was being watched.

Fran exited his unmarked vehicle and approached the man from behind. "Mr. Nico Novelli?"

"Yes?" Responded the man as he whipped around to see the man following him.

Detective Clavering pulled the front left portion of his jacket away from his body just enough for the banker to see his concealed badge. "I was wondering if I might have a word with you in private."

Novelli's mind raced. He was caught completely off guard, unsure what to do. "Ummm, what's this about?"

"I just have some questions I'd like to ask you, if you don't mind sir."

Novelli was still fairly new to America and her law enforcement system. He was having a hard time hiding the concern on his face. "Ummm, I guess so."

"Thank you sir! If you'd please, my car is over here...." Fran politely directed.

Fran escorted Mr. Novelli into his office and offered him a seat.

"Can I get you a cup of coffee Mr. Novelli?" Offered the New York detective.

"Yes please, with two sugars and a splash of cream if it's not too much trouble."

"No trouble at all, I'll be back in a minute."

"Thank you."

Fran nodded in confirmation, and left the office. Moments later, he returned, closing the door behind him. He gently placed the styrofoam cup of light tan, steaming liquid in front of his guest, then took his place behind his desk. Across from him sat a fifty-four year old rotund man of average height. He was balding and somewhat unkempt, sporting sparse stubble growth on his face. He seemed very uneasy as his gaze and attention drifted far away into the coffee cup he mindlessly stirred with a wooden stir-stick held firmly in his slightly trembling hands.

"Mr. Novelli, if you don't mind, I'd like to ask you a few questions about Mr. Giovanni Fedora and your relationship with him. I understand that you've worked closely with him for many years now," began the detective.

Novelli, who was already a nervous wreck, immediately dropped all eye contact with the detective, when the subject of his boss came up. "I-I-I really don't have much to tell you detective." Novelli stammered in a thick Italian accent. "I really shouldn't be talking to you at all sir."

"Mr. Novelli, I need you to understand, I didn't bring you in here because you are in any sort of trouble, I just want to get some information on Mr. Fedora," Fran responded calmly, trying his best to ease the mind of his visibly nervous guest.

"Look detective, I have a wife and family, I can't talk to you. I don't know where you got my name or my information, but I don't know anything."

Francis suddenly had an idea of what was troubling his guest. It was something he'd seen a thousand times before in his work involving the Mob. "Mr. Novelli,..."

"Yes Detective,..."

"Please call me Fran or Francis if you wish..." The detective paused for a few moments, then continued. "You are afraid of him aren't you?"

The man nodded and then exploded suddenly into a flood of uncontrollable sobbing.

"Blackmail? Extortion?"

Novelli nodded again, unable to control his emotions. "S-s-s-something like that...yes"

"We can help you, if you help us."

He tried to pull himself together as best he could, while the sympathetic detective handed him a box of tissues. "We?"

"I'm sorry, I normally have my partner Detective Lance Erikson here helping me, but he has already left for the day."

Novelli nodded in understanding. "Bu, bu, but if I help you," he stammered. "He will have me and my family killed. I really shouldn't be here. I need to get out of here. If word gets back to him that I was here, he will assume the worst and that will be the end of me and my family."

"Mr. Novelli," Fran pleaded. "I need you to trust me. I understand completely just how dangerous a man like Fedora can be."

"I don't think you really do, detective."

"There is a reason why I waited until you left the bank for the day, in an unmarked car to bring you in here, instead of coming into the bank, flashing my badge, during normal business hours." Fran tried his best to reason with the man seated across from him. We really need your help. There is no way we can stop him without your help."

Novelli momentarily calmed himself, and thought for a very long, silent moment. Novelli dabbed at his face and eyes with a tissue, then loudly blew his nose while the detective's words echoed through his mind. "It would be nice not to have to live in so much fear, for once." He thought to himself aloud.

Fran watched as something changed in Novelli's puffy, tear-soaked eyes. Novelli did his best to regain his composure. Still visibly nervous, after a long silent pause, punctuated with reflexive heaves, he finally responded. "Alright Detective, I will tell you everything as long as you promise that you didn't get any of this information from me."

"You've got yourself a deal, Mr. Novelli." Fran reached his hand across the desk to confirm the promise with a firm handshake. Fran explained the departmental procedures regarding informants. Following the completion of all the proper paperwork, a visibly less nervous Mr. Nico Novelli was ready to talk. "Since it is just me and you here, would it be alright if I record this conversation? Just to make sure I get every detail correct that you tell me? I promise to erase everything once everything is properly transcribed, and your identity hidden."

"That's fine, detective." Novelli nodded.

Fran produced a recorder from his desk drawer and loaded a fresh new cassette tape into the device, then pushed the red record and play button down, and watched the reels begin to spin. Novelli began with how he and Fedora first met back in 1964. The detailed recount of the early days of Euro Money Exchange Brokers was interesting, but certainly not all that remarkable. "...You see the two of us have very similar mindsets when it comes to money and finance. I just have a little more of a speculative mind than he does. We operated at a slight loss during those early years, but it wasn't enough to cause concern in either of us. We were building our business and in the process rebuilding my reputation."

"Your reputation?"

The man shamefully explained his very personal struggle with speculative gambling.

"Do you still find that to be a challenge now Mr. Novelli?"

Novelli's gaze drifted down to his shoes. "No."

Fran sensed that his guest wasn't being completely truthful in his response, but decided not to press the issue further, for the moment. He watched as Novelli's body language changed, once the conversation shifted away from his vices.

"Through our exchange brokerage, Fedora kept a watchful eye on how money moved globally. He kept tabs on nations and industries, while he positioned himself to cash in from each opportunity that presented itself. His loan sharking services became very lucrative for him. His own personal empire was growing faster and larger than ever. The man had no shame as he took advantage of the need or greed of everyone who sought out his advice and services."

"Is the brokerage and Lincoln National the only places that you've worked with Mr. Fedora?" Fran already knew some of the answer, thanks to his conversation with Cosimo, but wanted more information if possible.

Novelli offered a relaxed, slight chuckle. "No, not at all. I actually still retain administrative positions in several of his banks abroad."

"Hmmmm, exactly how many banks does he currently own?"

"He owns five.." Novelli then paused and quickly corrected himself. "I mean four now."

Fran played dumb as his guest confirmed what Cosimo had told him earlier. "Four?"

"Well it was five up until a few weeks ago."

"Oh?"

"Yes, two in Milan, one in Zürich, one in Geneva and then Lincoln National Bank, here in town. But, the one in Geneva was closed down by Swiss banking authorities a few weeks ago."

"Do you know why they shut down that Swiss bank Mr. Novelli?"

"No I don't. It's actually the only bank he owned that I didn't work at, detective."

Fran was surprised with Novelli's response. "Working so closely with Fedora all these years, you must have some idea what might have been going on at that bank."

"Well if I had to guess, it probably was similar to what I found at one of the Milan banks when I got there about a year and a half ago."

"A year and a half ago? So before you and Fedora came over here to Lincoln."

"Yes, that's correct. What I found there was absolutely disturbing, detective."

Fran stopped writing and looked up from his yellow notepad. "Disturbing?"

"Actually 'disturbing' is a bit of an understatement. The whole institution was a chaotic mess, everywhere I looked. Chaos in any business is never a good thing. In banking, it is disastrous. The only thing keeping that bank afloat, was foreign currency margins tied to black ops."

Fran remembered Cardinal Wexford mentioning Fedora and black money contracts. "Mr. Novelli, I hope you will forgive my ignorance, but what exactly are black ops?"

"Ahh, of course, detective, please allow me to explain. Black ops are a method used by banks to illegally export capital out of their home country. In the Milan bank, big money was moving out of the country daily."

"Is it common to have that much demand for those kinds of 'transfer' services in a bank?"

"No, not usually."

"Do you know why there was so much demand at that bank, at that time?"

"The most common reason would be tax evasion." Fran nodded in understanding, while Novelli continued. "I also found a lot of overdrawn accounts, far beyond what is legally allowed. Oh, and lots of theft..."

"Theft? You mean like bank robbers?" Queried Fran.

Novelli, chuckled. "No, nothing that brazen. You see, large amounts of money would be transferred from unsuspecting client's accounts to accounts owned by the Vatican Bank."

"The Vatican Bank?" Fran questioned, trying to maintain his composure.

"That's right, they would transfer money, minus whatever the current black market commission rate was at the time. That money would then be moved into an account owned by Fedora in his Swiss Finance Bank over in Zürich."

"And the bank's clientele didn't catch on, or protest any of this?"

"Occasionally one would argue a bounced check, when it shouldn't have, or their account balance was not reflective of their own records. They were simply directed to take their business elsewhere."

"That's it? Take your business elsewhere? How is that even a good business strategy?"

"Oh, it's not, many were completely dissatisfied by the bank's response. Those who chose to remain. spoke with a bank manager who apologized profusely, then blamed the errors on their computers."

"That's got to be the lamest excuse I've ever heard!" Interjected Fran.

Novelli nodded. "When my work was complete at the Milan bank. I was dispatched to his Swiss Finance Bank in Zürich, where things there were actually worse. The managing director there, was absolutely incompetent, and certainly had no business working anywhere near a bank. On top of that, the general manager spent a lot of time gambling stock, commodity and money markets. Losses were disbursed among several client's accounts, while winning profits were transferred into his own personal account."

"What the hell?!" Francis exclaimed, then just shook his head.

"But it wasn't just the manager, detective. Other department heads were doing the exact same thing, as did some of the reps from the Vatican Bank."

"Wait, the Vatican Bank was involved with this Zürich Bank too?" The detective questioned.

"Oh yes, but with the Zürich bank, things were a little different. You see, the Vatican Bank was actually a partial owner of the Zürich bank. The Vatican Bank had several accounts there. Every single one of them was deep in the red from all of their speculative losses."

"How on earth did they stay in business?"

"Losses were hidden in an offshore shell company that operated with over $30 million in losses."

"Jesus!" Fran could not believe what he was hearing. He then made a conscious attempt to calm himself once again.

"They've gotten away with so much for so long, I don't think anything will ever change."

Fran sat quietly stunned by what Novelli had just told him. Novelli gave him a few minutes to mentally process the information. "Shall I continue detective?"

Fran finished his notes and took a sip of coffee, and lit himself a cigarette. "Yes Nico, please continue."

"If you insist...So I presented my findings to Fedora. Upon his review, he instantly became furious."

"I can only imagine. So how many of those employees ended up getting fired?"

"Oh, he wasn't mad at them, he was mad at me, detective."

"You? I don't understand. You were only doing what he had asked you to do."

"True. But he didn't care about the illegal activities going on at his banks."

"Oh?"

"He then instructed me to send as much foreign money as possible to the Milan and Swiss banks. Knowing full well that both banks were absolute messes. I refused his request. Keep in mind that Fedora was not used to anyone telling him no. He quickly became angry and began shouting at me, 'how dare I challenge a man with his force of power and conviction. I completely lost my composure. I couldn't help but laugh at him, right in his face."

"Oh I'm sure he loved that..." responded Fran.

"He was not the least bit amused. His 'power and conviction' were the exact reason for my refusal to move the money he had requested. His 'force' and 'power' were nothing without his 'friends,' and I was not interested in tarnishing the reputations I had worked so hard to rebuild for myself and the business that I had helped create, and still had my name on it, just because he said so." Fran looked down at his notepad, and marked a big red asterisk near where he was writing, while Novelli continued. "But my protests were short lived, and certainly didn't change anything. Soon after that little dust up, I took over banking operations for both of those banks, mind you, against my own better judgment. Fedora then proceeded to use his working relationship with the Vatican Bank, to move his money from Italy to his Swiss banks, and beyond, all the while avoiding taxes. Fedora, Bishop Jonas Krivis and another man named Marco Ansios were all rolling in the cash, while the Italian financial sectors and government were hemorrhaging money badly."

"Did the Vatican, other than Krivis, know of any of these activities at that time?"

"Mmmm. It may have Fran, but really it's hard to say who exactly knew what and when."

"What do you mean by that?"

"Back in '67, the pope ordered audits of all Vatican wealth."

"Well then," interrupted Fran. "They must have known about all of this then."

Novelli gave a slight chuckle. "Nope, nobody had a damn clue."

"But how?"

"Pope Michael purposefully excluded the Vatican Bank from those audits. The exercise was pointless and impossible, given the secrecy among various sections within the Vatican. It was also around that same time that Krivis was appointed Secretary of the Vatican Bank by the pope. A position he had zero business being in, if you ask me."

"Why's that Mr. Novelli?" Fran already knew, but hoped his guest could elaborate further.

"Krivis is dumb as a rock, and cocky as hell. To this day he's still in way over his head. All he wanted to do was play golf, chomp on his damn cigars, drink his fancy scotch and chase anything in a skirt, oh and line his own pockets."

"So how the hell did he even get into a position in the Vatican Bank?"

"Oh he's a great liar, suck-up and con man, especially to all the right people in the Holy See. Especially that pope and his secretary priest, little guide dog of his. However, I'd have to say, the main man in the Vatican responsible for Krivis' appointment at that time was Pope Michael's number two in command, Archbishop Dante Leone."

Fran instantly broke into a coughing fit, choking on some water. He quickly shoved a piece of gum into his mouth, hoping to hide his facial reactions. The detective's thoughts raced. How could Cardinal Wexford refer him and his team to the man responsible for getting Krivis into the Vatican Bank? He thought to himself, doing his best to display his best poker face. "Archbishop Dante Leone, you say?"

"Yes, sir. I guess he and Pope Michael felt he'd be a valuable asset to their bank. It may have been poor judgment on their part, but knowing Krivis, it was more than likely they both got played."

"How's that?" Inquired the detective.

"About the time Krivis became bishop, the patriarch of New York unexpectedly passed away."

"I remember hearing about that." confirmed Francis, recalling Cardinal Wexford's information.

"Yeah, that was about the end of '67 if I recall correctly."

Francis nodded. "Yeah, that sounds about right."

"By the end of that year, Krivis was moving quickly through leadership positions at the Church's bank..." Novelli continued to reiterate what Cardinal Wexford had told Fran about Krivis, the Vatican Bank, and Fedora's personal and business relationships with other laymen in the Church's financial affairs. Fran was pleased to get further confirmation of what Wexford had told him, not that he ever doubted his words for even a second. "....I didn't like what Fedora was doing, but I knew my protests wouldn't do anything but be ignored, like before. It would certainly lead to another heated altercation. I decided instead to leave the brokerage firm in December of that year."

"Mr. Novelli, was Krivis and Fedora working together through all of this?"

"Hmmm, I don't think so." Novelli paused to reflect on his memory for a bit. "No, no, they couldn't have. They didn't even meet each other until sometime in the late spring of '69 I'd say."

"Are you sure?" Francis wanted further confirmation.

"Yes, yes, I'm sure. I remember now. They knew of each other, but had never met or worked together on anything at that point. They met just before Krivis was promoted to bishop and into his current position as Vatican Bank president. IItaly had also just changed their tax laws. The other incident of significance that happened that year, around that same time, was when Fedora met and started working with another banker named Marco Ansios."

The name instantly caught Fran's attention. He remembered Ansios was the bank president who inspected Benedetto's initial order of counterfeits before they went on to Vatican City. The detective had heard the name batted around during his surveillance of Fedora and his many conversations with Krivis. Of the three, Marco Ansios certainly kept the lowest profile.

"When Fedora met Marco Ansios, Ansios was still the assistant manager of Banco Generali in Milan..." Novelli informed the New York detective of Ansios' early days at Banco Generali in the mid 40s and his climb up the bank's management ladder.

"Fedora and the secular head of the Vatican Bank, Rinaldo Manna eventually got to know Mr. Ansios well. In their eyes, Ansios showed great promise and opportunity as he became a more influential employee at Banco Generali. Ansios was seen as a man that they could mold and perhaps at some point, even exploit through his lust for power and wealth. They were kind and accommodating, while friendships and trust were still being established.

"Fedora in his usual style, shamelessly took advantage of his friendship with Ansios. Something he had done time and time again with many others before him. Next thing anyone knew, Ansios, with the help of Fedora, became the new General Director of Banco Generali with all kinds of new privileges and authority he never had before. I'd say the entire process took just a couple of years from start to finish."

"If Ansios was already climbing the administrative ladder of his bank, why was he seeking Fedora's help?"

"Mmmm well, Ansios knew he'd get there eventually. Fedora just made it all happen sooner. Ansios was finally where he had wanted to be, for as long as he could remember. Ansios was happy, but he still wasn't satisfied. The sleepy town banker next moved into money laundering services for local Mafia families. Lira was illegally moving out of Italy, tax evasion, bribery, corruption, calling for wrongful arrests or hits on those who did him wrong or got in his way. He even had a hand in rigging the Milan Stock Exchange believe it or not. The man completely embraced the 'Godfather' Mobster lifestyle, while at the same time becoming one of the 'most trusted men of Vatican, Inc.'

"No one got in Ansios' way. No one in the Vatican protested. His roaring success was a boon for them, as large sums of money flowed into their coffers. Ansios didn't mind. His relationship with the Vatican Bank allowed him to break multiple Italian banking laws, over and over again, without fear of consequence."

Novelli watched as Fran began to shake his head in disbelief. "Are you alright detective?"

"Yes, I'm fine. It's just a lot to take in."

"That's more than understandable sir. Shall I continue?"

"Yes please Mr. Novelli, don't mind me..."

"Very well...1971 became a huge transitional year for all three of these men."

"Oh?"

"Fedora and Ansios tried hard to teach Krivis everything he now knows about banking. He wasn't a very good student. He still is an idiot, if you ask me. He knows just enough to get himself into trouble, but not enough to get himself out. It was shortly after the three of them met, that Krivis was promoted to president of the Vatican Bank. I couldn't help but laugh when I heard the news. Krivis in such a position would be an epic disaster. Even Fedora agreed with me, however, he found far less humor in the situation than I did. Soon after his new appointment, Krivis had invited Fedora to his lavishly furnished new office, and his beautiful, young secretary. He liked to keep several of these, witless young playthings 'working' around his office to stroke his ego. They would prance and flirt about as if they were his not so secret lovers or something. Fedora couldn't believe what he was seeing. You see, even Fedora knew better than to mix business with such pleasures. Then Krivis told Fedora that now he was only answerable to the pope, and was granted full powers at the Vatican Bank. Fedora and I laughed, we both knew he was full of shit."

"So he just invited Fedora to his office to just flaunt his shit?"

"Yes, and no...you see his stupidity had already managed to get himself into some big trouble with the Securities and Exchange Commission here in America for some violations that had caught their attention."

"Oh really?"

"Yep, the idiot thought it was a good idea to send some of the pope's money out to California. He was trying to convince the pope and his little priest secretary of the inconsequential nature of the situation, while begging Fedora to help him out of his mess. In that moment, there was an almost audible pop of the bishop's ego. Fedora felt compelled to remind the pompous fool that he was supposed to fire Rinaldo Manna and another very useful, influential layman in Vatican finance if he ever found himself in a position to do so. Krivis was now in such a position, and they were the two people who were best positioned to save his ass. Suddenly Krivis knew he was in way over his head. He couldn't afford word getting out about this blunder, or his own incompetence. Fedora now had Krivis, right where he wanted him...and Krivis followed him willingly from that point on."

"Mr. Novelli, do you know what the SEC was investigating?"

"I believe it had to do with Italian banks illegally exporting cash out of Italy at that time. Fedora and I found it all quite amusing."

"Oh?"

"Yeah, you see, the thing was that ALL Italian banks were engaged in these types of exports. These stupid Americans,..." Novelli suddenly caught himself, remembering who was sitting in the room with him. "Sorry, those are Fedora's words, not mine. However, both of us knew the Americans would never get anywhere in their investigation. Hell, the Italian government knew it was going on, and they couldn't stop it.

Once Italy changed its Italian banking laws, most of the exporting of cash out of Italy stopped. Fedora knew that any type of trial that came from it would expose the Vatican Bank as accomplices in numerous black money crimes. The fallout would damage the prestige and reputation of the Vatican Bank, pope, and church beyond repair. Fedora warned Krivis to stop, but Krivis ignored him. Despite Krivis' stupidity and vanity, he still remains extremely close to Ansios and Fedora."

Francis was a little confused, looking over his notes. "Mr. Novelli, you said you left your exchange business at the end of 1968?"

"Yes, that's right."

"If that's true, then how do you know all of this other stuff that has happened since?"

"Oh I did leave Euro Money Exchange at that time, but I stayed on to work at some of Fedora's banks. Besides, Fedora and Ansios weren't the only *uomini di fiducia* working in the Vatican detective."

"Please forgive me, but *uomini di fiducia*?"

"I'm sorry...the *uomini di fiducia* is a very exclusive group of five laymen that included Rinaldo Manna and the other man that Krivis wanted to fire, myself, Fedora, Ansios. We all worked intimately in Vatican finance with their officials. This situations gave me the perfect vantage point for all their activities."

"And you weren't worried about what was going on?"

"Oh it bothered me, but I was being paid well, and nothing they were doing had my name associated with it."

"I see, so you could easily divorce yourself from any type of trouble and responsibility Fedora and his friends could cook up."

"Exactly!" Novelli continued. "Now in April of last year, the three of them conspired to open Sierra Madre International Bank in Nassau, The Bahamas."

Mr. Novelli continued to explain Fedora's challenges with securing money for the purchase of Lincoln National, while Krivis and Ansios were busy trying to complete the sale of the Catholic Bank of Venice. The Venice bank was initially offered to Fedora. Fedora was interested, but he was not moving fast enough for the likes of Krivis. Then Archbishop Leone stepped in to stop the sale of the little Venice bank to Fedora, and the bank was sold to Ansios. The ink was well dried by the time the public learned of the sale eight months later.

"Do you know why they kept the sale hush hush for so long?" Responded Francis curiously.

"That I can't say, but it sure did upset a lot of people in Venice when the news finally broke. Of course by then, Krivis and the rest of them had already moved on to other things, despite Archbishop Leone telling him he was not to have any future involvement with

Fedora. The factual rumors were soon flying, keeping the press busy."

The detective had to work extra hard to contain his pride as Mr. Novelli explained the pair's foiled attempt to buy a huge Italian company using Benedetto's counterfeit bonds in West Germany. It was enough to confirm for Fran, that the Vatican did in fact receive their entire order of fake bonds. Fran wanted to dig a little more into the subject. "Do you know if there was any truth to the rumors of them actually having the counterfeit bonds?"

"Oh Yeah, they had them, but I have no idea how anyone caught wind of it..." Fran was absolutely giddy inside, as Novelli continued. He knew exactly how all that went down. He was even more impressed that none of them had a clue that it was all his doing. Fran's attention returned to Novelli as he continued to ramble, oblivious to what was going on in the detective's head. "...Shortly after that deal went south, Fedora and Krivis returned to Germany to retrieve the rest of the bonds that they had stored at other banks there. They couldn't chance any more of them being confiscated."

"Do you know where those bonds are now Mr. Novelli?"

"That I don't know. I am no longer privy to as much of the Vatican's activities as I once was."

"Hmmm. Do you know where all those counterfeit bonds came from?"

"To be honest, detective, no. I did my best to avoid any involvement in that one. I had seen plenty of their prior schemes, this one was far too risky for me."

"That's more than understandable, Mr. Novelli. You say you were involved with some of their other schemes?"

"I guess involved was not the best choice of words detective. I more or less just kept my head down, and did what I was told. None of their schemes were ever my idea."

"I see."

"The Krivis and Fedora screw up in Dachau is still haunting them, now."

"Hmmmm?"

"Fedora's most trusted and reliable business partner in the UK suddenly distanced themselves, and replaced their entire board of directors. Fedora suddenly became the fall guy for their own employee's incompetence. He was a convenient scapegoat for the company's self-preservation, which in turn pacified their shareholders.

"The ripple effect soon had Fedora gaining more enemies than friends. So he shifted his business strategy to well told lies, blackmail, and bribes. This allowed him to maintain great influence in many sectors of the European financial landscape especially in Italy. It was also time for him to turn his attention to Lincoln National here in New York."

"Ahhh, back on American soil." Fran thought to himself.

"Now there's a huge mess developing over there at Lincoln."

"A huge mess?"

"Yeah, Fedora's Finance Bank in Geneva was shut down a few weeks ago, and the Italian Finance Minister issued two warrants for his arrest."

"Was that one of the banks that you worked for?"

"No, that was his only bank that I didn't work at."

"Do you know what charges were on those warrants?"

"I've heard fraud, but that's all I know. Not long after the Geneva bank was shut down, Swiss bank inspectors showed up at Monrovia Monetary Group of Liberia."

"They were in Liberia?" Fran had learned all this from his conversation with Cosimo earlier.

Novelli chuckled a little. "No, the Liberian company was headquartered in Geneva."

"Do you know why they shut it down?"

"It was a shell company owned by Fedora, the Vatican Bank, and two other entities. When it closed, it was $45 million in the red and being backed by Fedora's Zürich bank."

"The bank you worked for…"

"Correct! The Swiss authorities gave Fedora and his friends forty-eight hours to shut down, or the bank in Zürich would be declared bankrupt. The Liberian bank closed immediately."

"And what happened to the negative balance?"

"It was transferred to a brand new bank in Panama that opened its doors with a negative $45 million balance on its books."

"So that's what happened to the $45 million Cosimo was talking about." Fran thought to himself, but he was still confused. "But how? I thought they were broke."

Novelli gave a slight chuckle. "Oh the transaction didn't involve the movement of any actual money detective."

"Wow! I just don't understand how they can do all this demented shuffling without getting caught." Commented a bewildered detective.

"It's a common thing in banking, especially for these guys. But I think the tide is turning whether any of them want to acknowledge it or not, especially for Fedora."

"What do you mean by that?"

"Remember when I was telling you about how Fedora wanted me to investigate the bizarre happenings at his Zürich bank?"

"Yes."

"Now keep in mind this was all long before the Swiss authorities got involved. It was then that I saw the writing on the wall, and have done whatever I could to try and distance myself from him and his dealings since..."

Suddenly Novelli became distant and quiet. Turning his gaze once again downward towards his shoes. "That is when he started blackmailing me."

"Mr. Novelli, I know this is difficult, but do you mind telling me exactly how he is blackmailing you?"

Novelli's gaze remained fixed as it drifted far, far away. It was obvious he didn't want to answer the question, but he did anyway. At this point, the Italian feared the Italian authorities far more than their American counterparts. He took in a deep breath and held it in for a while. When he finally spoke the shame could be heard in his trembling, fearful voice. "He threatened to use my old gambling habit to blackmail me. He said that he knew that I was back to my old habits, and was threatening to notify the head of the Bank of Italy."

"Was there any truth to his threat Mr. Novelli?"

Novelli straightened himself in his seat. "Absolutely not, but just the mere suggestion would ruin every bit of my reputation I had recovered since we opened Euro Money Exchange, and completely destroy any future I might have in banking. He yelled at me, and told me that I'd never be a 'real banker' because I stuck to my principles and integrity and my ignorance of blackmail. Soon after that he moved me to another department at Lincoln and hired someone else to take over the bank's international department. After all the years I had worked with him, the demotion at Lincoln really hit me hard."

The interview abruptly came to an end. Fran thought it odd that after everything Mr. Novelli had just told him, he suddenly didn't have anything else to say. Fran sensed that the man was holding something back, but decided it was best not to press the issue, for now. To be honest, the detective was actually grateful it was over. It was a lot for him to process, and it was going to take him a while to wrap his head around everything. He now had new eyes and ears to use in his surveillance work involving Fedora, Ansios and Krivis. Fran had one of his fellow department detectives give Mr. Novelli a ride to his home via an unmarked department vehicle. In the coming days, he would make contact with Cosimo and Cardinal Wexford regarding all of this new information. Fran gently removed the cassette from the recorder. He put the recorder away in his desk drawer, returned the tape to its case, and slipped the priceless recording into his jacket pocket.

Francis looked at his watch. He had completely lost track of time during the long interview with Novelli. "Shit," Fran thought to himself. "Peg is gonna be pissed at me. I'd better call her before heading home." Fran was worried. Not because he was late for dinner, but once again needed to ask his wife for another big favor. She would mercilessly haze him as he shamelessly begged for two versions of the Novelli notes, one for his European team, and one for the "official records" at the precinct with all Vatican information removed. This was going to set him back for quite a while with her, and they both knew it.

CHAPTER 25

Giovanni Fedora sat in his fine leather, high backed chair at his mahogany desk. The cold dreary day was on full display outside the window of his executive office suite. The deluge of rain that had assaulted the commuters that morning, had changed to impressively large snowflakes falling gracefully from the dark gray skies above. Clearly winter was not quite finished with her work, despite the passing of the vernal equinox the week before.

The world famous Italian banker and businessman sipped an exquisite cup of espresso from a fine china cup as he scanned through the headlines of a Milan business newspaper. The Milan Stock Exchange was booming. The lire was exchanging strongly against the US dollar. It was clear to the reader that news of his recent troubles in Switzerland, nor warrants for his arrest issued by the Italian Treasury Ministry, had phased the roaring economic sectors of Milan and beyond. He couldn't help but feel pleased and carefree, as he went about his morning. He recently had estimated that his net worth was somewhere in the neighborhood of $500 million. His own delusions may or may not have been stoked by the delusions of others in his orbit.

His long time employee and business partner, Nico Novelli suggested that the time was right for him to sell off one of his largest holdings in Milan. His biggest business rival in the region had just made him an incredible offer. Novelli's advice was sound, however, Fedora chose not to sell. Novelli's recommendation was laughed at and dismissed as was the majority of future forthcoming economic advice. Frustrated and ignored, Mr. Novelli would, from time to time as the months progressed, find himself in discrete meetups with certain New York detectives. His boss was a busy man. He remained oblivious of the covert actions of Novelli.

The detective team maintained their own surveillance on Mr. Fedora, installing bugs and 'taps in his home and work to fortify what Novelli was reporting to them. The operation was elaborate and extensive. Clavering found it curious that communications between Fedora and men like Krivis and Ansios became increasingly less frequent following the situation in Switzerland earlier in the year. It seemed that a new man, one unfamiliar to the detectives, suddenly seemed to be visiting and calling Fedora increasingly often. Who was this man? Fran had heard his name bantered about in conversations Fedora would have with others, but neither Hans or Friedrich in Germany, Cosimo in Rome or Wexford in New York City ever talked about this mysterious man named Gherado Fratello.

"Gherado! It is good to see you again, my friend." Fedora moved from behind his desk to greet his guest.

"It is always good to see you too, Giovanni. How have you been?"

Fedora motioned to his guest to take a seat. "Quite well, thank you. Can I get you something? Wine? Water? The espresso is exquisite, my friend."

"Water will be fine. Thank you."

"Of course...So what brings you to New York this time around?"

"Business, of course. But before we get into all of that, I am curious...Did you get the packet I sent you?"

"The P-2 membership card and information?"

"Yes. Did you have a chance to look it over?"

"I did, several days ago. Look Gherado, I am honored by your offer, but I feel I must decline. As I've said before, while I can appreciate the work you and your men do, I'm just not interested in joining your Masonic lodge. I'm sorry." Fedora grasped the document sized yellow envelope from his desk and reached out his hand to return it to its sender.

Fratello raised a hand to stop Fedora. "Keep it, just in case you need it some time. I understand and respect your decision. It changes nothing as far as our personal relationship is concerned Giovanni."

"I really appreciate that. So how are things with you?"

"Well, but busy, which brings me to the other reason for my visit."

"Oh?"

"I wanted to talk to you about South America. More specifically Argentina, if you don't mind."

"Of course. By the way, I must say, your work in returning Juan Peron to his rightful place of power last year, was quite impressive."

"Thank you, but to be honest, I couldn't have done it without the help of my P-2 network in that region."

"Regardless, your work is still impressive."

Fratello nodded in appreciation. "You know, Peron recently appointed me Special Counselor to the Embassy in Rome."

"I had not heard about that yet. Wow, not bad Gherado, not bad. So what are your concerns regarding South America, Mr. Diplomat?"

Fratello issued a prideful smile, then his body language changed to fit a more serious conversation. "I'm most concerned that Cuba, with help from Russia, is stoking the discontent of the populace towards their respective dictators and steering them directly into the arms of communism."

"Hmmm, yes...I can see how that could be a developing problem. What do you have in mind to remedy that?"

"Argentina has plenty of natural resources. They just lack the funds to develop them into something meaningful and lucrative. We need banks. We need investment and credit options and we need room to move into private ventures there."

Fedora thought about the situation for a moment, as Fratello further detailed the situation. "Have you talked with Marco Ansios yet?"

"No, you are the first one I've approached regarding any of this..."

"I'm sure Marco would be more than happy to get Banco Gererali established in South America, my friend. I'm sure Bishop Krivis will have the Vatican Bank on board too."

"How can you be so sure Giovanni?"

"Simple, South America already holds the largest number of Catholics per capita in the world."

"True."

"And Pope Michael is already living with the very real nightmare of losing more of his flock in other communist controlled parts of the world." Fratello nodded in understanding, as Fedora continued. "I tell you what, let me get him on the phone, and see what we can do to help you and the Argentinian people Gherado."

"That sounds perfect. Thank you."

"My pleasure."

Within a few minutes, Fedora's secretary announced that Marco Ansios was on line two. Fedora exchanged a few pleasantries with Ansios before patching him into the speaker phone. Marco Ansios in the past was an integral part of numerous business deals. Fedora's recent troubles in Italy and Switzerland may not have impacted financial markets, however, it did have a heavy impact on his friend, partner and protégé. Ansios was now even more skittish than ever. Ansios' greatest fear was the public finding out about his current and past dealings with Mr. Fedora.

"Giovanni?" Inquired Ansios with obvious nervousness in his voice.

"Yes Marco, how are you?"

Ansios cupped his hand over the phone's mouthpiece and began whispering into the phone coldly. "Why are you calling here?"

"Marco, is that any way to greet a friend and business partner?"

"I told you not to call me here at work Giovanni."

"Will you relax? I had to,...I have someone here who has a proposal you might be interested in."

Some of Ansios' nervous coldness shifted to cautious curiosity. "Oh? Who?"

"Gherado Fratello…"

As the initial concept was pitched to Ansios. The nervous Italian listened with guarded optimism. He liked what he was hearing, but wanted a few more details before fully committing to the plan. A meeting between Ansios and Fratello was arranged for the two of them in Rome, the following week.

The call terminated, and Fedora moved from behind his desk to get himself some water. Mid-pour, he turned to his guest, "Gherado, I was wondering, since you're going to Rome next week, would you mind doing me a favor?"

"Of course, my friend. What do you need?"

"Marco owes me some money. He's such a paranoid nervous wreck, whenever I visit or call him...I was wondering if you'd mind picking that up for me while you're over there?"

"Of course, consider it done."

Gherado Fratello returned from Rome after a couple of weeks to inform Fedora that Ansios was on board with the proposed South American developments. Fratello couldn't help but proudly brag that Ansios would soon be the newest member of P2. Fedora congratulated his guest with muted enthusiasm. The actions of either man were not surprising to Fedora.

"Please forgive my crassness, but did you get my money from Marco I requested."

"He said that he would pay you back a little at a time so that there would be no attention drawn or disruption to the booming Italian markets." Fratello confirmed, then continued. "I must say, you were right about his paranoia. He says that he doesn't even want those payments going directly to you. I told him that he could use my Swiss bank accounts to anonymously pay you back your money. He seemed relieved to have that option available. I hope that was alright with you."

"Yes, that's fine." Fedora responded in a fading tone. Fedora wasn't thrilled, but knowing Ansios as he did, he knew that that was the best he was going to get, for the moment.

Fedora was used to the nervousness of Ansios. But he never once expected it from Bishop Jonas Krivis. He too was now scared, and blatantly distancing himself from Giovanni Fedora. Fedora's recent troubles in Switzerland directly impacted Vatican finance departments. Krivis had already gotten an ass chewing from Cardinals Benoît and Leone, and others. Like Ansios, he too began to distance himself from Fedora in an effort to recover the sullied reputation of himself and his bank. Once again Fratello was dispatched to Rome. This time for a meeting with the Vatican Bank president. Krivis finally contacted Fedora to inform him that his bank would be happy to serve as fiduciary for Banco Generali's South America deals. Krivis was the final component needed for the deal to move forward.

The Italian press knew nothing of the newly brokered deal between Fratello, Fedora, Ansios and Krivis. The vultures from the press instead, went into a sudden frenzy, painting Fedora as the most dangerous Mafiosi in Sicily. Fedora had been close friends with the Sicilian Don of the Lanscano crime family for many years. The two men shared some fine wine and a hearty laugh as they discussed the blatant falsehoods being reported in the papers. Fedora, while he had done some work for various Mafia families in years past, his efforts were always 100% voluntary. He never once asked for, nor needed favors or "services" from them. Everyone knew that Fedora's financial institutions were first class banks catering to the aristocracy. Members of the Mob did like the finer things in life, but not for their financial needs. They were never fans of the kinds of attention that came with first rate banks. They preferred the lower profile, smaller banking establishments. It was nothing personal, it was just better for their "business" model.

Around mid-April, 1974, the Milan Stock Exchange suddenly took a nosedive. The exchange rate of the Lire reflected the economic trend. In New York, Fedora's Lincoln National Bank went public with its first quarter figures. The bank's stock was now trading sixty-six cents lower than it was the year before. The smiles and carefree days of prior months had given way to concern and anxiety as Fedora looked over the financial reports from his bank. Staring back at him was $40 million in losses. The pathetic two cents per share was actually a generous lie at best.

The man Fedora had hired to spite Novelli, Conner Gilmore, was the man with the brilliant plan for Lincoln's growing liquidity problems. Fedora gave him unrestricted access to all departments within the bank and an order to get the bank back in the black. Fedora wanted results, not details. His attention was needed in Europe, where he was quietly kicking himself for ignoring Novelli's advice to sell his largest Milan asset just a few weeks prior.

Gilmore, moved quickly from department to department, removing anyone who stood in his way. However, his efforts had nothing to do with cleaning up the bank, and everything to do with positioning himself to become the next chairman of the board and eventually Chief Executive. He would dine often with other prominent New York men in banking. Conversations frequently centered around the bleak situation at Lincoln National and how he was the only one who could save it. Back at the office, he continued to comb through banking records where many mistakes and improper dealings were discovered. These confidential indiscretions would also find their way into financial community discussions around the Big Apple.

Gilmore soon started looking into the bank's International Division. It was there that he found numerous illegal irregularities involving a Lincoln board member.. Novelli watched Gilmore from a distance as he violently confronted the man about his crimes and threatened to send his ass to prison. A few days later the man Gilmore accosted suffered a massive nervous breakdown that conveniently removed him from all bank business for the foreseeable future.

Novelli quickly realized that his replacement, Mr. Gilmore, had about as much intelligence and grace as an intoxicated bull rummaging through the bank's various departments. He was particularly stupid when it came to matters involving foreign exchange. In years past Novelli would have alerted Fedora of the situation. This would not be one of those times. Novelli had been knocked down too many times by Fedora over the years. He opted instead to just sit back and watch,

somewhat amused as Fedora's chosen replacement bumbled his way
through his days.

Fedora's attention was already consumed by a huge mess
developing in Milan. He got an urgent call from Lincoln's longest,
most successful, former CEO, that everyone fondly referred to as
"Pops." A man who was ousted in a hostile corporate takeover several
years before the Fedora arrived in New York City. "Pops" retirement
package insured a continued vested interest in the success of his
former bank long after his removal. An impromptu meeting with
"Pops," Fedora and Novelli was called to review the situation. Fedora
and "Pops" read through a report from an independent consulting firm
warning that Lincoln National Bank was on the brink of insolvency.
Fedora's stomach sank, they uncovered over $6 million in losses from
the fixed-rate sector, and over $30 million in additional undeclared
losses from over forty exchange contracts still outstanding.

Outraged, Fedora first confronted the accounting department
head. His pathetic yet legitimate defense was absolute ignorance of
the transactions. Fedora hauled the bank's publicly, self proclaimed
"Savior," Conner Gilmore into his office. He and "Pops" wanted
answers. Why were operations so sloppy? Novelli remained silent as
the man first tried to push the blame onto the sitting board president,
then back to the accounting department. It didn't work. It was now
clear that Gilmore was the problem.

Fedora immediately suspended Lincoln's massive currency
speculation and exchange operations in an effort to stem the
hemorrhaging of funds from his bank. Banks in London were caught
completely off guard. Just a week prior, they were clearing well over
£50 million worth of sterling daily through accounts connected to
the New York bank. Lincoln National Bank was now the first major
bank in the US to declare no quarterly dividend since The Great
Depression.

Fedora, "Pops," Novelli, with an attorney in tow, were called
to a meeting with the Comptroller and the Security and Exchange
Commission at the New York Federal Reserve Bank. After
consideration of mitigating efforts already initiated, the federal

authorities decided to allow Lincoln National to open its doors Monday morning after a recapitalization promise of $50 million was made from one of Fedora's holding companies in Liechtenstein and a fiduciary was assigned to take over Fedora's corporate voting powers. The Federal Reserve felt the move was warranted, given the rumors coming out of Europe regarding Fedora. The proposed fiduciary the Comptroller had in mind was initially Conner Gilmore. The four men representing Lincoln instantly protested. The Feds countered with another inappropriate suggestion. Finally the two parties agreed on a more suitable, relatively neutral man. Detective Francis Clavering knew the man as soon as his name was dropped. It was Nixon's former Treasury Secretary. The man with known ties to New York Mobster Luca Benedetto, and his friends in Munich.

A press release was quickly issued. Lincoln National's future was once again promising. A conflicting press release was issued the same day by Lincoln's sitting vice-chairman to a well-read New York paper that had many people confused, and many tongues wagging all weekend. Monday morning, as New Yorkers read the headlines of financial sections while drinking their morning coffee, Lincoln's sitting Chairman and Vice-Chairman were dismissed, and Novelli was offered his old position following Conner Gilmore's coerced resignation.

The drastic corrective measures brought welcomed stabilization to Lincoln's operations. The men of the Federal Reserve were satisfied with the bank's corrective moves. News spread fast following the public declaration by the comptroller that Lincoln National Bank would remain solvent. The bank's patrons, however, remained unconvinced as client after client visited the bank to withdraw funds, and close out their accounts at an alarming rate.

The former chairman of the FDIC quickly stepped in as the bank's new chairman and CEO. At this point the bank had already borrowed $1.2 billion from the Federal Reserves in order to keep it afloat. The Italian was not fond of the federal element hanging around his bank. However, he was not in a position to protest.

Fedora had no time to enjoy the carefree days of mid-summer. Satisfied that the Lincoln disaster in New York had been averted, it was time to address the liquidity problem in his two Milan banks. In a desperate campaign to salvage his Italian banking empire, he and Novelli worked together to develop the best strategy to save his two Milan banks. A proposal was submitted to the Bank of Italy for the merger of his two banks. Now all they could do was wait.

Fedora looked everywhere for help, while trying not to seem desperate. It was time for him to collect some long overdue debt and cash in on past financial favors. His first visit was to Banco Generali's chairman of the board, Marco Ansios. With all the turmoil swirling around Fedora, Ansios was none too pleased to see him walk through his office door.

"What are you doing here Giovanni?" Ansios greeted coldly in a hushed tone.

"My dear Marco, is that any way to greet an old dear friend?" Fedora responded sporting his sly signature smile, then lowered his tone slightly and winked. "It is good to see you too, my friend."

The uncontrollable twitch of Ansios' dark mustache did nothing to hide his nervousness and fear. "You should not have come here Giovanni."

"You must forgive me Marco, it is in extremely poor taste for me to show up here unannounced like this. I'm sorry."

The apology did nothing to comfort his nervous host. "Then why did you?"

Fedora sat back in the chair, and brought his fingertips together to a point in front of his mouth. "It seems that the arrangement you and Fratello had made has resulted in no money coming my way Marco. It's way past time for me to collect on my investment."

"Your investment?"

"Have you forgotten my generous efforts that helped put you behind that desk?"

"What?" It had slipped his mind, Ansios lowered his voice as he excused his brief ignorance...

"So Marco, what is the current return on my $18 million investment?"

"Oh that,...It's doing quite well, it was merged with funds from the Vatican Bank and other investors to purchase a network of companies."

Fedora was puzzled as he quickly scanned his memory. "Why is this the first I'm hearing about it, Marco?"

Ansios suddenly became even more nervous. "You know that my position here requires complete secrecy Giovanni."

"That's not good enough Marco, that shit may work with Krivis, and others..." Fedora instantly became heated. "I want a full audit of where and how my money is being used, Marco."

Fedora took a few minutes to regroup. He knew that it was unrealistic to demand such a report. Especially after showing up unannounced. Several days passed before Fedora made a return visit to the office. Fedora's presence was greeted by Ansios' secretary, Leonora Tocci, who displayed far more machismo than her cowardly boss who huddled silently in a corner of his office with all of the lights off. On the other side of the office door. She apologized and lied profusely for the absence of Mr. Ansios. The mortified banker shivered in fear until Fedora's car left the parking lot. Fedora's protégé feared that his own empire would soon become collateral damage as Fedora's troubles increased.

While Fedora was busy in Milan, Nico Novelli returned to New York ahead of him. When he arrived at Detective Francis Clavering's office, he looked like shit. Something wasn't right. It was obvious that the man hadn't slept in days.

"Would you like a cup of coffee Mr. Novelli?" Offered the seasoned detective, concerned.

Novelli responded in a shaky voice. "Yes, please."

Fran turned to a concerned looking Agent Erikson. "Lance, can you please bring our guest a cup of coffee,...oh, with two sugars and a splash of cream." Fran then looked at Novelli and issued an understanding nod.

"Yes, sir,...back in a second. Do you want one too, Fran?"

"Sure, why not."

Novelli issued a low toned "Thank you." As he took the steaming cup of coffee into his trembling hands from Lance.

Novelli explained that Lincoln National Bank was on life support, and its days were numbered. The two detectives who were tasked by Bayer to work alongside the Federal Reserve and SEC to keep an eye on Fedora were confused. "But I thought the Feds had stepped in to stop all that Mr. Novelli." Responded a confused FBI agent.

"They can't stop it, only slow the inevitable." Tears started flowing freely down Novelli's face.

Fran offered him a box of tissues. "What does this failure have to do with you sir?" Questioned Lance.

"Nothing detective,..."

"Then why are you so upset?"

"The failures and incompetence of my predecessor Conner Gilmore will all be blamed on me now that Fedora has reinstated me into my former position."

"But you aren't responsible for what happened when you weren't in that position Mr. Novelli."

"I know that, you know that, hell even Fedora and the Feds know that...but the public lynch mob, looking for someone to hang, doesn't know that detective. I will never be able to find work in this industry again." Novelli instantly bursted into uncontrollable sobs.

"Mr. Novelli, we will clear your name."

Novelli did his best to regain his composure. He dabbed at his eyes and nose with a tissue. "But how?"

"I'm not sure yet, but we will come up with a plan. I promise." Fran confirmed.

At a quarter to nine the next evening, a very upset and worked up Novelli dialed the home phone of Conner Gilmore across town.

"Nico, is that you?"

"Yes, it's me."

Gilmore was immediately uneasy about the call, especially coming in at 9 pm at night. "What can I do for you, sir."

"Listen Conner, I must be frank with you. I've just returned home from being at the SEC all day."

"Oh?"

"They questioned me for over five hours. Then they told me that you testified that I was the man setting amounts and rates for international exchange at the bank."

"What's that Nico? I can't hear you?" Shouted the man on the other line.

Novelli raised his voice louder. "I said that I was told that you testified that all the transactions that went through the Zürich bank were arranged by me, you know amounts, rates. Do you understand?"

"Why would I do that? You didn't do any of that Nico, I did."

"That's what I told them, but they don't believe me."

Gilmore was growing increasingly suspicions as the call went on. "Go back to the beginning, what exactly did you tell them Nico?"

"I told them that I didn't do anything. I wasn't involved in any of those transactions. I had no powers, as you very well know, and I resigned as vice-president and managing director of the Zürich bank way back in September of 1972."

"That's correct, but they wouldn't accept your statements?"

Novelli was becoming more distraught. "No."

"Listen, where are you now?"

"I'm calling from a payphone downtown."

"Do you have a number there?"

"What?"

"Give me the number there so I can call you back Nico."

"Can't you just tell me what happened? I really don't like this SEC shit."

"No, not on this line, Nico."

"Why not? It's a payphone."

"I'm not worried about your line kid, it's mine."

"Look man, I just want to know what you told them. I was really shocked by what they told me you said." Novelli looked nervously at Detective Clavering sitting across the table from him listening to the conversation on headphones in the interrogation room. Fran nodded at Novelli and quickly wrote down the phone's number. "There was this conversation between Fedora and myself a few months back..." Gilmore then went silent.

"Hello...Conner?" Novelli tapped several times on the phone's mouthpiece.

"Yeah, I'm still here. Listen, give me your number, so I can call you back in a few minutes. I just don't trust this line Nico."

"Fine, fine my number is..."

The three men in the room waited anxiously for a good ten minutes. Finally, the phone in the interrogation room rang. "Hello?"

"That's better." Responded a more relaxed Gilmore on the other end. "A few months back Fedora told me that all the Zürich deals were initiated by you when you were a consultant at that bank."

"He told you what? That is absolute bullshit Conner. I was never a consultant at that bank."

"Clearly we need to sit down and have a very serious talk, and soon."

"I don't need to sit down with you. Look Conner, all I want to know is did you testify that I arranged amounts, rates and everything else between Lincoln and Zürich?"

Gilmore was suddenly confused. "So you didn't have anything to do with any of this?"

"Nothing! How could I? I had no power in either bank."

"Then how did the Zürich deals take place Nico?"

"How the hell am I supposed to know! This is the first time I'm even hearing about this meeting between you and Fedora"

Gilmore gave a detailed account of the meeting, then the line went silent. A deep sigh could be heard on the other end of the line. "I think we are both in some very deep trouble here, Nico..."

The phone conversation between Novelli and Gilmore did a lot in the effort to clear Novelli's involvement. The two detectives immediately went to work looking deeper into Lincoln's foreign exchange transactions, hoping to find even more to help clear their informant's name. Federal Agent Lance Erikson came bursting through Fran's office door startling the detective seated at his desk.

"What the hell Lance?!" Fran yelled, grabbing his chest.

"Fran!" Responded the FBI Agent out of breath, while offering his partner the documents in his hands. "You are never going to believe what I found! Look!"

Fran took the papers from Lance's hands while still rubbing his chest with the other. "What's this?"

"Just read..."

Fran quickly scanned the documents. "Oh my God..." Fran muttered under his breath, then looked up again. "Lance, this is huge!"

"That's what I thought too! I think Mr. Novelli is going to be very relieved that we found this!"

"No doubt about it!"

"Do you mind if I hang onto this for a bit, so I can do it more justice than a quick glance."

"Of course...it took me a few times to grasp it all too. Take your time. I'm going to go grab a cup of coffee, you want one?"

Fran gave a slight chuckle. "Shit, I'm still trying to get my heart back into my chest...you asshole."

"Sorry about that,..."

"I will be fine..." Fran gave Lance a wink. "Thanks anyway."

Fran looked over the documents a few more times then looked at the wall clocks hanging on his wall. He got up to close his office door then dialed Cosimo's office number in Rome.

"...you're never going to believe what Lance just found!"

"What ya got?"

"Documentation on several foreign exchange transactions between Fedora's Swiss bank in Zürich and Lincoln National Bank."

"Oh really?"

"Yeah! They rigged the hyper-inflated exchange rates on deals, then used the huge profits gained from these deals to prop up the bank's poor earnings reports."

"Oh wow, send me that over as soon as you can, will ya? I'm going to have to let the boys know over in Zürich!"

"Absolutely! I will send it out today! How are things going over there?"

"Fedora doesn't have too much happening here in Rome, but over in Milan, he sure does."

"Oh yeah?"

"Yeah, the Bank of Italy just approved the merger of Fedora's two Milan banks."

"You mean the two banks that Novelli said were in deep shit?"

"Yep, those are the ones. Now it's one of the biggest private banks in the country. A bank that is deep in the red on day one."

Fran was puzzled. "So they let Fedora go from having two mid-sized, troubled banks, to now having one very large, very sick bank? In what world does that even make sense Cosimo?

"The logic behind it escapes me too, but I'm thinking that will be cleared up soon."

"Why's that?"

"My boss has been sending me over to Milan to assist the Treasury Minister and the Bank of Italy investigators with an audit."

"That's great to hear, but why now? They already approved the merger?"

"The only thing I can think of is now Fedora won't be able to hide anything in one bank, while we are looking at the other."

"I guess. But there's nothing to stop him from hiding shit in Zürich."

"Well now he only has one bank there. And with this shit you and Lance just found between Lincoln and Zürich, it seems he is running out of places to hide, if you know what I mean."

"Well, keep me posted on what you find over there."

"Only if you do the same my friend."

On August 9th, 1974, Richard Milhous Nixon resigned in disgrace as United States President amid pressure resulting from the Watergate scandal. Fedora was disappointed that he couldn't do more to help keep his long time friend in office. For the Italian banker, his own self preservation in New York and Europe took every minute of his time. Fedora was left scratching his head. For the first time ever in his career, nothing he did seemed to help turn things around.

Fedora was pleased that The Bank of Italy finally approved the merger of his two Milan banks. It was now time for the banking establishments of the region to rally round and help. Afterall if Fedora failed in Milan, it would be catastrophic for many others throughout Europe. Fedora approached the president of The Bank of Rome. This bank held a particularly large portion of Fedora's empire as collateral for outstanding loans. $128 million worth of lire was poured into the Fedora's bank. It was just a drop in a bucket. It was going to take a lot more than that to get it back from its troubled state.

Fedora worked hard throughout the month of August to find more help. He went back to The Bank of Rome with an offer to sell his large Milan holding company and his 51% controlling interest in his bank for 100 billion lire. The Bank of Rome countered with a 45 billion lire offer. By the first week of September, the state run Bank of Italy caught wind of their planned deal, and immediately halted all pending negotiations. Fedora was officially done.

The Italian state owned Bank of Italy seized Fedora's bank and handed over temporary control to its public holding company established by Mussolini in the '30s to rescue, restructure and refinance failed banks and private companies that had gone bankrupt during the Depression. An audit uncovered over $300 million in losses. Cosimo quietly informed Fran in New York that during the audit it was found that the Vatican Bank lost $27 million plus all of their shares in Fedora's bank. An Italian attorney, and good friend of Cosimo's, named Arturo Bartolone, was appointed to liquidate Fedora's bank on behalf of the Italian Treasury Minister and the Director of the Bank of Italy.

The press devoured the dirty laundry, gorging themselves like starved hyenas on the news. *Business Week* reported "The end for Giovanni Fedora in Italian banking, and the world." Fedora's holdings, credit, and reputation were gone, his empire was pillaged by the government of his home country without a penny of compensation offered to Fedora. The Bank of Rome instantly became collateral damage, as did many others.

"Clavering, call on line two..." Came a voice from somewhere in the busy precinct.

"Got it Jack, thanks!" The detective picked up the handset. "Detective Clavering here."

"Fran, it's Cosimo!" Came a hushed voice on the line. "Are you alone at the moment?"

Fran got up and closed his office door. "Yeah man, what's up?"

"We need you to do us a huge favor."

"Of course, my man, whatcha need?"

"We need you to make an arrest for us. I'll send you the arrest warrant and extradition papers."

"Alright, no problem. Who am I picking up for you?"

"We need you to pick up and detain Mr. Nico Novelli."

CHAPTER 26

Detective Francis Clavering returned the phone's handset slowly to its cradle. The only sound in the room came from the two ticking clocks on the wall labeled New York, and Munich/ Rome. "Novelli is going to hate me." Fran whispered to himself under his breath. He sat motionless, staring off into the distance that resided somewhere in his pen and yellow notepad laying in front of him, while his mind replayed the events of the last twenty months.

The ringing office phone startled him, yet didn't quite pull him out of his state of shock. "Detective Clav..." He responded in a shakey, distant voice.

"Fran?" Came a soft, assuring voice on the other end of the phone. "Is everything alright?"

"Oh, hey Peg..." His voice remained distant. "Yeah, I'm fine."

"Like hell you are! What's up?"

Fran held the phone to his ear, while running his fingers through his short, curly black hair. He explained the call from Cosimo. Peg too went silent, as she thought about the situation. "What are you going to do Fran?"

"Well it's not like I have much of a choice here Peg." He snapped. "Lance and I are going to have to go pick him up."

"No consideration for all the help he's been to your investigation?"

"None, this arrest warrant and extradition is coming from Switzerland. We can't even entertain a plea, a public defender or anything. This whole thing just makes me sick! He trusted me, Peg!"

"And you trusted him, Fran." She returned sharply.

Peg's words echoed through his head for a second, transforming his shock into anger. "You're right...I mean, yes he helped us, he helped us a lot. A few times, my gut sensed something was up...but I was so hungry for shit on Fedora and Krivis, I just let it slide. How could I have been such an idiot, damn it!"

"You can't kick yourself for this one Fran. Clearly he never intended for you guys to find out about Zürich."

"Yeah, I guess you're right. But I'm still going to be pissed at myself for a while."

"Well you better get over yourself by 7:00 tonight, mister." She scolded

"What?"

"Don't you remember? We have that dinner date tonight with..."

"...your sister and Jerry. I completely forgot about that."

"Yeah I know. I figured you would, that's actually why I called."

"Well I'm glad you did, thank you. I'll see you a little before six, love."

"Don't be late!" Peg warned half-heartedly as she hung up the phone.

Fran hung up the phone, and looked down at the notes from Cosimo's call. "Well, I guess we might as well get this over with." He thought to himself. He grabbed his coat, then went down the hall to fetch Lance.

"We're gonna do what?"

"Come on, I'll explain on the way..."

Two hours later, Lance followed Fran into his office, and sat down. Fran quickly dialed the phone.

"Hey Fran, did you get him?"

"I'm afraid not, Cosimo...he's gone."

"Gone?"

"Yep, without a trace."

"Shit!"

"Lance and I went to the bank, the staff there said he'd been out sick for the last few days. So we drove over to his home. The place was completely empty Cosimo. I don't know what you want us to do at this point, I'm sorry."

"It's not your fault Fran. Can you guys put out an APB for him? See if you can find him? He's got to be somewhere."

"Of course. Just keep me posted if you hear anything."

"Will do!"

In a nicely furnished villa on the outskirts of Milan, a phone rang on the third shelf of a bookcase made of beautiful bird's eye maple. Fedora looked up from his desk and glanced curiously at the source of the disturbance across the room. This particular phone in the office of Fedora's Milan vacation home had essentially remained untouched since its installation, with the exception of the occasional feather duster. In all of that time, never once did it ring. Only one person on the planet had the number to that phone.

Fedora walked across the room, picked up the phone, and slowly placed it to his ear. "Yes."

"You must go."

"Now?"

"Yes, they are coming for you tomorrow."

"Are you sure?"

"Yes, I have confirmation from judicial and law enforcement sources...do not set foot in Italy again, until you hear from me that it is safe to do so."

The line went dead.

3 AM the following morning, with three arrest warrants in hand, the Milan vacation home of Giovanni Fedora was raided. The heavy front double doors of the home were knocked in by a team of men conducting their mission with coordinated military precision. Every

room, and outbuilding on the property was methodically searched. The man they were looking for was gone without a trace.

The hunt was now on for Mr. Giovanni Fedora. He was now the most wanted man in all of Italy. Inside the walls of Vatican City, he was once the most sought after secular man. However, in recent months, he had become *persona non grata*. Pope Michael VI was briefed daily by his Secretary of State, Cardinal Benoît and his number two in command Cardinal Leone on Fedora's ever changing situation. With the update of each passing day, the Holy Father grew more and more distraught and depressed. The movement of Vatican investments from Italy to the United States, Switzerland, Germany and beyond during Pope Michael's reign had but three purposes,...increase profits, avoid taxes, and lower its profile in Italy. The Church and Holy Father were easily seduced by the *uomini di fiducia* through the promises of greater wealth. The most powerful and influential of those Vatican "men of trust" was Mr. Giovanni Fedora.

Much of the public believed that it was Pope Michael who was responsible for bringing Fedora into the Curia's inner workings. While the two men knew each other long before the beginning of Michael's papacy, the Pope's personal secretary, his advisors, his own Secretary of State, and others were convinced that Fedora was the answer to the Vatican's prayers. Even if no one in Vatican City ever prayed on the matter. It was because of them, that Pope Michael opened the bronze doors wide and personally escorted his friend, "the answer" inside. Fedona quickly made himself many "new friends" in Vatican City. All of them were ready, willing and eager to be a part of Fedora's criminal activities, while keeping the pope well insulated from what was really going on.

Every ounce of love and admiration Bishop Jonas Krivis had for Fedora publicly in the past, had grown cold and distant. If one was to actually believe the public statements of the Vatican Bank president. He was quoted in several articles that there was "...no way my bank could have lost money due to any type of relationship with Mr. Fedora. How could I? Truth is, I don't really know him all that well. The Vatican has not lost a single cent because of Mr. Fedora. Everything you might have heard is simply fantasy."

The Vatican Bank president seemed to frequently have a remarkably poor memory. It might have been a legitimate concern, if anyone actually believed him. The truth was that Krivis' "limited financial dealings" with Fedora were substantial and frequent from the time of their first meeting in the late 1960s up until just a few short weeks ago. Krivis was a man with many faults, but he was at least consistent. His lies, his disregard for disciplinary conversations with Cardinals Benoît and Leone, and his continued dealings with men like Giovanni Fedora and Marco Ansios were unrelenting. The financial losses to the Vatican Bank under Bishop Krivis' watch were impressive, and very real.

The morning sun of early October beamed through the windows of Fedora's New York office suite. He took a deep breath as he took in the beauty of the fall sunrise. The actions of the Italian Ministry of Justice out of Rome would force him to ground and focus his energies. He now had only Lincoln and the Zürich bank left to his name. It was time for the man, exiled from his home land to sit and quietly reflect on recent events and plan his next move.

Across town, the Board of Governors of the Federal Reserves called an emergency meeting. They had been alerted to the Italian government's actions against Giovanni Fedora over in Milan and Zürich. The proposed plan to save Lincoln National Bank just a couple weeks prior was now no longer an option. Fedora's failing empire had now reached America.

Following three days of meetings at the New York Federal Reserve, the Comptroller of Currency declared Lincoln National Bank insolvent and the FDIC seized control of the institution. "Biggest Bank Failure in US History!" was plastered all over newsstands in the Big Apple and beyond. In the morning, auditors stormed the building. By mid afternoon, the bank was auctioned off to a Euro-American bank and trust for $125 million. Fedora was legally forced into bankruptcy, and all of his remaining holdings were seized and prepared for liquidation. Just like that, Lincoln National Bank was gone.

It had been well over a month since anyone last saw or heard from Nico Novelli. His sometimes friend, business partner, and boss, Giovanni Fedora was now considered an imminent flight risk, considering what had happened in recent weeks in Milan. The bugs and 'taps placed in Fedora's Park Avenue apartment long ago by the surveillance team of Clavering and Erikson would become important tools in helping maintain eyes and ears on the man going forward.

The phone in Fedora's home office rang three times before he finally picked it up.

"Hello..."

"I see you made it out of Milan, safely."

"Yes, I owe you a debt of gratitude for that." Fedora responded humbly.

"My offer still stands if you need a place while all of this blows over. My men will take good care of you."

"I appreciate that. What are you hearing about what's going on in Italy?"

"I'm having a hell of a time controlling the situation there at the moment. There are men in that government, outside my control, who are more than determined to destroy you and scatter your ashes to the winds."

"Oh..." Fedora's tone did nothing to hide his sense of defeat.

"But I will continue to have my men help you where and when we can. As things progress."

"I really appreciate that, thank you."

Two months had passed since the Italian Treasury Ministry and the Bank of Italy raided Fedora's Milan bank, and one month since Lincoln National Bank was forced to shutter. The US Treasury Secretary was getting hammered by the public for the declining strength of the US dollar, and found a convenient scapegoat in the failed Italian banker and financier. In Italy, Arturo Bartolne, the attorney appointed to audit and liquidate Fedora's failed Milan bank had spent many long days combing through the records of what once was, not so long ago, two banks. The first report to surface was damning. Fedora's two Milan banks had been operating fraudulently since 1970. Documents were issued from Milan for the immediate extradition of Giovanni Fedora from New York City.

The Italian man living in New York stood at the large office window of his luxurious hotel apartment, staring off into dreary winter streets below, contemplating his future. In Italy, the hyenas and vultures sat drooling, waiting for their chance at his carcass. He decided his best option was to remain in the United States and face whatever fate might be handed down from a blind lady justice. He retained the services of disgraced former President Richard M. Nixon's law firm. The lawyers set to work right away fighting his extradition to Italy, claiming it was all nothing more than a conspiracy plot.

Fedora found that many close to him through the years had disappeared along with his power and his money. Bishop Krivis and Marco Ansios remained friends, but because of their respective positions remained distant. His only allies now were his friends in the Mob, and Gherado Fratello. Fratello, through his men inside the Roman Ministry of Justice, set to work right away, doing whatever they could to interfere with the extradition process. When impatient Italian authorities investigated what was taking so long with the paperwork, they found that the American Embassy in Rome claimed that they "knew nothing of the extradition request." Unable to leave Italy, Fratello made numerous visits to Fedora's office suite as the months progressed. On one visit, he presented an eighty page report filled with everything that was illegal about the Italian government's warrant, claiming Fedora was nothing more than their political enemy.

The crashing world of Giovanni Fedora decimated the Milan Stock Exchange. The close friendship and business associations of the past between Fedora and Banco Generali chairman, Marco Ansios was suddenly a huge liability for the banker and his bank. Ansios' paranoid nightmare had become his waking reality. The value of his bank's share dropped, as did the confidence and faith international financial sectors had had in him and Banco Generali in the past. Credit limits were cut, and loans from international sources were now gone. Time and options were running out. In Bano Generali's eleventh hour, a new, mysterious Milan Company entered the market and began purchasing bank shares. Confidence in Marco Ansios and his bank soon returned as millions of dollars worth of faith were poured into the bank in exchange for more shares.

It took a little time, but when the calendar finally flipped to 1975, Ansios' winter was beginning to grow less cold. His bank was well on the road to recovery. Fedora's fate was kept in a holding pattern, as Fratello's men went about their work. Everyone was so focused on Italian financial affairs, the sucker punch coming from the Swiss authorities out of Zürich blindsided everyone. The final flicker of remaining hope for Fedora's future was finally extinguished.

CHAPTER 27

Detective Francis Clavering sat at his desk, as the smoke from his cigarette swirled gracefully above him. He was deep into the latest information from Cosimo regarding the closure of Giovanni Fedora's final bank in Zürich. He mindlessly reached for the handset of the ringing black phone on his desk, placing it to his ear, and tucking it between his chin and shoulder.

"Detective Clavering."

"Fran?"

"Oh hey Peg, you're never going to guess what I just got from Italy..."

Peg listened intently, then responded. "Oh wow, love. That's great to hear."

"...You will get no argument from me. So what's up? Did I forget another dinner date or something?"

Peg chuckled. "No, nothing like that. I just wanted to let you know that John just called, and he needs to see you right away."

"John" was the code name the two of them used for Cardinal Wexford. Fran's curiosity was piqued. "Did he say what about?"

"No, he just said that it was urgent."

"Hmmm, I see. Can you please let him know that I will swing by on my way home from work."

"Of course love. I do hope everything is alright."

"Yeah, me too."

That evening Peg busily tidied up the kitchen after feeding the children. She waited to have her own dinner with her husband when he came home from work. She was just getting ready to run the bath when Fran came bursting through the door startling everyone.

"Goddammit Fran!" Interjected Peg clutching her chest. "Must you barge in here like that?"

Fran showed no remorse as he just stood there panting, with the biggest grin plastered on his face. He looked at his bride with excited eyes and an extended hand. "Look!"

Peg, suspect of what was handed to her, transformed from indignation to elation. "Is this for real love? For us?! Don't you dare mess with my head, Francis Clavering!"

"Yes ma'am, it's real! No messing, we're going to Venice!"

Peg squealed in delight, as she threw herself into her husband's arms. "My God honey, that's wonderful news! When?"

"That I will have to figure out once I get to the office tomorrow, but as soon as I can get the 'time off.' I will let Christopherson in on what's really going down regarding this trip."

Peg thought for a second. "Why do I get the feeling that this isn't just a vacation?"

"Because you know too much." Fran smiled, with a wink. "Cardinal Wexford said that Cardinal Leone called for an urgent meeting with Cosimo, Hans, and myself as soon as possible."

"Is Wexford going too?"

"Yes, he will be meeting us there."

In Venice, Cosimo's wife played hostess to the other two wives. The three women would shop and take in the sights while their men went on to meet with Cardinal Wexford at the Patriarchate of Venice. Wexford escorted the three detectives into an inner office chamber already occupied by two other cardinals seated across from each other talking. As the guests entered the room, they were greeted by the warm, welcoming smile of their host, Cardinal Chiaros Riluciani.

Following introductions, and appreciative compliments on the detectives' hard work, Cardinal Leone took control of the meeting. The toppling of a financial titan like Giovanni Fedora was commendable, and necessary. However, the financial damage sustained by the Vatican for its dance with a devil named Fedora was something that the Vatican public relations office was having a hell of a time keeping contained. For the three detectives, this was the first they'd heard of it.

A dark, heaviness came over the hearts of the men in the room when Detective Cosimo Angelo, through a mixture of sadness, pain and anger explained that five Italian investigators had already been brutally murdered because of their efforts in the Fedora case. Fran shook his head as he learned that one of the murders was a contracted hit carried out by one of Luca Benedetto's thugs. He was certain that D.A. Christopherson and his federal counterpart would be more than happy to hand Benedetto and his minion over to Italian officials after they were finished with them.

While Fedora was busy with his own self preservation in New York. The Vatican still remained financially in trouble. The cardinals and detectives listened intently as Leone continued to explain. The financial troubles of the Vatican remain unrectified, as men like Marco Ansios and Bishop Jonas Krivis proceeded with a more covert version of their "business as usual."

The warm, welcoming countenance and body language of Cardinal Riluciani hardened at the mention of Krivis and Ansios. Flashbacks of his own personal interactions with them, and the aftermath of their crimes, drew his attention away from the discussion in the room for a moment. What he had learned in the last three years, through his own efforts, and information given to him by Cardinal Leone left a remarkable disdain for the three men, in otherwise warm, loving hearts. Their diabolical scheme resulted in his beloved Catholic Bank of Venice being sold from Vatican control to Ansios', and the profiting of a cool $6.5 million for Krivis from his partners in crime. It was now clearer than ever to the Venice patriarch that nothing had changed in how any of these men conducted themselves since he first learned of them three years ago. Forgiveness for the unrepentant would have to come from God, as Riluciani held fast to his own bitterness, unwilling quite yet to let it go.

Cardinal Leone continued to explain the ongoing fiscal impact of Fedora's failed empire, and how it related to Marco Ansios, Bishop Jonas Krivis, the Vatican and beyond. "The Vatican Bank to this day, still receives huge sums of money from Ansios just so he can use the church's bank to commit wide scale international fraud."

"What kind of fraud?" Questioned Cosimo.

"One recent example I found was when the Milan Stock Market crashed right after Fedora's Milan bank was shuttered."

"Oh?" Responded the detectives in unison.

"In its eleventh hour, Ansios' Banco Generali was saved by an investor owned by a pair of companies over in Liechtenstein. On paper, those companies are owned by the Vatican Bank. However, they are actually owned by Marco Ansios."

"Does Krivis and others in his bank know that Ansios is illegally propping up the market share value of his own bank Dante?" Questioned Riluciani.

"It's no secret around there, I can assure you. They also have a very elaborate shell game going that extends far beyond European countries all the way to Panama and the Bahamas."

"Good God!" Erupted Fran before catching himself. The cardinals in the room were unphased by the outburst that reflected their own feelings of disgust. "Why the hell would he even go to all that trouble?"

"I suppose he's hoping those shares eventually regain their value at some point so he can unload them, would be my best guess, Francis."

"So how do we stop all this mess, Dante?" Questioned Cardinal Wexford.

"Much has already been done thanks to the work of these detectives." The other men in the room issued a look of extreme dissatisfaction with that response, before Leone continued. "That said, there is still a lot that remains to be done if we are to rid the church and world of these vipers. Fedora's world may be lying in ruins, but he is still a very dangerous man, especially now that he has absolutely nothing to lose. Karosis and Ansios are only slightly less dangerous. Extreme caution and secrecy must continue as we proceed forward."

"I agree with you cardinal," responded Fran. "I feel that without complete stealth in our operations and communications, we not only risk the success of our work, but also endanger every single one of our lives."

Leone nodded, then continued, "Riluciani, Wexford and Hans, you three are far enough removed from Rome, would you three mind serving as communication conduits going forward?"

The three men confirmed their commitment to the assigned tasks.

"The most challenging of all of this is keeping tabs on Krivis and Ansios' activities within Vatican City walls. I will take that on. Cosimo, you keep an eye on Ansios and Banco Generali. Fran, you keep up what you've been doing on Fedora. Finally, everyone, with every fiber of your being, pray. Pray for guidance, and more importantly for all of our safety. Pray like you've never prayed before in your lives!"

After the meeting was adjourned, the wives of the three detectives rejoined their husbands. The assembled became acquainted over a delicious, yet simple lunch of veal, green beans, pasta and wine hosted by Cardinal Riluciani. Following lunch, Leone and Wexford remained briefly, before rushing off to their next destinations. The remaining distinguished guests were treated to a personal tour of St. Mark's Basilica by the patriarch of Venice himself.

With the heaviness of the trip's true purpose behind them, Fran and Peg appreciated the hospitality of Cosimo, his wife, and the patriarch. Peg took in the entirety of the experience with great awe and wonder. The pair couldn't help but become intoxicated by the romance of Italy as they flitted and flirted about like young lovers, falling for each other all over again. Fran was appreciative that the tours, adventures, and provisions would provide plenty of fodder to satisfy the inquiring minds of his nosy cohorts back at the precinct.

A few weeks following their collective "vacation," they returned to their normal routines. They also had a renewed motivation for their work. It was a welcomed side effect of a well deserved vacation. Fran's office phone drew his attention away from his paperwork.

"Detective Clavering..."

"Fran, it's Cosimo."

"Hey man, what's up?"

"My men were working a tip over here that you might find interesting."

Fran got up to close his office door. "What da ya got?"

"We just picked up a man named Rinaldo Manna and another layman who works in the Vatican Bank under the direction of Krivis."

"Nice work! I'm guessing that you didn't pick them up for anything related to Krivis' dirty deeds."

"I have no idea what you're talking about Fran, Cosimo teased. The Italian Finance Police picked up the Vatican Bank's Secretary Inspector Rinaldo Manna, arrested him and withdrew his passport. Oh, and it just so happens that his son works with Ansios over at Banco Generali. The son claims to know nothing about money speculation in the upper executive levels of Banco Generali."

"Of course he doesn't, how convenient..."

"Wait, it gets better...this inspector guy, Manna, not only works in money speculation in the Vatican, he also worked closely with Nico Novelli in Fedora's now failed Zürich bank."

"Oh really?"

"...and he's being blackmailed by Fedora."

"Now that is very interesting, and finally something I can work with from my end. What is the nature of the blackmail?"

"Apparently this guy is a seasoned gambler..."

"Just like Novelli."

"Exactly! Turns out he and Novelli are quite similar, and quite close."

"I assume you've already asked him if he's seen or heard from him lately."

"Yeah, we did. Nobody's seen or heard from him in months."

"Of course. So what's the nature of the blackmail Fedora has on him?"

"Fedora keeps him under his thumb with threats of going public with his illegal operations at the Zürich bank."

"Sounds similar to what he was doing to Novelli."

"Yep."

Cosimo shifted the course of the conversation away from Novelli. "Hey Fran, do you remember about six months ago when I told you about Ansios' deputy manager at Banco Generali committing suicide?"

"Was that the one that was found at the rail yard with a suicide note in his pocket to his wife saying the missing $35 million from Ansios' bank was because of him?"

"Yeah, that's the one."

"What about him?"

"Krivis' boy just squealed that he and the director of the Swiss bank forced him to write out that confession before they had him suicided."

"Oh shit...Did he say anything else about it?"

"Basically the dead man took the blame, while the men who were actually responsible for the losses were given the task of recovering them."

"That's really fucked up Cosimo."

"Yeah it is."

The line went quiet for a good thirty seconds before Fran spoke again with a hint of sympathy and anger in his tone. "You said your guys picked up another man working closely with Krivis?"

"Yes, the other guy was his administrative secretary. Finance Police froze his assets and removed his passport too. He is also being blackmailed by Mr. Fedora."

"At least Fedora is consistent..."

"We already got him connected to three cases of banking law violations and a case of fraudulent bankruptcy. He first claimed that no one in the Vatican knew of Fedora or his crimes."

"Bullshit!"

"Then he claimed they'd been duped by the devil."

"...again, bullshit!"

"He finally dropped the bullshit and became quite amused when we asked him if it was just Fedora and Novelli playing these speculation games."

"Oh?"

"Seems that it has been going on for sometime, all over Italy. He claims that average to smallish banks easily move 50 billion lire daily. The bigger institutions like Fedora's and Ansios' move hundreds and hundreds of billions. As far as he was concerned, all Italian banks in Italy should be investigated."

"So he knew all of this was common in Italian banking, and he himself was up to his eyeballs in all kinds of criminal shit, yet he expects us to believe that he didn't know what was going on in his very own bank? How stupid does this guy think we are Cosimo?"

With everything that was happening in Italian finance, Bishop Jonas Krivis suddenly had a very big problem. Nobody had seen hide nor hair of Nico Novelli for months. Giovanni Fedora was now *persona non grata* within the Vatican Curia, while being sequestered in New York fighting his own extradition. The latest blow came with the recent arrests of the Vatican Bank's Secretary Inspector and Administrative Secretary by Italian officials. It was crucial at that point, that Vatican, Inc. remain in the speculation game. Their only remaining option was Marco Ansios.

Of the five Vatican *uomini di fiducia*, only one "man of trust" remained. That man was Marco Ansios. Ansios, by now, was a very busy man. He was recently bestowed the decoration of "Knight of Labor," by the president of Italy for his service to the country's economy the year prior. He became the new paymaster for Gherado Fratello's P2 Masonic Lodge. Finally, he slipped into Giovanni Fedora's role as the Mafia's Italian laundry man.

As Fedora's failure got smaller and smaller in the rear view, authorities were pressed harder and harder to come up with solid figures quantifying losses, especially when it came to the Vatican Bank. Swiss officials estimated the figure to be around $250 million, while Krivis' claim of "not losing a penny,..." amounted to another $50 million or more, and Roman and Swiss banks controlled by the Vatican contributed another $35 million to the loss column. The financial hits suffered by the Vatican, just kept rolling in as the investigators continued their work.

In Italy, Cosimo's close friend, Arturo Bartolone had completed his audit and liquidation of Fedora's empire and was ready to issue his report to their "Attorney General." Fedora had purposely looted his banks and was absolutely corrupt to his core. Back in New York, Giovanni Fedora deployed his few remaining loyal allies outside the Mafia. Gherado Fratello and his team of lawyers worked tirelessly fighting his extradition. While they were busy with their mission, Fedora occupied some of his time by defending himself in an interview with journalists from *Business Week* and plotting his revenge against enemies both real and imagined.

CHAPTER 28

In an office study deep within the maze of rooms, hallways, and secret passages sat a man alone. A rare moment of complete solitude, with nothing but his thoughts. The seventy-seven year old man was extremely distraught, and depressed. In his lifetime he had weathered much that would challenge him on a very personal level. Two World Wars, Indo-China conflicts that included the Korean and Vietnam Wars. Other tragedies like famines, droughts, floods, earthquakes, and disease would add to the psychological and physical burdens that would test any man's faith in both God and his fellow man.

Being elected the Holy Father of the Roman Catholic Church was the ultimate dream of many young priests during the youthful days of their ordination. For Pope Michael VI, his once beautiful dream, in recent years, had become a nightmarish, living hell. The man was old and tired. The last thirteen years of his papacy robbed him of vibrancy, youth and much of his own faith.

Not that many years ago, he endured rumors running rampant through the Curia of a homosexual affair with his long time personal secretary. The public airing of such sensational transgressions of the flesh took on an illusive life of its own. Nothing halted or slowed the spread and mutations of the information. It would move quickly, then linger, then change a bit, then move again. It was amazing that the stories managed to remain contained within the physical fortress of Vatican City's walls. Such gossip certainly provided sustained, gainful employment for those in the Vatican's public relations office. Only those in Pope Michael VI's closest inner circle knew there was no meat on those bones.

The most visible spiritual leader in the world, now had in his hands a very different church than what he had inherited from his predecessor Pope Phillip XXIII. The infiltration of communist, Mafia and clandestine elements were becoming metastasized cancers all through Europe, but it was especially aggressive in Vatican City. His beloved church was being destroyed from within, and under his watch. Pope Michael felt alone, lost and afraid.

Most of his waking hours, he had an entourage swarming about him constantly. Feeding him nourishment, and information, and assisting him with options and actions. Many who served in his cabinet since his papacy began in 1962, were honorable and loyal. However, more than a few would stab him like they did Caesar and take advantage of him. His leadership style favored intellect and ego, over heart, faith and spirituality. The mental and spiritual challenges of his past were compounded material problems that now lay at his feet.

His best years were well behind him. It was too late for him, he knew that there wasn't much sand left in his hourglass. The tears began flowing uncontrollably from his eyes as he contemplated the failure of his papacy, catching the Holy Father up by surprise. Through excruciating arthritic pain, the old man fell gracelessly to the floor and crossed himself. With his gaze fixed on Christ's crucifix hanging on his wall, he prayed for mercy and repentance for the past that now haunts him. He prayed for help, guidance and strength. It was too late to save his own legacy as pope. Only God in his mercy and power could fix this mess. The future of the Catholic Church, at that moment, was passed from the earthly to the divine.

Pope Michael wiped the moisture from his eyes with a soft, linen handkerchief embroidered with the Holy Father's personal coat of arms. He wincing as he struggled to get back to his feet. As he braced himself against a heavy desk, his eyes caught sight of something protruding from a pile of neglected works and projects.. He reached for the document to pull it from the stack. *The Third Secret of Fátima*, the Holy Father read aloud to himself. The aged man thought it curious to find the document on his desk, certain that it had been retired to the secret archives of the Holy Office long ago. He had read through the words of the Holy Virgin Mother as transcribed by her faithful servant Sister Lucy many years ago, yet he failed to release them to the public as per the instructions. Personally, he was never one to give much credence to seers or their messages in the past.

The Holy Father's glance then fixated on the calendar hanging on the wall. Seven years had passed since he last presided over the annual procession to *Cova da Iria* and the anniversary of Portugal's national consecration to the Immaculate Heart of Mary in Fátima, Portugal. He suddenly felt it was very important for him to attend the festivities this year. He dispatched a messenger to inform Cardinal Chiaros Riluciani in Venice of his decision. It was always the Venice cardinal who always coordinated the annual pilgrimage with great grace, passion and heart.

Cardinal Riluciani was delighted with the news. The annual Fátima pilgrimage had become a victim of divine politics during the previous pope's reign. Pope Phillip XXIII, who was also a former patriarch of Venice before being elected pope by his peers, was more than familiar with the annual Fátima pilgrimage. He'd even witnessed miracles of grace and healing, right before his own eyes while on official duties on behalf of the Holy Father. The future Pope Phillip remained unmoved by anything he had observed in Fátima.

Pope Michael had never once displayed any desire to meet with Sister Lucy in all of his years. He clinged to his own personal disdain for the patriarch of Lisbon. The recognition of the Holy Messenger of the Blessed Virgin as a prophetess did not sit well with this pope. The Lisbon diocese was cautiously optimistic that the Holy Father's attendance this year meant that *The Third Secret of Fátima* would finally be made public as the Blessed Virgin Mother had instructed long ago.

Cardinal Riluciani never understood the apathetic attitudes of the current pope, and more so of his predecessor. The jubilee of the Apparitions was, in their minds, a tradition of duty, not an event of spiritual significance. Nonetheless, the cardinal from Venice set to a most cherished labor of love, taking great joy in the planning and coordinating of events related to the pilgrimage.

The pope had communicated directly with Cardinal Riluciani his heart's intent. His travel coordinator, however, seemed to be kept in the dark of the pontiff's wishes. The on again, off again plans quickly became a source of great frustration. There were frequent heated exchanges between Venice and Rome over the coming weeks leading up to the event.

Ten short days prior to the annual celebration, it was finally announced to the public that Pope Michael would indeed make an appearance at the jubilee. The announcement caught many in the religious affairs office up by surprise. They were expecting the customary Papal letter addressed to Portuguese bishops for them to read aloud to the gathered faithful. This year, the Holy Father wished to speak to those who had made the trek to Fátima directly.

It was made clear that this pilgrimage of the Holy Father would have him arriving by plane in the morning around 9 am. Mass will be celebrated, followed by a few words for those gathered with their hearts full of faith. A more personal meet and greet with as many as possible before embarking for their return trip to Rome that evening. The Holy Father, who was no fan of the dictator running the Catholic state of Spain, purposefully opted to avoid any kind of side trip to Lisbon that might be mistaken for recognition or support of the man by the public.

Multiple meetings and ceremonies that were to take place over the course of the multi-day celebration, were suddenly called off. While Cardinal Riluciani remained grateful that this year, Pope Michael would do more than his usual impersonal address on papal parchment. To say that Cardinal Riluciani was disappointed with the changes in plans, was an understatement. All of his weeks of effort, energy and planning, were reduced to a quick round trip.

The morning of the jubilee, Cardinal Riluciani spotted the pope's traveling entourage as soon as they arrived. As they approached, from a considerable distance, the first person of the detail the cardinal recognized was the pope's big, hulking personal bodyguard. The six foot six, 220 pound man was hard to miss. Riluciani instantly became nauseous at the sight of him. Walking in front of the detail, clearing the way for the approaching pontiff was none other than Bishop Jonas Krivis.

The cardinal would not let his personal feelings towards the Holy Father's "personal travel companion" taint his heart nor the purpose for their visit to Portugal. Pope Michael had formally insisted on Sister Lucy be there during his visit. Sister Lucy, the seer, was a most uncomplicated, humble peasant woman. The gathered crowd of well over a million people, in all of their faith and poverty caught the visiting pontiff off guard. They had not come to see him, they had come to see her. He could not understand what possessed people to want to see such a simple girl.

The lessons of Fátima intended for the world included prayer and penance as the ultimate source of salvation from the ills of the modern world. The global devotion to the Most Blessed Immaculate Heart and the honor, love and praise of His Most Holy Mother was not to be restricted to just Fátima or Portugal. As the Holy Father looked across the sea of gathered people, humanity appeared united in love, devotion and praise. Pope Michael elected to ignore the prescribed intended message. For he personally felt that the push for global devotion of the Most Blessed Immaculate Heart bordered on the fanatical and was outside the doctrine and theology long established by the Catholic Church. The honor, love and praise of His Most Holy Mother, would be reduced to just "prayer and penance."

Following Communion and Mass, upon a raised platform before the Basilica, Sister Lucy became overwhelmed with devotion upon seeing Pope Michael VI before her. The Holy Father held out his arms to welcome her closer. Sister Lucy fell to the ground before his feet. She felt his hand gently rest on her head, and her apprehension vanished.

"Holy Father, I have urgent messages to deliver to you from Heaven. I must speak to you alone, in private." Sister Lucy repeated the request several times as the pope continued to smile and wave at the crowd, dismissing her words.

Through camera flash pops and cheers from adoring attendees, he responded trying not to break his forced smile for the photo opportunity. "This is not the time child. Whatever you feel you need to relay to me, please communicate through your bishop. He is a most obedient servant who has my complete trust."

A few feet away on the elevated stage, observing the exchange between Pope Michael and Sister Lucy sat Cardinal Chiaros Riluciani. He would have expected such coldness from the late Pope Philip XXIII, but never once did he anticipate this from the current pope. The cardinal became more and more incensed, as he watched Pope Michael wave off the "peasant girl" so rudely. In the cardinal's mind, this was not how a true messenger of heaven should be treated. Especially by the earthly leader of the Roman Catholic Church!

Cardinal sat with his anger for the remainder of his time in Fátima. For all of his energy and efforts in planning, the Fátima pilgrims would have been better served if the pope had just remained in Rome instead. Upon his return to Venice the events, exchanges and people of Fátima soon found a more healthy, creative vent. The humble heart of the cardinal with the characteristic warm smile was moved to sermon on the virtues and strengths of those written off by society as meek and powerless. Christ didn't move about in an open-topped Rolls Royce like the Holy Father did on his way to Fátima from the airport, he made his way on the back of a donkey. Christ's social circles were not those who stroked his ego. It was societal outcasts, the poor, the sick, the thieves and the prostitutes that gave his message legs that would reach hearts and minds. It was the down and out that helped him build his church, not the pharaohs and kings.

Back in Rome, the aging pope would continue to struggle with his own personal spiritual crisis. The coming months would fail to bring correction or stability for the pontiff. A noticeable increase in personal alone time was used to execute what little he could to hopefully save the future church from complete ruin. During his travels to Italy's northern regions, he would frequent the patriarch of Venice. In a packed St Mark's square the Holy Father sat quietly listening to the heartfelt sermons of Cardinal Riluciani. The message of humility and grace moved the pontiff deeply. He never once associated the message with his own recent pilgrimage to Fátima.

CHAPTER 29

In Italy, the press was not holding back their true feelings for Giovanni Fedora. He had endured bad press in the past. It was the price one must pay for being the most successful financier in the world. However, this time around, this assault was different. It hit hard and stung longer than it ever had before. This time it was personal, he no longer had his financial empire to hold him up or shield him. His might had been reduced to rubble in a matter of months. He had never once in his fifty five years on earth ever found himself in this type of situation. This was new, different, and most of all he didn't like it.

There were a few things he felt he needed to get off of his chest. For Fedora, a little self defense was in order. He sat for an interview with a reporter of one of the oldest newspapers in all of Italy. The Turin rag that began in the late 1860s was well respected for its journalistic integrity, and was well read beyond regional or country borders. At one point in the interview, Fedora changed the course of the conversation, from his past to his potential future. He hinted that maybe it was time to hire a ghostwriter to help him publish a tell-all book about the last ten years of Italian shame. Knowing the public's voracious appetite for names and the dirty laundry that came with it, it would be an instant bestseller flying off the shelves, all over Italy in no time. He already had a growing supply of enemies. A project like this, however, could very well get him killed too. Whether it was a teaser of a suggestion or not, only time would tell.

In New York, the press and the American legal system was still lagging far behind their Italian counterparts. A year had passed since the cracks in Lincoln National Bank began to show, at least to the ignorant outside world. The public was still fixated and growing more and more frustrated with the authorities' slow-walk of prosecutions connected to Fedora's American banking failure. *The New York Times* held the public on a string, stoking the public's outrage through the timely publication of the New York City Mayor smiling and shaking hands with Giovanni Fedora somewhere in Italy. The pictures were not from anything recent, but they certainly sparked an uptick in the number of papers sold. It was clear to their audience that George Orwell was right when he wrote *Animal Farm*... "All animals are equal, but some animals are more equal than others." The application of extradition laws, or rather the lack of enforcement of said laws, served to illustrate the point perfectly. Fedora's legal team was still fighting his extradition tooth and nail while he continued to issue statements, sit for interviews and rub elbows with global jet setters.

The public sarcastically applauded the long-awaited announcement that indictments were finally being made in the Lincoln National Bank failure case. The first indictment was a hefty thirty-two pages containing eighty-seven counts. Everything from perjury to wire fraud in foreign-exchange deals were included in the document. The case was huge. It would take months as teams of lawyers representing insurance companies, accountants, and others lined up on a mission to try and recoup some of their clients' losses. A case this big would certainly test the capacity and effectiveness of the US legal system in the coming months or even years.

The first verdict came from the US Attorney's Office of New York. They found Conner Gilmore, the man hired by Fedora to spite Novelli, culpable of fraud during his tenure at Lincoln. Nico Novelli, however, was still nowhere to be found. His indictment in conjunction with several other foreign-exchange traders, would not wait for him to resurface. Charges of falsification of documents, misapplication of funds, credits that were in excess of $30 million were filed. Then came more charges of defrauding the FDIC, the Board of Governors of the Federal Reserve, the Comptroller of Currency and more.

Giovanni Fedora hired his own team of legal representatives for the futile purpose of salvaging whatever they could from wreckage of the Fedora financial empire in Italy. In the US, a public relations man was also hired. He was convinced that it was a good time to send Fedora on a multi-state lecture tour for students attending universities.. The Italian financier was more than happy to speak, and share his financial knowledge with the next generation of bankers and businessmen about morals and corruption. The irony of him lecturing on said topics was laughable while his former senior executives from his failed New York bank were being arrested and charged back in New York City.

Conner Gilmore agreed to a plea deal. In exchange for leniency on his own guilty plea, he would provide evidence for the case against Fedora. Other foreign-exchange traders followed his lead. The *New York Times* published a candid interview with Giovanni Fedora, the man at Franklin National Bank's helm prior to and during its crash. "They want to blame me for all of this. They want to put me in prison, and keep me there for twenty years or more. I get these calls from voices I don't even recognize. They tell me suicide is my best option."

The Public Minister of Milan, who had initiated Fedora's extradition order, was growing restless. Ten months had already passed since the order was issued. There was still no estimate of when Giovanni Fedora would be returned to Italian soil. A meeting was requested with representatives from the US Department of Justice. They would accept no more delays in Fedora's extradition.

Elsewhere in Italy's economy, foreign-exchange speculation continued undeterred by the trials and tribulations of Giovanni Fedora. Marco Ansios' efforts to distance himself from the dark shadows of his mentor were working well. His scheme to stabilize Banco

Generali stock values in concert with the Vatican Bank was also starting to show dividends. His banking associates were impressed enough with his leadership that by the middle of November 1975, the Banco Generali Board Chairman was elected president of his bank. Little did they know at the time, their CEO, Marco Ansios was being blackmailed by his close associate Mr. Giovanni Fedora.

The Vatican declared publicly that they were experiencing a "serious budget deficit." A week into the new year, an Italian bishops' Conference was held in Rome. Numerous cardinals gathered from around the world for the event, including Leone, Wexford and Riluciani. The key topic of polite open conversation was the impact of the current Italian economic crisis on the public. In private, the dialogue was far more candid. The role Bishop Jonas Krivis and his close friend Fedora played in the current economic disaster could not be overlooked any longer. The Vatican was by no means an innocent victim or bystander in its current economic disaster. Many in attendance felt that Pope Michael VI should have removed Krivis from the Vatican Bank years ago when Fedora's financial troubles were just starting to surface. Here they were two years later with an even bigger mess, and Krivis still maintained his position as Vatican Bank president. The Italian press was now reporting over $100 million in Vatican losses thanks to their close relationship with Mr. Fedora. They would eventually admit to some losses as a result of Fedora's crashing empire, but never anything close to $100 million.

With the arrival of spring, came more bad news from Italy for Fedora.. New management officials from Fedora's former holding company issued a daunting report. Up until that point, the former owner, Fedora, was completely oblivious that Nico Novelli and his wife had repeatedly plundered his Swiss accounts. It began during the days when Novelli served as the director of Fedora's Zürich bank. By the end of 1974, Novelli had removed over $8.44 million from Fedora. Funds continued to flow into the Novelli's accounts from 1975 up until their disappearance. That blow hit Fedora hard. He'd always known that Novelli was a gambling addict, but never once did he peg him for a thief.

338

On the morning of September 8, 1976 Italian authorities demanded the arrest of Mr. Giovanni Fedora on a warrant for his extradition. He was booked and taken to the federal courthouse in Manhattan. With his attorneys in tow, he protested profusely. It only took the "competent and efficient" US Justice System two years to actually arrest him on what his legal team called "false charges' ' brought against him by the Italian courts. Fedora and his team of lawyers publicly declared that there was absolutely zero validity to the charges. Swearing that his net worth at that point in time amounted to $800,000, a mere fraction of what it once was. The judge moved the hearing to a date in December, then adjourned the court for recess, and the Italian fugitive was taken into custody. The following day Mr. Fedora posted the $3 million bail and was released on his own recognizance.

Sixteen days following the arrest of Mr. Fedora, his sometime business partner and employee, Nico Novelli surfaced in Venezuela. Acting under the direction of the US Department of Justice, he was being held in a jail cell until United States authorities could come to retrieve him. Detectives Francis Clavering and Lance Erickson volunteered for the task of bringing him back to US soil. Detective Clavering felt horrible several months back when Detective Cosimo Angelo called, asking him to arrest one of their key informants. That horrible feeling in the pit of his stomach was now gone. Now Clavering had to keep the rage deep within him from overriding his logical head and physical body. There was nothing he hated more than liars.

In the coming weeks, Novelli's Venezuelan lawyer would be in contact with his American counterpart in New York. The American man was the son of a well known, retired judge. The judge and Fedora had a common enthusiasm for the women with the beautiful ankles, blood red painted lips and evenings filled with laughter and fun that were never meant to last. It was also known in some certain circles that the judge was on the take and was a good friend to have if one was a mobster of sorts, and in trouble with the New York justice system.

For the son of this judge, the apple didn't fall too far from the tree. Thrilled that his boy was following in his footsteps. This lawyer was the judge's pride and joy. The lawyers of Venezuela and New York exchanged numerous conversations on behalf of their shared client. Things were going well, until the South American lawyer suddenly became deeply concerned. The credit of the company that Novelli shared with him was now on the verge of collapsing because of his partner's recent arrest. A loan of $700,000 worth of bolivars was made. The Venezuelan man took the money, mortgaged Novelli's house right from under him, and vanished, never to be seen again.

CHAPTER 30

Detectives Clavering and Erickson maintained their surveillance of the disgraced Italian financier. While Fedora was no longer being held in a jail cell, he most certainly was being imprisoned by the confines of the Big Apple's city limits. These newly imposed travel restrictions absolutely cramped his style. Suddenly, his "friends" were no longer as prestigious as they once were. Many of his former associates were suddenly nowhere to be found. Those who still owed him money were in hiding while the rest were running as far away from him as possible. The only people who seemed to remain steadfast by his side were mobsters from the local syndicate, and men like Gherado Fratello.

The two detectives saw a noticeable uptick in the frequency of visits and calls from Gherado Fratello and a new P2 sidekick. This "new acquaintance" seemed very knowledgeable about Italian Military Intelligence. He also seemed to have a great deal of information and impressive connections to people deep inside the Vatican. Lance would dutifully follow orders and ignore those Vatican details. His partner, on the other hand, quietly passed the information along to "other interested parties."

In the past, there were all sorts of rumors that Fedora had worked with several families in the Mafia's New York scene. His most significant ties to the mob were through the Lanscano crime family. Another guest whose frequency of visits had a very noticeable uptick was a thirty-six year old Mafia *caporegime*. He was third in line with the most powerful family in all of America. Giovanni Fedora may have been weakened, but he was never to be underestimated or counted out. He was still a very powerful man. He was still a very dangerous man.

FBI Agent Lance Erikson came running down the hall into Detective Clavering's office. "Fran, you are never going to believe what I just found!"

Fran took the documents from his partner's hands and quickly scanned them over quickly. Fran's gaze returned to Lance. "Fedora is one of four men involved in illicit drug trafficking between Italy, US, and Europe? And DC has known about all of this since Christ was a corporal? What fuckery is this Lance?"

"Keep in mind Fran that none of this has yet to be completely verified yet."

"Clearly you are satisfied enough with its validity to come running in here with it, Lance."

The FBI agent was caught a bit off guard with Fran's snarky remark. "What the hell is that supposed to mean Fran?"

Fran looked at the dates on the documents. "They've had this shit for a long time. Don't you even come running in here with this shit, then immediately start making excuses for those fuck ups in DC! Not after all that bullshit they pulled on the Vatican trip and that cover-up shit involving that Treasury clown. That shit still pisses me off!"

"I'm not going to make excuses for a single one of them, Fran. I'm just saying no one in DC will confirm that they have any hard evidence."

"Please tell me you're not buying that shit, Lance."

Lance looked away from Fran and softened his tone. "No, I'm not."

"You honestly think this is something new for Fedora? Or the Feds? Come on Lance, you're smarter than that!"

Following a more thorough review of the information, it was clear to both men that the US Intelligence Community had had intimate knowledge of all of Fedora's activities for a very long time. His involvement in numerous serious crimes in both Italy and the US were well documented in the papers Lance presented to Fran. It appeared that the rumors were true, he did have a very well established relationship with every single big name crime family operating out of New York City. It was also clear that he was absolutely involved in their major international drug trafficking operations.

The FBI and CIA knew it, and yet chose to ignore every single bit of the incriminating dirt they had collected on Fedora from the early '60s to the present. Clearly the Kennedy, Johnson, Nixon, nor Ford administrations were not interested in doing a damn thing about any of it. It was highly unlikely that the newly elected Carter Administration would do anything different. The best that the two detectives could come up with was that the Mafia, working with Fedora, would somehow, some way, keep Italy from the grips of communism. It was a most laughable excuse at best.

In Italy, Cosimo and Cardinal Leone continued to work together, covertly. Between the two of them, it was much easier to keep tabs on Marco Ansios and Bishop Jonas Krivis. It didn't take them long to discover that Ansios was in a round-about way selling himself highly overpriced shares of his bank. It was an insane scheme designed to increase Banco Generali's market worth, at least in the public's eyes. What he was actually doing was stealing 7.7 billion in lire and kicking back some of that money to the Vatican Bank. What appeared to be a $78,000 profit windfall for the Vatican Bank, was actually a $900,000 payment by Ansios to Krivis for the privilege of using the Vatican Bank's name and facilities. Not all of that payment made its way into the Vatican Bank's coffers. When Banco Generali's market share values artificially went up, he'd sell them off to one of his business rivals in Milan and pocket a cool $37 million for his efforts. This criminal dance happened over and over and over again, while Italian tax authorities and collectors were purposefully kept in the dark.

Bishop Jonas Krivis knew exactly what was going on. He was being paid handsomely to willfully approve every part of the operation. It was now clear that the Milanese Banker had assumed the responsibility of Vatican Finances in the wake of Giovanni Fedora's fall from grace and power. Marco Ansios was now secretly serving as both the pope's CFO, and the Italian Mafia's primary banker and laundry man.

Despite the efforts of his lawyers, his mafia friends and men like Gherado Fratello, the situation in Italy for Giovanni Fedora was not getting any better. A close personal friend of Detective Cosimo Angelo named Arturo Bartolone had been hard at work for the last six months, under the direction of the Italian Treasury Minister and the director of the Bank of Italy. Bartolone was meticulous as he went about the nightmarish job of teasing apart the mess of Fedora's financial affairs. He was also very cautious with whom he spoke about his findings. What he had uncovered over the many months of his investigation, convinced him that Fedora's banking activities absolutely showed criminal intent. The bankruptcy of his Milan bank was one of numerous examples. The bank's failure was not the result of any kind of bad business practices. Fedora and his management team had purposefully created a circumstance ripe for bankruptcy. The plundering started in 1974, possibly earlier. Bartolone's preliminary findings not only made it to the eyes and ears of his bosses, but also to his closest confidant on the Italian police force.

A black rotary phone rang in an office of a bustling New York precinct. "Clavering..."

"Hey Fran, it's Cosimo."

The detective got up and closed his office door, while continuing his conversation. "Cosimo, my man, what's new where you are?"

The Italian detective filled Fran in on the latest activities of Marco Ansios and Jonas Krivis.

"Wow, that's great work you guys are doing over there...keep it up."

Fran could hear concern in the Italian's voice. "Hey Fran, do you remember me telling you about my good friend Arturo Bartolone awhile back?"

"Is that the guy going through Fedora's stuff over there?"

"Yeah, that's the one."

"What about him?"

"Well I just had lunch with him. You should see the stuff he's digging up..." Cosimo filled him in on the details of Fedora's criminally fraudulent bankruptcy.

"That's amazing, I can't wait to read his reports. Arturo is a very bright and courageous man,..."

"Clearly, but he's also not stupid Fran. He knows the danger that comes with the work he is doing right now. He will do what he was assigned to do with the utmost integrity, but he's scared."

"Is that what he told you?"

"Mmmm, not exactly, not in those words...He just said that no matter what happens, he'll pay a high price for taking this job. I mean he knew that before he took the job, of course. He wasn't complaining. It was more like an understanding of the risks involved in his current work. He's not doing this for his own valor Fran, this one is for Italy. However, he feels like he is also making a lot of enemies for himself."

"Huh, did someone threaten him, or something?"

"Not from what he's told me so far...at least not directly anyway. I'm certain he would have told me if he did. He's done a hell of a job making sense of Fedora's purposeful chaos over here. You should see all the shit he's already uncovered. Everything from the parking of shares, buy-backs, and a lot of very perplexing transfers through a multitude of companies both legitimate and carefully disguised shell companies."

"That Fedora fuck sure has some nerve."

"What do you mean by that?"

"While he's been over there doing all of that shit, he's been over here lecturing aspiring young American businessmen and filling their heads with his version of the capitalistic dream. So why is Arturo coming at you with 'No matter what happens...' now?"

"Well he was approached recently by a Roman lawyer who had a very complicated offer to purchase Fedora's Milan bank out of bankruptcy. The deal was quite tempting. Even Italian banking authorities gave him their stamp of approval for him to buy it."

"So did he take it?"

"Hell no! The entire proposal had all the hallmarks of Fedora's past work. Arturo asked me to do a little digging into this lawyer guy."

"And..."

"It turns out, he was working for Fedora."

"Of course he was..."

"I worry about him, Fran. You know, Arturo is the Godfather of my children."

"I was not aware of that Cosimo. Is there anything specifically that has you worried?"

"Well he told me that the Prime Minister's office is putting a lot of pressure on the central bank over here to cover Fedora's debts."

"Isn't that the same bank and director that tasked Arturo to do the audit and liquidation in the first place?"

"Yes,...and after that lawyer guy didn't get anywhere with his proposal to Arturo, Fedora's team of lawyers came at him with allegations of embezzlement."

"...and..."

"Neither man has let the pressure and smears interfere with their work."

"Good."

"But my gut is still worried for his safety, Fran. He told me he keeps coming across references to a group called 'The 500.' I don't suppose you've come across that in any of your work?"

"I'm not sure, but please tell me more."

"It seems to be a list of black market clients. They seem to be very well connected exporters, if you will, who were moving currency out of Italy illegally. Fedora seems to have been using the Vatican Bank to fulfill some of that work for his clients."

"Interesting. Do we know who's on this list?"

"Arturo is having a hell of a time finding any actual names of individuals or companies. His best educated guess is that there are a lot of respectable public institutions on that list. Their funds flowed through Fedora's hands, and then straight back into the pockets of some of the directors of the same companies."

"So he knows what they are doing, but he doesn't know who they are yet? How the hell does that even happen?"

"Like I said he doesn't have the actual list, but he has made up his own list of about eighty names so far...Two of them were that Rinaldo Manna guy and the other secretary working with Krivis that we picked up a while back thanks to our work with 'Dolf.'" The New York detective immediately recognized Cardinal Leone's secret alias, as Cosimo continued. "Fran, he tells me that he has irrefutable evidence of Vatican Bank complicity in so many of Fedora's crimes."

"I completely understand your concern, all I can do is tell both of you to tread lightly and keep your heads on a swivel."

In both Italy and New York, Giovanni Fedora had exhausted his delay options. On June 25, 1977, the Italian authorities sentenced him *in absentia* to 3.5 years in prison on charges connected to the failure of the Milan bank. There were more black clouds looming on Fedora's horizon. That very same week, yet another former Lincoln National Bank senior official was indicted and agreed to a plea deal. Fedora couldn't shake the US Federal Grand Jury any longer as their investigation was now focused on him and his violations and involvement in the New York bank's collapse.

He knew he was losing this battle. It was time to tap into his "important connection" with Fratello, and his various puppets. One particularly helpful man was the president of the Roman division of the Italian Supreme Court. He submitted an affidavit on Fedora's behalf expressing great concern. His arguments were that if Fedora was to be returned to Italian soil, communism would take over the country, he would never get a fair trial, and it would most likely result in the untimely demise of Mr. Fedora. The only people who felt sorry for the failed banker were himself, his family and maybe the few men who still seemed to have his back.

At this point, Fedora was extremely dejected. He was desperate for both support and money. He decided to exercise a perverted version of the "free enterprise system" that was currently popular and effective in a democratic Italy. A massive blackmail smear campaign against Banco Generali's president Marco Ansios was initiated. Pamphlets and posters flooded the city of Milan with daunting accusations. Rumors of his former protégé's involvement in fraud, exporting of currency, falsifying of accounts, embezzlement and tax evasion were suddenly making the rounds. The next round of the smear campaign would reveal information about his Swiss bank accounts, and details of his illicit dealings with various Mafia connections.

Marco Ansios was now in the worst shape he'd been in in months. Fedora's blackmail campaign resulted in many sleepless nights and the formation of dark circles under his eyes. The chronically nervous man was now on the verge of a complete nervous breakdown. The public airing of his dirty laundry went far beyond the collection of monies owed. This was a personal vindictive assault. This was more like restitution in Fedora's greatest hour of need. Marco Ansios was now willing to do whatever was necessary to make all of the bad press stop!

Once again, he reached deeply into the pockets of his clients. $500,000 was swiftly moved from their accounts and into one owned by Giovanni Fedora. The payoff signaled the termination of Fedora's blackmail blitz, at least for now. The posters and publicity stopped instantly. Fedora was now pissed. The overly zealous efforts of the man Fedora hired to smear Ansios had unintended consequences for both of them. He only wanted to steal from his golden goose, not kill the damn thing.

The information circulating had now caught the attention of investigators with the Bank of Italy in Milan. The stonewalling director put in place by Fratello and his men had finally been removed by officials from the investigative branch of the Bank of Italy. Their next move was to use information revealed from Fedora's smear campaign to begin looking deeper into Banco Generali's operations. Every single exposed crime warranted a full preliminary investigation.

To the dismay of Marco Ansios, the chief investigator assigned to the case was an honorable and incorruptible man. The man had also been watching Ansios and his bank for years. These newly exposed details thanks to Fedora, were exactly what was needed to push much of their exhausted efforts. A few weeks after the smear campaign was halted, the corporate headquarters of Banco Generali was raided and numerous boxes of documents and records were seized.

The information from the smear campaign and news of the subsequent raid spread quickly through the financial community, globally. The value of Banco Generali's shares tanked instantly in response. Suddenly Fedora's blackmail and smear campaign were the least of Ansios' concerns. He was now in serious trouble. In a desperate attempt to plug the holes developing in his sinking ship, Ansios would divert more and more money in order to halt the collapse of his bank. The money came from a variety of bank branches in South America or from companies in Canada, Belgium and the United States.

The other major concern resulting from Fedora's poorly thought out scheme was the potential exposure of a Milan company called Financial and Commerce Services. It was a true Achilles' Heel for not just Ansios, but Fedora too. If these hot to trot inspectors ever dove into the particulars of that company, Banco Generali would collapse completely, Ansios would be thrown in jail, and Giovanni Fedora's extradition fight would be over and done.

Ansios' characteristic nervousness shifted to a constant state of agitation. He went about his day with an extremely short fuse. Back in New York, Fedora had stopped gloating about his extortion of Marco Ansios. The only hope for either man was sitting in the president's chair in the Vatican Bank.

Inspectors from the Bank of Italy hauled in the general manager of Banco Generali in for questioning. When they asked him who owned Financial and Commerce Services of Milan, his point blank response was the Vatican Bank. The inspectors took the information at face value, as they continued to dig deeper into Banco Generali's operations. They were particularly interested in the purchases, transfers, buybacks and parking of shares.

Ansios' one saving grace was that the inspector's jurisdiction stopped at the Italian border. The ongoing activities at his Luxembourg holding company and the millions of dollars borrowed through European markets were quickly funneled through banks owned by Bishop Krivis, and Ansios in Nassau and Manauga, Nicaragua. These banks would then issue unsecured loans worth millions to small Panamanian shell companies where and whenever they could. It was these foreign transactions that could potentially expose everything.

The investigators quickly became more and more frustrating as their access to information was denied and stalled. Marco Ansios steadfastly refused to breach the confidentiality of foreign collaborators and their transactions. His efforts worked for a little while, but eventually failed as their probe deepened. Inspectors soon learned that Financial and Commerce Services of Milan was co-founded by men on the board of a Vatican owned bank back in November of '71. Now one of those men was the managing director of Ansios' Catholic Bank of Venice. Financial and Commerce Services of Milan had Marco Ansios' fingerprints all over it. A little more digging revealed that it wasn't the Vatican Bank that owned the Milan company, but in fact Banco Generali.

Francis reached his hand towards the obnoxious sound coming from the bed stand next to his head. The clock next to the phone read 2:23 AM. "Hello." Answered the detective in a groggy tone full of sleep.

"Fran, it's Cardinal Wexford."

The detective still wasn't quite awake yet. "Who?"

"Cardinal Wexford."

The name suddenly registered in his brain, bringing him instantly to a fully awakened state. He detected concern in the caller's voice. "Cardinal Wexford? What's wrong?"

"I'm sorry to call you at this hour, but I just had to tell you, Cardinal Leone has been removed as Under Secretary of State and reassigned to another parish far away from the Vatican City... effective immediately."

CHAPTER 31

Cardinal Riluciani was a man who always firmly believed that nothing ever happened by chance. Everything was a purposeful part of God's master plan. The approval and opinions of us mortals was not required. In the early days of January, Cardinal Riluciani found himself sipping his tea as he reread the long address delivered to the faithful pilgrims of Fátima by one of his predecessors. The man who had penned those words would, in the two years that followed, go on to be elected Pope Phillip XXIII. The content of the address was clearly from a time when the former patriarch still had a great passion in his soul for the Fátima traditions.

Riluciani was deeply moved and inspired by the words of his late predecessor. As a large congregation gathered for the annual Feast of the Epiphany, men, women and children would flood Saint Mark's Basilica in Venice. It was on this occasion that they bore witness to the inspired words of his address. Their humble, yet smart, well read patriarch, was a most thoughtful and gifted orator. The words he chose to describe the pulsating sun as it set below the horizon during the miraculous events of 1916 and 1917 made many experience a renewed closeness to the Blessed Virgin and the Holy Spirit. Some even felt as if they had experienced the phenomenal events first hand through his carefully chosen words.

The Venice patriarch followed the lessons of the Fátima prophecies over the years. For the topic of penance was something near and dear to his own soul. Such a simplistic command from God himself via numerous pages of his written word. "It is an unwise endeavor to allow ourselves to be seduced by the whims and follies of new world customs and propaganda. They fill the heads of the materialistic with glorified dreams of their version of a 'well lived life.' A life full of gluttony, vanity, greed and lust. Their ways of fun and pleasure fill your days, steal your time and leave your soul tremendously empty and unfulfilled." It was the cardinal's opinion that the most endearing message received from the three messengers of Fátima was, "God does not promise that you will be happy in this world, but in the next one."

As we walk through our days, we are confronted with challenges of spirit and church. We must remain steadfast in our faith and our devotion to both Christ and the Blessed Virgin. It takes more than a quick periodical renewal of our faith on a certain day of the week, or a special occasion or tradition scattered throughout the year to sharpen, strengthen and test our spiritual weapons. The armor of God is necessary in our daily battles to defend the Catholic Church, and more importantly defend our own faith and salvation from the temptations of sin in our daily lives.

Since the days of the previous patriarch, Venice had always shared great reverence, tradition and connection with the faithful citizens of Fátima, Portugal. As the spring time tradition of 1977 approached, the faithful pilgrims of Fátima were filled with an even greater sense of anticipation. This year's gathering would commemorate the sixtieth anniversary of the miraculous apparitions.

This year's festivities, however, came and went with nary a mention from Pope Michael VI or anyone else in Vatican City. The Roman press seemed particularly harsh in their criticism of the church's nonexistent fervor for the event this year, adding that "... the Roman Catholic Church suppresses conversations about the one remaining secret of Fátima that still remains hidden from the people. Here this mystery persists long after it was supposed to have been revealed. What does it contain? Why has the church actively and willfully ignored the instruction of the Blessed Holy Mother, and heaven itself?"

Cardinal Chiaros Riluciani did not concern himself with the opinions and actions of Rome. He did not wish to participate in the cold display of his church's leadership. He made his own itinerary and arrangements for the momentous anniversary. Following his own personal traditions which closely aligned with those of his region. He was more than thrilled that this year's pilgrimage would be without the disastrously embarrassing pomp and circumstance of the prior year. The celebrations of the sixtieth anniversary continued long past the traditional end in years past. Cardinal Riluciani would make several more journeys to Fátima as the year progressed.

In the early part of July, he phoned a good friend of many years, who now lived in Fátima. The Marquess, since their initial acquaintance, had married into the high aristocracy of Portuguese society. He was hoping that she wouldn't mind making the arrangements for his upcoming visit. The Marquess was extremely humbled by the request. "I am not suited nor qualified for such a task, Your Eminence. I think it is better to make such arrangements through the Vatican." The cardinal instilled his own confidence in his beloved friend. Insisting that she was beyond qualified, and was the perfect woman for the job. Then his characteristically warm demeanor quickly turned jaded. "Besides, I wish for no business with Rome, spirituality or otherwise. I have come to learn that the Devil has taken up residence in the Vatican." Many were caught off guard by such an outburst from the "smiling patriarch." They were completely unaware of the infiltration of the Milanese mafia and the financial skulduggery that violently assaulted and pillaged the sanctity of Vatican City.

The visit was quick, yet genuine and heartfelt. While there, he preached of the beauty, the power and the mystery that comes from meditation of the Rosary. "It is through the Immaculate Heart of Mary that we find mercy for those stricken with afflictions of the mind, body, and soul. It is through the teachings of her son that we learn to summon the strength necessary to face situations that challenge us spiritually. Like Jesus in the Garden of Gethsemane, through his own nausea and anguish in knowing the horrors of what was to come, of what must be done, he knew the Heavenly Father would give him the strength needed in his hour of doubt and temptation. It was through Our Heavenly Father that Jesus found his courage, his strength. As it is said in the book of Luke 22:24 KJV 'Not my will but Thine be done.'"

Following the celebration of Mass, the Mother Prioress sent word to the visiting cardinal that Sister Lucy wished desperately to speak with him. The request caught the humble patriarch by surprise. Through a beaming smile, he responded that he'd be honored to exchange salutations with her. It was as if the Blessed Mother Mary herself had a hand in arranging the meeting between her messenger and her servant. The smiling patriarch in all of his humility and modesty would have never dreamed of requesting a conversation with someone so revered as Sister Lucy.

The two parties had never met, formally. They were, however, familiar enough with one another through their mutual acquaintance, the Marquess. The cardinal dismissed his own personal secretary Father Vincenzo Mancini prior to entering the meeting. "Please wait for my return in the lobby, this should only take a few moments."

Sister Lucy smiled with great reverence for the patriarch as he entered the room. "Holy Father, it is good to finally meet you after all these years."

The patriarch's cheeks instantly reddened. It had taken him a considerable time to get used to being called "Eminence" when he became a cardinal. Being addressed as "Holy Father" was just far beyond his humble nature. He gently corrected her with an unpretentious blush. The Marquess lingered for a moment unaware that the patriarch was fluent in Portuguese. She then quietly slipped away when the conversation became too personal in nature for her ears.

Two hours later, Cardinal Riluciani finally emerged from his meeting with Sister Lucy. Father Mancini had vacated his post after waiting for him in the lobby for over thirty minutes despite the directions of his patriarch. When Riluciani rejoined his entourage for a prearranged dinner, he was very late. He apologized for his tardiness, in a very withdrawn tone. He remained distant, not wishing to disclose any of the conversation he had shared with Sister Lucy. His face was ashen, and full of emotion. What little he ate was consumed quickly, void of conversation. His trademark smile felt forced. He looked like a man in some sort of emotional shock.

Father Mancini reminded his charge of a brief talk that was prearranged by one of the guests that had journeyed to Fátima with his group from Venice. "I'm sorry, I am unable to attend to that obligation at this time. It will have to wait until we return home. I'm sorry, I must return to Fátima, one more time, I must speak with the Madonna. Sister Lucy's words have left me feeling..." His voice went silent, failing to complete his sentence. After a moment, his gaze returned to his secretary, "Fátima will remain close to my heart for the rest of my days."

Upon leaving the eatery, on his way to Lisbon to catch his return flight to Venice, Cardinal Riluciani insisted on stopping in Fátima one more time. The normally warm, welcoming patriarch seemed oddly distraught. His attempts to hide his agitation were unconvincing as he purposefully avoided contact with anyone other than his escort, Father Mancini. The two men entered the chapel to recite the Rosary, then proceeded on their journey back to Venice.

Every morning at 5:00 AM, the cardinal was served his coffee by Sister Vittoria Falcone. She had worked as his personal assistant for almost twenty years. She followed this man from station to station, through his various posts and assignments over the many years. Other than his own family, nobody knew him like she did. His likes and dislikes. His routines and his habits. Her service was always received with heartfelt gratitude, never once did she feel taken for granted by him. While her attendance to the cardinal was her job, it quickly morphed into a labor of love and admiration filled with many moments of intimate conversation over morning coffee or a meal when he wasn't entertaining guests.

Several days passed since his return from Portugal.

"She should be known and honored more than she is, you know..." He began.

"Who Chiaros?"

"Sister Lucy." He responded in a far off tone. This was the first mention of her the cardinal had made to anyone since their two hour meeting in Fátima. Sister Falcone sat in silence as she listened to the reflective verbal muse of the patriarch. "She is an extremely blessed woman, Vittoria. Her work, her words in service of Our God and the Holy Mother...I wish more of the world would listen to her and follow her example."

"She is an inspiration. She has taught me much."

"The Holy Mother was with her during our conversation. I could see it in her eyes. I could hear it in her words. I could feel it in my heart."

"What did she say?"

"It is through her, guided by the Immaculate Heart of Mary, that the world will return to God."

"That is obvious Chiaros."

"Not to everyone, I'm afraid. She is an incredible woman. So strong, so devoted. She is an older soul, with an amazing memory. Her words are simple, yet clear and to the point. Did you know she turned seventy earlier this year, Vittoria?"

"One would never know it, Chiaros."

"She is so spry, for a woman her age. She lives so simply, and speaks with amazing conviction, and her words are so profound when she opens her heart to those who will listen. Sister Lucy of the Immaculate Heart of Mary is a most blessed gift to the world."

"Chiaros, I hope you won't think me too forward...what were your conversations about? Did the two of you speak of the apparitions?"

"I would never consider you too presumptuous Vittoria for asking such a question. We actually never discussed the apparitions." Cardinal Riluciani then became distant, and his tone softened.

"Mostly we spoke of the future. The future of the world, the future of the Church..."

Over the coming months, no other details would be revealed of his conversation with Sister Lucy. He would visit his home village with increasing frequency and stay with his brother, and his family. The direct interaction with Sister Lucy forever changed him. He would continue to be warm and approachable to those who sought his counsel. However, to those who knew him best, he seemed distant, concerned and often lost in thought. During one of his visits home, his sister-in-law commented on the lack of color in his cheeks and his elevated level of obvious distress. He simply excused himself and sealed himself in the guest room with his breviary without a single word. This would continue for several days. His hostess expressed concern for her guest. "Is the food not to your liking, Chiaros?"

"I'm sorry, my dear, your food is fine. I was just remembering the words of Sister Lucy last July. She told me...she told me..." He repeated himself multiple times, never once completing his thought verbally. As he departed their hospitality, his distress permeated his farewell. "We all find ourselves on this journey to join our Lord in Heaven. He will never abandon us, for it is him who showers us in mercy as we strive for our own piety."

On New Years Eve, Cardinal Riluciani delivered a sermon on resolutions:

"It is our future in Paradise that fills our hearts with so much hope as we go about our daily lives. What good does it do us to pursue that which is grand and materialistic, only to lose our own soul in the process? We must repent and live our lives according to the teachings of Jesus. 'Be prepared,' He tells us. 'For I will come upon you like a thief.' Shakespeare reminds us of our fate if we choose to ignore the words of Our Lord. In *Hamlet*, as his gravedigger sings while he goes about his work:

A pick-axe and a spade, a spade,

For and a shrouding sheet;
O, a pit of clay for to be made
For such a guest is meet.

Without Christ in our lives, death is a brutal end to a life lived, filled with earthly pleasures and sin. While none of us are perfect, our gracious God sacrificed his only son, so we don't have to be. For a Christian, death is only sad for those we leave behind. As we happily join our Father in our eternal home. As Hamlet gazed upon the lawyer's skull in reflection, we must consider that one day our own greatness in this life will soon mean nothing as our own skulls eventually become filled with dirt. Let us make good use of our deeds and our actions in the coming year. And promise God to go forward into the future doing his works as we try our very best to live by His example."

Via his Easter Morning sermon, Cardinal Riluciani finally revealed to the world a hint of his conversation with Sister Lucy. Mary's messenger greatly inspired his address:

"It is in the Gospel of John 20:1-9 that we find Saint Mary Magdalene visiting the tomb of Jesus. As we read through the Gospels of Matthew, Mark, Luke and John, of Jesus' Passion and Resurrection, it is the women who show themselves to possess bravery and character far greater than their male counterparts. For it is the women who bear witness at the foot of the cross. It is the women who receive and tend to his body following his crucifixion. It is the women who lay his body to rest in his tomb. It is the women who witness the resurrection at the tomb on Easter morning. It is the women who rush to tell the Apostles that Jesus has risen! It was not their place to preach like the disciples and Apostles. Their work is much more important. It is the women who Jesus has chosen to assist others in the sharing of his teachings far and wide. Since the days of Saint Mary Magdalene, Jesus has sent other women to witness and inform others of important lessons. Catherine of Sienna, Teresa of Avila, Bernadette, Lucy dos Santos, Armida Barelli. It is they who have received his words from on high to encourage priests and the pope, and all who will listen to their important messages.

"During an extended conversation with Sister Lucy last year, I never once thought of her as one who was below me. It was my honor to speak with this blessed sister who had witnessed the Mother Mary first hand and received her message and ensures the execution of her words. Who am I to dismiss the messenger of the Madonna? Who are any of us? The destiny that God has planned, lies before us. It is our duty to quiet ourselves and the outside world so we can not just hear his message, but listen and execute His will. It is not our position that will make us saints. It is our deeds, executed with the purest of hearts. It is our duty to recommit our faith through repentance, prayer and the reciting of the Rosary.

"Finally I feel that I must remind everyone that hell does exist. If we are not purposeful in our day to day lives, hell may very well be our eternity. There are many things that occupy our days that seem important in this world, but none are as important as asking God's only son to forgive us our sins. It is the only way to save our souls from the fires of hell. It is the only way we will be granted eternal life with our God in Paradise. It is not enough to just live a 'good life.' This message comes not only from Fátima, but from the Gospel of Matthew 16:26 ESV 'What will it profit a man to gain the whole world only to end up forfeiting his own soul?'"

CHAPTER 32

The sudden dismissal of Cardinal Dante Leone from Pope Michael VI's Vatican State Department came as a shock to many and a relief to others. While he was by no means a perfect man, he held his own when it came to doing what was right. He may not have been a resident of the Vatican any longer, but he still had his informers, and he still had influence. The only problem now was nobody inside the Vatican city state would be around to maintain a close watchful eye on Bishop Jonas Krivis like he had done.

For the covert team of detectives and cardinals, things became considerably more complicated. The best they could do now was to watch the Vatican Bank president via his associations outside the walls of Vatican City. Cardinal Leone, despite his new assignment, knew enough to keep the investigation moving forward. This major setback would do little to weaken the resolve of the team. Their work now remained more important than ever.

Confidential conversations continued between relevant parties. Detective Cosimo Angelo was hard at work assisting in the compilation of evidence in the ongoing Giovanni Fedora investigation. Things were progressing forward, but the slow pace quickly became a source of extreme frustration. Things finally picked up once a former managing director of the Bank of Rome was arrested on charges of suppression of evidence important to the Fedora investigation. After that, the investigation seemed to once again move forward at a more satisfying pace.

In South America, an incarcerated Nico Novelli would write of his many years of work with Giovanni Fedora. The autobiographical, self-exculpating account painted a very different image of Fedora's former employee and business partner than what had been discovered by investigators in New York and Europe during the ongoing investigation of Fedora. In this version of the story, Novelli portrayed himself as a reluctant, scared, subservient participant in Fedora's evil works. The writings of Novelli were picked up and published in well read weekly Italian business publications. The business periodical's managing editor just so happened to be a man who hated Fedora. He was on a personal mission to assist in the absolute destruction of the man, the myth and the legend: Mr. Giovanni Fedora.

Back in New York, Giovanni Fedora had a plethora of his own problems bubbling to the surface. Yet another former Lincoln National Bank employee was willing to testify against him. The information that he was providing to the Feds was absolutely damning. Fedora found himself in desperate need of silencing the man. A call went out to his friends in the Lanscano family. A small contracted "visit" resulted in a very real threat to life and limb of the man, his family and his lawyer. If the subject "voluntarily" decided to backtrack on his evidence, that would be the end of that. However, if he continued undeterred, follow up "visits" would need to be arranged.

The other brewing problem in New York was that Mr. Nico Novelli had been successfully extradited from Caracas. Fedora's former business partner and close friend was facing charges of his own related to the failure of Lincoln National Bank. There was no doubt in anyone's mind that a plea deal was on the table in exchange for the lethal testimony against his former boss and business associate. Mr. Novelli would also receive a "visit" similar to his former colleague from Lincoln with the damning evidence against Fedora.

Fedora's American legal team worked feverishly to do whatever they could to hinder the Italian courts still working on his extradition from the United States. The lawyers argued for a delay until US prosecutors were satisfied that Milan officials had sufficiently proven their case against their client. Prosecutors worked diligently to find evidence, while Fedora employed the services of Mafia and P2 members who worked just as hard to make evidence disappear.

Another effort deployed to keep Mr. Fedora's feet firmly on American soil came in the form of a contract for the the murder of the United States Assistant District Attorney, who just so happened to be the chief prosecutor for Fedora's extradition hearing. The mobster who took the $1,000 contract to rough up the witnesses from Lincoln National Bank was not interested in the $100,000 murder contract on the federal prosecutor. Someone else would have to be hired for that job.

In Milan, a federal judge ruled that despite the fact that Mr. Fedora was now a legal citizen of Switzerland, he should be returned immediately to Italy to face his crimes. He had already been sentenced the year before to 3.5 years *"in absentia."* Fedora knew there was more heading his way on the horizon. Regardless of what was going on with him legally in Italy, and the ongoing federal investigation in the United States, Mr. Fedora remained a relatively free man and went about his days in unimpeded luxury in the Big Apple.

On May 18, 1978 Giovanni Fedora's luck ran out. The New York Judge presiding over his extradition case had finally seen enough evidence to establish probable cause. The seventy-eight page declaration cited crimes of fraudulent bankruptcy in violation of Italian bankruptcy laws. Mr. Fedora would be heading back to Italy to face his fate. But of course the wheels of justice turn slowly. Italian authorities who were anxious to get their hands on Fedora, would have to wait until the prosecutors in New York were done with their case against him regarding the Lincoln National Bank failure.

Fedora, desperate for funds, decided to file a federal lawsuit on the man from whom he had purchased the New York Bank. Included in the charges was a breach of securities laws and fraud.

Most thought it was yet another futile effort exercised by the con man. However, Fedora had absolutely nothing to lose at this point. To everyone's surprise, Fedora and his lawyers, ended up winning their lawsuit and recovering $40 million of his funds, plus $400,000 in fees and another $80 million in punitive damages. The FDIC followed Fedora's lead and filed their own suit seeking restitution for their own losses related to the Lincoln National Bank collapse. They also piled on charges of breach of fiduciary duties and failure to properly vet Mr. Giovanni Fedora prior to selling him the institution.

A week later, "Pops," the former chairman of the board of Lincoln and two other men were indicted in federal court on fraud and co-conspiracy charges. Despite the hired threats against him, Nico Novelli would take a plea bargain in exchange for his own indictment.

Back in Italy, inspectors met with Marco Ansios a couple of times. At one of those meetings, Mr. Ansios, produced a letter from January, 1975 on Vatican letterhead. The letter showed a portfolio of shares held by the Vatican Bank for Financial and Commerce Services of Milan. The management and administration of the portfolio was under the direction of Marco Ansios on behalf of the Vatican Bank. The letter bore the signatures of Bishop Jonas Krivis and two of his chief accountants.

Investigators scanned the letter with the greatest of scrutiny. It seemed so odd to them that a copy of this document was nowhere to be found in the confiscated materials secured from their raid on Banco Generali months ago. They suspected that this letter had been produced in recent weeks with the full knowledge and approval of Bishop Krivis, however, they did not have the resources to prove their suspicions. With Cardinal Dante Leone no longer working in the Vatican's Secretary of State office, no one would ever be able to know one way or the other.

For the time being, Ansios, thanks to the help of Krivis, was no longer sweating buckets from the pressures of the Italian authorities. The recent frosty, antisocial demeanor of Mr. Ansios changed quickly to that of a man relaxed without a care in the world. With the utmost confidence that his greatest vulnerabilities had now been hidden from investigators, he decided that it was time to book a well deserved pleasure trip, mixed with a little business to South America himself and his wife. Once in South America, he finally felt like he could truly relax and forget the majority of his worldly troubles.

CHAPTER 33

The blaze from the huge fireplace inside the pope's private chamber grew larger and larger. The angry dance of the flames appeared almost sinister as it reflected off the lenses of the monsignor's glasses. The scent of paper on fire filled his nostrils, while pops and crackles randomly punctuated the silence, and the intense heat on the face and body of the pope's personal secretary caused him to retreat over and over again. He would return to feed the fire page after page from his hands, ensuring that every last one had burned completely. He watched with a distant gaze as the fire consumed the last of the personal papers of Pope Michael VI. It was the final earthly request made in the now late pope's hand written will.

In the days prior, Pope Michael VI retreated to his much beloved summer estate for a much needed reprieve from the day to day stresses of papal life and duties. As of late, he lamented what to do about the growing problems within his church caused by the financial mess created by his bank head, and his friends. He had heard an ear full from many prelates and laymen from the Holy See and beyond. He had made many grave mistakes.

The Vatican Public Relations Office did their best to control the narrative, but there was too much of the drama already in the public sector. The public press was merciless. Pope Michael VI remained extremely worried about the future of his church. He didn't have a clue what to do to fix the mess of mistakes and misjudgments. This retreat couldn't have come at a better moment, the Holy Father thought to himself.

The early August days were pleasantly warm, but not hot. The songs of birds and chatter of the estates' wildlife always brought the Holy Father peace and grounding. The scent of jasmine would carry on the breeze through open windows to fragrant his chambers. It was in that chamber on August 6, 1978 at 9:40 PM that he left this Earthly existence to be with his Heavenly Father.

At the twenty four hour mark, following the death of Pope Michael VI not much had been done yet to his body, and the evaluation of his legacy was still in the brains and pens of autobiographers. In the Holy City, there was an instant, palpable buzz. There was also a sudden plethora of activity as the body was prepared to lay in state, funeral ceremony and arrangements were considered, and travel itineraries made. Soon more than 115 cardinals, from every corner of the globe would ascend on the holy city of Rome. In addition to the religious customs to honor the late pope, the ritual of papal elections needed to be held for the selection of a successor.

The funeral procession to honor the late pope was the usual elaborate affair, filled with the traditions and practices appropriate for the occasion. The only thing extraordinary about this particular event was how remarkably unemotional and flat everything and everybody was. It was obvious, from the public's response, that Pope Michael VI's papacy was over long before the death of his physical body. There had been little communication from the late pope in the last decade to inspire, and uplift the people of his church. He was a man to respect, but not one to shower with affection and adoration.

The newspapers soon began buzzing with anticipation of the upcoming papal election in an environment that very much resembled a sports bookmakers scene from a Las Vegas casino. There were actual over and under odds posted on all of the eligible cardinals. However, what the press could not know or understand was that these conclave proceedings to elect the next pope would be very different than they were in the past. This exercise was going to be much more complicated than anyone had anticipated, especially for the participating cardinals.

Many years prior to his passing, as Pope Michael VI struggled with the state of affairs within his church, he decided to issue some drastic new rules for the conclave that would select his successor. The first rule was that upon his death, all cardinals employed within the Roman Curia would have to immediately resign their positions. The pope felt that this decision would, if nothing else, provide the next pope with a clean slate and was his postmortem effort to reduce nepotism within the Vatican as much as possible. The only exception to this rule would be Cardinal Benoît, Pope Michael's Secretary of State, who was now as per tradition, elevated to Camerlengo upon the death of the pope.

Pope Michael also handed down other new rules for this conclave. Any cardinal over the age of eighty would not be eligible for selection, nor would they be allowed to vote for the next pope. Pope Michael, during his days, had many disagreements with the over eighty crowd of cardinals. In his death, he had won his final argument with every single one of them. The cardinals affected by this strange new rule were absolutely incensed, yet compliant with the rules set forth by the late Holy Father.

There was a movement afoot among the electorate prior to the beginning of conclave, to select a pope that was more of the people, a truly holy man guided by God. One that was completely awash of the financial scandal that had brought so much shame to the Catholic Church in recent years courtesy of Fedora, Krivis, Ansios and their associates. The cardinals were searching for a man that truly recognized the down and out and was willing to distribute his power and authority among his peers and followers.

Twenty days after the death of Pope Michael VI, the conclave was finally ready to commence. Cardinal Benoît closed the chamber containing the 111 members of the College of Cardinals and secured it. The room would remain sealed until the white smoke billowed out of the chimney and was carried on the breeze over the waiting crowd indicating to those assembled in St Peter's Square and the rest of the world that a new pope had been selected.

Security both inside and outside of that chamber was amplified, ensuring that no one from the public or press would hint or release the identity of the newly selected Holy Father until the official announcement was made by the Vatican. The late pope was absolutely obsessed with secrecy. Every participating cardinal had to solemnly swear a personal oath of secrecy, not once, but twice. Violation of said oath would result in immediate excommunication from the church. There would be absolutely zero communication, verbal, written or otherwise to reveal the results of the voting cardinals. In a final step to ensure that there would be no discussion outside of the conclave, each cardinal was assigned a single occupant room, with frequent physical checks and roll calls taken. The entire policy and procedure resembled more of a penitentiary than a Holy Church of God.

The first day of the conclave came and went, without a single vote being cast. The cardinals remained locked in their stuffy, claustrophobic prison known to the rest of the world as the Sistine Chapel. The rest of Rome waited patiently as they baked in a late August heatwave that plagued all of Italy. The situation was the most uncomfortable, for those sealed inside of the conclave who were of a more advanced age.

The next morning following Mass and breakfast, the cardinals were seated in their assigned places. The quest for two-thirds votes, plus one was on. The next pope would need seventy five votes cast in his favor in order to be selected. Temperatures and emotions were running high as the first ballots were counted, checked, then rechecked three times. Following their counts and checks, each ballot was sown together by a silver needle and a long piece of red thread, then cast into the furnace and sprinkled with a powder that would turn the smoke some color other than white.

The initial vote resulted in:

Cardinal Adriano Russo	25
Cardinal Chiaros Riluciani	23
Cardinal Fausto Gallo	18

The remaining ballots were scattered among eight other contenders. None of which received more than twelve votes. The votes cast for the cardinals being considered were, for the most part, expected. Even speculators in the public sector had predicted numbers close to the first vote. The twenty three votes for Cardinal Riluciani, however, were an unexpected surprise for much of the electorate and the cardinal himself as he smiled and shook his head each time he heard his name called. He could not understand this sudden increase in popularity among his peers. There must be some mistake, he thought to himself. Surely the next round of voting will result in a correction of the tally.

The next round of voting was soon completed, and the results were tallied:

Cardinal Adriano Russo	35
Cardinal Chiaros Riluciani	30
Cardinal Fausto Gallo	15

The remaining votes were again scattered among other cardinal candidates in the room. The ballots were once again strung together and sprinkled with powder and black smoke billowed from the antiquated stove's chimney to the waiting crowd gathered in St Peter's Square.

Outside the conclave news reporters from around the world had gathered. They were reporting on the scene with the absolute conviction of authority and false confidence. It was as if they knew exactly what was going on within the locked chamber of cardinals.

Of course their loyal audience watched and listened as the talking heads remained ignorantly in the dark like everyone else outside the Sistine Chapel.

After a break for lunch, the third attempt to choose a new pope would begin. This time Cardinals Russo and Riluciani were almost equal. The patriarch of Venice was visibly upset by the results by now. The very real possibility that he may soon be elected pope weighed heavy on his mind. His fellow cardinals had done their homework on the eligible candidates. They wanted to select a man who would help strengthen their church. But why Riluciani? He was not a governing man. He was a man perfectly content with being a parish priest. The patriarch, for the life of him, could not understand this sudden burst in popularity. Those seated around him offered him their support and encouragement as best they could. Instilling their complete confidence in him as a leader of the Catholic church, should he indeed be elected.

The staff within the Curia were divided. On one hand they were very pleased that Cardinal Gallo would not become the next pope, but their most desired candidate was Russo, not Riluciani. Those content with business as usual within the walls of Vatican City, felt that the quiet demeanor of the patriarch of Venice would most certainly not give them any trouble, and would be easy to control. Others were not so sure about the cardinal as his popularity continued to grow.

Before returning from lunch, a very conflicted Cardinal Chiaros Riluciani retreated to his temporary quarters. He knelt and prayed for guidance, strength and courage to face the burden of the possible changes that seemed to be apparent in his current trajectory. He begged his Heavenly Father to consider someone other than him for the position, then concluded his prayer with the words, "Thy will be done Heavenly Father." Riluciani crossed himself and rose from his knees sweating.

The next tally of votes put the Venice patriarch within seven votes of the papacy. He placed his head in his hands as others could hear him mumbling "No, Please not me, no. I cannot be the one chosen by God." Cardinals sitting on either side of him saw his distress and placed their hands on his shoulders to comfort his anxious state. "God would not choose you, if you were not what his church and the world needs right now Chiaros." Remarked the cardinal seated next to him.

The final vote was cast, and white smoke floated from the chimney of the stove located within the Sistine Chapel, and the secured double doors swung open wide to the world with Chiaros Riluciani the newly elected pope of the Roman Catholic Church. Camerlengo Benoît entered the chamber and approached the newly elected pope.

"Do you accept your canonical election as supreme pontiff?"

Everyone watched and waited for the response. Riluciani sat silent for what seemed like an eternity. Then the man cleared his throat, and spoke. "While I feel this decision is a mistake, may God forgive every single one of you." Then he uttered loudly with a great smile, "*Accepto!*"

Benoît then asked, "By what name does Your Holiness wish to be addressed?"

Riluciani could then feel the Spirit of the Lord move decidedly within him, and through the characteristic smile that graced his glowing face. "Please call me Pope Phillip Michael the First!"

The new pope, unlike his predecessors and colleagues, never once dreamed that one day he would hold the highest position within the church. The dream of his new reality never once consumed a single thought in his head at any point in time in his life. He was a simple, quiet, humble man who served his parish with a pure heart, full of love for all who graced his presence. He did not seek the limelight. His sole desire was to help all, especially the poor, elderly and down trodden of his community.

From the conclave chamber, the new pope was escorted to the sacristy. The papal tailors worked feverishly to find a cassock that would fit his slender build. He was drowning in his newly vested garments, that were fitted as best they could given the circumstances. He emerged to greet each of his cardinals, they in return kissed Riluciani's hand, and then received a warm embrace by their new pope. One cardinal thanked him for accepting the will of God and his peers. The man was still unsure of his selection and future, joking that perhaps he should have declined the selection.

Outside the building the public waited with great anticipation for the introduction of the newly elected Holy Father. The newly vested Pope Phillip Michael I was escorted to the balcony with his interim staff.

"Attenzione." A booming voice silenced the waiting crowd that flooded St Peter's Square. "Our Heavenly Father has guided the hands and hearts of the Church's cardinals to select our new pope! The Church wishes to introduce *Carinalem Chiaros Riluciani!"*

The crowd's response was deafening. Cheers, smiles, praying, singing all could be observed throughout the assembly. Again, the loud speaker boomed, and the crowd quieted to listen.

"Cardinal Chiaros Riluciani has chosen the name Pope Phillip Michael the First!"

Again the crowd responded with cheers of love, joy and celebration for their new pope. Riluciani approached the edge of the balcony with a huge beaming smile. His blessings full of love and happiness seemed to touch everyone personally in St Peter's Square. Riluciani delivered a blessing to all those within the Vatican walls and beyond. The exuberant crowd exploded with happiness as they received the blessing of their new pope, Pope Phillip Michael I.

ACT 3

CHAPTER 34

He had been declining in health and mental capacity for several years already. The lackluster atmosphere of the events that he attended towards the end of his life served as more of an outward expression of his own personal daily struggle with debilitating depression. The death of Pope Michael VI didn't exactly come as a shock to many people. It was the timing of his departure from this earthly existence that created the most turmoil to the inhabitants of Vatican City.

As news of the deceased pontiff made its way around the world, Marco Ansios' phone began ringing off the hook. He became annoyed with the constant interruption to his South American celebratory vacation with his wife. The changes in his and many others lives and operations would, without a doubt, be happening soon. In his mind, there was no sense in speculating and fretting about the possibilities until Pope Michael VI's predecessor was elected and announced.

Never in a million years did the majority of the world anticipate that Cardinal Chiaros Riluciani would be elected the next spiritual leader of an eighth of the world's population, including Cardinal Riluciani himself. The press scrambled to become overnight experts on the relatively unknown man who had just become pope. For Marco

Ansios, he would have been happier if the College of Cardinals would have selected any one of the other 110 options to fill the vacant chair in Vatican City.

Marco Ansios knew personally, exactly what kind of man now sat in the pope's chair. He had already experienced first hand the wrath of the humble man, shortly after he took over the Catholic Bank of Venice back in the summer of 1971. He remembered the cardinal at the time taking his protests all the way to Rome in a futile attempt to return his favorite little bank back to the control of the diocese and ultimately the Vatican. Over the last seven years, Ansios learned a lot about the man. This man was fully committed to a life of personal poverty. His intolerance of questionable dealings involving anyone in the clergy were well known throughout Northern Italy.

From the makeshift remote office in his hotel suite in Buenos Aires, Marco Ansios began to immediately sell off shares of Financial and Commerce Services of Milan. As he proceeded to remove from his possession over 350,000 shares of the stock, Bank of Italy inspectors were watching his every move. It didn't matter to them that this sell off was happening remotely in another part of the world. The letter he presented from the Vatican regarding the company now seemed even more dubious, based on his actions.

The other problem that came from the election of this new pope was his absolute disdain for Bishop Jonas Krivis. After learning of the man's corruption and evil ways, there was no doubt in anyone's mind that his days were now numbered. It wasn't a matter of if Krivis would get the boot, but rather a matter of when. Along with his removal as Vatican Bank president, the entire fraudulent operations conducted by him and others would be exposed and come to an abrupt end.

"I hate to say it, Marco, but this pope is a very different animal than we've had here in the past."

"I thought you said he was harmless Jonas."

"I did, and he was...but that was before he became my boss."

"You told me everything was going to be ok Goddammit!"

"How was I supposed to know that these idiot cardinals would elect HIM?! It's not like it's my fault that he's now pope."

"I'm starting to think that you had more to do with it than you think Jonas."

"What the hell is that supposed to mean?"

"You've become very sloppy in your operations in recent years Jonas. Now both Giovanni and I have investigators all up our asses."

"Oh fuck off Marco. You two have gotten sloppy too. And it's not like the authorities up your guys' asses has really changed either of your operations all that much."

"Who the fuck are you kidding Jonas? Sloppy my ass."

"Oh? Who was knocking on my Goddamn door not that long ago looking for a letter that would take the heat off of you and your ownership of Financial and Commerce Services over in Milan?" Marco Ansios suddenly grew very quiet. He knew that Krivis was right. He had no one to blame but himself. "All I can say to you and Giovanni is that things are going to be very different around here from now on."

This new pope presented a very real, and very serious threat to the operations of Giovanni Fedora, Marco Ansios and especially Jonas Krivis. The investigation and audit of the Vatican Bank would result in many vacancies. Krivis wasn't the only man in the bank operating on borrowed time. Many of Krivis' staff had also been accessories to the crimes of both Fedora and Ansios for years. Krivis knew that the solution employed during his last encounter with Cardinal Riluciani would not be an option this time. Such a showdown this time around, would have him leaving the walled city of the Vatican this time.

This new pope lived and breathed by Jesus' ideology of a poor church that remained in dedicated service to the poor. His entire ethos posed a very real threat to the clandestine group known in some circles as Vatican, Inc. The extreme profiting that had become so commonplace over decades would stop under this new pope's regime. It would take a lot of work to bring his vision of the Catholic Church into reality. However, there was zero doubt in anyone's mind that a determined Pope Phillip Michael I would accomplish anything and everything he set out to do, in a most efficient manner.

Another likely problem for this new pope was the *Amministrazione del Patrimonio della Sede Apostolica,* or the APSA as the people of the Curia liked to call it. The APSA was created under the direction of Pope Michael VI who appointed his own Secretary of State, Cardinal Zacharie Benoît as department president. Their greatest source of income came from the rental of 5,000 apartment units that the Vatican owned outright. Over $1 billion in annual gross profits were made from the rental of those housing units. An even bigger source of profits for the APSA was a very robust daily stock speculation operation that would rival the over $1.2 billion grossed annually by the Vatican Bank under Krivis' watch. Bishop Krivis estimated that his bank was on pace to gross close to $2 billion by the end of 1978. Of course that figure would change drastically once Pope Phillip Michael I was done with it. Roughly 85% of those gross profits belonged to whoever happened to be the sitting pope.

Perhaps the biggest problem of all for the Vatican Bank were some of the actual accounts open in their institution. There were over 11,000 accounts on the books with the Vatican Bank. Only 1,650 actually belonged to the clergy and Curia employees within the Holy See. The remaining accounts were owned by diplomats, prelates outside of Rome and "other privileged citizens" like Giovanni Fedora, Marco Ansios, Gherado Fratello. These "privileged" politicians and businessmen would take full advantage of the bank's secrecy and services to move money illegally in and out of Italy without the detection of the Italian Tax Authorities.

If Jesus were to return to Vatican City in late August, 1978, what thoughts would be racing through his head given its current state? He whose "Kingdom was not of this earth..." would certainly be far more upset than he was when he purged the temple of the moneychangers of his time, as he roamed through the halls and facilities of the Vatican Bank and the APSA. He would scoff at the $1 million in profits collected off the sale of Vatican stamps and the collection of Peter's Pence that was deposited directly into the pope's pockets.

The fact was that if Jesus was to return to the Holy City today, he'd be arrested at St. Anne's Gate by the Swiss Guard and handed over to Italian authorities for prosecution. He most certainly wouldn't get far enough to learn of any of the crimes and schemes committed by anyone who was a part of Vatican, Inc.

The return of the Catholic Church to a church of the poor, would be a most monumental task. The new pope would have to first completely dismantle the Vatican Bank and the APSA. He would then have to decide what was to be done with all of the priceless art pieces and treasures in their possession. When the College of Cardinals elected their Colleague Chiaros Riluciani to the papacy, it was a clear message to everyone within the Holy See that there was extreme displeasure with the *modus operandi* and the deep rooted corruption that had infected the church for a very long time under its past leadership. The cardinals clearly wanted a very different future for their church. They set the smartest, most honest, holy and incorruptible man they had on a direct collision course with Vatican Inc.

CHAPTER 35

Detective Francis Clavering took his usual counter seat at his favorite New York City breakfast diner.

"Good Morning Fran, how's your day going?" Laura, the waitress, winked at him while chomping on her pink bubble gum and automatically pouring him a cup of coffee without him asking.

"Oh good morning Laura, not too much really..." Fran stretched a little in his seat trying to shake off the lingering sleep and stiffness from his body.

"You always say that, but I never believe you."

"Why's that?"

"In your line of work detective, I bet you've always got something interesting going on."

"Sometimes, but usually it's a lot of drudgery too. Ya know like watching, listening, waiting around and digging through records. I think that's the part that a lot of people don't understand about my work."

"Sounds like my work here," she winked at him, continuing to chew on her gum.

"Oh?"

"That's about all I do around here. I mean all day I watch, I listen and I wait on customers then shuffle through order tickets. Maybe I should give up waitressing and become a cop like you Fran." She issued a coy little joking smile. "So how's Peg?"

"She's great! She's keeping busy with the kids and her projects and social activities."

"That's great Fran. Please tell her hello for me Fran."

"Of course I will, Laura."

"So you gonna have your usual, or are ya gonna change it up on me?"

"Yes please, the usual. I'm starving!"

"Coming right up," She smiled and offered another wink and left to fetch his orange juice.

Fran dipped his whole wheat toast into the yolk of his runny, sunny side up eggs and took a large bite when his attention was drawn to the muted TV in the diner. Across the screen flashed the words "Pope Philip Michael I!" at the bottom of the screen along with an image of the man he and Peg had met on their recent trip to Venice. He turned to the busboy passing by with a half full bin of dirty dishes. "Hey Andy, would you mind turning that up for a minute, I want to hear this if you don't mind."

"Yeah man, no problem Fran."

The detective watched as the new pope greeted the world with bright eyes and his signature gleaming smile. Fran listened to the broadcast segment being reported from just outside the Sistine Chapel, in Vatican City. He finished his breakfast, paid his bill and began to make his way towards his work.

Francis hit the news stand before heading to the precinct. The headlines on all of the front pages read. "New Pope Elected!" He paid for his paper then continued on to his destination. Fran and Lance had been so engrossed in the Fedora drama that they somehow missed the news of Pope Michael VI's death. As soon as he got to his desk, he rang Cosimo over in Rome.

"Hey Cosimo, it's Fran."

"Hey Detective, how are things going over there in your part of the world?"

"Fedora's been keeping us busy over here. How's it going in your neck of the woods?"

"Fedora's drama has been keeping us busy over here too...and so has Ansios. You are so lucky Fran, you only have one guy on your radar, confined to one City, plus you have Lance to help you out... over here, these two are all over the place."

"I can only imagine."

"So what's up?"

"Well I was just having breakfast when the news said something about a new pope, and a very familiar one at that."

"Oh that? That's no big deal." Cosimo jested sarcastically.

"Yeah, I saw it on the news this morning and it's a headline on all of the newspapers this morning over here."

"Can you believe it? Cardinal Riluciani was elected pope in conclave the other night."

"I don't even think I heard that Pope Michael had passed away, I've been so caught up in Fedora's drama over here for weeks."

"Yeah, he passed, I'd say about three weeks ago. We've all been busy. Don't beat yourself up too much over this one Fran."

"Do you think there was any funny business regarding Pope Mike's death Cosimo?"

"I seriously doubt it. He wasn't the most beloved pope in history, but I really don't think someone did anything to arrange this meeting between him and his Heavenly Father. I mean the guy was 80 and in declining health, ya know."

"You have a point. But with everything we've learned about the Vatican, I just don't trust anyone around there anymore. Especially now that Cardinal Leone is no longer there."

"You will get absolutely no argument from me on that, Fran."

"So what else are you hearing over there?"

"Well it seems that nobody over here expected Riluciani to be elected pope. Those cardinals really threw everyone a curveball in that conclave."

"What do you mean Cosimo?"

"These people over here, especially the press, know almost nothing about our man who was just elected pope."

"That's really too bad, Peg and I thought he was an absolute delight when we met him during our visit."

Once all the pomp, circumstance, and celebration concluded, it was time for Riluciani to roll up his shirt sleeves and get started on what God had chosen him to do. He opened the windows to his papal study wide in a symbolic release of the dark, depressing atmosphere of the Roman Catholic Church under the leadership of his predecessor. The sunlight and fresh air accented with the delicate scents of rose, jasmine and other flowers flooded the chamber on the temperate August morning. The gardens and paths below beckoned him. The new Vicar of Rome who often described himself as a "man of simple means, who truly appreciated silence and the unsophisticated" suddenly found himself surrounded by Vatican grandeur and almost constant Curial blabber.

The "experts" whose job it was to keep the world informed on Vatican happenings, didn't quite know what to think about the Holy City's newest resident. These were the very same people who had completely failed to consider the possibility of Cardinal Riluciani becoming the next pope. To them he was the "Unknown Pope." He certainly wasn't unknown among his peers. It was their votes that signified a need to clean up the Vatican Curia and shake up their status quo. This new pope was seeking a complete revolt that would bring this church back to its roots. Back to the simple, honest, ideals and aspirations that Jesus had intended when he originally formed his church. The College of Cardinal knew exactly what they were doing when they sent this man to Rome. He was exactly what they wanted, and exactly what their church needed.

His first full day as pontiff was filled with the unfamiliar. He called Father Vincenzo Mancini in a desperate search for something familiar. His long time personal assistant in Venice could hear the loneliness in his conversation. Despite the cloud of homesickness that surrounded him, the first thing everyone noticed about this new pope was his warm and joyous smile. The public never had a leader like this "Happy Pope." His ability to communicate directly with media and his followers in a way they could understand, without talking down to them or insulting their intelligence was a refreshing change. His success as a pope would become quickly reflected in the public's response to him.

Early that afternoon, Riluciani took his lunch in the company of Cardinal Benoît. The man who served as Secretary of State since April, 1969, under Pope Michael VI. He was hoping to retire upon the election of his pope's successor. Riluciani kindly asked him to remain in his position for a while. The Holy Pontiff explained that this would be a temporary assignment until a suitable replacement could be found. Benoît reluctantly agreed. The two men then went about the many departments of the Roman Curia to reconfirm the various cardinals in charge. This was done with the understanding that their current positions were also temporary appointments. Clearly when Riluciani left Venice to attend conclave, he never anticipated these new responsibilities. It would take time for him to come up with a suitable list of people to make up his cabinet. As the Vatican staff got to know and understand their new pope, an odd dichotomy began to emerge. Some were anxiously welcoming of the inevitable changes, while others anxiously feared those changes.

At the end of his first full day as pope, Riluciani dined with his interim Secretary of State. He ordered him to immediately begin a full investigation and review of all Vatican financial operations. No department, congregation or section was to be excluded from this audit. He wanted special attention given to the Vatican Bank. Cardinal Benoît was instructed to go about his task with the utmost discretion, efficiency and accuracy. The information from Benoît's evaluation would be used to determine the appropriate actions and solutions necessary for resolution.

With the rising sun of the next day came Pope Phillip Michael I's first act of revolt. He absolutely declined the ceremonial Papal Coronation. He refused the *Sedia Gestatoria,* having no desire to be carried around on the shoulders of others in the pope's fancy chair. He would also decline the jewel encrusted tiara, ostrich feathers and six degree ceremony. The church with its lust from temporal power and the vanity displayed through its ridiculous display of deep seeded ritual was in that moment, instantly gone.

In place of the formal coronation, Pope Phillip Michael I presided over an informal mass in St. Peter's Square. The world's dignitaries were left feeling confused and uncomfortable as they mingled elbow to elbow with the general public without an ounce of regard to their worldly status or title. Some of the public vocally protested the presence of South American fascist dictators who had flown in for the muted special occasion. Following mass in private meetings he made his personal contempt for fascism known to all the dignitaries gathered.

The United States Vice President Water Mondale led an American delegation to attend the informal coronation. He presented the new pope with a copy of over fifty American newspapers announcing the election of Pope Phillip Michael I bound in book form. In addition to the newspaper clippings the American Vice President presented the Holy Father with a copy of Mark Twain's *Life on the Mississippi*. It was clear with the presenting of the second gift, that someone in the US State Department had done at least a little homework on the man who had become the new pope.

A few days later, Riluciani announced to his newly chosen diplomats that "The Vatican, in its sovereignty as a nation, had no goods to exchange with the world." With that official public declaration, Vatican Inc. was issued its death sentence. Its days of operation were now numbered. The news spread quickly through the financial hubs in Milan, London, Tokyo and New York. Speculators around the world went nuts with anticipation. Billions stood to be made, if they could successfully predict the direction the new Vatican leadership would take.

Those who had known Chiaros Riluciani for many years watched and waited, contemplating his next move. The central administrative body of the church, known as the Roman Curia, had been deeply engaged in an internal war for many years, long prior to the arrival of this new pope. Despite the various shortcomings of the previous pope, he had a certain knack for keeping such drama out of the public's view. Upon the arrival of this new pontiff, the internal war moved from the Curia to the papal apartments. His efforts to gain a better understanding of his new position within the church, he enacted his open door policy that was extremely effective back in Venice. In the Vatican, its success was questionable at best. The new Holy Father quickly grew tired of the bickering, bad mouthing, back biting and whining of his staff that seemed to get very little actual work done. After a few short days in Vatican City, there was nothing Chiaros Riluciani craved more than some true honesty and a really good cup of coffee.

In the early days of his papacy, Phillip Michael I was perceived as a humble mannered, simple man, full of all sorts of weaknesses. They quickly realized the errors in their judgment, as their "controllable pushover" removed every last one of his predecessor's Milan Mafia personnel. There was no Venetian counterpart to replace them. This new pope would not be a man held captive by his own Vatican Curia. Since his election, the Curia had been busier than they had been in many many years.

Members of Pope Michael VI's Curia wanted his memory and philosophies preserved and his traditions continued. Some in his Curia liked Cardinal Leone's heavy handed style, while others personally wished for him to affectionately burn in hell. In his role as Under Secretary of State, it was his job to maintain proper policy within Vatican City, and beyond. It was also the primary reason many in the Curia absolutely hated him. Pope Michael VI in an attempt to protect him from those who wished him harm, promoted him and made him the new patriarch of Florence. Cardinal Leone was now no longer a part of the Vatican Curia, and his protector was now dead. However, unbeknownst to many including the new sitting pope, it was him, Wexford and other men like them who conspired together to get Riluciani elected pope.

Because Chiaros Reluciani had done his best to avoid the Vatican through the majority of his career, he was the perfect man for the job in the eyes of Cardinals Leone, Wexford and others. He was a true outsider with very few enemies within the Curia, especially when compared to his colleagues who were eligible for the position. However, the void of adversaries, quickly filled as he began to settle into his new role within the church. It was his understanding that the function of the Curia was to bring his ideas and wishes to reality. Riluciani envisioned a more decentralized structure within the Vatican. He felt that the bishops of the Catholic Church should have more power and responsibility, on par with their superiors. He then instructed those in charge of his monthly salary to lower it by 50%.

As the new pope was getting fitted for his new vestments upon his election, members of the Roman Curia went to work right away. Like stealthy little soldiers in a battle, they were mobilized everywhere Riluciani had resided to secure the many notes, papers, and articles written by him. Items and documents deemed controversial in content were quickly sequestered from the public and placed in secret archives deep within Vatican vaults. Gone from public access were his writings on artificial birth control, his thesis and many other documents. The Vatican Curia effectively went about their task to help shape the public's version of the new pope that they wanted the world to see. Their efforts worked beautifully as the press, who knew nothing about the man before he was elected pope, began writing and reporting about a man who didn't really exist.

As the first few days passed of his papacy, the exchange between Riluciani and his temporary Secretary of State became more and more heated. It was the new pope's desire to melt the frosty demeanor of Cardinal Benoît. Benoît often responded with "Pope Michael would have said..." or "Pope Michael would have done..." It was annoyingly clear that many of his retained staff preferred the manners and styles of their prior boss over his.

While Riluciani was his own man, with his own style, he was no fool. There was no sense in reinventing the wheel completely from scratch. He liked to blend the successes of his predecessors, while learning from their mistakes on what not to do. He decided to fashion his own papacy with more inspiration from Pope Phillip XXIII and less from Pope Michael VI. After all Phillip was Riluciani's predecessor twice now, from his days in Venice and now his future in Rome. As the end of August, 1978 approached, he set out on a personal mission to revolutionize the Vatican Curia in his first 100 days as pope. In order to accomplish this, his first task would be to redefine the church's relationship with global capitalism.

Other hot button issues for the new pontiff were artificial birth control and the many deaths, especially in children, contributed to the scourge of malnutrition. To Riluciani, the two issues were closely related. He watched for years as members of his own family struggled to put food on the table, while the babies just kept coming. "Despite all of our prayers and absolute faith in God, He does not always provide." He was most perplexed by the harsh backlash he received from the senior leadership in the church. How can a religious establishment such as ours sit here and balk about the use of artificial birth control while we hold controlling interest in the primary pharmaceutical manufacturer of the birth control pill? He would set out to resolve that particular conundrum soon enough. For now he wanted to reach out a sincere, understanding hand to the people that capitalism, materialism and oppressive governmental regimes seemed to have forgotten. The financial exploitation and poverty he was so determined to stop led him on a crusade in opposition to several government entities in South America and certain elements within his own church.

Cardinal Benoît received correspondence that a US delegation was requesting an audience during the final week of October. Upon reviewing his calendar, he found a conflicting engagement for that week in Columbia to discuss the issue of birth control. After a few moments of contemplation, Riluciani instructed Benoît to cancel the Colombia trip and confirm the meeting with the Americans. He felt that over the coming weeks, it was important to concentrate his energies on getting his own house in order before broadening the scope of his work beyond Vatican walls. For now, his attention would remain fixated on the Vatican Bank and its administrative body.

CHAPTER 36

On the final day of August, 1978, Italy's largest, most read and respected economic newspaper addressed a substantial open ended letter to Pope Phillip Michael I. They proposed several very serious questions and suggested that it was a time for the return of papel oversight and intervention regarding the financial dealings that had gotten the Vatican in so much trouble in recent years. It was time for a return to something less chaotic and more morally correct. "Is it right for the Vatican Bank to be so deeply involved in market speculation?" "What about their assistance in all of the sketchy cash transfers from Italy to other countries?" "How about their role in helping Italian people and businesses evade taxation?"

Then the questions shifted to the cozy relationship between the bank and Mr. Giovanni Fedora over the years. They brought up a man who was essentially the secular "president of the bank" from '64 up until Krivis was appointed president by Pope Michael VI. This same secular Vatican Bank president served more recently as the managing director of Fedora's now failed bank in Milan. What about the numerous scandals involving the current sitting Vatican Bank president and the disgraced Italian financier Giovanni Fedora? Krivis also has other suspect relationships like the one with the head of the Chicago bank that handles all of the Catholic Church's American investments. It was clear that the author of the article had done his research. He even asked poignant questions about Bishop Krivis' Board of Directors position at a Banco Generali branch in Nassau, Bahamas. Their letter then closed with a final question. Why was the Catholic Church actively engaged in local and global investments for profits while committing multiple human rights violations, especially in third world countries?

There would be no official response to the onslaught of questions. Some in the Vatican Curia who objected to the activities of the bank and its president felt it was about time someone asked some real, hard questions. Others thought that the Church and its bank should work towards more investments for even larger gains. It was a very strange dichotomy for such a seemingly holy place.

The new pope read many articles from popular Italian publications that seemed sympathetic to the present financial problems plaguing the Vatican. Other articles discussed the myth of massive wealth held by the Vatican. After reading numerous articles and letters, pope Phillip Michael I now knew exactly what needed to be done. Even before his election, he knew of numerous grievances aired to Cardinal Zacharie Benoît. The Church's clergy were not ignorant of how Krivis was running the bank, his involvement with Fedora and Ansios, or the links between the APSA and Fedora. He had had his own personal run-in with the Vatican, Inc. machine and its shady deal which sold his beloved bank back in '72. At that time, there was a lot wrong with the structure and vision of the Vatican finance offices. Back then he was powerless to do anything about them. However, now things were very different.

A huge array of rumors began making their way through Vatican Village about the time Cardinal Riluciani came to see Leone, Benoît, the late pope and Krivis back in the early '70s. In Riluciani's futile attempt to halt the sale of his bank, words were floating that he confronted the Holy Father on the problem. The only response issued from the pope at the time was that "sacrifices were necessary for the

Church's financial recovery from damages caused by Krivis' friend Giovanni Fedora." The visiting cardinal, who was not satisfied with that action, was then directed to take up the matter with Bishop Krivis himself. The bishop offered his cardinal guest some of his finest scotch and a very nice cigar which were all declined, before he sat to listen to the complaints and concerns from Riluciani regarding the sale of his parish's bank. With a sip of his scotch and a long drag from his cigar, the only response issued from the Vatican Bank president was, "Your Eminence, surely you have something better to do than to come here and waste your's and my time today. I tell you what, Eminence, you go back to Venice and do your job, and I'll remain here and do mine." Following his comment, Krivis moved from behind his desk amid a large cloud of cigar smoke to escort his visitor from his office. Riluciani never forgot that incident nor that exchange. Now suddenly the cardinal with "nothing better to do" was in a position where he could remove his bank's president at any moment. Among the residents of the Vatican Village, a pool of sorts began to form as they tried to predict exactly how many more days would pass before Riluciani showed Krivis the door.

While Cardinal Benoît was busy with his audits of the Vatican Bank and the APSA, Riluciani thought it prudent to do a little digging of his own into the affairs of Vatican banking. Since his election, he'd been in constant contact with his most trusted advisor, Cardinal Dante Leone. Leone, in turn, remained in constant contact with Detectives Cosimo Angelo and Francis Clavering. The former Under-Secretary of State under this pope's predecessor had his own network of contacts and informants that reached far beyond the walls of Vatican City. Men like Gherado Fratello would have been most impressed and jealous of his scope and global reach. Riluciani learned through his confidant's Bank of Italy connections that there were some very concerning transactions between the Krivis' and Ansios' banks. Criminal charges were looming in the near future for Marco Ansios and his fellow directors. Implicated in these numerous serious crimes was the Vatican Bank. The primary perpetrators were Krivis, Rinaldo Manna and one other high ranking secular employee.

Leone's secret agenda that resulted in the election of his close friend as pope was his own personal mission to liberate his beloved church from the clutches of Vatican, Inc. He knew Riluciani would not succumb to pressure when the right action was required. He was a very cerebral man who considered all facts and recommendations presented. He was a very humble man with a gentle heart and stubborn commitment to a decision, once it was made. Leone provided important intelligence on the Bank of Italy's investigation to Riluciani, while P2 informants kept Gherado Fratello in the know in Buenos Aires. When necessary, information received by Fratello would make its way to Marco Ansios.

Many in and around the Church who parasitically depended on "business as usual" in and around the Vatican were suddenly becoming visibly more and more uneasy. Marco Ansios' vacation to South America with his wife for a victory vacation, suddenly made him feel like a fugitive on the run following the election of this new pope, The relaxing, refreshing fun in the sun moments at the beginning of his trip had now been replaced by a Milan banker now more jittery and nervous than ever. Every bit of news coming out of Rome, as far as he was concerned, was bad, very bad. Even his good friend Krivis called to inform him that his own days were numbered while serving under this pope. They all knew that Riluciani was working to completely dismantle everything they had built over the past years.

"Gherado, I think we should change our location tomorrow. We must keep moving. They will find us if we don't."

"My friend, you have nothing to fear." Gherado said calmly, lighting his fragrant cigar, as he took in the sights of tan skinned bikinis flitting and flirting about the resort. "Have another drink Marco, it will do us both some good."

Ansios motioned the scantily clad beautiful blonde waitress over, "A double scotch for me, miss. Gherado will you have anything?"

"I'll have another double shot of bourbon on the rocks. Thank you honey," as he looked her over longingly. He issued a deep lustful sigh as he appreciated the view as she sauntered away to fetch their beverages. A few moments after she disappeared into the crowd, his attention returned to his friend. "Marco, for God's sake, will you relax!"

"Gherado, how on Earth can you be so calm right now. We have a huge problem on our hands."

"What problem?"

"Jonas didn't tell you?"

"Tell me what? What the hell's got you so wound up?"

"This new pope has Krivis in his cross hairs. If he cans Krivis, his replacement will certainly find and expose the true relationship between Banco Generali and The Vatican Bank. Rest assured, replacing Jonas will not be the only change that this pope will be making."

"What the hell Marco! Why the hell didn't you bring this directly to my attention sooner?!"

"I thought you already knew!"

"Oh hell no! Shit, this IS bad, this is really bad. If the Bank of Italy and the finance ministers get wind of any of Jonas' shit, we are all going to rot in a cell somewhere."

The waitress returned a few minutes later with their drinks.

"It's about fucking time lady! Keep 'em comin', ya hear!" Gherado yelled at her, completely disregarding all manners.

"The Bank of Italy has already been looking long and hard for a connection they can pin on me for a while now. If Krivis is removed I wouldn't put it past Riluciani to flat out hand over every Goddamn piece of evidence that ever existed to the authorities. He will implicate us all. When that happens, we are all fucked!"

Gherado thought in silence for a few moments. Then with a sudden gleam in his eye, he snapped his fingers. "Here is what we are going to do, we will get one or two of our guys on the inside, offer them some big cash to 'work things out, or look the other way.'"

"Gherado," Ansios explained, visibly sweating now. "Have you ever had to deal with those men from the Bank of Italy?"

"No, not directly, why?"

"I hate them, you can't bribe them. Believe me, I've tried. They're incorruptible."

"The problem can and will be dealt with." Gherado said, rubbing his slightly stubbled chin thinking. "I assure you my friend, the problem can and will be resolved."

"Well you better get on it fast. I've heard rumors that they are almost done over there."

"Yeah I've heard that too from some of our guys inside the magistrate's office."

"Jonas informed me this morning that the investigation will be handed to some local judge named Armando Padovesi soon."

"Are you telling me that all this is already public Marco?"

"I can't say with any certainty, but Krivis is pretty sure Riluciani knows, and that's more disturbing than anything circulating around the public."

"Yes, I can see how that is a problem. You say Padovesi is the judge working this case?"

"Yeah, do you know him? Is he one of ours?"

"I do know him. Unfortunately, he is not one of ours."

"Shit! I was hoping for something of a break. Anything. Fuck!"

"Well I would strongly suggest that you stay out of Italy for a while Marco. Especially Rome until I can get this situation under control."

"I'm not planning on going anywhere near there anytime soon. But I do feel the need to unload some things, just in case, if you know what I mean."

"I trust your instincts Marco, but if I were you, with everything potentially on display for the world to see, I'd make sure those transactions are above board and legitimate. You know, i's dotted, t's crossed."

"Yeah, that's my plan. Now is not the time for playing games. If nothing changes from its current trajectory, my ass will be sitting in a cell somewhere. I wouldn't be surprised if yours wasn't sitting next to me."

"Marco, I know for the moment, the situation seems bad, really bad. But I don't want you fretting about any of this. Trust me. There is no way in Hell you are going to prison for any of this. That I can promise you."

"I trust you Gherado, I really do, but I just can't help being worried."

"Have another drink Marco. Go have a massage or a swim. Things WILL be ok."

CHAPTER 37

As the first week of his papacy came to an end, the new pope began to sense some indignation from his interim Secretary of State. Cardinal Zacharie Benoît was an 81 year old man who was tired and feeling his years and the burden of his responsibilities and position. He was only a year older than his previous boss. Benoît began the previous papacy as a part of the Roman Curia when both men were in their mid sixties. He didn't become Pope Michael VI's Secretary of State until 1969. Benoît's new boss was fifteen years his junior. This new pontiff was young, spry, healthy, and full of energy and life. By the way the man conducted himself and went about his days, no one would ever guess was actually sixty-five.

Pope Phillip Michael I decided to show some mercy to his reluctant old head of state. The pope lightened his load of responsibilities by removing him as the president of the Pontifical Council. Cardinal Zacharie Benoît desperately wanted a little less on his plate, however, this was not what he had had in mind. His position with the "Council" had him responsible for aggregating funds from all of the Catholic churches around the world. These funds would then be moved to poorer regions to assist other churches and organizations in their work to help the impoverished get back on their feet. Benoît's named successor was a cardinal from West Africa. He was also a longtime close friend and a like-minded colleague of Riluciani. He was a man of great faith in God and the church. He was a man of great integrity, honesty and transparency. He also knew first hand the struggles of the poor, and how to help them.

Pope Phillip Michael I found an interesting pattern forming as he went about his days. It seemed like suddenly nobody inside Vatican City claimed to know or even meet anyone who was a part of the previous pope's Milan Mafia. Ironically, many did know or were actually a part of the infiltration of the church by the Italian Mafia. Those who perpetuated those relationships freely and openly during Pope Michael's term quickly distanced themselves and denied ever meeting or knowing men like Fedora, Ansios or Fratello. Self preservation quickly became an increasingly important endeavor. Their little syndicate network of spies that remained in the new pope's temporary cabinet sent communications and intelligence constantly back to the papal apartments. They all knew who was next in this new pope's cross hairs.

Riluciani continued to be bothered by the papal entourage constantly buzzing about him, like flies that annoy a horse. His new staff were puzzled and somewhat put off by his manner and style. While he was committed to the work of his new job, he suffered tremendously from the absence of the familiar. He longed for his days of service to the community back in Venice. He also missed his attending staff back in Venice. Both the papal staff and pontiff were greatly relieved when Father Vincenzo Mancini and Sister Vittoria Falcone finally arrived from Venice. Other than his own family, nobody knew the Holy Father better than his personal assistant Falcone and personal secretary Mancini who had served Riluciani faithfully for years.

He was a simple and approachable man who didn't want to just be seen by his flock. He wanted to interact with them, he wanted to talk with them on their level without offending their intellect. He drew great inspiration for his point of view from the likes of Mark

Twain, Jules Verne and even the familiar classics like Pinocchio. His audiences embraced this relatable pope warmly, while bishops and cardinals of the Curia cringed at his odd, uncouth, and simple ways. Unlike his predecessor, he was comfortable interacting personally with reporters of the press. His ability to speak multiple languages fluently meant that he had no need for an interpreter. During his youth, he had aspirations of becoming a journalist, before being called to join the priesthood of the Church. Becoming a priest did nothing to curtail his passion to write in the least. Prior to becoming pope, he had already penned two books and published numerous articles. The media and public loved his familiar style, but his retained staff remained aloof. The constant censorship of Pope Phillip Michael I's "official" materials, documents and speeches that would become part of his official records and archives kept the Vatican Public Relations Department extremely busy. Speeches, sermons and more became censored, boring, formal lectures void of warmth and connection.

One afternoon, following his meditative walk through the papal gardens, Riluciani returned to his study. He thumbed through the mail left on his desk, until a copy of *Il Governo Guarda* caught his eye. He had never seen this publication before. Scanning the headlines, he called his personal cook and housekeeper into his study.

"Vittoria?" He called through the open door, into the other room. "Do you know where this paper came from?"

Sister Falcone entered the study and examined the publication.

"Your Holiness,..."

"Vittoria..." he responded with a 'please don't call me that' attitude.

Sister Falcone smiled broadly, knowing how much he hated such titles. "I just had to once, Chiaros..."

"Well I'm glad that's over with then." Riluciani responded relieved.

Sister Falcone continued with a slight smile looking at the paper in his hand. "I'm not sure where that came from, as far as I know, it was a part of today's mail. I'm sorry, but that is all I know of it."

"I didn't subscribe to this."

"I'm sorry Your Holi...I mean Chiaros, I don't have a better answer for you."

As his eyes caught an article of interest, his voice faded, while he continued to read the article.

"Thank you Vittoria, that will be all."

"Of course Holy Father." She didn't bother to correct herself this time, as she turned and left the chamber.

While he was puzzled as to how he was added to the publication's mailing lists. This edition of *Il Governo Guarda,* and the ones that would follow, gave this new pope useful, yet at times shocking intelligence. The editor had quite the knack for publishing scandalous stories that seemed highly accurate. Philip Michael became particularly engrossed with this mid-September issue. "The Vatican's Masons" headline captured his attention immediately. In the article was a list of over 100 members of Masonic Lodges who also held positions within the church. Philip Michael was well aware that the Roman Catholic Church long ago had decreed its opposition to Freemasonry. Involvement in Masonry was to result in immediate excommunication from the church. This pope's Curial staff sure liked to wave what was proper policy and procedure in his face constantly. Ironically, here was a perfect example of his predecessor and many of the same Curial staff, willing to ignore certain policies in the past whenever it served their purposes.

Philip Michael began hoping for the best, but bracing for the worst, as he began to read the article. The list included several laymen like Fedora, Ansios, Fratello, and a few others; these men were not of his concern. The majority of the men listed were cardinals, bishops and high ranking prelates. These were the men that Riluciani would need to strip of their titles and punish for their crimes against the church. Perhaps even more troubling was the fact that they had him almost completely surrounded. At the top of the list was none other than his own Secretary of State, Cardinal Zacharie Benoît. He immediately felt better about his decision to remove Benoît from several of his positions.

He let out a long vocal sigh of relief that two of his closest confidants, Cardinals Frates and Leone were nowhere to be found in the article. He closed his paper and immediately called Cardinal Frates and his personal secretaries Fathers Mancini and Barton to his office chamber. He then called Cardinal Leone so he could participate in the discussion from his office in Florence.

"Colleagues, thank you for making yourselves available at such short notice."

"Service to you is what we are here for Your Holiness."

Riluciani cringed a little at the formality, but smiled without correcting Father Barton in this instance. "There is some very disturbing news that has come to my attention, and it is very important that we correct this problem straight away."

"Of course Your Holiness, how can we assist you?" Replied Cardinal Frates.

Riluciani explained what he had just read to the assembled, then handed the article to Frates. Frates' face went wide-eyed in shock and disbelief as he read through the names on the list.

"Holiness, I knew it was bad, but I had no idea it was this bad."

Frates passed the article to Father Barton who had a similar reaction, then passed it on to Father Mancini to look over. The latter was less reactive to the list since he was still in the process of getting to know who was who in the Curial staff.

"I don't understand, you already knew about all of this? Is this list accurate?" Questioned Riluciani

Cardinal Leone chimed in. "Well Holiness, I do know that a similar list was quietly passed around in May of '76. Also given the reputation of the editor of that paper, I would not question the validity of this information Holy Father."

"So this is in no way a new problem within the Vatican?"

"Absolutely not, Holiness. I am only puzzled by why this list has surfaced now. Are they trying to influence some of the changes that are to be expected from a newly elected pope?" Questioned Frates.

"That's an entirely plausible thought Frates." deduced Leone.

"So what you are saying is that the press already knows of these church officials' involvement in P2?"

"Yes, Holiness." Responded Frates.

"For how long?"

"I'd say for at least two years now, Holiness."

"They've published this whole list before?"

"No Holiness," responded Leone. "A name here, an article there, never an entire list like this one."

"How did the Vatican respond to the articles and information in the past?"

"In typical Vatican fashion, Your Holiness...there was no response issued." Leone continued.

"During your time with Pope Michael, did he ever change or entertain the idea of changing the canon laws pertaining to clergy belonging to the Freemasons?"

"Holiness, he was being pressured from various groups, he was still considering changes when the Holy Father passed." Responded Frates. "Also, you should know that Cardinal Benoît was the one pushing hardest for the relaxation of those exact laws."

"I'm not all that surprised since his name is listed here in the article." replied the Holy Father. "Well we must make sure this list is accurate before we dismiss anyone from their positions and duties."

"We can cross reference the list with the Italian Government, Holiness." Suggested Frates.

"I don't understand," replied Philip Michael I.

Frates continued. "Under Italian Law, all organizations like theirs must have their membership lists registered as public record with the government."

"Oh really? I was not aware of that."

"Yes sir. It wouldn't be too hard to verify this list at all."

"Cardinal Frates, may I task you with following up on verifying the validity of this article?"

"Of course. I will get on it right away, Holiness. I should have something for you no later than tomorrow evening."

"Excellent, thank you.

"Since we are all gathered here," Cardinal Leone interrupted. "Holiness, have you seen the latest communication put out by the Italian Minister of Foreign Trade?"

"I'm not sure, cardinal, why do you ask?"

"Hang on the line while I go get my copy from the other room. I will be right back."

Upon returning, Cardinal Leone explained to his new pope, and the other assembled men a letter signed by the Foreign Trade Minister. Reluciani quickly realized that he too had recently received his own copy of that letter. Apparently it had been sent to all of the banks in Italy, confirming, and reminding all of them that the Vatican Bank was considered a foreign bank in the eyes of the government. Any transactions between Italian banks and the Vatican Bank were subject to the rules and regulations set by the Foreign Trade Minister's office. The letter went on to address the very real problem of currency abuse. Their biggest concern was the volume of Italian money being illegally transferred to other countries through the Vatican Bank.

The new pope produced the same letter brought to his attention by Cardinal Leone, then passed it around for the others to read.

"While the letter, on the surface, doesn't have anything to do with our P2 clergy, it does bring to light some of the activities of our church's bank and president." Commented Relucini.

The letter was without a doubt a response to the open letter that was addressed to him a few days after his election in a popular paper. The Italian Office of Exchange Control under the guise of the Minister of Foreign Trade reiterated that the Vatican Bank was a foreign bank. This distinction meant that the Vatican Bank ran by Krivis was required to abide by the same rules and regulations as any other bank outside of Italy. The article implored the new pontiff to rectify these currency manipulation abuses and the illegal transfers of monies out of Italy.

Following his meeting, Philip Michael I took some time to study the newspaper in even more detail. His eyes stopped when he saw the names of Ansios, Fedora and Krivis. He already had plenty of reasons to remove the president of the Vatican Bank, this article just added more fuel to the fire. He knew that P2 was Gherado Fratello's beast. After everything he had learned about these men over the last few years, none of these new revelations were all that shocking.

Philip Michael I already had a feeling of dislike and distrust for Krivis. He sat at his desk remembering his first face to face interaction with the man. Recalling the vanity and conduct of the man, as he sat across from him watching him puff on his cigar and drinking his scotch. The whole display was disgusting. The interaction between him and that young little secretary of his with her bosoms and legs on full display was far from appropriate. When Riluciani finally vocalized the complaints and protests of his congregation to the bank president. Krivis listened intently to him, then responded, "Eminence, I am certain that you must have better things to fill your day, don't you?" Then he continued after taking a drag off of his cigar. "I tell you what Cardinal Riluciani, you go back to your parish in Venice. You do your job, and I will stay here and continue to do mine." Without another word from either of them, the future pope was escorted out of the banker's office.

Philip Michael was not one to let his personal feelings for anyone cloud his judgment, but this situation was now beyond something personal. Ricluciani's distaste for Krivis was now far beyond anything personal. This pontiff was also not one to make knee jerk decisions, especially in disciplinary matters. He made some calls first. After confirming with Italian authorities that members of his church staff were in fact members of the P2 lodge. The new pope was now nauseous. How was he going to excise the Masonic and Mafia cancers from his church? Could he actually remove such influential groups from the Church? If he was successful in removing them, how would he keep them from coming back? The second part of his dilemma, of course, was dependent on the success of the first part.

Philip Michael became more and more disturbed by what he continued to learn about his beloved church. He was grateful for the loyalty of Frates, Leone, Mancini and Barton. He would lean heavily on the information and guidance from Cardinal Leone in the coming weeks. After his little meeting, he viewed many of his visitors with a greater level of scrutiny than he ever did before. The problem with Freemasons was their ability to seamlessly blend in with the rest of the population. They thrived best in an environment filled with secrecy and symbolism.

He was beginning to grow more comfortable with his newly elected role and what God had chosen him to do. It was also helpful knowing who could and could not trust among his staff. He was determined to correct the atrocities committed by his clergy. Also, while they were outside of his jurisdiction, he would lose no sleep in helping the Italian government shut down the operations of Fratello, Ansios, and Fedora.

Pope Phillip Michael I was an extremely busy man contending with important issues plaguing his Church. P2 spies were already scattered throughout Vatican City. Their work on behalf of their leader Gherado Fratello was suddenly becoming more and more important as the days passed. They worked hard funneling intelligence out of the Vatican and back to their Worshipful Master and eventually on to Marco Ansios and Giovanni Fedora.

CHAPTER 38

In a sunny and fun destination located on the outskirts of Buenos Aires, Argentina, Marco Ansios was not having a good time at all. All around him, everywhere he looked was new information coming his way, and every last bit of it was bad. His usual anxiety ridden manner had now morphed into a state of paranoid fantasy. Ansios was completely convinced that everything that Pope Phillip Michael I was now doing was motivated by a personal vendetta against him. Everything that was happening inside the Vatican Curia right now was payback for his dirty deeds that resulted in the takeover of the Catholic Bank of Venice. Why else would this new pope be conducting a complete audit of the Vatican Bank?

Everyone knew the true joy and smiles that were the hallmarks of the pope's personality; however, very few people on the planet had ever seen the more serious side of the new leader of the Catholic Church. Marco Ansios was one of the few who saw the anger and wrath Riluciani was capable of first hand. The man may have been relatively new to the rest of the world, but he knew exactly what he was doing when he organized countless protests with the clergy, staff and members of the Venice community in years past. The protests were relentless. Marco Ansios thought he would never see the day when they would finally stop.

The new owner of Catholic Bank of Venice at that time tried everything to bring the protests to a civil and immediate end. Nothing seemed to appease Cardinal Riluciani and his followers. Bishop Jonas Krivis told Ansios, "Everybody has a price." His friend in the Vatican Bank suggested a peace offering in the form of a large charitable gift endowment for his most favored pet project for the mentally and physically handicapped, thinking this donation might bring the protests and bad press to an end. It did not.

Riluciani threw the money back in Ansios' face, and told him to leave, and to take all of his dirty money with him. The patriarch of Venice then instructed his organized protesters to withdraw all of their funds and close out their accounts. Their money and business in the future would be managed by a crosstown rival. Ansios' new little goldmine of a bank was becoming a money pit thanks to the anger and efforts of one man. The same man who now sits on the pope's throne in Vatican City.

It has been said that time and tide waits for no man. The days of September marched on unsympathetic to the issues of Marco Ansios or any of his friends or associates. His nerves and paranoia became more and more exacerbated with each new day and the news that came his way out of Italy. His constant moving from one South American country to another did nothing to bring him peace. Only his closest confidant, Gherado Fratello, was his only source of the smallest sliver of hope.

Marco Ansios knew that whoever the new pope selected to replace Bishop Krivis as head of the Vatican Bank, would expose the true relationship between the Vatican Bank and Banco Generali for all the world to see. Many important laymen in senior administrative positions of the bank would soon be removed from their positions. Their replacements would then provide Pope Phillip Michael I with every bit of dirt uncovered. Then the information from his own internal probe would be passed along to investigators with the Bank of Italy. The very same investigative body working on behalf of

Italy's Finance Ministers would ultimately result in Marco Ansios spending the rest of his life in prison.

At this point, Marco Ansios had already embezzled over $400 million. The incredible irony of his scheme was how absolutely clueless the presidents and administrators of other banks seemed to be. While he was in the process of literally robbing banks by the dozen, others were constantly knocking on his office door. It was as if each one was trying to outdo the other for the privileged and prestigious opportunity of lending Banco Generali money.

The ongoing investigation underway by incorruptible men at the Bank of Italy did nothing to curtail the thievery of the man. As his bank heists started to reach their peak, he was informed by P2 Grandmaster of even more bad news. Through Fratello's network of men who worked in the Magistrate's office their investigation was almost finished. Fratello did his best to reassure the paymaster of his P2 Masonic lodge that solutions were in the works. Ansios remained cautiously optimistic.

Ansios was unsure of what Fratello had in mind, the details were never discussed. All he knew was that it needed to happen soon. It needed to happen before Bishop Krivis and others were removed from their positions at the Vatican Bank. He was hopeful that whatever Fratello's plans were, they would buy him some time to "take care of some business." Gherado Fratello sat and listened as an ever increasingly anxious Marco Ansios confided in him the worst of his fears. "I promise you Marco, your problems will be resolved, trust me."

Another man with growing concerns regarding what was happening inside the walls of Vatican City was Giovanni Fedora. He too was greatly concerned about the removal of Krivis as Vatican Bank president. Krivis would be just one of many problematic dominoes to fall. His removal followed by Ansios' imprisonment would negate whatever strategy remained in his long, drawn out extradition. His fight would be over. Many of Mr. Fedora's problems were quite similar to those of his protégé Ansios. He too sought the assistance of Grandmaster Fratello. He too was reassured that his problems would be resolved.

In New York, the case against Giovanni Fedora in the failure of Franklin National Bank was moving along well in the minds of investigators and prosecutors. The upcoming trial against him was going to be long and extremely complex. The New York DA and federal prosecutors were working in tandem; they were not interested in leaving anything to chance in their case against him. The details of the case being brought against him was impressive, it was clear that investigators had invested massive amounts of resources and manpower in their efforts. Even Fedora himself was impressed with some of their investigative skills.

On September 5, 1978, Mr. Nico Novelli was indicted. He immediately pled not guilty to all charges filed against him. He was then offered a plea deal, which he eagerly accepted. In exchange for his guilty plea on lesser charges of misapplication of bank funds and falsification of bank records he would help the prosecution with their case against Fedora. Novelli's sentence would be suspended until his work with prosecutors was complete.

One of the important strategies of Fedora's defense team in New York was the in-person testimony by Vatican Bank President, Bishop Jonas Krivis and two other cardinals from the Vatican Curia. It would be their most important job to help sway the jury in Fedora's favor. Pope Michael VI had already, reluctantly, given the approval for the three men to travel to America to deliver their testimony. Things had changed significantly since that time. Their ally pope was now dead, and his replacement was a man who had absolutely zero intention of helping Fedora nor any of his friends. Pope Michael VI's successor immediately withdrew the permissions granted for the Curial entourage to appear in any American court on Fedora's behalf. This sudden development left Fedora's defense team scrambling for another, hopefully just as effective defense strategy.

In Italy, multiple cases were building simultaneously against Fedora. Some of them were complex, others were much more simple and straightforward. The Italian authorities had already made it clear that they would not wait for their American counterparts to complete their long winded, drawn out legal process. They had already heard cases, made rulings and handed down sentences against him. They had more cases ready to be heard whether Fedora and his legal team were present or not.

A Milanese court had no interest in participating in Fedora's waiting game. They found him guilty of twenty three counts of mishandling almost 15 billion lira. The Milanese court then sentenced him to four years in prison and all of his assets were immediately frozen. This conviction, however, had absolutely nothing to do with the ongoing investigation by the Bank of Italy and Italian Finance Ministers regarding his Milan bank failures.

Fedora was suddenly in a very unfamiliar situation, one he had never experienced in all of his adult life. With all of his assets frozen in both the United States and Italy he became extremely uneasy and in a particularly foul mood. Fedora's American lawyers were still doing their best to stall his inevitable extradition back to Italy. Things were constantly changing, and it seemed like it was never for the better for Mr. Fedora. Other parts of Europe were now starting to line up with legal action. He was now wanted for questioning in connection with financial crimes elsewhere. They were ready to take their own legal shots at the disgraced Italian financier.

He was now all out of options. It was time for him to reach out to P2 leader Gherado Fratello for an infusion of cash, information and help.

"Fran, call for you on line 3..." came a voice from the hall.

"Thanks Jack!" Fran responded as he picked up the line. "Detective Clavering..."

"Hey Fran, it's Cosimo."

"Cosimo, my man, what's new in your world?" The detective queried as he got up to close his office door.

"A lot really."

"Oh yeah? Talk to me..."

"Fedora and Ansios have me running all over the Goddamn place over here."

"I can only imagine. Is your friend Arturo still working on his audit of Fedora's bank there in Milan."

"He is, as a matter of fact, I was just talking to him the other day about it. You wouldn't believe what an insane mess he has had to untangle."

"After digging into his failure over here, I can commiserate with some of what he is going through. Are you working with Arturo? Or do they have you working on other things?"

"No, he's on his own over there. They have me working with the Finance Minister's office and officials at the Bank of Italy investigating Ansios."

"That's great! How's that coming along?"

"Well, we now know all of the dirty details of how the Catholic Bank of Venice changed hands from the Vatican to Ansios a few years back."

"I bet Riluciani will be glad to see that."

"Yeah, and it definitely has Ansios', Krivis' and Fedora's fingerprints all over it..."

"...which isn't a surprise to anyone we know."

"It too is a big complicated mess. It's a lot for me to wrap my brain around some days. Despite all of that, the preliminary reports where we found a ton of gross irregularities have already been passed along to a local judge over here named Armando Padovesi."

"That's great to hear Cosimo! Do we know anything about that judge?"

"Yeah, Arturo has worked with him for years. He's a good man, with impeccable integrity, ethics, and a beautiful family."

"That's wonderful news. Looks like everything is heading in the right direction over there." Fran took a deep audible breath. "These three men sure weave a most complicated tangled web, don't they."

"That they do. That's why we had to split up our investigation efforts over here. We would have missed a lot of important information had we not."

"That makes a lot of sense, and I'm really glad you guys took that approach. So, what else is new over there Cosimo?"

"Oh shit, I almost forgot...I got a call from Leone."

"Oh yeah? How is he?"

"Well he'd rather be in the Vatican than Florence right now, but that's another story. He tells me that he's been in frequent conversations with Riluciani since he was elected pope."

"Nice! I talked to Wexford the other day too."

"Yeah? What'd he have to say?"

"He's pretty sure that once Riluciani gets his feet under him, Leone will be appointed his Secretary of State."

"Oh wow! That is some great news! I hope it's true. He seems like he's the perfect man for the job!"

"Did Leone say anything else?"

"He said that on day one Riluciani got his interim Secretary of State busy auditing all the financial nooks and crannies of the Vatican, including the Vatican Bank!"

"Well son of a bitch, that is some of the best news I've heard in months. Maybe now we can finally get somewhere with our investigation involving Krivis and that damn bank he's running."

"He also said that Riluciani wants to have another meeting with all of us soon, in Rome."

"Oh really? When?"

"They are thinking that all of the audits should be done in another week or two, so he's thinking maybe sometime around the 29th. Do you think you can get the time off?"

Fran quickly glanced at his calendar and cringed a little. That was only two weeks away. "I will see what I can do, and let you know as soon as possible. I know the importance of all of this, but damn I hate having to sneak around like this."

"I thought you said Christopherson knew what you were really working on over there under the cover of staying on the Fedora case?"

"He does, but coming from a man who rarely ever took time off, these trips are bound to raise some eyebrows around here. This dual life is really exhausting after a while."

"Tell me about it."

"So are you going to get in touch with Hans about the upcoming meeting?"

"Yeah, I will take care of that."

"Thanks. It will be good to see you guys again."

"Yeah, same here. Are you going to bring Peg again?"

"Yeah, it's easier to sell it as a vacation or family emergency, or whatever I come up with, if I don't leave her behind."

"That's true. I'm sure she won't mind."

"Are you kidding, she will be over the moon. I can hear her squealing with delight already." The two detectives shared a chuckle. "She had so much fun with your's and Hans' wife in Venice last time."

"Yeah, my wife wouldn't stop talking about it for days either."

"I wonder if Cardinal Wexford knows of the meeting yet?"

"I will find out soon enough, I'm sure Leone wouldn't leave him in the dark."

"Hey Cosimo, before you go, do you mind if I pick your brain a bit regarding Fedora?"

"Of course not, Fran, how can I help you?"

"Well he and his legal team are still over here playing their bullshit games. But I think he's starting to run out of options and tactics."

"Finally! It's about damn time."

"That's what I've been thinking since all this shit started... anyways, Lance and I have noticed he's suddenly been having a lot of conversations with some guy that I think is down in Argentina named Gherado Fratello. Have you ever heard of him? He sure knows a lot about our usual suspects, and the Vatican."

Cosimo went quiet for a moment. When he finally spoke, Fran detected a great deal of concern in the voice of his Italian counterpart. "Yeah I've heard of him. If he is now working with Fedora, we need to proceed with even more caution."

"Really? Why? Who is he?"

"He is the leader of a global Masonic group called P2."

"P2?" Fran scanned his memory for a moment. "Huh, I've never even heard of him or them."

"Fratello is a very dangerous and powerful man, Fran. He controls a lot of important and powerful men scattered throughout Europe, South America and the United States."

"I had no idea...like what kind of men are we talking about here?"

"Men from every industry imaginable. Military, government, judicial, law enforcement, media, and practically every sector of business. The list goes on and on, but you get the idea. I just read in an article the other day that he even has people in the Vatican, including Riluciani's current Secretary of State."

"Oh shit! Do you think Riluciani knows?"

"Yeah, I was talking to Leone about it. He just had a conversation with him about it yesterday as a matter of fact."

"That's good, and bad. So what does this Fratello guy do to keep all of these influential men scattered about the world?"

"The world is like his chess board, and he is this global chess master, moving his pieces around to do his own dirty work and the dirty work of others, as he sees fit. I am told that he was the one responsible for Juan Peron's return to power in Argentina a few years back."

"Wow, that is impressive."

"He's been known to work in concert and independently with major Mafia syndicates too. He is a hardcore fascist who has turned his P2 Masonic organization into a very real state within a state if you will."

"Do we know how he maintains all this control over these men of influence and power?"

"He's gathered his pieces through blackmail, favors, bribes and promises of position or advancement."

"Blackmail? I thought Novelli said that that was Fedora's MO?"

"Yeah, I remember him saying that too."

"So why would a master blackmailer like Fedora now seem to be such close friends with someone like Fratello all of a sudden?"

"Well Fedora is one of his lodge members. So are Ansios and Krivis according to what I read in that article."

"That's interesting, but still doesn't answer my question."

"My best guess is that he is now helping Fedora."

"From the conversations I've been hearing between him and Fedora, it sounds like he's helping Ansios too."

"Yeah, they both are in a lot of trouble at the moment."

"So what kind of help are we talking about here?"

"He controls some of the people working on the investigations over here. I'm pretty damn sure of it, now that you mention it. I'd bet good money that his men are the reasons why everything is moving so Goddamn slow over here, especially with the big cases we are building against Fedora and Ansios."

"Lance and I are hearing lots of whining from Fedora, now that his assets have all been frozen."

"Yeah, I've heard that too. That certainly gives another plausible explanation of why he's so buddy-buddy with Fratello all of a sudden. That also by extension, makes Fedora a very dangerous man. The only allies he has left now are his Mafia friends and Fratello with his P2 network. We need to be very careful as we go forward."

"Oh yeah, why's that?"

"Leone tells me that Fratello has spies pretty much everywhere... but then again, so does he."

"That's good to know...about both of them."

"Leone advised that we maintain our lowest profiles possible. After what you just told me Fran, that advice is even more important. Keep eyes and ears open wide, and mouths shut! We are still working against some extremely dangerous men."

CHAPTER 39

The new pope was a very different man than most of his predecessors. This pontiff was not interested in the ways and rituals of Rome. He longed for simple days filled with his own established ways and routines that had served him so well for the last sixty-five years. The papal staff could not understand his fussiness and refusal of the elaborate. Pope Michael VI wanted every bit of it and then some.

The Vatican staff and attendants did their best to accommodate him, but failed miserably at every turn. Everyone, especially the Holy Father, was relieved with the arrival of reinforcement staff, two of the most beloved members of his staff from Venice. The reunion of Riluciani with Sister Falcone and Father Mancini put everyone at ease. The pope's two closest attendants found themselves just as out of sorts back in Venice without their charge, as he was without them in Rome.

Sister Falcone had worked for or rather with him for nearly twenty years. She knew him better than anyone, his likes, his dislikes and his day to day routine. Her life had essentially become an extension of his over the years. She immediately dismissed the papal chefs from their positions. It was her job to cook for, clean for and fuss after the man she knew as Chiaros Riluciani. It was her job and duty that morphed into a labor of love and reverence for the man who had over the years become her closest friend within the church. She would often dine with him, keeping him company when he wasn't entertaining guests. They exchanged laughs, thoughts and tears over the years. She brought great peace to his spirit, even when she was pestering him like a caring mother to rest when he'd get too wrapped up in his work, or to take his medication for his low blood pressure.

A typical day in the life of this pontiff and his staff began early. At 4:30 AM every morning, Sister Falcone would bring a carafe of hot coffee to the study that adjoined his sleeping chamber. The alarm clock on his bedside table would chime every morning at 5 am. Its sole purpose was to ensure that Riluciani didn't oversleep. Once he had a little coffee in his system, he'd begin to prepare himself for his day. He'd bathe and shave while getting in a lesson or two of his latest language course via a cassette tape course. Next, he would make his way to a little private chapel for meditation, prayer and the reciting of his Breviary.

At 7 AM he would meet up with his two personal secretaries, Fathers Mancini and Barton. Father Barton served under the last pope. He was retained more for continuity than anything. Father Mancini, like Sister Falcone, had served Riluciani for many many years in Venice. He too seemed like a lost soul before joining him and Falcone in Rome. The three of them and the Holy Father would then join the other nuns and assemble staff for morning mass.

After mass, Sister Falcone would serve him his breakfast in his study. He would read through several Newspapers as he consumed his breakfast usually consisting of some fruit and a modest piece of bread and more coffee. The oppressive poverty of his younger years greatly impacted his simplistic palate and birdlike dietary habits. The remainder of his morning, until 10 am, was spent in silence as he prepared for the visitors on his schedule for that day.

His days between 10 am and lunch were the most relatively chaotic parts of his well regimented days. Pope Phillip Michael I would host his guests on the second floor of the Apostolic Palace. It was there that strict time constraints and routine would fall away as he ventured into deep, meaningful conversations with each of his visitors. The Curial attending staff would drive themselves insane trying to keep him on schedule, but this pope would not fit into their time restricted boxes. His appointments almost always ran over, throwing off the rest of his morning schedule as the morning progressed. Some may have considered his disregard for punctuality a rude gesture, but all was forgiven once their own meeting began. This pope was most skilled at making his guests feel not just heard, but listened to. He may not have agreed with everything discussed, but everyone felt like he genuinely listened to their wants, cares and concerns.

Riluciani would be served his lunch promptly at 12:30 pm. Unlike his predecessor, he'd often enjoy his lunch in the company of women. His niece and sister-in-law were frequent guests for a modest two course meal beginning with either pasta or minestrone soup followed by whatever Sister Falcone decided to make that day. If his lunch wasn't in the company of family, Sister Falcone herself would join him. Curial staff just shook their heads at this Holy Father's most unusual ways and habits. In all of their days, they'd never seen anything like it.

Following his lunch he'd retreat to the papal gardens for a walk. If the weather was nice, he'd sit on a slightly shaded bench with his nose buried deeply in one of his many treasured books. If the weather was less than desirable, he'd return to his study for his reading time. When he arrived for his appointment as patriarch in Venice many years ago, all he had with him were a few linens, a few sticks of furniture and several boxes of books. During his time in Venice the only thing that had changed about the man was the size of his personal library. His heart was filled with much joy as he was reunited with his most cherished material possessions. He appreciated Father Mancini bringing them with him when he made the trek from Venice to Rome. His most dog-eared, worn volumes were written by Mark Twain, but he also enjoyed the tomes of Sir Walter Scott, Jules Verne, Shakespeare, Dante Alighieri and Homer that also occupied his bookshelves.

No later than 4 PM each day, Riluciani would return to his office to quickly go over his schedule and visitors for the following day. Roughly thirty minutes later, he'd meet with members of his inner cabinet over chamomile tea served by Sister Falcone. This time was his opportunity to ensure the changes and actions he wished to implement in the church were progressing satisfactorily. Some in attendance appreciated his efforts, leadership and ideas for the future of the Catholic Church, others disagreed and whined like spoiled children about the disappearance of their elevated status and lifestyle in the church, which greatly affected their materialistic world.

Unless Riluciani had guests, dinner would be served at around 7:45 PM usually with Fathers Mancini and Barton in his company. When he wasn't entertaining, his dinner, like his lunch, was a simplistic dining affair, at times consisting of leftovers from the day before. He had no desire to mingle with the rich, and people of power with their stuffy ways, over expensive bottles of wine. His drinks of choice were coffee, tea and mineral water.

The remainder of his evening would consist of an update on current global and regional events via the televised news. He would then return to his office one final time to review and prepare for his guests and the events of the following day. This was usually done with his two secretaries and Sister Falcone to keep them in the loop. He'd leave his office to recite his final Breviary for the day, then retire to his sleeping chamber for the night sometime around 9:30 pm.

This was his usual routine, however, moments of spontaneity would find him throwing his own routine, and Vatican protocol to the wind. The Swiss Guards were kept on their toes when the mood for an extemporaneous strolls through Vatican gardens struck their new pope. Riluciani hated the Swiss Guard's kneeling before him without speaking as he approached. He would smile and actually help them to their feet, then converse with them openly and freely. He hastily did away with the ridiculous demands of Pope Michael VI. "I am not one who should be knelt to, I am not one deserving nor demanding of such treatment." He was not one to be waited on. Falcone and Mancini already knew this. Father Barton took a little longer to get used to it. The fact that this pope made and answered his own phone calls was the oddest thing for his secretary to grasp.

When he was in an especially playful mood he would go on mini excursions. The exploration of some of the Vatican's 10,000 rooms and hallways, and the 997 stairways. His favorites were the thirty secret stairway passages scattered about the Holy City. Sometimes he ventured alone, other times with the company of Father Mancini. Cardinal Benoît found this pope most annoying when he'd just appear in the Secretary of State's office completely unannounced.

Patience grew thinner with each passing day for this new pope who "did not know his place" and "his complete disregard of Curial and church protocols." This new pope seemed to be everywhere, and he had his fingers in everything that was going on with his church. Most alarming of all to the tenured, temporary staff was that he was making changes daily. Changes they very much disliked. It was only a matter of time before every last one of them would be off doing a different job, most likely in a different location.

Riluciani tried over and over again to reason with his traditionalist staff. However, it was nothing but a futile waste of time. Their world and traditions were not his. He had zero desire to participate in the pomposity of their existence. He much preferred to walk and talk freely with the public, for he felt that he was in no way a better man than any of them. He too was a sinner in the eyes of God. He had more serious and important things to devote his time and energy to, than the constant stroking of his own vain ego or anyone else's.

He'd receive correspondence daily, filled with every world problem imaginable. Many were inherited from the days when Pope Michael VI ran the church. Numerous groups approached him demanding change, accountability and transparency. He was attentive to all who sought out his advice, wisdom and leadership.

He quickly became an enigma to the press and media assigned to report on the Vatican. This Curial outsider, as far as they were concerned, came to Rome without any type of experience or reputation for foreign affairs. He was selected to bring something new and fresh to the old stale rooms and halls of the Holy City. The

College of Cardinals wanted him for exactly who and what he was: a man of humility, integrity and brilliance to lead the church away from a place of power, materialism and greed. The unintended irony was that this new relatable pope of the people was quickly becoming more and more celebrated and noble in the minds of the faithful Catholics scattered about the world.

Pope Phillip Michael I switched off the television showing the evening news, he had seen enough of the world's ills for the evening. It was time for him to retire to his study. While he was in the process of reviewing the next day's scheduled visitors he was joined by Fathers Barton and Mancini and Sister Falcone. The appointment he was anticipating most was at 10AM the next morning. He would be the first pope to welcome a leader of the Russian Orthodox Church to Vatican City. It was his desire to bring the major religions of the world together in some way, without compromising the discipline and teachings of the Catholic Church. Metropolitan Otravlen traveled with his delegation all the way to Rome from Leningrad to meet and congratulate the new pope.

The next morning at 10AM, many people filed into his second floor office in the Apostolic Palace. The Russian archbishop joined him for a brief private meeting. Shortly after that, the pope's two secretaries joined them, followed by the pope's Secretary of State, Cardinal Zacharie Benoît, and then the Russian archbishop's small entourage. There was a considerable cacophony of conversation as people and chairs moved about, and everyone settled into their positions. Sister Falcone served the Russian leader a hot cup of coffee in a fine china cup. Their guest was feeling parched and took a couple of sips right away while the other men were still getting settled into their seats. Sister Falcone quietly returned to the small coffee station to get another cup for the pope and other guests. She handed a cup to Cardinal Benoît, who passed the cup to Phillip Michael I who was just beyond the nun's reach. Otravlen began to talk and introduce his staff over the course of the next fifteen minutes. His final introduction was of his personal secretary of many years and a little bit of their history of working together.

The attention of everyone in the room was fixed on the speaking archbishop when suddenly he stopped talking, mid sentence. The delicate china cup in his hands fell to the floor, instantly shattering into a thousand pieces as it hit the hard floor. Sister Falcone let out a scream as she watched his face contort like someone suffering in silent agony. Everything after that seemed to happen in slow motion. The man's body slumped forward in his chair before falling to the floor with a great thud, the Russian made no effort to brace himself for the impact of the fall.

Father Barton immediately left the chamber to fetch medical personnel. Riluciani put down the cup of coffee in his own hand as he watched what was happening before him. Cardinal Benoît rushed to Otravlen's side trying his best to make the man as comfortable as possible as he writhed on the floor in pain. The cardinal was soon joined on the floor by the Holy Father. Both men immediately began to pray over him. The archbishop pulled the pope close to him and whispered something in his ear. Otravlen's secretary placed some nitroglycerine tablets in the pope's hand with instructions to place them under the archbishop's tongue. The archbishop used what remained of his strength and breath to pull the Holy Father close to him to once again whisper in his ear. The Holy Father looked up at the assistant, with great sadness in his eyes. I'm sorry, it is too late for such an intervention. Tears began flowing freely down the pope's face as he recited the absolution and last rites in Latin. Moments later the Vatican physician arrived. Nothing could be done but to declare the Russian Orthodox Metropolitan Otravlen deceased and noting the time of his passing.

The event weighed heavily on those assembled in the office. The Holy Father was so distraught he canceled all remaining appointments for the day. Sister Falcone retired to her quarters as one of the other nuns was dispatched to the office to clean up the spilled coffee and the shards of the china cup scattered about the floor. The remaining guests in the office, still in a state of absolute shock, were eventually dismissed by Cardinal Benoît. Father Mancini took an extra moment before he and the cardinal left the chamber themselves.

The body of the archbishop was moved to the physician's office accompanied by his longtime secretary. Following a cursory examination of the body, and a brief conversation with the dead man's assistant, it was announced that the forty-eight year old Russian religious leader had been a heavy smoker for many years and had already survived four heart attacks prior to the onset of this fatal one. Regardless of prior history, heart attack was the standard explanation for most sudden deaths at the Vatican. The body of the Russian archbishop was embalmed quickly after his death without a proper autopsy or a complete medical examination.

CHAPTER 40

The days following the passing of Russian Metropolitan Otravelen found Reluciani working with a greater sense of urgency as he went about his day. He had brief conversations with Cardinal Leone and Detective Cosimo Angelo about the events of that fateful morning leading up to the death of the Russian archbishop. They too perceived the events with a suspicious mind frame. Cardinal Leone had witnessed similar events during his tenure with Pope Michael VI. The remainder of his conversation with Cardinal Leone was more of a progress report of sorts on the now, well advanced, ongoing investigations into Vatican, Inc. and the Vatican Bank being executed by the top two men on Pope Michael VI's staff.

The preliminary information garnered from conversations with the two cardinals found its way into a speech delivered by the Holy Father on the 23rd of September in Rome. In attendance was the majority of the Curial staff and various secular authorities who had worked in the Vatican Bank for many years.

"I am still in the process of learning all of the jobs required of me for this papacy, I have decided to follow in the style of my predecessor Saint Tobias the Great. I will conduct myself in a compassionate and familiar style. I wish to maintain closeness with my subjects regardless of their rank or title. I will proceed with this style, but it is to be understood that I will retain authority granted me as supreme pontiff to entertain and exercise what is right against the wicked where I see fit to do so..."

The assembled audience was receptive to his message, occasionally nodding in agreement with his words. However, they remained completely ignorant of any kind of underlying message in his address. Those who sat on the stage behind him knew exactly what Pope Phillip Michael I was insinuating as they watched Bishop Jonas Krivis not so subtly squirm in his chair. Krivis' two secular administrators seated next to him also appeared increasingly uncomfortable as the pope's speech continued. All three men knew at that moment that they were finished. The only question that remained was who and what departments were next.

The following day, tongues were wagging, thick with rumors. A strange man had come to call the papal apartments. Speculated guesses consumed everyone until the man was actually identified. The rumors became worse as word spread that the mysterious man was actually the director of the Bank of Saint Mark in Venice. Had this new pope already found a suitable replacement for Marco Ansios and his Banco Generali?

The Bank of Saint Mark became the new official bank of the Venetian diocese several years back prompted by the Krivis, Fedora, and Ansios scheme that resulted in the secular takeover of the Catholic Bank of Venice. However, despite the tall tales circulating through Vatican City, this guest and visitor was a most innocent appointment. Chiaros Riluciani had invited the man to Rome for the sole purpose of closing his personal bank account. He knew that he'd never return to his beloved Venice now that he had become pope of the Roman Catholic Church. Riluciani had a healthy glow about him as he greeted and conversed with his guest, flashing his big signature smile constantly. His final instruction for his guest was to pass along what was left in his account to his soon to be appointed successor.

The truth of what was actually happening between the pope and his visitor never escaped the pope's office in the Apostolic Palace. The obsessed minds of those who remained soon spawned new rumors of what the new pope's plans were for his next victim, Mr. Giovanni Fedora. The walls surrounding Vatican City could not contain these rumors. Mr. Fedora's four year fight to avoid extradition would be over in the United States courts in a matter of days. He'd already been charged and sentenced twice by Italian federal courts despite his absence. The irony was that despite all of the rumors making the rounds, this new pope hadn't yet gotten around to the problems of Ansios and Fedora, but their turn was coming.

Pope Phillip Michael I took special notice of the date as he was writing it on a piece of paper awaiting his signature. His papacy began exactly one month ago today. He sat back in the chair of his desk for a moment of reflection. He was satisfied with what he had done so far. He had been a busy man. Any retained staff from the days when Pope Michael VI was alive, could attest to the work ethic of this new, younger pope. He had already accomplished some of the changes that he wished to make in his church. However, there was still so much to do, if he was going to accomplish everything that was on his agenda for his first 100 days as pope. As the audits and probes penetrated deeper and deeper into the inner workings of Vatican Inc, the corrupt and dishonest became more and more uneasy.

Phillip Michael I continued to be a thorn in the side of what was left of the Curial holdovers doing their best to cling to centuries old traditions. Their pomposity constantly resulted in heated exchanges terminated with the new pope reminding them that "Pope Michael VI is no longer the leader of this church, I am..." It was by far the most vain thing that Riluciani had ever let come out of his mouth, ever. However, it didn't come from a place of vanity. It came from a place of frustration. The constant comparisons and comments of what Pope Michael would have said or done was becoming like nails on a chalkboard to a man who possessed the patience of Job.

In other parts of the Vatican City, the radio and press corps put formal filler into the uncomplicated words of the Holy Father's speeches, lectures and sermons. Their changes created a body of official works that never actually existed. He always preferred to keep his jargon simple so the true meaning and message would not be lost or misconstrued to interpretation. Their words were not his. The public and media outside the Vatican City Walls were suddenly the true keepers of the Holy Father's true words and thoughts, not whatever the Vatican Public Relations men decided would go into this pope's official archives.

The following day, Pope Phillip Michael I finally received the highly anticipated, completed audits of both Cardinals Zacharie Benoît and Dante Leone. Riluciani had Father Mancini make a copy of Benoît's report to send to Cardinal Leone. Copies of both would also be sent off to Cardinal Wexford and the three detectives from Rome, Munich and New York. After his own thorough examination of the two reports he was now ready to make some very important decisions. What he was about to initiate would have global implications. He wanted to finally get the ball rolling prior to his upcoming meeting with Leone and the rest of the covert team.

The few evenings before the scheduled meeting, he had his typical simple dinner in the third floor dining room of the Apostolic Palace of Vatican City. Joining him for his dinner of broth, veal, green beans and a small side salad, were Fathers Mancini and Barton. He sipped his mineral water as the three men discussed the events and decisions to be implemented over the course of the coming days. This reluctant leader of the Roman Catholic Church knew his decisions were sound, but they still weighed heavily on his mind and physical modest frame.

Word of Pope Phillip Michael I's forensic audits soon reached Saint Nicholas' Tower and the office of Vatican Bank President, Bishop Jonas Krivis. Secrets were difficult to contain once they found themselves inside the walls of the Vatican. The American who had grown up in Al Capone's Chicago suburbs. The experiences of his youth, nor his graceless, rapid ascent through the ranks of the Vatican Banking structure, did not sufficiently prepare the six foot six, two hundred twenty pound bank president for the situations he was now being forced to face. It was visibly obvious that he had lost weight since the election of Pope Phillip Michael I. His usual extroverted, over the top vanity had been replaced by an introspective man with an extremely nasty attitude and a most rare moment of regret. It was now, some six years later, that his scheme to move the Catholic Bank of Venice into the hands of his friend Marco Ansios had come back and bite him in the ass, in the worst way possible.

Another man whose body was serving as a physical testament of the longer, harder working hours that came with the election of this new pope was Cardinal Zacharie Benoît. His elevated stress level was outwardly expressed by the significant increase in the number of cigarettes he smoked as the days of this papacy proceeded. He hated this pope's views on contraception. As the pope's interim Secretary of State, he was part of discussions on the topic and several others with the United States State Department. Later in that meeting, Pope Phillip Michael I handed him a list of Vatican personnel designated for appointments, transfers, and those who would be asked to resign. Benoît was an old, tired man, who was not well, but he still challenged Phillip Michael I on his decisions and selections. As he quickly looked over the list, he quickly realized that the common factor with all of them was that every last one of them was a fellow P2 Mason. Riluciani had found over 100 of them serving in a variety of positions in Vatican City. Cardinals, priests and a few laymen from every background. Their involvement with Freemasonry P2 was against Canon Law. His predecessor never did anything to change that law. Punishment for such an offense was immediate excommunication from the church.

In Buenos Aires the problems caused by this sitting pope just kept getting worse. The Chairman of the Board of Banco Generali and P2 Paymaster, Marco Ansios was looking rougher on the edges than ever with each passing day. He knew first hand how relentless Riluciani could become, if necessary. This man, as pope, was becoming a much bigger problem in Rome than he ever was in Venice. The situation was getting bad enough that even a man with great power and control over others like P2's leader Gherado Fratello was beginning to also show rare signs of concern too. He kept Ansios in the know regarding the ongoing investigation into him and his bank that started five months ago, thanks to an ill-conceived blackmailing dirty laundry campaign initiated by his close "friend" and associate Giovanni Fedora late last year. Fratello was also well aware of Pope Phillip Michael I's forensic probes into the Vatican Bank. Both Fratello and Krivis knew that the pope's probes would be willfully handed over to Italian banking authorities. Ansios was facing the imminent collapse of his bank followed by the remainder of his life in prison.

The mental capacity and patience of the P2 leader was beginning to wear thin as numerous men under his control were suddenly knocking on his door looking for help. His own self preservation would take precedence over the needs of any of the others. He also had the Bank of Italy investigating his own business dealings and financial empire. The very same financial empire he was actively embezzling over $1 billion from.

Back in New York, Mr. Giovanni Fedora was a wanted man on the streets of Milan. The cases against him already had charges relating to the fraudulent diversion of $225 million. Pope Phillip Michael I had already found his Mafia money laundering operation that was all made possible thanks to the cooperation of the Vatican Bank.

There were other "men of issue" for this pope to contend with, these were only slightly lower profile and priority then men like Ansio, Krivis, Fedora, Fratello and Benoît. It was now clearer than ever that this pope was prepared to resolve the issues that his predecessor would not, once and for all. It was exactly what the College of Cardinals had elected him to do. Today was the thirty second day of his papacy. He had made a lot of problems for a lot of men in a very short amount of time.

September 28, 1978 began like most others for Pope Phillip Michael I. Following his breakfast of fruit, a croissant and coffee, he returned to his study with a substantial list of things to be accomplished for the day. He was growing more and more impatient with Curial staff's constant efforts to undermine his authority and positions in the public media. A heated telephone exchange with Cardinal Benoît went on for some time regarding the public publishing of opinions that were definitely not his. He wanted answers. Where were all of these lies coming from?

He then vented his frustrations to Cardinal Frates. Riluciani respected his honesty and many years of wisdom that came from years and years of working in the Roman Curia. Cardinal Frates was one of the few men around him he could truly trust. Following a brief meeting to discuss pressing church issues occurring in the Netherlands, Lebanon and the Philippines, the pope's next meeting was with Cardinal Leveroni to discuss the removal of a problematic cardinal who was the current patriarch of the Chicago diocese. This particular patriarch, over the course of his thirteen year tenure, had become extremely corrupt in money matters. He also had a very public, ongoing love affair with a woman who seemed to also be benefiting financially from the bitter fruits of his corruption and his elevated position in the church. Riluciani was informed that there was no way in hell that the Chicago cardinal would vacate his position willingly. The Holy Father then issued an ultimatum. The cardinal could leave willingly "due to health issues," or be completely stripped of his power and position in a very public manner; the choice was his. Everyone in the Curia wanted to be a fly on the wall, but nobody there wanted to be the messenger of the pope's demands when they were delivered to their destination.

Cardinal Leveroni had worked hard for many many years to become one of the formidable movers and shakers of the Vatican Curia. The Holy Father had something else in mind for him.

"As I'm sure you already know, the people of Venice are most near and dear to my heart."

"Yes of course, Your Holiness."

"I want to send you to take care of my beloved Venice." Riluciani requested gently.

"Me?"

"Yes."

"I appreciate the consideration, Your Holiness, but there is still so much work that I have to do here in Rome. The bishops here, they need me..."

"I am moving you to Venice cardinal."

"You can't mean that."

"I most certainly do, Eminence."

"I appreciate the offer, but I'm afraid that I must decline your offer, Holiness."

"Decline?"

"I am needed here in Rome."

The pontiff remained firm but calm. "I believe it is my job to decide where my cardinals are needed, not yours, Eminence. I want you to go to Venice."

Leveroni was now growing more and more upset. "No."

"Cardinal, this is not something open for discussion. I've made my decision."

"I'm not leaving Rome."

"I see your oath of obedience means nothing to you, cardinal."

"I am a cardinal, a prince of the Holy Mother Church."

"I am the pope."

"Your Holiness certainly has a lot to learn."

Riluciani continued in an even toned manner. "I am learning a lot, every single day. Your relocation to Venice is not a request cardinal, it is an order."

Leveroni suddenly lost any remaining sense of self dignity. "I won't take orders from you."

"You willfully defy a direct order from the pope?"

"It takes more than a new wardrobe to make one a pope. It's more than walking around here smiling all the time, like you do. Thirty days ago you were a nobody in a far off quiet town preaching to empty pews and now you think you can rule the Roman Catholic Church. I'm staying exactly where I am."

"I may not be much of a pope, yet,...but you are going to Venice, Leveroni."

"I'd sooner go to hell!" The cardinal yelled at the seated pope.

"I'm sure that can be arranged."

In his fury, Cardinal Leveroni issued a few more verbally abusive shouts at the calm man seated across from him, then stormed out of the room without being formally dismissed. The last thing he wanted was to be out of sight and out of mind in a far away place like Venice. It was now more evident than ever that these two men would not see eye to eye anytime soon. One wanted what was best for his church, the other wanted what was best for himself. The Holy Father had numerous reasons for the reassignment, but the most important of all was his membership in Gherado Fratello's P2 Masonic lodge. The tantrum of Leveroni did nothing to change the mind of Riluciani. Leveroni could, like the cardinal in Chicago, could either accept the orders of his pope, or leave the Church all together.

The pope's next meeting was with Bishop Jonas Krivis. Phillip Michael I rose from his seat to shake the large man's hand as he entered the room and approached the desk of his private study.

"Bishop Krivis, thank you so much for coming. Can I get you some coffee?"

"No thank you, Your Holiness."

"Very well then, please have a seat."

This encounter between these two men was very different from the last time they met. "I understand that you are from the Chicago area of Illinois."

"That is correct, Holiness."

"How long have you been here in the Vatican?"

Krivis thought for a moment. "Mmmm, almost twenty years, I'd say."

"Wow, that is a long time to be away from home. Do you miss Chicago? Do you still have family there?"

"I do have some relatives still there. I try my best to visit them whenever I can."

"I'm sorry that the Church has kept you away from your home for so long, bishop."

"I sacrifice willingly, in service to God."

"What is it exactly that you do at the bank here in the Vatican?"

Krivis thought quietly for a moment before answering. "Mostly, I set policy."

"Policy? What kind of policy?

Krivis then shrugged and smiled, "To make money, I guess."

"Is that why you sold the Catholic Bank of Venice to your friend Marco Ansios for so little?"

Krivis squirmed in his seat uncomfortably. "Ah, er, well, we...I mean the Church received other favors in exchange for the low asking price."

"I see, and what about the bank's relationship with Banco Generali?"

Krivis suddenly began to visibly sweat. "Generali is a perfect partner for us. Our relationship goes beyond simple investment strategies. We often partner with them on projects that need funding."

"I see, and what exactly is the nature of these projects, bishop."

Krivis got quieter. "I don't ask that Holiness."

"You don't think it's important for the Church to fully understand the nature of all of their investments, Krivis?"

"Marco Ansios is one of the cleverest businessmen in all of Italy, Holiness. Your predecessor had remarkable trust in the man."

"And what about your other friend? I believe his name is Giovanni Fedora. Did Pope Michael trust him too?"

"Clearly the previous pope made a mistake in putting so much trust in Fedora. These things do happen from time to time."

"I am certainly all too familiar with the fallibility of a pope."

"Only on financial matters, Holiness."

"And what about your investments with Ansios?"

Krivis was only slightly relieved that the discussion shifted away from Fedora. "They are very complex."

"Do you honestly think it's wise to be so deeply involved with such complex investment operations?"

"Foreign banks do it all the time, Holiness."

"I feel the need to remind you, bishop, this is a Church, not a bank."

"I can understand that, but the Church can not function without the support of the bank, and the bank's function is to make money."

"This is a house of God, not a house of Rothschild."

"That it is, Holiness, but you can not run a Church, especially this Church solely on Hail Marys."

"I see," Riluciani paused for an extended moment, thinking. He then stands to escort Krivis from his study office. "Bishop Krivis, I appreciate you taking the time to meet with me today. I have enjoyed getting to know you better."

Krivis stands to leave, relieved that the meeting is over. "The pleasure is all mine Holiness."

"Your answers and comments should prove most helpful as I review the audit."

"The audit? What audit?" Krivis whipped around surprised.

"Oh, I'm sorry, I forgot to mention it. I asked Cardinal Benoît to conduct an audit of your bank." Riluciani moved from behind his desk to escort him to the door. "Thank you again for your time, it really has been a pleasure. Hopefully, we will be able to find you a place soon, closer to your home."

Cooler temperatures had finally given the people of Rome some relief from the stifling heat of Indian Summer. The Holy Father felt a need to decompress a bit after his meetings with Cardinal Leveroni and Bishop Krivis. He knew that his next meeting would be just as intense if not more so. He strolled aimlessly about the inner passageways of the Vatican in a quiet state of deep reflection. He didn't regret any of the decisions that he had already made, nor the ones that remained on his list for the remainder of his day. It was the emotional responses of those impacted by these decisions that wore on him heavily. The emotional protests changed nothing in his resolve to do what he knew to be right by his God, his Church and his fellow man.

At 3:30 PM, Riluciani returned to his study. He called Cardinal Leone on the phone. Leone was still in Florence, he planned to leave in the morning for the three hour drive to Vatican City. He promised to arrive in plenty of time for the meeting with his close friends Riluciani, Wexford and the three detectives. While he was talking to Leone, he had Father Mancini call Cardinal Frates to his study chamber. Upon the arrival of the latter, the three men discussed the events of the rest of the day and the next morning. Riluciani and the two cardinals then discussed the heated conversation the pontiff had had earlier with Cardinal Leveroni. Neither of the Riluciani's confidants were surprised by the resulting abusive confrontation. The intimate conversation then shifted to the subject of his next meeting. This one would be with his interim Secretary of State Cardinal Zacharie Benoît. Riluciani handed a copy of the designated transfers, removals and resignations to Cardinal Frates. Cardinal Leone already had his copy that had been sent to him the day before. Both cardinals liked the changes he was going to be executing starting that evening and long into the next day.

The meeting between Pope Phillip Michael I and Cardinal Zacharie Benoît began casually as the two men sipped on chamomile tea. The Holy Father spoke to Benoît in his native French with the skill and understanding of a native speaker. Reluciani hoped that this simple gesture would help put the excessively tense cardinal a little at ease as he sat before him smoking one cigarette after another. The chamomile tea didn't do a thing to soothe the nerves of the old man. Benoît caught the Holy Father off guard when he explained how impressed he was with his adjustment from humble patriarch of Venice to supreme pontiff of the Roman Catholic Church. Riluciani blushed a little and thanked him. Benoît explained that he was just as impressed with his skilled way of resolving issues and making difficult decisions, even if he didn't necessarily agree with his choices.

As the afternoon and conversation went on, the Holy Father and cardinal discussed the impressively detailed reports and issues surrounding the Vatican Bank. Unbeknown to the man sitting across from him, copies of these reports were already in the hands of investigators working in Italy, New York and Munich who just so happened to be in Rome, as they spoke. Benoît expressed his concerns regarding the reports and problems.

"Your Holiness, you must know by now that news of this internal investigation will make its way out of Vatican City and to the Italian press corps and beyond. We've already had a huge leak that has resulted in a highly accurate story that appeared recently in a *Newsweek* article in America. The article stated that 'Vatican sources' had stated that 'Bishop Krivis would be demoted to an auxiliary bishop and removed from his position at the bank.'"

Riluciani issued his signature smile before he responded. "Who does *Newsweek* say I should put in Bishop Krivis' place, cardinal?"

Cardinal Benoît shook his head in silence as he lit himself another cigarette. As the meeting and afternoon progressed, the pontiff made it absolutely clear that the American bishop would soon find himself in an auxiliary bishop's position with the New York diocese. Cardinal Benoît thought that it was an odd reassignment destination for this particular bishop. He knew nothing of the numerous conversations between the patriarch of New York and a few carefully selected others. Under the watchful eyes of Cardinal Wexford, his staff, and men outside the church like Detective Francis Clavering was a perfect place for this man.

Under the Holy Father's orders dictated to Cardinal Zacharie Benoît, Bishop Jonas Krivis would be removed the next day. He would take a temporary leave of absence while the diocese of New York found him a proper position. The pope already had a replacement in mind who would be named later. The departure of Krivis would be followed by his two secular administrators who also had close ties to Marco Ansios and Giovanni Fedora. They also just happened to be members of Fratello's P2 lodge. It was then announced that all associations with Banco Generali were to be suspended immediately once these three men were removed from the bank. The days of high ranking Curial personnel "looking the other way" for the sake of their own self-preservation had now suddenly come to an end. Cardinal Benoît requested a short break from the meeting so he could get some fresh air and fetch a fresh pack of cigarettes from his office. Riluciani obliged the elder cardinal's request.

During the short break, Cardinal Benoît alerted Krivis of the changes to take place the following day with scant detail. The Vatican Bank president immediately called Marco Ansios who was still hotel hopping about Buenos Aires. "I'm not going to be around here starting tomorrow, my friend. I'm sorry. It will serve you well to keep in mind that this pope is a very different man then the one before him. He is determined to make significant changes around here. Changes with huge, historic impact. I don't know what else there is to be said other than to wish you, Fedora, and everyone the best of luck in the days and weeks to come." Upon terminating the call, the bishop just sat in his office in reflective silence. The sweet, smokiness of his imported scotch suddenly tasted bitter on his tongue. He kept drinking it anyway as the clock on his wall continued to tick more pronounced in his ears than it ever had before.

Cardinal Benoît returned to the Holy Father's study with his fresh pack of smokes. The next topic of discussion between the two men was the pontiff's earlier decision to remove the Chicago cardinal. Benoît was most pleased about the removal of the Chicago cardinal. It had been a nagging problem for some time that Pope Michael VI never had the stones to resolve.

The conversation then transitioned to the topic of Cardinal Leveroni. Benoît was not surprised by Leveroni's push back regarding the patriarch of Venice appointment. "I will have a chat with him, Your Holiness. Perhaps I can persuade him to have a change of heart."

"I'd very much appreciate that Eminence. He was less than pleased with me when he stormed out of here this morning."

"Yeah, he does have a bit of a short fuse. But rest assured, I will have a talk with him."

"Thank you. My next appointment will be..." The Holy Father went one by one down his list moving or removing every single one of Cardinal Benoît's P2 brethren. It was as if someone came and overturned Gherado Fratello's chess board in the middle of an extremely intense, strategic game. The cardinal tried hard to maintain his best poker face. He didn't notice his own trembling hands giving away some of what was going on in his head. Benoît's hand was beginning to cramp as he made notes on the over 100 different men in the Curia and beyond who were moved, removed or replaced. The pope was nearing the end of his list, his Secretary of State was relieved that the end was now in sight.

"...and for the Vicar of Rome, I would like to appoint Cardinal Frates to that position."

Cardinal Benoît was surprised by this announcement. "Vicar of Rome, Your Holiness?"

"That is correct."

The cardinal quickly scribbled down the instructions. "And what about the current Vicar of Rome? What do you wish to be done with him?"

"He will be the new Archbishop of Florence starting tomorrow."

"And the current Archbishop of Florence?"

"Cardinal Leone, he will be my new Secretary of State, to replace you."

The old man sitting across from him suddenly stopped all writing and fidgeting. He sat perfectly still, in a state of suspended animation for what seemed like days. He was already smoking two packs of cigarettes a day before Riluciani was even elected pope. His arrival in Rome now had the old tired man smoking three packs or more on most days. He was already in poor health in the later years of Pope Michael VI's reign. This sudden increase in his daily habit did nothing to improve his current health concerns. Benoît was ready to retire long before the conclave of the previous month. Despite all of that, this announcement, this sudden change of job and position caught him completely off guard, as a full spectrum of mixed feelings filled his head and heart. He never expected this. His name was nowhere to be found on the list given to him earlier by the pontiff. He lowered his head a little and closed his eyes. His days of power and position in the Curia were now over. He had had numerous heated arguments with his replacement, Cardinal Leone over the years. The relationship between the Secretary of State and Pope Michael VI's number two in charge was definitely not a warm one.

Cardinal Benoît continued to study his notes. Riluciani laid his copy aside, and poured them both another cup of tea. He could tell by the cardinal's body language and facial expressions that he was thoroughly surprised by who would replace him the next day. Through his entire thirty-two days of service to this new pope, he had maintained a coolish and distant tone. Never once did he ever leave the formalities at the door. Riluciani tried his best to melt Benoît's frosty facade with his warm charm and genuine smile.

Pope Phillip Michael I finally spoke, pulling the cardinal's attention back into the room with him. "So Zacharie, what are your thoughts?"

Cardinal Zacharie Benoît was again caught off guard with the Holy Father calling him by his first name. The only person to ever do so in years was Cardinal Leone during their most heated conversations. "These are your decisions, Holiness. It is not my place to approve or disapprove."

"I understand that Zacharie, but that is not what I asked you. We've known each other for many, many years. I honestly want to know what you think."

Cardinal Benoît thought for a brief moment then issued a slight shrug of the shoulders. "Some of these decisions will be well received. I myself am more than pleased with some of them..."

"...and the others?"

"...in others these decisions will cause great surprise and disappointment, literally and figuratively. Some of these men in the Curia that you have chosen to move worked very hard to get you elected last month. I'm sure more than a few of them will feel deep betrayal by your actions. Many of these appointments go against the wishes of the late pope, Holiness."

The pope smiled warmly, then issued a slight chuckle, "I had no idea that the late pontiff was in charge of church appointments in perpetuity." Benoît just stared at him, maintaining his icy countenance, as Riluciani continued. "As for those feeling I betrayed them, I have said many, many times over the years, and especially in the last several weeks, I never once in my life sought to become pope. I never wanted this Zacharie, ever. I challenge you, name one person here that I promised anything if I were to be elected pontiff. This was not my desire, and it most certainly was nothing I had a hand in doing. These men here in the Vatican that I'm moving and replacing have forgotten their one true purpose: to serve God and help their fellow man. This place has become overrun with money changers. It is filled with corrupt men with hearts full of greed and lust for power. They are no better than their secular counterparts in Tokyo, London, Milan or New York. That is why I have made these decisions and changes."

"I see your point, Holiness, but it will be perceived as betrayal to your predecessor."

"Will they also think that I betrayed Pope Phillip XXIII? What about the pope before him? It is not my concern who they feel I have betrayed, Zacharie. My only purpose and guiding light is to not betray Our Lord, Jesus Christ, and the job he has chosen for me to do."

The meeting continued on for another couple of hours. Cardinal Benoît was exhausted by the time he got back to his office at 7:30 pm. He finally had a chance to examine the list and replacements thoroughly, without the watchful eyes of the pope upon him. As he read through it Benoît couldn't help but be impressed with this quiet, humble pope. It was clear that he had done his homework, and knew exactly what he was doing. With the precision of a most skilled surgeon, he had successfully removed every single P2 member from the Vatican Curia and replaced them all with non-P2 men. He hastily left his office, carelessly leaving his notes and papers scattered about his desk.

Following his long meeting with Cardinal Benoît, Riluciani was joined in his study by Father Vincenzo Mancini. The two men briefly discussed the pope's prior meeting. The Holy Father handed a copy of all of the changes that were dictated to Benoît just a few hours earlier. Please make sure that a copy of these changes gets to Cardinals Leone, Wexford and Frates in the morning. There was one more change that he wished to make that wasn't discussed with the departing Secretary of State.

"Vincenzo, would you please set up a phone meeting with the Archbishop of Milan at 8:45 PM."

"Of course Chiaros. Is there anything else you need me to do?"

"No, that will be all for now. I will call you if something else comes up."

"Very well, Chiaros.."

Father Mancini left the chamber. The reassignment of the man currently serving as Archbishop of Milan would be a helpful presence to him in the Vatican. While Riluciani had now successfully removed the P2 elements from the Curia, he now needed to remove any remaining elements of the Vatican Mafia. There was no one better for that job than the Archbishop of Milan who had done exactly that when he was appointed to fill the position vacated by the man who was elected pope in 1962.

At 7:50 pm, he was once again joined by Fathers Mancini and Barton. The three of them recited their final Breviary of the day before sitting down to dinner. Sister Falcone served a beef consommé, followed by a small salad, veal, a medley of sautéed summer vegetables and some herbed polenta. After serving the three men their dinner, Riluciani asked Sister Falcone to join them at the table for dinner.

The nun immediately blushed. "Holy Father, I must respectfully decline your offer."

Riluciani issued his welcoming trademark smile. "Don't be silly Vittoria, please join Vincenzo, Landon and myself for dinner. You work so hard every day. Please sit, I insist."

"As you wish Holi..."

Riluciani shot her a disapproving glance as he interrupted her. "Oh stop with the formalities Vittoria. You are among familiars here in this chamber."

Sister Falcone relaxed her demeanor and smiled at her charge. "Fine Chiaros." It felt odd for her to address him by his first name with others in the room, despite doing so countless times in private conversation over the last twenty plus years.

The assembled exchanged conversation and laughter as they enjoyed their meal and each other's company. Falcone served Fathers Mancini and Barton and herself some deliciously aged cabernet sauvignon while the pope sipped on his usual mineral water. To

Riluciani, this felt like a celebratory dinner with the most intimate members of his staff. They had accomplished a lot during their first thirty two days in Rome.

Shortly after 8 pm, Rilucinai returned to his study in a jovial mood. He was once again reviewing his notes from his hours-long meeting with Benoît. The buzzing phone on his desk made him glance at his wall clock displaying 8:45 PM. "Right on time," he thought to himself.

The thirty minute conversation was upbeat and full of hope and anticipation for the future of the Church. Before terminating the call, Rilucaini's final words to the Archbishop of Milan were, "Pray, my friend. Pray for me, and more importantly, pray for this Church."

The pope reviewed his appointments for the next morning. He was most excited to see his good friend Dante Leone and the others listed. He then went over a speech he had written to be delivered in the coming days on being disciplined with one's faith in Christ. It was a philosophy that served him well as he made difficult decisions over the last several days. Around 9:30 pm, he heard conversation in the hall outside his study door. Upon opening it, he immediately saw Fathers Mancini and Barton standing there briefly conversing just before they retired for the evening. He once again uttered the same words he had every night before retiring. *"Buona notta. A domani. Se Dio Vuole."*

"Good night Holy Father, until tomorrow, if God wishes it so." Responded the two priests, they then all went into their respective rooms for the night.

CHAPTER 41

At 4:30 AM the next morning, Sister Falcone entered Riluciani's study which adjoined his sleeping chamber, carrying a tray with a carafe of coffee as she had done every morning for the last twenty years. She left the tray of coffee on his study desk. She could see from under the door of his bedroom, that the light was already on and he was already up for the morning. She gently knocked, with a warm soft greeting. "Good morning Chiaros." She then turned and left the study.

A few minutes later, she returned to find that no coffee had yet to be poured. In all of their years, Riluciani had never once been late for his coffee. She could see that the light was still on in the next room. She walked quietly over to the door. She placed an ear against it, there was no sound coming from the other side. She knocked again, then listened for a response. The silence continued. Sister Falcone's knocks began to increase in frequency and force with each subsequent blow. Still, nothing could be heard coming from the room on the other side of the door.

She continued to knock, and called for him as she slowly opened the door. Her eyes immediately locked onto his form still in bed, sitting up. His hands were frozen in position in front of him, tightly gripping some papers that he had clearly been reading. His glasses were perched, cockeyed on the tip of his nose. Ready to fall off of his face. His head was slightly tilted to the right. His warm trademark smile was replaced by a horrifically, familiar expression. His lips were parted and the corners of his mouth were drawn back, showing his teeth in an agonizingly, contorted snarl. She felt his wrist for a pulse. True panic gripped her, as she realized from the cold stiff touch of his skin that there was no life, no pulse left in his body.

She ran from the room, in her horror-stricken state, then through the adjoining study and down the long hall, several doors away, to Father Mancini's room. Father Mancini didn't know what was happening, as he suddenly found himself being shaken violently awake by a fast talking, horrified Sister Falcone. "Vincenzo, Vincenzo wake up, wake up! Come, come quick! It's Chiaros!"

"What are you talking about? What is the meaning of all this Vittoria?"

"Will you shut up! Come quick! Hurry!" She cried as she pulled him forcefully from his bed.

Still half asleep, Father Mancini entered the pope's bedroom. "Look!" She directed.

He stood in the doorway for a moment in a complete state of shock. He did not want to believe that he was staring at the lifeless body of Chiaros Rilucini. The agony on the dead man's face, punctuated by the piercing stare of his open eyes was instantly burned into his mind. He pulled Sister Falcone tightly close to him, holding her as she burst into soul crushing, hysterical crying. His own body began to shake. He too wanted to break down from the flood of emotions coursing through him. It was difficult for him to stifle the emotions that were flooding over him.

He instantly recognized the papers clutched tightly in the dead man's hands as he began to do a visual inventory of the room. Sister Falcone continued to sob violently in his arms as she buried her wet face into his chest. He finished his survey of the room then gently tried to pry her away from his body slightly. "Vittoria," he said, his voice heavy with stifled emotion. "Listen, I must know, did you touch anything in this room, when you came in here this morning?"

She tried hard to suspend her absolute heartbreak for a brief moment so she could answer his question. "No," she stopped, her mournful heaves punctuating the silence as she recalled the events before she came to wake him. "No Vincenzo, the only things I touched were the door and knob, and his wrist to check for a pulse." She explained then burst into uncontrollable sobbing. "It hurts, Vincenzo. My heart…it hurts so bad."

"Sister Falcone, I know this is very difficult right now, but I really need your help." He grabbed her firmly by the shoulders, as she faced him. "I need you to go get Father Barton and have him come down here, right away. Do you think you can do that for me?" She nodded as tears flowed freely down her face. She ran from the sleeping chamber, leaving Father Mancini alone in the room with the dead body of Riluciani.

Sister Falcone and Father Mancini were the only two people to follow Riluciani from Venice. Sister Falcone was still beside herself with her emotions and grief for the man she had known for the last twenty years. The younger Father Mancini, stood there trying best to control everything flooding his heart and head. For him, grieving would have to wait. He did his best to subdue his own shattered heart and state of shock. He too had become very close to Riluciani over the years while in Venice. The former patriarch of Venice had become like a second father to the young priest, especially during the early years of his service to the Lord. Both Sister Falcone and Father Mancini searched their logical minds, through the free flowing tears streaming down their faces, to find some sort of reasoning or understanding of what had just happened. All that kept running through their heads was "Why God? Why him? Why now?"

Outside the papal apartments, some of the usual early birds noted the lights coming from the window of the pope's bedroom. It was nothing remarkable for this particular morning. It was something they had seen every morning since Riluciani had become pope. They were absolutely ignorant that on this particular morning things were different, very different. It was the job of the Swiss Guards to patrol and provide security inside Vatican City; they had failed to notice that those bedroom lights had actually been on all night long.

Father Barton was forcefully pulled into the room by the inconsolable Sister Falcone. He stared at the lifeless body sitting up in the bed. Riluciani's cold dead stare looked right through him and the agonizing grimace now haunted his psyche. He lowered his head, and crossed himself as he offered up a brief, silent prayer. This was now the second dead pope he had witnessed in as many months. His mind began to drift. This instance was absolutely nothing like the last. The death of Pope Michael VI was by no means a surprise when he finally entered his final slumber on August 8th. He was a tired, sick old man who's best days were already many years behind him. He passed peacefully, surrounded by beloved colleagues, friends and loved ones in the luscious garden surroundings of the papal summer retreat just outside of Rome. The final twenty-four hours of the life of Pope Michael VI were meticulously recorded with absolute detail and accuracy, complete with information on every single one of his long term health problems. Father Barton suddenly remembered in his mind, the time of the peaceful passing of the last pope was at exactly 9:40 in the evening.

The man who now lay dead before him had only been pope for thirty three days. It was clear that the man suffered an extremely painful death, alone. Cause of death and time were unknown. One of the shortest conclaves in the history of the church, had overnight become the shortest papacy in some 400 years. The last time something like his had happened, the man was pope for only seventeen days. That was sometime back in the early 1600s.

Father Barton's attention once again focused on the corpse before him. "We must notify Cardinal Benoît immediately." Everyone in the room knew that less than twelve hours earlier, Pope Phillip Michael I had relieved Cardinal Benoît of his position, and replaced him with Cardinal Leone as the new Vatican Secretary of State at the stroke of midnight. However, Leone, the man behind the movement to get Riluciani elected pope, was still in Florence. He was probably still asleep, completely unaware of the fate of his dear friend. The pending changes had not been announced to the public. The man who had wished to retire at the end of the last pope's term, and by those in the know, the now former Vatican Secretary of State was suddenly once again Camerlengo.

The now acting head of the Roman Catholic Church, arrived in the room just before 5 AM. Father Mancini watched Cardinal Benoît closely as he entered the room. Up until that moment, all who entered that chamber instantly displayed intense feelings of shock and grief. Cardinal Benoît crossed himself and stoically entered the room. He seemed remarkably unphased, with a distinctly cold lack of emotion. Father Mancini watched him as he walked over to the bedside of the deceased pope. Benoît's actions were deliberate and methodical.

He then exited the dead man's bedroom and made his way to the dead pope's desk in the adjoining study, and lowered himself into the Holy Father's chair. He opened the left bottom drawer, and removed some papers. It was clear that he already knew the exact location of what it was he was looking for. He gazed at the documents, satisfied with his acquisition, and set them aside on the desktop. He then imposed an absolute vow of silence to everyone in the room until further notice, especially to Sister Falcone.

The Camerlengo then immediately began to make a series of calls in rapid succession. The first call was to the Dean of the Sacred College, who was also the Head of Vatican Diplomacy. Next he called his deputy, the now dead pope's temporary number three in charge. Finally he dialed the Deputy Head of Vatican Health Services and the Head of the Swiss Guard. Then, without a single word, left Riluciani's study with all of the personal effects he had quietly lifted from the two rooms.

Father Mancini instructed Father Barton to remain in the room with Sister Falcone and the deceased man until he returned, then he too left the room. He paid no mind to Benoît's damned gag order. He had some calls of his own to make. His first call was to the man who had been Riluciani's personal physician for the last twenty years. The doctor could not believe his ears. The initial shock from the information, quickly morphed into a bombardment of rapid fire questions. Father Mancini had no answers for the senior physician. The doctor then told Riluciani's personal secretary he would be leaving immediately for Vatican City. The five and a half hour drive would give him plenty of time to think about what could possibly have happened so suddenly to a man who was in such great physical health. Father Mancini's next call was to Riluciani's dearest of kin. This was not the kind of news that those closest to the late pope should have to learn from the cold public media who thrived on sensationalizing these types of events.

Mancini's final call was to Cardinal Leone. "Sister Falcone and I found him this morning, Eminence." The initial weight of the news knocked Leone instantly to the floor. "No, no no no. Damn those who have done this! May their souls be forever tormented by what they have done to this beautiful, loving man and this damn poor excuse for a Church!" He prayed out loud and crossed himself. He held himself together long enough to finish the call. "I will be on my way to Rome soon. Whatever you do, do not leave his body alone at any time, especially until I get there. Do you understand?"

"Yes, Eminence."

"Also tell no one you spoke to me. If you must speak to anyone about anything, only speak to Cardinal Frates. That is all. I will be there in a few hours."

"Understood Eminence."

Cardinal Leone hung up the phone. Through the gut-wrenching sorrow now in his shattered heart, the completely broken man was openly sobbing as he returned to his room. There he prayed as he never had prayed before. He prayed for the spirit of his dearest friend, then he prayed for strength and guidance. He emerged from his private quarters now filled with grief driven conviction. Leone's thoughts immediately settled on Deuteronomy 32:35, "Vengeance is mine, and I will repay. In due time, their foot will slip; their day of disaster is near and their doom rushes upon them." Then he whispered to himself, "This vengeance will not be solely yours, oh

God, do with me what you will, as an instrument in your fight to destroy every last one of them..."

Cardinal Leone knew perfectly well that all of his efforts over the last few years to get his friend elected pope had now resulted in nothing but his murder. "Damn it, if I had not pushed this, he'd still be alive, I just know it. He never wanted any of this, he was perfectly happy there in Venice." Now that Riluciani was dead, so were all of the hopes and aspirations of the men who had elected him for the future of their church. All of his friend's plans, changes, new personnel and direction for the church were now in a state of suspended execution. Leone knew perfectly well that any pope's decisions that were yet to be made public, died with him, unless his successor chooses to adopt them as his own.

Cardinal Leone made two more calls before embarking on his journey from Florence to Vatican City. The first was to Cardinal Wexford and then to Detective Cosimo Angelo who was hosting Detectives Francis Clavering and Hans Kruck and their wives at his home. After delivering the tragic news, his instructions were simple. He wanted them to meet him there for their normally scheduled appointment. "It is most important that all of you act as if you know nothing of what I have just told you." Then he issued his final instructions. "Pray, pray like you never have before. It is moments like these that will test our faith the most. I will see you in a few hours."

Cardinal Benoît entered the papal study once again. There he saw Fathers Mancini and Barton and Sister Falcone seated in reflective meditation. He had no idea that Father Mancini had returned to the room just moments before him. The time had come for Cardinal Benoît to finally announce to the world the passing of Pope Phillip Michael I. As the information was disseminated, more hearts would be shattered into a million pieces. The coming days and weeks would test every sense of logic and faith possessed in their collective hearts, minds and souls.

Father Barton watched as two men entered the papal study unannounced. He immediately recognized them. He recognized them as the two men who had performed embalming services on Pope Michael VI's body just over a month prior. Father Barton thought it odd that the embalmers arrived to take possession of the body before the arrival of the Vatican Medical Doctor. Father Barton moved closer to Father Mancini who was still unsure exactly who the men were that had just entered the chamber.

Barton remembered the first time he ever saw them and started thinking about the events of the morning up until that moment. He leaned in even closer to Mancini now, and whispered even quieter. "Something's wrong, Vincenzo." He stopped for a second to choose his next words carefully.

Mancini's eyes suddenly went wide, as the words echoed through his head. "Are you sure about that?" He whispered back.

"Yes, yes, I'm very sure."

"Benoît didn't even come in here until just before 5 AM, Landon."

"Benoît only made three calls, correct?"

"As far as I know, yes."

"...and none of them were to the embalmers."

As the hour ticked away on the clock on the wall, the two embalmers waited patiently, like scavengers awaiting their opportunity at a corpse on the African savanna.

The physician chief from the Vatican Health Services Office finally arrived at 6 AM. Father Mancini watched him closely as he performed a rudimentary exam of Riluciani's body. He then quickly announced that the cause of death was acute myocardial infarction that occurred sometime around 11 PM the night before. Mancini, who was by no means any type of medical authority, was smart enough to know that such a diagnosis following such a limited external exam was medically impossible.

Father Mancini suddenly felt an urgent need to do whatever he could to stall the situation until Cardinal Leone arrived. It hadn't even been two hours since Sister Falcone had discovered Riluciani's dead body. Unless Leone drove from Florence like Mario Andretti, it would likely be another hour and a half until he would arrive in Vatican City. His mind raced as he tried to think of ways to everything that all seemed to be happening so quickly. Suddenly Sister Falcone returned to the bedroom of her charge. She threw herself across Riluciani's body sobbing. Benoît ordered her removed from the room at once. Mancini nodded at Barton as the two of them took as much time as possible to execute the Camerlengo's orders.

While the majority of the world rested peacefully, content in their ignorance, the imposed gag order by Benoît was absolutely pointless. The information spread like a raging wildfire out of control, touching every inch of Vatican Village. At 6:45 AM in a courtyard near Saint Nicholas' Tower, one of the members of the Swiss Guard found Bishop Jonas Krivis walking about. The guardsman recognized him immediately. He at first thought it odd to see the Vatican Bank president walking through the courtyard at such an early hour, but quickly dismissed it.

As Krivis moved closer, the guard called out to him in a rather cold, crude manner, "The pope is dead." The Vatican Bank president stopped instantly in his tracks, just staring at the man, still some distance in front of him. After a long silence, the guard approached the statue-like Krivis who was completely void of any reaction. The guard then reiterated "Papa Riluciani, he is now dead. He was found dead in his bed early this morning." The guard, unsure what more to do or say, nodded at Krivis and continued on with his rounds of the area.

At 7:20 AM at a small parish church in northern Italy, bells began to ring to announce the death of their native son. Seven minutes later, Cardinal Zacharie Benoît took to the Vatican Radio airwaves to announce to the world what had happened. "At 5:30 AM this morning, the private secretary of Pope Phillip Michael I went looking for the Holy Father, when he failed to arrive on time to recite his morning Breviary, in the small chapel located near his private apartment, as was his customary daily routine. His search was abruptly halted when he found Pope Phillip Michael I still in his bed, dead with the light still on in his sleeping chamber, as if he were still reading *The Imitation of Christ* that he still had clutched in his hands. The Vatican Health Services Physician was immediately dispatched to the pope's room where it was determined that Pope Phillip Michael I had passed away sometime around 11 PM the night before from a sudden acute myocardial infarction."

Outside the walls of Vatican City, in a home in Rome, three grieving detectives and their mournful wives huddled by a radio tuned into Vatican Radio. They were hoping to get more information about what had happened to their dear friend. All that was coming out of the Vatican at that point were lies, lies, and more lies. There was not even a single mention of Sister Falcone or Father Mancini whatsoever in the radio announcement.

Cardinal Benoît was a very busy and distracted man. Cardinal Leone first spoke with the head of the Swiss Guard upon his arrival. Then made his way to Father Mancini's private quarters for a detailed report of everything that had actually happened that morning. Father Mancini was greatly relieved when Cardinal Leone finally arrived. By the time the cardinal left the room, he had more questions than he had answers, he instructed Mancini to get a hold of Wexford and the detectives. "I want to meet with them right away. Have Wexford meet them at Saint Anne's gate and escort them into your office." Mancini nodded confirmation of his instructions.

Cardinal Benoît was none too pleased to see him as he bursted into his office unannounced.

"Cardinal Leone? What the hell are you doing here?"

"I should ask you the same question Zacharie. I believe you are sitting in my seat...Last I heard, as of midnight, I am now Pope Phillip Michael I's Secretary of State,..." as he waved before him a copy of the list that was dictated to Benoît the night before.

"Mmmm, well the situation has changed since the Holy Father dictated those changes, Dante."

"Why's that, because Chiaros is now dead?"

Benoît was surprised that Leone already knew. "Exactly."

"Well then, I guess that that would now make me Camerlengo now wouldn't it. Zacharie?"

Benoît answered smuggly. "Hardly, he only announced those decisions last night."

"Correction, he only made those announcements to YOU last night. There are enough around here who have known of them for days, some of us have known for weeks, Zacharie. I will be taking over immediately."

Benoît was surprised and instantly angered by Leone's words. "Like hell you will Dante! You have zero business here in the Curia anymore. Leave my office at once."

"I'm not going anywhere Zacharie. Riluciani made his wishes perfectly clear long before yesterday."

"Not to the public, he didn't."

"Shut the hell up Zacharie, and step aside."

"No! I will not, I am Camerlengo now Dante. Leave now or I will have the Swiss Guards come and remove you from Vatican City completely."

"Ha! I'd love to see you try."

Cardinal Benoît picked up the phone and began to dial, without another word.

"Fine, I will leave, for now..." Leone conceded. "However, this isn't the last of any of this, do you understand me?"

Cardinal Benoît waived off the threats of Leone and returned to his work.

Leone passed by the late pope's open study door. When he looked in, he could see Father Barton still in the room, as if he was guarding an assigned post. He could see the form of Sister Falcone still in the room with Riluciani's body. Suddenly he noticed the two strange men seated in the study office waiting patiently by the door. He walked over to Father Barton and asked in a hushed tone. "Who are these men, father?"

"Oh, those are the embalmers. They've been sitting there since about 5:30 this morning."

"Really?" Leone then walked over to the two men. "The two of you can leave now, I will let you know when we are ready for you and your services. Thank you."

One of the two men stood, "But cardinal..."

"Leave, now, before I call the Swiss Guards to have you removed from Vatican City completely."

The two men looked at each other confused, then without another word, did as they were directed.

The cardinal then returned to Father Barton. "How long has she been in there with him?"

"More or less since she found him." He was absolutely sympathetic to the grief-stricken woman in the other room. "May I go in and see him?"

"Of course Eminence. Take as much time as you need."

Cardinal Leone crossed himself as he entered the room. He looked about the room and at the body, then at her. He approached her with outstretched arms.

"H-h-h-he looks like he was in so much pain Dante when he went."

Leone looked at the dead man's face. His fixed piercing gaze was cold. Completely void of anything reminiscent of his dear friend. "That he does, Sister."

Through her tears she explained how she found him. "His glasses were almost falling off of his nose, and his papers were in his hands."

He quickly looked at the body, and around the room. "His papers?"

"Yes."

"What papers?"

"It was the list of names he had last night. He told me he was sending people home."

Leone thought for a moment. "Are you sure, Sister? Cardinal Benoît said on the radio that Father Barton found him, and he was reading *The Imitation of Christ*."

"Yes, I'm sure, without a doubt, he had his papers."

Leone quickly looked about the room. "But where are all of his things, Sister?"

"Cardinal Benoît removed everything, everything but his books this morning."

"Sister, did Chiaros at any time yesterday complain of any physical problems or pain?"

"No Dante, none at all."

"No chest pains or tightness? No shortness of breath?"

"No."

Leone then turns to the body of Riluciani. "You were wrong about the Holy Spirit. I regretfully was wrong about these men. I'm sorry old friend, I'm really really sorry." Tears began to flow once again down the cardinal's face as he turned back to Sister Falcone. "Sister, please pray for the both of us, and pray for this church." He crossed himself once again, and left the room. He instructed Father Barton to remain with her and Riluciani until he returned.

Cardinal Leone went down that hall to Father Mancini's office. He didn't bother to wipe the tears that still flowed down his cheeks. As he entered the room he saw the mournful, defeated faces of Father Mancini, Cardinal Wexford, and the three detectives seated in the room. Their faces were also wet with emotion.

"I wish I could say good morning gentlemen, but I just can't, not today. I wish we could take the time to grieve the loss of this great man right now, but that will have to wait for a bit." Everyone in the room understood where Cardinal Leone was coming from. "Father Mancini before I go any further, I want you to explain to us every single detail that you can remember from the last twelve to eighteen hours, especially everything that happened this morning if you don't mind. I think the minds of these detectives may come in very handy right about now."

Father Mancini reiterated the final hours of Chiaros Riluciani's life and the subsequent hours of the morning, the detectives sat listening carefully to every word. Scribbling down notes to themselves on their yellow note pads, not wishing to disturb the flow of the man and testimony.

He explained in detail how Sister Falcone had discovered the body, notified him and then Father Barton. He described the cold response of Cardinal Benoît when he entered the room. "Benoît entered and quickly looked around the room. He then quickly moved over to Riluciani's bedside. I watched him remove the notes from Riluciani's cold dead hands. The ones on transfers and new appointments that were supposed to go into effect at midnight. I watched Benoît stuff them into a pocket. Then I watched him pick up some items, then he left the room. He then went and sat himself in Riluciani's chair behind the desk, and opened the bottom left drawer. It was as if he knew the exact location of the pope's last will and testament. He added that to the rest of the personal effects that he had collected from the bedroom. He then made several phone calls, instilled a vow of silence to each of us, and then left the room. Then I also left the room, leaving Father Barton and Sister Falcone in the room, to make some calls of my own."

Everyone in the room was confused. There was nothing consistent with what Father Mancini had just told them and what Cardinal Benoît said earlier that morning on his Vatican Radio broadcast. Even the claim that Riluciani was reading *The Imitation of Christ* was false; that was one of only a few books from the pope's personal library that Mancini left behind in Venice. The collective minds of the detectives and the two cardinals started to race as they sat and listened. Every single man in the room independently came to the same conclusion. It was now clear to them that their friend did not die of a heart attack, and everything seemed to point to him being murdered!

CHAPTER 42

He was the first pope in over 100 years to die alone. It had been even longer since the last one was murdered, if one were to believe the official statements put out by the Vatican. As the people of the world began to mourn the death of the Holy Father, the Vatican was purposefully keeping every single point of possible truth from them. All who knew the real story now kept a close watch on Cardinal Zacharie Benoît's every move as he weaved a very complicated web of lies.

Cardinals Leone and Wexford and the three detectives who were in Rome to meet with the late Riluciani were now beginning to make a list of men who might benefit from the sudden, unexpected death of this pope. At the top of that list was Cardinal Zacharie Benoît, Bishop Jonas Krivis, Marco Ansios, Giovanni Fedora, and Gherado Fratello. Other considerations were the two corrupt administrators that worked closely with the three criminal bankers. Then there was the corrupt cardinal in Chicago and Cardinal Leveroni, who seemed none too pleased with his reassignment to Venice. All of these men stood to benefit from an application of the classic "Italian solution."

There was no shortage of motives or methods for a suspected murder. It would now be up to them to find the perpetrator, bring them to justice, and preserve their dear friend's legacy. The detectives went to work straight away brainstorming different plausible scenarios. If this was a case of murder, necessary for "business as usual" to continue for any of these men, this murder would have had to be done in complete stealth. Something high profile and dramatic like a public assasination in a public square, or some type of hit job to silence or stop him, would be a bad idea with all the investigations already underway in Italy, the United States and beyond. Something so public would only put the spotlight on them even more followed by a full scale investigation. None of these men were interested in that kind or that much attention on Vatican, Inc.

"I'm thinking the most efficient and effective way for them to accomplish what they wanted would be poison." Offered Detective Clavering.

"Poison?" A few of them responded in unison.

Fran continued with the trajectory of his thought. "Whatever they used would have to be effective and inconspicuous."

The possibilities were mind numbing to consider. Arsenic, strychnine, cyanide, mercury, polonium, death caps, belladonna, aconite, hemlock were all plausible possibilities. Suddenly an idea flashed into Cosimo's brain. "What about digitalis?"

"Digitalis? I don't know much about that one, Cosimo. What makes you think that might be a possible poisoning agent?" Questioned Clavering.

"Cardinal Leone, you said that every man on Riluciani's list for removal was a P2 member right?"

"That's right."

"And each of them were to be replaced by a non-P2 member, right?"

Leone started to understand where Cosimo was going with his theory. "That is correct Cosimo. I've also heard that all P2 members are required to carry a vial containing a lethal dose of digitalis on their person at all times. Just in case they are arrested and interrogated with no other way out."

The other men in the room agreed that was the best scenario to start with until they could rule it out. They would proceed while keeping their minds open for other plausible possibilities. Both Cosimo and Fran knew that two of their suspects had recently increased involvement with P2 leader Gherado Fratello. Fratello had all of the other possible suspects under his control too. The common denominator for all of the suspects seemed to be P2 and Fratello.

"Father Mancini, can I borrow your phone for a moment?" Fran asked.

"Of course detective, right this way."

A few minutes later, Clavering returned from the other room with a handful of notes and a little spark in his eyes. "Gentlemen, I just spoke with my medical examiner back in New York. He tells me that digitalis is actually a fairly common poison used in murder cases. It's a tasteless, odorless substance commonly used to treat cardiac conditions. It could be easily added to any food, drink or medication, completely unnoticed, until it was too late."

Cosimo was suddenly curious. "Did he say how much of it, and how long it would take to 'do the job'?'"

"My man says it would only take about half a teaspoon to kill someone Riluciani's size. If they used the liquid form, about fifteen to thirty minutes."

"Oh my God..." Father Mancini suddenly blurted out. As his mind suddenly began to race.

"What is it Vincenzo?" Leone questioned as everyone in the room looked at him with great concern.

"Remember a few weeks ago? The Russian Patriarch Otravlen that died in Riluciani's arms?"

"Yeah, I remember, what about it?"

"He died about fifteen minutes after he drank some of the coffee Sister Falcone served."

"Vittoria? She'd never do that to Chiaros." Commented Leone.

Wexford chimed in. "Certainly someone else in the room would have also drank some, Vincenzo."

"No, I remember it clearly, as if it were yesterday. She had only served the Russian and Chiaros their cups at the time before he collapsed."

"Are you sure?"

"Positive. I remember, he was in the middle of introducing one of his assistants, when he stopped mid-sentence. He had drunk almost the entire coffee in the china cup, when it suddenly crashed to the floor, just before he died."

"And Riluciani never drank from his cup?" Questioned Hans.

"No, I remember looking at him. He looked at the cup in his hands, still full of coffee then looked at Otravlen laying on the floor. He put the cup down on his desk. Now that I think about it, Otravlen's face looked like he was in great pain. He looked very similar to the pope's face this morning when we found him."

Fran piped in. "Did they do an autopsy on him?"

"No, the medical staff just said he died of an acute myocardial infarction and they took him away to be embalmed immediately..." Father Mancini's voice trailed off. "Wait, there's something else."

"What's that Vincenzo?" Questioned Leone.

"This morning, the embalmers, when they arrived at the pope's study. They arrived before the doctor even came in to examine the body."

"You said the doctor came in at 6 AM?" Questioned Hans.

"That's right."

"Do you remember what time the embalmers arrived?"

"It was about 5:20."

"Oh shit!" Fran exclaimed as everyone suddenly looked at him. "According to the 'official radio broadcast' they showed up before his body was even discovered by Father Barton! That is of course if we are to believe the official bullshit story that Cardinal Benoît put out on Vatican Radio this morning."

The eyes of everyone in the room went wide, and the minds of everyone in the room began to race as Mancini continued. "That's not all detectives. The men when they came in this morning, I knew I'd seen them before, I just couldn't place where. It was Father Barton who pointed out who they were. He said that in order for them to have arrived when they did, they would have been dispatched sometime between 4:45 and 5 AM!"

"Are you sure about that?" Questioned Cosimo.

"Yeah, I'm sure. But Cardinal Benoît didn't even come into the pope's study or bedroom until just before 5 AM. There's no way he could have called them within that fifteen minute window detective."

"You said he made several calls from Chiaros' phone in his study?"

"Yes."

"Were any of those calls to the embalmers?"

"No, none of them. I do know that one of the calls was to the Vatican Medical doctor."

"Was it the same doctor who showed up to examine Otravlen when he collapsed and died?"

Mancini's own mind was now racing. "The pair who embalmed the last pope were the same ones who came for the Russian's body a few weeks ago. They were also the same ones who showed up to Riluciani's study this morning...without being called."

"I think it would do us some good to haul that doctor and those embalmers' asses in here to answer some questions, Leone." Commented Fran.

Leone had Father Mancini call the doctor to his office immediately. When he entered the room, he wasn't prepared to see the five other men seated in the room. He recognized Cardinal Leone right away and issued a smile and greeting. "Doctor, I know you are a very busy man, but my friends and I have a few questions to ask you, if you don't mind."

"Of course."

"Doctor, you are the director of Vatican Health Services."

"That is correct, Your Eminence."

"For the record, everything that you say in this room is with the strictest of confidence, even the fact that you've been called here to meet with us."

"Of course, I understand."

"According to official statements from this morning, you determined the pope's cause of death this morning, is that correct?"

"Yes, he died of a myocardial infarction,...that is what is more commonly referred to as a heart attack, gentlemen."

"And you estimated that the approximate time of death was somewhere around 11 PM last night."

"Yes, probably while he was still awake."

"What makes you say that?"

"By the state of rigor mortis in the body. Also his glasses were still on, and the light by his bed was still on."

Mancini moved to comment, but was stopped abruptly before he could say a word by Cardinal Leone. "I see...did you by any chance see any evidence of some other cause of death?"

"Such as?"

"Oh, I don't know, just anything unusual."

"No, not at all."

"Did you see any evidence that that the pope may have been murdered?"

The doctor was taken aback by such a question. "Murdered? Of course not."

"Before examining the pope's body, and determining that he died of a heart attack, how often had you seen him before?"

"I had never examined him, not until this morning."

"Never?!"

"No, he just got here a few weeks ago."

"Have you ever spoken to the man who was his regular physician for over twenty years while he was in Venice?"

"Yes, I spoke to him last week as a matter of fact. He said that Riluciani was in excellent health."

"Have you spoken with his previous doctor since his death?"

"No."

"Did you ask anyone he was around the last twenty-four to forty-eight hours if he complained about any sort of symptoms consistent with someone about to have a heart attack. You know, like chest pains or shortness of breath?"

The doctor squirmed uncomfortably in his chair. "No, I figured that if something like that had happened, someone would have told me about it."

"So as far as you know, the Holy Father had no symptoms that might be common prior to such a massive heart attack?"

"That's correct."

Cardinal Wexford inquired. "So Doctor, may I ask you what you based your cause of death determination on?"

"Well, of course, in order to dispel all doubt, an autopsy and pathological exam would have to be done on him."

Wexford continued, "I think everyone in this room is aware of that, but that wasn't my question doctor. What exactly was the criteria that you used to determine that his cause of death was an acute myocardial infarction?"

The doctor paused for a moment prior to answering. "Well he died suddenly, while reading in his bed. And his skin was slightly pale. These things are consistent with someone who has suffered a heart attack."

"Doctor, is paralysis a symptom consistent with someone who is suffering a heart attack?" Questioned Leone.

"No, not to my knowledge."

"I understand that a heart attack is a very painful experience."

"That's correct."

"It usually starts with tightness in the chest, then severe pain along the left side and shoulder. Correct?"

"Yes."

"Would most people react to that pain and make some sort of attempt to get help, and possibly save their own lives."

"I would think so?"

"And you say that it was clear to you that this man was awake when this 'massive heart attack' happened."

"That seems to be the case since he was sitting up in bed, with his reading glasses on."

"There are alarm buttons on either side of the pope's bed in his room, either one is just a few centimeters away from him. Would a heart attack prevent him from pushing either one of those buttons doctor?"

"I don't see why it would."

"Even though the 'heart attack' was causing him excruciating pain, wouldn't he still be able to make an effort to reach for one of those call buttons?"

"I would think so."

"Did you see any evidence that he may have made such an effort, doctor?"

"No."

"Did you know that this man before he became pope was actually under the care of a cardiac doctor?"

"I was not aware of that. But that information is consistent with my diagnosis." The doctor suddenly started to feel a little more comfortable with this new information.

"He was being treated for low blood pressure."

The doctor's stomach sank. "Oh, I was not aware of that."

"Is it common for a man of his age, in 'excellent health,' with low blood pressure to suddenly die from a massive heart attack?"

"No, but it does happen sometimes."

"Given everything that we have just discussed, how can you surmise that the pope died of a heart attack doctor?"

"I...I um, well...He was the pope. It happened so suddenly. What else could it have been?"

"Last I checked sir, you are the doctor. I think that is a question that we should be asking you."

"Did you by any chance look for any evidence of poison?"

A look of shock came over the doctor's face with the asking of such a question. "Poison? Who on earth would want to poison the pope?"

Cardinal Leone then closed the interview, thanked the doctor for his time. "Doctor, we appreciate your time and expertise. We will be in touch if we have further questions. You are free to go sir."

"Thank you." The doctor left, grateful that he didn't have to answer any more of their questions.

Fran was the first to speak after the doctor left the room. "I sure hope to God that none of you ever have to be treated by that man."

Wexford couldn't help himself. "Dante, was he the same man that was treating Pope Michael?"

"Yes, for years actually."

"It's a miracle he actually lived as long as he did under his care."

Leone offered no argument. "Alright men, shall we get back to business?"

Mancini suddenly felt compelled to finally speak. "That doctor, he's lying. He said that when he walked in Riluciani had his glasses on and was reading in bed. By the time he got into the room, Benoît had already removed all of his things, Dante. He did look like he was reading the papers in his hands. I remember. How did he know that the pope died wearing his glasses?"

"You make a good point Mancini." Clavering commented.

"That's not all Fran. Sister Falcone was the first one to find him, then she came and got me, then I told her to go get Father Barton. Benoît didn't come in until close to 5. When he finally arrived, he was an iceberg, showing no emotions whatsoever."

"That is odd." Commented Cosimo.

"Vincenzo, you said that Benoît removed several items when he came into the room. Can you elaborate a little on what those items were?" Wexford queried.

"Benoît came into the study, and walked over to the open bedroom door, but he didn't walk in right away. He just stood there in the door frame for a short while, looking about the room. Then he walked over to Riluciani's bedside. I watched him pocket the papers clutched in the pope's hands."

"Papers?"

"Yeah, the ones with the list of transfers and removals." Mancini continued. "Then he placed Riluciani's glasses and the medicine bottle from his bedside table in his pocket. He then gathered up the pope's slippers, then left the room."

"Was there anything left on the bedside table after Benoît left the room?" Asked Hans.

"Just a glass of water and his beat-up old alarm clock. I recognized it from his days in Venice."

"But I thought you said Sister Falcone always got him up every morning at 4:30 AM with a tray of coffee?" Questioned Leone.

"She did, but he always set his alarm clock for 5 AM just before he went to sleep, just in case he overslept."

"Has he ever overslept?"

"Never, not for as long as I've known him."

"Did his alarm clock ring this morning?" Fran asked. "You said that Benoît came into the room just before 5."

"Now that I think about it, no."

"Do you know what time he usually went to sleep, Vincenzo?"

"He always retired to his bedroom around 9:30 PM, and because he always woke up so early, he'd go to sleep shortly after that."

"Do you know the last time was that anyone saw him alive?"

"Hmmm, well Father Barton and I were talking outside his study a little before 9:30 last night. He must have overheard us, because he poked his head out to say good night to us before going to bed for the night."

"Hmmm, I'm starting to think that Riluciani was killed long before 11 PM last night." Fran commented.

"What makes you say that Fran?" Inquired Wexford.

"He never set his alarm clock for the morning. And clearly he was awake when he died." The others in the room nodded in agreement with Claverings conclusion.

The information from the doctor, Mancini and Fran got Cardinal Wexford thinking out loud. "If it were poison, whoever did this would have to have all sorts of intimate knowledge of Vatican procedures following the death of a pope. They would have to know that there would be no autopsy. He would have to know that apostolic laws were under no obligation to require an autopsy. They also had to know that even though the death seemed suspicious, only a rather rushed cursory exam would be done, and that the official word would be whatever that quack of a doctor said, after his little bullshit exam."

Everyone in the room uttered in unison. "Cardinal Benoît!"

The heavy doors that lead to Saint Peter's Basilica were shuttered. Curia officials then had the Vatican flag lowered to half staff to honor the late pontiff. They then continued to bombard the public with lie after lie. Conversations, actions and events from the night before and earlier in the morning were carefully manufactured to fit their desired narrative.

Back in the Vatican, Camerlengo Benoît had a lot of work to do. He had no time nor patience for interference of any kind. Benoît was quickly becoming more and more agitated. He was quickly learning that it wasn't just Leone and Frates who knew about the changes dictated by Pope Phillip Michael I the night before. There were several new cardinal faces walking about the Curia who had arrived the day before, ready to take on their new assignments. A whole array of emotions filled their hearts and minds as their mood swung violently from one extreme to the other. Their elation for new positions, new opportunities and their optimism for the future of the church came crashing down as the news of the pope's passing permeated further and further beyond Vatican Village.

Benoît's desire for an immediate embalming of the pope's body was hitting all kinds of unanticipated snags. A growing number of cardinals and now the public were becoming more and more vocal in their demand for an autopsy of the late pope's body. Many suspected some sort of foul play was involved. If the mode of this murder was actually some sort of poison, the embalming process would mask it. Many were demanding the truth. They wanted to know what the real cause of this great man's death was, not whatever lies were coming from those left in charge of the church until the next pope was elected.

Cardinal Leone joined with Wexford, Frates and others as they barged once again into the Camerlengo's office. Benoît was in the middle of a conversation with Cardinal Leveroni when a parade of cardinals entered the room.

"Oh good, more help has arrived." Declared Benoît, trying to hide his annoyance. The cardinals entering the room were put off by his icy demeanor. "We need to schedule the funeral and prepare for the conclave."

"We need some answers first Zacharie." Began Frates.

"We can do all of that later. First we must..."

"No, we will do all of this now! The rumors are already beginning to swirl."

"Rumors? What rumors? I have no idea what you are referring to Frates."

"Oh something about the fact that his body wasn't found by Barton at 5:30, but by Falcone at 4:30 this morning for one." Mentioned Wexford.

"Or that he didn't die reading the *Imitation of Christ*, but rather secret papers Zacharie?" Mentioned another.

"I can't be responsible for rumors, gentlemen."

"Public newspapers are already showing far more respect and responsibility than you at the moment."

"By publishing lies that come from those who make their living off of discrediting the Vatican? Hardly." The Camerlengo scoffed.

Leveroni chimed in, "They're most likely the communists."

"Is Sister Falcone a communist, Leveroni?" Leone challenged bluntly.

Benoît jumped in, "Besides, Falcone will be on her way back to Venice soon."

"Well she's not at this moment, I just spoke with her. We know it was her that discovered his body this morning at 4:30."

One of the other cardinals was becoming increasingly impatient with the Camerlengo. "Benoît, what the hell is going on here?"

Benoît scanned the room before issuing his response. "I couldn't tell the public that a nun discovered his body?"

"So you lied to the press, and the world."

"Yes."

"And what of the bullshit about what he was reading in his hands Zacharie?" Leone challenged.

"Yes, that too."

"We all know the changes that went into effect at midnight."

Frates couldn't hold his tongue any longer. "How could you do this to him? To the Church?"

Leveroni rallied to the defense of Benoît "If we tell the truth, it will only make things worse gentlemen."

Leone turned to Leveroni. "You can't hide the truth."

"...why not?"

"You may be able to hide the truth from the public, for a little while, but we all know what really happened in that bed chamber this morning. We will not remain quiet." Leone continued.

"There are publications out there already saying he may have been murdered, Benoît. How the hell could you be so stupid?" Wexford was now pissed.

Leveroni responded, "Fine, we will issue a correction, explaining our mistake."

"Benoît is the mistake here." Wexford then turned to Leveroni. "That's not good enough, and you know it."

"We demand an autopsy immediately!" Interjected Leone.

Benoît responded. "It won't do any good, he's already been embalmed, Dante."

"No he hasn't."

"The embalmers arrived earlier this morning to take his body away to be embalmed."

"From what I have been told, those embalmers arrived at his study BEFORE the Vatican doctor this morning. Is that true?"

Benoît was starting to get nervous. His voice lowered slightly. "Yes, that is true."

"...and if we are to believe the official bullshit story you fed to the press, the embalmers arrived BEFORE his body was even "discovered" by Father Barton." Wexford challenged. "Now how the hell is that supposed to happen Zacharie?"

Benoît lit up a cigarette, trying to deflect the building anger of the men in the room. "It doesn't matter now. Like I told you, the embalmers have taken possession of his body."

"No they haven't."

"What are you talking about Dante? The body has been removed from his bedchamber."

"That is true, but I sent the embalmers away until we are ready for them and their services."

"You did what!?" Benoît was now absolutely incensed with Leone, as smoke flowed from his mouth with his response. "Where is the body now, Dante?"

"I instructed Fathers Barton and Mancini to dress him and move him into the Sala Clementina of the Papal Apartments. They were instructed to remain with the body until we can all reach a decision."

"There is no 'we' to reach a decision, I am the Camerlengo."

"Well actually Zacharie, the Camerlengo is me according to the pontiff's orders, and we all know it."

"Oh shut the hell up Dante. We're not going to get into that again."

"No! I will not. An autopsy will be done immediately!"

Leveroni jumped in. "No! There will not be an autopsy."

"Stay out of this Leveroni, shouldn't you be on your way to Venice by now?" Commented Wexford.

"Go to hell Wexford!" Leveroni then turned to the others. "There will be no autopsy!"

One of the other cardinals in the room couldn't help themselves. "...and why not?"

Leveroni continued. "Precedent."

"Precedent?! Is that the best you can come up with?" Remarked Wexford. "Frates, you are the expert in these things, what have you got to say about it?"

There was a long pause before Cardinal Frates finally responded. "I don't know."

Wexford continued. "Benoît has already lied to the public about the time his body was discovered, who discovered him and what the man had in his hands. The truth will get out, they will soon learn that you lied about the official cause of death too."

"There will always be rumors, Charles. There's nothing we can do to stop them." Benoît tried to reason.

"We can tell them the truth."

"The Vatican is not governed that way, Wexford."

"The Vatican is not governed on truth? I think that that has long been established by you and your little lap dog Leveroni here."

Leveroni moved closer to Wexford and grabbed him by the shoulder of his cossack. As he began to raise his fist, he was restrained by the other cardinals in the room. Cardinal Benoît tried to regain control of the situation. "That will be enough gentlemen! We need to set the dates for his funeral and conclave."

Leone was not ready to let him off so easily. "Zacharie, what happened to his things?"

"Pardon?"

"You know, his personal effects, his papers?"

"I had them removed. His watch, glasses, and pictures are all are being packaged up to be sent to his family."

"And his papers?"

"Oh, those were destroyed."

"Why?"

"I am Secretary of State, it was my decision. They were confidential documents, so I had them destroyed."

"And what about his medicine?"

"Medicine?"

"His medicine you removed from his bedside table?"

"I gave instructions to remove everything."

"No you didn't. We know that you removed his medicine, glasses, papers and slippers. Where are those things."

"They are gone."

"Then we will do an autopsy."

Frates was suddenly becoming hesitant of the idea. "But autopsies are so messy."

Leone looked him dead in the eye. "It's not nearly as messy as the possibility of murder."

Leveroni had regained some of his composure following Wexford's comments. "There will be no autopsy. How will we look?

472

How will the church look? An autopsy will only confirm their worst fears, it's not like they would believe the results anyway."

One of the cardinals chimed in from the otherside of the room. "I agree with Leone."

Frates responded sarcastically. "That Riluciani was murdered?"

"That an autopsy should be done to prove that he wasn't."

Frates tried to remain logical, given the situation. "We should begin a quiet, informal investigation, to see if an autopsy needs to be done."

"I say we carve the poor bastard up, prove he wasn't murdered, and be done with it."

The entire room went silent with the blunt, tactless remark. Nothing was to be done to the body until the growing group of gathered cardinals were satisfied that the pope had not been murdered. Further rudimentary investigation revealed the pre-dawn encounter between Bishop Jonas Krivis and one of the Swiss Guards on his early morning rounds. Krivis was also one of the men who was out of a job, as of midnight, according to the confidential papers. Everyone in the Vatican knew that the bank president was never an early bird. Sometimes even traditional bankers' hours were too early for him. It was odd that he'd be wandering about Vatican courtyards before the break of dawn. Especially on this particular morning. Adding to the suspicions of the encounter, was the well known fact that he did not live in Vatican Village. His private home was a good twenty minute drive from the gates of Vatican City. Krivis quickly became another person of interest in the investigation.

The public was growing more and more restless and skeptical of the official story which seemed full of lies. It was becoming increasingly clear that Vatican Curial officials had greatly underestimated the popularity of this new pope. The man had only been in office for thirty-three days. As the public filed by to view the body and give their last respects to the late pontiff, crying screams could be heard echoing through the chamber in which he lay. "Who has done this to you?" "Who has murdered you?" The Italian public especially, were well aware that lesser men than a pope were subjected to routine autopsies when they died, whether their death was suspicious or not. Italian law also stated that bodies were not to be embalmed until twenty-four hours after their souls departed. They could not understand why a man as important as a pope wouldn't be shown at least the same courtesy.

Benoît and his allies did their best to steam ahead quickly with traditions and procedures that had been established over the centuries, as suspicions continued to grow. Rumors were growing, stating that the Vatican was trying to cover up for the pope's unfortunate, accidental overdose of his medication. An autopsy would certainly dispel some of the rumors. However, the results could very well provide support for the theory of murder too. Certainly no one was believing their new smiling pope purposfully committed suicide. All who knew him prior to his arrival in Rome, knew that wasn't even a remotely plausible scenario.

Riluciani's long time physician wasn't buying any of the official story either when he spoke to the detectives and Cardinals Lone and Wexford. As answers were uncovered, more questions would surface. Why had the pope's personal effects been removed from the bedchamber? Were they stained with vomit as his body tried to expel some sort of poison? Shortly after Fathers Mancini and Barton moved Riluciani's body from his sleeping chamber, his last worldly possessions were removed from the nineteen rooms of the papal apartments. Boxes filled with his letters and writings, his book, and his pictures were all removed with the exception of a few momentos retained by his two secretaries. When all was said and done, it was as if Pope Phillip Michael I had never been there at all. Benoît had his staff remove all confidential materials, then the room was sealed. The room would remain sealed until Riluciani's replacement was elected.

Once again the group of cardinals marched unannounced into Cardinal Benoît's office.

Cardinal Wexford was the first to speak. "Cardinal Benoît, we have a few questions for you."

"Try to be brief, I'm a very busy man."

Leone was put off by his tone. "We want to discuss the death of a pope."

"All men die, even popes, gentlemen."

"It is one thing to die; it is quite another to be killed."

"No one killed the pope."

Leone was not going to let him off that easily. "Tell me about Pope Michael."

Benoît made an odd expression on his face before answering. "What? What are you asking Dante?"

"Tell me your thoughts on him."

"Well, he was a great pope. He was trained in Curial discipline. He was smart, a scholar, a man who cared deeply for the church, and carefully thought situations through prior to making a decision."

"In your opinion, what was his greatest contribution to the church during his reign?"

Benoît thought for a minute before answering. "I'd have to say his encyclical on birth control."

"I see. And what would you like to see in the next pope?"

"A man to walk as Michael did. One who will continue his work. A man of authority and discipline."

"What about a man of compassion?"

"Compassion is a trait for priests, not popes."

Wexford couldn't help himself. "It's clearly not for Secretaries of State."

Benoît brushed off the demeaning remark. "My function is to run the Church, gentlemen. Now if you will excuse me, I have a funeral and conclave to plan."

Leone continued. "Not until we are finished here Dante. So it is your function to run the Church, but you let Riluciani change the investiture ceremonies?"

Benoît grew annoyed with the question. "He changed a thousand year old tradition. He just threw it out like someone taking out the trash."

"...and you let him."

"He was the pope. What else was I to do?"

"...and as long as he was pontiff you had to obey?"

"Yes."

"What were his opinions on the birth control encyclical?"

"We would have eventually convinced him..."

"Convinced him of what?"

"That his predecessor was right."

"How exactly were you going to do that?" Chimed in Wexford.

"What do you mean by that?"

"He told you yesterday that he was removing you. You were to be packing your bags and departing Rome today Benoît."

"He never said that."

"Everyone standing in this room knows that he did say exactly that. They all have copies of his notes."

"And who was supposed to be your replacement Zacharie?" Challenged Wexford.

Benoît lowered his voice and his gaze as he gestured toward Leone. "You were."

"You returned later that evening, didn't you? To see him one last time."

"I saw him many times, Dante."

"You had just been removed. You went back to try and change his mind, didn't you."

Benoît's anger exploded. "He was going to destroy everything Pope Michael had done."

"...and you failed, didn't you?"

"He wouldn't listen."

"He had already made his decisions, and he took those decisions to bed with him, didn't he?"

"He was going to remove the best people in the Curia, Dante."

"But he was the pope, he had every right to do what he had done, and you had to obey."

"I did not have to obey."

"That's not what you said earlier." Commented one of the cardinals from the other side of the room.

"As long as he was alive, you were obligated to obey, weren't you?" Leone took a deep long breath. "So what was it, Zacharie? Was it his coffee? His beloved candies? His medication?"

"What are you talking about?"

"Where was the poison?"

"There was no evidence that he was poisoned."

"Certainly not after you destroyed it."

"What are you suggesting?"

"Oh I think you know exactly what I am suggesting Zacharie."

"Look Dante, no pope is more important than the Church. The Curia has certainly defeated greater men in the past than Riluciani."

"Is that so? And how were you going to stop him, Zacharie?"

"We buried him in paperwork."

"Paperwork that he made decisions on."

"Yes, but we told him no, time and time again. While we added even more to his work load."

"You burdened him in one month with every damn problem you could find. Shit that had been ignored for years by your precious Pope Michael. And then when he handed you a solution, you told him no..."

"He was wrong."

"It was his right to make the decisions he did."

"Mistakes in judgment have no rights."

"So Pope Phillip Michael was in error?"

"Yes, in everything that he said and did."

"Who the hell are you to judge the sitting pope?"

"He was no pope, Dante. He was just a simple country priest, put in that position by you and your allies. He was your pope, not ours."

"He was your pope, admit it. Just not the one you wanted."

"He would have destroyed the Church!"

"Who made you the Church's final arbiter Zacharie?"

"The Curia of the Church."

"He had just changed the Curia."

"I would have stopped him."

"He had just removed you. At that point, there was only one way for you to stop him, wasn't there? You murdered Chiaros Riluciani, didn't you."

CHAPTER 43

The group of cardinals concluded their confrontation with Cardinal Benoît. A few of them believed him when he denied killing the pope, others did not. Either way, everyone was convinced that if it wasn't him who figuratively pulled the trigger, he knew exactly who did and how. The investigative work would continue without the Camerlengo's assistance or interference. It was too late to save their dear friend, it was time to direct their attention to the future. The cardinals now had the important task of deciding who they wanted to serve as their next pope. They had already chosen the right man to lead the Church into a more desirable future, but the Vatican machine put an end to that in the most violent way possible.

At 6 PM on September 29th, 1978, the heavy doors of Clementina Hall were shuttered to the public. Cardinal Benoît looked worn out, yet visibly relieved that the embalming process was finally beginning. If the pope was poisoned, any evidence would be contaminated and masked by the embalming process. However, embalming fluid wouldn't hide any physical damage to heart and vessels if a heart attack were Riluciani's true cause of death. Before Father Mancini left the body to the embalmers, he reached over and closed the dead man's eyes for the final time. He then burst into tears as a flood of memories and emotions overtook him, practically knocking him to the floor. Father Barton came to his side, physically helping him walk out of the chamber.

The embalming process normally is a quick and routine process once started. Normally the blood is drained from the body and cleared with saline solution that is circulated throughout the body. The embalming fluids are then pumped into the body through the femoral arteries and other major veins of the body. It's a simple, straightforward procedure. There was nothing normal or routine about this particular case. Vatican officials insisted that no bodily fluids or organs were to be removed from the body. A sample would be all that was needed to put to rest some rumors or start some new ones. Three hours later the embalming was complete. The pope's excruciating grimace was contorted into an expression of tranquil peace. A cosmetic treatment of his face and hands came next. His hands were also repositioned from their tight grip of his papers to a prayerful pose complete with the placing of his rosary. With all that now done, Cardinal Benoît finally retired at the end of a very long day, just before midnight.

Benoît now felt that the church, and more importantly, the Vatican were once again under his control. The mass Curial exodus planned by Pope Phillip Michael I would never materialize. Instead, it was those closest to the Holy Father who would depart Vatican City. The emotionally and spiritually crushed Father Mancini and Sister Falcone after packing up the remaining earthly possessions of their beloved charge, would then begin to do the same with their own. Father Mancini would return to Venice, while Sister Falcone was sent even farther north to an obscure, quaint little convent far off the beaten path. Vatican, Inc. made certain that neither of them would be easily found by those with questions and suspicious minds. Father Barton would be the only one to remain. He was now destined to serve his third pope in a little over two months.

The cardinals may have relented, but the secular, uncontrolled press outside Vatican City would not. They continued to hound

Benoît. He tried to appease them by issuing a few corrections to his initial public statement. Admitting that the pope who was coherent, lucid and in perfectly good health in the days prior to the discovery of his dead corpse did not sit well. Benoît also admitted that Pope Phillip Michael I had given him complete instructions that were to be executed the next day; none of those instructions ever came to fruition. Benoît's actions and words only made the public more demanding of answers and an autopsy.

While the Vatican was its own sovereign, independent country, it remained greatly influenced by the laws and procedures that governed Italy. According to Italian law, embalming is not to be done until at least twenty-four hours post-death. Pope Michael VI was given this courtesy. His death was not dramatic or unexpected. It was not deeply steeped in suspicions of foul play and murder either. The public wanted answers. Their demands for an autopsy grew louder, followed by more questions. "Why was his body embalmed so quickly?" Unaware that if Benoît would have had his way, it would have been done within an hour or two of the discovery of his passing.

The Vatican press office tried everything they could think of to halt the constant bombardment from the public and media. Everything but the truth. The professional medical community called for the removal of Vatican Medical personnel and their prosecution for malpractice. What came out of the Vatican Press Corp ran the gamut between sensational to ridiculous. Tales of a perfectly healthy pope morphed into him being a long time sick, heavy smoker with one lung who survived multiple bouts of tuberculosis only to finally succumb to his fifth heart attack. Like Benoît, their efforts only made things worse. Why would the College of Cardinals elect such a sick man to be their supreme pontiff, only to let him die alone thirty-three days later? None of it made sense. The frustrated press would not be swayed by any of the official information put out by the Vatican. If the Holy City was not going to provide, their own army of investigative reporters would be deployed to find the answers that the Vatican was clearly not willing to give.

They would have their work cut out for them. The late Holy Father was a fabulous writer in his own right. He had penned numerous journal articles and opinion pieces and two books by the time he was elected pope. He would have had a brilliant journalistic career had he not been called by God to serve him and the Church when he was younger. Now he had become a victim of some of his would-be peers as they spun false narratives based on information from "highly placed Vatican sources" if one were to believe the press. These "sources" were nothing more than low-level priests and monsignors looking to stroke their own egos and a quick fifteen minutes of fame. They painted a great man as a simpleton. One who lacked culture and sophistication. Perhaps the most ironic of all was the fact that none of these "expert sources" had ever met Riluciani or stepped foot in the papal apartments. Besides dragging his name through the mud, they never once acknowledged Riluciani's numerous accomplishments he was able to complete during his brief papacy.

Less than forty-eight hours after his passing, the Vatican began a global broadcast showing the embalmed body of the Holy Father. The Curia was ill prepared for the huge flocks of people filing past the body as it lay in state. Officials were forced to move him to Samit Peter's Basilica in order to accommodate the ever increasing volume of people. They watched as 12,000 people per hour came to view and pray for the soul of their late spiritual leader and the future of their Church. The Curia were baffled and impressed. They just could not understand how a humble, unknown cardinal from way up north could amass such a large and devoted following in only thirty-three days.

The funeral for Pope Phillip Michael I was scheduled for October 4th. In addition to accommodating all of the people who came to pay their final respects, preparations were also needed for the conclave soon to follow on October 14th,. This event would draw 127 cardinals from around the world to join the twenty-nine who resided locally to attend the burial of the pope they had just elected only a few weeks ago, and elect yet another to replace him.

Benoît had his hands full, the Curial leader would not chance another Riluciani to be "chosen by God." This time, they wanted one of their own. This coming conclave would be nothing like the one that elected Phillip Michael I. That conclave was delayed as long as was legally possible according to Vatican laws. The next one would happen just ten days after the burial of the last. Curial staff hoped that the hype surrounding the new pope would distract the public's attention away from the suspicious death of Riluciani. The conclave could not come soon enough, as far as they were concerned.

By the first of October, the public pressure for an autopsy reached a fever pitch. Newspapers and reporters had often been critical of the Vatican over the years. The Curia would just ignore Church critics. They would not be governed by the court of public opinion. One reporter from Italy's most widely read paper published the headline, "Why no Autopsy?" He was known for his highly scandalous, yet accurate pieces exposing questionable financial dealings involving the Vatican. The press hit the mother lode when they connected the dirty dealings of Vatican Bank president, Bishop Jonas Krivis, failed global financier Giovanni Fedora and Banco Generali President Marco Ansios involving the Catholic Bank of Venice several years back. The former patriarch of Venice led vocal public protests, despite now having power to reverse or resolve the situation. It was leaked that the new pope was to remove Krivis soon. Was this pope murdered in order to keep men like Krivis and others like him in their positions within the Vatican?

An autopsy establishing the true cause of the pope's death was important for the factual historical records. If the cause of death was in fact a heart attack, the church would certainly have nothing to lose, and much to gain from the release of such information. The article went on to suggest that criminal elements within the Vatican had taken over the Holy City. No one believed that the pope's death was from natural causes with all of the devil's creatures now living in that city.

The press would not let Vatican officials hide their complicity in the murder of this pope behind some bogus claim that autopsies were not allowed according to Vatican policy. The public reminded them of the autopsy that was performed on Pope Pius VIII who died in November, 1930. The Vatican tried unsuccessfully to claim that it was never done and results were never released. Once again the press caught them in yet another lie. Ironically the case of Pope Pius VII followed the death of a seemingly healthy pope they had suspected to have been poisoned.

At 7 PM the night before the funeral of Pope Phillip Michael I was scheduled, the Curial leadership finally caved from pressure from the international governments outside of Italy. The gates of Saint Peter were closed off to the public, and four members of the Swiss Guard were ordered to stand guard at each of the corners of the catafalque on which Pope Phillip Michael I's corpse was being displayed. A group of 150 people who had traveled over 620 km from the town of Riluicani's birth in Northern Italy to pay their final respects to the man many had known personally were rudely kicked out, despite special permission granted to them by Vatican personnel. Instead, they were ushered into Saint Peter's Square, brokenhearted and bewildered.

Vatican officials then ordered everyone, including the posted guards, out of the chamber. A group of physicians was escorted to the pope's body. Large red screens were put up around the catafalque with adequate room to accommodate the doctors. The two hour exam performed by the doctors less than twenty-four hours before the scheduled funeral, judging by the reaction that followed from the Vatican, confirmed in the public's mind that the Holy Father had indeed been murdered.

The following day, over 100,000 people braved the pouring rain in Saint Peter's Square for the Requiem Mass. The connection established between this pope and the people of the world in a matter of only thirty-three days was remarkable. Over 1 million people joined the pilgrimage to the body of the late Holy Father between the time of his body's discovery until it reached its final resting place. The body was then hermetically sealed into nesting coffins made of cypress, lead and ebony, then placed in a marble sarcophagus in the crypt of Saint Peter between those which held the remains of Pope Phillip XXIII and Pope Michael VI.

At 1 PM, following the burial of Pope Phillip Michael I, Vatican officials released more lies. The two hour exam performed by medical professionals was skewed into a twenty minute routine check on the state of the body by the embalmers. It didn't take much to uncover the fact that none of the embalmers were actually present at the time of the exam. If this was truly an autopsy, and if foul play was not consistent with cause of death, surely officials would have released the information to silence those convinced that this pope was murdered. The Vatican Curial leadership continued through the remaining *Novemdiales* or period of mourning and continued into the *sede vacante* with a stoic attitude reminiscent of the Mafia's *omertà*. Their code of silence was poorly disguised as Vatican tradition and protocol. Their lies, especially over the last seven days, had destroyed every last bit of credibility they had recovered since their involvement in banking scandals.

The inquiring public finally came to the realization that they would never get the truth out of the Vatican. Those most troubled by the Vatican's behaviors and actions over the last week were those close enough to know the truth. They knew that Sister Falcone had discovered his body, they knew of the Curial staff changes contained in the papers he clutched in his hands as he lay dying in his bed. They knew of the violent protests and refusal of Cardinal Leveroni of his new assignment as patriarch of Venice. They remained sickened by the continued release of "official" lies even after the pope's burial. Many consulted with Cardinals Leone and Wexford. They could not remain quiet any longer. If the Vatican would not release the truth, they would. Leone and Wexford took the information and testimonials to the three detectives that had remained in Rome for the pope's funeral. All five men agreed that a deeper investigation was warranted.

It would now be up to the press to give the good people of the world the truth about what had happened. Leone and Wexford carefully selected the media sources for their long established reputations on delivering truth and not mincing, twisting and sensationalizing the information. There was no need for any embellishment of the information anyway, there was plenty of that coming straight from the Vatican sources already. The Vatican press officer once again found himself bombarded with questions surrounding the events of the last ten days. They were fine with the bombardment before as they controlled the material "leaked" to the press. However, now things were different. The truth had finally caught up with them. The distraction of a new pope was not going to happen soon enough to save them. The only response issued by the Vatican press office was that "The information spurring these questions are completely devoid of fact and foundation."

Inside the Vatican City walls, the men who made up the College of Cardinals were growing restless. They knew what had really happened. They were disgusted with the Curia's lies and propaganda. They were also incensed that because of the evil and dirty deeds of Vatican, Inc., they once again had to travel from around the globe for another conclave.

Cardinal Benoît unexpectedly found himself at the receiving end of the cardinals' collective fury. Some were unsure whether the Camerlengo actually murdered the pope, but they were all certain that he knew who did, and continued to do everything in his power to prevent that information from seeing the light of day. These senior ranking men of the Church wanted answers. The real answers.

"What are you covering up, and for whom, Benoît?" Challenged a cardinal from South America.

"That is enough of this ridiculousness gentlemen, we have important work to do." Benoît responded.

"We did our important work a little over a month ago, and you killed him." Delcared another.

"I killed no one."

"If it wasn't you, you know who did." Shouted the man from Canada.

Benoît ignored the comment. "Gentlemen please..."

"No, we want answers. Why are you feeding the press everything but the truth?"

"I gave them the truth!"

"Like hell you did Zacharie! The truth doesn't change every two seconds. What you gave them was the crap you wanted to be true."

"You think this job is easy? You think you can do better? Step into my shoes for a few minutes, you will see how truly thankless this job really is."

"Oh quit your bitching, Zacharie. You have no one to blame but yourself this time."

"Like hell I do. What is that comment supposed to mean?" Benoît challenged.

"You shouldn't even be Camerlengo right now, Leone should be. But you refused to step aside, like Riluciani had dictated the night before he was killed."

"He wasn't killed, and besides that Riluciani was wrong!"

"He was only wrong for you and your friends. He was right for us and our Church."

Benoît dismissed the last statement with a disingenuine, "What's done is done, can we now get on with the business of the conclave gentlemen?"

Two days before the conclave was scheduled to begin, the Vatican issued its final press release to address the controversy that lingered stubbornly around the late pope's death. "As we conclude *Novemdiales*, the Holy See wishes to convey their disappointment in those who have adulterated our period of mourning by the circulation of unchecked falsehoods and grave insinuations. In these times of great sorrow in the hearts of our Church we expected more decency and respect." The press secretary tried in earnest to draw the public back to the desired propaganda and away from the actual truth. Their lies continued to fail miserably. Everyone was now completely convinced that Pope Phillip Michael I was murdered.

CHAPTER 44

The international detective team's trip to Rome was nothing any of them could have anticipated. What was supposed to be a "working" vacation with colleagues, with a side of sightseeing with their wives, turned into a horrible nightmare, literally overnight on the evening of September 28th. Instead of their group's scheduled meeting with the pope to discuss criminal and corrective actions within the Vatican, they were now putting in long hours to investigate his murder, and determining why the Vatican was so hell bent on covering it up. The entire world sat in a state of suspended animation until Pope Phillip Michael I's successor was elected. The future remained uncertain until the Church's College of Cardinals completed the most important work of their lifetime. It was up to them to decide whether the next pope would be the second coming of Pope Michael VI or or the second coming of Pope Phillip Michael I.

The detectives kept themselves occupied while waiting out the results of the upcoming conclave. The investigative work had suddenly become very personal, more so than they ever thought was possible. Cardinals Leone and Wexford were very busy trying to uncover uncomfortable truths and influencing the future of Vatican political bureaucracy. They remained in constant communication with the detective team, assisting them as best they could.

The onslaught of Vatican clergy and staff who knew the real story continued to grow. These people also could not understand why the Vatican Press Corp had released nothing but lies since the discovery of the pope's dead body. The deception disgusted those in the know. These men and women wanted to assist in setting the record straight. However, that was a very dangerous endeavor for anyone inside Vatican City. They knew that there were eyes and ears everywhere. Clearly if they could kill the pope and cover it up, no one felt safe to protest or come forward.

The detectives began conducting interview after interview of individuals with direct knowledge or who personally witnessed events leading up to and following the death of Riluciani. These individuals were nervous, but they trusted Cardinal Leone and his leadership. It also helped that these investigators were independent of the Vatican and her criminal components. For people like Sister Falcone, Fathers Mancini and Barton and others they hoped and prayed for the success of these men to tell the world what really happened to the great man they knew, loved and respected.

As the detectives worked to compile testimonies and information, they were growing more and more puzzled and frustrated with the Vatican's unwillingness to cooperate. Repeated requests for Pope Phillip Michael I's death certificate were repeatedly ignored, then denied. It seemed that none of the medical doctors on the Vatican Health Services staff was willing to pen their name to any such official document. None of them were willing to take legal responsibility for the "official" cause of Riluciani's death, not without the confirmation that would only come from a full autopsy. Once the embalmers were done with him, it was too late for any of that.

None of the doctors on their staff ever saw him while he was alive. The only doctor to ever examine him, claimed that he died of an "acute myocardial infarction." That doctor's first interaction with the pope was when he examined his body as it lay dead in his bed. He knew nothing of his medications, conditions or medical history.

With the help of Hans, a world renowned cardiac specialist from Munich were consulted. In the physician's twenty-three years of specialty work in the field, he had never seen such a bullshit diagnosis, based on such a bullshit excuse for an exam and no prior knowledge of the patient's history. Another Munich specialist, this time a pathologist with over fifty years of experience, took his own shots at the quack doctor's claims. The 11 PM time of death wasn't working once he and detectives recreated the timeline of that early morning and the evening before. When a person dies, rigor mortis sets in between hours five and six under normal conditions. However, the temperature of the environment can speed up or delay the process. Rigor would, in most cases, be firmly fixed by the twelve hour mark, then slowly relax over the next twelve that followed. Without a temperature reading of Riluciani's internal organs like his liver, his time of death could only be approximated at best.

The last anyone saw him alive was a little before 9:30 on the night of the 28th. Since rigor was firmly affixed by the time Sister Falcone found him at 4:30 AM, and was beginning to relax by the time Fathers Mancini and Barton dressed him at 10 am, Rilucinai's death seemed to have occurred sometime between 9:30 and 10 pm. That also was consistent with the way the body was found, and the fact that his old beat up alarm clock didn't go off on the morning of the 29th.

The investigative team also learned of the identity of one of the doctors who was present during the body's examination the night before the funeral. He was a well known doctor from the Catholic University in the northern regions of Italy. It seemed suspect that the doctor mysteriously disappeared without a trace following the collective examination of Riluciani's body. The hunt was on to find him. "Famous doctors don't just vanish without someone knowing about it." Suggested Fran.

The investigative team gained great insight from an in depth conversation with the man who had been Riluciani's personal physician for the last twenty years. He also refused to believe anything that came out of the Vatican. He disclosed that when Father Mancini called him on the morning of the twenty-ninth, he just could not believe what he was hearing. Before the doctor left Venice, he gathered the late Holy Father's entire medical record to bring with him to Rome. The doctor and investigators poured over chest x-rays, numerous laboratory test results and electrocardiograms. There was every indication that the pope was in perfect health at the time of his death. There was certainly no sign of any type of heart condition. His only ongoing medical issue was a non-life threatening low blood pressure condition treated with minimal medical intervention. It was the best possible scenario for one who was expected to live a long life, full of vitality. The competence, detail, consistency of care and documentation was impressive. Nothing in it supported the ridiculous claims of Vatican medical staff. The fabricated information coming from the Vatican was now getting worse. The Venice doctor was livid as reports issued from the Vatican and press stated that Riluciani's long time medical doctor agreed with the Vatican medical personnel's diagnosis of acute myocardial infarction as Riluciani's cause of death. "How dare they defame me like that and tarnish my competence and reputation as a seasoned physician with their lies to cover up what they have done to this great man!"

The other odd component of this centered around Chiaros Riluciani's last will and testament. Why was it never made public? Vatican officials told his family and the public that one did not exist. Those who knew him the best, caught the Vatican in yet another lie. Riluciani's brother knew the will existed. While they never discussed the detailed content of the document, they did discuss it over lunch just a couple of weeks prior to his death, on one of his visits to Rome. Riluciani's niece also knew that her uncle was meticulous about keeping his will up to date. While he was patriarch of Venice, his last will and testament consisted of only three lines. Simply stating that everything was to be left to his seminary in Venice and named an auxiliary bishop to serve as executor. If the named executor moved or passed away, he'd simply cross out the name and put in his next choice. He was not a man obsessed with worldly, material possessions. However, the will of a pope goes far beyond just the distribution of physical assets. Spiritual and philosophical words and reflections regarding the state of the church and world and the future were often found written in such papal documents. This pope was a very different man. He was a revolutionary, and he was by far the most learned, accomplished writer the Vatican had seen in the modern era. How could he not have departing words penned for the good people of the world? People like Falcone, Mancini and Barton watched closely that fateful morning as Cardinal Benoît lifted papers, glasses, medication and slippers from the papal bedroom. Mancini was certain he saw Benoît remove the Holy Father's will from his desk drawer.

It was becoming more and more clear that Benoît was instrumental in the plot to murder the pope. His behaviors and actions were certainly consistent. Consistent in his efforts to cover up or obscure the truth. What a contrast this was from when Pope Michael VI passed away. Well over twenty-four hours had passed from the time of his death to when he was embalmed, consistent with the laws that govern the rest of Italy. This pope was embalmed a mere fourteen hours after they found him. Benoît, if he would have had his way, would have had it done even sooner. Why so fast? Also, how was it that the embalmers were called forty-five minutes "before Father Barton had discovered his dead body?"

Prominent Italian newspapers were now reporting that the embalmers were awakened at pre-dawn hours and taken from their homes to the Vatican mortuary at 5 AM by Vatican officials in black unmarked vehicles. Detective Clavering felt it was time to have a talk with these reporters about their information and sources. However, he remained less than optimistic about their success, after being shot down by New York reporter Robert Hinson and Peg in the past. Regardless, they had to try if they were ever going to solve the case of the murdered pope.

Hans suggested that they interview the embalmers too. After all it was they who were ordered to destroy the most telling evidence, before the true cause of death was determined. Who ordered them to violate Italian laws and why? What about the secret exam that was done on his body the night before the funeral? Who were those doctors? Where were they, and most importantly, what were their findings? Their claimed "embalming check" lie was quickly debunked. What were they doing to the body for an hour and a half? So many questions remained unanswered.

All three detective knew that their suspicions of murder were not dependent on establishing a motive. Of course that would not be an issue for this case. There was a motive everywhere they looked. Men like Benoît, Krivis, Leveroni and the corrupt cardinal from Chicago were certainly among the list of suspects. Being men of the cloth was not something they could use in their defense. If any of them was guilty, they certainly wouldn't be the first "holy men" to commit a horrible crime like murder.

Benoît was a sick, old man, ready to retire months if not years ago. The preservation of his position alone was most likely not enough for him to commit such a crime. However, he hated what Riluciani was doing to change the Church's traditions and shape its future. Did he have a vested enough interest in protecting his good men in the Curial staff from being removed? Were these situations enough to push someone like him, with retirement in his sites, to commit murder? All through history the Vatican and Curia had established and maintained a particular fondness and adherence to tradition and the status quo of the Church. Would the desired changes of this new "rogue pope," warrant his murder? Whether he actually killed Riluciani or not, he was already guilty of other crimes associated with his murder. Destruction of evidence, lying to the press and public, and the imposition of silence were just the beginning.

Leveroni had already demonstrated that he was a loose cannon when confronted. Was he level headed enough to formulate such a nondramatic method for murder? As far as the Chicago cardinal was concerned, very little was known about him by the detectives. However, there was no shortage of organized criminal elements and resources in that part of the United States. It seemed improbable, but at this point nothing was to be ruled out.

The case against Bishop Jonas Krivis was strong. Comparable to Benoît, he had motive and could access the pope at any given time.

The knowledge for access he gained from serving as Pope Michael VI's personal bodyguard for so many years would certainly come in handy for a man intent on such a dirty deed. What exactly was he doing wandering about the Vatican at such an early hour on the morning of September 29th? Everyone knew that that was not normal behavior for the man.

There were other potential suspects to be considered. Outside the Vatican and Church; the names of Marco Ansios, Giovanni Fedora and Gherado Fratello topped the list. All three had long established histories and capacity to commit murder to protect themselves and their interests. All three had plenty of motive too. While it was possible that the culprit was none of these seven men? The detectives would remain focused on them until additional information eliminated them from consideration. Whoever committed the murder was counting on the next pope to fill the Church's throne to discontinue what Pope Phillip Michael I had started. All seven desperately needed "the right man" to be elected for their own personal, individual benefits. All seven men were also in positions to influence the outcome of the next conclave.

The investigators next turned their attention to how such a crime could have been carried out. The city, state/country of Vatican City sits on 100 acres of land. There are six gate entrances scattered about the property. In the past, Swiss Guards maintained twenty-four hour posts just outside the papal apartments. Pope Phillip XXIII dismissed them from their posts during the overnight hours. Obviously, security was pretty loose at the time of Riluciani's murder. Ironically, he had more security surrounding him after he died than at any other time in his life. Both were situations that would benefit one who was intent on murdering the pope.

In a documented log, it was noted that the light in his bed chamber was still on at 10:30 PM the night of the twenty-eighth, by the chief officer in charge of the Swiss Guard. Other reports noted that that particular light was on all night long. That was consistent with the timeline rebuilt by the detectives. Most people came and went from the papal apartments via the elevator and a special key was required to access more exclusive areas of the complex. Many people had a copy of that key. The papal apartments could also be accessed through a hidden, little known staircase that was in close proximity to the apartments. Did the killer have a key? Did he know of this secret passageway?

Who ever the murderer was, his task was by no means anything complicated. He could have easily spiked his food, tea, coffee, water or medication. There was a host of over 200 lethal substances that could have been used to execute their mission and their man. In their per-meditation process, they would have had to have known that there would be no autopsy on the body, and that there was no doctor on duty late at night, or early in the morning.

As the detectives went about their work they considered the fact that Italy, as a country, had one of the lowest populations of coronary heart disease in the world. The diagnosis of Acute Myocardial Infarction just didn't make sense in a perfectly fit, native Italian. A man who had low blood pressure, never smoked, and the only alcohol he consumed was the wine he took with his communion. He was a moderate eater of a relatively bland diet, and exercised daily. His chosen modest lifestyle provided him the best possible cardiac health possible.

The man was under constant, competent medical supervision for years with clear chest x-rays and electrocardiograms absent of any type of heart weakness whatsoever. Death came for him so suddenly that his body instantly froze in space and time in what looked to be a very painful departure of his soul. As death came for him, he was not even afforded enough time or energy to push the call light just inches away from his hands. People don't just die like that, naturally. Especially men like Riluciani.

The men who elected him counted on, and looked forward to him having a very long papacy that would alter the church and world significantly. His two most recent predecessors had reigned for twenty years between them. Papal funerals and the subsequent conclaves were a very expensive endeavor for the church. Pope Michael VI's funeral and Pope Phillip Michael I's conclave racked up over $5 million in expenses for the Catholic Church.

The investigative team was fairly confident that one of their seven suspects held the answers to this murder mystery. While the perpetrator saw Riluciani as someone who was in the wrong place, at the wrong time...his murder was by no means anything random. It was clear that this particular murder was planned, and planned well. Complete with knowledge of exactly how the Curial leadership would respond postmortem.

When was this all planned? Was it in the days just after his election? Was it in the early days of his papacy as he began looking into the operations of Vatican, Inc? Maybe two weeks in when he learned of the Freemason's infiltration of the Church, especially the majority of the men who made up the Curial government? By his third week, he was ready to remove Bishop Jonas Krivis and his two accomplice secretaries from the Vatican Bank. The planning phase of his murder was not nearly as important as the timing of it's execution. For any of the men on their suspect list, another day or two would have been too late. Especially men like Cardinals Benoît, Leveroni, and Bishop Krivis.

At this point, much of what detectives had gathered was circumstantial evidence at best. Detective Clavering felt disheartened, frustrated and defeated that that would be the best their efforts could produce. For cases of murder, especially in Italy, circumstantial evidence was very common. Unless it was some sort of syndicate hit job, designed to extinguish a problem while serving as a warning to others contemplating similar violations of Mafia code, murderers liked to maintain a low profile. Detective Clavering was still operating under the mindset of the American legal system. He was visibly relieved to learn that in Italy circumstantial evidence had been sufficient to send many who were guilty to their own demise in numerous cases over the years.

While there was no shortage of criminal activity within the Holy City prior to Riluciani's arrival. The death of Pope Phillip Michael I was a high profile event. However, his murder was not. It had to appear natural and devoid of all dramatic incident and fanfare. Cardinal Benoît and the Vatican Curia failed miserably in their part of the murder plot. Their lies and actions backfired at every turn. Benoît and many on his staff were without a doubt 100 percent complicit in one of the most serious crimes of the century involving the Vatican. The detectives and the world would have to wait out the results of the impending conclave before narrowing down their list of possible suspects.

CHAPTER 45

There was a certain heaviness that came over Vatican City as the day of conclave drew closer and closer. The future of the Catholic Church was at a very unique, and historic crossroads. The next pope chosen by this College of Cardinals would have an enormous impact on both Church and global affairs. Whether the Church would return to the days and ways of Pope Michael VI or continue on the very different path set forth by his successor lay in the result of their vote.

Cardinal Leone found himself involved in many deep conversations about the future of the Church to which he had dedicated his life.

"Dante, do you remember a while back when I asked you if you'd ever consider a higher position? A higher office if you will?" Reminisced the cardinal from West Africa.

A senior cardinal from Belgium overheard the conversation, and decided to join them. "I agree with Hanru.We think you should be our next pope Dante."

"Me? I'm flattered. I can't believe that we are even having this conversation at the moment..."

"Will you please just listen to Jens and I? Look, the people of Africa, South America and most of Europe, they all want and need your leadership for the Church right now, my friend."

Leone remained silent for an extended moment. As a memory of his dear friend Riluciani caught him by surprise, and ran down his cheek. "I...um..." he caught himself before he lost complete control of his emotions. He took a big breath before responding. "I will think about it...but I feel that I must be honest here gentlemen. We just buried the last one. A man near and dear to all of us, and I feel that if I don't get to the bottom of who did it and how, there will never be justice for such a heinous act."

Hanru moved closer to Leone and wrapped his arm around his shoulder. "We all must live with that pain in our hearts, but we also must remember Dante, he is with God now. Those of us who have yet to be called by God the Father are not so fortunate, my friend."

"Hanru and I can both see it. You are a lot more like Chiaros than you know. Your faith is so, so strong."

"Believe me, my faith is nothing like his was. I have my moments where my faith completely fails me. Especially as I look at our Church today," Leone lowered his head and shook it in disapproving shame. "I often have my doubts..."

"As do most men who have walked this God given earth, my friend." Responded Jens.

"Most men who walk this earth are not contemplating the possibility of becoming pope."

"We had Chiaros, the man with more faith than any of us..."

"...and look where it got him. Look where it got us, Hanru."

"Perhaps we now need a man who is less confident in his faith, Dante."

"Well there's plenty of them around to choose from. What if I... we, choose wrong?"

"It was you who chose Riluciani, did you not?"

"I did."

"And were you wrong?"

"Yes and no..."

"Yes and no?" Echoed Jens.

"No I wasn't wrong, he was the right man for the job, but if I had not pushed him into the papacy that he did not want, he would still be with us today."

The cardinals watched as Leone continued with his very personal, internal struggle. "We all need to lean into our faith in times like these, Dante." Hanru advised.

"Faith? I need more than faith right now..."

"More?"

"Yes, now I need forgiveness more than I need faith. Forgiveness from my colleagues, from his family and those closest to him, forgiveness from the people of the Catholic Church, and most importantly, I need forgiveness from Chiaros' spirit and Our Heavenly Father." A tear streamed down the cheek of Cardinal Leone unchecked.

"You can't beat yourself up because of the darkness in the hearts of those who did this to him, Dante." Consoled Jens.

"I left him alone to die!"

"You were to be by his side the very next day! How were you to know that they would go to such extremes to maintain their dark grip of power over this Church."

"Why on earth would God make him pope, just to take him away from us in just thirty-three days?"

"Why does he ever let evil triumph at all, Dante?" Questioned Hanru.

"I guess those are questions that we will have to ask God when we finally meet him face to face."

"We are all instruments used by God in the fight against evil, my friends."

"Even men like Benoît, Leveroni, and..."

"Yes Dante, even men like them. Think of them as mirrors that show us what will become of us if we let their evil darkness consume us and rob us of what is our divine destiny."

"I have spent my entire life watching 'men of God' fall to their lust for power. I can't say that I'm all that much different."

"That isn't true, Dante, and you know it!" Responded a passionate Jens.

"Really? Have I not gained more and more power, and used it in order to gain more?"

"Yes, but..."

"Yes but...it was I who made Riluciani pope."

"And why was he your man?"

"Because he was different. He was the one of just a few men in this church that I knew power could not corrupt. He was a truly holy man." Leone then looked directly at his companion. "I am no Chiaros Riluciani."

"Perhaps he was too perfect for such a position. He was too perfect for this messed up world."

"I am not the man to fill his shoes."

"Alright, then if not you, who?"

"There are plenty of others to choose from, my friend. Anyone but me."

"Who should we choose? Leveroni? Frates? How about Benoît? Any one of them could be our next pope if you bow out of consideration."

"Benoît is too old, and sick. Leveroni is too full of himself and hot headed. He already has way too much power, if you ask me."

"And, what about Frates?"

"He's too weak, they will run his ass into the ground, while he's still thinking things over. None of those men should ever gain absolute power over this church."

"Listen, I spoke to Riluciani the day he died." Jens choked up a little from the memory. "He told me about his heated meeting with Leveroni. He also told me of his meeting with Benoît and what he was going to do about the situation in Chicago and with Krivis. He was sending them all home the next day...Riluciani was a man of his word, and a man of action based on those words...as we all know, that day never came for him."

Leone closed his eyes contemplating the past and the future for a moment. "It was me, I was wrong. I thought he could fix it."

"You weren't wrong, he was the one who could fix this church. That is exactly what he was doing...that's why they had to kill him." Jens confirmed.

"Damn it!"

"Look Dante, we all know it was you who ran Pope Michael VI's church. Benoît was too busy kissing his ass, I mean ring, to actually get anything done. That never became more obvious until Michael removed you and sent you to Florence. Everyone knew it, but no one knew it more than those two. You were Riluciani's closest friend, and you were slated to be his right hand man. The two of you were to be tasked with guiding this church into a future more befitting of what God wanted for His Church. Who else should we trust to avenge his death, and continue Riluciani's work?"

"Avenge his death?"

"I have one final question for you to consider Dante before I leave you...do you trust anyone else in that pool of possible popes to finish what Riluciani started?"

The conclave to select Pope Phillip Michael I's successor began early in the morning on October 15, 1978. Unlike the previous conclave, this one was extremely cold and hollow. As several cardinals jockeyed for the ultimate position of power, it was as if the influence of the Holy Spirit was forbidden anywhere inside the Sistine Chapel. The first day concluded without the selection of Saint Peter's latest successor. Emotions ran high throughout the day, leaving everyone exhausted. The results of the third casting of ballots were tallied. The front runners who emerged were Cardinals Leone and Frates. Leone was well on his way to securing his spot as the next pope. At the end of the day, Leone only needed five more votes in his favor to become the next pope.

The men, drunk on their power and positions within the Curia, suddenly became very concerned. Whoever killed Pope Phillip Michael I would have accomplished nothing should Leone end up getting elected. Leone would no doubt be the second coming of Pope Phillip Michael I. He already knew exactly what Riluciani had planned for the future of the church. He was inspired, motivated, and he was precisely the man to continue what his close friend had begun. Benoît would be packing his bags soon. Leveroni would be on his way to Venice. The problem cardinal from Chicago would find himself in a similar situation. Krivis and his corrupt secretaries would soon be gone from the Vatican Bank.

As the day came to an end, the election of Leone loomed as the inevitable successor to the throne of Saint Peter. Those who had chosen Riluciani were optimistic that Leone's vision and leadership would continue to shape the future of the Church in the right direction. Others viewed the exact same situation from a completely different perspective. Leone becoming the next pope would be far worse than anything that the last one could have become.

Sequestered in the privacy of Cardinal Benoît's office. Men like Leveroni, and others paced and plotted. "What about the Archbishop of Milan? He worked with Pope Michael for the longest time." Suggested Leveroni.

"He has withdrawn from consideration." Responded Benoît.

"This is news to me. He and I just discussed it yesterday."

"Leone has spoken with him since."

"Goddamn that Leone!" Leveroni shouted.

Benoît remained calm as he responded and lit himself another cigarette. "He is going to be the next pope, Ferinando. You might as well get used to it now."

"He is not pope yet." Responded another concerned cardinal from across the room.

Benoît continued. "He already has seventy votes, he only needs five more. I'm sure he can come up with what he needs by tomorrow morning."

"He will destroy this church!"

"We must find another Italian candidate." Called another voice from the room.

"There aren't any other Italians who can beat Leone."

"Then we need to look for someone outside of Italy."

"We've had an Italian pope for the last 500 years." Commented Benoît.

"I'd rather have a non-Italian pope than to have to kiss Leone's Goddamn papal ring!" Shouted an angry Leveroni.

The men sat in silence as they considered other possible candidates. Finally one of the cardinals broke the silence. "What about Lucjan Kułak? He already has nine votes."

"Kułak? The guy from Poland?"

"Yeah, that's the one."

"A Polish pope?! Are you mad?" Commented Benoît

Another cardinal chimed in at the suggestion. "The Austrians and Germans are already behind him."

"Isn't he a theological conservative?"

Benoît began to raise an eyebrow at the possibility. "Perhaps he's too conservative."

Leveroni couldn't help himself. "I'd rather we elect a heretic like Kułak than that damn Leone to the throne. Theology be damned!"

"It will take time to gather the support needed to get him elected." Considered Benoît. "It will take time that I'm sure we don't have."

"Do you think we can get Frates' men behind Kułak?"

"We have to, but again, it will take time."

"We don't have time, Leone only needs five votes!" Shouted Leveroni

"I'm sure Frates can hold the support of his men. Most of them are afraid of Leone, and those who are not, are afraid of Frates."

Benoît continued to think out loud. "How about we target his supporters who are still unsure? You know, those who are still kind of on the fence if you will?"

"What about the cardinal from Brazil?"

"Henrique?"

"Yeah, that's the one."

"He was a strong supporter of Riluciani's last time around. I think he's already firmly in Leone's camp."

"This is true," commented Benoît. "But I also think that he would be the most supportive of a non-Italian pope. Those are going to be difficult votes to move over to support Kułak. Both of them have a mutual respect and loyalty for each other that we can not dismiss, gentlemen."

In another office chamber located in the Vatican, the opposition was also hard at work strategizing.

"Cardinal Frates seems to be holding fast to his supporters, Dante." Reported Hanru, the cardinal from West Africa. "Wouldn't you agree, Jens?"

The Belgium cardinal responded. "To be honest, I'm actually quite surprised that he still wields that kind of influence anymore."

"I'm not surprised at all, actually..."

"What do you mean Dante?"

"One of the cardinals he has locked in told me that Frates is threatening him with content from the Vatican archives if he doesn't continue with his support of him."

Hanru was confused. "The archives? I don't understand.."

Leone continued. "Frates is one of the few men in the Curia with less than flattering information on many. If any one of them has ever even thought of any type of transgression, he has a record of it."

"He certainly has a knack for the art of 'moral persuasion.'" Commented Jens.

"Moral persuasion my ass!" Shot back Hanru. "I believe those in organized crime call that blackmail and extortion."

"We can still win, we only need to convert five more votes, Dante!" Encouraged Jens.

Once again the day passed without the successful election of a new pope. The frustration of Leone's camp was building. While his opposers stubbornly refused to concede in their efforts.

"I can't believe that we can't find five more votes." Remarked a frustrated Cardinal Leone.

"They certainly aren't going down without a fight."

The Brazilian cardinal entered the room. "Dante, please pardon my interruption, but the conclave has been deadlocked for the entire day."

"I know, I'm frustrated too Henrique, but I don't know what else to do." Commented Leone.

Henrique continued. "Well something has to give...we can't remain like this too much longer."

"What about the votes for Kułak? Doesn't he have like nine votes he's still holding on to?" Suggested Leone.

"Sigfried is holding tight to his men and the men from Austria. He won't budge, and neither will Frates with his conservatives." Interjected Jens.

"Damn it. We are so close."

Henrique reasoned. "As much as I hate to admit it, you are not going to get any more votes Dante. They have too much control over them at this point."

"Then what do you suggest Henrique?"

"We must come up with some kind of compromise. I spoke with Frates this morning, and he has suggested Kułak as a suitable compromise."

"A Polish pope?" Hanru could not believe his ears. "Can you believe such a proposal Jens?"

"All I can see is Benoît seething at the mere suggestion Hanru." The two men shared a chuckle and slight smile.

Henrique interrupted. "You know he has no connections with the Curia, right?"

"Then why would Frates throw his support behind him? That makes no sense."

"That's what's got me puzzled too, to be honest. All I know is that we will remain stuck at an impasse without either some of Frates' or Kułak's votes."

Everyone in the room knew that the South American was right. Leone thought to himself quietly for an extended moment. "Tell me about Kułak, Henrique."

"Don't you know him?"

"Not very well."

"I don't either." The South American then turned to the Belgium cardinal. "Jens, he's kind of from your part of the world. Certainly you should know a little more about him?"

"I know that he's taken a stand against the communists in Poland. He's also a vocal advocate for the citizens of his country. He pushes them to be politically engaged in movements for higher wages and better working conditions, things like that."

"Sounds like he would be a helpful ally for the people of South America as we continue to fight with our various dictators."

Leone liked what he was hearing so far, but still remained unconvinced. "Does anyone know what his take is on the Second Vatican Council?"

"He feels that it's important to have a more open Church, one that is welcoming of new ideas and a more open dialogue with other religions. He's absolutely committed to the Second Vatican Council."

"How do you know that Henrique?" Questioned Jens.

"I spoke to him, briefly, the other day."

"And you believe him to be true to his words?" Challenged Leone.

"That I can not say with any absolute confidence, Dante. There is no way for any of us to know what he will do once he puts on the Ring of the Fisherman."

"I knew with Riluciani..." Leone muttered to himself aloud.

"Look Dante, I don't like this any more than you do, but at this point there is very little we can do. Frates controls thirty of the votes and Kułak controls another nine. We need five of those votes. We all know that you won't accept Frates, and he won't accept you. Our only option at this point is Kułak."

Hanru voiced his frustration. "I can't believe how different conclave is this time around. When we elected Riluciani in August, all of us felt the Holy Spirit guiding and inspiring us."

"Hanru, that is definitely not the case with this conclave." Agreed Leone.

"The man who God chose, they murdered!" Commented Hanru, as he became upset. "Now He is left with the men we have remaining."

MONEY CHANGERS AND FALSE PROFITS

"I don't see a need for such a compromise. I don't trust Frates. We can keep him in limbo until he rots for all I care."

"Honestly Jens, I understand your passion, but that is hardly a suitable solution." The Brazilian then turned to Leone. "Look Dante, you are the only Italian that I will cast a vote for, if that is what you wish for me to do."

"I appreciate that Henrique..."

"...I can hold my loyalty until we all rot if you so desire. But at the end of the day, we must all consider what that will do to our Church."

"What are you trying to say Henrique?"

"Look, I don't like this impasse any more than you do Hanru, but if we withhold our support for the next pope, if it's not Leone, his authority from the world's perspective will be diminished, throughout his entire papacy." The cardinal chose his next words very carefully. "We won't be able to hide our absent support of the pope. The world will figure out fast that the next pope wasn't our first choice, or our second..."

"So you are asking me to walk away from the papacy Henrique."

"I won't tell you what you should do, Dante. You have my support regardless of what you decide to do."

"Is there any other way?"

"I'm afraid not."

Leone looked over at Hanru who was gesturing his disapproval of the proposal, when Jens broke the silence. "We can still win"

Leone then turns back towards Henrique. "I now understand how you have stood your ground so well among the oppressive governments in South America."

"That was a hell of a lot easier than this. There, I knew they were wrong, without question."

Leone remained lost in reflective thought as he ran his fingers over the irregular surface of the large cross that hung around his neck. "You know, Riluciani gifted me this cross many years ago, when we both were still archbishops." A tear formed and rolled down his cheek. This time he did nothing to reign in his emotions as the tears began to flow. "It is the most cherished thing I own. My God, I miss

that man! My heart will be forever broken for the rest of my days...
until we meet again. God willing..."

The three cardinals in the room began to shed tears of their own.
The man chosen by God was not even given a chance. All they could
do now was pray and mourn. All they had left was their faith in God.
They no longer had any faith in their fellow man, and certainly not
their colleagues. Leone then dried his eyes a little. He looked at Jens
and Hanru, then back at Henrique. "Kułak will be the next pope."

Jens and Hanru shook their heads in disagreement with Leone's
words. The South American then moved closer to Leone. Leone put
out his hand. Instead of shaking his hand, Henrique kneeled before
him and kissed Leone's ring. Leone looked at his ring, then at the man
before him puzzled. "This isn't the Fisherman's Ring, Henrique."

"It's a papal ring to me, Dante."

The West African repeated the gesture of Henrique, then the two
men left the room. It was now only the Belgium cardinal left with
Leone who felt a need to remind him. "Only five more votes, Dante."

"I understand that, but at what cost to the Church?"

"You would have made an excellent pope my friend."

Leone gathered his composure once again as he dried his face on
his handkerchief. "I was never meant to wear white, my friend." He
then smiled slightly. "Especially this late in the fall."

The following morning Cardinal Benoît began reading the
names on the ballots. "A vote for Cardinal Lucjan Kułak...A vote
for Cardinal Kułak...Cardinal Kułak...Cardinal Kułak..." A silence
came over the room for what felt like days. "The votes have all been
tallied. The final counted results are 103 votes for Cardinal Kułak and
seven abstentions." Cardinal Benoît walks towards Kułak. "Cardinal
Lucjan Kułak, do you accept your election as supreme pontiff?"

"I accept." The cardinal responded in a deep Polish accent.

"By what name do you wish to addressed, Holy Father?"

"Phillip Michael II..."

CHAPTER 46

Following the election of Pope Phillip Michael II, he was presented with the proposed changes that his predecessor announced on the night of his murder. He attended numerous meetings and conversations on a myriad of pressing problems. Fiscal information was presented from Leone, Frates, and others. Justification for the dismissal of the Chicago cardinal, and details on all of the Freemasons who had fully infiltrated the Vatican over the years. Kułak was the one man who had the power to bring Riluciani's plans to fruition. Everyone held their breath while they waited to see what this new pope, who was even more unknown than the last one, was going to do with his papacy.

It did not take long for the Curial powers that be to realize that the only thing that Pope Phillip Michael II shared with his predecessor was his chosen name as pope. Nothing that Rilucinai started in his thirty-three days ended up progressing any further. It became abundantly clear that the murder of Pope Phillip Michael I was the success those who plotted his demise hoped it would be. "Business as usual" soon returned to the Vatican and the Church with a vengeance.

Those whose heads who had previously been on the chopping block, were suddenly more cocky than ever.

Benoît remained Secretary of State, and quickly brought his new pope up to speed on issues of Curial traditions, protocol, and diplomacy. The men of the Chicago diocese were visibly frustrated and demoralized knowing the cardinal they despised would remain in his position. Bishop Krivis and his corrupt cronies all retained their positions at the Vatican Bank. They would engage in more criminal operations, now unimpeded. Banco Generali was suddenly enjoying their greatest success in the history of the bank. Marco Ansios walked about with a rarely seen smile on his face. His carefree demeanor was mirrored by Gherado Fratello, as the two of them pressed on with their schemes, wide scale theft, and fraud. They all knew full well that none of this would be possible without the protections and cover provided them by Krivis and the Vatican Bank.

This new pope, like Riluciani, was not a Curial pope. However, unlike his predecessor, he was not the type of man to shake up the status quo. He might have been able to ignore all of the wrongdoing against man, Church, and God that swirled around him; however, he could never claim ignorance or innocence. All of these men, especially Bishop Krivis were directly answerable to him. There was no way in hell that he could not know. As Kułak was getting settled in, Cardinal Leone sat down with him and revealed every last detail and fact of Krivis' criminal operations. This new pope's only response was no response at all. Leone was pissed. Frates, Leveroni and Benoît had saved their own asses, while pulling a fast one on him.

As the papacy of this Polish man developed and progressed, it became abundantly clear that the only thing consistent with this pope was his double standards. He talked a great talk, and the unwitting public glutted themselves with great gusto. His publically endearing style kept the masses distracted, while creating an ideal environment for even more rampant corruption. The constant public image campaign with Kułak as their frontman, was flashy and materialistic. He was more like a rock star on tour than anything nourishing and satisfying to the soul. To say that Vatican, Inc. was pleased, was an enormous understatement. This new pope was clearly the second coming of Pope Michael VI, but this time, with bells and baubles that paid dividends with compounding interest.

During the thirty-three days of Phillip Michael I's papacy, men like Marco Ansios and Gherado Fratello decided that their best strategy was to stay as far away from Italy as possible. The successful application of the Italian solution to the problem of an honest pope, and following the election of a "more understanding" successor was exactly what they needed. Fratello remained in Uruguay to continue his own plundering and manipulation of foreign leaders for personal gain of power and profit. Ansios felt it was finally safe for him to return home to Milan. He was the most free and easy he'd been in a very long time. He was grateful for the breathing space that came from the sudden demise of the pope with the warm characteristic smile.

The change in Marco Ansios, however, didn't last very long. The situation in the Vatican had very little effect on the ongoing investigation by the Italian Government. Riluciani had been dead only about a month when Ansios once again found himself in a state of panic. He was called to an urgent meeting by one of the inspectors working with the Bank of Italy in Milan. The twitch in his black mustache had returned to his face once again, this time more pronounced than ever before. The nervous banker responded to the inspector's questions with vague comments and words that contained neither admission nor denial of anything right or wrong. His gaze remained fixed on his shoes, the entire time. Never once making eye contact with his interviewer.

Despite his non-cooperative efforts, the inspection of Banco Generali by the men of the Milan division of the Bank of Italy was completed within only a couple of weeks. The documents and letters presented from Bishop Jonas Krivis and the Vatican Bank did not conceal the fact that Ansios was the true, rightful owner of the Financial and Commerce Services of Milan and other troublesome assets. The report revealed many hidden deals and details he and his banks had with the Vatican Bank, as well as his close working relationship with other ghost companies in recent years. Now, Marco Ansios had no other option but to rely even more on his connections with the Mafia, Vatican and P2 for assistance. As the findings of the Bank of Italy's report were making their way through the bureaucratic maze of the Italian government, Fratello and Ansios had already acquired copies via their network of P2 brethren. The news coming from Milan, and the Head of Vigilance was bad, very bad.

Things got even worse when Ansios learned via Fratello that the report was now headed for the desk of an investigating magistrate in Milan, who quickly ordered a full formal inquiry into all of Banco Generali's financial affairs.

"Do we know who the judge is going to be yet?" Questioned Ansios.

Gherado Fratello shuffled through the papers in his hands. "It's looking highly likely that this is now in the hands of Judge Ignazio Padovesi according to this report."

"Do you know him?"

"Yes."

Ansios displayed a visible look of relief. "Good."

Fratello didn't mirror Ansios' response, he just kept looking at the report. His voice grew quiet and less confident suddenly. "He is a very smart and talented judge."

"That's great news!"

"Actually it's not, I'm afraid."

"I thought you said he was very talented and smart."

"Oh he is. He's one of the best men I've ever seen in such a position."

Ansios failed to understand the problem. "So…?"

"He is also extremely incorruptible."

Ansios' stomach sank. "Shit! He's going to fuck up everything."

"No doubt about it, Marco. With this report in his hands, he will expose every last thing you've done, I'm afraid."

Ansios was expecting solutions and words of encouragement, not confirmation of his grim situation. He sat quietly thinking for a moment. His mustache failed to hide the trembling of his upper lip. "He's going to ruin everything. Are you sure there's no way to buy him off?"

Fratello too was feeling the same concern as his nervous banker. The thought of losing the bountiful flow of funds that found their way from the coffers of Banco Generali to him, was a very real possibility. "Some of our men have had him preside over their cases before. All I can say, is it didn't end well for them."

Judge Ignazio Padovesi suddenly became the one man who would, without a doubt, expose the corruption that men like Ansios, Krivis, Fratello and Fedora worked so hard to conceal. Ansios was as good as gone. Bishop Krivis would soon face public exposure of the absolute fraud he was. Fratello's significant flow of embezzled income would dry up quickly. This situation even posed a problem for Giovanni Fedora over in New York City. This development would create the most compelling argument to date for his immediate extradition to Italy from the United States.

In another part of Milan, a high profile investment banker and significant man of finance in Italy's capitalistic uprising, sat at his desk extremely worried. His true feelings and opinions of Fedora, his biggest nemesis of the region were no secret to anyone. The man was quoted in the media, just before Fedora's financial troubles started to become public, "Fedora should be completely destroyed, and his ashes should then be scattered to the wind." Fedora never once forgot, nor forgave the man. In Fedora's mind this man caused the destruction of his financial empire.

The man's hands shook as he returned the phone's handset to the receiver. He sat in quiet fear at his desk, trying to think of what to do next. This was the latest of several troubling phone calls he'd received in recent weeks. The threats were getting worse and worse. The banker thought the English speaking caller with a thick Brooklyn accent sounded familiar, but he couldn't place where he had heard it before.

The caller used horrific details to "persuade" the Milanese man that it would be in the best interest of him and his family to rescind the warrants issued for Mr. Giovanni Fedora's arrest. The man knew that anyone making these types of threats on behalf of Fedora was not to be taken lightly or dismissed. He'd seen a few brutal examples of those who did, first hand. Fearful for his own personal safety, and that of his family, he knew he had to do something. The following week, he had an intimate meeting with two of Fedora's representatives, his son-in-law and his Italian attorney in Milan. The men discussed the intimidating phone calls he had been receiving for weeks. Then the banking and investment man did his best to explain to Fedora's men that he had no power to do anything regarding any of the warrants. The matter was out of his hands, and out of his control. There was absolutely nothing that he could do. The banker felt much better following the meeting. The two men seemed to understand his situation. As the weeks passed by, he was confident that the information had reached the ears of Fedora.

One month later, the happy-go-lucky banker picked up the ringing phone on his desk. Horror gripped him tightly as he immediately recognized the man's deep toned Brooklyn accent. He hung up the phone, scared and unsure what to do next. It was clear that Fedora didn't believe a word of what was relayed to him. As he sat paralyzed with fear, the phone rang again, startling him. He slowly reached for the phone again and picked it up. All he could hear from the other end of the line was the panicked screams coming from his wife and children...

By the time he reached his home the fire was contained to just the foyer of their home by the firefighters, but the smoke and water damage was significant. He held his wife and children tightly. Tighter than he had ever done before. He was grateful that no one was injured, but he knew that his family was by no means safe. All that raced through his head were the numerous threatening phone calls he'd received over the past several weeks. He would send his family to distant relatives for their own safety. He would remain in Milan and work with the authorities to find the men who did this while repairs on their home were completed.

Several days following the fire that displaced the Milan investment banker and his family, another Milan man had a run in with some of Fedora's henchmen. This time, their target was one of Fedora's employees from one of his failed Milan banks. The Mafia hitmen for hire, claimed to be Fedora's "friends" from Staten Island. Fedora's former employee was instructed to stop all cooperation with the Italian government's investigation into his former boss' crimes. He was also instructed to retract deposition statements that helped their extradition case. Failure to abide by these warnings would get him two chopped off legs.

The weeks that followed the murder of Riluciani, Detective Francis Clavering remained in Rome to help out with investigative work. His wife Peg who had traveled with him to Rome was beside herself as she and the other detectives' wives mourned the loss of a great man whom they had had the privilege of getting to know personally. When they finally returned home from their vacation. Everyone around them couldn't help but notice a change in their personalities. They thought it was odd to see such sadness and defeat in them, especially after a vacation, but nobody was bothered enough to learn why. Nobody knew that they had been in Rome at the time of Riluciani's death, and returned following conclave. Clavering would continue to work with Cardinal Leone via Cardinal Wexford after he returned home. The murder of Chiaros Riluciani was a major set back that made the cardinals and detectives frustrated, yet even more determined to bring these evil men to justice.

In New York City, the detective along with his FBI partner, Agent Lance Erickson returned to their surveillance work of the disgraced Italian Banker. Clavering learned of the threats and intimidation going on in Milan on behalf of Fedora, through his Italian counterpart Cosimo. Through their work together, they found that the two men "from Staten Island" were contracted by Fedora. Information gathered from their most reliable syndicate informant lead them to another contracted hit ordered by Fedora. This one was a $10,000 hit job for the murder of the Assistant United States Attorney for the Southern District of New York who was the lead prosecutor in the Fedora case.

After learning of Fedora's recent rash of intimidation tactics over in Milan, an around the clock security detail was dispatched for the Attorney and his family. Fedora had nothing but hate in his heart for his Milan nemesis. However, he had absolutely nothing to do with the threatening phone calls and fire that occurred at his home. Fedora was pissed! A call was made to the hit men's boss immediately. "I don't know where that contract came from. It was nothing from me. Your guys are going to fuck everything up for me over there, and here too for that matter. No more, you hear!"

Through all of these intimidation tactics going on in Milan, the trial of the men responsible for the failure of Lincoln National Bank marched on, creating a lot of buzz in the New York press. An extradited Nico Novelli, with his plea deal, was now the star witness for the prosecution. He testified against "Pops," stating that he knew exactly what was going on at Lincoln. Novelli then testified that while he was manager of Fedora's bank in Milan, he was ordered repeatedly by Fedora to falsify earnings records. He was ordered to do more of the same in New York. Because of Novelli's testimony, "Pops" and a couple others were found guilty of conspiracy to falsify earnings data and sentenced to three years prison for each of them. The conviction didn't sit well with them. They all agreed that it should have been Novelli and Gilmore rotting in those cells and not them. Their personal opinions changed nothing. As Detective Clavering monitored the trial, it was blatantly clear that the US prosecution team knew nothing of Novelli's embezzlement of funds from Fedora's Italian accounts. In the mind of Clavering, a crime was a crime regardless of who the victim was.

Two weeks before Christmas, Fran was working at his desk. His attention was deeply focused on his work. The ring from the phone on his desk startled him.

"Detective Clavering." He answered as he mindlessly reached for the handset.

"Hey Fran, Cosimo here."

Fran's attention instantly shifted to the conversation. "Cosimo, my man, what's new? What can I do for you?"

"Oh you know, same shit, different day."

"Fedora and Ansios?"

"Of course, what else would we be doing these days?"

"Of course...so what's up?"

"Do you remember my telling you a while back about my dear friend Arturo Bartolone?"

Clavering sat quiet for a moment scanning his memory. "...the guy who's auditing and liquidating Fedora's shit over there in Milan?"

"Yep,...that's the one."

"Yeah, I remember, what about him?"

"I just wanted to give you a heads up, he's on his way to New York."

"Oh really? Tell me more..."

"He's got a meeting with federal officials over there. One of them is that Attorney from the SDNY."

"You mean the one that Fedora took out that $10,000 hit on?"

"Yeah, that's the one!"

"Oh shit! Do you think Fedora knows yet that he's coming to town?"

"I have no clue. I haven't heard anything suggesting that he does."

"At this point, I'd rather be safe than sorry. Thanks for the heads up! I will get a security detail on his ass as soon as he touches down."

"I'd very much appreciate that. He is a great friend, Fran. Never mind that he is doing some very important work over here, right now."

"No doubt about it. I actually look forward to meeting him. Don't you worry, I'm on it. I promise, I will make sure he stays safe over here, my friend."

"You're going like him, Fran. He's a lot like you."

"Me?"

"Yeah, but I'm not sure who's more stubborn, you or him!" The two detectives chuckled then terminated their call.

CHAPTER 47

Italian magistrate Ignzio Padovesi entered his office for the morning trying to shake off the cold of that frigid morning in early January. He hung his hat on the coat rack in his office, but he wasn't quite ready to give up his coat yet. He glanced at the thermometer hanging outside his office window. He read -5° C as he shivered then tried to rub some more warmth into his upper arms. The wind blowing down from the Alps and the Italian Great Lakes to the north gave the air an especially bitter bite that morning.

He poured himself a hot steaming cup of coffee, then cupped the mug in both hands. He gently blew on the surface as the steam and heat brought relief from the cold to his face and hands. He turned towards his desk, and took a sip of his brew. As his gaze turned towards his desk, he could see a thick document sitting there waiting for him. The next few days would be occupied by the contents of that report. He was finally starting to feel warm and comfortable once again. It was time to ditch his coat and get down to work.

The judge was meticulous as he made his way through the 500 page document. His note pad was full of scribbles, stars, arrows and underlined words of importance with page numbers for him to quickly reference. There were only five copies of the report created. The Italian government wished to keep the contents close to the vest until they were ready to make their move. No one outside of official investigative personnel had access to the information contained in that document. No one except for Gherado Fratello and Marco Ansios.

Regardless of either Fratello's, Ansios' or Padovesi's perspective as they all consumed the contents of the document, they couldn't help but be impressed by the effort and meticulous details of the information within. Fear and panic gripped Fratello and Ansios. This information in the hands of this judge was now a very big problem.

Magistrate Padovesi took two weeks to comb through the document. Once he was satisfied with his analysis, Padovesi rang the office of the Milan Tax Police. He ordered the lieutenant colonel in charge to have his men report to Marco Ansios' Banco Generali the next day. Every last criminal irregularity annotated in Padovesi's notes was to be fully investigated, quickly and quietly.

The deliberate efficiency was never again called into question. The stealthiness of the operation, however, was quite a different story. When the lieutenant colonel's men flooded the banking institution, they stood out like sore thumbs. They went about their work with laser focus and precision, while maintaining the highest degree of professionalism.

It only took a day or two for their presence and purpose to begin circulating through the local press. The news soon morphed into sensationalized rumors that Banco Generali President Marco Ansios and his entire Board of Directors were about to be arrested. Another rumor soon began to circulate that Italian government authorities had already withdrawn Ansios' passport. Ansios was an absolute mess. He chain smoked his way through the hours of each day as they passed. The possibility of losing his personal freedom consumed him, but for the moment that wasn't his biggest concern. Even more troublesome was if the rumors didn't die off soon, they would set off a public run on Banco Generali.

Magistrate Ignazio Padovesi received daily status updates compiled by the lieutenant colonel. He was pleased with the progression of their work thus far. It was Monday morning and he looked forward to a full summary from the previous week's worth of work. Padovesi was up early in anticipation of their findings. He kissed his wife goodbye, and loaded his young son into his car to take to school on his way to work. He walked his son to his class and gave him a big hug and kiss then returned to his car. He traveled down Via Maratori headed for his office. His attention drifted as he waited for the stop light to turn green.

A heavy thunk hit his back, just above his left kidney, followed by a snapping and tearing sensation as the bullet shattered his scapula and ribs, then tore through muscle, connective and lung tissue. He could suddenly feel the searing burn coming from the bullet lodged in his left lung. Padovesi instinctively grabbed his chest as the pain and impact knocked the wind out of him. He tried desperately to fill his lungs, as the air escaped through the bullet wound in his back. The warm salty, slightly metallic taste of blood filled his mouth. As he was beginning to fade, another bullet entered his neck, followed by an endless barrage of bullets that met the body of the trapped, unarmed, helpless magistrate.

When emergency personnel arrived, many of them immediately recognized the blood covered murder victim. The grim reality of what had just happened hit them like an out of control box truck. Investigative authorities quickly captured the gunmen responsible for the cold blooded, fatal assault. The five "guns for hire" quickly confessed to the crime, supplying full details of what had happened that fateful morning. A left wing extremist group claimed responsibility for the attack, but they had no motive. This was a situation that left investigators with more questions than answers.

Cosimo called Cardinal Leone and Detective Calvering in New York to inform them of the gruesome assassination.

"That's awful!" Exclaimed Fran in shock.

"A lot of my colleagues are really taking it hard too."

"I can only imagine...You say this was the work of leftist extremists?"

"Well that's who the gunmen said they were..." Cosimo's voice went quiet.

"Cosimo? Hello? Are you there?"

"Yeah Fran, I'm here. Sorry I just got to thinking...something's off regarding their confession..."

"What do you mean?"

"It just doesn't make sense..."

"What doesn't?"

"The group they are claiming to work for..."

"Why's that?"

"Everyone knows how extremely left leaning they are. Everyone also knows that magistrate, Fran. He is known nationally for bringing down the hammer of the law on many right wing terrorist groups." Clavering just let Cosimo run with his thought processes. "Why would such a group take out a guy who's body of work essentially aligns with their political stance?"

"I don't think I can offer you too much help here since I've never even knew of them before today. That said, given what you've just told me,...It does seem odd."

Once the press release and obituary were published, the motive coming from the assailants seemed to line up better to match their justification for the murder. It took a while for the dust to began to settle on this high profile murder case. Long after they had laid their beloved colleague to rest. It was time to get back to business. The Banco Generali case that Padovesi was deep in the middle of on the day he died, was now handed off to another magistrate.

Once again the Italian solution was successful. Marco Ansios soon found himself back in South America. This time in Peru which at the time, was deeply embroiled in a nasty civil war effort to help overthrow the Somoza dictatorship in Nicaragua. Ansios was wanting to establish a more robust banking operation in South America. He was ready to expand beyond the one Banco Generali branch already established in Lima. Ansios often used the Lima bank for his financial shell game schemes while Bishop Jonas Krivis and the Vatican Bank provided fiduciary services. Giovanni caught wind of what Ansios and Fratello were doing, and advised them against it. He then called Krivis and warned him to avoid any direct obligations with either of them other than serving a fiduciary role.

Ansios was completely under Fratello's control at this point. The P2 leader used him, his bank and his money to begin buying up South American newspapers with large distributions. Their plan was to use these news outlets to undermine the growth of communism in the country and the rest of South America. Once again Fedora tried to warn them. He knew that the fascists would be brutally unforgiving of their efforts, once they caught on. Fedora watched from his New York perch while Fratello over indulged his South American political friends to the extreme. The P2 Grandmaster then began buying into real estate schemes. Ansios and Fratello completely ignored Fedora's words of advice. Annoyed by what the failed banker had to say, the information flowing to him out of South America soon stopped altogether.

While both Fratello and Ansios stood steadfast by Fedora through his myriad of troubles in New York, Europe, and Italy. He watched as Fratello created a complex network of political and financial groups in many countries in the region. It was clear that they had no interest in his advice. It was time for him to stealthily move as far away as he could from anything involving them or South America.

Ansios attended a cocktail party at the beginning of February. As the drinks and conversation flowed, someone brought up the murder of Magistrate Padovesi that had occurred the month before. Ansios expressed sympathy for the man's loss and the impact his murder would continue to have on his widow and family, "...it's such a shame. I can't believe someone would do such a heinous thing. I spoke to him the day before the attack. He told me that he was going to have the case filed without taking any further action." Many who witnessed the conversation remained unconvinced of his sincerity. The coldness in his eyes gave away his true heart.

Cosimo continued his work with the Bank of Italy. He and the bank director in charge of the investigation were now more determined than ever that their efforts, the magistrate's death would not be in vain. The investigation of Marco Ansios and Banco Generali would proceed, but at a painfully slow rate of speed. It was suspected that whoever murdered Magistrate Ignazio Padovesi most likely also had a hand in the murder of Pope Phillip Michael I. The murder of the late pope bought them breathing room, while this latest murder bought them time.

Cosimo had the Bank of Italy call Marco Ansios in once again for questioning. He recalled the last time, shortly after the election of Pope Phillip Michael II. At that time, Ansios was a more exaggerated version of his normal anxious, fearful self as the Italian government's investigation was in full swing. Things were very different this time.

He was questioned extensively about Financial and Commerce Services of Milan. Investigators then shifted to the topic of Banco Generali's long established relationship and interactions with the Vatican Bank. Finally, they began to question him about Banco Generali's branch in Nassau, The Bahamas. The interviewers were fully prepared for the circular answers that weren't really answers they had received last time. It seemed that the death of Magistrate Padovesi created a certain air of invincibility about Ansios. His eyes were hard and cold as ice. The work and protections granted him by Gherado Fratello and his P2 brothers changed him from a nervous wreck to an arrogant, insufferable, and most unpleasant man. He sat in his seat, arms crossed, and flat out refused to answer any questions. At one point in the interview he became so annoyed and belligerent that he told the men seated across from him to "Go to hell."

The meeting revealed a lot to both Ansios and Cosimo. It was now clearer than ever that whoever was helping the Banco Generali president definitely had something to do with the murder of the Magistrate. Despite the cockiness of Ansios throughout his questioning, the meeting made it abundantly clear that the brutal killing of Padovesi had not resulted in the desired outcome. The Italian banking authorities still had him in their cross hairs.

Once again Marco Ansios returned to his protector and controller, Master Fratello, for help. Fratello did what he could to calm the Italian banker. Once again reassuring him that all would be fine, soon. Ansios believed and trusted his words and abilities to deal with this situation like he always had done so many times before. He had absolutely no reason to think otherwise.

Unbeknown to Ansios, Gherado Fratello had his own fires in need of his full attention. This was far more pressing and more personal than Ansios' ongoing problems. A man named Kristof Ricatto was becoming an ever increasing problem. He was a lawyer and journalist who produced a weekly publication called *The World Observer*. He had an extensive distribution list and had a knack for creating numerous pieces that highlighted allegations of widespread corruption in Italy business and government. He had a particular talent for stirring up impressive scandals that just so happened to be highly accurate. If one wished to know who was conning whom in Italy, he was the man to know. It was clear that Journalist Ricatto had unfettered access to highly classified personnel and information. His work was welcomed by the public, inspiring to other fellow journalists, and an absolute nightmare for those embroiled in the scandals he wrote about.

Ricatto had many key informants with the Italian Secret Service which held more power and secrets than any other agency within the Italian government. Ricatto was also one of Fratello's P2 members. The true Irony of the situation was that in the past, some of the most slanderous material published in *The World Observer* was actually provided to Ricatto by Grandmaster Gherado Fratello. Using systematic controlled leaks, Fratello created opportunities and situations that garnered him increasing levels of control and influence over his P2 members and other people of power around the world.

Sometime around the middle of the prior year, Mr. Ricatto decided to try his hand at a little blackmail. He had received documents detailing the theft of over $25 billion in oil tax revenue owed to the Italian Government. The man who had masterminded and ultimately profited from the scheme was none other than Gherado Fratello. Profits from his scam snaked its way through the hands of Giovanni

Fedora, then to the Vatican Bank and finally into Swiss accounts that were held in Fedora's failed Swiss Finance Bank in Zürich.

At the height of the scandal, Fratello had become a frequent visitor to the Vatican. He'd often be seen by Swiss Guards and others entering Vatican City through Saint Anne's Gate carrying large suitcases full of billions of lire stolen from the Italian Government. He covered his tracks by implicating the Finance Police General of Italy. He also held some Vatican Curia officials by the throat via one of their corrupt cardinals. The very same one who was removed from his position by Pope Phillip Michael I on the day he was murdered.

Ricatto was not aware of the late pope's intentions at the time, but he knew of the scandalous situation and began to produce teaser articles in his publication. As the information began to find its way to a more public audience, it was quickly stifled by a senator, a judge and a general who was working for the Italian Finance Police. In that moment, Ricatto may have been silenced, but he also discovered that it was far more lucrative for him to write about the Freemasons of Italy and the Vatican than any other topic. His articles began to be published in September, 1978 exposing the over 100 Freemasons residing in the Vatican. This certainly raised the eyebrows of both Riluciani and Fratello, calling them both to action. At the time, Fratello was more than aware of how dangerous Pope Phillip Michael I was to his P2 paymaster Marco Ansios. Ricatto and his articles had now become an even more dangerous problem.

Once the pope problem was resolved, Fratello turned his attention fully on Kristof Ricatto. The payoffs to keep him silent worked for a while. He finally felt that he had gotten an upper hand on the matter. However, Ricatto quickly learned just how important it was to Fratello to keep a very tight lid on certain information. *The World Observer's* publisher started to up the ante and demand more and more money to maintain his silence. Fratello grew frustrated and defiant, refusing to pay the extortionist's fees.

Ricatto began a torturously slow drip of articles exposing Grandmaster Gherado Fratello as the primary source of right wing fascism in Italy. The next article detailed his work as a communist spy during and after WWII. He exposed Fratello as the true former Nazi, ex-fascist, communist that he was. Ricatto fearlessly personified his position as an investigative journalist, revealing everything there was to know about Fratello and P2. His fellow P2 brothers felt completely betrayed by his actions.

On March 9, 1979, Vatican P2 Freemason and longtime Secretary of State, Cardinal Zacharie Benoît passed away. The man whom Pope Phillip Michael I had removed from his position the night of his murder had remained at all of his posts and positions until his own death six months later. Fellow P2 Freemason and Vatican Bank President, Bishop Jonas Krivis was constantly berated publically for bringing Mr. Giovanni Fedora to the Vatican, it was actually Pope Michael VI and Benoît who were truly at fault. Krivis' arrogance and stupidity provided men like Benoît and Fratello with a very convenient scapegoat. Pope Phillip Michael I had removed Benoît from both positions the night of his murder. Benoît made certain that those dictated changes never came to light or fruition. While his position as Secretary of State was extremely important to him, more important still was his position as head of the *Amministrazione del Patrimonio della Sede Apostolica,* or the APSA. It was the APSA that held the actual investment portfolio of the church, and was recognized as a central bank by The World Bank, International Monetary Fund and The Bank of International Settlements in Basel. It was Benoît and the APSA that actually had the long, deep involvement with Fedora that needed to be kept under wraps.

At the time of Riluciani's election, Benoît was a sick and tired old man. He already knew that he was seriously ill, he had been in declining health for years. His daily cigarette habit contributed considerably to his health issues. The rest and retirement that he so desired after the death of his beloved Pope Michael VI never found him. There was nothing he wanted more than to choose his successor, and Cardinal Leone was not going to be that man. There was no doubt in Benoît's mind that Leone would uncover the APSA scandal, and present it to Riluciani. This situation in conjunction with Riluciani's other changes in the Curia and Church was enough to provide significant motive for the murder of the pope. Did Benoît need to murder the pope in order to protect the future direction of the church and preserve the will of Pope Michael VI? Benoît had a front row seat to observe Riluciani's destruction of his church. Was the pope murdered for the "greater good of the Church?"

Benoît's reaction and behavior after learning of Riluciani's death seemed to indicate that he was either responsible or involved in the plotting of Pope Phillip Michael I's demise. Regardless, he was certainly a man suffering from a severe moral crisis. He didn't seem to concern himself with those who witnessed him destroying evidence, lying, imposing his vow of silence and speeding through the embalming process. Benoît had plenty of motive and opportunity to do the deed. If it wasn't him who murdered a perfectly health pontiff, he was certainly an accomplice. His actions and statements put out to the public meant that someone got away with murder. And once he became Camerlengo, upon the pope's death, he had complete control of the entire Church. Whatever Benoît's role was in that murder, his actions were 100% an effort to protect the Church. He was also the one man in the Vatican Curia who single handedly gave the murder conspiracy of Pope Phillip Michael I legs.

Ironically the time of Benoît own death, surrounded by close friends and relatives was meticulously recorded. His body was given a full diagnostic autopsy. His full health issues and cause of death were well documented and made available to the public. Vatican officials also honored the long standing Italian law by waiting well over twenty-four hours to have his body embalmed. In his death, he had been shown far more honor and respect than the late pontiff.

While the Vatican busied themselves with laying their longtime Secretary of State to rest, the Bank of Italy remained hard at work. Thanks to the work of their bank director, and the assistance of Detective Cosimo Angleo, the Department of Vigilance was nearing the completion of their work. Through their efforts, they had gathered more than enough evidence to justify the immediate arrest of Marco Ansios and the shutdown of Banco Generali. As Gherado Fratello and Ansios looked over the results of their investigation, their stomachs sank. There was absolutely nothing that could be challenged or refuted. There was nothing that would keep Marco Asnios' ass out of jail.

The problem of *The World Observer's* editor, Kristof Ricatto was becoming a bigger and bigger problem for Gherado Fratello by the day. He had just published his latest edition chock full of political scandals on the twentieth of March. The now disgruntled former P2 man had been divulging important intimate secrets regarding the clandestine organization since the beginning of the year. Fratello called Ricatto at his office in Rome.

"Kristof, it's Gherado, we desperately need to talk, can we meet? This can't continue, my friend."

"I agree. When would you like to meet?"

"How about tonight? Say 6PM?"

Ricatto looked at the amount of work piled on his desk, and released a deep sigh. "I'm afraid tonight's not going to work for me, I still have a lot of work to do."

"Mmmm, I understand. I'm sure you are very busy these days."

"That I am."

"Well how about tomorrow night then, same time?"

Ricatto looked at his calendar and schedule for the next day. "Yes, that looks a lot better for me."

"Great, how does *Ristorante Alfredo alla Scrofa* over on *Via della Scrofa* sound?"

"That sounds perfect. They have the best alfredo in all of Italy."

"I can't argue with you on that. See you tomorrow night!"

Ricatto stretched as he sat in his chair at his desk. He glanced at the clock hanging on his wall. "Wow, is it 9:00 PM already?" He muttered to himself. He glanced at his schedule for the next day, then tidied up his desk before he left his office for the evening. He walked a short distance down *Via Orazio* to where his car was parked. As he got in his car, a man approached him from out of the shadows, grabbed him by the hair on the back of his head, shoved the barrel of his P-38 revolver in his mouth and pulled the trigger twice. The gunman then shoved a rock into what was left of the dead man's mouth and left the scene. *Sasso in bocca* was a long established calling card of members from the Sicilian Mafia, Mr. Kristof Ricatto wouldn't be spilling any more secrets to the world.

Mr. Ricatto had a plethora of enemies both in and out of government. Authorities reported on his murder, but were completely lost on where to begin their investigaion. Mr. Gherado Fratello quietly read through his morning paper. As he read, it was clear that he would not be dining with his long established friend. He reached into the safe in his office wall and opened an old and worn black leather book containing the names of his P2 members. He found the entry listing Kristof Ricatto. He put a line through his name. Then next to his name, he wrote the word "deceased." No one ever claimed responsibility for the murder, and the case eventually went cold.

Gherado Fratello was more than pleased. He was relieved with the successful resolution to his most pressing problem. He paused for a moment, and took a deep breath. He could finally return his full attention to the problems of his paymaster Marco Ansios, and his pending arrest.

The obnoxious sound coming from the phone on Detective Clavering's bedside nightstand jolted him awake in the most unpleasant way. Instinctively, Fran reached toward the sound before it roused Peg from her slumber beside him.

"Hello,..." Fran muttered, still groggy.

Fran was immediately bombarded by rapid German-accented words that he did not understand.

"Whoa, whoa, whoa...Hans? Is that you?"

Hans quickly regained his composure before responding. "Yes Fran, It's me Hans."

Fran could here the panic in his German friend's voice. "Hans, what's wrong?"

"We have a huge problem! It's Cosimo..."

CHAPTER 48

Fran calmed Hans down enough to where he could understand him once again. "Now tell me again, slowly...what has happened to Cosimo?"

Hans took a deep breath. He continued to speak fast, but this time just a little slower and more deliberate in his words. "He's been arrested in Rome."

"Arrested? Oh shit, on what charges?!"

"Failure to disclose knowledge of a crime."

"What the hell kind of bullshit is that? Was he the only one they picked up?"

"No, they also picked up the director of the Bank of Italy that he was working for..."

"Interesting, I was just talking to him the other day about his work over there with that guy. They were really starting to get somewhere in that case too." Fran became silent for a minute as his mind continued to race. "I bet you money this has everything to do with the shit they've got on Ansios."

"I would not be the least surprised. Especially after someone knocked off the Magistrate who was handling the Ansios case."

"They did what?!"

Hans filled Fran in on the brutal murder of Magistrate Ignazio Padovesi.

"Oh wow! I had no clue. That's awful!" Fran's mind began to wander again. "So let me see if I have this straight. Someone knocks off the judge, and then a little over a month and a half later they throw Cosimo and that bank director working the same case in jail?"

"Ya."

"And all three parties were balls deep into the Ansios investigation over there..?"

"Correct."

"It sounds like things are getting a little too hot over there for Mr. Ansios, and someone is determined to make it go away."

"That's what I was thinking, Fran. But what are we going to do now? I don't know anyone else he's close with over there."

Fran had an idea flash before him, and smiled a little. "I do..."

"You do? Who? Leone?"

"No, but it probably wouldn't hurt to touch base with him too. I tell you what, you get in touch with Leone, and I will call you when I get into the office."

"Damn it Fran, don't leave me hanging like this."

"I will call you back in a few hours, Hans. I promise!"

Fran got an early start to his day. It was hard for him to go back to sleep knowing his friend and colleague was behind bars and being held in an Italian jail on bullshit charges. He glanced at the clock, it was still early, 5:30 AM, but he couldn't wait any longer.

"El lo..." came a groggy Italian accented voice from the other end of the line.

"Good morning, Arturo? It's Detective Francis Clavering from the New York Police Department."

"I'm sorry, who is this again?"

"It's Fran, I'm a good friend of Cosimo Angelo."

"Oh, I'm sorry Fran, I wasn't expecting a call so early. Is everything ok?"

"Well yes, and no. Do you have time to meet me for breakfast this morning so we can discuss it?"

"Yeah sure."

"Great! Would you like me to pick you up?"

"That would be great. I can be ready in an hour if that works for you."

"That will be perfect. See you then."

Over breakfast at Fran's favorite diner, the two men discussed their mutual friend and his work over the last several months. They both agreed that this had to be connected to the Ansios case. While Bartolone's own work was primarily focused on the Fedora case, and Cosimo's was on the Ansios case, there was much overlap between the two cases and the two of them shared information and collaborated often. Bartolone and Fran finished up with their breakfasts. Fran's Italian guest had an all day appointment with the Assistant United States Attorney from the Southern District of New York to discuss the Italian government's case against Fedora. The two agreed to meet up again for dinner to figure out what should, or could be done next regarding Cosimo.

By the end of the day, Fran had learned via Hans and Leone that the Roman Magistrate handling Cosimo and the bank director's case was well known for his right wing sympathies. He seemed to have had a bit of a change of heart. He decided to release the bank director on bail due to his advanced age of 67 years. Cosimo was not so fortunate. The judge was absolutely unwilling to dismiss the trumped up charges they had on him. He wouldn't even set a bail amount for his release. Everyone was frustrated, but they were not willing to give up the fight for their friend's freedom.

At first the two men were going to meet up at a restaurant for their dinner meeting. Clavering scratched those plans at the last minute. Fedora was too big of a name in New York City and the ongoing trial resulting from the Franklin National Bank failure was already the talk of the town. There were eyes and ears all over the Big Apple hoping to find an informative nugget on the case they could run with. Fran called Peg, the two of them decided instead to host Bartolone at their home that evening to discuss more of the Fedora case.

Peg was delighted and thrilled. She enjoyed entertaining. However, this was even better, as far as her investigative journalist brain was concerned. Typically her involvement with her husband's work only came second hand, from him. Either over dinner, or at night lying in bed together discussing the events of their day. Tonight she would get to sit in on their discussion. She looked forward to the change of pace.

"Fedora sure has made a mess of things over here at that bank here in town." Peg commented.

"I can't say that I'm all that surprised. You people are lucky, if you ask me."

"How's that Arturo?" Questioned Fran.

"You people only have one bank over here to comb through. Over there I have several banks to dig through."

Peg was confused. "I thought it was just the one over in Milan. No?"

"On paper it looks like one, but he merged his two failing banks into one big one not too long before it failed, so I have to go through pre and post merger records."

"What a mess. I don't envy you sir." She continued.

"It is pretty bad. Then there's his Swiss banks, and his co-mingling with Ansios and his bank, and the Vatican Bank...but it's the only way to get a full grasp of his situation." Fran just shook his head, as Arturo continued. "But I think things will be wrapping up soon."

"Oh, why's that?" Questioned Fran.

"After my many months of work, I finally have everything sorted out. I can finally put a dollar figure on his bank's failure over there."

"And that is?"

"257 billion lire."

"What does that equate to in American dollars?" Questioned Peg.

"Somewhere in the neighborhood of $300 million." Both Fran and Peg blinked and sat silently, open-mouthed in shock. Bartolone then suddenly went quiet, and looked down at his plate, and fiddled with his cutlery and peas nervously.

"Is there something wrong with the food Arturo?" Questioned Peg.

Their guest blushed slightly, as his attention returned to the present, then he answered. "I apologize for being so rude. No Peg, the food is delicious. I just want to say that I'm 100% committed to my work, but...well,...I, uh..." Bartolone closed his eyes and took a deep breath. "I've been getting phone calls back home."

"Phone calls? What kind of phone calls?" Questioned Fran.

"Awful, threatening ones."

"Does Cosimo know about this?"

"No, I've never told him."

Fran tried to reason with his guest. "But he's your best friend?"

"I know, I know, but I didn't want to worry him."

Fran tried to lighten up the conversation. "I hate to break this to you my friend, but he worries about you already. I could hear it in his voice when he called to tell me you were coming to New York."

"He did?" Bartolone was surprised to learn this.

"Yes, he did. He loves you like a brother, my man." Fran gave Arturo a minute to gather his thoughts. "Can you tell me more about these phone calls?"

Their guest had to admit to himself, being in New York, he felt the safest he'd been in months. He took a deep breath. "They started the first week of January. The next week I got four of them."

"What did the caller say?" Inquired Fran.

"I recorded some of them. One of them, the caller said, *'devi morire come un cano'* It still haunts me." While the man's focus drifted back into the peas on his plate.

Fran looked at Peg who shrugged her shoulders before she responded. "I'm sorry Arturo, our Italian isn't the best.

"Oh, yes, I'm sorry...of course. It means 'you should die like a dog.'"

"Was there anything else said during any of those calls?"

"Mmmm, mostly threats and insults, a few times there were bribes offered."

"I'd love to hear them sometime if at all possible. Do you remember if there was anything familiar about the voice?"

"It was definitely an American accent."

"Oh?"

"Yeah, I've heard similar styles of talking during my trip here."

The conversation continued well into the evening. It was an extremely fruitful evening. He detailed his work regarding Fedora that had consumed his waking hours of the last several months in Milan. Fran and Peg enjoyed getting to know the man so near and dear to Cosimo and his family. Before Bartolone left to return to Italy, he promised to bring Cosimo up to speed once his jail situation was resolved. In the meantime he'd make copies of the recordings to send over to Fran.

Bartolone's work with New York prosecutors was promising and productive for them too. It was exactly what they needed to put the finishing touches on their case against Giovanni Fedora. Ten days after his visit, Fedora was finally indicted. He was arrested and charged with ninety-nine counts of fraud, perjury, and misappropriation of funds in connection with the failure of Lincoln National Bank. He posted the $3 million bail immediately, then promised to report to the United States Marshal Office daily and was released. He then retained former law professor and US district court judge Andreas Stein to defend him in the upcoming trial. This was a small victory as far as Fedora was concerned.

It took two weeks to get the judge to set bail for Cosimo's release from jail. It was clear that if the judge had had his way, Cosimo would have still been in jail. Cosimo was happy to be out of jail, but he was immediately forbidden from his position with the Head of Vigilance and Bank of Italy director and their work investigating Ansios and his bank. Cosimo knew that there was more to what was going on, but he just couldn't put his finger on it. He would defy the judge's order and continue his work in stealth, just like his American counterpart had been doing for years over in New York.

Following his arraignment Fedora got a call from his arch nemesis, Claudio Dominez, in Milan. Fedora held tightly to the grudge that he had held against the man for the last six years following his failed corporate takeover that had the fingerprints of the Milan man all over it. Being unable to leave New York, Fedora invited him to his Regency Hotel suite. While he loathed his guest immensely, he had to play nice at least for a while. He did not want to give the Italian Government any new forms of ammunition for them to use against him in their case.

The repairs to his home following the recent fire were coming along satisfactorily. He was determined to return a sense of security and safety to his family and their home, once the construction was complete. Despite his past meeting with Fedora's lawyers and son-in-law, the threatening calls continued. Fedora apologized. He was sincere in his explanation that none of it was his doing. His guest, knowing of the well established reputation of Fedora, and his connections to certain mob affiliated families left him unconvinced.

Fedora again apologized and confirmed that he'd look into who might be threatening him and his family. In return he asked his guest to withdraw all the arrest warrants issued by the Italian government, and a 257 billion lire bail out for his Milan bank in exchange. Once again, like his previous conversations with Fedora's representatives, the man explained to Fedora that what he was asking of him was outside his control, and outside his circle of influence in the Italian government. Fedora didn't want to believe him, but he knew that his guest had his own long standing reputation for honesty and truthfulness. The conversation between Fedora and Domingez then shifted.

"That Goddamn liquidator working over there for the Bank of Italy, he is becoming a very big problem." Fedora complained.

The man was curious. "Who do they have working on it?" Questioned Domingez.

"That son of a bitch, Arturo Bartolone."

Domingez understood immediately. "He is very thorough in his work."

"He is doing great damage to me. I need to do something. I need him to disappear without a trace, and soon."

Domingez grew extremely uncomfortable with the tone and topic of the discussion. He knew Bartolone personally, and had much respect for the man. He had a difficult decision to make when he got home. Domingez was very aware of what happened to snitches and squealers.

Men working closely with Fedora had also placed a $100,000 contracted hit job for the Assistant US Attorney from the Southern District of New York. There was only one problem: they weren't in Italy. In Italy, the Italian solution was extremely successful as was recently demonstrated by Fedora's friend, Marco Ansio, and his problem judge, Ignazio Padovesi. In America, such a situation would have the opposite effect, and result in an acceleration of the prosecution's case against Fedora. The contract on the attorney's life was quickly retracted on Fedora's orders.

The first week of June, Arturo Bartolone began giving his sworn deposition to the judge presiding over Fedora's case in Palermo. There was so much to be covered, the deposition went on for weeks. A month into it, Fedora received some good news; the United States Federal Court Judge decided that he would not grant Italy's extradition request so he could face bank fraud charges levied against him by the Italian government. He was already facing similar charges in the American courts. As far as the American judge was concerned, the Italians could have him when the United States justice system was done with him.

As Giovanni Fedora's team of lawyers got to work on their client's defense, they were faced with a very rude awakening. In the four years since the Lincoln National Bank's collapse, the prosecutors in the US had been collaborating with investigators in Italy. Their work produced over 100,000 pages of meticulous notes and documents that would support his conviction. Italian investigator and auditor Arturo Bartolone presented to members of the US prosecution team and two special marshals who stood in as representatives for two of the Italian magistrates. At the conclusion of the first day of Bartolone's deposition, Fedora's lawyers were visibly worried.

Following his deposition, Bartolone met with the deputy superintendent of the Palermo Police Department, Carlo Manfredi.

The man was a long time police inspector, with special training by the American Federal Bureau of Investigation. His specialty was investigating crimes tied to the Mafia. Of particular interest to Bartolone was the investigator's information on the murder of a notorious Mafia enforcer who had done work for syndicate families like the Lanscanos in New York and their cousins in Palermo. On the murder victim's body at the time of his demise were checks and documents that provided the Italian goverment proof that Fedora was laundering heroin money on behalf of the Lanscanos and their relatives through the Vatican Bank and Fedora's now shuttered Swiss bank in Zürich.

Bartolone returned to his office later that afternoon. His next meeting was to be done over the phone with the head of Security Services in Rome, Lieutenant Colonel Rico Severino. The two men exchanged notes and connections regarding their individual investigations. Bartolone showcased Fedora's criminal banking practices, while Severino revealed his findings, connecting Fedora to P2 and its mastermind leader Gherado Fratello.

Bartolone had invested many months into his investigation, and several weeks into his deposition as the middle of July approached. On his final day of his deposition, Bartolone dropped a bombshell for prosecutors in the case against Fedora. His detailed testimony revealed the scam that resulted in the sale of the Catholic Bank of Venice back in 1972. When the Vatican Bank, with Bishop Jonas Krivis at its helm, sold the bank to Milanese banker Marco Ansios, Giovanni Fedora paid them both a "brokerage fee" of $6.5 million. No one knew it at the time, but that one event and the resulting backlash from the bank's patrons and religious leaders of the region, put the then patriarch of Venice, Cardinal Chiaros Riluciani, on his trajectory to become pope six years later.

The following day, Bartolone completed his deposition. He was relieved, knowing that all his hard work over the past many months was now officially entered into public record. All he had to do now was to come back the next day to answer any remaining questions from US and Italian prosecutors and Fedora's lawyers. Once all that was done, he would apply his signature to the record of his testimony.

Bartolone endured many long days since starting work on the Fedora investigation. Despite the job winding down, this day was no different. He phoned his wife around 11:30 PM to let her know he was on his way home. He felt bad when she told him that she still had dinner waiting for him when he got home. She heard his car pull into the driveway and went to open the upstairs bedroom window. She watched him get out of his car. The top button of his shirt was undone and his tie was loosely draped around the back of his neck. As he opened the back door of the car to retrieve his briefcase, she called to him, smiled and waved. He smiled instantly when he saw her, and blew her a kiss.

Out of the shadows, came a deep New York accented voice. *"Signore Arturo Bartolone?"*

The man automatically turned in the direction of the voice, *"Si."*

The discharge of four rounds fired from a Walther P-38 9 mm semi automatic pistol shattered the silence of the night followed by the gut-wrenching screams coming from Bartolone's wife through the upstairs window. The four bullets entered his chest at point blank range killing him instantly. After six death threats over the course of the last seven months, Arturo Bartolone lay dead in a pool of his own blood on his front lawn.

A manhunt for the killer immediately ensued. By 6:00 AM the next morning, "Carmine, The Exterminator," a well known associate of the Lanscano Crime Family in New York City, had made his way to Geneva, Switzerland. He was a cockroach exterminator by trade, and a human exterminator by calling. He had $100,000 more in his account than he had had the day before. The funds had been transferred from an account in Marco Ansios' bank belonging to Giovanni Fedora. Carmine, unbeknown to his target, had been stalking Bartolone for over a month before completing his contracted hit job. Less than twenty-four hours after the murder of Bartolone, his murderer was found with a bullet in his head and three in his chest.

Cosimo was overcome with emotion as he learned the news from Bartolone's grief stricken wife. Cosimo later called his American counterpart with the horrific news. The grief of Bartolone's family, friends and colleagues shifted to anger and disgust as newspapers and media outlets throughout Italy decided to give more attention to the murder of the number two man in command of the Lanscano Crime Family in New York than they did the murder of Arturo Bartolone here in his home land.

Lieutenant Colonel Rico Severino was being driven by his chauffeur in a blue BMW down the *Lungotevere Arnaldo de Brescia* in Rome on the morning of July 13, 1979. While enroute, a black Fiat 128 pulled up next to the Colonel's car and fired four rounds from a sawed off shotgun killing both men instantly. A far left anti-capitalism, anti-fascist group claimed responsibility for the killing. The killing of the Colonel came less than forty-eight hours after the brutal killing of Arturo Bartolone, and just four days after the two men met by phone to discuss Fedora's ties to the pseudo-Masonic organization P2.

One week later, Carlo Manfredi, the bank inspector known for his investigations into Mafia criminal activity in Palermo, was paying for his morning coffee at a local cafe on *Via Francesco Paolo Di Biasi* in Palermo. As he stood at the cash register, a man approached and fired off six shots in rapid succession into the crowded cafe, striking him and killing him instantly. He was another man closely associated with Arturo Bartolone. As the men went about their investigation into the inspector's murder, they found it remarkable that no one in the crowded cafe saw or heard anything. No one cared to claim responsibility for this particular murder either.

During the entire month of July, Giovanni Fedora was meeting with his team of lawyers to go over strategies for his defense. His attorneys were optimistic about the upcoming trial set to start in five weeks on September 10th in New York. When the news of the Bartolone murder finally populated the New York City news outlets, Fedora instantly appeared with his lawyers with a statement. "My love and sympathies go out to the wife, family and friends of Mr. Arturo Bartolone. I sincerely hope that this heinous act of cowardice against him is not somehow linked back to me. If that should end up being the case, I can promise swift and definitive legal action against the slanderous and defaming party or parties."

No one bought into the sincerity of Fedora's public statement. He had been complaining about the Italian Government's plot against him for well over two years. He even named Mr. Bartolone as the primary government agent working against him. Fedora's public opinion sounded threatening to say the least when he suggested, "there are a lot of men who should be afraid right now...very afraid."

There was no way in hell that all of Bartolone's years of work would just disappear. Men like Cosimo Angelo and Detective Francis Clavering were now more determined than ever to carry on what their friend had worked until his dying day to accomplish. His death would not be in vain. Whoever was responsible would be found and brought to justice. Despite the fact that Bartolone's deposition remained unsigned by the deposed, it became an even more powerful weapons for the prosecution in Fedora's upcoming trial following his brutal murder.

Bartolone's deposition reached far beyond detailing the crimes of Giovanni Fedora. Men like Marco Ansios and Bishop Jonas Krivis were also implicated in the sworn statements. Krivis, certain of the protections that were afforded him due to his position at the Vatican Bank, also hid behind the walls of Vatican City and denied everything. It was a tactic he used frequently in the past, just as he had when Fedora's financial empire crashed. He denied ever meeting Mr. Fedora which was a statement beyond laughable. Unlike his own reputation for falsehoods and bullshit, Arturo Bartolone was never one to make such damning accusations without an overwhelming amount of proof to back them up. The colleagues of Bartolone were not about to let any of those implicated by his work sully the character and name of the man they held with such great respect and fondness.

The key beneficiaries of the murders occuring throughout Italy in the last eleven months included Bishop Jonas Krivis, Marco Ansios,

Giovanni Fedora and Gherado Fratello. Those who continued to work in the Milan Palace of Justice were justifiably frightened to their core. The very idea that any one of them could be knocked off next began to wear on them physically and emotionally. After what had happened to Police Investigator Carlo Manfredi and Italian Security Services Officer Lieutenant Colonel Rico Severino, many who worked with or assisted Arturo Bartolone in his work developed a sudden case of amnesia when it came to anything related to the Giovanni Fedora case.

The man who was assigned to take over Bartolone's job following his untimely demise proceeded at such a ridiculously slow pace that his efforts were, for the most part, pointless. Just like when Cosimo Angelo and the bank director from the Bank of Italy's investigation into the crimes of Marco Ansios and his Banco Generali were arrested, this was yet another delay and interference tactic deployed by P2 allies. A new group of men had been installed in the Finance Police Offices. The new men in charge quickly concluded that Marco Ansios' responses and explanations given previously to investigators were suitable and legitimate. Between Fratello's men of P2, and Fedora's Mafia connections, none of these four men concerned themselves about Lady Justice coming for any of them anytime soon.

CHAPTER 49

Fran woke at his usual time of 5 AM to get ready for his work day. He was perfectly happy to let his bride and kids sleep in. They all looked so serene and peaceful as he quietly snuck into their rooms to give them all a kiss before he left the house. The weather in New York that last week of July was hot, sticky and unrelenting. Not wishing to heat up the house by cooking his breakfast, Fran opted to stop in at his favorite diner on his way to the office.

He sidled into his usual counter seat and waited for his waitress to come by on her rounds. She arrived with his cup of coffee in hand, already poured.

"Good mornin' Sunshine! How's the day treatin' ya so far?" She greeted with a big, huge smile, while chomping on her pink chewing gum.

"Good morning, Laura! So far so good, I can't really complain."

"That's great! How's Peg and the kids doin'?"

"Well the kids are out of school for summer, so they've been spending a lot of time at their Aunt and Uncle's. They love hanging out with their cousins."

"Ahhh yes, to be a kid again. Sure sounds better than our daily grind."

"No doubt. I'd do it too if I could figure out how to do that and get the bills paid."

They both chuckled and nodded. "...And Peg?"

"She's great. I don't know where I'd be without her."

"I do...you'd be in here every day...for three hots. So you havin' your usual?"

"Of course..."

"I swear one of these days you are gonna surprise me and change it up."

"Maybe someday, but not today."

"Sounds good, I'll get that order right in for ya."

"Thanks Laura."

"You're welcome, hon."

She scurried away to wait on another patron in the diner. Fran buried his face in the morning newspaper, and drank his coffee while he waited for his food. He didn't even notice DA Paul Christopherson walk in. Christopherson walked up behind him and clapped a hand on his shoulder firmly.

"Good morning detective!"

Fran startled a little. He was surprised to see him. "Good morning sir!"

"Mind if I join you, Francis?"

"No, not at all. Why don't we grab a booth so we can talk?"

"Sounds good."

Fran gathered his paper, coffee and silverware. Then he caught the waitress' attention. "Laura, if it's alright, we're gonna grab the booth over there in the corner. Oh, and can you bring D.A. Christopherson a cup of coffee when you get a second." She smiled and nodded to the two men, acknowledging Fran's request.

The two men settled into their places. Then Fran commented. "You must be busy these days, it seems like I haven't really seen you about the precinct in quite a while."

"Busy? Me?" Christopherson chuckled a little. "Yeah if I hear the name Giovanni Fedora or Lincoln National Bank ever again in my life, I think I'm gonna hollar!"

"Sure you are." Fran winked at the man. "You can't kid me, you live for cases like this sir."

"I'm getting too old for this shit, to be honest. This is probably one of the most significant cases of my entire career."

"No doubt about it. Mine too."

"Listen, since we are away from all those nosy guys down and around work, I just wanted to tell you that the work your and Lance have done for the Fedora case is absolutely incredible."

"Thank you sir." Fran lowered his head, a little embarrassed by the compliment.

"I mean it. The information you've managed to gather from Italy has helped our case enormously!"

"So I gotta ask you how's your 'side work' going? It seems like I haven't had an update in forever, especially since all of this Fedora stuff started piling up on my desk."

Laura brought over the men's plates of food, and frequently refilled their coffee cups. Fran detailed everything that had happened over in Italy and Vatican City since the election of Pope Phillip Michael I. Christopherson was shocked by what Fran was telling him.

"I must say, I'm extremely impressed, Francis."

"Why's that?"

"I can't believe that you've managed to keep all of that out of the mouths of all of those gossiping hens that like to stick their beaks in everybody's shit, if you know what I mean."

"I've been working for you for years, sir. It shouldn't come as a surprise by now."

"They always find out though, and once they do, the entire precinct knows, then it just spreads like a wildfire from there."

"Yeah, I know what you mean. But working with these fed heads, they got big heads and even bigger mouths."

"No doubt about it..."

"After all of the carnage over in Italy the last few weeks, it's now more important than ever to keep a low profile and a tight lid on operations over there, until it's time to round up all of these pieces of shit."

Christopherson's memory suddenly cycled back to six years earlier. "I can't believe that all of this is the result of you coming to my office that one morning with Bentley asking me to send you over to Munich."

Fran issued an uncomfortable, forced smile. "Yeah it's hard to believe how that one situation led us to where we are today." Fran's attention drifted off into the memory of that day. The lies that he and Bentley used to gain approval for that initial trip to Munich still gnawed at his conscience. There was nothing he hated more than a liar. He wanted to come clean, after all of these years, but this was neither the time nor place. The last thing he wanted was to piss off his D.A. in the middle of his favorite diner. He also didn't want to do anything to lose the trust and respect of a man whom he respected and admired for his honesty and work ethic. Fran's gaze drifted off into the broken runny yolks on his plate, as he mindlessly dipped his toast into them.

Laura passed by their table, noticing Fran fussing with his food, but not eating it like he usually did. "Something wrong with the food this morning, Sugar?"

Fran snapped back to the present. "What? Oh, uh, no. Everything's delicious as always Laura. Thank you."

"That's good to hear." She winked at him, then issued a nod at him, still chomping her gum. "Shall I top off your coffee, gentlemen?"

"That'd be great miss." Responded Christopherson. He too noticed the distance in his detective's attention as she walked away. "Are you sure everything's ok Francis?"

"Yeah, everything's fine..." The detective lied.

The D.A. didn't believe him, but decided that now was not the time to press the matter. He knew that his most talented detective would come to him in his own time if he needed to. "Listen, Francis.

I wanted to let you know, before anyone else, that once we wrap up this Fedora case, I'm going to hang it all up and retire."

The words hit Detective Clavering like a brick wall. He knew this day would come sooner or later, but it never entered his mind that that time had finally come. "Wow, are you sure?"

"Yeah, I'm sure. This is now a younger man's game. My 77 year old ass probably should have retired many years ago."

Fran raised an eyebrow. "77? Well you've put together an amazing body of work in your many years of service as the D.A."

"Well working with professionals such as yourself has helped keep me feeling younger than my years. That said, now I'm starting to feel my age. I feel the need to spend more time with my wife, kids and all those grandkids."

"Yes, those things are more important than anything we do at the office or in the field, if you ask me."

"Listen, Francis, I haven't submitted my retirement papers yet, so if you could do me a favor and keep this under your hat until I make the decision public."

"Of course sir. Your secret is safe with me." Fran had mixed feelings as Christopherson confided in him, a man who had lied to his face. "I must say,...it's going to be really different around here after you retire."

Christopherson played the compliment off with a rare display of modesty. "Bah...ain't no one around there gonna miss my grumpy old ass."

"How long are you gonna keep bullshitting yourself sir?"

The D.A. finally accepted the compliment. "Well thank you Francis. It's been my honor to work with you all of these years."

The two men finished up their food and conversation, and then headed to their respective offices. Fran suddenly remembered all of the department shuffling that happened after the Benedetto case was over. With Christopherson leaving, those that remained would be off to more demanding work in other departments or precincts. Fran discussed the retirement of Christopherson with Peg that evening. He too was unsure of what awaited him on the other side of the Fedora case.

Then the craziest idea popped into his head. "How about we move to Italy after this Fedora thing wraps up."

"Italy? Are you crazy?!" Peg shot back at him.

"Not at all. Why not?"

"I can't believe you're serious, Fran."

"I know it sounds nuts, but I want you to seriously consider it. Can you at least do that for me?"

"Fine...I guess. But I still think you're insane, Francis Clavering."

Giovanni Fedora had been strategizing with his lawyers in both the United States and Italy. His American legal team felt confident that they could work his defense for the best outcome possible. Fedora was not so confident about his legal situation in Italy. Even with men like Bartolone, Severino, and Manfredi removed permanently from the situation, he still remained worried about what those still determined to destroy him would do next.

It was time to persuade friends and colleagues that it was time to cash in on some long overdue favors. The Italian had a certain knack of convincing people that it would be in their best interest to be supportive of Fedora during his upcoming trial in New York. Once again, he reached into his bag of tricks for something very familiar: blackmail. He threatened those who declined or were still on the fence that he would reveal his highly coveted list of Italy's most rich and powerful people fully implicated in the illegal exportation of currency. The list was a Holy Grail of sorts, as far as the Italian Finance authorities were concerned. Many of their agents, including the late Arturo Bartolone, had uncovered numerous references to the infamous list as they went about their investigative work. The list was purported to contain a virtual who's who when it came to Italy's most powerful men. It wasn't just Fedora who used the legendary list as a tool in his bidding, others like Marco Ansios and Gherado Fratello also waved their copy of the list around to get what they wanted.

Fedora felt that the list, coupled with his blackmail tactics, was exactly what was needed to rebuild his reputation in Italian society circles. It would be the job of some very respectable blackmail victims to assist his legal defense team in convincing the jury and judge that he really was a good man and brilliant banker and staunch defender of capitalism who had become the victim of communists who created these wicked conspiracies that had been levied against him. The cracks in the banker's sanity were beginning to show.

A few weeks following the murder of Arturo Bartolone, Fedora received an urgent call from Marco Ansios. He was in New York and needed to meet with Fedora right away. Ansios was escorted into the office chamber of Fedora's high-rise hotel suite by Mrs. Fedora. He walked with a tense gait, clutching his trademark briefcase like a child holding a security blanket. The man looked like shit. Dark circles had formed under his eyes. It was clear that the man hadn't slept for days. His nerves were completely shot as displayed by his violently shaking hands, as he lit one cigarette after another.

"What the hell happened to you?" Questioned a very concerned Fedora.

"Thank you for seeing me on such short notice. I apologize for barging in here so rudely, unannounced." Ansios took a seat across from his host, and placed his closed briefcase on his lap. He could not stop his hands from shaking.

"It's quite alright Marco."

"Y-y-you were right Giovanni,..."

"Right? About what?"

"You were right about Gherado Fratello. What he has going on down in South America is nothing short of strange, and it has me scared to death."

"Scared? I thought he was helping you."

"He was, but now I don't have the slightest clue what he's doing. I'm not even sure if he knows what he's doing at this point. I'm scared, Gio, and I don't know what to do."

"I know he can be a very dangerous man to those who are no longer interested in being pawns in his global game of chess. Kristof

Ricatto is certainly a perfect and recent example of that, but I'm going to need more information if I am to help you in any way, my friend."

The shaking in Ansios' hands became even more accentuated. "I've been getting strange and threatening calls, and I'm pretty sure that he's having me followed. I had to get a fake passport just to get here this morning."

"Oh, that does sound serious." Fedora leaned forward in his chair. As he listened to his friend explain his concerns. Fedora finally responded. "Listen to me carefully Marco...Here is what you need to do. I want you to start selling off all of those newspapers that he had you buy up."

"O-o-ok..."

"If you can, sell them to independent parties. I'm sure you know who he has under his control down there better than I do. Try and sell them to those out of his control if you can. Do you think you can do that."

"Y-y-yes, I will do that." Ansios took in a deep breath, feeling only a little better after talking to his dear friend. "That man,...his, his..." It was all the man could do to keep from completely bursting into tears. "It's all just been too much."

Fedora did his best to comfort his friend. "We will get you through this my friend. I know things are not great at the moment, but hang in there. I will do what I can to help you. Just keep in mind that I can't leave New York until this damn trial is over."

"Trial? I'm sorry, Fratello's has had me spinning for weeks down in South America. I had no clue your case was heading for trial. When does it start?"

Fedora glanced at the calendar hanging on the wall. "Mmm, in about five weeks."

"Oh wow, that's going to be here before we know it. Is there anything that I can do to help."

"I want you to concentrate on getting those newspapers sold and dealing with your own shit for now. Don't worry about me. My lawyers say we are in really great shame."

"I'm glad to hear that Gio. Best of luck. I promise to keep you posted on my progress, and if anything changes."

"Please do, my friend...please do." The two men concluded their visit, and Marco Ansios departed the office suite.

Later that afternoon, Giovanni Fedora was seen by many people walking down 5th Avenue in New York City near the Hotel Pierre. He was a common sight in the neighborhood, his visits to his lawyer's office becoming more frequent as his trial date loomed nearer and nearer. He was in high spirits. Sporting a smile, he seemed to not have a care in the world.

Several hours later, in the office of Detective Francis Clavering across town, his phone began to ring.

"Detective Clavering."

"Clavering, listen to me carefully."

Fran struggled to recognize the voice on the other end of the line for a moment. "D.A. Christopherson?"

"Yeah, Francis, it's me. I think we have a problem." The man he had come to greatly admire over the years sounded very angry and even more concerned.

"What's that sir?"

"I just got a call from Fedora's lead defense lawyer,..."

"Yeah, and...?"

"Mr Fedora was supposed to meet with him in his office several hours ago, but he never showed up. He's in complete panic mode right now, and he fears the worst."

CHAPTER 50

Detective Clavering was curious as he listened to the concern in the D.A.'s voice as he explained the situation based on the information he'd just received from Fedora's lawyer. "How can a man as well known as Fedora, just up and disappear like that."

"I agree. Someone has to know something. Listen, I know we usually wait at least 48 hours on a missing persons case, but I want that son of a bitch found, and fast! His lawyer is on his way over here to meet with us as we speak. Can you get Lance and meet with us? Oh, and he doesn't need to know exactly how pissed off I am right regarding this."

"Of course sir, I will get Lance and we will be right there."

"Good. See you in a bit!"

When Detectives Clavering and Erickson arrived at the conference room, the room was already populated with their respective bosses, Inspector James Bentley and Federal Prosecutor Nathan Bayer. Seated next to them were D.A. Christopherson, Assistant D.A. Walter Thomas. Christopherson quickly took control of the meeting. He began by introducing their guest, Mr. Andres Stein, Giovanni

Fedora's lawyer. The man was upset, nervous and talking very fast as he explained the situation with Fedora.

"Has he ever been known to not show up for an appointment before?" Questioned Fran.

"No, never. Not without calling. He is always very respectful of people's time. Punctuality is something extremely important to him. Nothing angers him more than tardy people. He considers people who run late to be rude and disrespectful."

"Hmmm, I see. Have you spoken with anyone from his family yet?"

"No, not yet. I didn't want to alarm Mrs. Fedora at this point, but I am very worried."

The seven men sat around and discussed Fedora's activities and visitors over the last few weeks. Nothing out of the ordinary stood out to anyone. Unbeknownst to Mr. Stein, there were already two men in the room who more than likely knew Fedora better than he did. The two detectives seated in the room had been watching and listening to the man for the last several years. From their own observations, they had to agree with the lawyer this was highly unusual behavior for their man.

"Where could he have gone? He really shouldn't be that hard to find. It's not like his face hasn't been plastered all over this town in news print on every corner newsstand for years." Commented Lance.

Christopherson agreed with Lance's point. "We can start with having our men check local hospitals, just to rule those out. Then we can..."

A knock on the conference room door interrupted the D.A. in the middle of his sentence. The precinct officer poked his head into the crowded room. "Sorry to interrupt gentlemen, but Fran, you have a call on line three."

"Can you please take a message, I'm in a very important meeting."

"I tried that Detective. It's your wife. She said it's very urgent that she speaks with you at once. She was very insistent."

A sudden look of concern came over the detective's face, as he quickly scanned the other faces of the men seated in the room. Has something happened to Peg? One of the kids? His attention returned to the present. "I apologize, gentlemen. I will be right back."

The khaki clad man held the door for Clavering as he exited into the hallway. Upon exiting, before heading to his office to take the call, Fran turned to the officer. "Did she say what this was about?"

"No, she just said it was urgent, and it could not wait another minute."

"Ok, I will take the call in my office. Thank you."

Fran entered his office and closed the door behind him. He grabbed the handset and pushed the blinking button on the phone for line three. "Peg? What's wrong?"

"Fran, thank God! I'm so sorry to call you away from your meeting, but this just couldn't wait."

"I'm here love..."

"I just got a call from Robert, I guess he tried to call your office phone several times, but you were already in your meeting. He didn't want to leave a message, so he called me."

"Robert? Robert who?"

"Robert Hinson, remember, my friend...the investigative reporter from the *New York Times*?"

"Oh yeah, sorry, my memory didn't click without some context. What about him?"

"He just got a call from a woman claiming that they have kidnapped Giovanni Fedora and are holding him."

"Oh my God." The line went silent for at least thirty seconds.

"Hello? Fran? Are you still there?" Peg could be heard on the other end of the line tapping the mouthpiece of the phone.

"Yeah, I'm here. Sorry, I was just in a meeting with Fedora's lawyer. Listen, can you call Robert back and tell him to get his ass down here to the station ASAP?"

"Yeah, I can do that."

"Thanks love. I will explain everything later, I promise."

"Don't worry about me. Get back to your meeting. I will get a hold of Robert for you."

Fran hung up the phone and ran back to the conference room. He gave everyone a start as he burst into the room.

"Is everything ok?" Questioned Bentley.

Fran took a deep breath. "No, it seems that Mr. Fedora has been kidnapped."

Everyone in the room gasped. Then Bayer chimed in with a suspicious tone and attitude. "Your wife told you that? How the hell would she know something like that Fran?"

"She didn't..." The detective bit his lip as he altered the truth a little. "She just got an urgent call from a newspaper reporter friend of hers. He's the one who told me."

"Well we need to get him in here right away, Fran." Barked Christopherson.

"He's already on his way sir."

"Did he say anything else?" Questioned Bayer.

"No, he said he'd fill us in when he gets here."

Robert Hinson was finally escorted into the conference room after twenty minutes which seemed like an eternity. He entered the room out of breath, briefcase in hand. The luggage still had a few papers sticking out the sides of the case where it opened. The man continued with the weight and seriousness of the situation evident in his voice.

"I got a call about an hour ago from a woman claiming to be with a group called the Proletarian Citizens for a Greater Justice. They have kidnapped Mr. Fedora, and are holding him hostage."

Federal Prosecutor Nathan Bayer seized the moment and began rapidly firing off questions. "Who are they? Where are they from? What do they want? How do we know if he's even still alive?"

"Nathan, will you just cool your jets for a minute!" Interrupted the D.A. "Does anyone else know of this call besides you at this point Mr. Hinson?"

"No sir."

"...and this is the only call you've received from anyone on this matter so far."

"Yes sir."

"Good." Christopherson responded before turning to the rest of the men in the room.

"Lance, I want you to start digging...see what info you can find on that organization."

"Yes sir!" Responded the FBI agent.

"Francis, I want you to work on getting surveillance equipment set up on the phones of Mr. Hinson, and also the phones of Mr. Stein and the home phone of Mr. Fedora. In the meantime, Thomas and Bentley you two work on getting the judge's approval for those devices.

Each man in the room responded with a respectful "Yes sir" as the D.A. delegated assignments.

"What would you like me to do?" Responded Bayer, noticing that he'd been left without an assignment.

"If you can get us a little more help on this from the Federal level, that'd be great Nathan."

"Mr. Hinson, we're going to need to get this out to the public, so as soon as we can get a press release together on what we know so far, you will be the first to know. I want this all over the news. A man like Mr. Fedora," Christopherson paused. He wanted to choose his words carefully, "His face is recognizable anywhere. Someone had to see or hear something, somewhere."

"Bentley, please take the lead on this, and keep me in the loop."

"No problem, sir." Affirmed the Inspector.

"We will meet here again in the morning at 8 AM to update everyone and plan what comes next. If anything comes in sooner, let Inspector Bentley know and he will let me know. Is everyone clear on what they need to do?"

"Clear sir!" Echoed throughout the room.

"All right, let's get out there and find Mr. Fedora."

Chairs shifting away from the table made a terrible racket as some men stashed note pads, pens and effects into briefcases before closing and latching them. Christopherson got into an off-topic conversation with Bentley while the room cleared out. Fran soon returned to his office and got to work on phone surveillance devices and details. Everyone in the conference room with the exception of Mr. Stein and Mr. Hinson, already knew that Fedora's office had been tapped since the early days of the Fedora investigation. Getting one on the home phone wouldn't be a problem. As he was making a list, there was a knock on Fran's door frame. Fran looked up to see D.A. Christopherson standing in his doorway.

"Sir?"

"Francis, may I come in?"

"Of course sir, please do." Fran got up and motioned to a chair for him to sit, then he closed the door behind his visitor. "What can I do for you sir?"

"Thanks. I want you to get hold of your colleagues in Italy and the Church and see if they know anything over there in Italy."

"Will do, sir."

"Also see if you can get anything from your mob informants."

"Absolutely, sir."

"I want no stone left unturned. Do you understand?"

"100% sir."

"I want that damn bastard, son of a bitch found, and found alive! His trial is scheduled to start in five weeks, it can't happen without him, and I'm pretty certain that he's aware of that fact."

Fran caught something curious in the D.A.'s tone. "What do you mean by that sir."

"Listen, I wasn't going to say anything in front of the rest of them, and especially Mr. Stein, but I can't help but think this is some sort of stunt used by that slippery snake to escape facing justice in our courts."

"Yeah, that thought crossed my mind too. I will reach out to my guys in Italy, Munich, and the Mob. Trust me sir, we will find him. That I can promise you."

"Thanks, keep in touch. Call me at home if you have to."

"Will do, sir."

In almost no time at all, Fedora's face was plastered all over the front pages of Newspapers all over New York and Italy. The *New York Times'* front page displayed a large photo of the Italian with the headline "Fedora Missing!" In big bold lettering. The *New York Post* was a little more skeptical about the whole situation when they published his picture and their headline, "Has Fedora been kidnapped, or is this a scam?" Every article on the topic had some sort of quote from Fedora's lawyer, Mr. Andres Stein.

A week later, investigative reporter Robert Hinson's office phone rang. The woman's voice had a deep quality to it, like she was a seasoned cigarette smoker. Her thick Italian accent took a minute to comprehend. She claimed to be with a group called the Proletarian Citizens for a Greater Justice. She explained that "Mr. Giovanni Fedora was going to be executed by firing squad at dawn!" Then the line went dead. The dial tone on the line sounded louder in his ear than it ever had before.

Bayer went to work with Bentley and Thomas immediately. It was time to issue an FBI bulletin broadcast to every radio and television station for public assistance in finding the missing Mr. Fedora. Anyone with information was to contact the New York City Police Department or the Manhattan FBI office. Any informants would remain anonymous and all information would be held with the strictest of confidence.

Fran received a call from Cosimo. He reported that Fedora's lawyer in Rome got a call very similar to the one that Mr. Hinson received. Fran reported the information to D.A. Christopherson. They both thought it curious that Mr. Stein never mentioned the call that was received by his Italian counterpart. Fran knew from his past work with Cosimo and Bartolone that the two lawyers communicated often to strategize about their client's legal defense efforts. Why wouldn't they be in constant communication when the life of their shared client was at stake?

The weeks passed by slowly with very little telephone communication. Mr. Fedora's captors shifted their primary mode of communication to letters via the post office. Finally the day of September 10th arrived, it was the day the trial of Mr. Fedora was supposed to have begun. Mr Fedora had now been missing for over a month. By this time, his family, and lawyers had received over twenty large over-stuffed manila envelopes containing letters and photos of their hostage. The photos depicted Fedora with dirty, disheveled hair and salt and peppery shaded stubble on his face. Sometimes he'd be shown with a black eye in different stages of healing as indicated by the different shades of the discoloration from the bruising. He had dark circles under his other eye, and his face became more and more gaunt as the weeks progressed. Sometimes the pictures would show him with a busted lip, or a bloody nose or mouth. Fran noted that in those pictures, the blood was always dark and dry. Not fresh. The detective looked at the images closely trying to determine if the injuries were authentic, or the work of a make up artist. Every single postal communication was postmarked from either Brooklyn, New York or Newark, New Jersey. The letters in the envelopes told of horrific interrogations by his captors. Detective Clavering also noted that Fedora's wife and children didn't seem overly upset or concerned regarding the contents of the letters, nor the physical state of their beloved Giovanni Fedora.

A new package was received by Fedora's daughter and son-in-law who still resided in Italy. This time the captors decided to include a demand with the images of a beaten up Fedora. "If you value the life of your father, you will provide all facts and information related to his case and trial in your possession. A similar letter was sent to Fedora's Italian lawyer in Rome.

Eleven days later, Fedora's Italian lawyer received an overstuffed envelope with a Brooklyn, NY post mark. One of the pictures contained in the package depicted a very emaciated Giovanni Fedora holding a placard in front of his chest with the words *Il giusto processo lo faremo noi.* The true trial would be handled by his captors. They were requesting the names of corrupt politicians and businessmen who had engaged in crooked schemes with Fedora in the past. If these rag-tag vigilantes ever got their hands on such a list, it could prove to be most embarrassing to major Italian politicians, The Vatican, and large financial institutions.

Ten weeks had now passed since the kidnapping of Mr. Giovanni Fedora. The impatience of D.A. Christopherson was now wearing on him. He was now starting to think maybe he should have just retired already. Everyone who came in contact with the man couldn't help but feel the frustration of the old New York D.A. Nothing like this had ever happened in all of his years of service to the City.

Fran learned through his primary informant with the syndicate that he was pretty sure that Fedora wasn't even in the United States at this point. The idea gathered more traction when Cardinal Leone spoke to Cosimo about the situation. There were some fairly credible rumors floating about that Fedora had reached out to Bishop Jonas Krivis hoping that he could seek asylum within the walls of Vatican City. Despite the temper tantrum of Fedora, his request was denied.

Detective Clavering came bursting through the office door of Christopherson, completely out of breath.

"Francis Clavering?!" The older man shouted, grasping his chest. "What the hell?"

"Sorry sir, I should have called first...sorry..."

"Well now that you have my undivided attention, what is it?"

"Sir, I just got a call from my man in Italy. We're both pretty sure Fedora is currently in Italy."

"How the hell did he get over there undetected?"

"That part we have yet to figure out, sir. Anyway they just intercepted a courier on his way to the office of Fedora's Italian lawyer. This shit has the hallmarks of the mob all over it, sir!"

Christopherson looked slightly relieved and optimistic with the update. "Go on..."

"The courier they caught was the son-in-law of the most powerful Mafia Don in Sicily. They also just so happen to be the cousins of the Lanscanos Crime family."

"They Lanscanos? You mean the ones over in Jersey?"

"You got it!"

"The same Lanscanos that Fedora has been laundering dirty heroin money for since Christ was a corporal?"

"Yup!"

"And what did this man have on him at the time of his capture?"

"A message requesting a passport and lots and lots of cash!"

"Hmmmm, that's very interesting...who else knows of this information Francis?"

"Just you and me at this point, sir."

"Good, keep it that way. Do we know if Mr. Stein has been in contact with the Italian lawyer regarding any of this?"

"Not that I've seen or heard. Definitely not by phone anyway."

"It will be interesting to see if he mentions anything at our next strategy meeting."

"If he does know, it'd be rather stupid of him to say so...if you ask me."

"Stranger things have happened. Especially involving that piece of shit Fedora."

Fran raised an eyebrow, and nodded. "You will get no argument from me about that."

"Keep in touch with your guy in Italy. Come to me immediately when you learn anything new on this Francis."

"Will do, sir."

A few days later, the compound owned by the elder Mafia don near Palermo was raided by Italian authorities. Mr. Fedora was nowhere to be found. However, the entire operation proved to be too much for the old don in charge. The stress caused by the raid caused him to suffer a massive heart attack and he passed away en route to the hospital. The impact of the man's death reverberated throughout the syndicate regions and families, all the way to New York.

One week following the raid on the Palermo compound, an anonymous tip was called in to the Police Precinct from an anonymous citizen. Mr. Giovanni Fedora had been spotted on the corner of 10th Ave and 42nd St in New York City. "What the hell?" Thought Fran to himself. At first he didn't take the phoned in tip too seriously. After his various conversations with Cosimo over the last couple of weeks, Fran was damn sure that Fedora was still in Italy. The two detectives rushed to the scene, and were soon joined by others from the team investigating the Fedora kidnapping case. Fran could not believe what he was witnessing. He was thoroughly convinced that Fedora was still in Italy somewhere. Clearly this was not the case, as the situation unfolded. Before them, they found a very pale, emaciated man with a gunshot wound to his left thigh.

CHAPTER 51

Emergency personnel worked quickly to medically stabilize the Italian as best they could given his condition and the circumstances. They then loaded the fifty-nine year old man into an awaiting ambulance and quickly transported him to a local hospital. The high velocity penetrating wound to his leg was a significant injury. It quickly became clear to the physicians treating Mr. Fedora that this was not a recent injury. The injury was clean and expertly dressed. However, despite the best efforts of whoever was responsible for his care, the bullet remained lodged in the muscle of the man's leg and signs of serious infection were becoming more and more evident.

Fedora was in bad shape. By the time they got him to the trauma center, Fedora's breathing had become rapid and labored, as he floated in and out of consciousness. The infection coursing through his blood from the bullet and wound caused his fever to spike. He soon became delirious and began hallucinating. The doctors needed to get IV antibiotics started on him right away, and then get him prepped for surgery before the sepsis coursing through his body caused irreparable harm to his vital organs and their functions. He drifted in and out, completely unaware of anything that was happening around him. He felt like he was physically falling as his mind drifted.

Marco Ansios finally left his office. Fedora glanced at his wristwatch as he turned the knob to wind it. Thanks to the impromptu visit, he was now running behind schedule. He walked down 5th Ave, then hailed a cab. Soon, with the help of Donny Lanscano and a few others, he was fitted with a white wig, phony mustache and beard and large horn rimmed glasses. In the back of his mind he was sure that despite all this effort, someone would surely recognize him. Once the transformation was complete, he couldn't stop gazing into the mirror. He couldn't help but be impressed. Nothing in the face staring back at him looked familiar other than the color of his eyes. He was even more impressed that his new look perfectly matched the image on the fake passport in his hands. That evening, he and Donny boarded a red eye TWA flight from JFK to Vienna. Once they touched down, the two men were transported to Sicily. Their plan had gone off without a hitch. Certainly much better than anything they had anticipated. This particular trip had been planned for months.

Fedora found the whole situation quite amusing. While the world fretted about who was holding him captive and where, and whether he was safe or even alive, he was spending his days the most worry free he had been in many months. He casually sipped on his favorite wine and enjoyed the food, scenery and hospitality of the Santoro Family in their Sicilian Villa. The Santoro family was notorious in the southern region of Italy. They ruled Sicily similarly to their close cousins, the Lanscano Crime Family of New Jersey. Once in a while his thoughts would drift back to New York and the situation that awaited him should he ever return. His confidence in the talents and skills of his legal team remained high. However, he also knew that the Justice System in America operated very differently than it did in Italy. He actually relished the idea that back in New York, all the Americans could do was spin their wheels, they would not be able to do anything regarding his trial until he returned, if he ever returned.

Numerous images depicting a bloodied and roughed up hostage named Giovanni Fedora were created many weeks prior. They sat at the ready, waiting to be sent from various post offices around New York City and Newark, NJ at coordinated intervals. Everything was going brilliantly. Now they just needed to maintain their act and keep the authorities running in circles looking for him as long as possible.

As the weeks passed, the start date of the trial came and went. Fedora couldn't help but laugh as he imagined the anger and impatience building in the prosecution team while Mr. Fedora still remained nowhere to be found. The only changes in momentum for his adversaries came courtesy of the pre-planned, coordinated propaganda packets. The only question in Fedora and his host's minds were how long they could keep up their game.

Word had reached the Sicilian Villa via syndicate networks that there had been a shift in the efforts of city and federal investigators back in New York. The concern of the Lanscanos and now by extension, the Santoros was starting to become very real. As much as they loved and respected Fedora as one of their own, this kidnapping situation was suddenly beginning to attract far more attention for them than they had anticipated or wanted. Major players in the Santoro family were now becoming more and more uncomfortable with Fedora's presence in their home.

Fedora completely understood the seriousness of the present arrangement as the strategies of outside law enforcement agents looking for him changed. He reaffirmed his loyalty to his hosts and accomplices. No one would ever know of their part in any of this scheme. He also knew that he couldn't remain at the Santoro Family compound indefinitely. He was already beginning to think that he had already overstayed well beyond his welcome, even though his gracious hosts would never ever dream of saying so to his face. Fedora was beginning to feel restless anyway. It was time for him to explore his options and arrange for a change in scenery. Fedora, after downing a few glasses of delicious Italian wine, decided that it was time to call in a long overdue favor.

Fedora was normally a very proud man. He would never admit he needed help from anyone, especially someone as dim witted and arrogant as Bishop Jonas Krivis. He wasn't quite at the desperation point yet, but he knew that that could quickly change if other arrangements weren't made soon. The wine flowed through him, removing filters that he'd never admit existed otherwise. The office phone in Vatican City rang several times before Bishop Jonas Krivis finally picked it up. Krivis noticed right away the abnormally aggressive and salty demeanor of the caller. After all he had done over the years for various men in the Curia, and the boldness that came from the alcohol flowing through his veins, he was now feeling overly optimistic about his request for help. In all of the years the two men had worked together, Krivis had only denied him a handful of times. Krivis' response immediately angered Fedora. Pope Phillip Michael II wanted absolutely nothing to do with him.

While this pope was hardly the saint that his immediate predecessor was, as far as the public was concerned, he was the most holiest man to be elected pope in the 20th Century. The public relations campaign that began with the death of Phillip Michael I and continued over the last twelve months since had done wonders to fortify the reputation of the Catholic Church. Behind their fortress walls they hid their sins, while projecting the public image and propaganda they preferred to fill the hearts and minds of the devout. This was all done with the full knowledge that Fedora was the mastermind behind the majority of their scandals and troubles that resulted in the church losing millions and millions of dollars from its coffers.

"I'm sorry Gio, asylum is only reserved for select clergy. We are not going to be able to help you, I'm afraid."

Fedora became quite angered by that response. "Don't give me that bullshit Jonas. Both you and I know better than that, and so does the Curia and that dumb shit, fucking pope you guys got in there."

Krivis was caught off guard by the brash tone in his response. He'd never heard such a tone of disrespect towards a pope, even that last one whom he hated more than any other. "What the hell are you going on about?"

"All you have to do is spend an afternoon with Gherado Fratello to know exactly what I'm talking about Jonas."

"Fratello? What the hell does he have to do with any of this?"

"Plenty! All of sudden you guys come off at me with all these double standards?"

"Double standards? What double standards?"

"Nazi rat lines...does that ring any bells?"

"What?"

"You know, all those Nazi rat lines Fratello was running through the Vatican, with the full blessings of that Goddamn Pope Mathias."

"Wow, you had to reach back pretty far for that one, didn't you Gio? Those were different times, involving different men, and you know it."

Fedora ignored Krivis' comment and continued his rant. "Your precious Holy Mother Church and her fucked up leaders had no problems smuggling Hitler's butchers to safety after the war. You know, the ones who slaughtered so many of those Germans and especially the Yugoslavian Jews. You guys certainly had no problems taking the money looted from those they slaughtered in exchange for asylum, did you?"

"I still don't see the point you are trying to make here Gio."

"Your damn Holy Mother Church suddenly has a conscience? Nobody around there can be bothered to help me out a little in my time of need? Especially after everything that I've done for you and others in your Goddamn church!"

"Look Gio, you know I'd approve it in a second, but I can't. My hands are tied. It's not up to me. This pope was very clear on his decision. He's quite upset by the mess you've gotten yourself and us into lately."

"Bwhahahaha, you must be joking, right?"

"No, I'm afraid not. I'm beyond dead serious."

"So you're telling me that he's sore at me because I embarrassed the church and lost some money."

Krivis tried to reason with the intoxicated madman on the other end of the line. "Answer me this then Gio. Name me one sovereign country that would grant asylum to any man who had caused them to lose some $2 billion?"

"So if I lose your precious money because of a few miscalculations you guys are fine turning your backs on me, but if I kill tons and tons of Jews for the Reich, everyone around there would be welcoming me with open arms, right?"

"What?"

"You guys wouldn't even have any of that money to invest and lose had you not fleeced those Jews trying to save their own asses by converting to Catholicism. Not to mention the money still to be made when you guys turned around and took the money from Hitler's executioners in exchange for their asylum."

"You are a madman Gio, you know that?!"

"You think so? Let me ask you a question then. Had my actions resulted in the church raking in millions, instead of losing them, wouldn't we be having a very different conversation right now? Am I right?"

"Forget it Gio. This conversation isn't going to get you anywhere."

"It's ok, I already know the answer. If I killed Jews for the Reich or made money for the church hand over fist you guys would open the doors wide for me, just like Pope Michael did. Remember?"

"Pope Michael has been dead for well over a year now Gio, we've all moved on. It looks like you need to too."

"I know for a fact that Ansios and Fratello still come and go as they please; tell me I'm wrong."

"Yes, but they aren't asking for asylum."

"But if they did, would you turn them away too?"

"I don't know..."

"You don't know? They have been fucking you guys over and robbing the coffers of your bank, and you just let them do whatever they please. Then there's you just sitting up there in your damn tower, with your slutty little, empty headed whore of a secretary, so damn full of yourself. Does your stupid little pope know about all of that Jonas?"

"Oh shut the fuck up with your whiny bullshit."

It registered to the inebriated Italian that the last comment clearly struck a nerve with the Vatican Bank president. "Fine, I only have one more question for you. Tell me Jonas, who are the real gods of the Roman Catholic Church?"

"Gods?"

"Yes, gods. I bet you can't even answer me that, can you? I can..."

"I have no idea what you are talking about...gods..."

"Yes, the most powerful gods of all! Money and Power! Without those two, your church would be nothing right now. Nothing but dust!"

"My aren't we suddenly a blasphemous one."

"Call it what you want Jonas, but you know I'm right. If I were wrong, why the hell would the Vatican be holding onto all of that gold, silver, and treasures looted from those Jewish victims? What about the stuff all those people used to 'buy' their conversion to Catholicism trying save their own asses? It takes a special breed of greed to take their money and treasure, then turn around and offer all those Nazi killers who used the plundered loot of their victim's to fund their asylum and escape, doesn't it?"

"Give it a rest Gio. This pope isn't going to change his mind. Believe me, I'd help you out in a heartbeat if I could, but I can't." Krivis decided it was time to redirect the conversation. "Have you tried talking to Marco? Maybe he can help you."

Fedora calmed quickly with the change in exchange. "No, he's got his own shit he's in, and it's pretty deep too. Let's just say that he's working through some problematic situations, and leave it at that."

"I'm sure Fratello would be more than glad to help you out."

Fedora remembered the conversation he had with Ansios just before he left New York. "Nah, I think I'm going to steer clear of him for a while. I don't like what I'm hearing about him right now."

"Why, what are you hearing?"

"Oh, nothing..."

"I don't believe you Gio."

"It's not my business nor place to say, if you don't know already."

Krivis was curious, but not enough to press the matter. "So what are you going to do?"

"I'm not sure yet, but I will come up with something."

"I'm sure you will. You always do."

The call soon terminated. Fedora sat quietly in the ornately upholstered chair to think. He took another sip of his wine. The fermented liquid coated his tongue as it swirled around his mouth. The flavor had an unmistakable smoothness that only comes from years and years of aging. The hint of oak and cherry provided the perfect hint of sweetness to balance out the aroma and flavor. His quick jaunt to Sicily certainly reminded him of the days of his youth. The hustle, bustle and disgusting smells of New York City were nothing that he missed. As he reflected back on all of his years and what he had accomplished, he became aware of two things, he missed his freedom, and he missed his wife and family. He also knew exactly what was waiting for him should he return to New York.

As his mind wandered, Luxembourg populated his thoughts. The weather was perfect there year around, especially the winters. New York winters were harsh and bone chillingly cold. It was no place for a man in his golden years. Perhaps instead of returning to city life, a nice quiet country estate somewhere in Luxembourg would be a better option for a fifty-nine year old man to live out the rest of his days surrounded by his wife and family, especially those grandchildren. Fedora decided that Luxembourg sounded so much better than anything still waiting for him in the Big Apple. One of the younger Santoro men was dispatched from the family compound with a request for a new passport and lots and lots of cash. Fedora would send for his wife and family once he got himself established in their new home and country.

The excitement of a new future filled with novel adventures and possibilities was gaining some traction in Fedora's mind. One of the more senior family members entered the room, interrupting his daydream. The look on the man's face failed to conceal the concern on his face as he came closer to the Fedora seated out on the veranda taking in the fall colors of the Italian countryside.

"Giovanni, I'm sorry. I'm afraid I have some disappointing news."

"I more or less guessed, from the look on your face." Fedora opted to remain optimistic. "What's happened? Perhaps we can come up with a suitable alternate solution."

"I hope so, but I'm not so sure." Fedora's host was now purposefully avoiding making eye contact with his guest. "Our courier was intercepted on his return trip here."

Fedora tried to remain optimistic. "Did he have the passport and cash I requested on him at the time?"

"I'm afraid so."

Fedora's face now too displayed a similar expression of concern and disappointment. "Shit! How the hell did they even get tipped off to pick him up?"

"I have no idea. None of my men have uttered a peep, I'm certain of it. Who all have you talked to Giovanni?"

"I spoke with Krivis the other day, but that's it."

"Well clearly word got out somehow."

Both men became very concerned. The authorities, if they weren't already on to them, soon would be. They had to stick with the kidnapping scenario now, and accentuate it. If they failed to do so, there would be way too many eyes and ears looking their way, stirring up all kinds of questions as to what they had been up to in Sicily all these weeks. The two men sat quietly as they brainstormed for ideas.

Finally the slightly younger Donny Lanscano broke the silence. "Well, we could shoot you."

Fedora was completely caught off guard by the suggestion. "What the hell? You can't be serious? There must be a better solution than that!"

"I didn't say kill you Giovanni."

"Either way, I don't like this, nor where it's going. We must come up with a better plan."

"Well we better come up with something fast. Now that they have our courier, the authorities will be here soon. I'm sure of it. No matter what we decide to do, they can't find any trace that you were ever here, my friend."

"Agreed!"

"That said, no one is going to believe this kidnapping bullshit if you suddenly just waltz back into your New York City home or office with hardly a scratch on you. If you did that, they'd just start digging even more into your business and ours."

"But shooting me? Honestly, why can't you just rough me up a little like in the pictures."

"Why would your captors release you over that when they hadn't at any point in the ten weeks prior?"

Fedora hated the idea, but he knew that his host was right. He took a big deep breath, and slowly let it out. "I admit it, you're right, but I still don't like the idea." He sat in silence trying to come up with a better option, but none would come. "I guess I had better get started drinking if we're gonna do this shit."

"Drinking?"

"You don't think I'm going to be all in on this idea fully sober?"

"You've got a point."

"Well, if we are going to do this, I really hope you've got something stronger than this wine around here."

"I've got just the thing! I'll be right back."

The liquor was smooth and smoky. He drank the first two scotches relatively quickly. As he was drinking his third, he could finally feel the muting of his anxiety. His uneasiness once again began to ratchet up slightly upon the arrival of a friend of the family who was also a very accomplished physician. It would be his job to attend to the wound after the trigger was pulled and keep Fedora from bleeding out. As Fedora was sucking down his fourth scotch, the doctor explained to the gunman the best place and angle to fire the shot. They decided it was best to use the smallest caliber handgun they had on hand. They wanted to make every effort to avoid hitting Fedora's femur.

The report from the gun was more or less simultaneous with the punch of the bullet into the flesh of Fedora's right thigh. As the slug from the Jimenez JA-22 pistol entered his leg, the impact instantaneously knocked the wind out of him. At that moment, Fedora was fairly certain that a larger slug would not have hurt him any less than the pain he was feeling at that moment. The portions of his quadriceps muscle that remained intact in his leg immediately contracted, followed by the seering, burning sensation surrounding the bullet buried deep within his leg. The intense pain and the flush of adrenaline now coursing through his veins nullified the intoxicating effects of the scotch he drank earlier. Bright red blood immediately began spurting from the wound with every contraction of his heart. Fedora felt a wave of nausea come over him, followed by a sense of disorientation. The two men on either side of him grabbed him by the arms and laid him gently onto a nearby table. They held him down as the doctor quickly located the severed arteries and clamped them shut. There was now blood everywhere.

Once the bleeding was under control, The doctor administered an anesthetic into his leg to numb the pain. He then dug into the wound as best he could, but failed to find the .22 slug in his leg. There was no exit wound, so everyone knew that the bullet was still lodged somewhere in his leg. The doctor explained that this would most likely become a problem at some point. He then treated and bandaged the wound. The treatment and medication brought enough relief to the gunshot victim to where he could once again regain control of his breathing, however, the buzz from the scotch was all but gone.

"Goddamn, son of a bitch, that hurt!"

"Sorry about that Giovanni. I really do wish we had some other option."

"That's easy for you to say Donny."

"Well if it's any consolation, that was the hardest trigger I've ever had to pull, in all of my years. You really do mean a lot to this family."

Over the coming few days, they decided to move Fedora to another location. The doctor continued to do everything he could to control the man's pain. The wound was kept clean, and the dressings were changed regularly. Despite the doctor's best efforts, the .22 slug that remained in his leg was beginning to cause the wound to become infected. It was at that point that Fedora's game was up. Fedora now had no choice but to return to New York and face his fate, whatever it was going to be. Once again he was fitted with his white wig, phony facial hair and glasses. Once back in the United States, one of the Lanscano boys roughed him up a little and left him on a street corner.

Fedora was very weak at this point. For a few seconds he could hear the noises and commotion on the street around him, then everything went dark.

CHAPTER 52

The seasons were beginning to change from summer to autumn in Milan. Once in a while the winds would make a distinct shift and blow down from the Alps to the north or the Apennine Mountains to the southeast of the booming metropolitan city. The winds carried a certain chill that reminded the Milanese people that the summer season was now waning. Marco Ansios had way too much occupying his head to take any notice of the beauty of the seasonal visual cues or tactile sensations that ushered in the change of seasons.

The maneuvering of a few influential men under the direction of P2 Master Gherado Fratello was serving its purpose well. Detective Cosimo Angelo, who had been working on his case for some time, never returned to his investigative assignment following his release from jail back in April. Marco Ansios had received some additional good news recently regarding the Bank of Italy director that was arrested along with the detective at the time. The more senior Investigative Director with the Bank of Italy who was released on bail shortly after his arrest by a sympathetic magistrate considerate of his age, had decided it was best for him to resign from his position. Marco Ansios felt some weight lift from his shoulders as powerful, influential friends did what needed to be done in order to assist him. Their efforts were helpful to the corrupt banker's cause, however, it wasn't simply a noble gesture. At the end of the day it was more about those helpful men protecting their own asses and assets, than were dependent on him.

If there was ever a doubt in anyone's mind regarding the reach and power of P2 Master Gherado Fratello and his pseudo-Masonic brotherhood, there certainly wasn't now. Never had their influence been demonstrated more definitively. Agencies and authorities within the Italian Finance Ministry and the Bank of Italy which were bound by rules and governance were masterfully out manipulated by the lawless. The murder of the incorruptible magistrate, followed by the removal of detective Cosimo Angelo really slowed the momentum of the government's case. The recent resignation of the inspector was the third man of significance to be removed from the case. Marco Ansios hoped that this latest development would slow his case even further, or better yet, put an end to their months-long investigation involving him and his bank, all together. Either way, with these men out of the way, he could now devote his undivided attention to the removal of others seeking to harm him and his financial empire.

Marco Ansios was grateful to have one less problem on his plate. However, for him, it was synonymous with removing a pea from a dinner plate still fully loaded with food. Fratello's abilities and solutions brought some relief. However, Ansios never felt that Fratello's resolutions were absolute. There was a certain level of building desperation that created a new form of mental anguish for the tightly wound Milanese Banker. A constant feeling of foreboding consumed Marco Ansios. The last time his associates told him that "the problem would be taken care of", he had a nagging feeling that the problem was stalled, but not completely resolved.

The uneasy paranoia of Marco Ansios was outwardly evident by the presence of an around the clock, eight man security detail that accompanied him everywhere he went. He also felt it necessary to have his Alfa Romeo outfitted with security enhancements in the form of armor plating and bulletproof glass and tires. These heightened protections would be billed to the Banco Generali shareholders at the cost of a cool $1 million annually. It was evident by all of the blood running through the streets of Italy during the "Years of Lead," that magistrates and heads of state were clearly not as well protected as this banking man with very dangerous friends and enemies. He deployed the protective services of socialists, communists, Gherado Fratello and the men of P2 and his associates in the Mafia. They all served their purpose well. However, he was constantly haunted by the fact that any one of them could turn against him at any given moment with very little provocation.

His biggest fear, however, came from the Bank of Italy. They had already demonstrated their prowess to investigate questionable monetary situations in other parts of the country. If the Italian government ever got a wild hair up their ass to actually do the job that Italian taxpayers paid them to do, they would certainly discover that Banco Generali president, Marco Ansios, illegally owned shares of the bank he ran. These bank shares in his own personal portfolio were kept hidden in Panama, far from the prying eyes of the authorities in the Italian Finance Ministry. If they ever found out what he was really doing, Ansios' world would be destroyed.

Eight years ago he began moving shares around in order to hide certain investments from Italian authorities. He'd move shares from Nassau to Nicaragua, then on to Peru. Then they were sent to Panama, and Liechtenstein, and then finally back to Peru. The final destination for all of these illegal shares was a company in Luxembourg owned by the Vatican Bank and controlled by Ansios' friend Bishop Jonas Krivis.

Perhaps the truly mysterious thing here was how Ansios' illegal banking schemes remained undetected for so long. The Bank of Italy completed their most damning report long ago. A year later, the information still had yet to be released for public or professional scrutiny. The contents of that report were hardly anything obscure. A little digging and collaboration among just a few of the over 250 banks that lined up to pour millions into Banco Generali could have easily exposed Marco Ansios for the fraud that he actually was.

The lending practices of international markets in the '70s were, without question, extremely lax. There were no monitors or regulations in place. The only checks involved came not from central banking officials, but rather in the form of deposits of over $450 million in unsecured loans. These funds never ever made their way to any sort of banking institution. Instead they were deposited into Banco Generali Holdings, located somewhere in Luxembourg. The pouring of millions of dollars from international banks into Ansios' banks began over a year ago. There was no indication that anything would change anytime soon.

British banks were among those pouring money into Ansios' hands. The Milanese banker then moved the funds into companies owned by the Vatican and controlled by Krivis since 1971. That was when Marco Ansios and Giovanni Fedora placed Bishop Krivis on the Board of Directors of Sierra Madre International Bank, Nassau, The Bahamas. From the Vatican controlled Panamanian companies, the UK loaned money was sent on to Gherado Fratello. The P2 mastermind used British money to purchase Exocet Missiles for the Argentinians fighting the Falklands War. The nauseating reality was that British banks were funding the purchase of weapons that ultimately sent many of their own valiant fellow countrymen to early graves.

Ansios seized the opportunity and opened Banco Generali de América del Sud located in Buenos Aires, Argentina. Upon opening their doors, there was an eerie void of banking activity in the establishment, which would have raised serious red flags for most bankers or investors. Marco Ansios was not surprised and more importantly, he was extremely pleased by what he saw. This part of Ansios' banking empire was not there to serve the delightful people of Buenos Aires; it was there to assist the Argentinian government in their purchase of more missiles and weapons for their war efforts. Waiting in the wings were other South American regimes needing similar help with their own transactions to fortify their armies with weapons and munitions.

It was an extremely lucrative form of business. These men didn't care that the money they raked in hand over fist came soaked in the blood of many far removed from their schemes. Fratello netted $184 million from his brokered arms deals. The Vatican owned Panamanian company, on the other hand, ran up $486 million in debt. The only thing backing this insane amount of debt were copious amounts of extremely overvalued Banco Generali shares.

Milan magistrates felt it was time to call Mr. Marco Ansios in again for questioning. This time it wasn't men like the murdered magistrate, the detective or the inspector from the Bank of Italy that had successfully been removed from the equation. Ansios didn't like being questioned by them. Their questions were sharp, jagged and penetrating.

Ansios knew nothing of this new judge. Had he worked with any of the men who were working his case before? Ansios entered the room subdued and extremely nervous. His gaze was again firmly fixated on his shoes or the intricate patterns decorating the floor. His standardized response to most questions was his unwavering obligation to protect the banking secrecy of his loyal clientele. It quickly became evident to the Milanese banker being questioned that this new magistrate did not have any access to the prior work done by his predecessors working his case. This poor man was now starting back at square one. Ansios quickly dodged and out manipulated the conversation and the magistrate as the discussion was shifted away from the business of banking and on to the premier professional soccer team in Milan and the brilliant success they were having in their current season.

Despite there being a new idiot investigating his case, Marco Ansios was still not out of the woods. As the end of 1979 loomed, so did the exposure of his financial involvement in the Vatican owned companies that he controlled. This cozy arrangement involved over $500 million. The astronomical banking fantasies of Giovanni Fedora that inspired the other two bank presidents had yet to materialize. Suddenly, Ansios' long time advisor and mentor was in no position to assist him as he lay in a New York hospital under armed guard with a serious, uncertain prognosis for recovery.

Another imminent problem, unforeseen by these bankers and businessmen was inflation. This was a development that men like Ansios, Fedora, Krivis or Fratello could not foresee nor control. The value of the dollar began to rise against the lira. This was a particularly catastrophic development for Mr. Ansios.

A huge chunk of Banco Generali's assets in their investment portfolio were shares valued in lira, not the US dollar. The shifting of fiscal winds meant the value of those assets were unexpectedly dropping like a rock. Marco Ansios began to panic. He would have to act quickly if he was going to survive his newest problem which was an even bigger threat to his empire than the investigative efforts of the Italian government in his recent past.

It would now take Marco Ansios some 30 billion lira ($36.5 million) worth of trickery just to cover the overhead to keep his fraudulent empire afloat. "Overhead" was in the form of cash paid to media outlets and sources not controlled by Fratello's men for them to not report on the country's inflation situation. Marco Ansios made every effort possible to keep the public, and most importantly the socialists of the Christian Democratic Party, in the dark. This was imperative for the success of his operations through the continuation of money being lended to his bank. It would cost another 29 billion lira to keep the communists content. Suddenly everyone around Ansios seemed to have their hand out. The man with the biggest hands of all, raking in money hand over fist, was Gherado Fratello.

CHAPTER 53

Once Fedora was out of surgery and recovery, the patient was reunited with his frantically worried wife and family. Everyone was overcome with emotion from the reunion. In the strictest of confidence, he put their minds further at ease as he explained that the entire kidnapping situation was a fabrication, however, he didn't give any further details of where exactly he'd been for the last two and a half months. No one else, not even his lawyer was ever given this information.

The rest of the world waited, uncertain of the present condition or future fate of Mr. Giovanni Fedora. The prosecution had invested many months in building their case against him and anxiously awaited an update on the medical condition of their defendant. Everyone involved with the case breathed a huge, collective sigh of relief when medical staff finally announced that Mr. Fedora's surgery was a complete success and that they anticipated over the course of the next several weeks that he'd make a full and complete recovery. Their optimism continued to grow as the days progressed. New reports on the improvements in Fedora's condition were issued regularly, leading to a more positive prognosis over the coming days and weeks.

District Attorney Paul Christopherson, upon the advice of his detective Francis Clavering, requested an around the clock, armed security detail to stand guard outside Fedora's hospital room. This maneuver was carefully framed as a gesture of good faith, caution and concern for the safety and protection of the defendant as he lay recovering in his hospital bed. They didn't want the last group or some other copycat nefarious party to take advantage of his compromised medical condition to pay him a visit, determined to finish him off.

The reality was that the men who stood guard outside Fedora's hospital room were actually members of the US Marshal's office. Everyone on the prosecution team, especially Christopherson, following confidential consultation with Detective Clavering, now saw Fedora as an extreme flight risk. The D.A. was not thrilled about the delay of the trial caused by this kidnapping stunt by Mr. Fedora. While he was frustrated, he couldn't help but be pleased when a new date was set for the trial's start.

Christopherson was most pleased that the trial would start soon. Mr. Fedora continued to recover from his injury and infection over the coming few weeks. During that time, many bedside interrogations were conducted. Fedora detailed the events surrounding his abduction and how he was kept in a dark, dank, windowless room during his ten week absence. It was when he tried to escape, that his captors decided to shoot him in the leg. They tended to the wound as best they could for a while before dumping him on a busy New York street corner without any explanation.

After a few weeks, his health had improved enough to consider his release from the hospital. He was given complete examinations to ensure that he was physically and psychologically fit to stand trial, and then he was discharged from the hospital. Fedora was outraged as he was handcuffed and released not to the comfort of his home, but to a federal correctional facility. The D.A. felt that following the defendant's little stunt, a more fitting wardrobe for Mr. Fedora's upcoming trial consisted of a jail jumpsuit and handcuffs instead of one of Fedora's custom tailored Italian suits.

Fedora was outraged! "I was kidnapped you moronic goons! You have no business treating me this way!" Fedora vocally protested continuously. Nobody listened or cared as he continued with his tantrums, except his lawyer. It was highly probable that even he would not have cared, had he not been paid to do so by his client. The judge eventually relented, and Mr. Fedora was released from the confines of his jail cell, against the many objections of both teams of lawyers that made up the prosecution, on a $3 million bond. The prosecution and NYPD soon were pleased to discover that they no longer needed to devote numerous man hours keeping tabs on Mr. Fedora. On the rare occasions when he decided to travel from his home or office, the local press reporters and paparazzi were now buzzing about him every chance they got.

The first week of November, a major Italian newspaper published a scathing article about how former New York judge, turned high profile lawyer, Andreas Stein was essentially forced to represent Mr. Fedora for his trial. Mr. Stein failed to reveal to US prosecutors his knowledge of a major meeting that took place among high profile Mafia leaders in Sicily. These Sicilian Mafiosi were rumored to be close associates of Mr. Fedora. For those in the know, the information was factual. Mr. Stein knew of the meeting scheduled for the second day of August. Coincidentally the gathering was slated to occur during the exact same time Mr. Fedora was reported to have been kidnapped.

As the days continued to march on, D.A. Christopherson and the Chief US Prosecutor were working hard to make sure everything was properly prepared for the upcoming trial. They were diligent in their work. They were determined to make every single charge filed against Mr. Fedora stick hard and fast. There would be no dismissal of anything nor any kind of technicality as far as they were concerned.

Christopherson urgently summoned Detective Clavering to his office following a meeting with his federal counterpart. Upon entering the D.A.'s office, he directed Fran to have a seat across from him, and handed him some papers. He gestured at the papers while he finished up a phone conversation. His detective visually consumed the information. Fran's eyes went wider and wider as he continued to read what was handed to him. Finally Fran returned his attention to his host upon the conclusion of his phone call, puzzled and concerned.

"Where the hell did you get this?"

"The Chief US prosecutor who is working with me just handed it to me this morning. I am aware that showing this to anyone outside the prosecution team goes against protocol, but I had to speak to you about it right away!"

"Well unless he got information directly from you, based on what I've been telling you, I have no clue where this information came from. I can tell you, without a doubt, he didn't get any of this information from me."

"What about Lance?"

"No, I've been very careful to keep any of my side work from him."

"Forgive me Francis, but if you don't mind me asking, who else here knows of your side work besides me?"

"Only you, Bentley knows whatever you've told him and Cardinal Wexford sir, oh and Peg."

"Hmmm, I see. It appears that you aren't the only one here doing some secretive side work my friend."

"This wouldn't be surprising if one of the Fed men found the money laundering connection between Fedora and prominent Italian Mafia players. That's everywhere, if one knows where to look."

"I agree, but that's not what this says, Francis. This is money laundering for powerful Italian's that are not associated with the Mafia, as far as I can tell."

"Yeah, that is interesting."

"Can you do me a favor and contact your man in Italy. See what he knows about this and these men. Oh, and can you confirm that the Italians mentioned here are not Mafia men?"

"Absolutely sir!" Fran confirmed with a bit of a sly smile. "But now I too need to ask a favor of you."

Christopherson picked up on the loaded comment. "And that is...?"

"I want to know, if possible, how your prosecution partner learned of these Italian money laundering clients and how exactly they are associated with the Vatican. I'd really like to know who's been over there digging around like I have, because we both know that it isn't that fuck up Nathan Bayer."

Christopherson nodded and smiled. "You definitely got that right."

"I mean, I can confirm that the Feds have CIA operatives all over the world. A couple of them helped Hans and I get surveillance equipment and a tech on that first trip, when I first followed Benedetto over to Munich."

"That's right, I'd forgotten about that."

"This looks to me like the Feds aren't as opposed to digging into Vatican connections after all. Bayer is so full of shit after all that shit he gave us when it pointed back to Benedetto and Mafia men."

"I can't say. Maybe at the time there was a problem. Those were different times, under a different administration."

Fran thought for a moment. "Yeah, maybe. If you're right, I'm honestly curious when and why that changed. Because we both know that none of this or the past shit has anything to do with any sort of religious protocol or practice of the Vatican or Catholic Church."

Christopherson gave a nod of confirmation. "I will see what I can come up with for you Detective, and let you know."

"Thank you sir, and I will do the same."

As the new trial date approached, there was a lot of buzz in the media and public building. Media tycoons seized the opportunity, taking full advantage of the public's fanatical fascination with Fedora and anything Mafia related since Francis Ford Coppola's *The Godfather* movie came out in '72. A month prior to the trial, a five part series began to run in one of London's most read newspapers. The initial article entitled "The Italian Who Hustled the World," showcased Fedora's Mafia connections. The end of that article included the tale of his recent kidnapping and his return to New York back in October. The drama of the narrative was punctuated by the bullet wound in his leg. It also served as a very effective reminder to him and others in the know, that it'd be in their best interest to keep their mouths shut. That opening article also included a quote from a New York Lawyer, well known for his defensive representation of key Mafia figures in the syndicate. This man had nothing to do with Fedora's upcoming trial. However, the two of them had a friendship that went back at least five years. The truly amazing part was that despite all of the hours and hours of surveillance collected by authorities working on various cases, never once was there ever a mention of Mr. Fedora by anyone involved with organized crime. Detective Clavering knew first hand the extent that Mr. Fedora took to cover his tracks when it came to his Mafia connections.

On January 11, 1980 a new sixty-nine count indictment was filed against Mr. Giovanni Fedora. This new one superseded the previous ninety-nine count indictment filed against him previously. His trial would begin a mere twenty-six days later. Fedora's defense lawyer through his client's connections felt it was time to call in some favors to aid in his defense. Two Curial cardinals and Vatican Bank President, Bishop Jonas Krivis were called to testify for the defense.

With only two weeks remaining before the trial date, the judge assigned to the case was very impressed with the ability of Fedora's lawyer, Andreas Stein, to get three Vatican holy men to take the witness stand. The plan hit a snag, however, when Vatican policy prohibited them from appearing in New York in person. Stein had to shift gears significantly in order to obtain what could be some of the most important testimony to the defense of his client. Mr. Stein, accompanied by the chief US prosecutor, would now have to travel to Rome in order to obtain the videotaped testimonies for the upcoming trial. D.A. Christopherson put in a persuasive argument that he should be included in the trip to Rome, but was ultimately denied.

Jury selection for the trial had finally begun. The fact that the men and women of the jury were to be sequestered during the entire trial was proving to be a major problem as selected participants were removed one by one from the pool of potential jurors, unable to fulfill their civic obligation for one lame reason or another. The jury still had not been fully selected by the time Stein and his American Federal counterpart were scheduled to depart for Rome.

The two lawyers arrived in Rome just two days before the scheduled trial to videotape the testimony of the key character witnesses for the defense. Upon their arrival, the federal prosecutor sat patiently waiting inside the US Embassy located in Rome. Stein headed off to the Vatican to meet with his three witnesses before returning with them to be recorded. Stein's absence went on far longer than was expected. Something wasn't right.

Fedora's lawyer arrived at his scheduled appointment, and was escorted into the Vatican Bank president's office chamber by his beautiful, young secretary with all of her assets on full display for everyone to see.

"Your Excellency," she muttered in a soft, sweet seductive tone as she escorted the American into the room. "Mr. Andres Stein is here to see you."

"Thank you my dear." Krivis smiled and winked at her. "That will be all."

Stein couldn't help himself as he watched the secretary's form leave the room and close the door behind her. His attention then turned to the man seated behind the desk who was smiling at him behind a thin veil of cigar smoke. "Mr. Stein, welcome! Can I get you a scotch? Straight or on the rocks?"

"None for me, thank you bishop."

"Please, call me Jonas."

"Thank you. You can call me Andreas if you wish."

"Very well, Andreas, please have a seat."

"Thank you. I just wanted to meet with you and the two Curial cardinals briefly before we went over to the US Embassy to record your testimonies, if that's alright."

"Oh yeah, about that..." The bishop took a swig of his scotch, followed by a good hearty drag from his cigar. The smoke gracefully flowed from Krivis' mouth as he spoke. "There seems to be a bit of a problem regarding all of that, I'm afraid."

Stein suddenly became extremely concerned. "A bit of a problem?"

"Yes, it seems that our Secretary of State has decided to nix the Vatican's approval for all the video stuff."

"He did what?!" Stein summoned every bit of his character in order to maintain his professional composure in that moment.

Krivis appeared completely unconcerned by the seriousness of this last minute development. "Yeah, he told us that we weren't allowed to provide any kind of testimony that might be helpful in Mr. Fedora's case. I'm sorry."

The American lawyer was now livid. "You couldn't call and tell me this before we left New York?"

"No actually, he just told us this morning, I'm afraid."

"Shit! Shit! Son of a Bitch!" Stein racked his brain trying to figure out what to do next. He momentarily calmed himself. "Did he offer any kind of explanation for the sudden change in decision?"

"He just said that this type of situation would set a most disruptive precedent. There has already been a lot of unfortunate, unfavorable publicity in Italy, and especially around Rome regarding these sworn depositions."

"Bad press? That's it? That's his reasoning?"

"Well, that paired with the fact that the US Government does not give diplomatic recognition to the people of the Vatican."

"So bad press with a side of grudge is what I'm getting here, am I correct?" Stein fired off in a snarky tone.

Krivis responded to the barbed remark with a simple, "That is correct."

Mr. Stein made several further pleas for the Vatican's cooperation in Fedora's defense, only to be met with continued disappointment. Several hours later, a defeated looking Andreas Stein walked back into the US Embassy in Rome. His hair was unkempt, sticking up randomly in multiple directions. His tie was undone and sloppily draped about his neck. His jacket was off and slung over one arm, while holding his briefcase in the other. The top two buttons of his fine linen shirt were open and the sleeves were unbuttoned and rolled up to his elbows. He looked like he'd been roughed up by some street thugs, except there was no blood or bruises.

"What the hell happened to you?" Questioned the federal prosecutor, concerned.

"They changed their minds. The Vatican Secretary of State decided this morning that he wasn't going to allow the testimonies of their men to go forward."

His traveling partner could suddenly comprehend the disappointment and defeat Mr. Stein was feeling at that moment. "I'm sorry. Even though we are working against each other, I can understand what a devastating blow this must be for the defense of your client's case."

"Thank you, I appreciate that."

Mr Stein was unsure exactly how his client would receive the disappointing news. His flight back to New York was anything but pleasant. On the occasion when he would doze off, he'd be jolted awake by nightmares of an irate Fedora screaming at him because of his failure, even though he had nothing to do with the Vatican's decision. He was not looking forward to meeting with his client the next morning.

Fedora's response did not disappoint, the man was pissed. Stein listened to the man's rant, grateful that his anger was appropriately directed at the source of his disappointment and not at him. He personally knew the man that had become Pope Phillip Michael II's Secretary of State six months following the death of Cardinal Zacharie Benoît. He liked the pope's pick, at the time. However, at the moment he was strongly having second thoughts. This pope, unlike Pope Michael VI, never sought out Fedora for his advice on anything.

Fedora suspected that the decision of the Secretary of State had been influenced more by Bishop Jonas Krivis than would ever be admitted. Fedora, through his various sources within the Vatican Curia, soon learned that Pope Phillip Michael II had already given his approval for the three Curial men to give their sworn statements. It was the Secretary of State alone who acted to pull the plug at the last minute. His reasoning was two fold: If Fedora was found guilty, the three high ranking Curial prelates of the Church would certainly be branded as liars. This would then open the Vatican doors wide for the Italian magistrates with their own ongoing investigations. This would then lead to the discovery of violations of the 1929 Lateran

Treaty between the Holy See and the Kingdom of Italy. This was an important treaty that granted a cardinal immunity from arrest in Italy. The Vatican Inc. machine could not operate under those conditions. Just four hours before the videos were to be recorded, the Secretary of State overrode the decision of his pope. At this point, it didn't matter. Without those three testimonies, the defense was sent scrambling as attempts were made to come up with new ways to demonstrate Fedora's credibility. Stein failed miserably. Whoever rendered the decision had effectively sealed the future fate of Mr. Giovanni Fedora.

While all of the drama surrounding the Vatican situation in Rome was happening, Fedora got a call from Marco Ansios who was now in Zürich. The caller was distinctly calmer than he was the last time the two men talked, which happened to be on the same day that he was "kidnapped." Fedora thought the calmness of his friend was oddly uncharacteristic, as he listened to him ramble on like a madman.

"Did you sell off those South American papers like I told you?"

"No, I uh, well..." Ansios suddenly got very quiet, and stumbled with his words. Fedora was disappointed to learn this, but decided not to interrupt his caller. "Fratello had me via Banco Generali issue large loans to Italy's most well read newspaper."

Fedora was confused. "Did he say why?"

"He told me his second hand man in P2 sat on the paper's board of directors. With the shared control of that paper, no one in Italy would dare do anything nefarious to him or me. This is my last chance to truly defeat the men who wish to destroy me and my legacy, like they did to you." Ansios instantly regretted revealing his true feelings through that last statement. He was pleasantly surprised that he wasn't met with some sort of explosive tirade from a man he knew had a serious temper once provoked.

Perhaps in another time and place, Fedora may have scolded his protégé for not listening to him, but that would not be the case today. Fedora just remained quiet and listened, knowing full well that despite Ansios' best efforts and anything that Fratello had up his sleeve, neither of them would be able to control the fickle and free flowing press, especially in Italy. Fedora could now see clearly that Ansios was on a direct collision course with his own destruction. Fratello had Ansios right where he wanted him. Fedora knew Fratello's ego needed feeding regularly. Through his control and manipulation of his P2 Paymaster, he would seek revenge on a publishing world that seemed to take great satisfaction in giving him nothing but a cold shoulder.

Ansios shifted the topic of conversation. With all of the drama surrounding Fedora's kidnapping and upcoming trial, he knew nothing of Ansios' more recent business operations. As his friend informed him of the new Banco Gererali de America del Sud headquartered in Buenos Aires and explained its primary function with an abundance of excitement. Fedora didn't share in his friend's enthusiasm. He sat bewildered that Ansios could not see what was absolutely obvious to him. Ansios was now in far more trouble than he could ever possibly imagine.

CHAPTER 54

On February 6, 1980 the trial UNITED STATES OF AMERICA, APPELLEE, v. GIOVANNI FEDORA, DEFENDANT-APPELLANT began. The defendant entered the courtroom dressed to impress, as per his usual. His custom designed, custom tailored Giorgio Armani suit was crafted with the finest of fabrics and materials available. He was escorted into the room and to his seat by his lawyer Mr. Andreas Stein. He was to face sixty-nine criminal charges arising from his involvement in the collapse of Lincoln National Bank.

The first several days were filled more with formalities than substance as it related to the trial and the charges levied against Mr. Fedora. As the trial entered its second week, word had reached Gherado Fratello in Italy through some of Fedora's close friends in Washington, DC. Fedora's situation was not good. The very same Catholic Church who sought out his financial advice repeatedly for decades, and profited handsomely from it, had now completely turned their backs on him at the worst moment possible.

Mr. Stein informed the trial judge of the disastrous trip to the Vatican he and the Chief US Prosecuting Attorney had made. The judge appeared visibly disappointed. He was actually looking forward to hearing what some of the important men of the Vatican had to say about the defendant, and their experiences with him. D.A. Christopherson then got up and informed the court that the diligent work of his men in the NYPD, had uncovered the plot that Mr. Fedora had, in fact, faked his own kidnapping. A ten week escapade that allowed him to leave the United States for destinations in southern Italy last August through half of October. An audible buzz immediately began to spread through the courtroom, as many sat stunned with the evidence presented by D.A. Christopherson. The judge who previously had some sympathy for Fedora and granted bail while he awaited his trial was absolutely pissed off when he heard the news. He immediately revoked the $3 million bail and release of Fedora, and he was immediately ordered to federal prison. From this day forward, Giovanni Fedora would be forced to trade in his fancy Armani suits for the latest prison jumpsuit and handcuff fashion provided by the American taxpayers. Christopherson was pleased as he had accomplished the first of his missions for this trial. Fedora's little kidnapping stunt, and the freedoms he relished since his return would be his last, at least until lawyer, jury and judge were finished with him.

"Order! Order! Order in the court!" The judge struck the sounding block with his gavel several times trying to quiet the crowd still buzzing inside his courtroom as they reacted noisily to the shocking revelations of the D.A. and the actions of the judge that followed. Once order was restored, he nodded to the federal prosecutor, "Counselor, the prosecution may begin."

The federal lawyer then turned toward the men and women of the jury and began to speak. "Ladies and gentlemen of the jury, the defendant in this case, an Italian financier, is alleged to have controlled an international group of banks and corporations in the early 1970s. The prosecution wishes to demonstrate that the financial machinations of Mr. Giovanni Fedora were indeed massive, complicated and unscrupulous, wreaking financial havoc on banking and financial institutions as well as economic and personal tragedy upon other persons involved. Partially as a result of his conduct,

Lincoln National Bank, in which Fedora owned a controlling 22% of the outstanding stock, and Fedora was a sitting director on the bank's board and an executive committee member, was declared insolvent on October 8, 1974.

The prosecution wishes to file on this day, January 11, 1980, a sixty nine count indictment against Fedora. The first count charges Fedora with conspiracy to defraud the United States and various departments and agencies, and scheming to defraud both Lincoln and the United States by misapplying $15 million of bank funds in October, 1972. The prosecution wishes to call to the stand Mr. Nico Novelli."

Detective Francis Clavering sat in the courtroom gallery accompanied by his wife Peg. The sight of Novelli as he approached the witness stand absolutely nauseated him. He could not believe that the prosecution was going to use the testimony of such a man to make their case. There was nothing Fran hated more than a liar, and this man approaching the witness stand was the biggest one he'd met in years. Through Novelli's convincing lies, the detective and his partner, FBI agent Lance Erickson and others were completely sympathetic to his fears and situation. At least until his lies and own crimes like embezzlement were revealed by his Italian partner Cosimo.

Peg could feel the emotion quietly welling up in her husband as he silently squeezed her hand very tightly in his as if it was in some sort of vise. The strength of the grip varied depending on what was going on in the courtroom. She knew exactly what was going through his head as his grip became uncomfortably constricted to the point that it was becoming painful. She too watched with great displeasure, what was happening inside that courtroom. She understood completely the reasons behind the disdain her husband felt for this particular witness. She instinctively patted his hands with her free hand in a silent comforting gesture as Novelli placed one hand on the Holy Bible, and then raised the other solemnly swearing to tell the whole truth. "...so help me God."

Novelli testified that in October, 1972, one of Fedora's Milan banks had insufficient monetary resources needed to complete the purchase of Lincoln. Fedora, with the assistance of Novelli, arranged a system where Lincoln would accept $15 million in the form of what appeared to be a time deposit into a subsidiary of Banco Generali in Milan. The majority of people in the courtroom were completely ignorant of the significance of Marco Ansios' bank in this scheme, however, Fran, Peg and Christopherson certainly were not. The $15 million in questionable funds were then released to Fedora's bank in Zürich via an oral contract releasing Ansios' and his bank from all liability regarding repayment. Following a bribe of the general manager of Ansios' bank, the funds were then moved to one of Fedora's Milan banks under a secondary fiduciary contract. None of these details were ever documented in Lincoln's records. From these actions, the prosecution charged Fedora with wire fraud and misapplication of bank funds. Fedora's defense counsel tried to argue against the charges but were unsuccessful as the judge deemed their points of contention were irrelevant to the case.

The next seven counts levied against Fedora by the prosecution stemmed from him making secret payments to Lincoln senior officer Conner Gilmore. These subtle bribes served as the motivation behind Gilmore's repeated practice of entering falsified information into Lincoln's books. Additional wire fraud charges were imposed on Fedora from those illegal bribes paid to Gilmore. Gilmore, within days of being hired, was immediately placed on Lincoln's board of directors. His primary purpose at the bank was to expand Lincoln's foreign exchange trading capacity. A payment of $100,000 suddenly appeared into Gilmore's account located in a Swiss bank owned and controlled by Fedora. Gilmore was then permitted to speculate freely in foreign currency for his own benefit, with a guarantee against losses from Fedora. Gilmore netted gains of $476,000 which were deposited into his own personal Swiss accounts and then wired to Lincoln. He then sent these funds on to accounts he owned in Montreal, Canada.

Novelli further testified that Gilmore, who was bribed by Fedora, faithfully did as he was instructed. He documented fictitious foreign exchange transactions in order to demonstrate Lincoln's profits.

Because of these actions, Fedora was further charged with causing false entries (through his bribes to Gilmore) to be made in Franklin's books, reports and statements. These falsified documents concealed $30 million in foreign-exchange losses through the illusion of profits in other fabricated foreign-exchange transactions. These falsified statements of Lincoln were then submitted to other United States financial institutions in order to obtain loans and extensions of credit to Lincoln amounting to $35 million.

Detective Francis Clavering carefully watched the defense's cross-examination of Nico Novelli. Even though they were batting for the other team, he took great satisfaction in knowing that Novelli's treachery would not remain hidden from the public, even if it did hurt the credibility of the prosecution's key witness. The defense demonstrated that Novelli was by his own admission a liar and a cheat of the highest order. While Novelli and Gilmore lined their own pockets with accumulated and embezzled wealth, Fedora lost millions. The defense then continued to chip away at the integrity of Novelli by bringing up his eight hour, lie infested testimony to the Securities and Exchange Commission a few years back. Stein then brought up the fact that Novelli continued to work for and with Fedora after falsely accusing him of raping his wife in December of 1973. What man in his right mind does that? The accusations were part of an ill-fated plot to extort money from the defendant. Novelli was asked point blank if he hated Fedora, and that was the reason for him to bear false witness against his former business partner and employer. Novelli responded with an emphatic "no", and then was suddenly overwhelmed by his emotions that sent the trial into recess for the evening, much earlier than had originally been planned.

Prior to the start of the trial, Stein had every intention of calling Fedora to take the witness stand in his own defense. That idea was promptly scrapped once counsel and the courtroom learned of Fedora's fake kidnapping scheme. The prosecution repeatedly hammered the defense on the abduction hoax, and Fedora's defensive counsel was unable to successfully recover from that point forward. As much as the defense wanted to blame the Vatican's last minute nixing of key witness testimony, the most damaging blow to their case was a result of Fedora's own stupidity and pomposity in action. Fedora was charged with perjury as his lies to the United States Securities and Exchange Commission were exposed. Charges of wire and mail fraud came from his manipulative scheme with respect to the purchase and sale of Lincoln stock. Prior to the prosecution resting its case, D.A. Christopherson added a few new charges of perjury, bail-jumping and falsifying a kidnapping stemming from Fedora's abduction escapade.

The prosecution then tried to seal the deal on their case by presenting suppressed evidence. Financial statements were presented to the judge and jury, however, the federal lawyers failed to properly explain the significance to their case against Fedora. Stein did his best to object to the admission of the evidence in a last stitch effort to protect his client. The objections were denied, and the defense counsel was subjected to rude, volatile reprimands by the presiding judge. Stein demanded a public apology from the judge, but none came. As Stein was further degraded while doing his professional duty, the contrast in treatment of the US Government's counsel versus the defense's became absolutely blatant. The bias in treatment by the presiding judge caused Stein to enter a motion for mistrial. The motion was denied.

The prosecution finally presented their closing arguments for their case. "This case is about Lincoln National Bank. This case is about rampant conduct of the most fraudulent order. It's about deceptive corruption and a most extreme criminal use of power. It is our hope as prosecutors that we have demonstrated to the men and women of the jury that Mr. Fedora, at the time of his purchase of Lincoln National Bank, used funds illegally obtained from his own and other Swiss and Italian banks. Mr. Fedora then embezzled money, misapplied Lincoln National Bank's funds, and finally falsified bank earnings reports to cover up his criminal actions." The chief attorney for the United States then turned so he could address both the judge and jury. "Your Honor, the prosecution rests."

The case was then passed into the hands of members of the jury. As they deliberated, Giovanni Fedora pondered the current situation. Things did not have to be this way. His mind drifted back to a point before the trial began, when Fedora was offered a plea deal. All he had to do is plead guilty to a single count, and the remaining counts would have been dropped. He'd be looking at a maximum sentence of about two years. In exchange for the court's leniency all he needed to do was provide testimony against the man who had just delivered closing arguments for the Federal Government's case against him. In the defendant's mind, the government was the true criminal Mafia in the United States.

It was a tempting offer, but nothing that ever remotely interested the Italian banker. As far as he was concerned, the charges against him were wrong. The money he used to purchase Lincoln National Bank was his, and he had proof. The deposits that he placed into Marco Ansios' subsidiary bank were not fiduciary at all. Even the late Italian liquidator Arturo Bartolone included that fact in his sworn deposition. Bartolone also reported that Fedora's Milan bank was already in the process of repaying the funds legitimately loaned to him so he could purchase the New York bank in Manhattan. He was absolutely certain that no one would believe anything an admitted liar like Nico Novelli had to say against his former business partner and boss. Giovanni Fedora was wrong.

The court decided to dismiss only three of the many counts against Mr. Fedora. At the conclusion of the six week trial, the jury went into deliberations for six days. At 11:00 AM on March 27, 1980, Mr. Giovanni Fedora stood dressed in his jail jumpsuit and handcuffs as the foreman stood, vocally cleared his throat and then read the jury's verdict.

"The men and women of this jury find the defendant guilty on all sixty-four of the original charges except one, and all three of the new charges stemming from his kidnapping hoax in October, 1979."

The presiding judge then began to speak. "I'd like to thank the men and women of the jury for their hard work over the last several weeks. Mr. Giovanni Fedora has been found guilty by a jury of his peers on sixty-seven counts of fraud, conspiracy, perjury, falsifying bank statements and misappropriation of funds. Sentencing will be scheduled for May 15, 1980 at 10:00 AM. While Mr. Fedora awaits his sentencing, he is to remain in the custody of the Metropolitan Correctional Center until that day and time." The judge then rapped his gavel hard on its sounding block.

Detective Francis Clavering couldn't help but smile after the verdict was read aloud. He hugged and kissed his wife in a personal, private celebration of victory. All of his and Lance's hard work here, and assistance from Cosimo, Hans and others had finally led to justice finally being served to a man who truly deserved it. He had some mixed feelings when he learned that Mr. Fedora was no longer the newest resident at the Metropolitan Correctional Center of Manhattan. Another Southern District of New York judge had sentenced Nico Novelli to seven years in prison and a fine of $20,000 for his own crimes. Novelli was then entered into a classified location within the Witness Protection Unit on the third floor of the downtown Manhattan correctional facility. Clavering understood the leniency that came from his accepting the plea deal offered by the prosecution in Fedora's case, but he didn't like it one bit.

Francis Clavering kissed his wife one more time as they left the federal courthouse, before he headed back to his office. Upon his arrival, he took to the phone immediately. His first call was to his Italian counterpart Cosimo Angelo in Rome. He then called Hans Kruck over in Munich. His final call was to Cardinal Dante Leone in Florence. He then grabbed his jacket from the coatrack and left his office. The final announcement, he decided to make in person. He entered the office chamber of Cardinal Charles Wexford with a proud, beaming smile on his face.

"Good afternoon Francis! It looks like someone has some good news."

The smile remained as the detective responded. "I do sir! I just had to come over here and tell you personally! Mr. Giovanni Fedora was just convicted of all but one of the counts we had against him!"

"Praise God Almighty! That IS some great news Francis! I can't even begin to tell you how impressed, and proud I am of you and your team of men."

"Well thank you cardinal, I appreciate that but in all honesty, my team consists of men like you and Cardinal Leone too. You contributed greatly to our work." Fran got really quiet. "Cardinal Riluciani contributed the most. God rest his beautiful soul."

Both men crossed themselves, then Wexford spoke again. "Believe me Francis, we tried so hard, for so many years to get rid of the cancers in this church with no success to show for it...then one day, after many many hours of prayer, you show up out of the blue to my office, and a few years after that, here we sit, while Giovanni Fedora sits in a jail cell across town. Thank you, for everything you've done!"

"Well.." Fran blushed a little, "I hate to break this to you cardinal... but you, Cardinal Leone and the late Holy Father are part of our team. We could not have done any of this without the help of the truly holy men of this church, so we thank you too!"

Cardinal Wexford just smiled. "Honestly, I can't believe we got him convicted. Here in the US of all places."

"Oh, we aren't done. The only thing we have left now for Fedora is his sentencing which will be in about six weeks. After that, he will be shipped off to Italy so they can take a crack at him."

"Amazing!"

"Oh, and we are also still investigating Marco Ansios and trying to figure out a way to get to that dirty bishop ya got taking up space in that Vatican Bank."

"I have no doubt in the future of your success, Francis. I will continue to pray for you and your men."

"Thank you. Please pray for all of us, sir. Including you and Cardinal Leone. We still have a lot of work to do."

"No doubt about it, but that doesn't mean we can't celebrate how far we've already come on this journey."

For the next forty nine days, word of Fedora's conviction traveled like a wildfire out of control. Borders and oceans didn't even begin to slow it down. Media sources of all modes profited handsomely as they continued to fan the flames in the direction that bloated their profits best. They needed to keep the story in the forefront of the world's mind while they waited for the day his sentence would be handed down by the judge.

On the ninth floor of the downtown Manhattan Metropolitan Correctional Center, Giovanni Fedora sat alone in his cell with nothing but his thoughts. He knew that the United States Justice System was about to sentence him, and wash their hands of him within the next two days. After that he would be handed over to the goons of the Italian Justice system for more of the same. Fears for the future that awaited him upon his return to Italy were overwhelming. No sleep would find him, as anxious thoughts raced unrelenting through his head. The clock in his cell displayed 2:45 AM. He got up from his bunk to take a piss. As he washed his hands, he looked at his tormented, God forsaken reflection in the polished metallic mirror in front of him. His hair was disheveled and the dark circles beneath his eyes were well pronounced features. He ran his hands over the salt and pepper stubble that accented his face, while more thoughts permeated his mind. He returned to his bunk and carefully removed the sharp new blade from the disposable plastic safety razor that he was issued earlier the prior day, and laid it aside. He swallowed hard multiple times, making a face at the overwhelmingly bitterness that remained on his tongue. Then softly uttered to himself, "I hope my family will forgive me."

Five days after his sixtieth birthday, he drew the blade firmly across his left wrist, then his right. He watched as the dark blood began to flow from his veins into a wastepaper basket. Minutes later, a guard passed by his cell on his hourly headcount rounds. He saw Fedora seated on the edge of his bed holding his hands, mesmerized by the sight of his own blood flowing out of his wrists and into the trash can. The guard fumbled frantically trying to find his key to unlock the door to Fedora's cell, while he radioed for help. As the door to the cell finally swung open, Fedora slumped over unconscious in his bed. Staff members transported him immediately to the prison infirmary, as his condition continued to deteriorate. An ambulance was dispatched to take him to the New York Infirmary at the Beekman Downtown Hospital. En route to the hospital, Fedora's heart stopped.

CHAPTER 55

The world seemed to have stopped spinning for Giovanni Fedora since day one of his trial. For those who had a long history of association with the failed banker, however, time continued to march on unimpeded. Gherado Fratello continued his work with the dictatorial regimes of South America in a way that bordered on evil madness. As he sat in his remote office in Italy, he was keeping tabs on the Fedora trial in New York through the Italian press and his P2 sources scattered throughout the eastern United States. For the moment, there wasn't much that could be done. Help would have to wait until the trial was over.

Since he already had his attention focused on the United States, it was time for him to subtly address one of the glaring problems going on there named President Jimmy Carter. Fratello began to work closely in conjunction with the Republican National Committee to elect a more suitable man to reside at 1600 Pennsylvania Avenue, Washington, DC. Former Hollywood actor and California state governor Ronald Reagan was a more suitable man for the presidency of the United States of America, in his not so humble opinion. Fratello employed his network of P2 men from television, radio, newspapers and magazines globally. Especially in Italy.

Fratello's office phone rang. He lowered the newspaper in his hands and reached for the handset. "Hello?"

It was one of his many press sources in New York on the other end of the line. He was talking fast, and he was talking nonsense. "Fratello, it's Fedora! He's attempted suicide in his cell!"

It took a minute for the words to register in the P2 leader's head. "What? Slow the hell down! Where? When?"

"A guard found him in his cell this morning a little after 3 AM with his wrists slashed." The man frantically reported.

"Slashed his wrists? That's odd. Such a barbaric way to end things. Why didn't he just use the digitalis issued to him when he joined the lodge?"

"I don't know?"

"Where is he now?"

"Last I heard he was transported to the Beekman Downtown Hospital."

"Then he must be still alive!"

"I haven't heard officially that he has died, yet."

"Interesting,...well keep tabs on the situation, and let me know right away if anything changes!"

"Will do, sir!"

Paramedics followed by Emergency Room staff began Cardiopulmonary Resuscitation on Mr. Fedora immediately. They were persistent in their efforts to revive the sixty year old failed Italian banker. It took several hours for them to successfully stabilize his cardiac rhythm. And admit Fedora to the hospital where he remained in critical condition. His precarious state of health had nothing to do with what physicians described as the "simple lacerations" found on bilateral wrists, and everything to do with some mysterious cardiac issues. His prognosis was bleak at best. Death was waiting patiently for him just outside the door to his hospital room.

Medical professionals continued to scratch their heads. For a man his age, he was in great health. He'd never had any sort of heart problems ever in his life. It was clear to attending doctors that his presenting grave condition was not due to the slashing of his wrists with a blade from his safety razor. Something else was going on here.

Three days later, a hospital spokesman held a press conference. Fedora's condition was deteriorating. For the moment, he remained in critical, yet unstable condition. It was clear that he had no desire to continue living on this planet. He refused to help the medical personnel working so hard to keep him alive. He refused to cooperate when he was conscious. He refused to tell them what medications he took prior to cutting his wrists. For the time being Fedora remained in critical, yet unstable condition.

As the hospital spokesman was wrapping up his portion of the press conference, and preparing to take questions from the journalists that had gathered, he suddenly stopped speaking as he heard distinctive alert tones come over the hospital public address system, followed by a calm clear voice. "Code Blue room 463 ICU... Code Blue room 463 ICU." A sudden look of panic came over the spokesman, as it registered in his brain that Giovanni Fedora had now flat-lined upstairs in his ICU bed. "I'm sorry, I have to go now. We will issue more information as we get it. Thank you." He gathered all of his notes, and ran back into the hospital and straight for the stairwell. He skipped every other step as he climbed up level after level of stairs arriving finally in the ICU located on the hospital's fourth floor.

There was a lot of loud, busy commotion going on all around Giovanni Fedora, but it sounded like it was far off. "Hmmm," he thought to himself, "they must be working on another patient nearby." Suddenly he was surrounded by absolute silence. He was surrounded by a darkness like he'd never seen before. He consciously tried to blink his eyes several times hoping they would quickly adjust to the darkness that consumed him. He held his arms out around him, hoping to feel for a wall or anything. He took a few steps into the emptiness and still felt nothing. He could hear the echo of his footsteps like he was walking on dark cobblestones down a long dark tunnel. He could hardly see anything in front of him. His hands guided his movement forward. Suddenly he came upon a vision of his wife and three children. They were fearful and full of an overwhelming sorrow deep in their hearts. He recognized the form of his daughter as she began to speak. "Papa, please don't leave. You must stay. Please come back. For us, for your grandchildren, for yourself, you must come back. You must fight." As the words of his family continued to echo, Fedora felt himself being pulled quickly and forcefully back through the dark dank tunnel from which he had just come. Suddenly, he opened his eyes and gasped, forcing a huge volume of air to fill his lungs.

"We have a heartbeat!" He heard a man shout, confused by what was happening all around him. When hospital staff stabilized him once again, he remembered the vision of his family coming to him as the end loomed near. He knew they were right, he had faced and survived far more adversity in his life than this. His stubbornness morphed into a more cooperative state. He revealed to the medical staff that prior to slashing his own wrists, he had ingested four bottles of digitalis and ninety benzodiazepine pills.

As hospital staff worked diligently to administer a proper antidote to Mr. Fedora. People who were intimately involved in his criminal trial were immediately updated. They exhaled audibly when they heard the news. All parties involved were relieved to finally hear some optimistic news regarding Fedora's condition. Judge and counsel from both sides once again began to look towards the future in preparation for Fedora's sentencing.

Fran called Cosimo and updated him on Fedora's condition. "He's not quite out of the woods yet, but he's better than he's ever been since they drug his ass into that hospital. It's looking like he's going to make it!"

"That is great to hear, Fran!"

"I agree. But I must admit that I'm getting tired of this son of a bitch's dramatic bullshit."

"Yeah he certainly knows how to wear folks like us out, doesn't he?" Cosimo chuckled. "First the kidnapping hoax bullshit, now digitalis and benzos. I'm afraid to ask what's next."

"No doubt." Fran agreed, then expressed the thoughts going through his head aloud. "For the life of me, I can't figure out how the hell he managed to get access to those drugs. Especially in quantities like that. The security maintained at the MCC is tighter than a drum."

"Digitalis isn't really all that surprising, now that I think about it."

"Four bottles doesn't surprise you?"

"Mmmmm, I suppose it depends on the size of the bottles, maybe. But not that particular poisoning agent."

"Why's that?"

"You said Fedora's been in close association with Gherado Fratello for a while, right?"

"Yeah..."

"...and even more so since just before his financial empire began to crumble, right?"

"That's right."

"I'd bet you money he's one of Fratello's P2 men now, especially now that Krivis and Ansios are no longer interested in helping him. He's only got the Mafia and P2 left to help him now." Cosimo continued to think out loud.

"I'm sorry Cosimo, you've lost me."

"Don't you remember? That time when Novelli was telling us about his days when he was involved with P2?"

Fran physically convulsed slightly as the sound of Novelli's name reverberated in his ears like nails drug across a chalkboard. "What?"

"You don't remember Novelli telling us that all P2 members were required to carry a lethal dose of digitalis on their person at all times? It's their ultimate insurance measure should any of them suddenly find themselves in a situation where they were being forced to divulge secrets critical to the operations of their organization."

"I'd completely forgotten about that."

The two men brainstormed how difficult it would be to smuggle four bottles of digitalis into the MCC in downtown Manhattan. The two men recalled the last time they had a discussion that involved digitalis and Fedora. That was shortly after the death of Chiaros Riluciani. As the conversation progressed, the two detectives agreed that getting the drug through the security in place at the MCC would be far more difficult than getting it into the papal apartments in late September back in 1978.

After a consultation with Fedora's attending physicians, the judge presiding over Fedora's trial felt comfortable with rescheduling his sentencing just shy of four weeks in the future. Fedora continued to improve, and he was growing stronger with each passing day. Finally the morning of June 13, 1980 arrived.

The judge met privately with the defendant prior to sentencing him. Once again he was dressed in his prison jumpsuit and handcuffs. "Mr. Fedora, do you have any desire or willingness to make any sort of restitution for your criminal actions?"

Fedora just sat, completely unmoved by the question. He refused to make any sort of eye contact with the man who held his fate in his hands. He raised his head enough to look out the window, before issuing his cold, simple response. "No."

The judge looked upon the man seated before him, only slightly surprised by his answer. "Very well then, I have made my decision."

The two men returned to the overcrowded courtroom. He rapped on his gavel a couple of times to silence all of the chatter that had reached a crescendo when they reentered the courtroom. Once order was restored, the judge began to speak. "Mr. Fedora, please stand." Fedora came to his feet, as the sound of his handcuffs clamoring against the armrests of his wooden chair punctuated his efforts. He stood there before his accusers, and before the public completely emotionless, as the judge proceeded to speak. "Ladies and Gentlemen, before you stands Mr. Giovanni Fedora. A man who through his life has no doubt achieved impressive status in the business world, and certainly on the global business stage. He used his elevated status for criminal purpose and personal gain with absolute lack of any remorse what-so-ever. I hereby sentence Giovanni Fedora to three twenty-five-year prison terms, and one twenty-four year term, to be served concurrently. You are hereby fined $207,000 and the costs incurred by the prosecution." The judge rapped his gavel hard on the sounding block. Fedora turned slightly towards his daughter and issued a slight smile before a jail guard approached him to escort him away.

The prosecuting attorney for the US Southern District of New York spoke to the press soon afterward. "I believe this is the most severe sentence ever handed down for any sort of white-collar crime. It is a demonstration that those who willingly commit these types of crimes, even if the perpetrators are rich and powerful, they will be caught and vigorously prosecuted to the fullest extent of the law."

Later that day, Fedora's attorneys issued the defense's response to his sentence. Fedora's reign of power was now officially over. Sympathy only came from his closest family members. It was as if overnight, nobody in the world seemed to give a damn about the man who once dominated and at times even controlled much of the global financial world.

CHAPTER 56

It was a surreal day for the men in blue at the New York City Police Department. It was also a day that no one thought would ever come. Everybody who had ever worked with D.A. Paul Christopherson was pretty sure that the man would remain in his position until his dying day. That certainly was his intention, but health issues began to take a greater toll on his ability to do his job effectively. He was too much of a professional to proceed in his life's work, with less than satisfactory results. It was time for him to hang it all up. He had announced months ago that he intended to retire once the Giovanni Fedora trial was officially over. Within a few days following the sentencing of Fedora, he would leave it all behind for good.

Detective Francis Clavering, could feel the loss looming as the epic era of D.A. Christopherson came to an end. Fran thought back to the early days of the Luca Benedetto case. They sure had been through a lot together over the years. He shifted uncomfortably as he remembered the lies he and his boss told him so many years ago, just to follow a gut feeling. There was nothing he hated more than a liar. Christopherson held the same sentiment. He wanted so badly to get the deception off of his chest. He was running out of chances to do so, but he refrained. He didn't want the man whom he loved and respected so dearly to occupy his final day of work chewing his ass out over something that happened so long ago, even if the ass chewing was well deserved. The thought of Christopherson's disappointment in him as a person and as a professional was something he just could not bear. He held way too much respect for the man. Fran's confession would have to wait for another, more appropriate time.

Fran issued a smile and a slight chuckle as he remembered the day he walked into Luca Benedetto's disgusting headquarters, Frankie's Lounge to serve him Christopherson's subpoena. Pouring that mug of beer all over the bar top, leaving the mug upside down in a puddle, then slapping the document into the hand of the raging Mafia gangster whose head was about to explode. All the years that Christopherson through Bentley gave him liberty to play off his hunches, no matter how insane they seemed at the time. Fran would never consider trading in a single minute. There certainly were a lot of moments filled with intense drama, below the belt laughs, demoralizing frustration, absolute heartbreak, and fulfilling satisfaction. No one could have predicted all the twists and turns of the last several years. The dead ends and brilliant breakthroughs all led to the termination of Fedora's criminal career, followed shortly by his own professional one. There would never be a more appropriate, impressive or satisfying time for him to ride off into the sunset.

Christopherson called Fran to his office one last time. As Clavering entered the room, the gravity of the moment hit him hard. He wanted to cry, but fought back the emotions flooding his mind as he caught sight of all of the boxes packed and stacked so neatly beside the D.A.'s desk. The walls, shelves and desk top were all bare, empty of all of the memorabilia, honors, and mementos that had been awarded to Christopherson over his many years as district attorney. Christopherson welcomed him in and gestured for him to close the door behind him. Christopherson got up from the large brown leather chair and moved from behind his desk. He reached out his arms and gave Fran a big bear hug in a rare show of emotion. The embrace was followed by expressions of gratitude for all of their accomplishments, a few regrets for the things that didn't quite work out as planned and the few things that had to remain unfinished. He was proud of his detective's work ethic, especially his perseverance in the Vatican matter. He was most impressed that Fran never once went about his work in order to feed his own ego. He did what he did because it was the right thing to do. He didn't feel the need to take credit for his successes, only his mistakes. He preferred to work in the shadows. His secret work with the men in Germany and Italy, investigating crimes involving the Vatican, were perfect examples of that. The two men returned to their respective seats, and continued to talk.

"Francis, I just want you to know that I wish we could keep the 'Rackets' team intact. The quantity and quality of work done was far beyond anyone's expectation. It was an experimental situation from the start whose time has run its course. With me leaving now, I'm sure whoever fills my shoes will have their own ideas to contribute to how they want to run this department."

Fran didn't like what he was hearing, but there wasn't a damn thing he could say or do about it. "I understand sir."

"That said, this department no longer has room for you, I'm afraid. The department only allows us three sergeants, and there aren't any openings at this time."

Fran nodded without the words registering. "I know that too, sir."

"Listen Francis, I want to assure you that you will end up in the right place, to serve the department and public in the best way possible."

"I appreciate that sir."

"How's your old uniform fitting these days?"

Fran was completely caught off guard by the question. "Um, ah, they fit just fine sir."

"Good! So the bad news is that you will need to return to uniformed duty for the next six months."

"If that's my new assignment sir, so be it." Fran was unsure exactly where this conversation was headed. "But I must ask why?"

"Give me a second, I'm getting to that. You're being reassigned to work with Ralph Lynch."

"Ralph Lynch? I've never heard of him sir."

"I'd be surprised if you had. You've been a very busy man, and so has he. He's been working hard as special counsel investigating corruption within the NYPD. Governor Carey has just appointed him D.A. for Queens County to replace the corrupt D.A. over there that has just been arrested. Lynch is a good man, I know you are going to like him. He actually came to me a few weeks ago, in search of competent, incorruptible men with solid experience. Of course your name immediately came to mind."

"Thank you sir."

"He needs you to establish and run a rag-tag team of investigators for him once your six months in uniform is over. There's only one thing..."

"What's that?"

"It's a sergeant's position Francis."

"But sir, I'm not a sergeant."

"You are now, son! Congratulations!" Christopherson pulled open a desk drawer to retrieve several sets of sergeant's chevrons and documents from an otherwise empty drawer and handed them to his detective with the proudest of smiles.

Fran never saw the promotion coming as he stood there overwhelmed and beaming with pride. "Wow, really?! I can't believe it sir. This has to be the best possible going away gift you could have ever given me, sir."

"Bah...it's not because of me Francis, it's because of all of your hard work over these last several years. It also helps that you passed the Sergeant's Exam a while back with the highest score ever recorded!"

"I did? Wow, honestly, I've been so busy, I almost forgot that I took the damn thing. Thank you sir! I will wear these stripes with honor and pride!"

"I have no doubt that you will. Now get out there and get some work done!"

"Will do, sir. I will do everything in my power to make you proud, sir!"

"You already have, son! It has been an honor to work with you, detective!"

"The honor is all mine, sir. I hope you have a great retirement, you deserve nothing but the best sir! Go kiss all those grandbabies!"

Nobody in the Manhattan NYPD could argue against the promotion of Detective Clavering to Sergeant. Of all of the men in the department, none were more deserving. However, none of them were excited to see him leave their precinct for Queens. It didn't matter that the entire rackets team was now being disbanded and their skills and talents distributed to new assignments in other stations and precincts in the area and beyond. It wasn't just Christopherson who was having a surreal day.

Clavering had to get used to wearing blue starched shirts and ties once again, after all of the years of more casual attire. He had to admit, he looked good in stripes, even if he hated wearing the starch and tie. He reported for his new assignment with the 102nd precinct located in Queens. He looked forward to November when he could ditch the street gig and get back to the detective work he loved so much. The street beat quickly had him missing his days of fighting organized crime, the six month wait would be worth it in the end. The next time he would work in a detective's division, he'd take on the role of a sergeant in charge within the office of the new Queens district attorney.

Six weeks into his new street assignment he got a call from Bentley. The grand jury had completed all of their remaining work connected to the Fedora case, and an official press conference had been called in connection to the Fedora's kidnapping hoax. Since Clavering's hard work had been so instrumental in the case, Bentley wanted Clavering featured on the platform at the time of the announcement of new indictments. Fran hated the spotlight, but because it was Christopherson's final ride, he could not say no.

Fran arrived an hour before the press was to show up. Everyone was there: Inspector Bentley, Assistant DA Walter Thomas, FBI Detective Lance Erickson and his Federal Prosecutor of a boss

Nathan Bayer. Sgt. Clavering caught Bayer's eye as he arrived. He motioned to the sergeant to come over to him.

Bayer knew of the connections that Fedora had with the Vatican. The fact that prominent men of the Vatican were unable to come to Fedora's defense failed to diminish the public's fascination with the subject. As Clavering approached Bayer, he was pulled in closer to have a private conversation. "Detective, I'm sorry, I mean Sergeant, there is something very important that I need to say to you before this press conference kicks off."

"Yeah?" Clavering was not interested in anything Bayer had to say to him. He had already lost all respect for him after he hijacked the trip to the Vatican to confront Krivis so many years ago. It was a stunt that was unforgivable as far as the sergeant was concerned.

"Under no condition..." Bayer ordered. "Are you to talk to reporters at any point in time. There will be no mention whatsoever of Fedora's involvement with the Vatican. Do you understand?"

Fran could not believe the stones on this clown. He just sneered at him, with much disdain. "You aren't my boss Nathan. I will talk to whoever I want." Fran then turned and walked away.

Fran had no intentions of talking to the press anyway, but that fact had nothing to do with any sort of directive that came from a shithead like Bayer. Even though he was now retired, as far as Fran was concerned, this was still part of Christopherson's final moment in the spotlight.

As the press conference went on, Fran stood at the rear next to his former partner FBI Agent Lance Erickson. As the two of them stood and listened to the words of Bentley and Christopherson, Fran took great personal pride in knowing that justice had been truly served in the Fedora case. Bentley then shifted away from their announcements to take questions from the press. Not a word regarding the Vatican was mentioned. Fran was relieved when all of the drama was finally over. He was ready to get back to Queens. He was ready to get back to work. He shook Lance's hand and bid him farewell. "Don't be a stranger, my man!"

As he was starting to leave, one of the other detectives formerly from Christopherson's office ran towards him. "Hey Fran?"

Fran turned to see who was calling him. "Oh hey Jordan, how the hell are you? Damn, it's been a while, hasn't it! Where do they have you working these days?" Fran reached out to shake the man's hand.

"I'm great, thanks! Yeah, they moved me over to the Bronx for now."

"That's great to hear, Jordan. You're going to kick some ass over there, I'm sure of it."

The man was a little embarrassed by the remark. "I hope so..."

"Of course you will Jordan, I'm certain of it."

"Well thank you. Hey Fran, I was wondering if you wouldn't mind doing me a favor?"

"For you, of course! What do you need?"

"I got a friend of mine who's a reporter for the *Wall Street Journal* here. He's been following the Fedora situation, and he has a few questions. Would you mind talking to him?"

"Sure, no problem. I'd be happy to."

Jordan brought the man over and briefly introduced the two men and then departed. "Thank you for taking some time to speak to me today, Sergeant."

"It's my pleasure."

The reporter's questions were focused on the surveillance work and maneuvering around language barriers more than anything. Fran simply stated that he had a lot of help from colleagues in Europe to assist him with his work and left it at that. There was never a mention of the Vatican at all. There was nothing in that conversation that would cause Bayer to lose his shit. Fran was relieved to finally turn the page, and never deal with Bayer ever again.

He stopped in at his favorite diner on his way to work for some breakfast. One of the regulars tossed him a section of a newspaper, folded to display the article. "It looks like you made the paper this morning, Fran." Mentioned the man patting him on the back as he was leaving.

Fran read the article in silence as he dipped his toast into the runny yolks of his eggs, and washed it all down with occasional sips of his coffee. "What the actual hell is all of this?" He muttered to himself under his breath.

The story appeared in the *Wall Street Journal* with quotes from Fran about his surveillance work in the Fedora case. The article then shifted gears and went on full of rhetorical comments like, "It remains unclear why federal prosecutors like Nathan Bayer have failed to investigate Fedora's connections to the Vatican. Our own sources close to the investigation in Europe have confirmed that a high ranking man of the cloth within the Vatican has been a suspected accomplice in Fedora's crimes now for many years."

Fran had barely reached the desk in his new precinct in Queens before the federal attorney was on the line yelling at him. "Goddamn it, Clavering! I told you not to talk to reporters, you son of a bitch!"

"Oh shove it up your ass, Nathan! You can tell me whatever the fuck you like, but you aren't my boss! I don't answer to you. That reporter asked me some legit questions. He never once brought up you, or the Vatican."

"Do you have any idea what your bullshit in this article is going to cost me?!" Bayer was absolutely livid as he continued his tirade.

Fran had heard enough. "I will say it again. I did not talk to him about any of the shit you're ranting about Nathan! None of it, I have no idea where he got that information from, but it wasn't from me, so fuck the hell off already!"

"I only have one more thing to say to you, Francis Clavering! Let me be very clear, you will never get out of that uniform again, that I can promise you. You hear me? You will spend the rest of your Goddamn days in that fucking uniform!" Then the line went dead.

Fran slammed down the handset on the phone. It took a while for him to calm himself after the call was terminated. He was never one to hide behind the protections provided him by men like Bentley or Christopherson in the past. But things were very different now. He was now in a new precinct, with a new crew. No one knew him well enough yet to fight off Bayer or at least have the sergeant's back at the moment.

A few weeks passed, and Fran had forgotten about the whole dust up with Bayer. He went about his business as he always did, with great professionalism and integrity. One afternoon, Fran was summonsed to DA Ralph Lynch's office. "Good afternoon Francis."

"Good afternoon Sir."

"I called you in today to discuss your future position within our department."

"Yes sir!" Fran was having a hard time containing his excitement.

"I have decided that I'm going to select another sergeant to head up my organized crime investigation division. For now I'm going to need you to remain on the beat. I'm sorry."

Fran's heart sank. He didn't even know how to respond other than to say that he appreciated even being considered for the assignment. His words were empty. He was no career beat cop. He was a highly decorated detective with numerous awards for his work with the Manhattan Precinct. His talents and skills were being wasted working the street beat writing parking tickets, busting dope pushers, junkies and street thugs. Fran finished up his shift, and swung by Bentley's office before heading home. Bentley knew something was wrong as soon as he saw Fran.

Fran explained everything that had happened since the day of the press conference. "Listen Bentley, I don't expect you to intervene in my situation. I'm not here for that at all. All I want to know is if you can some how find out if Bayer is the reason why Lynch is denying me the position?"

"I will see what I can do Fran. And if it helps a little, he's making a big mistake passing you over. He will live to regret that, believe me."

"I appreciate that." The compliment did little to lift the sergeant's spirits.

"For now get on out of here, I will be in touch as soon as I find out anything."

"Thank you sir."

It took a few days for Bentley to get back to his former detective. The news was not good. The inspector found out that Nathan Bayer had been close friends with Ralph Lynch for years. A little digging uncovered a conversation between Bayer and Lynch where Bayer advised the new district attorney assigned to Queens that he'd be making a huge critical mistake if he place Francis Clavering in charge of his organized crime division. "Clavering has a big mouth, he likes to talk to the press."

The heaviness of defeat weighed on him as he went about his work. He had poured his soul into his profession, only to be done in by an incompetent piece of shit like Nathan Bayer. He didn't know what his future would entail, but he'd quit before serving the remainder of his career as a beat cop. He started to discuss his options with Peg. She was sympathetic to his situation, comforting him as best she could. She suggested private security work, but that was of no interest to him.

"How about private investigative work Fran?" She suggested. "It's what you love most, besides, you're really good at it."

He liked the idea a little better. "Mmmm, maybe. Let me think about it."

"You know the best part about private work, don't you?"

"What's that?"

"You will never have to deal with that asshole Bayer ever again, Fran."

Fran was shocked to hear his wife curse. She did have a point. Private work would certainly have less bullshit bureaucracy to deal with. "We will see. I'll think about it."

One depressing day followed another. Peg was beginning to worry about the man she loved. She wanted the old version of her husband back. She missed the end of the day recaps shared during intimate moments between the two of them. Something had to change, somehow. She could not live with him like this until the day he retired.

She heard his car pull into the drive. She steadied herself for the evening ahead, not at all looking forward to him in his depressed state. He startled her as he burst through the door talking fast and full of excitement. He had the biggest smile she'd seen on his face in weeks.

"Honey, I love you so much! You're never going to believe this!" He lifted her in his arms and swung her around as he kissed her repeatedly. "We're moving to Italy!"

CHAPTER 57

On the American side of the Atlantic, the US Government finally concluded their dealings with convicted financial fraudster Giovanni Fedora. Despite all of the times he had helped men like Krivis, his directors, and Ansios over the years, there were no lifelines coming his way from any of them. Their betrayal was understood, yet painful nonetheless. They were only slightly better off than he was at the moment. The only good news that came out of Milan was that Fedora's true betrayer, Nico Novelli was finally extradited on a warrant that had been on the books for five years. He was now facing conspiracy charges of his own. His plea deal arrangements in the United States would do absolutely nothing for him now in Italy. It would be the only time Fedora would be in agreement with the Italian prosecutors and legal system.

As both the court of appeals and Supreme Court of the United States denied his requests for a retrial, Giovanni Fedora was out of options in the American Courts. Fedora was soon moved to a federal prison facility located in Springfield, Missouri. During the first several weeks of his incarceration there, he remained in frequent contact with Gherado Fratello. His Mafia family from New York was now distant and not as easily accessible as they had been when he was in the MCC. There would be no relaying of information between them through the various inmates that would come and go from the facility. Fratello was now the only person to remain steadfast by his side. Loyalties such as those from a man like Fratello never came without a price.

The chilly weather of mid-fall began to grip the midwestern states. The people of the United States had decided that they had had enough of President Jimmy Carter's policies and administration after only four years. On November 4, 1980, former Hollywood actor and California Governor Ronald Reagan was elected to become the 49th President of the United States. Gherado Fratello continued to build his close working relationship with the newly elected President. His strategy was working better than he could have hoped as he had received an invitation to be among the honored guests at the Reagan inauguration on January 20, 1981 in Washington, DC. Fedora wished to capitalize on the relatively new friendship between the two men. Now that his convictions in association with the Lincoln National Bank failure had been confirmed in the American courts, Giovanni Fedora asked Fratello if he could arrange a meeting between him and the soon to be installed President.

In Italy, there were also new government leaders from the 1980 autumn election to contend with. Prime Minister Arnaldo Forlani and his administration were members of the right-wing Christian Democracy Party. A newly appointed magistrate went to work right away in Milan, Italy. He had only been on the job for a few weeks before he became perplexed and concerned. For the life of him, he could not figure out why the wheels of justice had been turning so damn slowly for so damn long. There had been absolutely no action taken on information from the 1978 investigative reports issued by the Bank of Italy's Financial Police. The Italian justice system had decided to sit on the information for two years, despite the scandalous details revealed in the records. There was certainly more than enough evidence presented to warrant immediate action. The magistrate ordered Marco Ansios to immediately surrender his passport. Further action and criminal charges would soon follow.

Ansios wasn't the only man in the magistrate's cross hairs. This new prime minister was on a hell bent mission to root out corruption in all areas of the Italian government. This change in leaders was especially bad news for the men in Vatican City. While government officials couldn't do anything about the debauchery among various members of the clergy, two of Bishop Jonas Krivis' high ranking Vatican Bank directors were not men of the cloth. Both men soon found themselves in the custody of Roman authorities, and at the mercy of the diplomatic relationship between the two sovereign countries. They were facing charges of complicity in connection with the banking crimes of Giovanni Fedora who had recently been convicted in the American courts. Gherado Fratello flexed some muscles and pulled a few puppet strings that resulted in the restoration of Ansios' passport after a few months. The P2 leader, however, would not extend such generous assistance to either of Krivis' men. As far as he was concerned, they were the Vatican's responsibility.

Fratello's beneficial efforts, however, were short lived. Now that the long established, strategically placed informants in their communication network were dismantled, Marco Ansios was having a hard time remaining a step ahead of the authorities. Such uncertainty found him becoming more reliant on the protections provided by Bishop Krivis and the Vatican Bank. The relationship between him and the Vatican was no longer what it once was. There would be no more covering up of Ansios' criminal antics, no matter how much incentive he or Fratello threw at Krivis to keep him looking the other way. The withdrawal of Vatican support left Marco Ansios in a very unfamiliar situation. He was now in a position of seclusion and extreme vulnerability. All he had left now was Gherado Fratello, P2 and maybe a few Mafia connections.

The situation with Ansios kept worsening as the new year was just getting started. Italy's new Treasury Minister also looked over the 1978 Bank of Italy's reports with great scrutiny. He felt compelled to protect the Catholic Church at all costs. Following a brief meeting with Pope Phillip Michael II's Secretary of State, he quickly crafted an advisory letter. The Vatican should immediately cease all support or activity in connection with Mr. Marco Ansios and Banco Generali. The directive was given to Bishop Jonas Krivis and was promptly and purposefully ignored. As the situation with Ansios deteriorated, Krivis would later claim ignorance that any sort of directive or advisory had ever been given. At that point it didn't matter anyway. There was no possible way for the Vatican to sever any sort of financial ties it had with Banco Generali or its president since the Vatican actually owned and had controlling interest in the bank headquartered in Milan.

As this newly installed batch of men proceeded deeper into their work, they became increasingly more troubled by what they were uncovering. As much as they tried, it was becoming harder to dismiss the fact that the Vatican, Fedora, and Ansios had been conspirators in many shady dealings for an impressive number of years. Krivis' lay administrative officials were left hung out to dry. Unlike Vatican clergy, they were not afforded the privileges of immunity from the prosecution by the Italian government. The two directors would remain incarcerated on conspiracy charges stemming from their extensive histories with either Marco Ansios, Giovanni Fedora, or both. Their only hope for self preservation was spilling their guts. Between the two of them, there wasn't much that they didn't know. One man served on multiple boards of directors in Fedora's banks in other parts of Italy and Europe for years, while the other, at the time of his arrest, was the current managing director of Ansios' Catholic Bank of Venice.

Gherado Fratello worked tirelessly to assist his paymaster puppet, while the Italian authorities continued to make significant progress in their investigation into his clandestine state within a state P2 world. There was rumored to be an extensive list of Catholic men of authority scattered throughout the Italian government and the business world who were also part of his pseudo-Masonic brotherhood. A series of articles soon began to circulate in newspapers throughout Italy to remind Catholics that it was forbidden to be a Mason and a Catholic in good standing, according to Cannon Law. The segregation between Masonry and Catholicism was nothing new, especially in Italy. Ansios and Fratello thought that the sudden media interest in the combined topics seemed oddly random.

Many long standing P2 brothers were not fond of the new, increasing attention focused on "good Catholics" and Masonry. The entire premise of a clandestine organization like P2, was to operate in stealth. Fratello increasingly found his attention drawn away from his own affairs and onto those within his lodge. He had to reel in more control of his men before any form of real trouble could take hold within his ranks. Gherado Fratello no longer had the liberty to devote his assistance to the one man who needed his help now more than ever, Marco Ansios.

The new men working in Italy's government and the Bank of Italy were not Fratello's stooges. Another round of conveniently timed murders of key people involved with scandalous investigations was out of the question. That card had already been played. The arrests of Bank of Italy director and Detective Cosimo Angelo last March had bought them some time. They were even more optimistic when the same bank director resigned his position six months later. They purposefully kept Detective Cosimo Angelo busy fighting for his own freedom and career through the many bogus charges levied against him. Fratello and Ansios couldn't have been more pleased with the effectiveness of their tactic.

However, now the situation was completely different. Italy had a new Prime Minister. He campaigned heavily that if elected, he would end the corruption that had plagued the judicial and political systems of Italy for so many years. Soon after his election, all of the men controlled by Fratello were removed with surgical precision. The new men were there to do the people's work. They went to work right away on the high profile cases against Giovanni Fedora and Marco Ansios. They were impressed with the quality and scope of the earlier investigative work. None of them could understand what prompted the removal of Detective Cosimo Angelo from the case, nor the charges levied against him almost two years prior. The charges were bogus, and both the detective and the new men of the administration knew it. The charges were immediately dropped, his record was expunged. Detective Cosimo Angelo could hardly contain himself when he was promptly reinstated to the case.

Sergeant Francis Clavering was busily typing up some reports from his prior day's work in the 102nd precinct in Queens. The obnoxious ringing of his desk phone just added to the noisy cacophony of his work environment. He really missed the days of having his own private office back in the Manhattan Precinct. It was just as loud and busy there, but at least he could close his office door once in a while for some privacy and solitude when he needed it. He would have been fine if this was just a temporary inconvenience, but thanks to that piece of shit, Bayer, his current situation was no longer something temporary.

"Sergeant Clavering," he muttered in a monotone as he absent mindedly picked up the phone.

"Sergeant?" Came the voice on the other end of the line in a familiar, distinct Italian accent.

It took Fran a second to register the voice issuing the one word response. "Cosimo? Is that you?!"

"Yes sir! How the hell are you?"

"I'm...ah...fine." Fran paused, then sighed.

"When did you make sergeant?

"Mmm, a few weeks ago, when Christopherson retired."

"That great!" Cosimo detected something was off about his American friend. "You sure don't seem too happy about it though."

"It's a long story, I'm sure you don't have the time for all that bullshit right now." Fran had no desire to get into it with the new precinct eyes and ears all around him. "How the hell did you get this number?"

"I called your old office, and they gave it to me."

"Those bastards...they are going to blow my cover over here." The two men laughed. Fran appreciated the relief from the mundane, rat-race career he was now stuck in. Fran explained the changes that had transpired since the Fedora trial wrapped up, Christopherson's retirement and his promotion and transfer with key details purposefully left out.

Cosimo could still detect that all was not right with Fran, but knew better than to probe any further. "Wow, you have been busy."

"What about you, my friend? It seems I haven't talked to you, Hans or anyone since Fedora's sentencing over here. What's new in your world?"

Suddenly there was a lot of excitement in Cosimo's voice. "Hmmm, let's see...did you hear that we got a new prime minister over here in Italy?"

"No, I hadn't heard. We got a new president too."

"Yeah, I heard about that. I can't believe you guys put a Hollywood actor in there."

"He can't be any worse than that last one, but that's a whole other story."

"We're doing a lot better with our new administration too. This new guy is hell bent on rooting out the corruption that's been going on over here for years in the courts and financial sectors!"

"That's some great news Cosimo!"

"Hang on, it gets even better. Remember when that Bank of Italy director and I got arrested a year ago in March?"

"How the hell could I forget that?" Fran was getting pissed just thinking about it.

"Well guess what?"

"What?"

"The new administration also thought it was bogus bullshit! They dropped all of the charges and removed everything from my records!"

"That's wonderful news Cosimo! Congratulations!"

"Hang on there my friend, it gets even better!"

"I'm listening..."

"They reinstated my investigative position as Head of Vigilance with the Bank of Italy!"

"Well son of a bitch! That is some great news, my friend. Believe me, no one deserves that after all the shit you've been through."

"Thanks! They got me back on the job immediately."

"Damn, that's the best news I've heard in weeks!"

"Yeah, well I started reviewing some of the more recent stuff, and you won't believe what I found."

"Yeah? What ya got?"

"Remember that Fedora kidnapping hoax that went down just before his trial over there?"

"Of course, how could I forget? I have never seen Christopherson so pissed off about anything ever!"

"I remember that part too. Well I think Gherado Fratello had his fingers in some of that situation over here."

"You don't say?" Fran's brain began to race. He quickly scanned the personnel of the precinct. One of his new detective friends caught his eye as he was walking by. "Hey Cosimo, can you hang on a second?"

"Sure, no problem."

"Great, I'll be right back." After a brief hold, Fran came back on the line. "Listen Cosimo, I want you to call me back on another line, if you don't mind."

"Sure, I'll call you back in five."

Several minutes later Fran found himself in a more familiar setting. He appreciated the detective letting him use his office for a more private conversation. Impatiently he waited for Cosimo to call him back. He wanted to hear more about the Fratello connection to the Fedora kidnapping hoax. He also wanted to tell him about the shit that recently went down with Bayer.

Finally the phone rang. "Sergeant Clavering."

"Fran, it's Cosimo..."

"Cool, listen I want to hear all about that new shit you've uncovered, but first I gotta tell you about my current situation."

Fran detailed everything that had happened since the press conference. Cosimo could not believe what he was hearing. The talents and skill of the newly promoted beat sergeant were a blatant waste of resources as far as the Italian was concerned. He could hear the displeasure and frustration in Fran's voice. The cogs in Cosimo's brain began to turn as he continued to explain the recent developments.

"Hey Fran, what if you came over here?"

"I can't, they got me too busy, besides I haven't been here long enough to put in for any vacation time yet."

"I wasn't talking about for a vacation. I meant to give me a hand."

The words rattled around inside Fran's brain for a moment. "Are you insane? How would that even work?"

"You take an extended leave from your current position, and then come over here to Italy and work with me."

"You can't be serious?" Fran couldn't believe what he was hearing. The idea sounded wonderful.

"I'm 100% serious Fran! Since they reinstated me to my former position, I'm surrounded by investigators who are certainly competent, however, they are also completely clueless about all the historical baggage that goes along with this investigation. If you know what I mean."

"Yeah, I can relate. After working with Lance all that time, God love him, don't get me wrong, he was great at what he did, but he was also in the dark about so much of what I was doing. It made my job a lot harder than it needed to be."

"No one knows more about the whole story regarding men like Fedora, Ansios, Krivis and Fratello than you do Fran. I mean look at all we've done since we first met back in '73. Look, I'm absolutely thrilled to finally be back to working my old position, but I'm faced daily with the frustration of having to bring people up to speed with every damn thing we've done for the last eight years."

"These new guys will let you bring me on, just like that?"

"Yes! I can frame it in such a way that you'd be serving as a professional expert consultant of sorts."

"But I know nothing about Italian laws, and you already know exactly how much my Italian sucks."

Cosimo laughed as he remembered the last time he tried to teach Fran a few Italian words and phrases. "I could cover you regarding Italian laws, but you're right, your Italian is pretty lousy. You're right, maybe this isn't such a great idea," Cosimo joked.

"You're serious?" Fran must have asked him at least twenty times. "Don't bullshit me, Cosimo."

"100%! You've got the skills, talents and knowledge that we could use over here right now."

Fran still couldn't believe such an offer was sitting right in front of him. "Of course, I'd have to run all of this by Peg."

"As you should, but if what my wife told me about their antics on some of your visits, I honestly don't think that will be a problem."

"I tell you what, let me see what I have to do to get some extended leave around here. After my conversation with my old boss a few weeks ago that probably won't be a problem. But that's a story for another time. Give me a few days and I will let you know what Peg and I decide."

"That sounds great! I honestly hope it all works out!"

"Me too!"

"We will talk soon."

Fran hung up the phone. His mind was now high on hopeful optimism. In his heart of hearts, he hoped that Peg wouldn't be too salty about the move, if he could get all of the details worked out. As he remained seated in the detective's office, he decided to make one more call before returning to his desk.

"Inspector Bentley."

"Hey Inspector, it's Fran."

"Sergeant Clavering! How are you? Better than the last time we spoke, I hope."

"Mmmmm, I'm ok, and hopefully getting better soon."

"That's a step in the right direction." While Bentley missed working with Fran, he always wanted to see him doing well in all of his endeavors. "So Fran, what can I do for you?"

"Well I just got a call from my friend Cosimo over in Italy." Fran proceeded to explain the situation in full detail over the course of several minutes. The discussion soon shifted to the extended leave situation. Fran didn't want to invent another lie like he and Bentley did so many years ago with Christopherson. It didn't matter that both men's respect for D.A. Lynch was zilch following the whole Bayer bullshit that killed his future career with the NYPD. Regardless of the circumstances, Fran still hated lying.

"Yeah, just ask for a year of leave." Bentley advised. "If you need more at the end of that time, just extend it."

"Thanks, I will do that!"

"This sounds like a great opportunity for you Fran! I'm excited for you!"

"Thanks! I just hope that Peg is on board with the move."

"She loves you Fran, and she's so dedicated and supportive of you. I'm sure the two of you and the kids will be fine. I only have one more directive to give you, Sergeant."

"What's that Inspector?" The two men laughed, and then Bentley got serious and very quiet.

"Please be careful over there. It would crush me if anything were to happen to you. We all know how dangerous these men can be."

"We will all be careful sir! I promise!"

Fran hung up the phone and sat there smiling. He was now in the best mood he'd been in in weeks. He returned to his desk and immediately began to fill out the paperwork for his year long sabbatical. He didn't include any details about where or what. Bentley was right, it was none of their damn business. His next two stops were his supervisor's office, and then D.A. Lynch's office. His supervisor was hesitant to grant the leave. Fran was a great street cop, and he was proud to have him on his team. Lynch did not share the same sentiment, especially after Bayer filled his head with lies and garbage. Lynch hardly had a word to say; he was happy to have this big mouth out of his hair for a while.

CHAPTER 58

It didn't take very long for the people of Italy to realize that the newly installed Prime Minister and his administration were not a bunch of slouches. They hit the ground running, with efficiency and fervor not seen in many, many years. They were ready and determined to tackle the problems and issues that had been stuck in the system for what seemed like a century. The days of slow walking investigations and meritless court delays were over. It would take several months, and numerous long days to work through the backlogged work. The taxpayers were pleased with the new sense of urgency and efficiency that came with competence and integrity. Those whose names appeared on the dockets failed to share the public's enthusiasm.

One of the biggest trials that seemed to be going nowhere for the longest time was the case against Giovanni Fedora. The excuses and delays were tired and worn out. The American legal system had convicted and sentenced him over six months ago, yet he still hadn't been extradited to face his fate in Italy. He'd already been convicted on some of the charges by Italian judges despite his absence. What were they waiting for? The Italian authorities and people were out of patience, and Mr. Fedora was now out of delays.

The new judge assigned to the Fedora case, was a surprisingly fair magistrate, as far as the defendant was concerned. Fedora's biggest problem wasn't the authorities or their case against him, it was actually his legal counsel. His lawyer was a stupid hack whose best strategy was for Fedora to take an insanity plea. There was no way in hell Fedora was going to use any sort of mental impairment as his primary defense. He wanted to fire the man, but that was no longer an option. The Italian government was ready to move forward. There would be no more delays.

The case was short and to the point. Two weeks later, Mr. Giovanni Fedora was convicted of some of his lesser crimes, and fined $25,000. He was then sentenced to thirty-six months in prison. That sentence would begin immediately and be served concurrently with the term he was presently serving in the US.

Sergeant Francis Clavering finally, successfully uprooted his entire family from all that they had ever known. The transition from the New York hustle and bustle to a city and country steeped with centuries of history, culture and traditions was a thrill of a lifetime. The sites, customs and food were nothing like they were in the "New World." Fran took it as a good sign when all of the logistics of the last several weeks turned out to be a lot simpler than he and Peg had anticipated. The most complicated and time consuming part was obtaining their travel visas. Once they were approved, all that was left to do was to pack up some essentials for the year and begin learning Italian.

Peg and the children took to their new culture right away. The kids loved their new school and began making new friends right away. Thanks to Cosimo's wife, Peg also began to expand her own social circle. None of the Claverings could understand the Italian's fascination with their old, boring American culture.

While Fran's Italian was slower to come along than his family's, he fit in with Cosimo's investigative team immediately. They would laugh and tease him about his Italian, but they remained impressed by this new man's depth of knowledge and investigative talents. In some ways, it was as if he'd been working in Italy for many years. Fran and Cosimo just smiled and shrugged, as they collectively decided that maintaining a few secrets for the time being was a good idea.

Even though his work with the NYPD was over and Christopherson had retired, Fran still had a borderline obsession with Giovanni Fedora. It was on par with his preoccupation with Bishop Jonas Krivis. His interest in Marco Ansios and Gherado Fratello were only slightly less. Cosimo noticed that his new partner seemed a little out of sorts.

"Is something wrong Fran?"

Fran caught himself as his thoughts wandered. "I'm sorry, please forgive my rudeness. I'm just not used to this."

"I can only imagine. Leaving behind home, extended family and friends must be a jarring experience."

"No, it's not that."

"Oh?"

"Nah, this is actually fun. We are all absolutely enjoying everything. It's just that I've...well, for so many years been doing so much work in the shadows, back in New York. It's just weird, yet a welcomed change of pace to finally be able to be working so openly."

"I can understand that. But to be completely honest, I have to operate in the shadows over here too."

"But you don't have a corrupt government official watching and waiting for you to step out of line, just so he can destroy any potential future career you might have."

Cosimo could hear the bitterness in his friend's words. "Believe me, we have a lot more corruption than meets the eye. I too must operate with some secrecy."

"You don't have higher-ups destroying your career."

"No, here we have criminal elements who would rather kill you than sabotage your career. The Italian solution is a very real occupational hazard around these parts. As has already been demonstrated by the demise of so many good men like Riluciani and my friend Arturo Bartolone, just to name a few." Cosimo got really quiet as memories of his childhood friend and the late pope filled his head.

"I'm sorry, you are right. I'm naive to think things are really all that different here. I will say, however, I'm pleased as punch to actually have a real partner who understands everything that has happened since the beginning."

"Yeah, I agree, that is really nice. Around here it's hard to know who to trust. Even those I do trust, I still don't tell them everything."

"Ahhhh, so you were withholding evidence, eh?" Fran winked and smiled, jokingly. "I guess they were right to throw your ass in jail a while back."

"Oh shut the hell up Fran."

"Sorry, I couldn't help myself. You left that door wide open, my friend."

"Yeah, I guess I did."

"All joking aside, I'm extremely happy that this all worked out."

"Yeah, me too."

The two detectives were requested to accompany a pair of magistrates when they called in a doctor for questioning. It was suspected that the man had had ties to Fratello and his P2 network and needed more information. As the interview unfolded, their suspicions were confirmed. What they didn't anticipate was the detailed knowledge the physician had of Mr. Fedora's alleged kidnapping several months prior. As the man continued to talk, it became abundantly clear that this was the very same physician who tended to the gunshot wound Fedora had sustained in his leg during his kidnapping. The investigators in the room already knew how badly he had failed at his job. His patient almost died under his care. Keeping the wound from getting infected was nearly an impossible feat outside of a hospital environment. Fearful of being slapped with charges of malpractice and losing his medical license, he made the difficult decision to rat out his P2 ring leader and brethren to save his career. Two hours later, he had explained every detail of Gherado Fratello's involvement in the Fedora abduction hoax. They now had exactly what they needed to move further forward with more of the Fedora and Fratello investigations.

The rush of adrenaline felt good as it coursed through Fran's veins. He was thrilled to assist the Italian finance police in the raid of Gherado Fratello's office and private villa. What began as a quest for more evidence that connected Fratello to Fedora's kidnapping hoax quickly unfolded into something far beyond anyone's imagination. The opening of Fratello's safe became a very literal, modern day Pandora's Box. The secrets contained in dossiers, government reports and documents were absolutely scandalous.

The most damaging information of all was found in a worn brown case, tied shut with a knotted sturdy red string, and the word "fragile" embossed into the leather lid. Investigators carefully opened it to find a registry of sorts listing all 962 members of P2. Important men from all around the globe were listed, but the majority of them were Italian. There were two members of the Italian President's cabinet, members of parliament, members of the Italian secret service, High ranking men of the military, diplomats, industrialists, bankers, journalists from the most respected publications in Italy, rock stars, and members of the American Republican Party.

Cosimo scanned his work environment carefully as he found several well known investigators that he had known for years on the list. The raid was far more revealing than anyone could have anticipated. The list alone was a veritable who's who of global power players and pillars of Italian society.

It was now clear that Gherado Fratello was operating a parallel state within a state, and had complete control of a good portion of Italy's government. While the raid was successful and revealing, the team failed to apprehend the P2 mastermind. It was clear that someone in the tight knit team had successfully tipped him off with just enough time for him to flee. A global all points bulletin was issued, and he was soon arrested in Geneva trying to withdraw $50 million from one of his Swiss accounts. By the time Fran and Cosimo had traveled to Geneva to transport Fratello back to Italy, he had escaped from jail and vanished. Rumors quickly began to fly that he was now in Uruguay. He was successful in his escape, but the damage to his P2 organization was catastrophic.

Fran and Cosimo sat at their desks pouring over some of the contents retrieved from Fratello's safe. Cosimo suddenly slammed his clenched fists hard on his desk. The outburst startled Fran. When he looked over to see what was the matter, he saw tears streaming down the face of his friend. "What's wrong?"

"That, that fucking son of a bitch!" Cosimo was enraged. Through gritted teeth. "So help me God, if I ever get close enough, I'm gonna kill that fucking bastard myself!"

Fran was completely clueless about the source of Cosimo's rage. "Who?"

Cosimo could no longer speak as his emotions overwhelmed him. He just handed some papers over to Fran and pointed. As Fran read, the name of a notorious New York Mob hit man caught his eye. This was the contract ordered by Giovanni Fedora for the killing of Cosimo's close friend Arturo Bartolone. "Oh my God, Cosimo. I don't even know what to say."

Cosimo lost any remaining sense of emotional control. "I miss him, Fran. So much every Goddamn day. We'd been friends since childhood. He was the godfather of my children. So help me, if I ever get that fucking Fedora in my sites, I will take him out myself, I don't give a shit what happens to me after that."

Fran knew that Cosimo meant every word he uttered through the cascade of tears and heartbreaking emotion. He would have to keep a close eye on his new partner in the future should Fedora ever walk among them. The desire to avenge the death of such a dear friend was more than justified. However, Fran reasoned that such action would not bring Arturo Bartolone back, and worse yet, it would result in the imprisonment of a very valuable man in Italian law enforcement. Such fiery passion was never a good thing in their line of work, even if it was justified.

Cosimo, with the help of Fran, finally regained his composure. It would take a few more days for them to comb through the overwhelming amount of evidence produced from the raid. They passed along their findings to the magistrate appointed to Fedora's case. Cosimo felt only slightly better when the Italian judge charged Fedora with the murder of Arturo Bartolone. Fedora also was slapped with charges of complicity in the Mafia's $600 million per year heroin trade between the US and Italy.

Many were hit hard by the Fratello raid. The entire Italian government practically collapsed as it was rocked with one scandal after another. The true irony was this relatively new administration, which campaigned and had already begun to deliver on its promises to end deeply entrenched corruption, had managed to destroy itself in the process. The corruption was so entrenched that the Italian people felt it was best to just fire everyone and start all over.

The case against Marco Ansios' suddenly had new evidence, and new eyes. The case against the Milan banker roared full steam ahead. Marco Ansios, now that the P2 network was dismantled, was truly caught by surprise when Cosimo and Fran showed up to Ansios' office to arrest him and transport him to a Lombardy prison a few short weeks following the Fratello raids.

Fratello was nowhere to be found. He took refuge in South America while he assessed the damage, regrouped and planned what to do next. Many of his minion puppets were suddenly left without their puppet master, and more importantly, left to fend for themselves. A scant few came to the aid of Marco Ansios, but what he really needed was the help of Bishop Jonas Krivis and the Vatican. His timing could not have been worse.

All of Vatican City suddenly was preoccupied with matters more important than Marco Ansios. At a recent gathering in the middle of Saint Peter's Square, a madman had managed to get close enough to the Holy Father to fire off several shots from his handgun. This broad daylight, assassination attempt occurred, despite the best efforts of the world renowned security services of Swiss Guards. The health of their beloved pope weighed heavily on the minds of many, regardless of their chosen religion.

While the world prayed for the pope's survival and recovery, Marco Ansios became obsessed with his own survival. Ansios had his sons go to Bishop Jonas Krivis' office to implore him to admit publicly that he'd been cooking the Vatican Bank's books for many years. The many years of personal and professional relationships suddenly meant nothing. Krivis had no intention of becoming the scapegoat for either him or Fedora. He continued to work from his high tower office, just as aloof as ever. "If I were to entertain such an insane notion, it would only serve to tarnish the image of the church and bank. It certainly would not relieve you from any sort of consequences resulting from our collective actions. Both Marco and I both know at this point that our problems are his problems."

Ansios was hurt and disappointed. However, he couldn't argue against Krivis' point. Banco Generali and the Vatican Bank had been intertwined for far too long. The last two years of financial dealings were especially damning. If the truth ever got out, the wrath of global financial sectors and the entire country of Italy would all come crashing upon them and both their institutions.

At this point all of the charges levied against Ansios were for illegal currency exporting offenses. This part of Ansios' operations had never had any involvement with the Vatican Bank. Krivis felt his best strategy, for the moment, was to abandon Ansios entirely until the dust settled from his trial. If everything worked out satisfactorily, they could at that point revisit their usual business relationship and practices.

Marco Ansios sat in his cell awaiting trial for charges of fraud and illegal exportation of capital levied against him by the Finance Police and the Bank of Italy. He wasn't used to being so alone. He had now been abandoned by anyone who had ever helped him for the last decade and beyond. Everyone was focused on saving their own hides; no one was coming to rescue him. It was now up to him to save his own ass. He sent a message through the prison system for the two arresting officers, he wished to see them, he was willing to talk.

CHAPTER 59

Fran and Cosimo sat in a locked chamber inside the Lombardi prison. The room was cold and absent of all décor, and the furnishings consisted of a simple metal table, a few chairs, and a few ashtrays. As the two men waited for the guards to escort Mr. Marco Ansios into the room, Fran couldn't help but be taken back to the time when he and Hans traveled to the prison in Saltzburg to interview Dr. Karl Schwartz in the early years of the fraudulent securities investigation. He reflected upon some of the other key transitional moments in his journey up to that moment. His heart started to race, and his stomach tightened as the moment he and Bentley lied to D.A. Christopherson flooded his memories. He had gotten a call from Bentley just a few days ago. He was sad to hear that D.A. Christopherson was no longer the man he once was. He was starting to decline mentally and physically. The news filled Fran with concern and sadness. He promised his old boss that he'd touch base with the former D.A. soon.

Fran's attention returned to the present as the clanking of keys, handcuffs and shackles announced the arrival of Ansios into the room. Although Fran knew quite a bit about the Milan banker, this was the first time he'd ever actually seen him in anything other than

JANE M. BELL

photographs. Ansios was led into the room by a pair of guards and took his seat across from the two detectives. His hair was uncombed and it was clear he hadn't shaved for at least two days. His rotund body was dressed in typical prison garb with his prisoner number on displayed across his chest and back. The anxiety level in the room ratcheted up the moment he entered the room. He waited for the guards to leave, knowing that P2 had eyes and ears everywhere. He also knew that these two men were not part of the organization. He wanted no witnesses, not even a lawyer, to this conversation. Now it was only the two detectives and hewho remained in the room.

"You got any smokes?" Ansios asked in a dry, raspy voice.

Fran took the fresh green pack of Salems from his shirt pocket and shook a cigarette loose from it, then offered the man a light. Ansios seemed to become calmer after he took a few deep drags. It was the first cigarette he'd had in days. Cosimo did not have as much patience with the prisoner as Fran did. "You wished to see us?"

Ansios shifted in his chair, then cleared his throat. "Yes."

The man explained for hours the oppressive power and control Gherado Fratello had over him. He had been completely convinced that without Fratello's protections he would have already been a dead man several times over. The Milan banker was then pressed to reveal all that he knew about Fratello, P2 and Giovanni Fedora.

"You must understand gentlemen, I am nothing but a cog in the wheel of the deceptive ways of others. To be frank, I don't even own Banco Generali, I am essentially stuck there at the service of others."

Nobody in the room was buying his bullshit, but Fran wanted to keep him talking, hoping he'd break or slip at some point. Over the course of several hours, Ansios spoke of many powerful people. A few of them, the banker would have considered close friends up until a few weeks ago. The activities he spoke of ranged from the sketchy, to those which were downright illegal. He then admitted to paying $30 million in blackmoney bribes to the Socialist Party of Italy for "political protection services."

Sometime around 3 AM, Fran asked him. "If what you say is true, then you must tell us who it is that actually controls you, Marco?"

Ansios was exhausted. "I'm sorry, I can not tell you anything more."

Fran and Cosimo by now had heard plenty. Three days later Ansios retracted every last statement he had made to the two detectives. Word had gotten out that Ansios was singing from his jail cell. However, the content of his conversations remained speculative. Ansios' wife was now receiving threatening phone calls from irate power politicians in Rome and beyond. They would pull their influential strings. They would make sure that Ansios would spend the rest of his days rotting away in that prison cell after what he had done. The power of rumors, not the actual conversation, had put the man's family in danger.

The following week, Ansios sat in his prison cell after finishing his breakfast. Part of his established morning routine, long before the days of his incarceration, was a quick read through of the newspaper. His stomach instantly began to sour as the headline caught his eye. "FEDORA CHARGED WITH BARTOLONE MURDER!" The article went on to detail additional charges issued from the presiding magistrate. The more he read the more upset he became. In addition to being charged with the Arturo Bartolone murder, Fedora was now accused of being a key figure in the Sicilian Mafia's heroin trade.

Ansios moved slower than usual, shaving and getting ready for the day's court trial. He contemplated the very serious collateral impact Fedora's new charges would have on his own troubles. Ansios was quick tempered as he went through his day. Media reporters circled him as he exited the Roman courthouse trying to get a statement or sound bite to twist and regurgitate to their masses. They were aggressive and persistent, like sharks when they get the scent of blood in the water.

That evening Ansios sat alone in his cell. The late night hours passed by, with louder than usual ticking coming from the clock on the wall. His mind was full of worry, and would not let sleep find him. He glanced over at the clock. "3:15 AM," he muttered to himself. He took a deep breath, and got up from his bunk. He downed a handful of barbiturates then slashed his wrists. With little to no appetite the day prior, his empty stomach protested the assault of the pills and he began to retch. That soon went away as he focused on the dark red blood flowing with a macabre grace from his veins.

A few hours later, Ansios was in a Lombardy hospital getting his stomach pumped. Fran suggested to medical staff to immediately check for digitalis in Ansios' system. Fran had already seen this show a few months before with Fedora in New York. Fedora came pretty close to dying before he finally disclosed what he had taken. Fran did not have the patience nor the desire to see a repeat of the Fedora drama show.

As the world began to wake up and get ready for their day, word of Ansios' suicide attempt spread like wildfire. The media played up the seriousness of the situation, and compared him to his friend Fedora. Those who really knew him just shook their heads. None of them thought for a second that the Milan banker was serious about ending his own life with that lame ass attempt. Many knew, especially those who were fellow P2 brethren, that if Ansios had really wanted to kill himself he would have just taken the lethal dose of digitalis he had on him at all times, even in a Lombardy prison cell.

The magistrate didn't care that Ansios was laying incapacitated in a local hospital bed under 24 hour armed guard. The following day, the trial against him continued. Ansios would recover enough to return to the courtroom after a few days. A week and a half after his suicide attempt in his prison cell, Marco Ansios stood before the court as the magistrate read his verdict. "Mr. Marco Ansios, you are here by convicted of all charges brought against you." He was sentenced to four years in prison and fined 16 billion lire. Ansios' lawyer immediately filed an appeal, and he was out on bail within a few days. The next morning he returned to the Banco Generali Board of Directors to a rousing, standing ovation, and his fellow directors reconfirmed him as their chairman. Many from around the world, including Fran and Cosimo could not believe what they had just witnessed. How could the Bank of Italy allow a man convicted of numerous banking crimes to return to his position in Italy's largest bank? The only explanation for those intimate with the situation was that a few P2 sleeper personnel still remained within the Bank of Italy. Men from the Italian financial regulating body would not go against the power of P2, despite the very vocal protests of Banco Generali's own general manager.

The one man who seemed to have played his cards perfectly throughout this entire situation was Bishop Jonas Krivis. The prior working relationship between the two banks immediately roared back to business as usual. But things were no longer what they once were. What neither man could have anticipated was that while everyone was preoccupied with Ansios' very public trial, Pope Phillip Michael II quietly commissioned a panel of fifteen cardinals to study the finances of the church. What began as a quest to find ways for the church to increase its revenue, soon uncovered that the Vatican Bank had over $1 billion in unsecured loans to Ansios' banks in Peru and Nicaragua, with nothing to back them. The Peruvian bank manager was growing more concerned by the day as he was pressed by Vatican cardinals from the pope's commission. It was now clear that none of these cardinals knew a thing about this financial situation. Who would pay off these debts should the Vatican default on its loans? The concern was legitimate, however, there were no real answers.

Ansios was more focused on salvaging his own life and money to concern himself with the Vatican's problems, despite all of the frequent calls coming from the staff of his own bank. Krivis, once again played the innocent, none of this was of his doing. His two lay administrators that were arrested and jailed recently served as timely and convenient scapegoats. Krivis' ways of deception had come a long way since his earlier days of working in the Vatican Bank. The only time in all of these years his job was ever in any sort of jeopardy was the brief thirty three days of Pope Phillip Michael I's papacy. At that time, Krivis was considered the Catholic Church's most malignant and prolific cancer. The murder of the last pope meant that the cure for the church's biggest problem was also dead. Krivis remained in his position in the Vatican Bank, now more cocky than ever.

Pope Phillip Michael II became very impressed with Krivis, as he explained his work to the Holy Father over the years. Like Pope

Michael VI, this pope saw little wrong with the way this man ran his Bank. Krivis had become very skilled at hiding multiple schemes and documents. No one knew of the Vatican's offshore companies scattered around South America and other parts of the world. Every last one of them operated for the mutual benefit of Banco Generali and the Vatican Bank. One of the aces Marco Ansios kept hidden up his sleeve was the biggest fraud between the two of them called the "Letters of Comfort."

For those who believed the Vatican still had any sort of functional moral compass, there was no comfort to be found in those letters. Marco Ansios kept in his briefcase a document on official Vatican letterhead postdated 1 September, 1981. The document confirmed that Krivis and his bank had control of five Panamanian companies, plus a bank, and one company each in Liechtenstein and Luxembourg. The letter substantiated that the Vatican Bank currently owed $907 million to a Peruvian bank alone. At the bottom of the letter was the forged signature of one of Krivis' imprisoned administrators.

The directors of Ansios' bank were becoming increasingly uneasy with the large amount of debt they were carrying on their books. When they presented their concerns to Ansios he put forward a sincere face as he listened to their concerns, then addressed their fears with a reassuring air of confidence. Having the Vatican Bank and the Catholic Church listed as guarantors on loans, was the best kind of insurance a bank could ask for.

What Ansios failed to disclose to anyone was a copy of another letter tucked in his briefcase. This letter had been given to Krivis in exchange for the Vatican guarantor document. It was dated five days prior to the guarantor letter, and relieved both Church and her bank of any responsibility for repaying any of those loans. Krivis' bank was absolved in secret for the loans it was about to admit were their responsibility. Perhaps the most ironic part of all of this was that it was created and signed on the third anniversary of the election of Chiaros Riluciani as pope. The one man on a mission to eliminate this kind of corruption from the Vatican and Church.

However, there was a major flaw in their scheme. It didn't matter if their misstep was intentional or not. These criminal fraudsters completely failed because the letter that relieved the Church of responsibility for those loans, had zero legal standing. The matter was never put to a vote before Banco Generali's directors or shareholders. The document also never made its way into the public domain.

Despite all of Krivis' chicanery, his work somehow continued to impress Pope Phillip Michael II. The two men had developed a distinct friendship thanks in part to their professional proximity and ethnic heritage. Lithuania and Poland were geographical neighbors with a lot in common. Krivis had the ear of the one man who ensured his job security. The deception of Pope Phillip Michael II had served its purpose well. On the third anniversary of the previous pope's murder, Jonas Krivis was promoted to a position that essentially made him the mayor of Vatican City. He would maintain his position and duties with the Vatican Bank as he was automatically elevated to the rank of archbishop. He was now only one promotion away from obtaining the scarlet zucchetto he had been longing for since his early days as a priest with the Chicago diocese. Krivis' journey to become a cardinal was now closer than it had ever been in his life.

The Vatican would continue to vilify men like Giovanni Fedora and Marco Ansios, and describe them as evil, wicked and deceiving. However, the most deceiving man of them all continued to walk the grounds of Vatican City as its new mayor. Archbishop Jonas Krivis went to great lengths to control and twist the information that the pope received. He and a handful of others did what needed to be done to preserve their jobs, positions, and way of life. The Vatican Inc. machine would continue to lie, cheat, and embezzle from anyone. The pope and the walls of Vatican City provided him great protections from prosecution for his criminal activities with the evil and the wicked. He worked gracelessly hard for the pope's protections. He was well protected, however, he was by no means a controlled man.

While in the process of righting his own ship, Gherado Fratello received a request from the United States. Giovanni Fedora was hoping to capitalize on the power of Fratello and his new close relationship with President Ronald Reagan. He was in desperate need of a presidential pardon which he believed Fratello was positioned to accomplish on his behalf. Fratello, at the moment, was also a very busy man but made a few calls to key members of the Reagan Administration. That was all he had time for before he had to return to his own pressing problems.

Reagan denied the pardon request without reason or comment. Next Fedora turned to a man with whom he had been close to from many many years, former President Richard Nixon. Fedora was hoping that he could cash in on the monetary contributions he had made to his campaign a few years back. The response from Nixon was far more painful and personal. Nixon was in the process of rebuilding his own reputation. The last thing he needed at the moment was to sully his recovering reputation through any sort of close association with a man like Fedora. Fedora was quickly running out of options.

For Fratello, the disastrous fallout that came from the public airing of the P2 membership list and dirty laundry meant that the power that he had gained through years and years of infiltration in Italy and beyond were now beginning to collapse. Master Gherado Fratello was now forced into exile, using Uruguay as his headquarters to assess his situation and regroup. The one man who was key to the recovery of the great Fratello empire of power and wealth was Marco Ansios. It was an odd turn of events. Fratello now needed Ansios more than Ansios would ever need him. This form of vulnerability could never be revealed to anyone, especially Marco Ansios.

Fratello had worked hard in the past to protect his P2 paymaster. He had wielded great control over the man for a very long time. Certainly long before there was ever a hint of any of his current financial troubles. Now that the majority of Fratello's European assets were frozen, he was desperate for money. Once Ansios was reinstated as chairman of Banco Generali, Fratello began tightening the screws on his paymaster. He began extorting large sums of cash from the chronically nervous Milan banker.

Long before the public learned about P2 and the scandals that destroyed the Italian government and political system, Marco Ansios was trying to find a way to sever ties with P2 and Gherado Fratello. "Protection for a price" was now more of a liability than an asset. He just wanted relief from the suffocating control of Fratello. He wasn't interested in divulging P2 dirt like some who had sought to break away in the past. The grisly hit job that ultimately silenced Kristof Ricatto when he tried to use Fratello's tactics against him immediately came to mind.

In the office of his private villa on the outskirts of Milan there was a phone attached to a phone line separate from the main house line. The only person on the planet with the number to that line was Gherado Fratello. On occasion when Ansios was late with a deposit or transfer of funds, he would receive a reminder call. If Ansios' wife or one of his children happened to pick up that phone while he was away, he would say Riluciani called.

The master of blackmail chose his tactics wisely to instill the most fear in order to maintain his control of an individual. His chosen code name was purposeful and effective. Only he and Ansios knew for sure the true meaning behind the late pontiff's name. Was it to instill obedience and loyalty by way of fear? Or a not so gentle reminder of the windfall that came with the critically timed demise of an honest pope. Regardless of the cloaked meaning behind the chosen code name, funds flowed freely and frequently.

Fratello was now the most wanted man in all of Italy. His ability to help or protect Ansios was now extremely limited. Ansios knew that the protection money he paid Fratello was actually for the salvation and protection of the P2 leader. Despite this dynamic shift in their situation, $500 million continued to move from Banco Generali to a destination in South America.

Ansios started to avoid his calls as they increased in frequency. The phone attached to the P2 master's private line would be left to ring unanswered. Once in a while, his family would pick it up and say he was either ill or away. Fratello, the keeper of so many secrets and information on so many people, had at his disposal the ultimate secret that would instantaneously send the already chronically nervous man into fits of anxious terror. The master blackmailer would not be denied. At this point it was too late for Ansios. Calls to Ansios' villa phone from "Riluciani" suddenly became more and more frequent.

As fall was starting to wane and the Italian people began to prepare for the Christmas holiday season, Marco Ansios took it upon himself to appoint a new deputy chairman to the Banco Generali board of directors. The public image of the bank was in really bad shape thanks to events and mishaps in the earlier months of 1981. This new deputy chairman's primary purpose was to overhaul the public image of Banco Generali. Many on the board of directors whose personal financial futures were dependent on the continued plundering of their own Milan bank were not pleased with Ansios' new appointment.

Ansios for once in his life was trying to do the right thing and clean up the image of his bank, as well as his own reputation in the process. What was good for Banco Generali and its president, was seriously bad news for many, including his P2 puppet master. Ansios had worked hard to convince this new man to join their ranks despite his own personal reservations. Four weeks later the new public relations man was blindsided as he was asked to clear out his office and not return. Ansios was dismayed, but had no choice in the matter. He had learned from others caught in Fratello's P2 web that failure to dismiss the new man would soon result in the man's death. Ansios would not have the blood of a man who had done nothing wrong on his hands. The now former deputy chairman of the Banco Generali board of directors would never know that by firing him, Marco Ansios had actually saved his life and would now have to come up with another plan for removing the stranglehold Fratello had over his personal and professional life.

CHAPTER 60

Detective Francis Clavering sat at his desk immersed in his work. He hardly even noticed the phone ringing on the other desk in the shared office space.

Cosimo instinctively reached for the handset. *"Buongiorno, parla il detective Angelo..."* Following a few words from the caller, Cosimo continued. "Cardinal Leone, it's so good to hear from you again. It's been ages since we last talked."

Fran looked up from his papers curiously once the identity of the caller was announced.

The two Italians exchanged a few more words then the call was transferred to the speakerphone. "Cardinal, there's another man here who wishes to say hello."

"Oh?"

Fran couldn't help but smile. "Your Eminence! Detective Clavering here!"

The two detectives could hear the joy in Leone's response. "Francis? Francis Clavering? My what a most pleasant surprise! What are you doing here in Italy?"

"I'm just here giving Cosimo a hand with his work for a while."

"Really? That's wonderful news. You two make an awesome team. Italy must be glad to have you."

"Mmmm, some are." Responded Fran in an unpretentious tone. "Others, not so much."

"So cardinal, what can we do for you on this fine day?"

"Ahh yes, sorry, I got a little side tracked there. Before I get into all of that, I want to commend you two on the fine work you've done, and continue to do on the Fedora stuff! I must admit, I'm most impressed. I can't wait until he finally gets shipped over from that US prison so Italy can finally serve their justice."

"Well thank you sir!" Responded the two men, slightly in unison.

"I've heard that you've been up to your eyeballs with the Marco Ansios case."

"Damn, the man still has his sources, doesn't he." Commented Fran.

Cosimo added. "Yeah, we've both been working at that since Fran arrived several months back."

"Keep up the good work gentlemen. So, back to the reason for my call, I'm wondering if you two know anything about some letters that were recently sent to Vatican higher-ups from the Banco Generali shareholders over in Milan?"

Cosimo scanned his recent memory, then looked at Fran. "No, I haven't heard anything about those. Were these letters recent?"

"Interesting. They were recently sent, but were dated a little over a year ago."

"That is weird, what do the letters say?" Questioned Fran.

"It seems that the Catholics over in Milan who also happen to be Banco Generali shareholders are none too happy about the unscrupulous relationship between Ansios' and Krivis' banks. They were looking for some intervention from the pope."

"Cardinal, do you know if these letters ever got any traction in the Vatican when they were first issued?" Inquired Cosimo.

"I can tell you for a fact that they never made it to the eyes of this pope."

"What makes you so sure of that?" Asked Fran as he lit himself a cigarette.

"If it had, that damn Jonas Krivis would not have been promoted to archbishop a few months back."

"He was what?!" The two detectives exclaimed.

Fran then continued. "Please tell us you're kidding Eminence."

"I only wish I were, gentleman, believe me. That never would have happened under my watch!"

"There's got to be a reason for whoever sent them to be making another attempt. Was there any kind of post mark on them?" Cosmio thought out loud.

"Now that I think about it, it is rather odd that 'Catholic shareholders' are the ones pissed off about all of this. I thought it was common knowledge that the biggest shareholder of Banco Generali is the Vatican Bank."

"Yeah I remember reading about that in court documents, and the stuff seized from the Fratello raid. When all the information was finally put together, it clearly laid out the cozy relationships between Ansios, P2, Fedora, the Mafia, and the Vatican."

"So if I'm understanding what you've just said, cardinal, the Vatican is essentially partners now with P2 and Fratello now."

"I'm afraid so. Chiaros is probably rolling in his grave as we speak." Leone went quiet on the line. "He would have stopped all of it, had they not murdered him."

No one could explain the sudden reappearance of the letters. The inner workings of the Roman Curia once again did what it did best. The documents were promptly destroyed before the pope ever saw them. All the outside world would ever know is that the Vatican simply had no interest in addressing the problem.

Marco Ansios had a problem, a gigantic, and very serious problem. He was hemorrhaging a lot of money. There was no way he could sustain the outflow of $1.3 billion. Political groups like the Italian Christian Democrats, and the Communist Socialists wanted their share, followed by the military regimes of Argentina, Uruguay, Paraguay and Poland. Behind all of that, were a few individuals. The line was long, and every single one of them had their hands out. The one man, however, who always pushed his way to the front of the line was Mr. Gherado Fratello.

In order to keep up with demands, Ansios had no choice but to resort to inventive methods of thievery. Fratello was increasingly demanding when it came to his funds. He was also very controlling of how and to where Ansios' other money should flow, especially for those South America Countries. Ansios, at the direction of the P2 Master, brokered a deal for the Argentinian junta when they needed Exocet missiles from France for the Falkland War against the British. Ansios would then take other stolen funds, and combine it with money from Catholic offering plates to secretly and illegally send money to aid solidarity in Poland.

One of the individuals who would frequent Ansios' office was a trusted P2 man of many years. One morning he visited Ansios' office, seeking his payout with a side of conversation.

"I don't really understand what you are so worried about, Marco."

"Mmmm, I'm worried about Krivis."

"Krivis? Why would you worry about him? He's got that damn pope eating out of the palm of his hand, now more than ever, especially since he got promoted."

"Oh, it's not the pope that concerns me. That pope has never had a problem with Krivis. Krivis is the one sending loads of money to the pope's homeland. That pontiff doesn't even care where the money comes from."

The man nodded his head in agreement. "This is true. He's certainly no Riluciani."

Ansios made a slightly uncomfortable face, then caught himself before answering. "Thank God."

"God had nothing to do with it, my friend. Well God may have gotten him elected, but we had other plans."

"What do you mean?"

"Oh, nothing." The man shifted the direction of the conversation rather quickly.

"No, I'm more concerned with the Vatican's Secretary of State than I am this pope." Replied Ansios

"Mmm, I've heard that he's not too fond of Krivis."

"That's the biggest understatement I've heard in ages. I think that man enjoys finding shit he can nail on Krivis."

"Well there's no shortage of that shit around there." Responded the man with an off tone.

Ansios thought for a moment, then answered. "I don't think the ease of his quest makes it any less noble of a cause for that man."

"Mmmm, maybe."

"My biggest concern is if that Secretary gets to chatting with any of those financiers over there in New York."

"New York?" Questioned the man, confused and clueless about what the man was talking about.

"Yeah, they are the ones kissing Krivis' ass, and sending money over to Poland. If that were ever found out, the Vatican would collapse."

Ansios' guest scoffed. "The Vatican? Collapse? You are a mad man Marco. You can't be serious."

"I am serious. More serious than I've ever been on anything." The topic of the conversation caused Ansios' anxiety to ratchet up visibly. He lit himself a cigarette to help calm his nerves. The cigarette bobbed erratically in his lips as he continued to speak while he shook his hand to extinguish a match. "Shit that last transaction sent $20 million over to Poland alone. I think when all is said and done, $100 million will find its way over there, if they can keep it a secret. However, if they get caught, it would mean the end of Krivis, Pope Phillip Michael II and the end of Solidarity."

"Interesting, who else have you discussed this with Marco?"

"I've only loosely spoken to the former Prime Minister, but to be honest, I'm still unsure exactly where his loyalties lie quite yet. If situations here in Italy go where I think they are headed, that combined with the exposure of the Polish deals, the Vatican will crumble. Whatever is left of it will have to move far far away from Rome. Perhaps an office complex in Washington, DC, near the Pentagon or something."

"Wow! You really think that it's that serious of a problem?"

"I do. We should all be worried, my friend. Very worried."

Marco Ansios would continue to worry about what was happening in the Vatican, even though there was very little he could do about it. Krivis still maintained his attitude of stupid arrogance, accented with moments of faux competence. He'd purposefully ignored numerous bits of sound advice graciously given to him by Ansios, Fedora or both of them in the past. Krivis always thought he knew better. He did whatever he wanted, whenever he wanted.

As spring was approaching, Archbishop Krivis sat for a rare interview with a popular Italian publication. This interview came only seven months after the Vatican and Krivis uncovered that Marco Ansios had stolen over $1 billion from them, then left them with the tab to cover him. This was also just eight months after Krivis' friend, Marco Ansios was fined $13.7 million and sentenced to four years in prison. The public may have believed the official story coming from the Vatican, but there were a few who knew exactly what went down.

The article quoted Krivis, "Marco Ansios is a great man, well deserving of our trust. We have no reason to doubt the man's integrity, nor do we have any future plans to part with our shares of Banco Generali. We also have other investments with this group like The Catholic Bank of Venice which is doing quite well as we speak."

As the detectives, and Cardinal Dante Leone read the article, they couldn't help but to be reminded of the last time Krivis said similar words about one of his friends. That was back in April of 1973, when the idiot FBI man, Nathan Bayer, hijacked Fran's trip to the Vatican to impress his boss, and ended up stepping on his own dick. Back then, as Krivis was being half-heartedly questioned about a $1 billion counterfeit security bonds scheme involving US mobsters, he was fully singing the praises of the genius financier, who was "well ahead of his time" in the world of banking, Mr. Giovanni Fedora. The very same financial genius who was now sitting in a US prison for crimes related to the biggest bank failure in American history. The very same archbishop who now claims he hardly knew the man nor had much interaction with him, had every intention of testifying on behalf of Fedora's defense not that long ago. The only thing that stopped him was the Vatican's Secretary of State. A decision that even overrode the approval of the pope at the time.

Ansios' bigger problem was a particular deputy chairmen sitting on his board of directors. This man had been with Banco Generali just as long as Ansios. He always had his ambitions set on becoming the bank's president/chairman. During Ansios' recent incarceration, suicide attempt and trial, he decided to sieze the opportunity and overthrow the sitting chairman. He failed miserably. The man, however, would not be discouraged so easily. Once Ansios returned to Banco Generali boardroom, the would-be usurper hit him hard with many difficult questions about the numerous loans made to various ghost companies that had Vatican affiliation. Ansios would shift the confrontations around asking the man what knowledge or authority he had to question the integrity of the Vatican or what they deemed to be right or wrong. The public shaming of the deputy chairman failed to discourage his efforts.

One late April morning the deputy chairman was out walking and conversing with his bodyguard near his Milan home. Suddenly a barrage of gun shots came from behind the two men. The Banco Generali man was struck instantly in both legs, and collapsed to the ground. The bodyguard instinctively turned around, drew his .357 magnum, killing one assailant instantly, as the other ran off. As the bank man lay in his hospital bed recovering from the botched assassination attempt, it was discovered that the attacker, killed by the bodyguard, was a Roman hit man closely connected to the Sicilian Mafia. Marco Ansios had paid the man $530,000 to neutralize the deputy chairman problem.

By May 1982, even more pressure was applied to Mr. Ansios. Now he was facing scrutiny from the regulators of the Milan Stock Exchange. They were asking for a complete and independent audit of all of Banco Generali's banking records and a complete listing of all of the bank's publicly held shares. Ansios ran to the Vatican desperate to have Pope Phillip Michael II address the $1 billion loan debt that had them listed as a guarantor. The pope knew nothing of these money issues that were the result of Fratello, Krivis and his own schemes. Ansios was kept far, far away from the pope but Krivis promised to present the issue to the Holy Father, employing his usual skillful, treacherous means to bamboozle the pope.

Krivis returned to Ansios a few days later with a signed promise from Pope Phillip Michael II that if the Vatican could be liberated from their debt, Marco Ansios would be granted full control of the intricate workings of Vatican finances as he helped restore them to their more prestigious status. Ansios' heart sank as he read the letter. The offer was more than generous, however, it did nothing to rectify his dilemma at this moment. What he really needed was the Vatican to cough up the money they owed him and his banks, not a perpetual rubber stamped business as usual approval from the pope.

As the end of May approached, the Bank of Italy contacted Marco Ansios and his entire Banco Generali board of directors in Milan. They too were seeking full audits and disclosure of all foreign lending Banco Generali had on their books. Although Ansios vehemently protested the request, the directors quickly silenced their chairman's protests and voted 11-3 to comply with the order.

Ansios was now in a precarious situation. He was being pressured from every angle imaginable: officials with the Milan Stock Exchange and the Bank of Italy, Mafia clients, pissed off stockholders, rebellious directors of his board, and a Vatican/pope uninterested in making good on their $1 billion debt. It was a lot coming at him, all at once.

Marco Ansios had intimate knowledge of all of the Vatican's financial secrets going back at least ten years. He had sat back and watched the Vatican's net worth blossom from $3 billion back in the days of Riluciani's brief papacy, to now over $10 billion. The more he thought about it, the more irate he became with the Vatican shirking of legal financial obligation to him and his bank. Especially since they benefited the most from those now missing millions.

If the Vatican wasn't going to do the right thing, Marco Ansios' only other option for salvation was his symbiotic relationship with his P2 Master. Gherado Fratello needed the banker's money, and Ansios needed protection that only Fratello could provide. Ansios knew that Fratello's reign over his minions was not what it was since the authorities raided his Italian villa, whether the P2 leader wanted to believe it or not. Still, the man had his connections and influence. Ansios once again needed Fratello to pull on the puppet strings connected to the power elite of Italy. What the banker absolutely did not need was a parasitic Gherado Fratello coming to him once again for another hand out, yet that is exactly what happened.

Gherado Fratello, was still a wanted man in multiple countries, especially Italy. He was now the world's most sought after fugitive. The man thought to be hiding somewhere in Uruguay strolled right into Marco Ansios' office wearing a most sophisticated disguise. He pushed his way past the protesting secretary and straight into the fourth floor office of Marco Ansios. The Milan banker had no clue who he was, and instructed the man to make an appointment with his secretary seated in the other room. Fratello turned slightly as if to leave then whispered under his breath, "Riluciani."

Ansios' eyes widened in shock. "Fratello?!"

"Hello Marco." The man turned around once again and flopped himself into a seat across the desk from his bewildered host, who just issued his trademark sly smile and nodded.

"What the hell are you doing here?"

"I'm in need of a little help, my friend."

"That's interesting, because so am I." Ansios explained everything happening with his bank.

Fratello sat and listened intently to the man's lament. "Yes, I can see how these problems are starting to get increasingly out of hand."

"So you will help me?"

"Yes, I don't want you to worry about any of that any longer."

Ansios took in a deep breath, held it, then let it out slowly in relief. "Oh God, thank you!"

"Let me first finish up with this latest arms deal for Argentina, then my attention will be all yours, my friend."

Marco Ansios had alway played second fiddle to whatever Fratello decided was his priority. With authorities from multiple agencies now watching him so closely, he no longer had the luxury of just handing over the funds Fratello needed whenever he demanded them. While Fratello was busy playing the arms dealer at the height of the Falkland war, Banco Generali was on the verge of collapse. Time was running out for both the Argentinians and Marco Ansios.

"Marco, listen carefully, I need you to leave Italy, and head to London, by way of Austria, are we clear with those instructions?"

"But I am constantly being watched Gherado. Besides if I leave the country I will officially be a fugitive."

"I've been wearing that badge for a few months now. It's not so bad." Fratello issued another sly smile. "I will set you up with a disguise and passport through one of my guys, alright?"

Ansios really hated the idea, but he no longer had any other option, besides he already knew what happened to men who told Fratello no. Begrudgingly, the banker agreed to do as he was being instructed.

"Excellent! I will meet up with you there, once this is over we will tackle all of your problems together."

"Fine, when do you want me to do all of this? I'm going to need a little time to get everything together."

Fratello looked at the calendar hanging on the wall. "Mmmm will a few weeks be enough? Say June 17th?"

Ansios also glanced at the calendar, "Yeah, that will work, and your guys will be in touch for arrangements, disguise and passport?"

"Absolutely."

The pressure and problems continued to grow by the day. Despite everything that seemed to be working against him, Marco Ansios remained impressively calm. If it weren't for the promises of Fratello, he would have already had a nervous breakdown. In a few days, he'd be making his way to London as he was instructed. He had to believe that everything would work. It had to. It was his last thread of hope, and the only thing keeping him sane at the moment.

Ansios' secretary, Leonora Tocci, strolled into his office to remind him of his appointment later that day. She couldn't help but notice him being in such a calm, almost upbeat mood. He even brought her a small bouquet of flowers that morning for her desk. It was nice to see her boss smiling, and carefree for a change.

Mrs. Tocci escorted a medium build, fit man with dark hair, beard, mustache and glasses into Ansios' office. "Mr. Ansios, Mr. Harding is here to see you."

"Thank you Mrs. Tocci, please hold my calls until this meeting is over."

"Yes sir." She turned on her heels and left the two men in the room.

"Mr. Marco Ansio? My name is Oliver Harding." Introduced the man with a distinct accent.

Ansios rose from his chair and extended his arm to shake his guest's hand. "It's nice to meet you sir. Do I detect a bit of an accent?"

The man fidgeted a little, slightly embarrassed. "Yes sir. You have a sharp ear."

"Thank you, Mr. Harding. I'm afraid my..."

"Please call me Oliver." Interrupted the man.

"Alright, Oliver, I'm afraid my secretary hasn't briefed me too much about you, or the purpose of our meeting this afternoon."

Oliver smiled. "I'm afraid some of that is my fault. I didn't give her very many details. I'm sorry."

"No problem, Mr. Harding, I mean Oliver, what can I do for you?"

"I'm an American author working on a book project on modern day Italian banking systems and practices."

"Mmmm, I see. Yeah, I may know a few things about some of that."

"From what I've heard, I thought you might. That's why I needed to meet with you today."

The interview was going well. Ansios remained calm and jovial as the two men exchanged conversation and a few laughs. Ansios fielded questions about Banco Generali, the Milan Stock Exchange, and other topics pertinent to banking. In the back of his mind, Ansios was beginning to think something like this would be a great way to resurrect his image and reputation after he returned from his upcoming trip to London.

"Mr. Ansios, if you don't mind, I'd like to change gears a bit and ask you some questions about The Catholic Bank of Venice."

There was an immediate shift in Ansios' body language and tone. "The Catholic Bank of Venice?"

"Yes sir, if you don't mind. I read in a recent article that you owned that bank too, is that correct?"

The banker shifted uncomfortably in his chair. "Yes, that is true."

"Would you mind telling me how you came to own one of the Vatican's banks?"

As if someone had flipped a switch, the composed Milan banker once again became nervous, agitated and very suspicious. "What did you say this book was about again?"

"Italian banking."

"I don't believe you Mr. Harding."

The American swallowed hard. "You don't?"

"No, not for a second. Who are you really?"

"Oliver Harding, independent author from the States."

"Who has sent you here? Who has sent you against me?"

"Nobody sir. I am just trying to gather information for my book project."

"You are full of shit Mr. Oliver. Who told you to do this? Was it Gherado Fratello?"

"I've never met Gherado Fratello, I don't even know who that is sir."

Ansios didn't even register his guest's response. "Goddamn it, I always have to pay and pay. What do you want? How much do you want?"

"I don't want anything but your time and some information sir." Harding did his best to stay calm despite his host's shift in mood.

"Listen to me carefully Mr. Oliver Harding, or whoever the fuck you are. You will not write that damn book! Do you understand me?! I will tell you nothing more. Don't ever contact me or my office again, EVER! NOW GET OUT!!!"

Harding gathered his papers and briefcase hastily in his arms and exited the building quickly. He walked with quick steps for about three blocks, then turned a corner. He then entered the side door of an unmarked van parked by the curb. Once inside, he immediately began to pull at his beard separating the itchy latex from his face.

"Well that escalated rather quickly, wouldn't you say Fran?" Commented Cosimo.

"Yeah, for a minute I wasn't sure exactly what he was going to do, or if I was going to make it out of there."

"Peg sure set you up with some great questions."

"Yeah she did. I only wish I could have gotten more out of him for Leone."

"Yeah that was a bit of a bust, I'd say."

"I wouldn't quite say that."

"Oh?"

"Well I think it's safe to say that Fratello is extorting the man in a very bad way, and he seems quite tired of it."

"Yeah, I picked up on that."

"Sounds like Fratello isn't the only one either."

Cosimo nodded in agreement. "He sure didn't want to talk about Riluciani's old bank or the Vatican did he?"

"Shit, I'd still be sitting in his office talking to him, had I not brought that up."

"Man did he turn fast."

"An innocent man doesn't act like that Cosimo."

"I agree."

The day after his interview with the undercover detective, Ansios disappeared without a trace. He had only eleven more days until he was scheduled to be back in court to appeal the Italian Government's ruling. As word of his disappearance got out, Banco Generali's stock value dropped precipitously causing a $137 million decline in their market value. To add insult to injury, with many unanswered questions about the bank's foreign share holdings, a run on the bank ensued.

A few days later, with an altered appearance and forged passport in hand, Marco Ansios boarded an airplane for Gatwick Airport in London, by way of Austria. Upon arrival, he checked into room

1054 of a residential hotel near the Thames River waterfront. The room was simply furnished with all of the basic comforts. He placed his signature briefcase on the desk near the window, unpacked his suitcase, then called his wife. His mood was good, and his tone was upbeat. "Incredible things are happening my love, this will resolve everything!" He reported.

Two days later, as Fran and Cosimo were starting to wrap up their work for the day, there was a sudden flurry of phone calls coming into the *Commissariato Polizia*. The two detectives and their colleagues rushed quickly to the Banco Generali Headquarters in Milan. Upon their arrival, they immediately saw a cloth draped corpse laying on the cobblestone in front of the building. They approached the body, and Fran crouched down and pulled back the drape. Staring back at him were the cold dead eyes of a woman he had met just the week before.

Fifty-five year old Leonora Tocci, the longtime secretary of Marco Ansios lay dead in a small pool of her own blood. The two men looked up the building's facade to see double windows open wide from a fourth story office suite. Fran led Cosimo up to the office as fast as their legs would carry them. There were already many people swarming about the office.

Suddenly Cosimo yelled loudly, *"Fermati tutti!"* Everyone instantly froze in their tracks. "We need to get every single fingerprint there is in this place immediately!"

"But sir, it was a suicide." Commented one of the investigators.

"I don't care, I want this place dusted from top to bottom."

The team processed the scene with the strictest of protocols. A note was found on Miss Tocci's desk simply stating "He should be damned, again and again!" Once they collected all of the evidence, the body was loaded into the coroner's vehicle and driven away. Technicians would spend their evening developing photos and organizing information for the detectives to start sifting through the next morning.

The next morning, June 18, 1982, at 7:30 AM, a young employee of a London Newspaper walked his usual morning commute along the footpath beneath Blackfriars Bridge. He paid little attention to the wrought iron arches decorated in pale blue and white. A bright orange rope tied to a pipe on the north arch caught his eye against the backdrop of pastel colors. Unsure of what he saw, he leaned over the low walled structure for a better look, then froze in his tracks. Above the water of the Thames River, from that orange rope hung a man's body with a thick knotted rope tied around his neck. He looked away, shaking his head, not wanting to believe the horror of what he had just discovered. He walked a little closer to the northern arch and onto a nearby terrace to get a better look. From there, he could see the eyes of the dead man, still partially open and locked in a cold absent stare. The waters of the Thames lapped gently at his feet.

As the panic of the grisly discovery fully registered in his brain. He ran as fast as he could to the newspaper office where he worked. His coworkers noticed him looking pale and nauseous; he almost fainted. He instructed one of his colleagues to immediately call Scotland Yard.

CHAPTER 61

Fran and Cosimo got to the office early, they wanted to get started digging into to the suicide case of Marco Ansios' late secretary Leonora Tocci. The two men had just sat down to their desks with a fresh hot cup of coffee when Cosimo's phone started ringing. It was Hans calling from Munich. Fran and Cosimo had spoken with him the night before regarding the odd death. Hans was talking a mile a minute, and was difficult to understand through his German accent.

"Hans, slow down, I can't understand a word you're saying." Requested Cosimo, as he transferred the call to the speaker phone box.

"I'm hearing all kinds of things from Interpol coming out of London! They found a body hanging from Blackfriars' Bridge. They think it might be Marco Ansios'!"

"Oh my God!" Exclaimed Fran.

"Are you sure?"

"I'm pretty sure, but they are having a hard time identifying the body."

"Alright, we will be on the next flight there, can you meet us there?"

"Yeah I will meet up with you two as soon as I can."

"Great! See you in a few hours."
"Will do!"

Within thirty minutes the Thames River Police had cordoned off the area. They positioned one of their river boats under the Number One arch of Blackfriars' bridge. They immediately ruled the death a suicide. Oddly, no one took any pictures of the body or scene. As the River Police moved closer, they estimated the man to be in his sixties. He was heavyset, and of average height. He had an advanced receding hairline and what was left of his hair was black as night. The body was clothed in an expensive business suit that was oddly contorted and disheveled. The suit had shrunk, especially in the arms and legs, after being submerged in the river waters during the recent high tide.

After cutting the man's body down, they gently laid him down on the deck of the police boat. At Waterloo Pier, Murder Squad Detectives took possession of the cold, stiff corpse. While they waited for the city coroner to arrive, they took some pictures of the body, complete with the hangman's noose still tied around his neck. Investigators were puzzled when their initial examination found numerous large rocks crammed into the pockets of the man's pants. They also found a couple of bricks broken in half and stuffed into his mis-buttoned jacket. Then they found a large chunk of cement stuffed down the front of the man's pants. Once all the bricks and other materials were removed they figured they weighed well over ten pounds.

As the forensic team began removing the man's personal effects. They found two wallets containing a mixture of British, Swiss, Italian, Austrian and American currency worth about $50,000 USD. On his wrist, a gold Patek Philippe watch estimated to be worth about $15,000 had stopped running at 1:52 AM. Another gold timepiece was found in the inside pocket of his jacket. It had stopped at 5:49 AM. Other items found in his pants pockets included a ring, a pair of gold cufflinks, four sets of eyeglasses with three cases, a few photos, a pencil and some papers. Among the papers was an Italian passport with the name Urbano Rivera, and portions of an address book with contact information for people in Italy, London, and the Vatican. The rest of the address book was never recovered.

When the coroner arrived two hours later, the body and personal effects were transported to London's Milton Court Morgue. They had the corpse stripped, as was normal routine procedure. Everyone thought it was odd that the man was wearing two pairs of underwear. By the time they took his fingerprints, blood samples for a toxicology screening and prepared the body for autopsy, Fran, Cosimo, and Hans had arrived. Fran first noticed that Ansios had shaved off his distinctive mustache and dyed his hair since he last saw him, the week before. The alterations in his appearance were not enough to conceal his identity from these men. They quickly identified the corpse as sixty-two year old Marco Ansios.

While they waited for information from the medical examiner, they decided to lend a hand to the detectives of Scotland Yard. Together they found a residential hotel room registered to Mr. Urbano Rivera not too far from where Ansios' body was found. The room was tidy and his luggage was neatly stacked. A bottle of barbiturates was found near the sink. As Fran and Cosimo looked around the room, they became acutely aware that Ansios' signature briefcase was nowhere to be found. In all of their face to face encounters, never once was he without that briefcase. Fran and Cosimo wanted the room completely dusted for fingerprints. "For a suicide?" Protested the investigators before agreeing to the forensic procedure. Both sets of investigators took pictures of the room and combined them with the copies of images taken of Ansios' body and effects at the coroner's office.

Fran, Hans and Cosimo could not believe that the River Police failed to take any pictures of the scene where the body was found. Then the three men parted ways with local law enforcement for a while to discuss what had been found so far. They headed over to Blackfriars' bridge to see if they could find anything. They quickly found the remaining portion of the bright orange colored rope still tied to the wrought iron underpinnings of archway number one. Fran made his way to the surface of the bridge. Cosimo and Hans watched in horror as Fran climbed over the parapet, then started down a narrow twenty-five foot ladder attached to the side of the bridge.

"Fran? What the hell are you doing?" Inquired Hans.

"Just checking something out."

"Please be careful up there." Yelled Cosimo, worried. "I don't want to have to be the one to tell Peg something happened to you."

"I will, I promise. I certainly don't want you to have to do anything like that..."

Hans and Cosimo watched with great concern from the footpath below, as Fran made his way over a three-foot gap in the construction scaffolding and on to where the rope had been secured to the bridge. Fran tried unsuccessfully to untie the rope from the bridge with his free hand as he held tight to the scaffolding with the other. Eventually he made his way back to the bridge's surface and rejoined his colleagues.

Fran was tired and sweating. He had rust all over his hands, feet and clothes after climbing on the ladder and scaffolding. Fran took a few minutes trying to brush away some of the rust that had gotten on his hands, feet and clothes. "Shit, Peg is going to be pissed at me." He muttered. The rust wasn't that easy to get off. "There's no fucking way that that fat ass hung himself from that bridge!"

"There sure is a lot that doesn't seem right about neither this case nor the one back in Milan involving his secretary yesterday."

"I mean, I'm not in that bad of shape, and it was a challenge for me."

"Yeah, we noticed." Commented Hans.

The three men eventually made their way back to the coroner's office. The official report would have to wait a few more days for the toxicology results, however, the preliminary coroner's results was suicide.

"Suicide? Are you sure?" Questioned Cosimo.

Fran turned to the medical examiner. "Sir, if you don't mind, I have a few questions."

"Of course, detective."

"I assume you examined the dead man's hands."

"I did."

"Did you find anything? Some sort of residue perhaps."

"No, his hands were completely clean."

"Nothing under his fingernails?"

"No, nothing I'm sorry."

"Ok, thank you sir." Fran then turned to the lead detective on the case. "Sir, I was wondering if you and your men had found the source for the rock, brick and cement materials found in his pockets."

"Yes, as a matter of fact we did. The materials match items we found on a construction site about 275 meters east of where the body was found."

"I see." Fran now had more questions. "Do you mind if we examine Ansios' personal effects one more time before we head home?"

"Certainly, right this way gentlemen."

Fran, Cosimo and Hans closely examined Ansios' polished dress shoes. Then the clothing that had been carefully cut away from the man's body. The London investigators remained in the dark regarding what the three detectives were hoping to find. There were no signs of rust or cement residue on any of the evidence collected. Something just wasn't right.

The information from this case, when combined with the incident involving Ansios' secretary the evening before, left them with more questions than answers. However, they didn't have to dig too deeply into either case for it to became abundantly clear that neither Marco Ansios nor Leonora Tocci committed suicide. There wasn't much more they could do in London. Fran and Cosimo were now itching to get back and find out what the Milan team of investigators had uncovered so far from the Tocci suicide case.

The three men decided to take in a late lunch before heading back to their respective home countries. During their meal, they'd brainstorm their own theories.

"Are any of you guys buying that Ansios traveled well over the equivalent of six football pitches on his way to kill himself that night?" Questioned Hans.

"How long is a football pitch?"

"Mmmm, about 105 meters, that'd be about 115 feet for you yanks." Responded Cosimo.

"Ah, so about fifteen feet longer than an American football field." Fran remembered back to his football playing days of high school and college. "That's a pretty good trek, if you ask me."

"Don't forget half of that trek he'd somehow be carrying all that shit in his pockets plus about five and a half kilograms of rocks, bricks and cement."

"That was a lot of rocks and stuff." commented Hans.

"These investigators have to be an impressive kind of stupid if they think that that fat man, in the dead of night committed suicide by scrambling about under that bridge like I did after his casual stroll carrying twelve pounds of that shit shoved in his pockets." Fran's tone was particularly snarky. "I wonder when it was exactly that he shoved that big chunk of cement down his crotch?"

"I'd say the fact that there were no signs of cement or rust on Ansios' hands definitely answers some of those questions for us." Commented Hans.

"What I really want to know is where the hell his briefcase has disappeared to?"

Many in the Italian banking world already knew about the $1.3 billion hole in Banco Generali. They also knew that the information was about to be released to the rest of the public. Millions had been withdrawn from the bank Ansios ran for so many years. Within a few days of the "suicides" that would claim the lives of Mrs. Leonora Tocci and Mr. Marco Ansios, there was a heavy run on withdrawals at Banco Generali. On the heels of that was a run on the Vatican Bank. Those who knew of Generali's dire situation, also knew about Ansios and his bank's long established relationship with Archbishop Jonas Krivis and the Vatican Bank. Within a few days of Ansios' death in London, Banco Generali collapsed completely and was shuttered.

The only one convinced that the Milanese banker hung himself from BlackFriers' bridge was the coroner from London. Those who knew him the best, knew that this was a case of murder, not suicide. Ansios' oldest son, who served as the family's spokesman, wanted the authorities to investigate further. He poked another hole in the suicide theory the British investigators when he told Fran and Cosimo how terrified the man was of heights. Who did it? Was it the relatively new socialist political group in Italy? Ansios did have documents that would expose the black-money bribery schemes rampant in numerous Italian political groups, including this new one. That was one theory. Another possibility was the mercenaries Ansios hired shortly after he got out of jail. They were actively extorting huge payments from the banker for their services. Corruption in Italy in the early 1980s was a high-stakes game. In the United States, judges and politicians could be bought off for $1 million. In Italy the cost was at least three times more expensive. The millions and millions that Ansios would pay for control of and power over various men ultimately lead to his death.

There was no shortage of plausible theories. The number of people who had motive and means to kill Mr. Ansios were endless. However, none of their possible culprits seemed to fit as far as Detective Francis Clavering or his partner Cosimo Angelo were concerned. Something in Fran's gut had him feeling like they were missing something, something big. Fran tried his best not to bring his work home with him. However, this one was quickly becoming a bit of an obsession for the New Yorker.

Fran had often found that bouncing ideas off of Peg was helpful in the past. The only thing that Fran knew for sure was that Marco Ansios did not commit suicide, regardless of what the British coroner had to say about it. With the suicide option dismissed, and his death certainly wasn't an accident. The only thing left was murder!

Fran approached Peg from behind and gave her a kiss on the neck as she washed the evening's dishes. "Honey, I know you're busy." He removed her soapy hands from the dish water in the sink, and placed them in his, then spun her around to face him. "Would you mind looking over some of the pictures I brought back from London."

"More sightseeing, Mr. Clavering?" She teased.

"If you call looking at the tide soaked corpse of a balding fat man 'sightseeing' then yes. And might I add you're a little insane, my love." He smiled, lifting her gently then kissing her.

She returned the smile, "You sure have a nice way of being convincing. Is this the technique you typically use at work?"

"No, but it has been effective in the past around here, maybe I should." He winked.

Peg couldn't help but giggle at the idea. "Sure, hon, I don't mind taking a journalistic view of what you got. Just let me finish these dishes first."

"Here, let me finish those, while you go take a look."

"Well, if you insist, how can I say no to that?" She kissed him, and then turned to walk over to the kitchen table. She shuffled through all of the pictures brought back from London.

"What did you say the name of that bridge was?"

"Blackfriars' bridge," came Fran's voice from the other room.

"Blackfriars'? No kidding? That's interesting?"

"No kidding, interesting how?"

"I remember taking a course in college where we studied the middle ages. The Blackfriars were monks who operated monasteries in England during the middle ages."

"Yeah, so?"

"In the middle ages, the Blackfriar brotherhood provided sanctuary for embezzlers, swindlers and thieves of that era."

Fran raised an eyebrow, "You're right, that is interesting. For me, when I think of 'Blackfriars' all that comes to my mind is Vatican clergy."

"That bridge sure has some nice architecture. I really like the pretty light blue and white colors," she commented.

"You wouldn't think so if you had to climb around the iron structure underneath it."

"You did what, Francis Clavering?!"

"Shit!" Fran's voice came, cursing from the other room. "I wasn't supposed to tell you that! Well it wasn't like Hans or Cosimo were going to do it."

671

"So of course you had to."

"Well how else were we going to prove that it wasn't a suicide?"

"Oh I'm sure there are a million other ways that come to mind."

Once again her attention turned to the images in her hands. She began to lay them out on the table then took a step back to look at everything. "You know Fran, from everything I'm seeing in this picture, none of what was found on his body seems random. You know those Mafia hitmen always leave some sort of message in the way the carry out their murders?"

"Oh, you mean like the rounds fired into the mouth of that guy Kristof Ricatto, followed by the rock placed into his mouth when he was spilling all kinds of P2 secrets in his newspaper a while back?"

"Yeah, exactly."

"Yeah, around here they call that *sasso in bocca*. They like to do that to guys who talk too much."

"Interesting. Your Italian is getting better, I..." She began to tease. Suddenly she stopped mid-sentence, and ran over to the living room bookcase. She pulled a thicker volume of the *World Book Encyclopedia* from the shelf and started going through its pages frantically, then stopped. Peg then looked up at her puzzled husband. "I think I know who killed Ansios!"

CHAPTER 62

The same day as Marco Ansios' supposed suicide, the military dictator appointed president by the Argentinian junta was ousted. The top military brass were not happy with the way the Falkland war effort was going. All blame for the South American country's strategic problems quickly shifted to the shoulders of Marco Ansios' cold, dead corpse. He was 100% to blame for everything that was going wrong in Argentina. They were completely unsympathetic that the Italian banking authorities had been watching the man's every move up until the day of his suspicious death. It would have been impossible for him to divert the funds needed for a strategically important arms deal without being caught.

Argentina needed the help of Gherado Fratello, but they would have to wait in line. The general elections in Italy were approaching quickly. It was a critical moment for the future of Italy, P2 and Master Gherado Fratello. P2 and its leader still had a great deal of power and money. They had the means to control the landscape of Italian politics and beyond despite Fratello being an international fugitive harbored in far off Uruguay, with the majority of his assets frozen. If P2 members failed to be elected, all would be lost.

Key people who remained in strategic positions made sure that all investigative work into P2 activity and personnel would be suspended until after the election was over. The Christian Democrat Party had five candidates listed on ballots who were also part of Fratello's P2 network. Having multiple horses in multiple races, Fratello liked his organization's odds. In June 1983, the Italian people selected several P2 men. Fratello and his men were pleased with the election results.

As fall was approaching, the Argentinian Junta were not ready to surrender to the British quite yet. They were certain they could win both the war and the island. They just needed more weapons for their military. Once again they reached out to their steadfast arms dealer, Gherado Fratello. He would make sure that the mistakes of the past would not be repeated. Now that his long-time paymaster was six feet under, Fratello's had to execute this particular arms deal himself. He deployed the help of a former Italian Secret Service officer and P2 loyalist. Knowing that the delays in Ansios' actions lead to catastrophic results for the Argentinians last time, this deal would be expedited. Things were not as tight lipped as they were when Marco Ansios was running the show.

Fratello called Geneva Switzerland, like he had done so many times before. He needed to move the remainder of his $55 million from the private, numbered account that Marco Ansios had set up for him ages ago. As the years progressed, well over $100 million had been funneled through that account before being transferred to Fratello's account in Uruguay. But there was an issue with his account, his typical money transfers were suddenly being declined. The bank's staff informed him that he would have to appear in person in order to complete his transaction.

Before leaving South America, Fratello grew out a mustache, then dyed his salt-and-peppery locks brown. With a fake passport in hand, he boarded a flight that would take him from Buenos Aires to Madrid, and then on to Geneva. Upon arrival at his destination, he checked into a local hotel. He would enjoy the hotel's bar and spa while he waited for his other party to arrive.

The next morning, accompanied by his P2 legal confidant, he walked into the Swiss Union Bank of Geneva. Fratello was politely asked for identification, and promptly presented the fake passport that matched his altered appearance.

"It will take us a few moments to prepare your funds for you sir. In the meantime, please have a seat."

"Thank you miss." Responded Fratello before taking the seat next to his lawyer.

The two men sat and waited patiently, without a care in the world. While they were discussing where they should have dinner that evening, a plain clothes law enforcement officer approached and promptly arrested the international fugitive and his companion. As they were led out of the bank in handcuffs Fratello was kicking himself for ignoring the sage advice of Giovanni Fedora. Fratello had just learned a most valuable lesson the hard way; there really was no such thing as an anonymous bank account, not even in Switzerland.

Working off of intelligence received from "Five Eyes" a plan was formulated quickly. The trap deployed by Italian banking officials had been executed perfectly! Once the Swiss bankers were alerted that the true owner of that account was the late Marco Ansios, the account was immediately frozen. Fratello's final Swiss asset was now gone.

As Gherado Fratello was being transported to maximum security prison in Geneva, the extradition process began right away. Fratello's protests were ignored. So were his claims that he was the victim of political persecution plotted against him by left wing political factions in Italy. As far as the Italian authorities were concerned, that particular tactic was tired and overused by his friends Giovanni Fedora and Marco Ansios. The same Italians who had been waiting years on Fedora's extradition were all out of patience.

Two days into October, another top executive from Banco Generali was suicided out the same fourth story window of the bank's Milan headquarters building as Ansios' secretary had been weeks earlier. This incident prompted the wife of the slain Milan banker to speak to the press. The paper printed her passionate claims that her late husband had not committed suicide under the Blackfriars' bridge in London. He was actually murdered and placed there by men of the Vatican trying to cover up their own financial crimes and imminent bankruptcy. Some thought the woman had gone mad from the grief of losing her husband. However, those in the know saw great plausibility in what she had to say. Her theory was surprisingly sound for a woman who was clueless to her husband's affairs.

If she was correct, it would not be the first time someone who threatened the financial operations of Vatican, Inc. had been done in. Many still had fresh memories of what had happened to the last pope who was going to expose and stop the pillaging of over $1 billion from the Vatican's coffers by Ansios. The number of people who rejected the Vatican's official account of events continued to grow over the last five years. The irony here was that the late Milan Banker was still near the top of the list of possible suspects for those convinced that the perfectly healthy Pope Phillip Michael I was murdered just thirty-three days into his papacy.

Since Riluciani's death, an additional $400 million had been removed from the Vatican's coffers and placed into Ansios'. At the time of the Milanese banker's death, he was a very busy laundry man. He had fully taken over all Mafia money laundering operations from his now imprisoned mentor, Giovanni Fedora. He also was moving money from Banco Generali to Vatican accounts and then on to Switzerland on behalf of Gherado Fratello and his minions. He cleaned cash for kidnappers, drug and arms dealers, bank thieves and those with more material assets like jewels and art pieces. His clientele were a hodgepodge of high ranking Mobsters, average Joe murderers and right-wing terrorists.

Fran and Peg had had numerous conversations about Marco Ansios. Those conversations had become more frequent since they moved to Italy. By Fran's calculations, since the days of the Fratello raid, and the public exposure of P2 that followed, Fratello needed Ansios and his money far more than Ansios needed Fratello. Why would a man with a plethora of frozen assets kill off his cash cow and only remaining source of funding? Fratello leaned heavily on Ansios, or rather his money, while brokering critical arms deals for the Argentinian military.

"You're nuts!" Fran proclaimed loudly. "Do you know that? Absolutely nuts!"

"I'm also right, love." Peg shot back her cute, yet annoying characteristic look.

Fran just waved her theories off. "Hardly."

"Alright, Mr. Detective, let me ask you a few questions."

"Fine...let's see what you got."

"Are you buying the London coroner's report that Ansios comimtted suicide by hanging himself from that bridge?"

"Hell no!"

"...and since his death, the Italian government has halted all investigative efforts into his case, and fast-tracked his case through the courts."

"Well it is hard to convict a dead man ya know."

"True, but doesn't it seem odd to you that their court system now seems unconcerned with a lack of credible evidence for their case?"

"What do you mean?"

"Consider the fact that some of their witnesses have suddenly gone missing, and those who do show up are blatantly perjuring themselves. You and I both know that if this was still a 'real' case where they needed to convict Ansios, they wouldn't be so careless and sloppy."

"I suppose. Maybe they don't buy the Ansios suicide bullshit either. They have every right to be scared if they suspect he was murdered."

"Look, I think we can both agree that Marco Ansios was suicided. Just like that other exec."

"Suicided, yes. Just like that guy and his secretary, from her fourth story office window."

"Right? And who did you say found her 'suicide note?'"

"That other Generali executive that tried to kick Ansios out as chairman and take over his bank, while he sat in jail."

"That's right, the same man who is still hobbling about on crutches and recovering from his own botched assassination attempt."

"Who knew that there were so many deadly occupational risks associated with a career in banking?"

"In Italy? After all the crap Fedora pulled back in New York, you honestly can't be that shocked."

"True. Alright Ms. Reporter, it's my turn to ask you some questions."

"Shoot."

"So at the time of Ansios' death, Fratello had already been on the run for several months, right?"

"From what you've told me, correct." Peg quickly turned the tables on the conversation. "Where was his last known whereabouts when your fat little banker supposedly hung himself?"

"Buenos Aires."

"Oh, you mean like in the capital of Argentina?"

"Yeah."

"What were the colors painted on that bridge where they found him?"

"White and light blue." Fran failed to see her point.

"Did you know that the colors on that bridge match the Argentinian flag?"

"What?"

"Go look, it's right there in the encyclopedia at the end of the hallway Fran."

"Yeah, but..."

"Then there's the bricks and cement found stuffed in his clothes and down his pants."

"Yeah, so?"

"Bricks and mortar, sounds like the work of Masons to me."

"Mmmm, maybe." Fran was starting to see her point.

"Finally there is the bridge itself. What was the name of that bridge again?"

"Blackfriars'? That's just what they call that part of London, Peg."

"Look beyond the obvious, love. What does friar make you think of?"

"Monks, priests, the Vatican?"

"Mmmm maybe, especially if we go off of what Ansios' wife was saying. Killing off a shady loan source could be an effective way for the Vatican to make certain loans vanish without them repaying them."

"After what they did to Riluciani, I certainly wouldn't put it past any of them. Especially Krivis. So what comes to your mind when you think of that bridge?"

"A ritualistic brotherhood."

"Masons?" Peg nodded. "But Fratello was in Argentina."

"Since when has he ever done his own dirty work? Did he kill that journalist that was spilling P2 secrets himself a while back?"

"Of course not."

Peg was absolutely convinced that the bizarre scene under that bridge in London, was one of the ritualistic Masonic executions she'd read about during her days as a journalist. Fran remained skeptical.

Fran had a hard time arguing with her logic. He would hold on to Peg's theory for now. At least until something more plausible came along. He loved the way her mind worked, yet hated it too. He looked forward to proving her wrong, even if it didn't happen very often. Her investigative mind was just as sharp as it had ever been.

From his close association with Marco Ansios, Fran and Cosimo were confident that Fratello knew exactly what had happened to Banco Generali's missing millions. Fratello knew where all of the bodies were buried, when it came to Banco Generali's schemes. However, something wasn't quite right in Fran's mind. If he did in fact know these things, why would he risk capture trying to withdraw the $55 million from Ansios' Swiss account? Was he that desperate for money, now that his assets were frozen, and his P2 paymaster was dead? It was either arrogance, or desperation. Either way, it was a stupid error for a man who controlled some of the most powerful men in the world.

While Gherado Fratello was awaiting his trial, he was nothing short of a model prisoner. He got along well with the men in the maximum security facility. The staff had favorable interactions with the P2 leader too. A little over a week before his scheduled hearing in the Italian courts, he escaped from the Swiss prison. The papers were saying that he had bribed a corrupt prison guard with $10,000 for his assistance in the escape. That explanation didn't sit right with Fran or Cosimo. Why would a prison guard take what equated to a mere four months worth of his salary, in exchange for eighteen months in a prison cell, and the loss of a very lucrative career for so little money.

The escape was elaborate in its execution. It involved numerous vehicles, a helicopter, and finally a P2 associate's yacht that would take the international fugitive from Switzerland to France, then on to Monte Carlo before reaching his final destination in Uruguay. It left many in the Italian government scratching their heads and very displeased with their Swiss counterparts. All they knew for sure was if the Italian authorities ever got their hands on Gherado Fratello again, the number of charges against him would completely destroy the P2 leader. Extortion, blackmail, drug and arms smuggling, conspiracy to overthrow the legally elected government of Italy, political espionage, and illegal possession of state secrets were just some of the charges levied against him. The world's most wanted man was even accused of masterminding several terrorist bombings and the murder of Princess Grace of Monaco. Despite all of the political and legal troubles mounting in Italy, the junta who ruled over the Argentinian people were steadfast in their support of the P2 leader. A lifetime of loyalty was exchanged for their much needed weapons of war.

The other thing that happened the day after Marco Ansios's death, was the Bank of Italy appointing commissioners to clean up the mess of his imploded bank. Fran and Cosimo were assigned to accompany Italian banking officials for a meeting with Archbishop Jonas Krivis and other Vatican banking officials in Rome. Italian banking officials presented letters that documented the Vatican Bank's control over numerous ghost companies that took out over $1.4 billion in unsecured loans from Banco Generali. Krivis responded promptly with Ansios' letter absolving the Vatican from all debts. His guests wanted nothing more than to tell their host exactly what he could do with those letters. Instead, Krivis quickly reminded his guests that they held no power within the sovereign state of Vatican City, regardless of which country they represented. Their visit to the Holy City was merely a gesture of courtesy.

It would be a cold day in hell before the Italian Treasury Minister would see Krivis or his bank make good on their outstanding debts. The Italian banking officials would not be thwarted, just because Krivis had shown them the door. Authorities began to chip away at the machine that was the Vatican Bank. Their targets were now the laymen of the Vatican Bank. They were pleased with their progress as they rounded up twenty-four men, and quickly prosecuted them on charges connected to the failure of Giovanni Fedora's bank in Milan. One of the men of particular interest to Fran and Cosimo was Krivis' former top administrator.

As the months progressed, the screws continued to tighten. More and more would be uncovered about the Vatican Bank under the leadership of Krivis. As the volume and criminality of their banking scandals began to reach the public sector, Krivis found the accusations more difficult to dismiss. The Italian government announced that neither the Bank of Italy nor Milan's newest bank Nuovo Banco Generali would be burdened with the Vatican Bank's defaulted loans issued to them from the now defunct Generali Holdings in Luxembourg.

The public's response globally was harsh and deafening. The treasury ministers would direct their animosity to the Vatican Bank and Archbishop Jonas Krivis. It was their professional, roundabout way of telling Krivis that he could shove his damn letters up his ass. The men in charge of Vatican Public Relations and even Pope Phillip Michael II himself needed to get a grip on the situation and fast. They would visit Krivis' office to confront him several times. The last thing the Vatican needed now was another scandal.

In an effort to appease the public's growing criticism, the pope ordered Krivis to pay $250 million as a good faith settlement of the ghost companies' debts. It was a start, but the people would not be satisfied with such a small offering to satisfy over $1.3 billion in Vatican debt. Krivis was reluctant, but he had no choice. He had to do as he was directed by his bank's one and only shareholder. The bigger problem, that nobody, including Pope Phillip Michael II knew was that pockets of the Vatican Bank were not as deep as the world had been led to believe. The vast wealth and gold reserves held by the Vatican were legendary, however, they were also mythical. Krivis' bank had, at most, $200 million in liquid assets. After making the payment commanded by His Holiness, the Vatican bank was in desperate need of money. With Marco Ansios now dead, they would now have to seek funding in the real world markets. That would be a huge challenge now that the public knew of their billions of dollars in defaulted loans.

For the moment, the Holy City's most valuable asset was its prestige. The value of that asset had been on a steep decline ever since Pope Michael VI appointed Krivis president of Vatican Bank. It was one of the biggest mistakes that the late pontiff had ever made. Many took advantage of the arrogance and stupidity of the bank president. His closest friends like Giovanni Fedora and Marco Ansios were also not above taking advantage of the Krivis' weaknesses, after all, they were the ones who had taught the pompous idiot everything he now knew about banking. Ansios paid the Vatican Bank, or rather Krivis, $20 million for the letters of comfort. Ansios knew that the letters were meaningless in the financial world outside Vatican City. He also knew that it was an offer Krivis could not refuse.

The men of the Vatican public relations office and the pope would have several more meetings with Krivis. They needed to come up with a way to appease the angry public, while increasing Vatican revenue. The Pope would capitalize on the 1950th anniversary of the redemption of Jesus, he declared 1983 to be "Extraordinarily Holy Year." The public's fickle outrage would shift from the Holy City, back to Italy's treasury minister quickly.

They may have successfully pacified the public, but the treasury ministry was not quite finished with the Chicago native. They had enough proof to open up a formal investigation into the events and transactions that lead to the collapse of Banco Generali. Marco Ansios was by no means an innocent bystander in the failure of his bank. That being said, the Italian government would not sit back and allow a derelict like Krivis to use his late friend as a scapegoat to cover up his own crimes and scandals.

In light of these developments, the Vatican Curia relieved Krivis from his position as head of the papal bodyguard detail. Krivis also had to give up his personal living quarters in Rome, and return once again to the confines of Vatican City. This was a move that seriously cramped the style of this particular "Holy Joe." He would still enjoy his scotch, cigars and women, but the days of flaunting his own self-importance at the Roman golf courses and country clubs were now over. Any venture by Krivis outside the protective walls of Vatican City would result in his immediate arrest.

The Vatican Curia worked diligently to intercede any and all efforts by Italian authorities to serve Krivis or other bank officials with judicial paperwork. They demanded that all proper diplomatic protocols be followed at all times. $1.3 billion in unpaid Vatican loans was by no means a reason to abandon all forms of formal decorum. If papers were to be served anywhere in the Holy City, for any reason, they would have to go through the Italian Ambassador to Vatican City. The Vatican did its best to run interference on behalf of their bank and staff, but they could not stop the Italian government's formal investigation; it was time for them to look into the actions of their bank president. Reluctantly, a Curial commission of inquiry was formed, and Vatican Bank attorneys conducted an inquiry of their own. Krivis failed to help his own cause as he quickly joined the chorus of Vatican bank lawyers, from his lofty office atop St. Nicholas' tower, to emphatically declare that the Vatican would never admit any knowledge of, or accept any responsibility for the missing billions. There would be no reparations coming from their coffers.

CHAPTER 63

Word of Krivis' conundrum made its way to the United States. From his prison cell in Springfield, Missouri, Giovanni Fedora voraciously consumed media content focused on financial matters. He was particularly interested in the drama in Italy and the antics of Archbishop Jonas Krivis. "That stupid fool." Fedora thought to himself out loud. Fedora's friend, former business partner and reluctant apprentice, often thought he knew better than men like himself and Ansios. The know-it-all with the big mouth, had now become a virtual prisoner within the confines of Vatican City in order to avoid his own arrest. As Fedora enjoyed coffee and much welcomed conversation with the priest serving as the prison's chaplain, the topic of Krivis came up one afternoon, he knew that Krivis was now on his own. There would be no Ansios, Fedora or even Fratello coming to rescue him. Fedora turned his far off gaze back to the priest. "Please tell him that I hope he can somehow find a little humility for once. I also hope that he can somehow, some way find peace."

The P2 paymaster, Marco Ansios, was now dead. Archbishop Jonas Krivis continued in his position at the Vatican Bank, however, his role was diminished. He didn't like working under the watchful eyes of the papal appointed commission, but he was in no position to protest. Vatican City had become his chosen prison. The accommodations were nicer than anything the Italian government had waiting for him outside the Holy City. Gherado Fratello was once again on the run far far away from Italy, and most likely somewhere in South America.

The attention of Detectives Francis Clavering and Cosimo Angelo was once again directed to the United States. Giovanni Fedora, was still using every trick in the book to avoid his extradition. The Italian government and courts would not tolerate any more delays. He had already been indicted in a Palermo court with over seventy other men, including the Mafia Don of the Lanscano Crime Family operating out of Sicily. Detective Francis Clavering knew the Lanscano family well from his years working in "Rackets" under the leadership of D.A. Christopherson and Inspector Bentley for the NYPD.

Fedora faced new charges of conspiracy for his involvement in their $600 million heroin-trafficking trade that flooded many American cities with the dope. The Mafia cartels had not seen this much unwanted attention from the Italian government since the days of Mussolini. It quickly became the most intensive legal action against the Mafia in all of Italian history. The Italian prosecutors were diligent in their work. Their case was tight as a drum. By the end of numerous trials, only indictments dismissed were the ones against Giovanni Fedora.

Cosimo violently crumpled up the newspaper he was reading and threw it forcefully at a wall in his smallish office space. He was pissed by the judge's dismissal. "That Goddamn son of a bitch!"

Fran was startled by his partner's uncharacteristic outburst. "What's wrong?"

"How can that fucking monster keep getting away with this shit?" A lot of pain could be heard in the detective's words, as he slammed his clenched fists down hard on the papers covering his desk.

Fran remained level headed, and spoke calmly. "He's currently rotting in a Missouri prison cell, Cosimo. I'd hardly say he's gotten away with anything.

"Not here, he's not."

"Cosimo, I know that that man is a huge part of the most painful chapter in your life. But nothing we do here now will bring Arturo back."

"I know." A tear ran down Cosimo's cheek. "It still hurts Fran, it hurts my heart, right here." Cosimo grabbed at his chest.

"I wish I could tell you that that goes away. It doesn't, you just learn to live with the pain, my friend. Try to flood your mind with the best of memories from the past."

"That's what hurts Fran!"

"He was a special man. I'm glad I got the opportunity to meet him when he came to New York. You were very special to him too. The way his face lit up when he spoke of you was unmistakable."

"He was the Godfather of my children, and I was for his too."

"Look Cosimo, I want to nail every possible thing we can on him, but this one was a rare dud. The lawyers failed to deliver anything that would stick. The judge had no choice but to throw out those charges Cosimo."

Cosimo just sat there a while in silent contemplation of the American's words. "You really believe that Fedora is innocent in this case?"

"In this particular instance, I do."

Cosimo's only response was to shake his head.

"Listen, I may not know Ansios, Fratello, or even Krivis as well as you do, but I do know Fedora. I've personally listened to thousands of hours worth of wiretap surveillance on him and the Lanscanos back in New York. In all of those hours, Fedora's name never came up once. I'm not saying that Fedora is an innocent man, by any stretch of the imagination, but I honestly think he is in this particular situation."

"But we know he's involved with the Mafia, Fran."

"Involved, yes, but he's no Mafioso, Cosimo. Even the prosecutors back in the States have trouble with that one."

"What do you mean?"

"Are you sure you want me to go into that right now Cosimo?"

"Yeah, go ahead Fran."

"I'm not even 100% convinced that Fedora had anything to do with the murder of your dear friend."

Cosimo's anger instantly began to rise with that statement. "How can you even say that? He had everything to gain from the murder of Arturo, Fran."

"Mmmm I guess, for a bit. But consider the timing of the murder, Arturo was already done with his investigation. All of the evidence he found was meticulously detailed in his reports."

"That's the way he did everything, Fran."

"I don't doubt that. He was even done with his sworn deposition, right?"

"Yeah, he just needed to come back the next day to sign it." Cosimo was overcome with emotion as he finished his sentence.

"That's right. Now think about it from Fedora's perspective for a minute."

"I'd rather not."

"I know he's a rightful sore subject with you, but please bear with me here for a moment."

"Fine."

"If either of us were standing in Fedora's shoes, intent on using the Italian solution to eliminate a problem, don't you think the deed would have been done much sooner? Why would he wait until everything was already wrapped up? The only thing missing was a 'bow,' his signature."

Cosimo didn't want to admit it, but Fran was right. Fedora was one of the most dangerous men to ever come from Sicily. Every last one of his accusers were either dead or hidden in witness protection programs in various countries. Even his hired hit man, sitting in the confines of a New York prison wouldn't utter a single word against Fedora. It was easier for Cosimo to grasp the idea that Fedora had had Bartolone killed than to think that his true killer might be still running around free somewhere.

A few weeks had passed since Fran and Cosimo's emotion filled exchange. The winters in Rome were much less dreary and bitter than they were back in New York City. Nonetheless, the final month of winter was a welcome change of seasons in Rome. Fran had received a call from Deputy Chief Bentley back in New York.

"Deputy Chief? When did all that happen?" Commented Fran.

"Oh several months ago."

"Well congratulations on your promotion seems long overdue Chief!"

"Thank you."

It was good to hear his old boss' voice once again. The two men exchanged pleasantries and stories. The only thing Fran really missed about New York was working with Bentley, Christopherson and Cardinal Wexford. As Bentley updated Fran, it was now more clear than ever that leaving New York was the best decision he'd ever made.

"Say Fran, do you remember that hitman guy contracted to kill Arturo Bartolone that was convicted a while back?"

"Yeah, of course I do. What about him?"

"Well, I thought you should know, he's dead now."

"What? How? I thought he was serving time at the Metropolitan Correctional Center there in Lower Manhattan."

"Mmm, well he was, the official story is he fell to his death from the roof of the MCC."

Fran's mind started to drift a bit. "Did he fall, or was he thrown or pushed?"

"The reports just say that he fell, why do you ask?"

"We are noticing an uptick in murders lately where the killer or killers want it to look like suicide."

"Really? That's odd."

"Yeah, so far we're up to three in the last eight months or so."

"I will dig a little more and let you know if I find anything like that."

"I'd appreciate that."

The topic of conversation shifted away from work once again. Fran became concerned when Bentley told him that their retired D.A., Christopherson was not in the best of health. "Please give him my best next time you talk to him."

"I will."

"Thank you."

Giovanni Fedora was no longer the man he once was. The man who *Forbes* used to call a "Legendary Financial Titan" and "Immaculate Global Banker," now had other labels. None of them were flattering. Hc had fallen hard and fast in recent years. Now he bore the moniker of "the Sicilian who bankrupted the Vatican" and a "high ranking power mafioso" who commanded respect in the syndicate. Some sources even went so far as to informally incriminate him with contracting the killing of Pope Phillip Michael I. Fedora was certainly on a short list of possible suspects by those who rejected the Vatican's official story, but there wasn't enough to substantiate the accusations.

One summer day, Fedora was visited at the Missouri prison by two men from the Reagan administration. The first man was the Executive Director for the President's commission on organized crime, and the other was an assistant US attorney for the government. They had evidence connecting Fedora with organized crime.

Fedora had very little patience with these Neanderthal types. "I'm already spending the rest of my life in prison, what more do you want from me?"

The attorney was first to respond. "Mr. Fedora, we're not here for anything like that."

Fedora remained suspicious. "Oh?"

The other man continued. "No, my commission knows full well of your history. We were wondering if you'd come to Washington, DC next month to teach us the procedural details of money laundering."

"Me?" Fedora perked up. Getting out of his drab accommodations for a while, regardless of where or why, would certainly be a most welcomed change. "Yeah, I could do that."

Once he got to DC, he quickly realized that everyone in the DEA, FBI and presidential commission thought that money laundering was the same as hiding money, rather than a process of cleaning dirty money made by illegal means like drugs, murder for hire, or extortion. These men knew nothing about international monetary systems. He did his best to educate them on how large sums of money were laundered. The information went right over their heads. They decided to abruptly end Fedora's teaching when he informed them that laundered monies were taxable. They didn't like the idea of the IRS being used to funnel dirty money around the world, while others considered the amount of tax revenue lost to money laundering. Clearly the latter had not heard a damn word Fedora had told them. As he was returning to his prison cell in Missouri, Fedora gave up all hope on this administration's ability to stop the flow of dirty money in the US. He also in that moment gave up all hope for a pardon from President Ronald Reagan.

Cosimo and Fran were a mixed bag of emotions as they left an unexpected meeting with the chief of inspector's office. Fedora had finally conceded his final efforts against extradition. He would finally be returning to Italian soil to face his fate in person.

"It's about damn time!" Fran exclaimed.

Cosimo echoed Fran's tone in his response. "This is some great news!"

"I can't argue with that gentlemen," responded the chief. "I want you two men to go over to the States and bring him back for us."

Fran was elated about the assignment. Cosimo was a mixed bag of emotions. He wasn't sure he would be able to keep his emotions in check. It would take everything in him to remain level-headed enough in the presence of Fedora to keep from strangling him with his own bare hands.

Fran noticed a slight contortion in his partner's face. He knew exactly what was going through Cosimo's head. He quickly cleared his throat and responded to the man's orders. "Thank you sir, we'd be more than happy to get him over here safely for you."

"Thank you Fran, Cosimo." The chief confirmed. "You two have been working so hard for so many years on his case, I thought it was only fitting."

"We can appreciate that."

"I will have my secretary call you when arrangements are made and your itineraries are ready."

"Perfect!"

The two detectives soon returned to Cosimo's office. Cosimo promptly closed the door behind him. Fran could see the tears in his eyes, just waiting to drop. "I don't think I can do this Fran."

"Yes you can, Cosimo. You have to, for Arturo."

"I will kill that man, with my own hands, the first chance I get."

"No you won't. The coward has already wasted too many people's time, energy and money, including ours. It is time for him to face justice and his fate here in Italy."

"But Fran, I..."

"You sitting in prison for killing that man won't solve a damn thing. It most certainly won't bring Arturo back Cosimo, and you know it."

A couple of weeks later, the two detectives boarded a plane for the States. They touched down at LaGuardia Airport in New York. They had a purposeful, extended layover. They wouldn't be flying on to Springfield, Missouri until the next day. Fran and Cosimo took a cab over to his old precinct on Leonard Street. They caught Deputy Chief Bentley by surprise as they walked through his office door, unannounced.

"Francis Clavering! What the hell are you doing here?"

"Just visiting..."

"Yeah sure you are." The two men laughed.

"Chief, I'd like you to meet Cosimo Angelo, my partner from Italy."

Bentley shook the man's hand. "It is so good to finally meet you Cosimo. Fran has told me many things about you over the years. I must say, I'm most impressed!"

"Well thank you sir." Cosimo responded with a slight blush of embarrassment.

The three men chewed the fat for a bit. They talked about cases, promotions and family. Fran knew Bentley was a very busy man, and needed to get back to his work. The detectives cut the visit short. He had two more important stops to make before their day was over.

Cardinal Wexford was just as surprised as Bentley was to see the two men. He couldn't believe what all had transpired since the last time they saw each other, just days after the murder of Riluciani. The tenacity of these men, Hans included, was impressive and appreciated. Before Fran and Cosimo left, Cardinal Wexford prayed with them, asking God to continue to guide them and hold them safe for whatever was next in their still dangerous journey.

Their final stop was to the home of retired D.A. Christopherson. The two men were quietly escorted to the man's bedroom by his wife. Fran could see that the man had lost a considerable amount of weight. The cancer that coursed through Christopherson's body had stolen the vigor of the man he once was. It was difficult for Fran to see the man who held such an honored and respected place in his heart in this condition. He felt bad for waking him from his sleep.

As he and Cosimo came through the door, the frail man opened his eyes. The man perked up and a smile instantly came to his face as he recognized one of the faces. "Francis? Francis Clavering? What the hell are you doing here?"

"Oh we were just in the neighborhood, sir."

"Bullshit!"

Fran couldn't help but smile as the spirit of the man he knew and loved returned. "Somehow, I knew you weren't gonna believe that."

"Not for a second. How the hell are you?"

"I'm great..."

"How are Peg and the kids? Are you all still in Italy?"

"Yes, and everyone is doing great. Sir, I'd like you to meet my friend and partner Cosimo Angelo from Italy."

"It's a pleasure to finally meet you detective! I've heard many impressive things about you over the years."

Again Cosimo again blushed slightly as he thanked the man for the compliment.

"So what brings you gentlemen to the States?"

"You wouldn't believe me if I told you sir."

"Try me..."

"We're here to take Giovanni Fedora back to Italy."

"No shit? Finally! It took long enough."

"Yeah he finally gave up his fight."

"That's some of the best news I've heard in quite a while gentlemen."

The two detectives told the D.A. of the drama surrounding Marco Ansios and his mysterious death. As the topic of discussion shifted over to Archbishop Jonas Krivis, Fran got quiet. The old man could see something was weighing heavy on his detective's mind.

"Is something wrong Francis?"

Fran's thoughts drifted back to the early days of the Benedetto case. The lies he and Bentley told the D.A. that had led him to where he was today, still ate at his conscience. "I, uh..." Fran paused for what felt like hours. "It's nothing sir, just some jet lag. I will be fine." Fran knew he was running out of time to confess his lies to the man. That said, he didn't want some of his final memories of the old man to be of him chewing his ass out over twelve year old lies. Fran continued to sit there in silence.

Christopherson detected something was off with his detective, but decided not to press the issue. He decided to shift the conversation to another topic. "Look Francis, you are an incredible detective, husband and father. No matter what bullshit Bayer pulled or other obstacles got in your way, you were always determined to do whatever needed to be done. I'm so sorry that piece of shit Bayer fucked up your career over there in Queens."

"It all turned out alright, sir."

"There was never any doubt that it would in my mind. However, his actions were still inexcusable, Francis." Fran just nodded in response. "You know what you have to do now, don't you?"

"What's that sir?"

Christopherson grabbed Francis by the hand, and looked directly into his eyes. "Finish it!"

"Finish it?"

"Yes, get Fedora's ass back to Italy and have their courts finish him off. Then go get that son of a bitch Krivis! You hear me?!"

"Yes sir! We will! That I can promise you sir."

"Good!" Christopherson quietly reflected for a moment, proud of his detective.

Fran figured that this could very well be the last time he'd see his old D.A. alive. Fran didn't want the visit to end, but the man was visibly getting tired in his weakened state. It had been a long day. Tomorrow he and Cosimo would travel on to Missouri, and escort Mr. Giovanni Fedora to his date with lady justice in Italy. Francis Clavering would go forward from this day with renewed purpose, thanks to the push by his old D.A.

CHAPTER 64

Once Cosimo got a hold of his personal emotions, the flight home was long, but pleasant. He would remain professional, but he absolutely hated the man. Cosimo was not interested in idle chitchat with the man responsible for the murder of his best friend. Prison life had aged Fedora quickly. Long gone was the suave, debonair man Fran had only seen on the television and in print.

Cosimo couldn't stomach a conversation with Fedora. Fran on the other hand, wanted to know more about the mysterious man he'd been following for years. Fedora was a virtual Dr. Jekyll and Mr Hyde. During the flight, Fran was introduced to the intelligent, and charming side of the man with numerous fascinating tales to tell. It was easy to see how people could be innocently lulled into his evil con games. Fran already knew about the darker side of the man.

Fedora was treated very differently from other men imprisoned in Italy as they awaited their trials. Because of his long suspected history with powerful Mafia families, authorities thought it best to keep the failed businessman and banker in a women's correctional facility in the Lombardi region of Italy. Their reasoning was based on safety more than anything, he was isolated from much of the female inmate population the majority of the time. This was a two pronged strategy to also limit his ability to interact or communicate with his Mafia friends on the outside.

The novel arrangements had its pros and cons. Fedora had missed seeing the female form he appreciated so much during his years in a Springfield, Missouri penitentiary. Also the guards in Lombardi were friendly, kind and respectful. A far cry from their American counterparts who treated him like a dog. The food was also better, but the facility was much older than the more modern prisons in America. The worst part about the Lombardi prison were the winters. No matter what the staff did, it was always frigid and drafty in those antiquated prison cells.

Two short days after Fedora had returned to Italian soil, he was sitting in a courtroom in the Palace of Justice. His lawyers protested loudly about not having enough time to prepare. The judge, nor anyone else, wanted to hear their concerns. "Counselor, you've had years to prepare with your client. Since before he was incarcerated in the United States." There would be no delays, for any reason. Fedora was facing a myriad of charges stemming from the fraudulent bankruptcy of his Milan bank and the Bank of Rome that failed after trying to bail out his bank.

The Italian con man appeared for the first few days and sat through opening arguments and procedures. The whole circus bored him to tears, so he opted to stay in his prison cell. For several weeks, Fedora had no interest in what was happening in that courtroom. He would not return until damning reports and secret internal documents from the Bank of Rome were introduced as evidence.

The defense countered that the bankruptcy of Fedora's Milan bank was because of the embezzlement by his staff. They successfully demonstrated that Mr. Nico Novelli, his wife and a handful of friends had fortified their personal Swiss bank accounts with over $60 million of Mr. Giovanni Fedora's money. The prosecution took great interest in the exculpatory evidence. Not because of what it contained, but rather how Fedora and his legal team obtained the information. It became abundantly evident to the defendant and his counsel that the outcome of the trial had been predetermined long before the trial ever began. On March 15, 1985, Giovanni Fedora was sentenced to twelve years in prison for the fraudulent bankruptcy of his Milan bank and the Bank of Rome. Fedora's only break during the trial came during his sentencing. The prosecution wanted him locked up for fifteen years.

The fraudulent bankruptcy trial demonstrated perfectly why Fedora fought his extradition from the United States for so many years. The power players in Italian business and government who felt wronged by Fedora were not interested in any sort of actual justice. They only wanted Fedora to disappear for the rest of his days. They were not concerned about how they accomplished their objective.

Next up for Fedora and his lawyers was the trial for the murder of Mr. Arturo Bartolone. Several years had already passed since the government-appointed liquidator was gunned down on his front lawn while his wife watched in horror from their upstairs bedroom window. In those many years various media outlets would produce extensive content related to the Bartolone murder and eventual trial. On May 8th, Fedora observed his sixty-fifth birthday in his prison cell. He was visited by his wife. He missed her, and relished the moments they had shared together. She was deeply troubled by the things she had been reading in the press about him. The information shocked her conscience. Fedora worked very hard his entire life to keep his true world and alter ego hidden from her. She just couldn't believe that the love of her life was capable of the crimes reported in the press.

The following day, Francis and Peg Clavering accompanied Cosimo Angelo, his wife and children, and many others from all parts of Italy to the Palace of Justice in Milan. They were all gathered there for the dedication of the Arturo Bartolone Law Library. It was a somber, yet respectful event for Cosimo, and his family, and the widow of the slain government investigator. Cosimo found some peace in knowing that his dear friend would not be forgotten by current and future generations who would choose to follow in his footsteps.

In the coming weeks, Giovanni Fedora would meet frequently with his lawyer in the Lombardi women's prison to strategize their defense for the upcoming murder trial of Arturo Bartolone. This trial would be unlike anything he had ever been through before in either Italy or America. These charges were all based on circumstantial evidence. Hearsay was admissible in Italian courts, as was indirect proof of innocence or guilt.

Sitting in the gallery for much of the trial, was Bartolone's good friend Cosimo Angelo. Sitting next to him was Detective Francis Clavering. Clavering was curious about the Italian legal system and the use of ambiguous evidence. "This shit would never fly in D.A. Christopherson's office, when he was there." The detective thought to himself disapprovingly. The prosecution worked hard to demonstrate that Giovanni Fedora had the motive and connections needed to kill Bartolone. Conviction was easy when the evidence was vague.

As Fran listened to the trial in the gallery, some of the information used was from the Lincoln National Bank trial in New York. He remembered that particular hearing well, after all it was much of his and FBI Agent Lance Erickson's work that was used by the prosecution in that trial. But something wasn't right in the way it was being presented by the prosecution in Italy. Fran's suspicions grew stronger when Fedora's defense lawyer introduced a sworn affidavit that confirmed that Fedora and Bartolone's paid hitman, who had died the winter before trying to escape from the Metropolitan Correctional Center in Manhattan, had never met or spoken with each other.

Fran decided it was time for him to do a little bit of digging. He knew that Cosimo would be of no help to him. He had already convicted Fedora of the murder of his friend in his mind. Fedora was guilty of plenty of crimes. He was already facing the remainder of his life in prison. However, one thing Fran could not stand was gung ho prosecutors who would essentially frame criminals for something that they didn't do, in order to make themselves look good to the public. That was the kind of shit that men like Federal Prosecutor

Nathan Bayer would pull. Men of integrity, like D.A. Christopherson would never pull something like that.

It didn't take long for Fran to discover that Fedora's primary Italian nemesis, who was quoted in Italian media that "Fedora's ashes should be scattered about the surface of the earth" had actually contracted a hit-for-hire on Giovanni Fedora in the past. Fran was becoming more and more uncomfortable with what he was uncovering. The final straw was when the defense presented yet another affidavit from an inmate who had done time in the MCC New York prison facility at the same time as Bartolone's supposed hired hit man. This sworn statement claimed that Giovanni Fedora had absolutely nothing to do with the murder of Arturo Bartolone.

Following a few short weeks of independent side work, Fran finally discovered the truth. The information made him angry and unbearable to live with. He had no idea what to do with the information now that he had found it.

Peg had had about all she could take of her husband. "Fran, you can't just sit with that information you've uncovered. You've got to tell someone, and soon. This animosity has made you a miserable ass to live with, no matter how much the kids and I love you."

Fran knew she was right, he had been the biggest ass the last week and a half. "I have no idea who to tell, Peg."

"Ummm, Cosimo should be the first one on your list, Fran."

"Cosimo? I can't. It would be just reopening a deep, deep wound that's almost healed over."

"But Fran, you have to. Put yourself in his shoes, he's gotta know, love, even if it hurts. The truth here is important."

Fran took a deep breath and sighed. "You really think I should tell him? He's going to hate me. He may not even believe it?"

"If you show him what you showed me, he will believe you. Maybe not right away, but he's a smart, level headed man. I mean, isn't that why the two of you work so well together?"

"Yeah, I guess. But, I'm not sure how he will take the information. I don't think this is something that I should do at work."

"Then invite him over here and tell him, love. I will take the kids out for some gelato and shopping."

"Fine."

Three hours later, Cosimo was seated in an overstuffed chair in the Clavering home. All he knew was that Fran had something very important to tell him, but he had no idea what. His anxiety was growing as he watched and waited. Fran paced the room searching for the best way to say what he needed to say.

Finally Fran stopped, took a deep breath, and broke the awkward silence. "Cosimo, I know this is going to be hard for you to hear, but I've found hard evidence that Giovanni Fedora was not responsible for the murder of Arturo Bartolone."

Cosimo took a few moments to process what Fran had just said. "How can you say that after sitting next to me in that courtroom all of these months Fran?" A tear flowed down his cheek, as his voice cracked with his response.

"That's just it, I have been listening to that trial. Those prosecutors are out to get him despite there being evidence that would exonerate him."

"There is no such evidence Fran!"

"I'm sorry, I know this is shocking and upsetting, but hear me out. Please!"

Cosimo didn't want to listen, but he knew the type of detective Fran was. He would not be saying such things just to say them. "Fine. I'm listening."

"Thank you." Fran went into detail about the prosecution's twisting of information from the Lincoln National Bank trial, and the sworn affidavits. "Cosimo, Fedora did not have Arturo killed... Nico Novelli did."

"Novelli?! How the hell did you come up with that one Fran?"

"Look Cosimo, I know that Fedora is guilty of plenty of things, but the murder of your friend was not one of them. Look..."

Fran handed Cosimo some papers he had Bentley send him from New York. It clearly documented the transfer of money from Fedora's account to the account of Bartolone's killer. "This doesn't prove anything, Fran. If anything, it confirms that Fedora did have him killed."

"Yeah, I thought that too, at first, but look who authorized it."

Cosimo looked. "Novelli?"

"Yeah!"

"Novelli did it as directed by Fedora."

"Nope, he couldn't have."

"Why?"

"Look at the date Cosimo. Fedora couldn't have ordered the hit on your friend because he was in jail at that time! That son of a bitch Novelli who made us feel sorry for him for being blackmailed by Fedora, fucking got away with everything! He framed Fedora for the murder he hired out, while embezzling millions from him. Now that piece of shit is an American Citizen, living the dream in the witness protection program somewhere over there!"

Cosimo's eyes went wide as every last thing Fran had said started to click in his head. "Fran, we have to do something! Fedora can't wrongly take the hit for Arturo's murder!"

Over the course of the next twelve weeks, Fran and Cosimo would visit Giovanni Fedora at the Lombardi women's prison. Fedora understood that none of what the two detectives presented exonerated him from his other crimes, but he did appreciate their efforts to help get the murder charges dismissed. The defense lawyers presented the new findings to the judge as Fedora and the two detectives clinged to their sliver of hope. In the end, Nico Novelli marching into that courtroom and admitting to the world that he was the one who contracted to have Bartolone killed would not have mattered. Like the fraudulent bankruptcy trial, this one too was rigged against the former Italian mogel. Justice had turned her back on Mr. Fedora once again. On March 18, 1986, Giovanni Fedora was found guilty for the murder of Arturo Bartolone, and was sentenced to life in prison.

At 8:30 AM on March 20th, Fedora had his breakfast and coffee like he had always done since he arrived at the women's prison in Lombardi. He staggered through the door that separated his sleeping area from his bathroom. As he slumped to the floor, he yelled his final words. *"Mi hanno avvelenato con il mio caffè!"* As he was loaded into an ambulance, he slipped into an irreversible coma as the lethal dose of potassium cyanide coursed through his body. That afternoon the hospital priest recited his last rites. At 12:02 the next morning, Giovanni Fedora succumbed to the poisonous cyanide that had been stirred into his coffee the morning before.

CHAPTER 65

The news of the sixty-five year old's death traveled quickly around the world. It didn't matter if the people loved or hated the man, the public had a hard time believing the news. The rumors of both suicide and murder spread like an out of control wildfire. Suicide was certainly a plausible possiblity. If that were the actual cause of his death, it would not have been his first go at it. Clearly he was more successful with this attempt than when he slashed his wrists and ingested digitalis back in New York. Did he finally succeed with this attempt like his lifelong hero Socrates, many centuries before him?

His family came forward immediately. His oldest son quickly became the family's public voice of contention, especially regarding the theory of suicide. This was a clear case of murder, and they knew it. The family was not about to allow their beloved patriarch's death become a circus swirling with lies about suicide. They remembered what the court of public opinion did to his close friend Marco Ansios. They would make every effort to not let that happen to their Giovanni Fedora.

Was this a case of murder like his family insisted? There was certainly no shortage of former friends, lovers, and enemies who could make the list of creditable suspects. There was also a plethora of people who would come forward with newsworthy nuggets to claim their fifteen minutes of fame. Integrity was not on the minds of the news sources. They had employed a quantity over quality mentality regarding what they put in print regarding Fedora. They didn't even bother to verify the authenticity of many of these acquaintances before unleashing their stories to the public domain.

Giovanni Fedora was an enigma. The man rose from humble beginnings to become the world's richest, most powerful man. Yet in his final years of life, his entire global empire came crashing down and he spent his final years incarcerated. The man's life made for a fascinating story. For many years, while he was at the pinnacle of success in the financial and business worlds, he remained relatively obscure to the general public. That all changed when rumors of loan sharking and his close association with a world famous Mafia crime family began to circulate.

His notoriety really came to a head in 1972 following Hollywood's release of the first of *The Godfather* movies. Soon after that, the world quickly developed an insatiable appetite for anything that would reveal more of the hidden underworld of a glamorized Mafia lifestyle. Giovanni Fedora perfectly embodied the Mafia persona long before it became popular in the cinema. He had the style, the money, the power and the women. The only thing he didn't have was the family. That all changed when he started laundering massive amounts of dope money for the Lanscano crime family.

The media would capitalize greatly on the public's fascination. So many pieces were hitting the media so fast, it was hard to keep up. Every last one of them liberally sensationalized the myth, drama, crime and mobster connections. Only those who truly knew Giovanni Fedora for years were able to separate fact from fiction.

Fran and Cosimo immediately notified Hans and Cardinals Leone and Wexford of the news of Fedora's death. It only took a few days until Detectives Francis Clavering and Cosimo Angleo were bombarded by a constant barrage of phone calls both at work and occasionally at home. Most of the calls at Fran's home were from former colleagues from his days working the "Rackets" bureau back in New York. A few news outlets tried to get exclusive quotes and sound bites. Fran just waved them off rudely. He was not interested in contributing to their material, just so that they could twist and manipulate it to fit their narratives. That lesson, learned the hard way, cost him his future career as a detective back in New York City, thanks to Nathan Bayer. The call from Bentley wasn't all that surprising. The two men had spoken several times since the Claverings had moved to Italy.

The frenzy finally began to fade the following week. Fran and Cosimo were in a weird phase of operations. They would spend their days cataloging and filing numerous documents that had come from the Fedora investigation over the years. It was a staggering amount of material. It seemed that Fran's work with Cosimo and the Italian government was soon coming to an end.

"Are you going to go back to the states, Fran?"

"I don't know, to be honest, I haven't even thought about any of that. I mean I knew the end would come eventually, but I definitely wasn't expecting it to be right now."

"Now that Ansios and Fedora are dead, there's only Fratello and Krivis left."

"It's really incredible what all has transpired since we all started on this journey." Fran reminisced.

"Certainly nothing I could have anticipated." Cosimo responded. "So much has happened, and so many have been lost along the way."

Fran just nodded as a memory of Chiaros Riluciani came to the forefront of his mind. "Yeah, I wonder what Riluciani would think about all of this?"

"Mmmm, he'd still be disappointed in his church, but then again if he were alive, all of this would be completely different."

"That's true." Fran confirmed. "If only..."

"If we do keep at this, it's certainly not going to get any easier."

Fran agreed with his partner. "Nope, I'm sure Fratello is off hiding somewhere in South America."

Cosimo sighed loudly. "Yeah that would be my guess."

"I mean, I know Krivis is a stupid, arrogant fuck, but do you honestly think he's dumb enough to ever step foot out of Vatican City again so we can nab him?"

"Mmmm, maybe. If he did, it would have to be for a damn good reason."

Fran remembered back to his first encounter with Krivis. "Well the man does love to golf. You taught me that, my friend, so many years ago."

"That he does. Somehow I just don't see Pope Phillip Michael II putting a country club and golf course in Vatican City, just for an idiot like Krivis."

"True, I mean we both know the Vatican is strapped for cash these days, right?"

"Right."

"Seems to me the Vatican could use a new tourist attraction these days. All those green fees certainly would help refill their coffers and restore their public image."

"Hmmmm, I wonder what Riluciani would think of your idea?"

"It's far better than the bullshit that's been happening around there since they killed him."

"True," Cosimo agreed. "I guess at this point it doesn't really matter. I mean Krivis may now be a prisoner of Vatican City, but he's far from suffering. He's still got his scotch, cigars, and women."

Fran raised an eyebrow and nodded. "You aren't wrong there. That young, sexy little secretary he's got working up there in that tower of his is definitely not hard on the eyes."

"No she's not...I mean for a man who is a prisoner trapped in the world's smallest country, he's not suffering too much."

"Not with that kind of eye candy sashaying about the office! Do you even think she knows how to type?"

"Fran, knowing what you know about Krivis, do you honestly think he hired her for her typing abilities?"

The rest of the day was relatively uneventful, yet still somehow exhausting. The two detectives had always been meticulous with their paperwork, even if they hated every minute of it. That evening

Fran was glad to finally get away from his work and out of his head. It had been a while since he spent some quality time with Peg and the kids. He very much enjoyed his dinner listening to the children talk about their day at school. After dinner, Fran helped Peg clean up the dinner dishes and get the kids settled in for the night.

Finally the two of them had a moment to themselves. It was one of the things they both made a point of doing more often since coming to Italy. Back in New York, Peg often played second fiddle to Fran's work life. She never complained about his long, odd hours, even if she had every right to. After all, if it wasn't for her, he'd never have given up his successful career in the private sector for his lifelong dream of public service. His dedicated, almost obsessive detective work for men like Bentley and Christopherson was appreciated by superiors and colleagues, and never once were his efforts ever taken for granted. Well not until a piece of shit FBI prosecutor sabotaged his future career did his level of commitment to his work finally let up. Fran was still a man of principle and integrity, but he was no longer willing to sacrifice his valuable time with his family.

Fran put on some music. Then walked over to Peg seated on the couch reading a magazine. Gently he took her hand in his, "Would you care to dance, my love?"

"I don't think I've ever heard such a stupid question in my life Francis Clavering." She rose from the couch, chuckled then smiled.

The pair exchanged conversation as they moved gracefully about the room. "So how was your day?"

Peg closed her eyes to remember, as Fran pulled her body closer into his. "Nothing too extraordinary, really."

Fran looked into her eyes as she spoke. "Why am I suddenly having a hard time believing that?"

Peg played off his comment with a slight shrug. "Hmmm, I don't know."

"What did you do today?"

"Well let's see, I did a little shopping with Cosimo's wife." Fran closed his eyes and pulled her in closer, and continued to listen without saying a word. "Then we had lunch in the cutest little *ristorante.*"

"What did you have for lunch?"

"Nothing too fancy, just some *Cacio e Pepe* and a side salad."

"That really sounds delicious. You may have to take me there some time."

"The Pecorino Romano they used was amazing."

"It sounds like it, yum."

"After lunch, I had a doctor's appointment, and then I came home."

"Doctor's appointment? I didn't know you were going to the doctor today. Is everything alright?"

"Yeah, I'm fine, but I will be even better in about thirty weeks..." She grinned.

"Thirty weeks? Why, what's happening in thirty weeks?" Fran's mind raced, clueless.

Peg was amused. She couldn't help but smile as she watched him try to figure out what she was trying to tell him.

"Come on love, won't you help me out a little here? What's happening in thirty weeks?"

Peg couldn't help but smile. "That's when you and I will be bring home your next son or daughter, love!"

"Are you serious?!?!" He pushed her away a little to get a better look in her smiling eyes. He failed miserably at hiding his overwhelming sudden joy.

"Absolutely, 100%!" She confirmed.

"My God, that is wonderful news!" He lifted her from the floor, swung her around and kissed her before gently returning her feet to the floor. "Have I told you lately that I love you?"

Peg immediately began to hum a few bars of the catchy tune before responding. "Yeah, you may have mentioned that a time or two before, but don't let that stop you from saying it again." Then she kissed him.

They agreed to break the news to their children over breakfast the next morning. It seemed like a fun thing to do before they shuffled off for their school day. This evening would be for just the two of them.

The two lovers spent their evening waltzing about the living room, enjoying the moment and each other without a care in the world.

The moment and mood was interrupted by an unexpected knock on the front door. Fran looked at Peg, "Are we expecting anyone, hon?"

"Not that I know of."

"Well excuse me for a minute. Save my place. I will be back in a moment." He winked and issued a huge smile.

When Fran opened the door, he immediately recognized the man standing on the stoop as Fedora's lawyer. He and Cosimo had gotten to know him quite well during the latter months of Fedora's murder trial. At the man's feet sat a rather large box. There were no markings on the box anywhere, but there was an impressive amount of tape used to seal the thing shut.

"Can I help you?"

"Detective Clavering, please forgive my manners. I apologize for showing up so late and unannounced, but it was urgent that I deliver this box to you."

Fran looked again at the large box, curious. "What's in it?"

"I have no idea sir. I was just ordered by Fedora to give it to you should anything happen to him. Clearly something has happened to him, so um, well, here we are."

Fran looked at the man and the box now more puzzled than ever. "Why didn't you just bring it to me at the office tomorrow morning?"

"He was specific with his instructions. He wanted it to be delivered to your home sir."

Fran helped the man lift the surprisingly heavy, awkward box. The two men carried it into the living room and placed it onto the coffee table. There was very little further conversation. The man apologized to Fran one more time, and then to Mrs. Clavering. He then handed Fran one of his business cards, then abruptly left without another word.

Peg was more confused than her husband by what had just happened. "Who was that? And what's with this gigantic box sitting here?"

"That was Fedora's lawyer. Fedora ordered him to give it to me, if anything ever happened to him." Fran looked at her then back at the box, then turned to head for their bedroom.

"Aren't you going to open it Fran?!"

"Not tonight."

"Clearly it's something important, or he would not have brought it over here so late, and unannounced."

"Oh I'm sure it's important, but I'm not opening Fedora's version of Pandora's box tonight, I'm going to bed. Would you care to join me, my love?"

"How can you just dismiss your curiosity like that Fran? What if it's some sort of urgent business?"

"Mmmm, I don't know. I just feel like tonight you are my urgent business, not whatever's in Fedora's big ol' box over there."

CHAPTER 66

The next morning, Fran and Peg were up a little earlier than normal. Peg made a hearty breakfast for everyone. Fran helped get the children ready for their school day. As they filed through the living room on their way to breakfast, all three of them became extremely fascinated with the mysterious box that appeared during the night.

"Wow, that's a really big box! It's not Christmas. Nobody has a birthday soon. What is this?"

"That's just daddy's work, kids. Now come eat your breakfast please."

"Fine." Responded their oldest son as his stomach began to growl loudly.

The children forgot all about the box as they approached the table. "Pancakes!" They all said in unison. "On a school morning! Wow, this is great! Thanks mom!"

"You're welcome kids!" Peg shot Fran a glance, followed by a smile, then a wink. Fran then pulled her in close to whisper something in her ear, then kissed her. "Ewww! The youngest boy protested. "Not during breakfast!"

Infectious giggles and chatter broke out amongst the kids as they buttered and poured syrup on their hotcakes. Fran then nodded at Peg. "Kids, your dad and I just wanted you to know that in about seven months you guys are getting another brother or sister!"

The middle sister squealed with delight upon hearing the news. "Really mom! That's great! I can't wait to meet him or her! I can't wait to help you with the new baby mom!"

The two boys echoed with their excitement. "Me too!"

Following breakfast, Fran cleaned up the dishes and kitchen. Peg loaded the children into the car and drove them to school. While they were gone Fran called Cosimo to inform him he'd be late coming in that day.

"Is everything ok? You are never late for work Fran."

Fran chuckled, "Yeah, everything's fine around here. I will tell you all about it when I come in."

Cosimo grew suspicious of Fran's uncharacteristic behavior, but decided not to press the issue. "Alright, I will let the supervisor know. See you when you get here."

Peg returned from chauffeuring their children to school. "I think that went over well."

"I'd say it did. I was a little worried about how it was going to go over, considering what happened the last time you were expecting."

Peg quickly changed the subject. She really didn't want to talk about her last pregnancy and miscarriage. "Well Detective Clavering, shall we finally open Fedora's box?"

"Yes, ma'am!"

Fran took his knife from his pocket and cut carefully through the ridiculous amount of tape sealing the box shut. As he lifted the box's flaps, he saw lots and lots of crumpled newspaper and a sealed envelope sitting on top. The envelope had "Detective Francis Clavering" written across it in very elegant handwriting.

Fran opened the letter and began to read aloud:

Dear Detective Francis Clavering,

If you are reading this letter, I, Giovanni Fedora, am now dead.

No matter what is said about me in the public sector, you must know that I did not take my own life. I may not have not have conducted myself in the most honorable or honest of ways during my life, but I sincerely appreciate your efforts to clear my name of the murder of Mr. Arturo Bartolone. He and I may not have seen eye to eye, but he was a brilliant man doing honest, meticulous work that even a man like myself could appreciate.

As a dying wish, I hope that you could please share the information you found and exonerate me of that crime, with my family and his. I want them to know, once and for all, that I had no part in that murder! Regardless of what the Italian courts might have to say about it.

I know you have invested many years of your life into your work investigating me, and by extension, a few others. You and I may not have been on the same side of the law, but I can respect the honesty and integrity of the hard work that you have done over the years. As I'm sure you already know, there is no shortage of crooked colleagues in your line of work. May the contents of this box serve you well as you go forward into the future.

Sincerely,
Giovanni Fedora

Fran and Peg exchanged curious shrugs. He then carefully returned the letter to its envelope. The couple carefully continued to dig through the crumpled newspapers to find yet another sealed box tightly sealed with even more tape.

Fran took out his pocket knife again. "This is getting ridiculous...I feel like this is some sort of sick joke stringing us along..."

"Somebody sure didn't want whatever's in there gone through very easily."

"...and without it being obvious."

The inner box contained yet another letter. This one was addressed to Giovanni Fedora in nice handwriting that was different from Fedora's letter. Fran opened and unfolded the one piece of stationary contained inside. He cleared his throat once again and began to read:

My Dearest Brother Giovanni,

I hope this box finds you well. If you are receiving this, obviously the worst has happened to me. Please know that I did all in my power to deploy everything that you've taught me over the years. Your friendship, tutelage and help have always been invaluable to me and my family. All I can say is thank you for everything you've ever done for all of us.

I'm sure as you go through the stuff in this box, you will find much that is familiar to you. They are of no use to me now. You always gave me a hard time about my "pack rat" ways. The stuff in this box still holds great power and value even though I'm now dead. I hope these things will somehow help you and your future. I have always trusted your judgements and opinions. Feel free to do with them what you will.

Best of luck, my brother,
Marco Ansios

This box contained reams and reams of papers and an astonishing number of cassette tapes with names and dates. Fran curiously took a small stack of the papers off the top of the stack. He scanned the documents somewhat quickly as he fanned through them. Suddenly his eyes went wide as he realized what he was holding in his hands.

"Shall I go get the cassette player Fran?" Peg offered.

Fran just stood there in a state of disbelief, not registering a word his wife had just said.

"Fran? Are you ok?"

"What, dear?"

"I asked if I should run upstairs and get the cassette player?"

"What? Oh, uh, yeah. You do that, I gotta call Cosimo and get his ass over here right away!"

Fran was very cryptic during his call. He didn't want to chance anyone at work knowing a thing about what was sitting in his living room. The two men who were responsible for the contents of that box were now both dead. Secrecy moving forward would be extremely important in order to keep everyone safe!

About an hour later, a very confused Cosimo Angelo arrived at the Clavering household. "Sorry it took me so long, Fran. What's the meaning of all of this? Why are you suddenly acting so strange?"

Fran escorted his partner into the room with papers and tapes scattered about. "Look!"

Cosimo scanned the room. "It's just a bunch of papers and tapes. Where did all this come from?"

"This was delivered to our home last night by someone we both know."

"Who?"

"Fedora's lawyer."

Cosimo was still confused. Again he looked around the room. "What is all of this?"

"This, my friend, is the contents of Marco Ansios' briefcase."

"No shit?"

"No shit!"

"Oh my God! How much have you gone through so far?"

"Nothing really. As soon as I realized what it was, I called you to come over." Fran then handed the two letters to Cosimo to read.

Cosimo looked up from the second letter with a sudden look of terror in his eyes. "Fran, with those two now dead, this is some very dangerous stuff."

"No doubt about it. First we need to figure out what all we have here. Then we can figure out what to do next."

"From the looks of it all, that's going to take a while with the two of us."

"Well technically four of us."

"Four?"

"I'll help!" Peg interjected.

Cosimo issued a smile, but remained confused. "That's great Peg, thank you. But, who's the fourth person?"

Fran grabbed his wife's hand and placed them both on her stomach. "This little person is coming along for the ride!"

"Peg, you're expecting?"

She issued a beaming smile, unable to hide her extreme joy any longer. "Yes, sir!"

"That's great news! Congratulations to your entire family!"

"Thank you Cosimo!" She returned.

"You obviously haven't told my wife yet. I know she would have told me as soon as I got home last night."

"No, I only found out yesterday afternoon after our lunch date."

"I promise I won't tell her. I will let you deal with all that ridiculous carrying on she does when she finds out someone is expecting a new *bambini o bambino*." The three exchanged a laugh.

The attention of the three soon returned back to the contents of the box.

"Shall I put on a pot of coffee before we start digging into this stuff?"

"That would be great Peg, thank you!" Responded Cosimo.

"No problem, back in a second, gentlemen!"

Every evening after work Cosimo would follow Fran home after their days at the office to sort through and catalog all of the documents. While the two men were away at work, and the children were at school, Peg would begin to transcribe the many hours of taped conversations between Marco Ansios and others. When she was done, the conversations that were in Italian would be gone through thoroughly by Cosimo to ensure accuracy in their translation. It would take almost three months for them to get through everything. Once that monumental task was complete, they divided the materials and transcripts into four piles. Two of the piles were for Fedora and Ansios. The information in them would be used later posthumously to clear them of some of their crimes. The other two piles were for Gherado Fratello and Archbishop Jonas Krivis.

When all was said and done, the two detectives and Peg stepped back for a minute to admire their collective body of work.

"I can't believe that Ansios had all of this shit on everyone." Commented Cosimo.

"Me neither, but I'm sure as hell glad he did."

"Well now, thanks to him, I think I am now completely fluent in Italian." Peg smiled.

"Me too."

"It's about damn time, Fran!" Teased Cosimo. Cosimo took a deep breath. "So, now what do we do with all of it?"

"Mmmm, that's a good question." Fran quietly contemplated for a moment what they should do next. "I think first we should expand our little circle a bit, before all of that is decided."

"Ummm, what do you mean by that Fran? We can't go barging into my boss' office with this stuff. That would be like walking into our own suicides, kinda like Ansios did in London."

"I don't mean like that Cosimo. I think before we do anything further, we need to discuss all of this stuff with Hans and Cardinal Leone."

Cosimo agreed Hans and the good cardinal needed to be let in on the information they now had. If anyone would know what to do with the information it most certainly would be Cardinal Leone. Cardinal Leone was out of the country conducting church business, and wouldn't return to Florence for another four weeks. The information was important, but neither man felt it was an urgent matter. They knew Krivis was hiding somewhere in Vatican City, and Fratello was probably doing the same somewhere in South America.

Hans and Cardinal Leone arrived in Rome for a mid-summer dinner party hosted by Claverings. Peg was no longer able to hide her growing baby belly. The two out of town guests were happily surprised to see that Peg was now with child. They also harassed Fran relentlessly for forgetting to tell them about it.

"How on earth could you forget to tell us something like that Fran!" Teased Hans. "This has to be one of the happiest anticipated events of your lives."

"It is, but I, I mean we have been busy, to be honest."

"Busy? With what? What on earth could be so consuming to overlook something like that Fran?" Questioned Cardinal Leone.

Fran caught Cosimo and Peg's eyes, then nodded. "Follow us gentlemen, and let us show you."

The two men were escorted into the room that would eventually become the baby's nursery. The room had several card tables in it covered with papers and tapes. The men were confused upon entry.

"What is all of this?" Questioned Hans.

"All of this gentlemen, is the recovered contents of Marco Ansios' briefcase."

The two guests looked upon the display with curious wonder. "Where the hell did you guys get all of this?" Inquired Leone.

"You wouldn't believe me if I told you."

"Try me..."

"I got all of this from Fedora's defense lawyer at the end of last March when he paid me a visit one night."

"And you've been sitting on it for the last four months?" Commented Hans.

"Not exactly," interjected Cosimo. "It has taken us the last several months just to go through all of it."

"That's right gentlemen. This is the real reason why Peg and I invited you here tonight."

Hans and Leone began carefully looking through some of the documents and transcripts. The hour was getting late, but no one was leaving the Clavering home anytime soon. Neither guest could believe what they were seeing. Every bit of information recovered from that briefcase was damning and irrefutable.

"All of these contracts and papers with Krivis' signatures on them are originals! I remember seeing some of them when I was working in Pope Mike's Secretary of State office with Zacharie Benoît."

"You do?" Fran couldn't help but be impressed.

"Yes, you have enough here to have that son of a bitch jailed in multiple countries, gentlemen." Leonc added.

"I don't doubt that, but that chicken shit has been hiding in Vatican City for a while now. He knows we're gonna nab him if he ever steps foot out of there."

"Well what do you know?" Commented Leone. "That idiot isn't as stupid as I thought he was, but he's still plenty stupid not to be played."

Cardinal Leone soon turned his attention to the other pile labeled "Fratello." As the cardinal read through several of the documents, he became more and more distraught. He held a few of the documents in his hands. "This right here," he commented as he waved some of them in the air. "Gentlemen, I tell you what, I will help you flush out that damn Fratello, on one condition."

"What's that?" Commented Fran.

"If we ever get our hands on him, his ass is mine! He and I have some very important, unfinished business to discuss!"

"You got it, cardinal!" Everyone in the room instantly agreed to Leone's terms.

"I will also help you guys get Krivis out of the Vatican too. That won't be nearly as difficult as luring Fratello out of hiding, but I still have some resources and connections that will certainly come in handy."

The three detectives were curious exactly what the cardinal had in mind, but it was now long past midnight. Those details would have to be worked out some other time. Before departing they agreed that all communications would go through Hans or Peg at the Clavering home. None of this was to be discussed anywhere else. It was an important detail necessary to keep every last one of them safe.

CHAPTER 67

The morning of late August had a distinct feel of autumn in the air. Summer was in her final days. Only a few of the trees and vineyards in Rome and the surrounding Italian countryside had begun to change their wardrobe. The displays of early fall foliage were beautiful with its rich, warm breathtaking colors. Everything that had transpired over the last five months made it seem like summer had just started.

Peg called Fran at the office mid morning to tell him she'd have lunch ready for him and Cosimo around 12:30 PM. When the two men arrived a little after noon, they were famished from their morning's work. Conversation was exchanged as the three of them passed around a tureen of warm soup and a platter of ham and cheese sandwiches. Peg told them that she had received a call from Hans about mid morning, and needed to speak to Fran and Cosimo somewhat urgently.

After lunch, Fran rang Hans from the bedroom phone, then Cosimo got on the extension in the living room.

"Fran, we picked up Gherado Fratello last night on the south side of Munich. He was trying to get some money out of an account over there."

"That's great news. I can't believe he got caught doing that again. He's either desparate or stupid."

"Probably quite a bit of both, I'd say." Hans responded.

"Have you called Leone yet?"

"No, not yet. I was going to call him right after I heard from you."

"I will call him as soon as I get off the phone. Let's see what he wants to do with him. In the meantime don't let that jackass bribe any guards over there."

"We have some of our best men assigned to guard detail. Rest assured, you have nothing to worry about. There will be no escaping this time, I promise."

"Good! I'll be in touch soon."

Next Fran called Cardinal Leone's office. The patriarch of Florence was surprised by the call. "That was quick. I was certain he would be more careful this time, considering what happened last time."

"That's what I was thinking. Things must have really gone sideways in his operations since Ansios' death."

"Yeah that had to be one of his more stupid moves."

"Do you really think he had Ansios killed?"

"At this point, if I had to guess, yes."

"It just seems like a very stupid move for a supposedly smart man." Commented Cosimo.

"Oh, Fratello isn't a smart man. He overplayed his hand thinking Ansios would be an easy man to replace. Clearly he was wrong, and perhaps by now he knows that."

"I remember Fedora commenting that Fratello wasn't the smart man the world was led to believe." Commented Fran. "He clearly underestimated the importance of his paymaster he had wrapped around his little finger."

"I'm sure he figured he had another sucker waiting in the wings. Looks like Ansios' waterlogged shoes weren't so easy to fill." Added Cosimo.

"So cardinal, how do you want to handle our situation over in Munich?"

"Well I know what I'd like to do to him, but that wouldn't look good for a man in my position."

"I'm not even going to ask."

"Oh, you can ask all you want, but you will never get an answer from me." Leone thought quietly for a moment. "Let's meet up in Munich, how about on Thursday. Does that work for you two?"

"Yeah, that will be fine. We will be there."

"Great! I have some ideas, but we can discuss those further when we get to Germany next week."

"Perfect. We will see you then!"

Fran called Hans back to let him know the plan. They all agreed that letting Fratello stew in his jail cell for a few days was hardly suitable punishment for his crimes, but it was a start. Their flights were booked and their bags were packed. They had no idea what Leone had in mind. They weren't sure how long they would be gone, but they would not return to Italy until their mission was complete.

Two days before Fran and Cosimo were scheduled to leave, Peg called Fran at the office distraught and crying.

"Fran, I need you to come home."

"What's wrong, love?"

"I'm starting to have contractions."

"Contractions?! Already? I thought the doctor said you had another ten weeks?"

"He did. I called him, he wants me to come into his office right away."

"Hold tight, I will be right there."

Fran slammed down the handset, grabbed his coat and hat, and headed for the door.

"Is everything ok Fran?" Questioned a concerned Cosimo.

"It's Peg, she's having contractions."

"So soon? But her due date is weeks away!"

"I know, the doctor wants to see her right away!"

"Go, and keep me posted on how she's doing."

"I will call you later!"

Fran drove like a bat out of hell to the house. The concern on his face was unmistakable. Peg decided at that moment that her loving husband was quickly becoming more annoying than her contractions. "Fran, will you calm down!"

"Just relax honey, we will be at the doctor's office soon!"

The way he was carrying on ensured relaxation would not be coming any time soon. Peg just took another deep breath and let it out slowly until her pain subsided once again. There were moments she thought punching him might do them both a world of good, then thought better of it. It'd probably be best to at least wait until he wasn't driving the car anymore.

The doctor examined her, then sent them over to the hospital for more observation. Several hours and a few bags of IV fluids later, Peg's contractions had finally stopped and the two of them returned home exhausted. Dutifully Fran escorted her to the bedroom and helped her into her nightgown and then into bed. Both of them were exhausted from the experience, and promptly fell asleep.

Fran woke about an hour and a half later. He sat on the side of the bed for a moment watching Peg as she slept. She looked so peaceful. Nothing like she did earlier that day. As he was getting ready to go downstairs to prepare something for dinner, he saw his half packed suitcase across the room. He then left the room and quietly closed the bedroom door behind him.

Once downstairs he picked up the phone and began to dial. "Cosimo, it's Fran."

"Thank goodness. My wife and I have been worried sick about you guys all day! How's Peg?"

"She's fine. She's upstairs sleeping right now."

"So they stopped her contractions?"

"Yes, they think she wasn't drinking enough water and that's what triggered those early labor pains."

"Thank God that's all it was!"

"It certainly makes me feel a little better. Needless to say, the doctor has ordered her to stay in bed for the next few days so she doesn't do too much and trigger those contractions again."

"I'm just glad everything's alright with her."

"Me too." Fran suddenly got really quiet.

"Fran, are you still there?"

"Yeah, I'm here, just thinking."

"Oh?"

"Yeah, I'm thinking that I shouldn't go on that trip to Munich with you guys."

"You need to stay with Peg, Fran. I'm pretty sure Leone has an idea about what he wants to do with Fratello."

"Are you sure? I mean I really do want to go."

"Stay home Fran, we can handle this. I promise we will call you often and keep you in the loop of what's going on."

Cosimo could hear the relief in Fran's voice. "Thank you my friend! I don't know what I'd do if she lost another baby while I was off in another country like last time. I owe you guys one!"

"No, you owe your attention to your wife right now. Stop worrying about us."

"Again, thank you! But you guys better promise to call me. Don't you dare leave me out of those strategy meetings."

"We'd be very stupid to even consider something like that."

Fran sighed. "Good, that makes me feel so much better."

"I will see you at the office tomorrow morning."

"Sounds good. Just call me if anything changes."

"Will do."

"Say Fran, would you like me to update Hans and Leone about your situation?"

"Would you? I'd really appreciate that. I still have to figure out something to feed these kids."

Cosimo laughed at the thought. "Good luck there. I'm pretty much useless in the kitchen."

"I'm not far behind you, my friend. Good night."

"Night."

Peg woke up some time later to the sound of pots and pans banging about the kitchen. She was still tying her robe closed as she entered the kitchen. "What the hell are you doing to my kitchen Francis Liam Clavering!"

Fran had an embarrassed, sheepish half grin on his face. "What the hell are you doing up?"

"Well it's not like I could sleep through all of your racket. What are you making anyway?"

"Just some pasta and vegetables, would you like some?"

"I guess, it smells alright." She looked skeptically around him and into the pot he was stirring and wrinkled her nose. "Sure, I'm famished!"

After dinner, Fran cleaned up the kitchen and put away the dishes. He then went up to their bedroom. Peg walked in as he was unpacking his suitcase. "Honey? What are you doing?"

"Unpacking."

"Why?"

"I'm not going to Munich on Thursday."

"But you have to. They need you, love."

"No they don't. Fratello is Leone's mission, not mine."

"But Fran."

"No Peg, I'm not leaving you here after what happened today! There will be no more discussion on the matter, my love. Hans, Cosimo and Leone are more than capable of handling things there with Fratello."

Peg didn't like his response, but she knew that there was no way she'd ever get him to change his mind. "Fine, but I still think you should go, Fran."

"Even Cosimo agrees that I shouldn't."

"Now you guys are just ganging up on me."

Fran walked over and took her into his arms. "Listen Peg, I won't deny that this trip is very important to me."

"Then you should go." Peg interrupted.

"No, I can't."

"Is this about what happened last time?"

"Absolutely! I'd never be able to live with myself if something like that ever happened again while I was away. So you can just stop asking. Yes that trip is important to me, but you, my love, and this child are the most important to me right now." Then he kissed her tenderly.

"I can already see that you've already made up your mind. You worry too much, you know that."

"Well, that is my job. You'd be pissed at me if I didn't."

"Yeah, I guess. It was kinda nice having you there with me at the hospital, well except for the times I wanted to reach over and strangle you." Peg smiled, with a wink, then she kissed him.

Thursday morning Fran drove Cosimo to the airport. He would be included in frequent calls over the coming days. Fratello was stubbornly confident that his current situation was only a temporary inconvenience no different than his imprisonments many times before. Hans, Cosimo, Fran and Cardinal Leone were determined that Fratello would never be released to the free world ever again.

CHAPTER 68

The thunderous deluge violently impacted the outer exterior of St. Nicholas' Tower in Vatican City. The winds that whipped and stirred the dark, menacing clouds were unrelenting. The skies were threatening even more rain as residents kept a concerned, watchful eye on the rising Tiber River that flowed through Rome. The freak torrential storm caught many unprepared after so many weeks of warm, picture perfect, late summer weather.

The clock on the wall bonged once announcing 10:30 AM this Monday morning in late August. However, if one had to guess based on the weather and other visual cues outside, they might think it was late afternoon or early evening on a day deep in the winter months. Archbishop Jonas Krivis sat alone in his office. His desk was covered in papers, photos and other items as he briefly read through some of the contents of a large thick manila envelope that had arrived by special courier earlier that morning. He was completely oblivious to the raging storm outside his office windows. On this morning, the scotch and cigar smoke he would take into his body were more medicinal than pleasurable and satisfying.

He sat in the sparsely lit room primarily illuminated by the lamp on his desk and the occasional flashes of lightning from the stormy skies outside. His fingers tapped and fidgeted anxiously as he read through the proposal in his hands. He didn't like the options he was being offered. Whoever put this together did so with many years of knowledge to back it. In another time and circumstance, he would have consulted with a trusted friend to discuss what he should do, or just ignore the proposition outright. However, this deal was not like any he'd ever seen before during his tenure as Vatican Bank president. This time, the decision was all on him.

Krivis swallowed another oversized double shot of his scotch followed by a long, deep drag from his smoldering cigar. He then picked up the handset of his desk phone. Slowly and deliberately he pushed each button as he dialed the phone number listed in the manila envelope's letter addressed to him. Very few words were exchanged during the call. Krivis wrote a few notes in the letter's margin, then a few moments later, he was gone.

Detective Francis Clavering opted not to go into the office that Monday morning. He knew that his team was busy putting Leone's plan in motion that day, and confronting Gherado Fratello in his Munich jail cell. He wanted to stay close to home just in case they needed any help. His anxiousness waiting for an update call would look very suspicious to any of his officemates, had he gone into work that morning. As he watched the storm rage outside the large living room window, he was actually glad he didn't have to be out in the angry weather that morning.

He hated being in the dark and removed from all of the action and excitement. However, the prior week's events involving Peg and the baby shifted his priorities significantly. It certainly made his decision to stay home an easy one. He had absolute faith in his team; besides he was only a phone call away should they need him for anything.

Fran anxiously picked up the phone on the first ring. Peg was upstairs reading. She decided to come downstairs when she heard the phone ring. After the last four plus months, she too was heavily invested in the operation that was about to go down in Munich. She waited patiently in the kitchen fixing herself a snack until Fran got off the phone to update her.

She heard Fran terminate his call and walked into the living room just in time to see him grab his coat and hat. "Where are you going?"

Her voice surprised him, he did not hear her come down the stairs. He whipped around to see Peg standing there with a half eaten ham and swiss sandwich in her hand. "What? Oh I need to go grab something."

"In this weather? Are you insane?"

"Yeah, it's pretty bad out there. I probably should go up and change into my boots." The two of them went back upstairs together so Fran could change his footwear.

"Was that one of the guys?"

"Yeah, they need me to go pick up something that they need."

"I really don't like you going out there right now. Is it something that can wait until this storm lets up a little?"

"No, this is kinda urgent, love. Besides, this storm isn't going to calm down for hours." Fran walked over to her. He took her into his arms, pulled her body close into his, mindful of her pregnant belly and kissed her. "Don't worry about me, love. I promise I will be careful out there."

"You promise?"

"I promise." He smiled and took her by the hand and escorted her back downstairs. "Now go sit down, read your book and finish your sandwich."

His promises did little to ease her mind as loud thunder roared in the clouds above their home, but she did as he instructed.

Thirty minutes later, Fran pulled into a relatively empty parking lot. There were only four other cars, despite it being almost lunch time. He walked to the *ristorante* entrance of the Santa Romano Golf Club doing his best to shake off as much of the rain as he could from his coat and hat before entering. He remembered the last time he had been there, some thirteen years ago with Hans, just hours after he had met Cosimo for the first time. Fran scanned the mostly empty room. A room that on any other normal August day would be teaming with locals enjoying a light lunch, before hitting the links for an early afternoon round of golf. In the distant corner booth, Fran could see the big hulking form of a man dressed in all black except for the starched stiff white collar at his neck. As Fran walked towards the familiar booth, Krivis threw back the rest of his scotch and motioned to the buxom waitress to bring him another.

Fran approached the table, "I see you've decided to do the honorable thing for once in your life Jonas Krivis."

"That's archbishop or Your Excellency to you, Clavering."

"Really Jonas? I can think of a few other words I'd rather use myself, but I prefer not to use such language in mixed company."

The waitress came to the table and placed a fresh double scotch on the rocks in front of the archbishop. She then turned to Fran. "*Signore,* can I get you something to drink?"

Fran smiled at the young lady. "Yes please, a cola would be great."

She nodded and smiled. "I will be right back."

"Thank you."

Fran's attention once again turned back to Krivis. It was obvious that Krivis was already pretty tipsy and absolutely miserable. He had zero desire to be there, but after viewing the sampling of documents, some of the photographs and the letter he'd received from the detective that morning, he was left with very few options. Krivis decided that this meeting situation worked best for him.

Fran sat down at the table somewhat across from Krivis. "To be honest Jonas, I was surprised to hear from you so soon. I figured you'd drag this shit out for days or weeks."

"Your letter was clear. You left me with very few options."

"I did, didn't I?" Fran smiled smugly. "So you prefer to turn yourself in like this instead of making a huge public spectacle of us dragging your ass out of the Vatican?"

Krivis laughed. "I hate to disappoint you detective, but there's no way in hell you would have dragged my ass out of the Vatican."

"Oh? Then why are you here Jonas? Why aren't you still cowering in your stupid tower inside the protective walls of Vatican City, like the real chicken shit that you are?"

Fran's tone immediately angered the archbishop, causing him to raise his voice. "Listen here you fucking son of a bitch."

The waitress returned with Fran's cola. She immediately felt uncomfortable as she interrupted Krivis' verbally assaultive tirade. "Can I get you gentlemen anything else?" She responded in a quiet, fearful tone.

"No miss," Fran responded in a reassuring polite voice. "That will be all for now. We will let you know when we are ready to order."

The waitress looked at Fran with an odd look, confused by his tone after observing Krivis' face which had turned various shades of red as he stifled some of his anger. "Ok, I will come back in a little while to check on the two of you."

"That'd be great, miss, thank you."

Fran grabbed one of the menus the waitress had left for them on the table. He opened it up and began to read through the lunch options. He frequently glanced over the top of the menu at the seething expressions on the archbishop's face. "So are we having some lunch this afternoon Jonas or are we going to get on with this shit?"

"I'm not fucking hungry!"

"Really? You used to love coming to this place every chance you got back in the day Jonas."

Krivis had heard enough from the smug American detective. "We can go, but first I have to take a piss." He responded in an indignant manner.

Fran issued a confident, yet suspicious nod. He too was ready to get on with the business of finally arresting the man he had been after for well over a decade now.

When he saw Krivis emerge from the men's room, Fran got up from booth seat. He looked down at his money clip as he pulled it from his pocket. Fran placed a few lira on the table to pay for the drinks. As the detective was reaching for his soaked coat and hat, he looked up, and saw the fleeting image of Krivis disappearing through the double doors that lead to the restaurant's kitchen about seventy five feet away.

"Goddamn it!" Fran yelled then began to run after him. "Krivis, you're not doing yourself any favors!"

Fran barreled through the swinging double doors, but failed to see Krivis anywhere. "Which way did he go!" Then looked around quickly at all of the startled kitchen staff. They silently pointed. "*Grazie!*" Fran exclaimed as he quickly ran out the kitchen's back door to see Krivis driving off through the pouring rain in a golf cart he had stolen.

Fran finally found another golf cart and took off after the archbishop. He looked around through the torrential rain, but couldn't see his cart anywhere.

"That stupid son of a bitch! Damn it, if he gets away, there's no way I'll ever be able to face the guys on the team ever again," Fran thought to himself.

Finally he saw it, just as clear as day. The tracks of Krivis' golf cart had been imprinted in muddy grass. Fran floored the accelerator, tearing off as fast as the cart would go across one of the open fairways of the golf course. All around him the rain continued to assault him and obscure his vision. Then came the blinding flashes of lightning followed a few seconds later by deafening claps of thunder.

Krivis' tracks finally lead the detective to a sizable outbuilding. Fran unholstered his gun from under his rain soaked jacket. He ran through the door closest to the archbishop's abandoned cart. It was dark inside the building. As his eyes began to adjust to the lower level of light, he could see the warehouse was a virtual maze filled with all kinds of lawn care equipment, broken golf ball washers, unserviceable carts and other obscure equipment. He passed by pallets stacked high with numerous bags of grass seed, as he cautiously made his way further into the building. He could see a trail of Krivis' oversized wet footprints with each flash of lightning that came through the building's skylights and high windows. As he proceeded further still, Fran's nose suddenly began to burn as he passed by several pallets stacked high with bags and bags of fertilizer. He was smart enough to know how dangerous it was to follow the exact path of Krivis. Suddenly Fran jumped as the room was filled with blinding light, and deafening thunder as the ground shook beneath his feet. A bolt of lightning had just struck one of the big trees just outside the building. He waited a few moments for his eyes to readjust to the dark before he moved any further into the building. Finally after another brilliant flash of lightning, he saw the hulking silhouette of Krivis just standing in a large puddle of rain water in a distant part of the building. Fran kept his gun aimed at center mass as he slowly approached his target.

"This piece of shit is not going to run off on me again." Fran thought to himself as he advanced silently, closer behind his target. Finally he was close enough, "Jonas, put your hands up where I can see them, and turn around slowly!"

Krivis just stood there motionless, and silent with his back to Fran and his arms down at his sides.

"Come on Jonas, you and I both know that this ends here, now!"

"Yes Clavering, it does!" Krivis broke his silence, yet remained motionless with his back turned to the detective. "You think you're pretty smart, don't you, detective."

"Well my friend, I've only been following your crooked ass for about thirteen years now."

"Thirteen years? You're full of shit Clavering!"

"Am I Jonas? Where shall I start? Your meetings with Dr. Schwartz? Your reams and reams of fake securities you got from Benedetto and his crew? I can go on."

"Fake securities?" Krivis paused for a few seconds. The man couldn't believe what he was hearing. He quickly whipped around where he stood to look Fran in the eyes. His hands remained down by his sides.

Clavering held his firearm steady, with the archbishop in his sights and his finger ready on the trigger. "Put your Goddamn hands up, then don't move another inch Jonas!"

"You sure didn't do a damn thing to stop any of it."

"Oh, I wouldn't say that. You know Jonas, I gotta say, that was a pretty ballsy move you and Fedora tried to pull with some of those fakes over in Dachau a few years back. The fake name you used was a nice touch. I bet you didn't know that I was the one that fucked that whole thing up for the two of you. I have it all you know. What I sent you in that packet was just a small sampling of what I've got. We both know that there's no one left to help your sorry ass now. Ansios and Fedora, the only friends you probably ever had, are now dead."

Suddenly there was a bright flash of lightning and instantaneous booming clap of thunder, followed by the flash from the barrel of a handgun. Fran instantly dropped his weapon as he was thrown back against the wall by the impact of the round entering his left shoulder knocking the breath out of him. He grabbed his now dead arm and winced as a searing pain began to burn deep in his shoulder. Dark red blood began to flow from the wound in his shoulder. "Fuck that hurt!" Fran shouted once he caught his breath again.

"Oh, I'm just getting started with you, you piece of shit!" Krivis shouted at the detective. "You've fucked up every Goddamn thing! It's fuckers like you who have cost me my cardinal's rank." Krivis lowered the highly polished silver gun in his hands, now that the detective had been successfully disarmed.

Fran winced as he took a deep breath. "Oh I think you pretty much fucked that one up yourself, you idiot."

"Shut the fuck up!" Fran didn't have a chance to brace himself for the forceful impact of the right cross as it impacted his jaw.

Fran knew the impact would have been far greater and more on the mark had Krivis not been so drunk. He needed to keep Krivis talking while he tried to figure out how he was going to get out of his current mess. "That's a pretty nice gun you got there. Is that a Beretta?"

"Yeah, it's a 92s, first edition. It was a gift from the company a few years back. They sent it to me when the bank bought a bunch of their stock."

"That's a nice little piece. Do you mind showing me a closer look at it?"

As Krivis got closer, Fran tried to kick the hand gun from his grip, but missed. Krivis pointed the gun at Fran's head, and Fran closed his eyes and dropped to the ground, as the loud report of a shot left his ears ringing. He opened his eyes to see a bullet wound in Krivis' chest and his huge body falling to the ground with a thud. Fran winced in pain as he tried to look around the dark warehouse. Krivis suddenly tried to reach for his gun once more.

"Leave it Krivis!" A familiar voice came from out of the dark shadows.

"Peg?!"

Out of the shadows came Peg with a handgun aimed right at Krivis' face as he lay on the dirty floor. She walked over and kicked the silver Beretta far from Krivis' reach.

"Peg?" Fran couldn't believe what he was witnessing. "What the hell are you doing here?"

"I might ask you the same damn thing Mr. Francis Liam Clavering! 'Picking something up for the team,' I see." She said as she walked over to Fran, while keeping her gun aimed at the archbishop.

"Well I didn't exactly lie."

"Technically, no. But you weren't exactly truthful either."

Krivis moaned in pain. "You stupid fucking bitch!"

Fran grimaced in pain as he struggled to get back on his feet. He walked over and punched Krivis as hard as he could in the mouth. "Now listen here you mother fuckin' piece of shit! Don't you ever speak to my wife like that again!" Fran then kicked him as hard as he could in his ribs. Then he reached for the archbishop's neck with his only functional hand. Fran forcefully ripped the stiff white collar from his neck and threw it in the puddle of rain water a few feet away, and stomped on it. Krivis groaned in pain one more time, then went silent.

Peg felt Krivis' cold clammy neck for a pulse, then looked up at her husband still standing over him. "He's dead, Fran!"

"Sit down Fran, I don't want you to move any more."

"Yes ma'am."

She made a crude compress from the cleanest rags she could find. She pressed on the bullet wound firmly. Fran immediately recoiled in pain. "Hold this as tight as you can on the wound. I will be right back." Fran focused on each painful breath until she returned a few minutes later.

"An ambulance is on the way, we're going to get you to the hospital."

"Peg, I don't think I've ever loved you as much as I do right now. You saved my life!"

"Yeah I did, didn't I?"

"But how did you even know I was here?"

"You're not as slick as you think you are, mister." She then issued a smile. "You'd never believe me, even if I told you."

"Try me."

"Alright, since we got nothing else to do for a while. Right after you left this morning, the phone rang."

"Was it Cosimo? Hans?"

"Will you shut up! Ya know Krivis was right to pop you in the mouth."

"Oh you saw that?"

"Yup, anyway, it was Krivis' secretary on the line."

"That two-bit little slut?"

"I'd hold your judgment if I were you. That 'two-bit little slut' actually saved your stupid ass."

"Say what?"

"After Krivis called you this morning."

"Wait, you knew Krivis called me this morning?"

"Ummm, not initially. But I figured it out when his secretary called."

"Oh?"

"I guess Krivis had left his office without telling her. She saw that the light on the phone line was no longer lit so she went in to have him sign some papers. As she walked in, she became very concerned. It was way too early in the day for his scotch decanter to be almost nearly empty, and she knew that Krivis had left his office recently."

"How the hell did she know that?"

Peg giggled a little. "Actually I thought it was kind of brilliant how she figured that out. His cigar was still smoldering in the ashtray on his desk."

"Oh wow, that was pretty damn smart."

"She looked at the papers scattered on his desk. Then she saw the letter from you with our number on it and this country club written on the paper."

Fran shivered slightly as he got a chill, then recoiled in pain. "Go on."

"Anyways, when she moved from behind the desk, she struck her leg hard on the half opened lower drawer. She saw a very nice black box lined with red velvet with the imprint where a Beretta handgun and clip used to be."

"Oh wow."

"So she called our number to warn you, but you'd already left the house."

Suddenly Peg made an uncomfortable face and put her hand on her belly.

Fran instantly became worried. "Are you ok, love? God I hope the contractions are back again."

"No," Peg laughed. "The baby just kicked me really hard, that's all."

"Phew. Still it was pretty stupid for you to put your's and the baby's lives in danger like this."

Peg just shot him a sideways look. "I'd be careful if I were you."

"But I'm sure as hell glad that you did." He pulled her close and kissed her.

They could now hear the approaching sirens in the distance. Soon there was a flurry of activity as they loaded Fran into an ambulance and took him to the hospital. Peg stayed behind a few more minutes. Some of the police officers immediately recognized Fran and were puzzled by the scene they had walked into. Peg explained to the police and coroner why Archbishop Jonas Krivis was lying dead in a small pool of his own blood mixed with rainwater.

That evening Cosimo called the Clavering home to update them on what was happening in Munich. Cosimo was surprised to hear his wife's voice on the other end of the line. The entire team became deeply concerned as she explained that Fran had been shot and was now in surgery at the hospital. She had very few details to relay. "I'm just here to watch the children until Peg comes home, and pray."

Next Cosimo called the hospital and had Peg paged. Cosimo, Hans and Leone got on the line. Peg told them that Fran had made it through surgery fine and was now sleeping off the anesthesia in recovery. Cardinal Leone said a quick prayer for his full recovery. Peg thanked the cardinal, then she told them all that Krivis was dead and that she and Fran would fill them in later with all of the details.

Cardinal Leone then told her that Gherado Fratello was also dead. The three of them had had a brief conversation with the man earlier that afternoon. The cardinal presented him with a similar package as the one that was sent to Krivis that morning. A few hours ago, guards found the man dead in his cell after he ingested the lethal dose of digitalis he had on him at all times.

Peg was stunned, yet relieved by the news. She promised to update Fran as soon she could. Once her husband was discharged from the hospital and was feeling up to having company, they wanted to have them all over for dinner. "I do believe gentlemen that we all deserve to celebrate everything we've accomplished over these past many years!"

CHAPTER 69

A week had passed, and most of the world seemed to have returned to normal. Fran was well on the road to recovery. The papers around the world were full of stories surrounding the bizarre shooting death of Archbishop Jonas Krivis in a warehouse of a Roman golf country club. Fran and Cosimo's coworkers were very careful and respectful in their statements to inquiring press reporters not to reveal the role Fran or Peg had in the incident.

The Vatican's Secretary of State and Public Relations offices went to work right away. They worked feverishly to bury Krivis and all of the evidence from his many years of criminal activities Cardinal Leone had presented to them. There seemed to be a suddenly increasing global chaos developing around the world. The news of Fratello's suicide in a Munich jail cell was a virtual tsunami as various powerful global leaders who suddenly found themselves arrested by the same military they once commanded.

The men all gathered in the living room of the Clavering home. There was much laughter and chatter coming from the kitchen and dining room as the wives of Hans and Cosimo assisted Peg with the food in the kitchen and setting the table in the dining room. The table was beautiful and inviting and the food looked and smelled delightful. As everyone made their way over to the table, Cosimo walked around and filled everyone's glass with wine.

Once all were seated, Fran looked at Cardinal Leone. "Your Eminence, would you please do us all the honor of blessing this food and this occasion?"

"It would be my honor Fran." Cardinal Leone stood before them all, as they all took each other's hands. "Shall we pray?" Everyone crossed themselves and bowed their heads. "Oh Heavenly Father we gather here in celebration of this collective group's triumph over unimaginable evil not just in the Catholic Church, but in the greater world as we know it. We pray for the souls of the great brave men like Papa Chiaros Riluciani, Arturo Bartolone, and so many others who were struck down by the hands of truly evil men during this journey. We hope that we have brought honor to you and your spirit with our efforts. We pray for the souls of those whose faith may have wavered after witnessing the wickedness and disgrace these men have brought on you and the Holy Church. It is our hope that they find peace and understanding as they find their faith once again. We ask that you bless and guide all of us from this moment forward as we continue to do work that honors you and your teachings. Please continue to bless us all with your love, protection, and forgiveness, as we move on to whatever future you may have planned for us in the future. In the name of the Father, Son and Holy Ghost, Amen."

"Amen." Everyone uttered in unison as they crossed themselves one more time.

Then Fran stood up at the head of the table, and raised his wine glass in his right hand. "I'd like to propose a toast to His Holiness, Papa Chiaros Riluciani, even though he'd hate us for calling him that right now." Everyone in the room smiled and nodded in agreement as they clinked their glasses together and sipped from their wine glasses.

"Finally a toast to another man who went about his work with the greatest of honor, hard work, passion and a truest example of professional integrity I have ever witnessed in my entire career, regardless of the contrary pressures around him. To our brother Arturo Bartolone."

"Hear, hear." Echoed throughout the room as once again wine glasses came together to honor one of the fallen.

The food was delicious, and the conversations light hearted and joyful. The main course of chicken, green beans and pasta was served. Fran had just taken a bite of his chicken when the telephone in the living room began to ring. He dabbed at his mouth with his cloth napkin, "I'll get it, excuse me," he announced, then left the room.

A short while later, Fran returned from the other room. Peg watched him as he returned to the head of the dinner table. Everyone noticed the smiles and good spirits the man had had all evening were now gone. They could tell by Fran's body language and facial expressions that the call was not to deliver good news.

Peg watched him as he once again took his seat across from her. "Who was that honey?"

Everyone suddenly looked at him with great concern. "Oh, that was Deputy Chief Bentley calling from New York...He says that D.A. Christopherson's health has taken a turn for the worse. They think he only has a few more days, maybe a week left to live."

"Oh God, I'm so sorry to hear this news Fran." Cardinal Leone took his hand to offer him comfort. "I will pray for his comfort, peace and soul."

"Thank you cardinal."

"We all will Fran."

"Thank you, all of you. I really appreciate that." Fran patted his open right hand on his heart to express his gratitude for their collective support.

The evening continued on with a certain air of heaviness. Fran knew the old D.A. had been very sick for a very long time. Fran was actually surprised the old man had hung on as long as he had. Fran firmly believed that the only reason the cancer hadn't taken him yet, had everything to do with the man's orneriness. "Those types just don't give up that easily." Fran thought to himself.

A few days following the dinner party gathering, Fran, Peg and the kids flew back to New York. The kids couldn't wait to tell their cousins about all of their adventures in Italy. Fran and Peg drove to the Christopherson home. Fran sat quietly in the parked car for an extended moment with his eyes closed.

"Do you want me to go in with you?"

Fran just sat silently next to her and nodded. Trying to maintain control of the emotions flowing through him. He took her hand in his. "Would you please? I still have to tell him about that lie Bentley and I told him before he goes. I just can't live with that for the rest of my life."

"Of course, love." She gently squeezed his hand. "Come on, I'm sure he can't wait to see you."

Mrs. Christopherson soon escorted them into the room. He looked so peaceful as he lay there with his eyes closed. Fran took his frail hand in his, and the old man opened his eyes to see his detective standing there with his left arm in a sling.

In a scraggly old voice, the old man began to instantly yell at Fran. "Goddamn it, Clavering, I told you to be careful over there!"

"I was careful sir!"

"Bullshit, you know, you never were very good at lying, you son of a bitch!" Then the old man smiled and winked at Fran. Christopherson then looked over at Peg. "Mrs. Clavering, please excuse my manners, I'm not usually so rude in mixed company."

Peg smiled at the old man. "Please sir, call me Peg. Oh and don't worry about the language sir, Fran says that kind of stuff a lot, especially lately when he bumps his shoulder just right."

The three of them smiled and chuckled for a few minutes. Christopherson noticed Peg's pregnant belly and couldn't help but comment. "I see you weren't very careful in multiple ways Francis." Christopherson teased, as they all smiled. "Congratulations to both of you!"

"Thank you, sir." Peg and Fran responded.

"So Bentley tells me you finally got that Goddamn Krivis and the rest of his cronies."

"We did, sir."

"Good! It's about damn time! Now have a seat and tell me all about it."

Fran looked at Peg, then back at the old man. "Everything?"

"Yes, everything! And don't bullshit me like you and Bentley did with that cockamamy crap when you wanted to follow Benedetto over to Munich!"

Fran just looked over at Peg, then back at the old man. "Wait, you knew we lied to you?"

"Sure did. You can't lie to me, son."

"Damn it! That lie has been eating me up for all of these years."

"I know." Christopherson just looked at him and smiled.

"You really are a son of a bitch, you know that?"

"Yup, always have been...always will be."

"Why didn't you say anything? Why didn't you do anything about it? Why didn't you chew our asses out instead of letting me go to Munich, knowing that we lied to you about all of it?"

"Fran, you were the best detective I had on the force. Your instincts were never wrong, you did your work with honor and pride. I knew you had never lied to me or anyone else in that department before. I figured if you were lying to me, there had to be a damn good reason for doing so. So tell me Fran, was I wrong?"

Fran shrugged his one good shoulder. "Mmmm, I guess not. I can't believe I've had all of those sleepless nights haunted by that damn lie, while all along you fuckin' knew. Damn it!"

"It certainly kept you from tellin' any more of them, now didn't it, son?"

"Yeah, it sure did." Fran loved the man too much to stay angry at him.

"Good, then it all worked out alright in the end." Christopherson smiled. "Now have a seat and tell me how you brought ever last one of those mother fuckers down!"

"Are you sure, sir? This might take a while."

"Absolutely. You know me, I have always loved a good story."

"Alright, you asked for it."

Peg interrupted Fran as he was clearing his throat. "Shall I leave and come back later?"

"Sure, I'll call you at your sister's when I'm through here."

She kissed her husband and left. "It was nice to see you again, D.A. Christopherson."

"The pleasure was all mine Peg. You've certainly got your hands full with this one." Christopherson smiled and winked at her, before she turned and left the room.

"So you already know quite a bit about Giovanni Fedora and all of his bullshit from your prep and trial. So I will skip all of that."

"That's fine."

"So by the mid 1970s, Marco Ansio and Bishop Jonas Krivis had partnered on multiple criminal schemes. They were running massive money laundering operations through their banks and their offshore ghost companies for years. But Krivis overplayed his hand, so he came up with a fake securities scheme."

"That's where Benedetto came into the picture."

"Exactly! Now Cardinal Leone worked in the Vatican's Secretary of State office and knew of all the shit that Krivis, Ansios and Fedora were involved in. Leone and his friends hatched a plan and got Rilucini elected as pope, and to get rid of Krivis and the whole lot. His plan worked brilliantly until thirty three days into his papacy they poisoned him."

"Those bastards! Who killed him exactly?"

"Well that was the big question. Every single one of them had motive and means."

"After they killed him, they thought they were in the clear. That pope they got in there now is as useless as the gum stuck on my shoe. And he's definitely not a good man."

"Really? I would have never guessed."

"Yeah their public relations department is something else, but that's a whole other story. Anyway, they carried on about their business less impeded than ever before."

"No surprise there."

"So when they fially got Fedora's ass over to Italy they immediately had his trials for his fraudulent bankruptcy and the murder of Cosimo's friend."

"Yeah, I remember reading about that."

"Well they used a good portion of material from your case."

"They did?" Christopherson perked up with pride.

"Well sort of, but they twisted a bunch of your hard work around in unethical ways to fit what they needed to convict him."

"The bastards!"

"I knew what was going on wasn't right, but neither Cosimo nor I had any power to refute any of it."

"So they wrongly convicted him of fraudulent bankruptcy?"

"Yes, and no. They had more than enough to convict him on legitimate charges. I have no idea why they twisted your work and threw it in there. The whole thing just pissed me off, to be honest."

"Me too."

"So after the bankruptcy case, came Fedora's trial for the murder of Cosimo's friend Arturo Bartolone."

"He was a great man."

"Yes he was, but get this. The stuff they were saying in that trial didn't make sense. Fedora and his lawyer had evidence that would have cleared him, but the judge wouldn't allow it. The three of us figured out who actually ordered the murder of Bartolone and framed it on Fedora."

"Was it anyone I know?"

"Yeah, it was Nico Novelli!"

"No kiddin'?"

"Nope. Anyways the courts once again were stacked against Fedora, and he was convicted of the murder."

"Damn!"

"Right after that, Fedora was poisoned in his prison cell. That was about six months ago."

"Damn, that sucks. So with Ansios and Fedora now dead, all you had to deal with was Fratello and Krivis?"

"Yup. They were also the most difficult to bring to justice."

"Clearly."

"So about a week after Fedora was poisoned, his lawyer showed up at my house one night with this huge box."

"Oh?"

"I guess both Ansios and Fedora had an agreed upon 'dead man's switch' should anything happen to either of them."

"Really? Interesting..."

"So the lawyer brings me this box filled with every last bit of incriminating evidence Ansios carried around on him in that damn briefcase of his."

"But I thought you said that the briefcase disappeared the night they found him hanging from that bridge?"

"The way he carried that thing suggested he had some very important shit in there. To be honest, I'm not sure what exactly was in the one they found the day he died, maybe copies of the original documents."

"I see. In some ways that was pretty smart, even if it still got him killed."

"Yeah that's kind of what sucks about it all. I mean they all deserved to go to prison for the rest of their lives, but Ansios and Fedora wanted to make certain that the last two remaining wouldn't get away with anything."

"Interesting. So what all was in there?"

"There were the letters and recorded conversations setting up the counterfeit securities deal."

"Nice!"

"And there were all the documents and tapes proving that Fratello was the one who contracted Riluciani's poisoning with digitalis."

"Really?"

"That's unfortunate, but impressive with his level of infiltration."

"You don't know the half of it. Ansios even had some pictures Fratello had given him of Pope Phillip Michael II naked in some health spa somewhere."

"Good God! Now that's some shit."

Fran didn't want to say goodbye, but he could tell the old man was tired and fading.

"Thank you Francis for coming all this way to come see me. I know I don't have much time left. But at least now I can die in peace knowing I played a small part in all of that."

"Small part sir? Don't you go bullshitting me now." Fran smiled and gave him the longest hug before he left.

"I will see you on the other side, Francis."

"Yeah, hopefully not too soon, my friend."

"Nope, not with that new baby coming soon. Please give my love to Peg and your beautiful family."

"I will, I promise."

"...and God Dammit, be careful wherever you end up! I don't want to be chewin' your ass again anytime soon."

Fran hugged Christopherson one more time. "I love you, you grumpy old man."

"I love you too, son. Thank you for everything."

Fran departed knowing, yet satisfied that that would be the last time he'd see the old man alive.

CHAPTER 70

The evening following Fran and Peg's visit with Christopherson, Fran and Peg laid in bed together talking. Peg did her best to snuggle up close to her husband. Her growing belly made something previously so simple, now almost impossible. The best she could manage was to lay on her side, more or less with her back to him. He pulled her pregnant body close to his as best he could with his good arm. It was awkward, but still each other's touch felt comforting.

"I can't believe that asshole knew this whole time!"

Peg just laughed at him. "And here I thought you knew him better than anyone. Damn did he have you fooled."

"It's not funny."

"Yeah it is."

"My conscience has been suffering with that guilt all these years, and you just sit there and laugh at me. This pregnancy is making you a cold hearted..."

"Careful there mister."

"Uh, woman."

Peg just smiled, then issued an evil laugh. "You're weak, Clavering...soft. Especially in that head of yours. Hardened New York cop, my ass. More like stupid if you ask me."

Fran couldn't believe what he was hearing out of her mouth. "Peg? You can't really mean all that?"

Peg decided to tease him a little more, now that she had him going. "I meant every damn word of it."

"What? I had no idea you felt this way."

"Well it was pretty stupid of you to try and take Krivis down by yourself. You almost got your stupid ass killed. Dumb ass!"

Fran kind of turned away from Peg slightly. She could feel him soften his embrace of her. He didn't like the barbed words coming from her mouth. He just laid there silent next to her. Peg didn't really mean it to sound so harsh, but she had wanted to call him out on his stupidity which had almost gotten him killed, pretty much since the day it happened.

"Am I wrong, Clavering?"

"No. You're not." Now more than ever, he hated it when she was right.

Finally she reached over to hold him awkwardly, and kissed him. He pulled away slightly from her kiss. "Wow, you're a sensitive one tonight aren't you?"

He just laid there silent as her jagged words stuck in his head.

"Bah, I didn't mean it, love. Well most of it."

"...most of it?"

"I did mean the part about your stupid ass almost getting yourself killed. I'm sure your former New York buddies down at the precinct would love to hear about a 'two-bit slut' and your rotund pregnant wife saved you from certain death."

"I guess that's fair."

He pulled her close to him once again, wrapping his arm around her, then his hand came to rest on her belly. The baby kicked hard and moved under his hand. "See even the baby thinks that was pretty stupid."

"Now you two are just ganging up on me."

"You really think we should let up on you that easily after almost losing you?"

"Fine, I guess I deserve it. But I still say that that secretary is a slut!"

"She was very nice on the phone with me."

"You'd have a different opinion if you saw her."

"You've met her?!"

"Yeah, she flirted with me a few times."

"Flirted with you? Really? What's she look like?"

"Mmmm, beautiful flowing strawberry blonde hair. Great figure! Tits out to here. Sweater cut down to hear, tiny skirt slit up to here. Then there were those heels."

"You're just making all that up."

Now it was his turn to tease her. "No I'm not. Ask Cosimo sometime. In front of his wife would be even better."

"Alright, that's enough."

Fran pulled her close once again. "I'm just teasing you...for the most part."

"I bet she can't shoot like I can."

"Mmm, I'd guess she hardly knows one end of a gun from the other. That was a hell of a shot you got him with, by the way."

"Thank you."

"Yeah, you're a hell of a shot, and you can type."

"What the hell is that supposed to mean?"

Fran just chuckled. "Oh that's just a joke Cosimo and I were talking about awhile back after we went to Krivis' office. We were pretty certain that Krivis didn't hire that secretary for her typing skills."

"You two are terrible."

"You know, now that I think about it, I should talk to Cosimo."

"About?"

"Now that she's out of a job with her boss dead, we really could use a new secretary at work."

"Oh, you!" She reached over and hit him hard with a pillow.

"Ouch!"

"That didn't hurt."

"Not my head, my shoulder."

"Oops, sorry, I forgot about that."

The two of them were exhausted from all of the events of the last two weeks. Once they finally found a comfortable position, sleep found them both quickly. Fran had a fitful sleep. He had one of the many recurring nightmares since the Krivis incident. However, this one was different from any of the ones he had had before. This time it wasn't Peg in his dream, but Christopherson. In this scene Christopherson shot Krivis instead of Peg. Suddenly Fran bolted straight up in his bed sweating and out of breath.

"Honey, are you ok?"

Fran turned to her with a tear running down his cheek. "Christopherson just died."

"Oh honey," she reached to hold him. "I'm so sorry."

Fran just sat on the side of the bed with his head in his hand. A cascade of tears and emotion came over him. There was no way to stop it, even if he wanted to. The pain he felt in his heart was something he'd only felt two times before. The first time was when his father passed so many years ago, and the second when Riluciani passed more recently.

The phone on the nightstand began to ring. Peg looked over, 3:48 AM read the clock on the nightstand next to the phone. "I'll get it." Peg announced.

There was a short exchange, "I'll tell him. We are both so sorry for your loss. Please give our love to Mrs. Christopherson, and tell her to reach out to us if there's anything she needs. Goodnight."

"Rest well my old friend, until we meet again." Fran whispered through the pain of his broken heart.

On September 28, 1986 Paul Callum Christopherson passed away peacefully in his sleep. Over the coming days people would descend upon New York from around the world to publically honor and eulogize the well respected, honorable man. Cosimo, Hans and their wives flew in from their respective parts of the world for the services. Cardinals Wexford and Leone presided over the mass and funeral services for the late District Attorney. The ceremony was full of much laughter and even more tears. It was clear that that man left an indelible mark on the lives of many. He was a man who would never be forgotten.

Over the coming weeks, time would stretch and compress in odd ways. Fran and Peg returned with their children to Italy, unsure what exactly the future held for them. Fran would just be working at his desk when tears would just start falling on his paperwork. He was out of sorts and wondered about like a lost soul at times. Peg, Cosimo and even Bentley would remind him often that it was ok for him to embrace the grief he was feeling so deep in his soul. Fran found great comfort in their support.

Fran was upstairs deep asleep for what seemed to be the first time in weeks. Peg went in. He looked so peaceful as he slept. She felt bad for having to wake him from such a restful slumber.

"Fran?" She said softly in a calm voice

Fran stirred and stretched as he pulled her in close to him. "Yes love."

"I'm sorry to wake you."

"It's ok honey, come lay here with me."

"I don't think I can right now." Fran woke up a bit more, and sat up slightly to look at her. "I just wanted to let you know, my water just broke."

It took a few moments for her words to register in his brain. Then suddenly Fran burst into a furry of panicked chaos. "Oh my God honey, when? Are there contractions? How far apart? Shit, I gotta get you to the hospital."

Peg slapped him firmly across the face. "Will you calm down? My contractions are far apart and barely hurt at this point, we have lots of time."

"But, honey?"

"Fran, trust me, this baby isn't going to just come flying out of me any second now. Dang, you act like you've never seen a woman give birth before."

The last three were so long ago, most of Fran's memories were a blur. A lot had changed since their last child was born. "It will be interesting to see how these Italians go about this birthing business compared to the American doctors."

Fran was beside himself. "How can you be so damn calm right now? We should have left for the hospital twenty minutes ago."

"Fran we have to wait for Cosimo and his wife to get her and watch the kids first." She paused then turned her gaze upward. "Lord help me if he's going to be like this through my entire labor!"

Fran threw her small suitcase in the car so they could leave as soon as the Angelos got there. Upon their arrival the ladies were jovial, calm and chatty. Fran and Cosimo watched with nervous anxiety as the two women talked and exchanged advice over a cup of tea.

"I think they are doing this on purpose, just to make us crazy Fran."

"That's exactly what I was just thinking."

An hour later, they finally arrived at the hospital. For the next twenty six hours Peg would labor and push with Fran right next to her. He became more and more uncomfortable as the contractions became more and more forceful and painful. Fran did everything he could to be supportive of his wife, as the constant feeling of failure came over him. He hated seeing his wife endure so much pain, while he just sat there helpless, unable to do a damn thing about it. It made him feel slightly better in a somewhat comical way as she yelled at him things that would make the foulest mouthed sailor blush. Fran was impressed by her vulgar vocabulary. He definitely saw Peg in rare form that day. He was pretty sure that even ol' Christopherson might have turned red hearing her words as she labored through the day.

On October 15, 1986 Francis and Margaret (Peg) Clavering welcomed a handsome and strapping baby boy. He weighed in at seven pounds ten ounces and measured eighteen inches long. He had a full head of dark brown curly hair, just like his mother. His eyes and facial features were mirror images of his father. Peg watched her husband's face as he held the baby in his arms for the first time. Tears ran down Fran's face as he was overcome with pride and joy.

"See Fran, I told you you were a big ol' softy." She teased.

Fran just ignored her comment, and issued a beaming smile. "He's beautiful Peg, just beautiful."

"Yeah, he is pretty good looking if you ask me." Peg chuckled. "Ya know, he looks just like you."

"No wonder he's so good looking."

"You're a brat Francis."

A few days after Peg was discharged, arrangements were made for the baby's christening ceremony. They agreed that they wanted Cardinals Leone and Wexford to perform the blessed ritual at Leone's Florence parish. In a highly unusual deviation from tradition, the new parents asked Hans and his wife, and Cosimo and his wife to be the child's godparents. "It would be our honor Fran, Peg." they both confirmed.

The ceremony began and Cardinal Wexford turned to Hans and his wife. "Mr. and Mrs. Hans Kruck, do you turn to Christ, repent your sins, and renounce all evil?"

"We do."

Cardinal Leone then turned to Cosimo and his wife. "Mr. and Mrs. Cosimo Angelo, do you turn to Christ, repent your sins and renounce all evil?

"We do."

Cardinal Wexford then continued speaking to the four of them. "Do you believe and trust in God the Father who has made Heaven and Earth"

All four of them responded, "I believe and trust in Him."

Cardinal Leone then spoke. "Do you believe and trust in His son, Jesus Christ who redeemed mankind?"

Again all four responded, "I believe and trust in Him."

Wexford then asked the final question. "Do you believe and trust in His Holy Spirit who gives life to the people of God?"

Their final response was issued. "I believe and trust in Him."

Cardinals Wexford and Leone then dipped their hands into the holy water and poured water on the baby's head, then together said, "We baptize you, Christopherson Riluciani Bartolone Clavering in the name of the Father, Son and Holy Spirit! Amen!"

Peg, Fran and many in the congregation crossed themselves. The parents and godparents were then given a lit candle, which they held together in their hands.

Wexford was suddenly flooded with emotion. He cleared his throat, then spoke. "This candle represents Jesus as the light of this world."

Leone didn't bother to wipe away the tear as it ran down his cheek. His voice cracked a little when he finally began to speak. "May this beloved child shine brightly as a light in this world to fight against the sins and the devil, like every single one of his namesakes." Through tears, both Cardinals Wexford and Leone raised their hands to bless the child, his parents and his godparents.

ABOUT THE AUTHOR

Maybe it was inevitable that I became a writer. Growing up, the constant tap tap tap ding of my grandmother's manual typewriter surrounded me as she constantly worked on a myriad of writing projects.

I grew up just south of Modesto, California, and graduated from Ceres High School. My College career began at Modesto Junior College, where I developed an interest in psychology and began working in a locked mental facility. In 1988 I began my 20 year career with the United States Army Reserves where I served as an Armorer, Drill Sergeant, and Combat Medic Instructor.

After earning my AA from Modesto Junior College, I completed my four-year degree at Sonoma State University where I earned my BA in Psychology with Distinction, and did Post-Graduate studies in Neurobiology. For postgraduate work I divided my time between Sonoma State University and the San Francisco VA Medical Center at Ft Miley where I worked in a schizophrenia research lab.

Following my graduate work, I worked in the medical field as an Obstetrics Technician at a local hospital.

Today I make my home just outside of Modesto, California with my two sons, daughter, two dogs and a cat. In my spare time, I serve as a docent at Columbia State Historic Park in the Sierra foothills east of Modesto, and I am a proud member of the Columbia Gold Diggers Granny Basketball Team.

http://www.janembell.com
https://www.facebook.com/JaneMBellAuthor
https://www.instagram.com/jane_m_bell_author/
https://twitter.com/JaneMBellAuthor

CHARACTER MAP

Law Enforcement

New York City: NYPD (Manhattan County)

Paul Callum Christopherson – Manhattan County District Attorney

Walter Thomas – Manhattan County Assistant District Attorney

Inspector James Bentley – Commanding Officer of the Manhattan Racketeering Bureau

  Francis Liam Clavering – New York City Detective

  Margaret "Peg" Clavering – Wife of Francis Clavering

Chief Joel Wallace – Strikeforce Commander Dept of Justice/FBI

Nathan Bayer – Federal Prosecutor

Lance Erickson – FBI agent Partner of Detective Francis Clavering

Germany/Rome:

Hans Kruck – Detective with Munich Police Department

Friedrich Behrens – Rome Expert working in Munich Police Department

Cosimo Angelo – Italian colleague of Frederich and Hans from Rome

Mafia Mobsters and Associates:

US/New York:

Alessandro Moretti (Uncle Al) – Underboss of Moretti Crime family

  Luca Benedetto – NYC Mafia Caporegime of Moretti Crime Family

  Gordon "Gordo" Davies – frequent accomplice of Benedetto

Europe:

Hugo Franz – Munich	**Gunther Straussen** – Munich
Dr Karl Schwartz – Austria	**Duncan Hughes** – London
Mateo Taverna – Italy	

Catholic Church/Vatican:
Giancarlo Volonté aka Pope Michael VI
    Father Lance Barton – personal secretary of Pope Michael VI
Cardinal Zacharie Benoît – Vatican Secretary of State
Archbishop Dante Leone – Vatican Under Secretary of State
Cardinal Chiaros Riluciani – Patriarch of Venice
    Father Vincenzo Mancini – personal secretary of Chiaros Riluciani
    Sister Vittoria Falcone – personal assistant of Chiaros Riluciani
Cardinal Charles Wexford – Patriarch of New York
Rinaldo Manna – Senior Layman/Chief Administrator of the Vatican Bank

International Bankers/Businessmen:
Bishop Jonas Krivis – President of the Vatican Bank and Board of Directors Sierra Madre International Bank, Nassau, The Bahamas

Marco Ansios – Owns Banco Generali, Milan; Catholic Bank of Venice and co-owns Sierra Madre International Bank, Nassau, The Bahamas; co-owns Financial and Commerce Services of Milan with Vatican Bank

Giovanni Fedora – Owns Lincoln National Bank, New York; 1 bank in Zurich, Geneva, and 2 in Milan, and co-owns Sierra Madre International Bank, Nassau, The Bahamas

    Men of Lincoln National Bank:
      Nico Novelli
      Conner Gilmore
      "Pops"

Gherado Fratello – Grand Master of P2 Masonic Lodge

25636949R00461